THE FIFTH QUEEN

Praise for *The Fifth Queen*:

'The whole struggle between Katharine and Cromwell for the King seems told in shadows – shadows which flicker with the flames of a log fire, diminish suddenly as a torch recedes, stand calm awhile in the candlelight of a chapel: a cresset flares and all the shadows leap together. Has a novel ever before been lit as carefully as a stage production? ... *The Fifth Queen* is a magnificent bravura piece' Graham Greene

'*The Fifth Queen* ... is like Eisenstein's *Ivan*: slow, intense, pictorial, and operatic. Plot is both its subject and its method. Execution is its upshot and its art ... It must be read with the whole mouth – lips, tongue, teeth ... For prose, it is the recovery of poetry itself' William Gass

Ford Madox Ford was born in Kent in 1873. His first published works were fairy stories. In 1898 he met Joseph Conrad and they collaborated on several works, including the novels *The Inheritors* and *Romance*. He published over eighty books in total, *The Fifth Queen* appearing in three parts during the period 1907–8. In 1915 he published *The Good Soldier*, which he regarded as his finest achievement. In the same year he enlisted in the army, in which he served as an infantry ... *Parade's End*, the culmination of his experiences during the First World War, was published in four parts ... He moved to Paris in 1922 and ... *lantic Review*, whose c ... thers, James Joyce, Ezra ... s later years he divided hi ... merica. Ford Madox Ford also publish ... mes of autobiography and reminiscence, including *Return to Yesterday* (1931) and *It was the Nightingale* (1933), and a final characteristically personal and ambitious volume of criticism, *The March of Literature*. He died in Deauville in 1939.

A. S. Byatt was born in 1936 and educated at York and Newnham College, Cambridge. She taught at the Central School of Art and Design, and from 1972 to 1983 was a lecturer in English and American literature at University College London, becoming a senior lecturer in 1981. She has broadcast regularly on the BBC and contributed to many newspapers and weeklies. She has also written critical studies of Iris Murdoch, Wordsworth and Coleridge, and edited George Eliot's *The Mill on the Floss* for Penguin Classics. Her highly acclaimed books include: *Shadow of a Sun*; *The Virgin in the Garden*; *Still Life*, winner of the Silver Pen Award; *Possession: A Romance*, winner of the 1990 Booker Prize and the 1990 *Irish Times/Aer Lingus* International Fiction Prize; the novella *Angels and Insects*; *The Matisse Stories*; *The Djinn in the Nightingale's Eye*, a collection of fairy tales; *Babel Tower*; *Elementals*; and *The Oxford Book of English Short Stories*, of which she is the editor. A. S. Byatt was awarded the CBE in 1989.

FORD MADOX FORD

THE FIFTH QUEEN

With an Introduction by
A. S. Byatt

PENGUIN BOOKS

PENGUIN BOOKS

Published by the Penguin Group
Penguin Books Ltd, 27 Wrights Lane, London w8 5tz, England
Penguin Putnam Inc., 375 Hudson Street, New York, New York 10014, USA
Penguin Books Australia Ltd, Ringwood, Victoria, Australia
Penguin Books Canada Ltd, 10 Alcorn Avenue, Toronto, Ontario, Canada m4v 3b2
Penguin Books (NZ) Ltd, Private Bag 102902, NSMC, Auckland, New Zealand

Penguin Books Ltd, Registered Offices: Harmondsworth, Middlesex, England

The Fifth Queen first published 1906, *Privy Seal* first
published 1907, *The Fifth Queen Crowned* first published 1908
Published in one volume as *The Bodley Head Ford Madox Ford* 1962
Published in Penguin Books as *The Fifth Queen* 1999
1 3 5 7 9 10 8 6 4 2

Introduction copyright © A. S. Byatt, 1984
All rights reserved

The introduction by A. S. Byatt first appeared
in *The Fifth Queen*, published by Oxford University Press 1984

Printed in England by Clays Ltd, St Ives plc

CONTENTS

2000-6714

INTRODUCTION

BY A. S. BYATT

'Ford's last Fifth Queen novel is amazing. The whole cycle is a noble conception—the swan song of Historical Romance—and frankly I am glad to have heard it.' So, somewhat ambiguously, wrote Joseph Conrad (to whom *The Fifth Queen* is dedicated) to John Galsworthy in 1908. Ford's Tudor novels have often been discussed as a nostalgic exercise in an already outdated form. I think that their ideas, and their techniques, are much more interesting than that. For Ford, the past—the English past, the European past, his own past—was an integral part of present experience and understanding. This is not to say, either, that he uses the Tudor Court as an allegorical portrait of Edwardian England or of Ford Madox Ford. He was more subtle than that.

Ford published eighty-one books between 1891 and 1939, when he died. His father, Francis Hueffer, was German; his English grandfather was the painter, Ford Madox Brown. Ford grew up in Brown's house amongst artists and artistic debate; Graham Greene sees the imposing figure of Ford Madox Brown with his irascibility, fear of plots, enthusiasm, and melancholy behind the looming figure of Henry VIII in these novels. Ford's early books include a life of Brown, a study of Rossetti, and a book on the Pre-Raphaelites; in 1905 he published a monograph on Holbein. Some of the great set-piece descriptions in *The Fifth Queen* are reminiscent of the composition—and lighting—of Madox Brown's historical paintings of Chaucer at the court of Edward III, or Oliver Cromwell—talking to Milton and Marvell or brooding on a white horse amidst farmyard muddle. (Compare Thomas Cromwell on his barge, the carefully composed interior portrait of Anne of Cleves, the farmyard muddle surrounding Mary Hall or Lascelles.) Katharine Howard herself is often described

vii

stretching out, or dropping her arms, in hope or despair, like a posed figure 'caught' by the painter at a historical crisis. Ford preferred Brown's historical paintings to his 'decorative' work. 'As a Teuton, I like to think—and I feel certain—that whatever of Madox Brown's art was most individual was inspired by the Basle Holbeins.' The virtue of Brown's best work derived from 'the study of absolute realism and of almost absolute minuteness of rendering'.

This word, 'rendering', is a central word in Ford's many and varied discussions of the art of the novel. During the period of his collaboration with Conrad, the two of them discussed the techniques of narrative, the importance of 'accurate letters', and developed a set of ideas which Ford referred to, on the whole, as Impressionism. 'We saw', he wrote in his memoir of Conrad, 'that Life did not narrate, but made impressions on our brains. We in turn, if we wished to produce on you an effect of life, must not narrate but render ... impressions.' Their masters were Stendhal, Maupassant, and above all Flaubert, with his insistence on *le mot juste*—a crafted, exact, descriptive language from which the author, both as rhetorical stylist and as moral commentator, should be absent. In English, both novelists turned to Henry James, who in his essay on 'The Art of Fiction' (1884) spoke of 'the air of reality (solidity of specification)' as 'the supreme virtue of a novel' and used the word 'render' and the analogy with painting to illustrate his meaning. 'It is here that the novelist competes with his brother the painter in *his* attempt to render the look of things, the look that conveys their meanings, to catch the colour, the relief, the expression, the surface, the substance of the human spectacle.' 'Rendering' tends to be concerned with evoking surfaces, especially visual surfaces. In Ford's work it usually carries moral connotations of authorial reticence, non-interference, impersonality. Here his ideas can be related to Eliot's idea of the impersonal poet, Joyce's retired artist-God, paring his fingernails. While he admired their desire for accurate recording of natural objects, Ford mistrusted the moral fervour and nostalgic medievalizing of Ruskin and the Pre-Raphaelites. All this helped to shape his highly visual 'historical Romance'.

His book on Holbein, unlike his book on Rossetti or his life of Brown, is written with moral and aesthetic passion. He opposes Holbein to Dürer on its first page in a way that directly prefigures the opposition of the two forces that battle for the soul of Henry VIII (and England) in the *Fifth Queen* novels. The painters are 'the boundary stones between the old world and the modern, between the old faith and the new learning, between empirical, charming conceptions of an irrational world and the modern theoretic way of looking at life'. Dürer 'could not refrain from commenting upon life, Holbein's comments were of little importance'. It seems that Dürer is greater. 'Dürer had imagination, where Holbein had only vision and invention—an invention of a rough-shod and everyday kind.' But it is Holbein whose accuracy Ford is praising. Praising Samuel Richardson's 'craftsmanlike' approach to the novel, Ford said he was 'sound, quiet, without fuss, going about his work as a carpenter goes about making a chair and in the end turning out an article of supreme symmetry and consistence'. He compared Richardson to 'the two supreme artists of the world—Holbein and Bach'. He had already compared Holbein to Bach in the Holbein book itself, after praising Holbein's depiction of Henry VIII as 'an unconcered rendering of an appallingly gross and miserable man'. 'Holbein was in fact a great Renderer. If I wanted to find a figure really akin to his I think I should go to music and speak of Bach.'

Ford, it seems, was interested in Holbein's art and in Henry VIII's court and the politics of Thomas Cromwell because of their 'realism'—and the word 'realism' draws together here both moral attitudes and aesthetic priorities. In the *Fifth Queen* novels Katharine Howard is presented as a virtuous, highly intelligent woman who wishes to reverse the political and religious changes worked by Thomas

Cromwell, Lord Privy Seal—to reintroduce the old faith, feudal values, monastic virtues. This figure bears little relation to what evidence we have about the real Katharine, although Ford teases the reader delicately and inconclusively about the truth of his Katharine's early relations with her alarming cousin, T. Culpepper. Ford himself was a Roman Catholic, of a kind (with more or less fervour at different times of his life), and liked to refer to himself as a 'radical Tory'. He argued for the independent smallholder, old continuities, aristocracy, against the depersonalizing effects of modern machinery and democracy. This has led critics of *The Fifth Queen*, almost universally, to see Katharine as its heroine. Arthur Mizener's comment, in his biography of Ford, *The Saddest Story*, is typical. 'In the end Ford's romantic need to turn her into an impossibly ideal figure makes her unconvincing.' Robert Green, who wrote a good and thoughtful book on Ford's 'prose and politics', noticed that Ford, in his non-fictional writings, praised Cromwell as a 'genius' and 'the founder of modern England', but says that he is portrayed in the novels with 'near-total disfavour'. Ford 'attempts to vilify' Cromwell, and idealizes Katharine's idealism. I think this view, both of what Ford intended to do, and of what he achieved, arises from a kind of stock response to the 'historical Romance' as a genre, and from a failure to appreciate Ford's scrupulous 'rendering' of his world and his characters' consciousness.

It is very illuminating to look at the books, collected as *England and the English*, that Ford was publishing during the same years as the Tudor trilogy. *The Spirit of the People: An Analysis of the English Mind* appeared in 1907 in the same year as *Privy Seal*, and a year before *The Fifth Queen Crowned*.

In this book, Ford claims that England's greatness 'begins with the birth of the modern world. And the modern world was born with the discovery of the political theory of the Balance of the Powers in Europe'. *The Fifth Queen* is concerned with sex, love, marriage, fear, lying, death, and confusion—it is also concerned with the idea of the balance of power as a real force in men's lives. The Ford of *The Spirit of the People* leaves us in no doubt about his admiration for the Cromwell who was 'the founder of modern England'. He describes Henry VIII's ministers as 'Holbein's type', the 'heavy, dark, bearded bull-necked animal, sagacious, smiling, but with devious and twinkling eyes'. He goes on:

And indeed a sort of peasant-cunning *did* ... distinguish the international dealings of the whole world at that date. Roughly speaking, the ideals of the chivalric age were altruistic; roughly speaking, the ideals of the age that succeeded it were individual-opportunist. It was not, of course, England that was first in the field, since Italy produced Machiavelli. But Italy, which produced Machiavelli, failed utterly to profit by him ... England *did* produce from its depths, from admist his bewildering cross currents of mingled races, *the* great man of its age; and along with him it produced a number of men similar in type and strong enough to found a tradition. The man, of course, was Thomas Cromwell, who welded England into one formidable whole, and his followers in that tradition were the tenacious, pettifogging, cunning, utterly unscrupulous and very wonderful statesmen who supported the devious policy of Queen Elizabeth—the Cecils, the Woottons, the Bacons and all the others of England's golden age.

The Tudor age, Ford said, was 'a projection of realism between two widely differing but romantic movements'. That is, the feudal-Catholic times were romantic because of the altruism, heroism, and chivalry of their ideals. In Ford's view, the post-Stuart times, the days after William III and the glorious Revolution, were paradoxically 'romantic' in a deeper sense than the 'picturesque' romanticism of the Stuart cause.

For in essentials the Stuarts' cause was picturesque; the Cromwellian cause a matter of principle. Now a picturesque cause may make a very strong and poetic appeal but it is, after all, a principle that sweeps people away. For poetry is the sublime of common-sense; principle is wrong-headedness wrought up to the sublime pitch—and that, in essentials, is romance.

Consider this opposition: 'the sublime of common-sense'/'wrong-headedness wrought up to the sublime pitch'. It has much in common with the opposition, in these novels, between Cromwell and Katharine—the realistic Machiavellian with his belief in England, the King, the health of the country, and the in many ways 'wrong-headed' Katharine, unprepared to come to terms with the greed of the nobles who have acquired the lands of the dispossessed monasteries, the venal nature of servants, or the distress of Margaret Poins who cannot be married in Katharine's restored Roman Catholic dispensation. There is a further twist to this opposition. Later in *The Spirit of the People* Ford blames Protestantism for 'that divorce of principle from life which, carried as far as it had been carried in England, has earned for the English the title of a nation of hypocrites'. Katharine's Catholicism is like the 'female' Catholicism which Ford says these islands have discarded: the female saints, the Mother of God, 'an evolution almost entirely of the sentiments and of the weaknesses of humanity'. Katharine calls on the saints and on the Virgin throughout this book. But she also calls on the great classical moralists for what Ford would have called 'principles', and Throckmorton sums her up, in this context, shrewdly, as a Romantic puritan as well as a romantic Catholic woman: 'in all save doctrine this Kat Howard and her learning are nearer Lutheran than of the old faith.' (We remember that Ford, in his Holbein book, describes Holbein's portrait of Katharine's 'bitter, soured and disappointed' uncle, Norfolk, as 'rigid and unbending in a new world that seemed to him a sea of errors' and pointed out that it was Norfolk who said, 'It was merry in England before the new Learning came in.') Katharine's appeal to Henry is essentially romantic: they speak of the Fortunate Isles and bringing back a golden age. And her morals have the absolute quality of Ford's 'principle', against which the despairing cynicism of Cicely Elliott is set. Cicely Elliott says, 'God hath withdrawn himself from this world', and to Katharine 'Why, thou art a very infectious fanatic ... But you must shed much blood. You must widow many men's wives. Body of God! I believe thou wouldst.' And Katharine does not demur. She will kill out of her righteous principle as Cromwell will out of his expediency. In *The Spirit of the People* Ford remarks in parenthesis, contrasting his versions of Catholicism and Puritanism, 'I am far from wishing to adumbrate to which religion I give my preference; for I think it will remain to the end a matter for dispute whether a practicable or an ideal code be the more beneficial to humanity.'

A novel, Ford wrote, was 'a rendering of an Affair: of one embroilment, one set of embarrassments, one human coil, one psychological progression'. That the world of this novel is seen through Katharine's eyes more than any other has tended to make her appear to be a 'heroine'; but this, as I suggested earlier, is partly the result of Ford's attempt at what he called authorial 'Aloofness'. I believe she is morally judged, but she is judged by juxtaposition (another favourite term of Ford's, who admired Stendhal and Jane Austen for their gifts of dramatic juxtaposition of incidents which changed the reader's view of what had gone before). The moral work is done by the reader. We do not see so much of Cromwell, or Throckmorton, as we do of Katharine, and the King, passionate, bewildered, cunning, desiring virtue, dangerous, generous, cruel, is seen almost— not entirely—from the outside, a looming body at the end of dark corridors, behind doors. We guess at their motives, with Katharine, but not through her view of them. In his later masterpieces, *The Good Soldier* and *Parade's End*, Ford used bewildered innocent minds to depict the muddle, the horror, the endless unsatisfactory and painful partiality of knowledge of human motive, of what has 'really' happened, or why. This novel is not so subtle, but it is recognizably by the same man. Ford as a writer was always preoccupied with the effect of lies, and the nature of worry and anxiety—they are his great themes, public and private. *The Good Soldier* and *Parade's End* are inhabited by grand, terrible liars. In *The Fifth Queen*, Udal's little lies run into Throckmorton's politic and murderous ones, as the sexual lies of Tietjens' wife in 1914–18 run into the public lies behind the Great War. In *The Spirit of the People* Ford wrote that the English are 'a nation of hypocrites' *because* Protestant virtue divorced principle from life. In *The Fifth Queen* he displays the workings of the divorce.

The 'solidity of specification' of the world of this novel is its great virtue. Ford claimed to have spent ten years before these novels were written working on a book on Henry VIII, whose private papers had just been published.

I worried about his parentage, his diseases, the size of his shoes, the price he gave for kitchen implements, his relation to his wives, his knowledge of music, his proficiency with the bow ... But I really know—so delusive are reported facts—nothing whatever. Not one single thing! Should I have found him affable, or terrifying, or seductive, or royal, or courageous? There are so many contradictory facts; there are so many reported interviews, each contradicting the other ...

He used his 'facts' supremely well. He is at ease with clothes, food, rooms, roads, hangings. The world of this novel is largely an indoor world, dark, artificially lit, a world of staircases, spyholes, hangings that conceal listeners, alleys where men lurk with knives, walls that close people in. This both mirrors the confusions of Katharine's 'affair' and the new world of Tudor England.

Holbein's lords no longer ride hunting. They are inmates of palaces, their flesh is rounded, their limbs at rest, their eyes sceptical or contemplative. They are indoor statesmen; they ideal in intrigues; they have already learnt the meaning of the words 'The balance of the Powers' and in consequence they wield the sword no longer; they have become sedentary rulers.

In the context of this observation, from Ford's Holbein book, it becomes easier to see why the archaic outdoor scenes are so moving. In the brief days of her happiness with Henry Katharine is portrayed out of doors, hunting, in the North, amongst farmers and peasants. In the marvellous scene in the stable yard (designed by Holbein) the old knight, survivor of a world of chivalric action, amongst the already outdated armour, drops his lance. Roy Strong, in *The Elizabethan Image*, wrote of the importance to the Tudors of the nostalgia for chivalry. In *When Did You Last See Your Father?* he wrote of the genuine historical and human concerns of Victorian historical painting. Ford understood—and rendered—both.

A word, finally, about the language. Ford believed—in the interest of excluding the writer from the reader's experience of the affair rendered—in plain words, current language, common speech. He distinguished three English languages: 'that of the Edinburgh Review which has no relation to life, that of the streets which is full of slang and daily neologisms and that third one which is fairly fluid and fairly expressive—the dialect of the drawing-room or the study, the really living language.' Nevertheless, in 1903 he wrote to H. G. Wells, advocating that we should learn from the Elizabethans to use current slang. 'If you will reconsider the matter you will see that slang is an excellent thing. (Elizabethan writing is mostly slang.) And as soon as practicable we should get into our pages every slang word that doesn't (in our selective ears) ring too horribly . . . we must do that or we shall die; we and our language.'

He uses Tudor language in the *Fifth Queen* novels with *this* kind of vitality—a pleasure in accuracy and sharpness, not a distant strangeness. His heroes and heroines tend to be excellent Latinists—Katharine Howard is related to Valentine Wannop in *Parade's End*. Ford's prose has the flexibility and elegance of a good Latinist and the roughness and brilliance of a writer interested in the quiddities of the vernacular. It is proper that his comic character should be

Magister Udal, looking back, like Katharine, to the Golden Age of Latin, unaware that he will be remembered as the father of the drama in the 'vulgar tongue' he so despises.

THE FIFTH
QUEEN

THE FIFTH QUEEN

PRIVY SEAL

THE FIFTH QUEEN CROWNED

THE
FIFTH QUEEN
and how she came to court

To
Joseph Conrad

PART ONE

THE COMING

I

Magister Nicholas Udal, the Lady Mary's pedagogue, was very hungry and very cold. He stood undecided
in the mud of a lane in the Austin Friars. The quickset
hedges on either side were only waist high and did not
shelter him. The little houses all round him of white daub
with grey corner beams had been part of the old friars'
stables and offices. All that neighbourhood was a maze of
dwellings and gardens, with the hedges dry, the orchard
trees bare with frost, the arbours wintry and deserted.
This congregation of small cottages was like a patch of
common that squatters had taken; the great house of the
Lord Privy Seal, who had pulled down the monastery to
make room for it, was a central mass. Its gilded vanes
were in the shape of men at arms, and tore the ragged
clouds with the banners on their lances. Nicholas Udal
looked at the roof and cursed the porter of it.

'He could have given me a cup of hypocras,' he said,
and muttered, as a man to whom Latin is more familiar
than the vulgar tongue, a hexameter about 'pocula plena.'

He had reached London before nine in one of the King's
barges that came from Greenwich to take musicians back
that night at four. He had breakfasted with the Lady
Mary's women at six off warm small beer and fresh meat,
but it was eleven already, and he had spent all his money
upon good letters.

He muttered: '*Pauper sum, pateor, fateor, quod Di dant
fero*,' but it did not warm him.

The magister had been put in the Lady Mary's household by the Lord Privy Seal, and he had a piece of news as to the Lady's means of treasonable correspondence with the Emperor her uncle. He had imagined that the news—which would hurt no one because it was imaginary—might be worth some crowns to him. But the Lord Privy Seal and all his secretaries had gone to Greenwich before it was light, and there was nothing there for the magister.

'You might have known as much, a learned man,' the porter had snarled at him. 'Isn't the new Queen at Rochester? Would our lord bide here? Didn't your magistership pass his barge on the river?'

'Nay, it was still dark,' the magister answered. The porter sniffed and slammed to the grating in the wicket. Being of the Old Faith he hated those Lutherans—or those men of the New Learning—that it pleased his master to employ.

Udal hesitated before the closed door; he hesitated in the lane beyond the corner of the house. Perhaps there would be no barges at the steps—no King's barges. The men of the Earl Marshal's service, being Papists, would pelt him with mud if he asked for a passage; even the Protestant lords' men would jeer at him if he had no pence for them—and he had none. He would do best to wait for the musicians' barge at four.

Then he must eat and shelter—and find a wench. He stood in the mud: long, thin, brown in his doctor's gown of fur, with his black flapped cap that buttoned well under his chin and let out his brown, lean, shaven and humorous face like a woodpecker's peering out of a hole in a tree.

The volumes beneath his arms were heavy: they poked out his gown on each side, and the bitter cold pinched his finger ends as if they had been caught in a door. The weight of the books pleased him for there was much good letters there—a book of Tully's epistles for himself and two volumes of Plautus' comedies for the Lady Mary. But what among his day's purchases pleased him most was a medallion in silver he had bought in Cheapside. It showed on the one side Cupid in his sleep and on the other Venus fondling a peacock. It was a heart-compelling gift to any wench or lady of degree.

He puckered up his deprecatory and comical lips as he imagined that that medal would purchase him the right to sigh dolorously in front of whatever stomacher it finally adorned. He could pour out odes in the learned tongue, for the space of a week, a day, or an afternoon according to the rank, the kindness or the patience of the recipient.

Something invisible and harsh touched his cheek. It might have been snow or hail. He turned his thin cunning face to the clouds, and they threatened a downpour. They raced along, like scarves of vapour, so low that you might have thought of touching them if you stood on tiptoe.

If he went to Westminster Hall to find Judge Combers, he would get his belly well filled, but his back wet to the bone. At the corner of the next hedge was the wicket gate of old Master Grocer Badge. There the magister would find at least a piece of bread, some salt and warmed mead. Judge Combers' wife was easy and bounteous: but old John Badge's daughter was a fair and dainty morsel.

He licked his full lips, leered to one side, muttered, 'A curse on all lords' porters,' and made for John Badge's wicket. Badge's dwelling had been part of the monastery's curing house. It had some good rooms and two low storeys —but the tall garden wall of the Lord Privy Seal had been built against its side windows. It had been done without word or warning. Suddenly workmen had pulled down old Badge's pigeon house, set it up twenty yards further in, marked out a line and set up this high wall that pressed so hard against the house end that there was barely room for a man to squeeze between. The wall ran for half a mile, and had swallowed the ground of twenty small house-holders. But never a word of complaint had reached the ears of the Privy Seal other than through his spies. It was, however, old Badge's ceaseless grief. He had talked of it without interlude for two years.

*   *   *   *

The Badges' room—their houseplace—was fair sized, but so low ceiled that it appeared long, dark and mysterious in the winter light. There was a tall press of dark wood with a face minutely carved and fretted to represent the portal of Amiens Cathedral, and a long black table, littered with large sheets of printed matter in heavy black type, that diffused into the cold room a faint smell of ink. The old man sat quavering in the ingle. The light of the low fire glimmered on his silver hair, on his black square cap two generations old; and, in his old eyes that had seen three generations of changes, it twinkled starrily as if they were spinning round. In the cock forward of his shaven chin, and the settling down of his head into his shoulders, there was a suggestion of sinister and sardonic malice. He was muttering at his son:

'A stiff neck that knows no bending, God shall break one day.'

His son, square, dark, with his sleeves rolled up showing immense muscles developed at the levers of his presses, bent his black beard and frowned his heavy brows above his printings.

'Doubtless God shall break His engine when its work is done,' he muttered.

'You call Privy Seal God's engine?' the old man quavered ironically. 'Thomas Cromwell is a brewer's drunken son. I know them that have seen him in the stocks at Putney not thirty years ago.'

The printer set two proofs side by side on the table and frowningly compared them, shaking his head.

'He is the flail of the monks,' he said abstractedly. 'They would have burned me and thousands more but for him.'

'Aye, and he has put up a fine wall where my arbour stood.'

The printer took a chalk from behind his ear and made a score down his page.

'A wall,' he muttered; 'my Lord Privy Seal hath set up a wall against priestcraft all round these kingdoms——'

'Therefore you would have him welcome to forty feet of

my garden?' the old man drawled. 'He pulls down other folks' crucifixes and sets up his own walls with other folks' blood for mortar.'

The printer said darkly:

'Papists' blood.'

The old man pulled his nose and glanced down.

'We were all Papists in my day. I have made the pilgrimage to Compostella, for all you mock me now.'

He turned his head to see Magister Udal entering the door furtively and with eyes that leered round the room. Both the Badges fell into sudden, and as if guilty, silence.

'Domus parva, quies magna,' the magister tittered, and swept across the rushes in his furs to rub his hands before the fire. 'When shall I teach your Margot the learned tongues?'

'When the sun sets in the East,' the printer muttered.

Udal sent to him over his shoulder, as words of consolation:

'The new Queen is come to Rochester.'

The printer heaved an immense sigh:

'God be praised!'

Udal snickered, still over his shoulder:

'You see, neither have the men of the Old Faith put venom in her food, nor have the Emperor's galleys taken her between Calais and Sandwich.'

'Yet she comes ten days late.'

'Oh moody and suspicious artificer. Afflavit deus! The wind hath blown dead against Calais shore this ten days.'

The old man pulled his long white nose:

'In my day we could pray to St Leonard for a fair wind.'

He was too old to care whether the magister reported his words to Thomas Cromwell, the terrible Lord Privy Seal, and too sardonic to keep silence for long about the inferiority of his present day.

'When shall I teach the fair Margot the learned tongue?' Udal asked again.

'When wolves teach conies how to play on pipes,' the master printer snarled from his chest.

'The Lord Privy Seal never stood higher,' Udal said. 'The match with the Cleves Lady hath gained him great honour.'

'God cement it!' the printer said fervently.

The old man pulled at his nose and gazed at nothing.

'I am tired with this chatter of the woman from Cleves,' he croaked, like a malevolent raven. 'An Anne she is, and a Lutheran. I mind we had an Anne and a Lutheran for Queen before. She played the whore and lost her head.'

'Where's your niece Margot?' Udal asked the printer.

'You owe me nine crowns,' the old man said.

'I will give your Margot ten crowns' worth of lessons in Latin.'

'Hold and enough,' the printer muttered heavily. 'Tags from Seneca in a wench's mouth are rose garlands on a cow's horns.'

'The best ladies in the land learn of me,' Udal answered.

'Aye, but my niece shall keep her virtue intact.'

'You defame the Lady Mary of England,' Udal snickered.

The old man said vigorously, 'God save her highness, and send us her for Queen. Have you begged her to get me redress in the matter of that wall?'

'Why, Providence was kind to her when it sent her me for her master,' Udal said. 'I never had apter pupil saving only one.'

'Shall Thomas Cromwell redress?' the old man asked.

'If good learning can make a good queen, trust me to render her one,' Udal avoided the question. 'But alas! being declared bastard—for very excellent reasons—she may not——'

'You owe me nine crowns,' old Badge threatened him. He picked irritably at the fur on his gown and gazed at the carved leg of the table. 'If you will not induce Privy Seal to pull down his wall I will set the tipstaves on you.'

Master Udal laughed. 'I will give thy daughter ten crowns' worth of lessons in the learned tongues.'

'You will receive another broken crown, magister,' the

younger John said moodily. 'Have you not scars enow by your wenching?'

Udal pushed back the furs at his collar. 'Master Printer John Badge the Younger,' he flickered, 'if you break my crown I will break your chapel. You shall never have license to print another libel. Give me your niece in wedlock?'

The old man said querulously, 'Here's a wantipole without ten crowns would marry a wench with three beds and seven hundred florins!'

Udal laughed. 'Call her to bring me meat and drink,' he said. 'Large words ill fill an empty stomach.'

The younger John went negligently to the great Flemish press. He opened the face and revealed on its dark shelves a patty of cold fish and a black jack. With heavy movements and a solemn face he moved these things, with a knife and napkins, on to the broad black table.

The old man pulled his nose again and grinned.

'Margot's in her chamber,' he chuckled. 'As you came up the wicket way I sent my John to turn the key upon her. It's there at his girdle.' It clinked indeed among rules, T-squares and callipers at each footstep of the heavy printer between press and table.

Magister Udal stretched his thin hands towards it. 'I will give you the printing of the Lady Mary's commentary of Plautus for that key,' he said.

The printer murmured 'Eat,' and set a great pewter salt-cellar, carved like a Flemish pikeman, a foot high, heavily upon the cloth.

Udal had the appetite of a wolf. He pulled off his cap the better to let his jaws work.

'Here's a letter from the Doctor Wernken of Augsburg,' he said. 'You may see how the Lutherans fare in Germany.'

The printer took the letter and read it, standing, frowning and heavy. Magister Udal ate; the old man fingered his furs and, leaning far back in his mended chair, gazed at nothing.

'Let me have the maid in wedlock,' Udal grunted

between two bites. 'Better women have looked favourably upon me. I had a pupil in the North——'

'She was a Howard, and the Howards are all whores,' the printer said, over the letter. 'Your Doctor Wernken writes like an Anabaptist.'

'They are even as the rest of womenkind,' Udal laughed, 'but far quicker with their learning.'

A boy rising twenty, in a grey cloak that showed only his bright red stockings and broad-toed red shoes, rattled the back door and slammed it to. He pulled off his cap and shook it.

'It snows,' he said buoyantly, and then knelt before his grandfather. The old man touched his grandson's cropped fair head.

'*Benedicite*, grandson Hal Poins,' he muttered, and relapsed into his gaze at the fire.

The young man bent his knee to his uncle and bowed low to the magister. Being about the court, he had for Udal's learning and office a reverence that neither the printer nor his grandfather could share. He unfastened his grey cloak at the neck and cast it into a corner after his hat. His figure flashed out, lithe, young, a blaze of scarlet with a crowned rose embroidered upon a chest rendered enormous by much wadding. He was serving his apprenticeship as ensign in the gentlemen of the King's guard, and because his dead father had been beloved by the Duke of Norfolk it was said that his full ensigncy was near. He begged his grandfather's leave to come near the fire, and stood with his legs apart.

'The new Queen's come to Rochester,' he said; 'I am here with the guard to take the heralds to Greenwich Palace.'

The printer looked at him unfavourably from the corner of his dark and gloomy eyes.

'You come to suck up more money,' he said moodily. 'There is none in this house.'

'As Mary is my protectress!' the boy laughed, 'there is!' He stuck his hands into his breeches pocket and pulled out a big fistful of crowns that he had won over-night at dice, and a long and thin Flemish chain of gold. 'I have enow to last me till the thaw,' he said. 'I came to beg my grandfather's blessing on the first day of the year.'

'Dicing. . . . Wenching . . .' the printer muttered.

'If I ask thee for no blessing,' the young man said, 'it's because, uncle, thou'rt a Lutheran that can convey none. Where's Margot? This chain's for her.'

'The fair Margot's locked in her chamber,' Udal snickered.

'Why-som-ever then? Hath she stolen a tart?'

'Nay, but I would have her in wedlock.'

'Thou—you—your magistership?' the boy laughed incredulously. The printer caught in his tone his courtier's contempt for the artificer's home, and his courtier's reverence for the magister's learning.

'Keep thy sister from beneath this fox's tooth,' he said. 'The likes of him mate not with the like of us.'

'The like of thee, uncle?' the boy retorted, with a good-humoured insolence. 'My father was a gentleman.'

'Who married my sister for her small money, and died leaving thee and thy sister to starve.'

'Nay, I starve not,' the boy said. 'And Margot's a plump faggot.'

'A very Cynthia among willow-trees,' the magister said.

'Why, your magistership shall have her,' the boy said. 'I am her lawful guardian.'

His grandfather laughed as men laugh to see a colt kick up its heels in a meadow.

But the printer waved his bare arm furiously at the magister.

'Get thee gone out of this decent house.' His eyes rolled, and his clenched fist was as large as a ham. 'Here you come not a-wenching.'

'Moody man,' the magister said, 'your brains are addled with suspicions.'

The young man swelled his scarlet breast still more

consequentially. 'This is no house of thine, uncle, but my grandfar's.'

'Young ass's colt!' the printer fulminated. 'Would'st have thy sister undone by this Latin mouth-mincer?'

Udal grinned at him, and licked his lips. The printer snarled:

'Know'st thou not, young ass, that this man was thrown out of his mastership at Eton for his foul living?'

Udal was suddenly on his feet with the long pasty-knife held back among the furs of his gown.

'Ignoble...' he began, but he lost his words in his trembling rage. The printer snatched at his long measuring stick.

'Down knife,' he grunted, for his fury, too, made his throat catch.

'Have a care, nunkey,' the young man laughed at the pair of them. 'They teach knife-thrusts in his Italian books.'

'I will have thy printer's licence revoked, ignoble man,' the magister said, grinning hideously. 'Thou, a Lutheran, to turn upon me who was undone by Papist lies! They said I lived foully; they said I stole the silver cellars....'

He turned upon the old man, stretching out the hand that held the knife in a passionate gesture:

'Your Papists said that,' he appealed. 'But not a one of them believed it, though you dub me Lutheran.... See you, do I not govern now the chief Papist of you all? Would that be if they believed me filthy in my living. Have I not governed in the house of the Howards, the lord of it being absent? Would that have been if they had believed it of me?... And then....' He turned again upon the printer. 'For the sake of your men.... for the sake of the New Learning, which God prosper, I was cast down.'

The printer grunted surlily:

' 'Tis known no wench is safe from thy amorousness. How many husbands have broken thy pate?'

The magister threw the knife on to the table and rose, frostily rustling in his gown.

'I shall bring thee down, ignoble man,' he said.

'If thou hast the power to do that,' the old man asked suddenly, 'wherefore canst not get me redress in the matter of my wall?'

The magister answered angrily:

'Privy Seal hath swallowed thy land: he shall not disgorge. But this man he shall swallow. Know you not that you may make a jack swallow, but no man shall make him give back; I, nor thou, nor the devil's self?'

'Oh, a God's name bring not Flail Crummock into this household,' the young man cut in. 'Would you undo us all?'

'Ignoble, ignoble, to twit a man with that Eton villainy,' the magister answered.

'A God's name bring not Privy Seal into the quarrel,' the young man repeated. 'None of us of the Old Faith believe that lie.'

'Keep thy tongue off Cromwell's name, young fool,' his grandfather said. 'We know not what walls have ears.'

The young man went pale: the printer himself went pale, remembering suddenly that the magister was a spy of Cromwell's; all three of them had their eyes upon Udal; only the old man, with his carelessness of his great age, grinned with curiosity as if the matter were a play that did not concern him. The magister was making for the door with the books beneath his arm and a torturing smile round his lips. The boy, with a deep oath, ran out after him, a scarlet flash in the darkening room.

Old Badge pulled at his nose and grinned maliciously at the fire beside him.

'That is thy deliverer: that is thy flail of the monks,' he croaked at his son. The printer gazed moodily at the fire.

'Nay, it is but one of his servants,' he answered mechanically.

'And such servants go up and down this realm of England and ride us with iron bridles.' The old man laughed dryly and bitterly. 'His servant? See how we are held—we dare not shut our doors upon him since he is Cromwell's servant, yet if he come in he shall ruin us, take

our money that we dare not refuse, deflower our virgins ...
What then is left to us between this setter up of walls and
his servants?'

The printer, fingering the T-square in his belt, said,
slowly, 'I think this man loves too well that books should
be printed in the Latin tongue to ruin any printer of them
upon a private quarrel. Else I would get me across the
seas.'

'He loves any wench much better,' the old man answered
maliciously. 'Hearken!'

Through the wall there came a scuffling sound, thumps,
and the noise of things falling. The wall there touched on
the one that Cromwell had set up, so that there was bare
room for a man to creep between.

'Body of God,' the printer said, 'is he eavesdropping
now?'

'Nay, this is courtship,' the old man answered. His head
leaned forward with a birdlike intentness; he listened with
one hand held out as if to still any sound in the room.
They heard footsteps from the floor above, a laugh and
voices. 'Now Margot talks to him from her window.'

The printer had a motion of convulsed rage:

'I will break that knave's spine across my knee.'

'Nay, let be,' the old man said. 'I command thee, who
am thy father, to let the matter be.'

'Would you have him ...' the printer began with a snarl.

'I would not have my house burnt down because this
Cromwell's spy's body should be found upon our
hands. ... To-morrow the wench shall be sent to her
aunt Wardle in Bedfordshire—aye, and she shall be
soundly beaten to teach her to love virtue.'

The young man opened the house door and came in,
shivering in his scarlet because he had run out without
his cloak.

'A pretty medley you have made,' he said to his uncle,
'but I have calmed him. Wherefore should not this
magister marry Margot?' He made again for the fire. 'Are
we to smell always of ink?' He looked disdainfully at his

uncle's proofs, and began to speak with a boy's seriousness
and ingenuous confidence. They would tell his uncle at
Court that if good print be the body of a book, good
learning is even the soul of it. At Court he would learn
that it is thought this magister shall rise high. There good
learning is much prized. Their Lord the King had been
seen to talk and laugh with this magister. 'For our gracious
lord loveth good letters. He is in such matters skilled
beyond all others in the realm.'

The old man listened to his grandson, smiling
maliciously and with pride; the printer shrugged his
shoulders bitterly; the muffled sounds and the voices
through the house-end continued, and the boy talked on,
laying down the law valiantly and with a cheerful voice.
... He would gain advancement at Court through his
sister's marriage with the magister.

Going back to the palace at Greenwich along with the
magister, in the barge that was taking the heralds to the
King's marriage with Anne of Cleves, the young Poins was
importunate with Udal to advance him in his knowledge
of the Italian tongue. He thought that in the books of the
Sieur Macchiavelli upon armies and the bearing of arms
there were unfolded many secret passes with the rapier
and the stiletto. But Udal laughed good-humouredly. He
had, he said, little skill in the Italian tongue, for it was but
a bastard of classical begettings. And for instruction in the
books of the Sieur Macchiavelli, let young Poins go to a
man who had studied them word by word—to the Lord
Privy Seal, Thomas Cromwell.

They both dropped their voices at the name, and,
another gentleman of the guard beginning to talk of rich
men who had fallen low by the block, the stake, and
gaming, Udal mentioned that that day he had seen a
strange sight.

'There was in the Northern parts, where I governed in
his absence the Lord Edmund Howard's children, a certain
Thomas Culpepper. Main rich he was, with many pastures
and many thousands of sheep. A cousin of my lady's he

was, for ever roaring about the house. A swaggerer he was, that down there went more richly dressed than earls here.'

That day Udal had seen this Culpepper alone, without any servants, dressed in uncostly green, and dragging at the bridle of a mule, on which sat a doxy dressed in ancient and ragged furs. So did men fall in these difficult days.

'How came he in London town?' the Norroy King-at-Arms asked.

'Nay, I stayed not to ask him,' Udal answered. He sighed a little. 'Yet then, in my Lord Edmund's house I had my best pupil of all, and fain was I to have news of her. . . . But he was a braggart; I liked him not, and would not stay to speak with him.'

'I'll warrant you had dealings with some wench he favoured, and you feared a drubbing, magister,' Norroy accused him.

The long cabin of the state barge was ablaze with the scarlet and black of the guards, and with the gold and scarlet of the heralds. Magister Udal sighed.

'You had good, easy days in Lord Edmund's house?' Norroy asked.

II

THE Lord Privy Seal was beneath a tall cresset in the stern of his barge, looking across the night and the winter river. They were rowing from Rochester to the palace at Greenwich, where the Court was awaiting Anne of Cleves. The flare of the King's barge a quarter of a mile ahead moved in a glowing patch of lights and their reflections, as though it were some portent creeping in a blaze across the sky. There was nothing else visible in the world but the darkness and a dusky tinge of red where a wave caught the flare of light further out.

He stood invisible behind the lights of his cabin; and the thud of oars, the voluble noises of the water, and the crackling of the cresset overhead had, too, the quality of impersonal and supernatural phenomena. His voice said harshly:

'It is very cold; bring me my greatest cloak.'

Throckmorton, the one of Cromwell's seven hundred spies who at that time was his most constant companion, was hidden in the deep shadow beside the cabin-door. His bearded and heavy form obscured the light for a moment as he hurried to fetch the cloak. But merely to be the Lord Cromwell's gown-bearer was in those days a thing you would run after; and an old man in a flat cap—the Chancellor of the Augmentations, who had been listening intently at the door—was already hurrying out with a heavy cloak of fur. Cromwell let it be hung about his shoulders.

The Chancellor shivered and said, 'We should be within a quarter-hour of Greenwich.'

'Get you in if you be cold,' Cromwell answered. But the Chancellor was quivering with the desire to talk to his master. He had seen the heavy King rush stumbling down the stairs of the Cleves woman's lodging at Rochester, and the sight had been for him terrible and prodigious. It was Cromwell who had made him Chancellor of the Augmentations—who had even invented the office to deal with the land taken from the Abbeys—and he was so much the creature of this Lord Privy Seal that it seemed as if the earth was shivering all the while for the fall of this minister, and that he himself was within an inch of the ruin, execration, and death that would come for them all once Cromwell were down.

Throckmorton, a giant man with an immense golden beard, issued again from the cabin, and the Privy Seal's voice came leisurely and cold:

'What said Lord Cassilis of this? And the fellow Knighton? I saw them at the stairs.'

Privy Seal had such eyes that it was delicate work lying to him. But Throckmorton brought out heavily:

'Cassilis, that this Lady Anne should never be Queen.'

'Aye, but she must,' the Chancellor bleated. He had been bribed by two of the Cleves lords to get them lands in Kent when the Queen should be in power. Cromwell's silence made Throckmorton continue against his will:

'Knighton, that the Queen's breath should turn the King's stomach against you! Dr. Miley, the Lutheran preacher, that by this evening's work the Kingdom of God on earth was set trembling, the King having the nature of a lecher . . .'

He tried to hold back. After all, it came into his mind, this man was nearly down. Any one of the men upon whom he now spied might come to be his master very soon. But Cromwell's voice said, 'And then?' and he made up his mind to implicate none but the Scotch lord, who was at once harmless and unliable to be harmed.

'Lord Cassilis,' he brought out, 'said again that your lordship's head should fall ere January goes out.'

He seemed to feel the great man's sneer through the darkness, and was coldly angry with himself for having invented no better lie. For if this invisible and threatening phantom that hid itself among these shadows outlasted January he might yet outlast some of them. He wondered which of Cromwell's innumerable ill-wishers it might best serve him to serve. But for the Chancellor of the Augmentations the heavy silence of calamity, like the waiting at a bedside for death to come, seemed to fall upon them. He imagined that the Privy Seal hid himself in that shadow in order to conceal a pale face and shaking knees. But Cromwell's voice came harsh and peremptory to Throckmorton:

'What men be abroad at this night season? Ask my helmsmen.'

Two torchlights, far away to the right, wavered shaking trails in the water that, thus revealed, shewed agitated and chopped by small waves. The Chancellor's white beard shook with the cold, with fear of Cromwell, and with curiosity to know how the man looked and felt. He ventured at last in a faint and bleating voice:

What did his lordship think of this matter? Surely the King should espouse this lady and the Lutheran cause.

Cromwell answered with inscrutable arrogance:

'Why, your cause is valuable. But this is a great matter. Get you in if you be cold.'

Throckmorton appeared noiselessly at his elbow, whilst the Chancellor was mumbling: 'God forbid I should be called Lutheran.'

The torches, Throckmorton said, were those of fishers who caught eels off the mud with worms upon needles.

'Such night work favours treason,' Cromwell muttered. 'Write in my notebook, "The Council to prohibit the fishing of eels by night."'

'What a nose he hath for treasons,' the Chancellor whispered to Throckmorton as they rustled together into the cabin. Throckmorton's face was gloomy and pensive. The Privy Seal had chosen none of his informations for noting down. Assuredly the time was near for him to find another master.

The barge swung round a reach, and the lights of the palace of Greenwich were like a flight of dim or bright squares in mid air, far ahead. The King's barge was already illuminating the crenellated arch at the top of the river steps. A burst of torches flared out to meet it and disappeared. The Court was then at Greenwich, nearly all the lords, the bishops and the several councils lying in the Palace to await the coming of Anne of Cleves on the morrow. She had reached Rochester that evening after some days' delay at Calais, for the winter seas. The King had gone that night to inspect her, having been given to believe that she was soberly fair and of bountiful charms. His courteous visit had been in secret and in disguise; therefore there were no torchmen in the gardens, and darkness lay between the river steps and the great central gateway. But a bonfire, erected by the guards to warm themselves in the courtyard, as it leapt up or subsided before the wind, shewed that tall tower pale and high or vanishing into the night with its carved stone garlands, its stone men at arms, its lions, roses, leopards, and naked boys. The living houses ran away from the foot of the tower, till the wings, coming towards the river, vanished continually into shadows. They were low by comparison, gabled with false fronts over each set of rooms and, in the glass of their small-paned windows, the reflection of the fire gleamed capriciously from unexpected shadows. This palace was called Placentia by the King because it was pleasant to live in.

Cromwell mounted the steps with a slow gait and an arrogant figure. Under the river arch eight of his gentlemen waited upon him, and in the garden the torches of his men shewed black yew trees cut like peacocks, clipped hedges like walls with archways above the broad and tiled paths, and fountains that gleamed and trickled as if secretly in the heavy and bitter night.

A corridor ran from under the great tower right round the palace. It was full of hurrying people and of grooms who stood in knots beside doorways. They flattened themselves against the walls before the Lord Privy Seal's procession of gentlemen in black with white staves, and the ceilings seemed to send down moulded and gilded stalactites to touch his head. The beefeater before the door of the Lady Mary's lodgings spat upon the ground when he had passed. His hard glance travelled along the wall like a palpable ray, about the height of a man's head. It passed over faces and slipped back to the gilded wainscoting; tiring-women upon whom it fell shivered, and the serving men felt their bowels turn within them. His round face was hard and alert, and his lips moved ceaselessly one upon another. All those serving people wondered to see his head so high, for already it was known that the King had turned sick at the sight of his bedfellow that should be. And indeed the palace was only awake at that late hour because of that astounding news, dignitaries lingering in each other's quarters to talk of it, whilst in the passages their waiting men supplied gross commentaries.

He entered his door. In the ante-room two men in his livery removed his outer furs deftly so as not to hinder his walk. Before the fire of his large room a fair boy knelt to pull off his jewelled gloves, and Hanson, one of his secretaries, unclasped from his girdle the corded bag that held the Privy Seal. He laid it on a high stand between two tall candles of wax upon the long table.

The boy went with the gloves and Hanson disappeared silently behind the dark tapestry in the further corner. Cromwell was meditating above a fragment of flaming wood that the fire had spat out far into the tiled forehearth. He pressed it with his foot gently towards the blaze of wood in the chimney.

His plump hands were behind his back, his long upper lip ceaselessly caressed its fellow, moving as one line of a snake's coil glides above another. The January wind crept round the shadowy room behind the tapestry, and as it quivered stags seemed to leap over bushes, hounds to spring in pursuit, and a crowned Diana to move her arms, taking an arrow from a quiver behind her shoulder. The tall candles guarded the bag of the Privy Seal, they fluttered and made the gilded heads on the rafters have sudden grins on their faces that represented kings with flowered crowns, queens with their hair combed back on to pillows, and pages with scolloped hats. Cromwell stepped to an aumbry, where there were a glass of wine, a manchet of bread, and a little salt. He began to eat, dipping pieces of bread into the golden salt-cellar. The face of a queen looked down just above his head with her eyes wide open as if she were amazed, thrusting her head from a cloud.

'Why, I have outlived three queens,' he said to himself, and his round face resignedly despised his world and his times. He had forgotten what anxiety felt like because the world was so peopled with blunderers and timid fools full of hatred.

The marriage with Cleves was the deathblow to the power of the Empire. With the Protestant Princes armed behind his back, the imbecile called Charles would never dare to set his troops on board ship in Flanders to aid the continual rebellions, conspiracies and risings in England.

He had done it too often, and he had repented as often, at the last moment. It was true that the marriage had thrown Charles into the arms of France: the French King and he were at that very minute supping together in Paris. They would be making treaties that were meant to be broken, and their statesmen were hatching plots that any scullion would reveal. Francis and his men were too mean, too silly, too despicable, and too easily bribed to hold to any union or to carry out any policy. . . .

He sipped his wine slowly. It was a little cold, so he set it down beside the fire. He wanted to go to bed, but the Archbishop was coming to hear how Henry had received his Queen, and to pour out his fears. Fears! Because the King had been sick at sight of the Cleves woman! He had this King very absolutely in his power; the grey, failing but vindictive and obstinate mass known as Henry was afraid of his contempt, afraid really of a shrug of the shoulder or a small sniff.

With the generosity of his wine and the warmth of his fire, his thoughts went many years ahead. He imagined the King either married to or having repudiated the Lady from Cleves, and then dead. Edward, the Seymour child, was his creature, and would be king or dead. Cleves children would be his creations too. Or if he married the Lady Mary he would still be next the throne.

His mind rested luxuriously and tranquilly on that prospect. He would be perpetually beside the throne, there would be no distraction to maintain a foothold. He would be there by right; he would be able to give all his mind to the directing of this world that he despised for its baseness, its jealousies, its insane brawls, its aimless selfishness, and its blind furies. Then there should be no more war, as there should be no more revolts. There should be no more jealousies; for kingcraft, solid, austere, practical and inspired, should keep down all the peoples, all the priests, and all the nobles of the world. 'Ah,' he thought, 'there would be in France no power to shelter traitors like

Brancetor.' His eyes became softer in the contemplation of this Utopia, and he moved his upper lip more slowly.

Now the Archbishop was there. Pale, worn with fears and agitation, he came to say that the King had called to him Bishop Gardiner and the more Catholic lords of the Council. Cranmer's own spy Lascelles had made this new report.

His white sleeves made a shivering sound, the fur that fell round his neck was displaced on one shoulder. His large mouth was open with panic, his lips trembled, and his good-natured and narrow eyes seemed about to drop tears.

'Your Grace knoweth well what passed to-night at Rochester,' Cromwell said. He clapped his hands for a man to snuff the candles. 'You have the common report.'

'Ah, is it even true?' The Archbishop felt a last hope die, and he choked in his throat. Cromwell watched the man at the candles and said:

'Your Grace hath a new riding mule. I pray it may cease to affright you.'

'Why?' he said, as the man went. 'The King's Highness went even to Rochester, disguised, since it was his good pleasure, as a French lord. You have seen the lady. So his Highness was seized with a make of palsy. He cursed to his barge. I know no more than that.'

'And now they sit in the council.'

'It seems,' Cromwell said.

'Ah, dear God have mercy.'

The Archbishop's thin hands wavered before the crucifix on his breast, and made the sign of the cross.

The very faces of his enemies seemed visible to him. He saw Gardiner, of Winchester, with his snake's eyes under the flat cap, and the Duke of Norfolk with his eyes malignant in a long, yellow face. He had a vision of the King, a huge red lump beneath the high dais at the head of the Council table, his face suffused with blood, his cheeks quivering.

He wrung his hands and wondered if at Smithfield the

Lutherans would pray for him, or curse him for having been lukewarm.

'Why, goodman gossip,' Cromwell said compassionately, 'we have been nearer death ten times.' He uttered his inmost thoughts out of pity:—All this he had awaited. The King's Highness by the report of his painters, his ambassadors, his spies—they were all in the pay of Cromwell —had awaited a lady of modest demeanour, a coy habit, and a great and placid fairness. 'I had warned the Almains at Rochester to attire her against our coming. But she slobbered with ecstasy and slipped side-ways, aiming at a courtesy. Therefore the King was hot with new anger and disgust.'

'You and I are undone.' Cranmer was passive with despair.

'He is very seldom an hour of one mind,' Cromwell answered. 'Unless in that hour those you wot of shall work upon him, it will go well with us.'

'They shall. They shall.'

'I wait to see.'

There seemed to Cranmer something horrible in this impassivity. He wished his leader to go to the King, and he had a frantic moment of imagining himself running to a great distance, hiding his head in darkness.

Cromwell's lips went up in scorn. 'Do you imagine the yellow duke speaking his mind to the King? He is too craven.'

A heavy silence fell between them. The fire rustled, the candles again needed snuffing.

'Best get to bed,' Cromwell said at last.

'Could I sleep?' Cranmer had the irritation of extreme fear. His master seemed to him to have no bowels. But the waiting told at last upon Cromwell himself.

'I could sleep an you would let me,' he said sharply. 'I tell you the King shall be another man in the morning.'

'Ay, but now. But now....' He imagined the pens in that distant room creaking over the paper with their committals, and he wished to upbraid Cromwell. It was his

policy of combining with Lutherans that had brought them
to this.

Heavy thundering came on the outer door.

'The King comes,' Cromwell cried victoriously. He
went swiftly from the room. The Archbishop closed his
eyes and suddenly remembered the time when he had
been a child.

Privy Seal had an angry and contemptuous frown at his
return. 'They have kept him from me.' He threw a little
scroll on to the table. Its white silence made Cranmer
shudder; it seemed to have something of the heavy
threatening of the King's self.

'We may go to bed,' Cromwell said. 'They have devised
their shift.'

'You say?'

'They have temporised, they have delayed. I know
them.' He quoted contemptuously from the letter: 'We
would have you send presently to ask of the Almain Lords
with the Lady Anne the papers concerning her pre-contract
to the Duke of Lorraine.'

Cranmer was upon the point of going away in the joy of
this respite. But his desire to talk delayed him, and he
began to talk about the canon law and pre-contracts of
marriage. It was a very valid cause of nullity all the doctors
held.

'Think you I have not made very certain the pre-contract
was nullified? This is no shift,' and Cromwell spoke
wearily and angrily. 'Goodman Archbishop, dry your tears.
To-night the King is hot with disgust, but I tell you he
will not cast away his kingdom upon whether her teeth be
white or yellow. This is no woman's man.'

Cranmer came nearer the fire and stretched out his lean
hands.

'He hath dandled of late with the Lady Cassilis.'

'Well, he hath been pleasant with her.'

Cranmer urged: 'A full-blown man towards his failing
years is more prone to women than before.'

'Then he may go a-wenching.' He began to speak with

a weary passion. To cast away the Lady Anne now were a madness. It would be to stand without a friend before all nations armed to their downfall. This King would do no jot to lose a patch upon his sovereignty.

Cranmer sought to speak.

'His Highness is always hot o'nights,' Cromwell kept on. 'It is in his nature so to be. But by morning the German princes shall make him afraid again and the Lutherans of this goodly realm. Those mad swine our friends!'

'He will burn seven of them on to-morrow sennight,' Cranmer said.

'Nay! I shall enlarge them on Wednesday.'

Cranmer shivered. 'They grow very insolent. I am afraid.'

Cromwell answered with a studied nonchalance:

'My bones tell me it shall be an eastward wind. It shall not rain on the new Queen's bridals.' He drank up his warm wine and brushed the crumbs from the furs round his neck.

'You are a very certain man,' the Archbishop said.

Going along the now dark corridors he was afraid that some ruffling boy might spring upon him from the shadows. Norfolk, as the Earl Marshal, had placed his lodgings in a very distant part of the palace to give him long journeys that, telling upon his asthma, made him arrive breathless and convulsed at the King's rooms when he was sent for.

III

The shadow of the King kept hands from throats in the palace, but grooms were breaking each others' heads in the stables till towards morning. They fought about whether it were lawful to eat fish on a Friday, and just after daybreak a gentleman's oarsman from Sittingbourne had all his teeth to swallow for asserting that the sacrament should be administered in the two kinds. The horses were watered by ostlers who hummed the opprobrious song about Privy Seal, called 'Crummock.'

In the hillocks and lawns of the park round the palace Lutherans waited all night to welcome their Queen. They lit small fires on the turf and, standing round them, sang triumphal hymns. A Princess was coming from Cleves, a Lutheran; the day-spring from on high was visiting them; soon, soon now, the axe and the flail should be given into their hands.

In the dawn their boats could be seen pulling like water-beetles all across the pallid river from the Essex shores. They clustered in grey masses round the common steps.

A German horse merchant from the City pulled a putrid cat out of the river mud and held it over his head. He shrieked: 'Hic hocus pocus,' parodying the '*Hoc corpus meum*' of the Mass. The soldiers of the Duke of Norfolk were unable to reach him for the crowd. There were but ten of them, under a captain, set to guard the little postern in the side wall of the garden. Towards ten o'clock the Mayor of London came by land. He had with him all his brotherhood with their horses and armed guards in a long train. The mayor and his aldermen had entrance into the palace, but the Duke had given orders that men and horses must bide in the park. There were forty battles of them, each of one hundred men.

The great body came in sight, white, shining even in the grey among the trees along the long garden wall.

'Body of God,' the captain said, 'there shall be broken crowns.' He bade his men hold their pikes across, and paced unconcernedly up and down before the door.

The City men came down in a solid body, and at sight of the red crosses on their white shoulders the Lutherans set up a cry of 'Rome, Rome.' Their stones began to fly at once, and, because they pressed so closely in, the City bowmen had no room to string their bows. The citizens struck out with their silvered staves, but the heavy armour under their white surcoats hindered them. The Lutherans cried out that the Kingdom of God was come on earth because a Queen from Cleves was at hand.

An alderman's charger was struck by a stone. It broke loose and crashed all foaming and furious through a tripe stall on which a preacher was perched to hold forth. The riot began then. All in among the winter trees the City men in their white and silver were fighting with the Lutherans in their grey frieze. The citizens' hearts were enraged because their famous Dominican preacher had been seized by the Archbishop and spirited into Kent. They cried to each other to avenge Dr Latter on these lowsels.

Men struck out at all and sundry. A woman, covered to the face in a fur hood and riding a grey mule, was hit on the arm by the quarterstaff of a Protestant butcher from the Crays, because she wore a crucifix round her neck. She covered her face and shrieked lamentably. A man in green at the mule's head, on the other side, sprang like a wild cat under the beast's neck. His face blazed white, his teeth shone like a dog's, he screamed and struck his dagger through the butcher's throat.

His motions were those of a mad beast; he stabbed the mule in the shoulder to force it to plunge in the direction of the soldiers who kept the little gate, before in the throng the butcher had reached the ground. The woman was flogging at the mule with her reins. 'I have killed 'un,' he shrieked.

He dived under the pikes of the soldiers and gripped the captain by both shoulders. 'We be the cousins of the Duke of Norfolk,' he cried. His square red beard trembled beneath his pallid face, and suddenly he became speechless with rage.

Hands were already pulling the woman from her saddle, but the guards held their pikes transversely against the faces of the nearest, crushing in noses and sending sudden streaks of blood from jaws. The uproar was like a hurricane and the woman's body, on high, swayed into the little space that the soldiers held. She was crying with the pain of her arm that she held with her other hand. Her cousin ran to her and mumbled words of inarticulate tenderness, ending again in 'I have killed 'un.'

The mob raged round them, but the soldiers stood firm enough. A continual cry of 'Harlot, harlot,' went up. Stones were scarce on the sward of the park, but a case bottle aimed at the woman alighted on the ear of one of the guards. It burst in a foam of red, and he fell beneath the belly of the mule with a dry grunt and the clang of iron. The soldiers put down the points of their pikes and cleared more ground. Men lay wallowing there when they retreated.

The man shouted at the captain: 'Can you clear us a way to yon stairs?' and, at a shake of the head, 'Then let us enter this gate.'

The captain shook his head again.

'I am Thomas Culpepper. This is the Duke's niece, Kat,' the other shouted.

The captain observed him stoically from over his thick and black beard.

'The King's Highness is within this garden,' he said. He spoke to the porter through the little niche at the wicket. A company of the City soldiers, their wands beating like flails, cleared for a moment the space in front of the guards.

Culpepper with the hilt of his sword was hammering at the studded door. The captain caught him by the shoulder and sent him to stagger against the mule's side. He was gasping and snatched at his hilt. His bonnet had fallen off, his yellow hair was like a shock of wheat, and his red beard flecked with foam that spattered from his mouth.

'I have killed one. I will kill thee,' he stuttered at the captain. The woman caught him round the neck.

'Oh, be still,' she shrieked. 'Still. Calm. Y' kill me.' She clutched him so closely that he was half throttled. The captain paced stoically up and down before the gate.

'Madam,' he said, 'I have sent one hastening to his dukeship. Doubtless you shall enter.' He bent to pull the soldier from beneath the mule's belly by one foot, and picking up his pike, leaned it against the wall.

With his face pressed against his cousin's furred side, Thomas Culpepper swore he would cut the man's throat.

'Aye, come back again,' he answered. 'They call me Sir Christopher Aske.'

The red jerkins of the King's own guards came in a heavy mass round the end of the wall amid shrieks and curses. Their pike-staves rose rhythmically and fell with dull thuds; with their clumsy gloved hands they caught at throats, and they threw dazed men and women into the space that they had cleared before the wall. There armourers were ready, with handcuffs and leg-chains hanging like necklaces round their shoulders.

The door in the wall opened silently, the porter called through his niche: 'These have leave to enter.' Thomas Culpepper shouted 'Coneycatcher' at the captain before he pulled the mule's head round. The beast hung back on his hand, and he struck it on its closed eyes in a tumult of violent rage. It stumbled heavily on the threshold, and then darted forward so swiftly that he did not hear the direction of the porter that they should turn only at the third alley.

Tall and frosted trees reached up into the dim skies, the deserted avenues were shrouded in mist, and there was a dead and dripping silence.

'Seven brawls y' have brought me into,' the woman's voice came from under her hood, 'this weary journey.'

He ran to her stirrup and clutched her glove to his forehead. 'Y'ave calmed me,' he said. 'Your voice shall ever calm me.'

She uttered a hopeless 'Oh, aye,' and then, 'Where be we?'

They had entered a desolate region of clipped yews, frozen fountains, and high, trimmed hedges. He dragged the mule after him. Suddenly there opened up a very broad path, tiled for a width of many feet. On the left it ran to a high tower's gaping arch. On the right it sloped nobly into a grey stretch of water.

'The river is even there,' he muttered. 'We shall find the stairs.'

'I would find my uncle in this palace,' she said. But he muttered, 'Nay, nay,' and began to beat the mule with his fist. It swerved, and she became sick and dizzy with the sudden jar on her hurt arm. She swayed in her saddle and, in a sudden flaw of wind, her old and torn furs ruffled jaggedly all over her body.

IV

The King was pacing the long terrace on the river front. He had been there since very early, for he could not sleep at nights, and had no appetite for his breakfast. When a gentleman from the postern gate asked permission for Culpepper and the mule to pass to the private stairs, he said heavily:

'Let me not be elbowed by cripples,' and then: 'A' God's name let them come,' changing his mind, as was his custom after a bad night, before his first words had left his thick, heavy lips. His great brow was furrowed, his enormous bulk of scarlet, with the great double dog-rose embroidered across the broad chest, limped a little over his right knee and the foot dragged. His eyes were bloodshot and heavy, his head hung forward as though he were about to charge the world with his forehead. From time to time his eyebrows lifted painfully, and he swallowed with an effort as if he were choking.

Behind him the three hundred windows of the palace Placentia seemed to peer at him like eyes, curious, hostile, lugubrious or amazed. He tore violently at his collar and muttered: 'I stifle.' His great hand was swollen by its glove, sewn with pearls, to an immense size.

The gentleman told him of the riot in the park, and

narrated the blasphemy of the German Lutheran, who had held up a putrid dog in parody of the Holy Mass.

The face of the King grew suffused with purple blood.

'Let those men be cut down,' he said, and he conceived a sorting out of all heresy, a cleansing of his land with blood. He looked swiftly at the low sky as if a thunderbolt or a leprosy must descend upon his head. He commanded swiftly, 'Let them be taken in scores. Bid the gentlemen of my guard go, and armourers with shackles.'

The sharp pain of the ulcer in his leg gnawed up to his thigh, and he stood, dejected, like a hunted man, with his head hanging on his chest, so that his great bonnet pointed at the ground. He commanded that both Privy Seal and the Duke of Norfolk should come to him there upon the instant.

This grey and heavy King, who had been a great scholar, dreaded to read in Latin now, for it brought the language of the Mass into his mind; he had been a composer of music and a skilful player on the lute, but no music and no voices could any more tickle his ears.

Women he had loved well in his day. Now, when he desired rest, music, good converse and the love of women, he was forced to wed with a creature whose face resembled that of a pig stuck with cloves. He had raged overnight, but, with the morning, he had seen himself growing old, on a tottering throne, assailed by all the forces of the Old Faith in Christendom. Rebellions burst out like fires every day in all the corners of his land. He had no men whom he could trust: if he granted a boon to one party it held them only for a day, and the other side rose up. Now he rested upon the Lutherans, whom he hated, and, standing on that terrace, he had watched gloomily the great State barges of the Ambassadors from the Empire and from France come with majestic ostentation downstream abreast, to moor side by side against the steps of his water-gate.

It was a parade of their new friendship. Six months ago their trains could not have mingled without bloodshed.

At last there stood before him Thomas Cromwell, unbonneted, smiling, humorous, supple and confident for himself and for his master's cause, a man whom his Prince might trust. And the long melancholy and sinister figure of the Duke of Norfolk stalked stiffly down among the yew trees powdered with frost. The furs from round his neck fluttered about his knees like the wings of a crow, and he dug his Earl Marshal's golden staff viciously into the ground. He waved his jewelled cap and stood still at a little distance. Cromwell regarded him with a sinister and watchful amusement; he looked back at Privy Seal with a black malignancy that hardened his yellow features, his hooked nose and pursed lips into the likeness of a mask representing hatred.

This Norfolk was that Earl of Surrey who had won Flodden Field. They all then esteemed him the greatest captain of his day—in the field a commander sleepless, cunning, cautious, and, in striking, a Hotspur.

A dour and silent man, he was the head of all the Catholics, of all the reaction of that day. But, in the long duel between himself and Cromwell he had seemed fated to be driven from post to post, never daring to proclaim himself openly the foe of the man he dreaded and hated. Cranmer, with his tolerant spirit, he despised. Here was an archbishop who might rack and burn for discipline's sake, and he did nothing. . . . And all these New Learning men with their powers of language, these dark bearded men with twinkling and sagacious eyes, he detested. He went clean shaved, lean and yellow-faced, with a hooked nose that seemed about to dig into his chin. It was he who said first: 'It was merry in England before this New Learning came in.'

The night before, the King had sworn that he would have Privy Seal's head because Anne of Cleves resembled a pig stuck with cloves. And, shaking and shivering with cold that penetrated his very inwards, with a black pain on his brow and sparks dancing before his jaundiced eyes, the Duke cursed himself for not having urged then the immediate arrest of the Privy Seal. For here stood Cromwell, arrogantly by the King's side with the King graciously commanding him to cover his head because it was very cold and Cromwell was known to suffer with the earache.

'You are Earl Marshal,' the King's voice drowned Norfolk's morning greeting. He veered upon the Duke with such violence that his enormous red bulk seemed about to totter over upon the tall and bent figure. A searing pain had shot up his side, and, as he gripped it, he appeared to be furiously plucking at his dagger. He had imagined Chapuys and Marillac, the Ambassadors, coming upon guards with broken heads and sending to Paris letters over which Francis and his nephew should snigger and chuckle.

'You are Earl Marshal. You have the ordering of these ceremonies, and you let rebels and knaves break heads within my very park for all the world to see!'

In his rage Norfolk blurted out:

'Privy Seal hath his friends, too—these Lutherans. What man could have foreseen how insolent they be grown, for joy at welcoming a Queen of their faith,' he repeated hotly. 'No man could have foreseen. My bands are curtailed.'

Cromwell said:

'Aye, men are needed to keep down the Papists of your North parts.'

The two men faced each other. It had been part of the Duke's plan—and Cromwell knew it very well—that the City men should meet with the Lutherans there in the King's own park. It would show the insolence of the heretics upon whom the Privy Seal relied, and it might prove, too, the strength of the Old Faith in the stronghold of the City.

Henry rated violently. It put him to shame, he repeated many times. 'Brawling beneath my face, cries in my ears, and the smell of bloodshed in my nose.'

Norfolk repeated dully that the Protestants were wondrous insolent. But Cromwell pointed out with a genial amusement: 'My Lord Duke should have housed the City men within the palace. Cat will fight with dog the world over if you set them together.'

The Duke answered malignantly:

'It was fitting the citizens should wait to enter. I would not cumber his Highness' courtyards. We know not yet that this Lady cometh to be welcomed Queen.'

'Body of God,' the King said with a new violence: 'do ye prate of these matters?' His heavy jaws threatened like a dog's. 'Hast thou set lousy knaves debating of these?'

Norfolk answered darkly that it had been treated of in the Council last night.

'My Council! My Council!' The King seemed to bay out the words. 'There shall some mothers' sons rue this!'

Norfolk muttered that he had spoken of it with no man not a Councillor. The King's Highness' self had moved first in this.

Henry suddenly waved both hands at the sky.

'Take you good order,' he said heavily into the lean and yellow face of the Duke. 'Marshal these ceremonies fitly from henceforth. Let nothing lack. Get you gone.' An end must be made of talk and gossip. The rumour of last night's Council must appear an idle tale, a falsehood of despairing Papists. 'The Queen cometh,' he said.

With the droop of the Duke's long arms his hat seemed to brush the stones, his head fell on his chest. It was finished.

He had seen so many things go that he loved. And now this old woman with her Germans, her heresies—her children doubtless—meant the final downfall of the Old Order in his day. It would return, but he would never see it. And under Cromwell's sardonic gaze his head hung limply, and his eyes filled with hot and blinding drops. His face trembled like that of a very old man.

The King had thrust his hand through Cromwell's arm, and, with a heavy familiarity as if he would make him forget the Council of last night, he was drawing him away towards the water-gate. He turned his head over his shoulder and repeated balefully:

'The Queen cometh.'

As he did so his eye fell upon a man tugging at the

bridle of a mule that had a woman on its back. He passed on with his minister.

V

In turning, Norfolk came against them at the very end of the path. The man's green coat was spotted with filth, one of his sleeves was torn off and dangled about his heel. The mule's knees were cut, and the woman trembled with her hidden face and shrinking figure.

They made him choke with rage and fear. Some other procession might have come against these vagabonds, and the blame would have been his. It disgusted him that they were within a yard of himself.

'Are there no side paths?' he asked harshly.

Culpepper blazed round upon him:

'How might I know? Why sent you no guide?' His vivid red beard was matted into tails, his face pallid and as if blazing with rage. The porter had turned them loose into the empty garden.

'Kat is sore hurt,' he mumbled, half in tears. 'Her arm is welly broken.' He glared at the Duke. 'Care you no more for your own blood and kin?'

Norfolk asked:

'Who is your Kat? Can I know all the Howards?'

Culpepper snarled:

'Aye, we may trust you not to succour your brother's children.'

The Duke said:

'Why, she shall back to the palace. They shall comfort her.'

'That shall she not,' Culpepper flustered. 'Sh'ath her father's commands to hasten to Dover.'

The Duke caught her eyes in the fur hood that hid her face like a Moorish woman's veil. They were large, grey and arresting beneath the pallor of her forehead. They looked at him, questioning and judging.

'Wilt not come to my lodging?' he asked.

'Aye, will I,' came a little muffled by the fur.

'That shall she not,' Culpepper repeated.

The Duke looked at him with gloomy and inquisitive surprise.

'Aye, I am her mother's cousin,' he said. 'I fend for her, which you have never done. Her father's house is burnt by rioters, and her men are joined in the pillaging. But I'll warrant you knew it not.'

Katharine Howard with her sound hand was trying to unfasten her hood, hastily and eagerly.

'Wilt come?' the Duke asked hurriedly. 'This must be determined.'

Culpepper hissed: 'By the bones of St Nairn she shall not.' She lifted her maimed hand involuntarily, and, at the sear of pain, her eyes closed. Immediately Culpepper was beside her knees, supporting her with his arms and muttering sounds of endearment and despair.

The Duke, hearing behind him the swish pad of heavy soft shoes, as if a bear were coming over the pavement, faced the King.

'This is my brother's child,' he said. 'She is sore hurt. I would not leave her like a dog,' and he asked the King's pardon.

'Why, God forbid,' the King said. 'Your Grace shall succour her.' Culpepper had his back to them, caring nothing for either in his passion. Henry said: 'Aye, take good care for her,' and passed on with Privy Seal on his arm.

The Duke heaved a sigh of relief. But he remembered again that Anne of Cleves was coming, and his black anger that Cromwell should thus once again have the King thrown back to him came out in his haughty and forbidding tone to Culpepper:

'Take thou my niece to the water-gate. I shall send women to her.' He hastened frostily up the path to be gone before Henry should return again.

Culpepper resolved that he would take barge before

ever the Duke could send. But the mule slewed right across the terrace; his cousin grasped the brute's neck and her loosened hood began to fall back from her head.

The King, standing twenty yards away, with his hand shaking Cromwell's shoulder, was saying:

'See you how grey I grow.'

The words came hot into a long harangue. He had been urging that he must have more money for his works at Calais. He was agitated because a French chalk pit outside the English lines had been closed to his workmen. They must bring chalk from Dover at a heavy cost for barges and balingers. This was what it was to quarrel with France.

Cromwell had his mind upon widening the breach with France. He said that a poll tax might be levied on the subjects of Charles and Francis then in London. There were goldsmiths, woolstaplers, horse merchants, whoremasters, painters, musicians and vintners. . . .

The King's eyes had wandered to the grey river, and then from a deep and moody abstraction he had blurted out those words.

Henry was very grey, and his face, inanimate and depressed, made him seem worn and old enough. Cromwell was not set to deny it. The King had his glass. . . .

He sighed a little and began:

'The heavy years take their toll.'

Henry caught him up suddenly:

'Why, no. It is the heavy days, the endless nights. You can sleep, you.' But him, the King, incessant work was killing.

'You see, you see, how this world will never let me rest.' In the long, black nights he started from dozing. When he took time to dandle his little son a panic would come over him because he remembered that he lived among traitors and had no God he could pray to. He had no mind to work. . . .

Cromwell said that there was no man in England could outwork his King.

'There is no man in England can love him.' His distracted eyes fell upon the woman on the mule. 'Happy he whom a King never saw and who never saw King,' he muttered.

The beast, inspired with a blind hatred of Culpepper, was jibbing across the terrace, close at hand. Henry became abstractedly interested in the struggle. The woman swayed forward over her knees.

'Your lady faints,' he called to Culpepper.

In his muddled fury the man began once again trying to hold her on the animal. It was backing slowly towards a stone seat in the balustrade, and man and woman swayed and tottered together.

The King said:

'Let her descend and rest upon the seat.'

His mind was swinging back already to his own heavy sorrows. On the stone seat the woman's head lay back upon the balustrade, her eyes were closed and her face livid to the sky. Culpepper, using his teeth to the finger ends, tore the gloves from his hands.

Henry drew Cromwell towards the gatehouse. He had it dimly in his mind to send one of his gentlemen to the assistance of that man and woman.

'Aye, teach me to sleep at night,' he said. 'It is you who make me work.'

'It is for your Highness' dear sake.'

'Aye, for my sake,' the King said angrily. He burst into a sudden invective: 'Thou hast murdered a many men ... for my sake. Thou hast found out plots that were no plots: old men hate me, old mothers, wives, maidens, harlots ... Why, if I be damned at the end thou shalt escape, for what thou didst thou didst for my sake? Shall it be that?' He breathed heavily. 'My sins are thy glory.'

They reached the long wall of the gatehouse and turned mechanically. A barge at the river steps was disgorging musicians with lutes like half melons set on staves, horns that opened bell mouths to the sky, and cymbals that clanged in the rushing of the river. With his eyes upon them Henry said: 'A common man may commonly choose his bedfellow.' They had reminded him of the Queen for whose welcome they had been commanded.

Cromwell swept his hand composedly round the half horizon that held the palace, the grey river and the inlands.

'Your Highness may choose among ten thousand,' he answered.

The sound of a horn blown faintly to test it within the gatehouse, the tinkle of a lutestring, brought to the King's lips: 'Aye. Bring me music that shall charm my thoughts. You cannot do it.'

'A Queen is in the nature of a defence, a pledge, a cement, the keystone of a bulwark,' Cromwell said. 'We know now our friends and our foes. You may rest from this onwards.'

He spoke earnestly: This was the end of a long struggle. The King should have his rest.

They moved back along the terrace. The woman's head still lay back, her chin showed pointed and her neck, long, thin and supple. Culpepper was bending over her, sprinkling water out of his cap upon her upturned face.

The King said to Cromwell: 'Who is that wench?' and, in the same tone: 'Aye, you are a great comforter. We shall see how the cat jumps,' and then, answering his own question, 'Norfolk's niece?'

His body automatically grew upright, the limp disappeared from his gait and he moved sturdily and gently towards them.

Culpepper faced round like a wild cat from a piece of meat, but seeing the great hulk, the intent and friendly eyes, the gold collar over the chest, the heavy hands, and the great feet that appeared to hold down the very stones of the terrace, he stood rigid in a pose of disturbance.

'Why do ye travel?' the King asked. 'This shall be Katharine Howard?'

Culpepper's hushed but harsh voice answered that they came out of Lincolnshire on the Norfolk border. This was the Lord Edmund's daughter.

'I have never seen her,' the King said.

'Sh'ath never been in this town.'

The King laughed: 'Why, poor wench!'

'Sh'ath been well schooled,' Culpepper answered proudly, 'hath had mastern, hath sung, hath danced, hath your Latin and your Greek . . . Hath ten daughters, her father.'

The King laughed again: 'Why, poor man!'

'Poorer than ever now,' Culpepper muttered. Katharine Howard stirred uneasily and his face shot round to her. 'Rioters have brent his only house and wasted all his sheep.'

The King frowned heavily: 'Anan? Who rioted?'

'These knaves that love not our giving our ploughlands to sheep,' Culpepper said. 'They say they starved through it. Yet 'tis the only way to wealth. I had all my wealth by it. By now 'tis well gone, but I go to the wars to get me more.'

'Rioters?' the King said again, heavily.

' 'Twas a small tulzie—a score of starved yeomen here and there. I killed seven. The others were they that were hanged at Norwich . . . But the barns were brent, the sheep gone, and the house down and the servants fled. I am her cousin of the mother's side. Of as good a strain as Howards be.'

Henry, with his eyes still upon them, beckoned behind his back for Cromwell to come. A score or so of poor yeomen, hinds and women, cast out of their tenancies that wool might be grown for the Netherlands weavers, starving, desperate, and seeing no trace of might and order in their hidden lands, had banded, broken a few hedges and burnt a few barns before the possé of the country could come together and take them.

The King had not heard of it or had forgotten it, because such risings were so frequent. His brows came down into portentous and bulging knots, his eyes were veiled and threatening towards the woman's face. He had conceived that a great rebellion had been hidden from his knowledge.

She raised her head and shrieked at the sight of him, half started to her feet, and once more sank down on the bench, clasping at her cousin's hand. He said:

'Peace, Kate, it is the King.'

She answered: 'No, no,' and covered her face with her hands.

Henry bent a little towards her, indulgent, amused, and gentle as if to a child.

'I am Harry,' he said.

She muttered:

'There was a great crowd, a great cry. One smote me on the arm. And then this quiet here.'

She uncovered her face and sat looking at the ground. Her furs were all grey, she had had none new for four years, and they were tight to her young body that had grown into them. The roses embroidered on her glove had come unstitched, and, against the steely grey of the river, her face in its whiteness had the tint of mother of pearl and an expression of engrossed and grievous absence.

'I have fared on foul ways this journey,' she said.

'Thy father's barns we will build again,' the King answered. 'You shall have twice the sheep to your dower. Show me your eyes.'

'I had not thought to have seen the King so stern,' she answered.

Culpepper caught at the mule's bridle.

'Y' are mad,' he muttered. 'Let us begone.'·

'Nay, in my day,' the King answered, 'y'ad found me more than kind.'

She raised her eyes to his face, steadfast, enquiring and unconcerned. He bent his great bulk downwards and kissed her upon the temple.

'Be welcome to this place.' He smiled with a pleasure in his own affability and because, since his beard had pricked her, she rubbed her cheek. Culpepper said:

'Come away. We stay the King's Highness.'

Henry said: 'Bide ye here.' He wished to hear what Cromwell might say of these Howards, and he took him down the terrace.

Culpepper bent over her with his mouth opened to whisper.

'I am weary,' she said. 'Set me a saddle cushion behind my shoulders.'

He whispered hurriedly:

'I do not like this place.'

'I like it well. Shall we not see brave shews?'

'The mule did stumble on the threshold.'

'I marked it not. The King did bid us bide here.'

She had once more laid her head back on the stone balustrade.

'If thou lovest me...' he whispered. It enraged and confused him to have to speak low. He could not think of any words.

She answered unconcernedly:

'If thou lovest my bones ... they ache and they ache.'

'I have sold farms to buy thee gowns,' he said desperately.

'I never asked it,' she answered coldly.

Henry was saying:

'Ah, Princes take as is brought them by others. Poor men be commonly at their own choice.' His voice had a sort of patient regret. 'Why brought ye not such a wench?'

Cromwell answered that in Lincoln, they said, she had been a coin that would not bear ringing.

'You do not love her house,' the King said. 'Y' had better have brought me such a one.'

Cromwell answered that his meaning was she had been won by others. The King's Highness should have her for a wink.

Henry raised his shoulders with a haughty and angry shrug. Such a quarry was below his stooping. He craved no light loves.

'I do not miscall the wench,' Cromwell answered. She

was as her kind. The King's Highness should find them all of a make in England.

'Y' are foulmouthed,' Henry said negligently. ''Tis a well-spoken wench. You shall find her a place in the Lady Mary's house.'

Cromwell smiled, and made a note upon a piece of paper that he pulled from his pocket.

Culpepper, his arms jerking angularly, was creaking out:

'Come away, a' God's name. By all our pacts. By all our secret vows.'

'Ay thou didst vow and didst vow,' she said with a bitter weariness. 'What hast to shew? I have slept in filthy beds all this journey. Speak the King well. He shall make thee at a word.'

He spat out at her.

'Is thine eye cocked up to that level?... I am very hot, very choleric. Thou hast seen me. Thou shalt not live. I will slay thee. I shall do such things as make the moon turn bloody red.'

'Aye art thou there?' she answered coldly. 'Ye have me no longer upon lone heaths and moors. Mend thy tongue. Here I have good friends.'

Suddenly he began to entreat:

'Thy mule did stumble—an evil omen. Come away, come away. I know well thou lovest me.'

'I know well I love thee too well,' she answered, as if in scorn of herself.

'Come away to thy father.'

'Why what a bother is this,' she said. 'Thou wouldst to the wars to get thee gold? Thou wouldst trail a pike? Thou canst do little without the ear of some captain. Here is the great captain of them all.'

'I dare not speak here,' he muttered huskily. 'But this King...' He paused and added swiftly: 'He is of an ill omen to all Katharines.'

'Why, he shall give me his old gloves to darn,' she laughed. 'Fond knave, this King standeth on a mountain a league high. A King shall take notice of one for the duration of a raindrop's fall. Then it is done. One may make oneself ere it reach the ground, or never. Besides, 'tis a well-spoken elder. 'Tis the spit of our grandfather Culpepper.'

When Henry came hurrying back, engrossed, to send Culpepper and the mule to the gatehouse for a guide, she laughed gently for pleasure.

Culpepper said tremulously: 'She hath her father's commands to hasten to Dover.'

'Her father taketh and giveth commands from me,' Henry answered, and his glove flicked once more towards the gate. He had turned his face away before Culpepper's hand grasped convulsively at his dagger and he had Katharine Howard at his side sweeping back towards Cromwell.

She asked, confidingly and curiously: 'Who is that lord?' and, after his answer, she mused, 'He is no friend to Howards.'

'Nay, that man taketh his friends among mine,' he answered. He stopped to regard her, his face one heavy and indulgent smile. The garter on his knee, broad and golden, showed her the words: '*Y pense*'; the collars moved up and down on his immense chest, the needlework of roses was so fine that she wondered how many women had sat up how many nights to finish it: but the man was grey and homely.

'I know none of your ways here,' she said.

'Never let fear blanch thy cheeks till we are no more thy friend,' he reassured her. He composed one of his gallant speeches:

'Here lives for thee nothing but joy.' Pleasurable hopes should be her comrades while the jolly sun shone, and sweet content at night her bedfellow. . . .

He handed her to the care of the Lord Cromwell to take her to the Lady Mary's lodgings. It was unfitting that she should walk with him, and, with his heavy and bearlike gait, swinging his immense shoulders, he preceded them up the broad path.

VI

Cromwell watched the King's great back with an attentive smile. He said, ironically, that he was her ladyship's servant.

'I would ye were,' she answered. 'They say you love not those that I love.'

'I would have you not heed what men say,' he answered, grimly. 'I am douce to those that be of good-will to his Highness. Those that hate me are his ill-wishers.'

'Then the times are evil,' she said, 'for they are many.'

She added suddenly, as if she could not keep a prudent silence:

'I am for the Old Faith in the Old Way. You have hanged many dear friends of mine whose souls I pray for.'

He looked at her attentively.

She had a supple, long body, a fair-tinted face, fair and reddish hair, and eyes that had a glint of almond green—but her cheeks were flushed and her eyes sparkled. She was so intent upon speaking her mind that she had forgotten the pain of her arm. She thought that she must have said enough to anger this brewer's son. But he answered only:

'I think you have never been in the King's court'—and, from his tranquil manner, she realised very suddenly that this man was not the dirt beneath her feet.

She had never been in the King's court; she had never, indeed, been out of the North parts. Her father had always been a very poor man, with an ancient castle and a small estate that he had nearly always neglected because it had not paid for the farming. Living men she had never respected—for they seemed to her like wild beasts when she compared them with such of the ancients as Brutus or as Seneca. She had been made love to and threatened by such men as her cousin; she had been made love to and taught Latin by her pedagogues. She was more learned than any man she had ever met—and, thinking upon the heroes of Plutarch, she found the present times despicable. She hardly owed allegiance to the King. Now she had seen him and felt his consciousness of his own power, she was less certain. But the King's writs had hardly run in the Northern parts. Her men-folk and her mother's people had hanged their own peasants when they thought fit. She had seen bodies swinging from tree-tops when she rode hawking. All that she had ever known of the King's power was when the convent by their castle gates had been thrown out of doors, and then her men-folk, cursing and raging, had sworn that it was the work of Crummock. 'Knaves ruled about the King.'

If knaves ruled about him, the King was not a man that one need trouble much over. Her own men-folk, she knew, had made and unmade Kings. So that, when she thought of the hosts of saints and of the blessed angels that hovered, wringing their hands and weeping above England, she had wondered a little at times why they had never unmade this King.

But to her all these things had seemed very far away. She had nothing to do but to read books in the learned tongues, to imagine herself holding disquisitions upon the spiritual republic of Plato, to ride, to shoot with the bow, to do needlework, or to chide the maids. Her cousin had loved her passionately; it was true that once, when she had had nothing to her back, he had sold a farm to buy her a gown. But he had menaced her with his knife till she was weary, and the ways of men were troublesome to her; nevertheless she submitted to them with a patient wisdom.

She submitted to the King; she submitted—though she hated him by repute—to Cromwell's catechism as they followed the King at a decent interval.

He walked beside her with his eyes on her face. He spoke of the King's bounty in a voice that implied his own power. She was to be the Lady Mary's woman. He had that lady especially in his good will, he saved for her household ladies of egregious gifts, presence and attainments. They received liberal honorariums, seven dresses by the year, vails, presents, perfumes from the King's own still-rooms, and a parcel-gilt chain at the New Year. The Lady Rochford, who ruled over these ladies, was kind, courteous, free in her graces as in the liberties she allowed the ladies under her easy charge.

He enlarged upon this picture as if it were a bribe that he alone could offer or withhold. And something at once cautious and priestly in his tone let her quick intuition know that he was both warning her and sounding her, to see how far her mutinous spirit would carry her. Once he said, 'There must be tranquillity in the kingdom. The times are very evil!'

She had felt very quickly that insults to this man would be a useless folly. He could not even feel them, and she kept her eyes on the ground and listened to him.

He went on sounding her. It was part of his profession of kingcraft to know the secret hearts of every person with whom he spoke.

'And your goodly cousin?' He paused. The King had commanded that a place should be found for him. 'Should he be best at Calais? There shall be blows struck there.'

She knew very well that he was trying to discover how much she loved her cousin, and she answered in a low voice, 'I would have him stay here. He is the sole friend I have in this place.'

Cromwell said, with a hidden and encouraging meaning, her cousin was not her only friend there.

'Aye, but your lordship is not so old a friend as he.'

'Not me. Call me your good servant.'

'There is even then my uncle.'

'Little good of a friend you will have of Norfolk. 'Tis a bitter apple and a very rotten plank to lean upon.'

She could not any longer miss his meaning. The King's scarlet and immense figure was already in the grey shadow of the arch under the tower. In walking, they had come near him, and while they waited he stood for a minute, gazing back down the path with boding and pathetic eyes; then he disappeared.

She looked at Cromwell and thanked him for the warning, '*quia spicula praevisa minus laedunt.*'

'I would have you read it: *gaudia plus laetificant,*' he answered gravely.

A man with a conch-shaped horn upturned was suddenly blowing beneath the archway seven hollow and reverberating grunts of sound that drowned his voice. A clear answering whistle came from the water-gate. Cromwell stayed, listening attentively; another stood forward to blow four blasts, another six, another three. Each time the whistle answered. They were the great officers' signals for their barges that the men blew, and the whistle signified that these lay at readiness in the tideway. A bustle of men running, calling, and making pennons ready, began beyond the archway in the quadrangle.

Cromwell's face grew calm and contented; the King was sending to meet Anne of Cleves.

'Y' are well read?' he asked her slowly.

'I was brought up in the Latin tongue or ever I had the English,' she answered. 'I had a good master, one that spoke the learned language always.'

'Aye, Nicholas Udal,' Cromwell said.

'You know all men in the land,' she said, with fear and surprise.

'I had him to master for the Lady Mary, since he is well disposed.'

' 'Tis an arrant knave tho' the best of pedagogues,' she answered. 'He was cast out of his mastership at Eton for being a rogue.'

'For that, the worshipful your father had him to master,' he said ironically.

'No, for that he was a ruined man, and taught for his victuals. We welly starved at home, my sisters and I.'

He said slowly:

'The better need that you should grow beloved here.'

Standing there, before the bushes where no ears could overhear, he put to her more questions. She had some Greek, more than a little French, she could judge a good song, she could turn a verse in Latin or the vulgar tongue. She professed to be able to ride well, to be conversant with the terms of venery, to shoot with the bow, and to have studied the Fathers of the Church.

'These things are well liked in high places,' he said. 'His Highness' self speaks five tongues, loveth a nimble answer, and is a noble huntsman.' He surveyed her as if she were a horse he were pricing. 'But. I doubt not you have appraised yourself passing well,' he uttered.

'I have had some to make me pleasant speeches,' she answered, 'but too many cannot be had.'

'See you,' he said slowly, 'these tuckets that they blow from the gate signify that the new Queen cometh with a great state.' He bit his under lip and looked at her meaningly. 'But a great state ensueth a great heaviness to the head of the State. *Principis hymen, principium gravitatis.* ... 'Tis a small matter to me; you may make it a great one to your ladyship's light fortunes.'

She knew that he awaited her saying:

'I do not take your lordship,' and she pulled the hood further over her face because it was cold, and uttered the words with her eyes on the ground.

'Why,' he said readily, 'you are a lady having gifts that are much in favour in these days. Be careful to use those gifts and no others. Meddle in nothing that does not concern you. So you may make a great marriage with some lord in favour. But meddle in naught else!'

She would find many to set her an evil example. The other ladies amongst whom she was going were a mutinous knot. Let her be careful! If by her good behaviour she earned it, he would put the King in mind to advance her. If by good speeches and good example—since she had great store of learning—she could turn the hearts of these wicked ladies; if she could report to him evil designs or plots, he would speak to the King in such wise that His Highness should give her a great dower and any lord would marry her. Or he would advance her cousin so that he should become marriageable.

She said submissively:

'Your lordship would have me become a spy upon the ladies who shall be my fellows?'

He waved his hand with a large and calming gesture.

'I would have you work for the good of the State as you find it,' he said gravely. 'That, too, is a doctrine of the Ancients.' He cited the case of Seneca, who supported the government of Nero, and she noted that he twisted to suit his purpose Tacitus' account of the soldiers of that same Prince.

Nevertheless, she made no comment. For she knew that it is the nature of men calmly to ask hateful sacrifices of women. But her throat ached with rage. And when she followed him along the corridors of the palace she seemed to feel that each man, each woman that they passed hated that lord with a hatred born of fear.

He walked in front of her arrogantly, as if she were a straw to be drawn along in the wind of his progress. Doors flew open at a flick of his finger.

Suddenly they were in a tall room, long, and dim because it faced the north. It seemed an empty cavern, but there were in it many books upon a long table and at the far end, so that they looked quite small, two figures stood before a reading-pulpit. The voice of the serving man who had thrown open the door made the words 'The Lord Privy Seal of England' echo mournfully along the gilded and dim rafters of the ceiling.

Cromwell hastened over the smooth, cold floor. The woman's figure in black, the long tail of her hood falling almost to her feet like a widow's veil, turned from the pulpit; a man remained bent down at his reading.

'*Annuntio vobis gaudium magnum,*' Cromwell's voice uttered. The lady stood, rigid and straight, her hands clasped before her. Her face, pale so that not even a touch of red showed above the cheekbones and hardly any in the tightly-pursed lips, was as if framed in her black hood that fastened beneath the chin. The high, narrow forehead had the hair tightly drawn back so that none was visible, and the coif that showed beneath the hood was white, like a nun's; the temples were hollowed so that she looked careworn inexpressibly, and her lips had hard lines around them. Above her head all sounds in that dim room seemed to whisper for a long time among the rafters as if here dwelt something mysterious, sepulchral, a great grief or a great passion.

'I announce to you a master-joy,' Cromwell was saying. 'I bring your La'ship a damsel of great erudition and knowledge of good letters.'

His voice was playful and full; his back was bent supply. His face lit up with a debonnaire and pleasant smile. The lady's eyes turned upon the girl, forbidding and suspicious; she remained motionless, even her lips did not move. Cromwell said that this was a Katharine of the Howards, and one fit to aid her Ladyship and Magister Udal with their erudite commentary of Plautus his works.

The man at the reading desk looked round and then back at his book. His pen scratched upon the margin of a great volume. Katharine Howard was upon her knees grasping at the lady's hand to kiss it. But it was snatched roughly away.

'This is a folly,' the voice came harshly from the pursed lips. 'Get up, wench.' Katharine remained kneeling. For this was the Lady Mary of England—a martyr for whom she had prayed nightly since she could pray.

'Get up, fool,' the voice said above her head. 'It is proclaimed treason to kneel to me. This is to risk your neck to act thus before Privy Seal.'

The hard words were aimed straight at the face of Cromwell.

'Your ladyship knows well I would fain have it otherwise,' he answered softly.

'I do not ask it,' she answered.

He maintained a gentle smile of deprecation, beckoning a little with his head and with his eyes, begging her for private conversation. She lifted Katharine roughly to her feet and followed him to a distant window. She seemed as if she were an automaton without will or independent motions of her own, so small were her steps and her feet so hidden beneath her stiff black skirts. He began talking to her in a voice of which only the persuasive higher notes came into the room.

At that time she was still proclaimed bastard, and her name was erased from the list of those it was lawful to pray for in the churches. At times she endured great hardships, even to going short of food, for she suffered from a wasting complaint that made her a great eater. But starvation could not make her submit to the King, her father, or to the Lord Cromwell who was ruler in the land. Sometimes they gave her a great train, strove to make her dress herself richly, and dragged her to such festivals as this of the marriage with Anne of Cleves. This was done when the Lord Privy Seal dangled her before the eyes of the Emperor of France as a match; then it was necessary to increase the appearance of her worth in England. But sometimes the King, out of a warm and generous feeling of satisfaction with his young son, was moved to behave bountifully to his daughter, and, seeking to dazzle her with his munificence, gave her golden crosses and learned books annotated with his own hand, richly jewelled and with embroidered covers. Or when the Emperor, her cousin, interceded that she should be treated more kindly, she was threatened with the block. Of late Cromwell had set himself to gain her heart with his intrigue that he could make so smooth and with his air that could be so gentle—that the King found so lovable. But nothing moved her to set her hand to a deed countenancing her dead mother's disgrace; to smile upon her father and his minister, who had devised the means for casting down her mother; or to consent to relinquish her right to the throne. So that at times, when the cloud of the Church abroad, and of the rebellions all over the extremities of the kingdoms, threatened very greatly, the King was driven to agonies of fear and rage lest his enemies or his subjects should displace him who was excommunicated and set her, whom all Catholics regarded as undergoing a martyrdom, on his throne. He feared her sometimes so much that it was only Cromwell that saved her from death. Cromwell would spend hours of his busy days in the long window of her work room, urging her to submission, dilating upon the powers that might be hers, studying her tastes to devise bribes for her. It was with that aim, because her whole days in her solitude were given to the learned writers, that he had sought out for her Magister Udal as a companion and preceptor who might both please her with his erudition and induce her to look kindly upon the New Learning and a more lax habit of mind. But she never thanked Cromwell. Whilst he talked she remained frozen and silent. At times, under the spur of a cold rage, she said harsh things of himself and her father, calling upon the memory of her mother and the wrongs her Church had suffered—and, on his departing, before he had even left the room she would return, frigidly and without change of face, to the book upon her desk.

So the Privy Seal talked to her by the window for the fiftieth time. Katharine Howard saw, before the high reading pulpit, the back of a man in the long robes of a Master of Arts. He held a pen in his hand and turned over his shoulder at her a face thin, brown, humorous and deprecatory, as if he were used to bearing chiding with philosophy.

'Magister Udal!' she uttered.

He motioned with his mouth for her to be silent, but pointed with the feather of his quill to a line of a little book that lay upon the pulpit near his elbow. She came closer to read:

'*Circumspectatrix cum oculis emisitiis!*' and written above it in a minute hand: 'A spie with eyes that peer about and stick out.'

He pointed over his shoulder at the Lord Privy Seal.

'How poor this room is, for a King's daughter!' she said, without much dropping her voice.

He hissed: 'Hush! hush!' with an appearance of terror,

and whispered, forming the words with his lips rather than uttering them: 'How fared you and your house in the nonce?'

'I have read in many texts,' she answered, 'to pass the heavy hours.'

He spoke then, aloud and with an admonitory air:

'Never say the heavy hours—for what hours are heavy that can be spent with the ancient writers for companions?'

She avoided his reproachful eyes with:

'My father's house was burnt last month; my cousin Culpepper is in the courts below. Dear Nick Ardham, with his lute, is dead an outlaw beyond sea, and Sir Ferris was hanged at Doncaster—both after last year's rising, pray all good men that God assail them!'

Udal muttered:

'Hush, for God's dear sake. That is treason here. There is a listener behind the hangings.'

He began to scrawl hastily with a dry pen that he had not time to dip in the well of ink. The shadow of the Lord Cromwell's silent return was cast upon them both, and Katharine shivered.

He said harshly to the magister:

'I will that you write me an interlude in the vulgar tongue in three days' time. Such a piece as being spoken by skilful players may make a sad man laugh.'

Udal said: 'Well-a-day!'

'It shall get you advancement. I am minded the piece shall be given at my house before his Highness and the new Queen in a week.'

Udal remained silent, dejected, his head resting upon his breast.

'For,' Cromwell spoke with a raised voice, 'it is well that the King be distracted of his griefs.' He went on as if he were uttering an admonition that he meant should be heeded and repeated. The times were very evil with risings, mutinies in close fortresses, schism, and the bad hearts of men. Here, therefore, he would that the King should find distraction. Such of them as had gifts should display those talents for his beguiling; such of them as had beauty should make valuable that beauty; others whose wealth could provide them with rich garments and pleasant displays should work, each man and each woman, after his sort or hers. 'And I will that you report my words where either of you have resort. Who loves me shall hear it; who fears me shall take warning.'

He surveyed both Katharine and the master with a heavy and encouraging glance, having the air of offering great things if they aided him and avoided dealing with his enemies.

The Lady Mary was gliding towards them like a cold shadow casting itself upon his warm words; she would have ignored him altogether, knowing that contempt is harder to bear than bitter speeches. But the fascination of hatred made it hard to keep aloof from her father's instrument. He looked negligently over his shoulder and was gone before she could speak. He did not care to hear more bitter words that could make the breach between them only wider, since words once spoken are so hard to wash away, and the bringing of this bitter woman back to obedience to her father was so great a part of his religion of kingcraft. In that, when it came, there should be nothing but concord and oblivion of bitter speeches, silent loyalty, and a throne upheld, revered, and unassailable.

Udal groaned lamentably when the door closed upon him:

'I shall write to make men laugh! In the vulgar tongue! I! To gain advancement!'

The Lady Mary's face hardly relaxed:

'Others of us take harder usage from my lord,' she said. She addressed Katharine: 'You are named after my mother. I wish you a better fate than your namesake had.' Her harsh voice dismayed Katharine, who had been prepared to worship her. She had eaten nothing since dawn, she had travelled very far and with this discouragement the pain in her arm came back. She could find no words to say, and the Lady Mary continued bitterly: 'But if you love that dear name and would sojourn near me I would have you hide it. For—though I care little—I would yet have women about me that believe my mother to have been foully murdered.'

'I cannot easily dissemble.' Katharine found her tongue. 'Where I hate I speak things disparaging.'

'That I attest to of old,' Udal commented. 'But I shall be shamed before all learned doctors, if I write in the vulgar tongue.'

'Silence is ever best for me!' the Lady Mary answered her deadly. 'I live in the shadows that I love.'

'That, full surely, shall be reversed,' Katharine said loyally.

'I do not ask it,' Mary said.

'Wherefore must I write in the vulgar tongue?' Udal asked again, 'Oh, Mistress of my actions and my heart, what whim is this? The King is an excellent good Latinist!'

'Too good!' the Lady Mary said bitterly. 'With his learning he hath overset the Church of Christ.'

She spoke harshly to Katharine: 'What reversal should give my mother her life again? Wench! Wench!...' Then she turned upon Udal indifferently:

'God knows why this man would have you write in the vulgar tongue. But so he wills it.'

Udal groaned.

'My dinner hour is here,' the Lady Mary said. 'I am very hungry. Get you to your writing and take this lady to my women.'

VII

The Lady Mary's rooms were seventeen in number; they ran the one into the other, but they could each be reached by the public corridor alongside. It was Magister Udal's privilege, his condition being above that of serving man, to make his way through the rooms if he knew that the

Lady Mary was not in one of them. These chambers were tall and gloomy; the light fell into them bluish and dismal; in one a pane was lacking in a window; in another a stool was upset before a fire that had gone out.

To traverse this cold wilderness Udal had set on his cap. He stood in front of Katharine Howard in the third room and asked:

'You are ever of the same mind towards your magister?'

'I was never of any mind towards you,' she answered. Her eyes went round the room to see how Princes were housed. The arras pictured the story of the nymph Galatea; the windows bore intertwined in red glass the cyphers H and K that stood for Katharine of Aragon. 'Your broken fortunes are mended?' she asked indifferently.

He pulled a small book out of his pocket, ferreted among the leaves and then setting his eye near the page pointed out his beloved line:

'*Pauper sum, pateor, fateor, quod Di dant fero.*' Which had been translated: 'I am poor, I confess; I bear it, and what the gods vouchsafe that I take'—and on the broad margin of the book had written: 'Cicero sayeth: That one cannot sufficiently praise them that be patient having little: And Seneca: The first measure of riches is to have things necessary—and, as ensueth therefrom, to be therewith content!'

'I will give you a text from Juvenal,' she said, 'to add to these: Who writes that no man is poor unless he be worthy of ridicule.'

He winced a little.

'Nay, you are hard! The text should be read: Nothing else maketh poverty so hard to bear as that it forceth men to ridiculous shifts. . . . *Quam quod ridiculos esse* . . .'

'Aye, magister, you are more learned even yet than I,' she said indifferently. She made a step towards the next door but he stood in front of her holding up his thin hands.

'You were my best pupil,' he said, with a hungry humility as if he mocked himself. 'Poor I am, but mated to me you should live as do the Hyperboreans, in a calm and voluptuous air.'

'Aye, to hang myself of weariness, as they do,' she answered.

He corrected her with the version of Pliny, but she answered only: 'I have a great thirst upon me.'

His eyes were humorous, despairing and excited.

'Why should a lady not love her master?' he asked. 'There are examples. Know you not the old rhyme:

' "It was a lording's daughter, the fairest one of three,
   Why lovéd of her master. . . ." '

'Ah, unspeakable!' she said. 'You bring me examples in the vulgar tongue!'

'I babble for joy at seeing you and for grief at your harsh words,' he answered.

She stood waiting with a sort of haughty submissiveness.

'I would you would delay your wooing. I have been on the road since dawn with neither bit nor sup.'

He protested that he had starved more hideously than Tantalus since he had seen her last.

She gave him indifferently her cheek to kiss.

'For pity's sake take me where I may rest,' she said, 'I have a maimed arm.'

* * * *

He uttered her panegyric, after a model of Tibullus, to the Lady Rochford and the seven maids of honour under that lady's charge. He was set upon Katharine's enjoyment, and he invented a lie that the King had commanded a dress to be found for her to attend at the revels that night. The maids were already dressing themselves. Two of them were fairheaded, and four neither fair nor dark; but one was dark as night, and dressed all in black with a white coif, so that she resembled a magpie. Some were curling each other's hair and others tightening stay-laces with little wheels set in their companions' backs. Their bare shoulders were blue with the cold of the great room, and their dresses lay in heaps upon sheets that were spread about the clean floor—brocades sewn with pearls, velvets that were inlaid with filagree work, indoor furs and coifs of fine lawn that were delicately edged with black thread.

The high sounds of their laughter had reached through the door, but a dead silence fell. The dark girl with a very long bust that raked back like a pigeon's, and with dark and sparkling eyes, tittered derisively at the magister and went on slowly rubbing a perfumed ointment into the skin of her throat and shoulders.

'Shall he bring his ragged doxies here too?' she laughed. 'What a taradiddle is this of Cophetua and a beggar wench.' The other maids all tittered derisively at Udal.

The Lady Rochford, warming her back close before the fire, said helplessly, 'I have no dresses beyond what you see.' She was already attired in a bountiful wine-coloured velvet that was embroidered with silver wire into entwined monograms of the initials of her name. Her hood of purple made, above her ample brows, a castellated pattern resembling the gate of a drawbridge. She, being the mistress of that household, and compassionately loved by the ladies because she was so helpless, timorous, and unable to control them, they had combined to comb and perfume her and to lace her stomacher before setting about their own clothing. White-haired and with a wrinkled face, she appeared, under her rich clothes, like some will-less and pallid captive that had been gorgeously bedizened to grace a conqueror's triumph. She was cousin to the late Queen Anne Boleyn, and the terror of her own escape, when the Queen and so many of her house had been swept away, seemed still to remain in the drawing-in of her eyes. In the mien of the youngest girls there, there could be seen a strained tenseness of lids and lips as though, in the midst of laughter, they were hearkening for distant sounds or the rustle of listeners behind the tapestry. And where a small door came into one wall they had pulled down the arras from in front of it, so that no one should enter unobserved.

Lady Rochford addressed herself to Katharine with limp gestures of protest:

'God knows I would help you to a gown, but we have no more than we are granted; here are seven ladies and seven dresses. Where can another be got? The King's Highness knoweth little of ladies' gowns or he had never ordered one against to-night. Each of those hath taken the women seven weeks to sew.'

Udal said with a touch of anger, since it enraged him to have to invent further, as if the one lie about the King were not enough: 'The Lord Privy Seal commanded very strictly this thing to be done. He is this lady's very diligent protector. Have a care how you disoblige her.'

The ladies rustled their slight clothing at that name, turned their backs, and looked at Katharine above their shoulders. The Lady Rochford recoiled so far that her skirts were in danger from the fire in the great hearth; her woebegone, flaccid face was suddenly drawn at the mention of Cromwell, and she appeared about to kneel at Katharine's feet. She looked round at the figures of the girls.

'One of these can stay if your ladyship will wear her dress,' she flustered. 'But who is tall enow? Cicely is too long in the shank. Bess's shoulders are too broad. Alack! God help me! I will do what I can'—and she waved her hands disconsolately.

Cold, fatigue, and her maimed arm made Katharine waver on her feet. This white-haired woman's panic seemed to her grotesque and disgusting.

'Why, the magister lies,' she said. 'I am no such friend of Privy Seal's.'

Swift and wicked glances passed among the girls; the dark one threw back her head and laughed discordantly, like a magpie. She came with a deft and hopping step and gazed at Katharine with her head on one side.

'Old Crummock will want our teeth next to make him a new set. He may have my head, tell him. I have no need for it, it aches so since he killed my men-folk.'

Lady Rochford shuddered as if she had been struck.

'Beseech you,' she said weakly to Katharine. 'Cicely Elliott is sometimes distraught. Believe not that we speak like this among ourselves.' Her eyes wandered in a flustered and piteous way over her girls and she whimpered, 'Jane Gaskell, stand back to back with this lady.'

Katharine Howard cried out, 'Keep your gowns for your backs and your tongues still. Woe betide the girl who calls me a gossip of Privy Seal.'

Cicely Elliott cast her dark head back and uttered one of her discordant laughs at the ceiling, and a girl, hiding behind the others, called out, 'What a fine ——!'

Katharine cried, 'It is all lies that this fool magister utters. I will go to no masques nor revels.' She turned upon Lady Rochford, her face pallid, her lips open: 'Give me water,' she said harshly. 'I will get me back to my pigsties.'

Lady Rochford wrung her hands and protested that her ladyship should not repeat that they were always thus. Privy Seal should not visit it upon them.

The magister blinked upon the riot that his muddling had raised. He called out, 'Be quiet. Be quiet. This lady is sick!' and stretched out his hands to hold Katharine on her feet.

Cicely Elliott cried, 'God send all Crummock's informers always sick.'

'Thou dastard!' Katharine screamed aloud. She tried to speak but she choked; she grasped Udal's hand as if to wring from him the denial of his foolish lies, but a sharp and numbing pain shot up her maimed wrist to her shoulders and leaped across her forehead.

'Thou filthy spy,' the dark girl laughed wildly into her agonised face. 'If there had never been any like thee all the dear men of my house had still breathed.'

Katharine sprang wildly towards her tormentor, but a black sheet seemed to drop across her eyes. She fell right down and screamed as her elbow struck the floor.

PART TWO

THE HOUSE OF EYES

I

A GRAVE and bearded man was found to cup her. He gave her a potion composed of the juice of nightshade and an infusion of churchyard moss. Her eyes grew dilated and she had evil dreams. She lay in a small chamber that was quite bare and had a broken window, and the magister ran from room to room begging for quilts to cover her.

It was nobody's affair. The Lord Privy Seal, her uncle, the Catholics, and the King were still perturbed about Anne of Cleves, and there were no warrants signed for Katharine's housing or food. All the palace was trembling with confusion, for, when the Queen had been upon the point of setting out from Rochester, the King was said to have been overcome by a new spasm of disgust: she was put by again.

The young Earl of Surrey, a cousin of Katharine's, gave Udal contemptuously a couple of crowns towards her nourishment. Udal applied them to bribing Throckmorton, the spy who had been with Privy Seal upon the barge, to inscribe on his lord's tablets the words: 'Katharine Howard to be provided for.' Udal made up his courage sufficiently to speak to the Duke, whom he met in a corridor. The Duke was jaundiced against his niece, because her cousin Culpepper had fallen upon Sir Christopher Aske, the Duke's captain who had kept the postern. It had needed seven men to master him, and this great tumult had arisen in the King's own courtyard. Nevertheless, the Duke sent his astrologer to cast Katharine's horoscope. He signed, too, an order that some girl be found to attend on her.

Udal filled in the girl's name as Margot Poins, the granddaughter of old Badge, of Austin Friars. Even among these clamours his tooth watered for her, and he gave the order to young Poins to execute. The young man rode off into Bedfordshire, where his sister had been sent out of the way to the house of their aunt. He presented the order as in the nature of a writ from the Duke, and amongst Lutherans in London a heavy growl of rage went up— against Norfolk, against the Papists of the Privy Council, and, above all, against Katharine Howard, whom they called the New Harlot.

Katharine, having taken much nightshade juice, was raving upon her bed. The leech became convinced that she was possessed by a demon, because the pupils of her eyes were as large as silver groats, and her hands picked at the coverlets. He ordered that thirteen priests should say an exorcism at the door of her room, and that the potion of nightshade—since it might inconvenience without dislodging the fiend inhabiting her slender body—should be discontinued.

Udal sought for priests, but having no money, he was disregarded by them. He ran to the chaplain of the Bishop of Winchester. For the clergy upheld or ordained by Archbishop Cranmer were held to be less efficacious in matters of witchcraft and possession. Just then Cromwell had triumphed, and Anne of Cleves was upon the water coming to the palace.

Bishop Gardiner's chaplain, a fat man, with beady and guileless eyes sunk in under an immense forehead, imagined that Udal's visit was a pretext for overhearing the words of rage and discomfiture that in that Papist centre might be let drop about the new Queen. For Udal, because Privy Seal had set him with the Lady Mary, passed amongst the Papists for one of Cromwell's informants, and it amused his sardonic and fantastic nature to affect mysterious denials, which made the fiction the more firmly believed and gave to Udal himself a certain hated prestige. The chaplain answered that in the present turmoil no such body as thirteen clergymen could be found.

'But the lady shall be torn in pieces,' Udal shrieked. Panic had overcome him. Who knew that the fiend, having torn his Katharine asunder, might not enter into the body of his Margot, who was already at her bedside? His lips quivered with terror, his eyes smiled furiously, he wrung his hands. He swore he would penetrate to the King's Highness' self. Udal was a man who stuck at nothing to gain a point. He had heard from Katharine that the King had spoken graciously to her, and he swore once more that she was the apple of the King's eye, as well as a beloved disciple of Privy Seal's.

'Be sure,' he foamed, 'they shall be avenged on a Gardiner and his crew if you let her die.'

The chaplain said impassively: 'God forbid that we, who are loyal to his Highness, should listen to these tales you bring us of his lechery!' They had there a new Queen, their duty was to her, and to no Katharine Howard. The bishop's clergy were all joyfully setting to welcome the lady from Cleves, they had no time to waste over a leman's demons. It overjoyed him to refuse Privy Seal's man a boon on the plea of loyalty to the new Queen. Nevertheless, he went straight to the presence of the bishop, and told him the marvels that Udal had reported.

'The man is incontinent and a babbler,' the chaplain said. 'We may believe one tenth.'

'Well, you shall find for once how this wench is housed and where,' his master answered moodily. 'God knows what we may believe in these days. Doubtless the Nuntio of Satan hath a new plot in the hatching.' Making these enquiries, the chaplain came upon the backwash of Udal's reports that the King loved some leman. Some lady, somewhere—some said a Howard, some a Rochford, some would have it a Spanish woman—was being hidden up, either by the King, by the Duke of Norfolk, or by Privy Seal. God knew the truth of these things: but similar had happened before; and it was certain that the Cleves woman had been for long kept dangling at Rochester. Perhaps that was the reason. His Highness had his own ways in these matters: but where there was smoke, generally fire was to be found. The chaplain brought this budget back to Bishop Gardiner. Gardiner swore a wild oath that, by the bones of the Confessor, they had unmasked a new plot of Satan's Legate, the Privy Seal. But, by the grace of God, he would counter-plot him.

Udal, who had started all these rumours, had run to get the help of a Dean of Durham, with whom formerly he had had much converse as to the position of the Islands of the Blest. He never found him; the palace was in confusion, with the doors all open and men running from room to room to ask of each other how far it might be safe to be extravagant in their demonstrations of joy at the coming of the new Queen.

All night long, from about dusk, the palace rang with salvos of artillery, loud shouts and the blowing of horns: the windows glowed duskily now and again with the light of bonfires that leapt up and subsided. Margot Poins, who was used to rejoicings in the City, set the heavy wooden bar across the door in Katharine Howard's room, turned the immense key in the rusty lock, and opened to no knocking until the day broke. There were shouts and stumblings in the corridor outside and the magister himself, very intoxicated and shrieking, came hammering at the door with several others towards one in the morning.

Katharine could walk by noon to the lodging that had at last been assigned to her by Privy Seal's warrant. The magister, having got himself soundly beaten the night before, was still sleeping away the effects of it, so she and Margot stayed for an hour in solitude. Voices passed the door many times, and at last a Master Viridus entered stealthily. He was one of the Lord Cromwell's secretaries, and he bore a purse. His name had been Greene but he had translated it to give a more worshipful sound. His eyes were furtive and he moved his lips perpetually in imitation of his master; wore a hooded cap, and made much use of the Italian language.

'Bounty is the sign of the great, and honourable service ensureth its continuance,' he said in a dry and arrogant voice. 'This is my Lord Privy Seal's vails. My lord hath gone to his own house.'

He presented the purse of gold, and peered round at the room which, following the warrant, had been assigned by a clerk from the Earl Marshal's office.

'I thank your lord, and shall endeavour to deserve his good bounty,' Katharine said. The nightshade juice being left two days behind she had the use of her eyes and much of the stiffness had gone out of her wrist.

'Your ladyship had much the wiser,' he answered. He lifted the hangings and, under pretence of examining into her comfort, peered into the great Flemish press and felt under the heavy black table to see if it had a drawer for papers. Cromwell had been forced, following the King's command, to give Katharine her place. But he had no love for Howards, and already the maids of the Lady Mary were a mutinous knot. Viridus was instructed to keep an attentive eye upon this girl—for they might hang her very easily since she was outspoken; or, having got her neck into a noose, they could work upon her terror and make her spy upon the Lady Mary herself. None of the Lady Mary's women were housed very sumptuously, but in this room there were at least an old tapestry, a large Flemish chair, a feather bed in a niche like an arched cell over which the hangings could be drawn, and a cord of wood for the fire. He hummed and hawed that workmen must come to bring her better hangings, and a servitor be found to keep her door. A watch was to be set on her; the women who measured her for clothes would try to discover whom she loved and hated, and the serving man at her door would report her visitors.

'My lord hath you very present in his mind,' Viridus said.

She was commanded to go on the Saturday to the house

in Austin Friars, where my lord was preparing a great feast in the honour of the Queen.

Katharine said that she had no dress to go in.

'A seemly decent habit shall be got ready,' he answered. 'You shall sit in a gallery in private, and it shall be pointed out to you what lords you shall speak with and whom avoid.' For '*com' è bella giovinezza*' . . . How beautiful is youth, what a pleasant season! And since it lasted but a short space it behoved us all—and her as much as any— to make as much as might be whilst it endured. The regard of a great lord such as Privy Seal brought present favours and future honours in the land, honours being pleasant in their turn, when youth is passed, like the mellow suns of autumn. 'Thereby indeed,' he apostrophised her, 'the savour of youth reneweth itself again and again . . . "*Anzi rinuova come fa la luna,*" in the words of Boccace.'

Her fair and upright beauty made Viridus acknowledge how excellent a spy upon the Lady Mary she might make. Papistry and a loyal love for the Old Faith seemed to be as strong in her candid eyes as it was implicit in her name. The Lady Mary might trust her for that and talk with her because of her skill in the learned tongues. Then, if they held her in their hands, how splendid a spy she might make, being so trusted! She might well be won for their cause by the offer of liberal rewards, though Privy Seal's hand had been heavy upon all her kinsfolk. These men of Privy Seal's get from him a maxim which he got in turn from his master Macchiavelli: '*Advance therefore those whom it shall profit thee to make thy servants: for men forget sooner the death of a father than the loss of a patrimony*'—and either by threats or by rewards they might make her very useful.

She had been minded to mock him in the beginning of his speech, but his dangerous pale-blue eyes made her feel that if he were ridiculous he was also very powerful, and that she was in the hands of these men.

Therefore she answered that youth indeed was a pleasant

season when health, good victuals and the love of God sustained it.

He surveyed her out of the corners of his eyes.

'Seek, then, to deserve these good things,' he said. He stayed some time longer directing her how she should wear her clothes, and then in the gathering dusk he dwindled stealthily through the door.

'It is to make you like a chained-up beast or slave,' Margot said to her mistress.

'Why, hold your tongue, coney, after to-day,' Katharine answered, 'the walls shall hear. I am a very poor man's daughter and must even earn my bread if I would stay here.'

'They could never tie me so,' Margot retorted.

Her mistress laughed:

'Why, you may set nets for the wind, but what a man will catch is still uncertain.'

It was cold, and they piled up the fire, waiting for some one to bring them candles.

A tall and bulky figure, with a heavy cloak cast over one shoulder in the Spanish fashion, but with a priest's cap, was suddenly in the doorway.

'Ha, magister,' Katharine said, knowing no other man that could visit her. But the firelight shone upon a heavy, firm jaw that was never the magister's, on white hands and in threatening, steadfast eyes.

'I am the unworthy Bishop Gardiner, of Winchester,' a harsh voice said. 'I seek one Katharine Howard. Peace be with you in these evil days.'

Katharine fell upon her knees before this holy man. He gave her his blessing perfunctorily, and muttered some words of the exorcism against demons.

'I am even cured,' Katharine said.

He sent Margot Poins from the room, and stood in the firelight that threw his great shadow to shake upon the hangings, towering above Katharine Howard upon her knees. He was silent, as if he would threaten her, and his brooding eyes glowed and devoured her face. Here then, she thought, was the man from the other camp descending secretly upon her. He had no need to threaten, for she was of his side.

He said that a Magister Udal had reported that she stood in need of Christian aid, and, speaking Latin with a heavy voice, he interrogated her as to her faith. The times were evil: many and various heresies stalked about the land: let her beware of trafficking with them.

Kneeling still in the firelight, she answered that, so far as was lawful, she was a daughter of the Church.

He muttered: 'Lawful!' and looked at her for a long time with brooding and fanatical eyes. 'I hear you have read many heathen books under a strange master.'

She answered: 'Most Reverend, I am for the Old Faith in the old way.'

'A prudent tongue is also a Christian possession,' he muttered.

'Nay there is no one to hear in this room,' she said.

He bent over her to raise her to her feet and holding before her eyes his missal, he indicated to her certain prayers that she should recite in order to prevent the fiend's coming to her again. Suddenly he commanded her to tell him how often she had conversed with the King's Highness.

Gardiner was the bitterest of all whom Cromwell had to hate him. He had been of the King's Council, and a secretary before Cromwell had reached the Court, and, but for Cromwell, he might well have been the King's best minister. But Cromwell had even taken his secretaryship; and he was set upon having Privy Seal down all through those ten years. He had been bishop before any of these changes had been thought of, and by such Papists as Katharine Howard he was esteemed the most holy man in the land.

She told him that she had seen the King but once for a little time.

'They told me it was many times,' he answered fiercely. 'Should I have come here merely to chatter with you?'

There was something sinister and harsh even in the bluish tinge of his shaven jaws, and his agate-blue eyes were sombre, threatening and suspicious.

She answered: 'But once,' and related the story very soberly.

He threatened her with his finger.

'Have a care that you speak truth. Things will not always remain in this guise. I come to warn you that you speak the King with a loyal purpose. His Highness listens sometimes to the promptings of his women.'

'You might have saved your journey,' she answered. 'I could speak no otherwise if he loved me.'

He gazed involuntarily round at the hangings as if he suspected a listener.

'Your Most Reverence does ill to doubt me,' Katharine said submissively. 'I am of a true house.'

'No house is true save where it finds its account,' he answered moodily. He could not believe that she spoke the truth—for he was unable to believe that any man could speak the truth—but it was true she was poorly housed, raggedly dressed and hidden up in a corner. Nevertheless, these might be artifices. He made ostentatiously and disdainfully towards the door.

'Why, God keep you,'—he moved his fingers in a negligent blessing—'I believe you are true, though you are of little use.' Suddenly he shot out:

'If you would stay here in peace your cousin Culpepper must begone.'

Katharine put her hand to her heart in sudden fear of these men who surrounded her and knew everything.

'What hath Tom done?' she asked.

'He hath put a shame upon thee,' the bishop answered. He had fallen upon Sir Christopher Aske: he had been set in chains for it, in the Duke's ward room. But upon the coming of the Queen the night before, all misdemeanants had been cast loose again. Culpepper had been kept by the guards from entering the palace, where he had no place. But he had fallen in with the Magister Udal in the courtyard. Being maudlin and friendly at the time, he had cast his arms round the magister's neck claiming him for a loved acquaintance. They had drunk together and had started, towards midnight, to find the chamber of Katharine Howard, Culpepper seeking his cousin, and the magister, Margot Poins. On the way they had enlisted other jovial souls, and the tumult in the corridor had arisen. 'These scandals are best avoided,' the bishop finished. 'I have known women lose their lives through them when they came to have husbands.'

'I could have calmed him,' Katharine said. 'He is always silent at a word from me.'

Gardiner stood pondering, his head hanging down. His eyes, hard and blue, flashed at her and then down again at the floor.

'They told me you were the King's good friend,' he said, resentfully. 'Your gossip Udal told my chaplain, and it hath been repeated.'

'They will talk where there are a many together,' Katharine answered; 'the magister is a notorious babbler and will have told many lies.'

'He is a spy of Privy Seal's and deep in his councils,' Gardiner answered gloomily.

A heavy wind that had arisen hurled itself against the dark casement. Little flaws of cold air penetrated the room, and the bishop pulled his cap further down over his ears.

'My Lord Privy Seal would send my cousin to Calais where there is fighting to come,' Katharine said.

Gardiner raised his head sharply at Cromwell's name.

'You speak sense at the end,' he muttered. To him too it had occurred that if she was to be the King's peaceably, this madman must begone. If Cromwell wished this lover of this girl out of the way, the reason was not obscure.

'A man of his hath been here this very day,' Katharine said.

'Privy Seal learned whoremastering in Italy,' Gardiner cried triumphantly. 'He saw signs that his Highness inclined to you. Have a care for your little soul.'

'Why, I think Privy Seal had no such vain imagination,' Katharine answered submissively. She would have laughed that the magister's insane babblings should have raised such a coil; but Gardiner was a man esteemed very saintly, and she kept her eyes on the floor.

'Give thou ear to no doctrines of Privy Seal's,' he answered swiftly. 'Thy soul should burn: I will curse thee. If the King shall offer thee favours for thy friends come thou to me for spiritual guidance.'

She opened amazed and candid eyes upon him.

'But this is a folly,' she said. 'A King may regard one for a minute, then it is past. Privy Seal would not bring me up against the King.'

He flashed his gloomy blue eyes at her, suspecting her, and still threatening.

'I know how Privy Seal will plot,' he said passionately. 'Having failed with one woman he will bring another.'

He clenched his hands angrily and unclenched them: the wind moaned for a moment among the chimney stacks.

'So it is!' he cried, from deep down in his chest. 'If it were not so, how is there all this clamour about his Highness and a woman?'

'Most Reverend,' she said, 'there is no end to the inventions of Magister Udal.'

'There is none to the machinations of the fiend, and Udal is of his councils,' he said. 'Be careful, I tell you, for your soul's sake. Cromwell shall come to you offering you great bribes. Have a care I say!'

She attempted to say that Udal had no voice at all in Privy Seal's councils, being a garrulous magpie that no sane man would trust. But Gardiner had crossed his arms and stood, immense and shadowy, in the firelight. He hissed irritably between his teeth when she spoke, as if she interrupted his meditation.

'All the world knows Udal for his spy,' he said, sombrely. 'If Udal hath babbled, God be thanked. I say again: if Privy Seal bring thee to the King, come thou to me. But, by the Grace of Heaven, I will forestall Privy Seal with thee and the King!'

She forbore to contradict him any more; he had this maggot in his head, and was so wild to defeat Privy Seal with his own tool.

He muttered: 'Think you Privy Seal knoweth not the King's taste? I tell you he hath seen an inclination in him towards you. This is a plot, but I have sounded it!'

She let him talk, and asked, with a malice too fine for him to discern:

'I should not shun the King's presence for my soul's sake?'

'God forbid,' he answered. 'I may use thee to bring down Privy Seal.'

He picked up a piece of bark from a faggot beside the fire and rolled it between his fingers. She stood looking at him intently, her lips a little parted, tall, graceful and submissive.

'You are more fair-skinned than any his Highness has favoured before,' he said in a meditative voice. 'Yet Cromwell knows the King's tastes better than any man.' He sank down into her tall-backed chair and suddenly tossed the piece of bark into the fire. 'I would have you walk across the floor, elevating your arms as you were the goddess Flora.'

She tripped towards the door, held her arms above her head, turned her long body to right and left, bent very low in a courtesy to him, and let her hands fall restfully into her lap. The firelight shone upon the folds of her dress and in the white lining of her hood. He looked at her, leaning over the arm of the chair, his blue eyes hard with the strenuous rage of his new project.

'You could take a part in an Italian interlude? A masque?'

'I have a better memory of the French or Latin,' she answered.

'You do not turn pale? Your knees knock not together?'

'I think I blush most,' she said seriously.

He answered, 'You will be the better of a little colour,' and began muffling his face with his cloak.

'See you, then,' his harsh voice commanded. 'You shall see their Highnesses at Privy Seal's house on the Saturday; but they shall see you at mine on the Tuesday. If you are good enough to serve the turn of Privy Seal, you may be good enough to serve mine. The King listens sometimes to the promptings of his women. I will teach you how you may bring this man down and set me in his place.'

She reflected for a moment. 'I would well serve you,' she said. 'But I do not believe this fable of the King, and I have no memory of Italian.' She talked of being the Lady Mary's servant, or that she must get her lady's leave.

His brows grew heavy, his eyes threatening and alarming beneath their heavy lids.

'Be you faithful to me,' he thundered. Even his thin and delicate hands seemed to menace her. 'Retain your obedience to your Faith. Your duty is to that, and to no earthly lady before that.'

Her eyes were cast down, her lips did not move. He said, harshly, 'It will go ill with you if it become known to Cromwell I have visited you. Keep this matter secret as you love your liberty. I will send you the words you shall say by a private bearer. After, maybe, his Highness shall safeguard you, I admonishing him. But the Lady Mary shall bid you obey me in all things.'

He opened the door and put his head out cautiously. Suddenly he drew it back and said in Latin, 'Here is a spy.' He did not flinch, but advanced into the corridor, keeping his back to the servitor whom already Master Viridus had sent to keep her door. Gardiner fumbled in his robes and pulled out his missal. He turned the pages over, and, speaking in a feigned and squeaky voice, once more indicated to her prayers against the visitations of fiends. Reading them aloud, he interspersed the Latin of the missal with the phrases, 'You may pray to God he have not seen my face. Be you very silent and secret, or you are undone. I could in no wise save you from Cromwell unless the King becomes your protector.' He finished in the vulgar tongue. 'I pray my prayers with you may have availed to give you relief. But a simple priest as myself is of small skill in these visitations. You should have sent to some great Churchman or one of the worshipful bishops.'

'Good Father Henry, I thank you,' she answered, having entered into his artifice. He went away, feigning to limp on his right knee, and keeping his face from the spy.

At the corner of the corridor Margot Poins, an immense blonde and gentle figure in Lutheran grey, stood back in the hangings. The Magister Udal leant over her, supporting himself with one hand against the wall above her head and one leg crossed beneath his gown.

'Come you into my room,' Katharine said to the girl; and to the magister, 'Avoid, man of books. I will have no maid of mine undone by thee.'

'*Venio honoris causa*,' he said pertly, and Margot uttered, 'He seeks me in wedlock,' in a gruff, uncontrolled voice of a great young girl's confusion, and immense blushes covered her large cheeks.

Katharine laughed; she was sorely afraid of the serving man behind her, for that he was a spy set there by Viridus she was very sure, and she was casting about in her mind for a device that should let her tell whether or no he had known the bishop. The squeaky voice and the feigned limp seemed to her stratagems ignoble and futile on the part of a great Churchman, and his mania of plots and counter-plottings had depressed and wearied her, for she expected the great to be wise. But she played her part for him as it was her duty. She spoke to the girl with her scarlet cheeks.

'Believe thou the magister after he hath ta'en thee afore a priest. He hath sought me and two score others in the cause of honour. Get you in, sweetheart.'

She pushed the girl in at the door. The serving man sat on his stool; his shock of yellow hair had never known a comb, but he had a decent suit of a purplish wool-cloth. He had his eyes dully on the ground.

'As you value your servitorship, let no man come into

my room when I be out,' Katharine said to him. 'Saving only the Father Henry that was here now.'

The man raised expressionless blue eyes to her face.

'I know not his favours,' he said in a peasant's mutter. 'Maybe I should know him if I saw him again. I am main good at knowing people.'

'Why, he is from the Sheeres,' Katharine added, still playing, though she was certain that the man knew Gardiner. 'You shall know him by his voice and his limp.'

He answered, 'Maybe,' and dropped his eyes to the ground. She sent him to fetch her some candles, and shut the door upon him.

II

The Queen came to the revels given in her honour by the Lord Privy Seal. Cromwell had three hundred servants dressed in new liveries: pikemen with their staves held transversely, like a barrier, kept the road all the way from the Tower Steps to Austin Friars, and in that Lutheran quarter of the town there was a great crowding together. Caps were pitched high and lost for ever, and loud shouts of praise to God went up when the Queen and her Germans passed, with boys casting branches of holm, holly, bay and yew, the only plants that were green in the winter season, before the feet of her mule. But the King did not come. It was reported to the crowd that he was ill at Greenwich.

It was known very well by those that sat at dinner with her that, after three days, he had abandoned his Queen and kept his separate room. She sat eating alone, on high beneath the dais, heavy, silent, placid and so fair that her eyebrows appeared to be white upon her red forehead. She did not speak a word, having no English, and it was considered disgusting that she wiped her fingers upon pieces of bread.

Hostile lords remarked upon all her physical

imperfections, which the King, it was known, had reported to his physicians in a writing of many pages. Besides, she had no English, no French, no Italian; she could not even play cards with his Highness. It was true that they had squeezed her into English stays, but she was reported to have wept at having to mount a horse. So she could not go a-hawking, neither could she shoot with the bow, and her attendants—the women, bound about the middle and spreading out above and below like bolsters, and the men, who wore their immense scolloped hats falling over their ears even at meal-times—excited disgust and derision by the noises they made when they ate.

The Master Viridus had Katharine Howard in his keeping. He took her up into a small gallery near the gilded roof of the long hall and pointed out to her, far below, the courtiers that it was safe for her to consort with, because they were friends of Privy Seal. His manner was more sinister and more meaning.

'You would do well to have to do with no others,' he said.

'I am like to have to do with none at all,' Katharine answered, 'for no mother's son cometh anigh me.'

He looked away from her. Down below she made out her cousin Surrey, sitting with his back ostentatiously turned to a Lord Roydon, of Cromwell's following; her uncle, plunged in his silent and malignant gloom; and Cromwell, his face lit up and smiling, talking earnestly with Chapuys, the Ambassador from the Emperor.

'Eleven hundred dishes shall be served this day,' Viridus proclaimed, seeming to warn her. 'There can no other lord find so many plates of parcel gilt.' His level and cold voice penetrated through all the ascending din of voices, of knives, of tuckets of trumpets that announced the courses of meat and of the three men's songs that introduced the sweet jellies which only Privy Seal, it was said, could direct to be prepared.

'Other lordings all,' Viridus continued with his sermon, 'ha' ruined themselves seeking in vain to vie with my lord.

Most of those you see are broken men, whose favour would be worth naught to you.'

Tables were ranged down each side of the great hall, the men sitting on the right, each wearing upon his shoulder a red rose made of silk since no flowers were to be had. The women, sitting upon the left, had white favours in their caps. In the wide space between these tables were two bears; chained to tall gilt posts, they rolled on their hams and growled at each other. From time to time the serving men who went up and down in the middle let fall great dishes containing craspisces, cranes, swans or boars. These meats were kicked contemptuously aside for the bears to fight over, and their places supplied immediately with new. Other serving men broke priceless bottles of Venetian glass against the corners of tables, and let the costly Rhenish wines run about their feet.

This, the Master Viridus said, was intended to point out the wealth of their lord and his zealousness to entertain his Sovereigns.

'It would serve the purpose as well to give them twice as much fare,' Katharine said.

'They could never contain it,' Viridus answered gravely, 'so great is the bounty of my lord.'

Throckmorton, the spy, enormous, bearded and with the half-lion badge of the Privy Seal hanging round his neck from a gilt chain, walked up and down behind the guests, bearing the wand of a major-domo, affecting to direct the servers when to fill goblets and listening at tables where much wine had been served. Once he looked up at the gallery, and his scrutinising and defiant brown eyes remained for a long time upon Katharine's face, as if he too were appraising her beauty.

'I would not drink much wine with that man listening at my back. He came from my country, and was such a foul villain that mothers fright their children with his name,' Katharine said.

Viridus moved his lips quickly one upon another, and suddenly directed her to observe the new Queen's headdress, broad and stiffened with a wire of gold, upon which large pearls had been sewn.

'Many ladies will now get themselves such headdresses,' he said.

'That will I never,' she answered. It appeared atrocious and Flemish-clumsy, spreading out and overshadowing the Queen's heavy face. Their English hoods with the tails down made the head sleek and comely; or, with the tails folded up and pinned square like flat caps they could give to the face a gallant or a pensive expression.

'Why, I could never get me in at the door of the confessional with such a spreading cloth.'

Viridus had his chin on the rail of the gallery; he gazed down below with his snaky eyes. She could not tell whether he were old or young.

'You would more prudently abandon the confessing,' he said, without looking at her. 'My lord is minded that ladies who look to him should wear such.'

'That is to be a bond-slave,' Katharine cried indignantly. He looked round.

'Here is a great magnificence,' he uttered, moving his hand towards the hall. 'My Lord Privy Seal hath a mighty power.'

'Not power enow to make me a laughing-stock for the men.'

'Why, this is a free land,' he answered. 'You may rot in a ditch if you will, or worse if treasonable actions be brought home to you.'

Down below, wild men dressed in the skins of wolves, hares and stags ran round the tethered bears bearing torches of sweet wood, and a heavy and languorous smoke, like incense, mounted up to the gallery. Viridus' unveiled threat made the necessity for submission come once more into her mind. Other wild men were leading in a lion, immense and lean as if it were a fawn-coloured ass. It roared and pulled at the golden chains by which the knot of men held it. Many ladies shrieked out, but the men dragged the lion into the open space before the dais where the Queen sat unmoved and stolid.

'Would your master have me dip my fingers in the dish and wipe them on bread-manchets as the Queen does?' Katharine asked in a serious expostulation.

'It were an excellent action,' Viridus answered.

There was a brazen flare of trumpets so that the smoke swirled among the rafters. Men with brass helmets and shields of brass were below in the hall.

'They are costumed as the ancient Romans,' Katharine said, lost in other thoughts.

Suddenly she saw that whilst all the other eyes were upon the lion, Throckmorton's glare was again upon her face. He appeared to shake his head and to bow his immense and bearded form. It brought into her mind the dangerous visit of Bishop Gardiner. Suddenly he dropped his eyes.

'You see some friends,' Viridus' voice asked beside her.

'Nay, I have no friends here,' Katharine answered.

She could not tell that the bearded spy's eyes were not merely amorous in their intention, for such looks she was used to, and he was a very vile man.

'In short,' Viridus spoke, 'it were an excellent action to act in all things as the Queen does. For fashions are a matter of fashion. It is all one whether you wipe your fingers on bread-manchets or on napkins. But when a fashion becometh general its strangeness departeth and it is esteemed fit for a King's Court. Thus you may earn your bread: this is your duteous work. Observe the king of the beasts. See how it shall do its duty before the Queen, and mark the lesson.' His voice penetrated, low and level, through all the din from below. Yet the men dressed like gladiators advanced towards the dais where the Queen sat eating unmoved. The lion before her growled frightfully, and dragged its keepers towards the men in brass. They drew their short swords and beat upon their shields crying: 'We be Roman traitors that war upon this land.' Then it appeared that among them in their crowd they had a large mannikin, dressed like themselves in brass and running upon wheels.

The ladies pressed the tables with their hands, making as if to rise in terror. But the mannikin toppling forward fell before the lion with a hollow sound of brass. The lean beast, springing at its throat, tore it to reach the highly smelling flesh that was concealed within the tunic, and the Romans fled, casting away their shields and swords. One of them had a red forked beard and wide-open blue eyes. He brought into Katharine's mind the remembrance of her cousin. She wondered where he could be, and imagined him with that short sword, cutting his way to her side.

'That sight is allegorically to show,' Viridus was commenting beside her, 'how the high valour of Britain shall defend from all foes this noble Queen.'

The lion having reached its meat lay down upon it.

Katharine remembered that Bishop Gardiner said that her cousin must be begone. She tried to say to Viridus: 'Sir, I would fain obey you in these things, but I have a cousin that shall much hinder me.'

But the applause of the people below drowned her voice and Viridus continued talking.

Let it be true that the Queen, being alone, showed amongst their English fineries and nicenesses a gross and repulsive strangeness. But if their ladies put on her manners she should no longer be alone, and it would appear to the King and to all men that her example was both commended and emulated. It was a matter of kingcraft, and so the Lord Privy Seal was minded and determined.

'Then I will even get myself such a hat and tear my capons apart with my fingers,' Katharine said.

'You had much the wiser,' he answered.

The hall was now full of wild men, nymphs in white gowns, men bearing aspergers with which to scatter perfumes, and merry andrews, so that the floor could no longer be seen. A party of lords had overset a table in their efforts to get to the nymphs. The Queen was schooled to go out behind the arras, and the ladies, laughing, calling to each other and to the men at the other tables, and pinning up their hoods, filed out after her.

'I shall do my best to please your master and mine,' Katharine said. 'But he must even help me, or I can be no example to emulate, but one at whom the finger of scorn is likely to be pointed.'

Viridus paused before he led his charge from the gallery. His pale-blue eyes were more placable.

'You shall be well seconded. But have a care. Dally with no traitors. Speak fairly of your master's friends.' He touched her above the left breast with a claw-like finger. 'The Italian writes: "Whoso mocketh my love mocketh also mine own self." '

'I mock none,' Katharine said. 'But I have a cousin to be provided for that neither you nor I shall mock with much safety if he be sober enough to stand.'

He listened to her with his hand upon the door of the gallery: his air was attentive and aroused. She related very simply how Culpepper had besieged her door —'He came to London to help me on my way and to seek fortune in some war. I would that a place might be found for him, for here he is like to ruin both himself and me.'

'We have need of good swordsmen for an errand,' he said, in an absorbed voice.

'There was never a better than Tom,' Katharine said. 'He hath cut a score of throats. Your lord would have sent him to Calais.'

He muttered:

'Why, there are places other than Calais where a man may make a fortune.'

Something sinister in his brooding voice made her say:

'I would not have him killed. He hath made me many presents.'

He looked at her expressionlessly:

'It is very certain that you can not serve my lord with such a firebrand to your tail,' he said. 'I will find him an errand.'

'But not where he shall be killed,' she said again.

'Why,' he said slowly, 'I will send him where he will make a great fortune.'

'A great fortune would help him little,' she answered. 'I would have him sent where he may fight evenly matched.'

He laid his hand upon her wrist.

'He is in as much danger here as anywhere. This is not Lincolnshire, but an ordered Court.'—A man drew his sword with some peril there, for there were laws against it. If men came brawling in the maids' quarters at nights there were penalties of losing fingers, hands, or even heads. And the maids themselves were liable to be whipped.—He shook his head at her:

'If your cousin hath so violent an inclination to you I were your best friend to send him far away.'

It was in his mind that if they were to breed this girl to be a spy they must keep her protected from madmen. Something of mystery in his manner penetrated to her quick senses.

'God help me, what a dangerous place this is!' she said. 'I would I had never spoken to you of my cousin.'

He eyed her solemnly and said that if she were minded to wed this roaring boy they might both, and soon, earn fortunes to buy them land in a distant shire.

III

The young Poins, in his scarlet and black, drew his sister into a corner of the hall in which the gentry of the Lords that were there had already dined. It was a vast place, used as a rule for hearing suitors to the Lord Privy Seal and for the audit dinners of his tenantry in London. On its whitened walls there were trophies of arms, and between the wall and the platform at the end of the hall was a small space convenient for private talk. The rest of the people there were playing round games for kissing forfeits

or clustered round a magician who had brought a large
ape to tell fortunes by the *Sortes Virgilianæ*. It fumbled
about in the pages of a black-letter Æneid, and scratched
its side voluptuously: taking its own time it looked at the
pages attentively with a mournful parody of an aged sage,
and set its finger upon a line that the fates directed.

'Here's a great ado about thee,' Poins said, laughing at
his sister. 'Thy name is up in this town of London.'

He had come in the bodyguard of the Queen, and had
made time to slip round to old Badge's low house behind
the wall in order to beg from his grandfather ten crowns
to pay for a cloak he had lost at cards.

'Such a cackle among these Lutherans,' he mocked at
Margot. 'Heard you no hootings as your lady rode here
behind us of the guard?'

'I heard none, nor she deserveth none,' Margot
answered. 'For I love her most well.'

'Aye, she hath done a rape on thee,' he laughed. 'Aye,
our good uncle hath printed a very secret libel upon her.'
He began to whisper: Let it not be known or a sudden
vengeance might fall upon their house. It was no small
matter to print unlicensed broadsides. But their moody
uncle was out of all fear of consequences, so mad with
rage. 'He would have broken my back, because I tore thee
from his tender keeping.'

'Sure it was never so tender,' Margot said. 'When was
there a day that he did not beat me?' But he would have
married her to his apprentice, a young fellow with a
golden tongue, that preached every night to a secret
congregation in a Cripplegate cellar.

'Why, an thou observest my maxims,' the boy said,
sententiously, 'I will have thee a great lady. But uncle
hath printed this libel, and tongues are at work in Austin
Friars.' It was said that this was a new Papist plot. Margot
was but the first that they should carry off. The Duke and
Bishop Gardiner were reported to have signed papers for
abducting all the Lutheran virgins in London. They
were to be led from the paths of virtue into Catholic

lewdnesses, and all their boys were to be abducted and sent into monasteries across the seas.

'Thus the race of Lutherans should die out,' he laughed. 'Why they are hiding their maidens in pigeon-houses in Holborn. A boy called Hugh hath gone out and never come home, and it is said that masked men in black stuff gowns were seen to put him into a sack in Moorfields.'

'Well, here be great marvels,' Margot laughed.

He shook his red sides, and his blue eyes grew malicious and teasing:

'Such a strumpet as thy lady,' he uttered. 'A Papist Howard that is known to have been loved by twenty men in Lincoln.'

Margot passed from laughter into hot anger:

'It is a marvel God strikes not their tongues with palsy that said that,' she said swiftly. 'Why do you not kill some of them if you be a man?'

'Why, be calmed,' he said. 'You have heard such tales before now. It is no more than saying that a woman goes not to their churches to pray.'

A young Marten Pewtress, half page, half familiar to the Earl of Surrey, came towards them calling, 'Hal Poins.' He had black down upon his chin and a roving eye. He wore a purple coat like a tabard, and a cap with his master's arms upon a jewelled brooch.

'They say there's a Howard wench come to Court,' he cried from a distance, 'and thy sister in her service.'

'We talk of her,' Poins answered. 'Here is my sister.'

The young Pewtress kissed the girl upon the cheek.

'Pray, you, sweetheart, unfold,' he said. 'You are a pretty piece, and have a good brother that's my friend.'

He asked all of a breath whether this lady had yet had the small-pox? whether her hair were her own? how tall she stood without high heels to her shoon? whether her breath were sweet or her language unpleasing in the Lincolnshire jargon? whether the King had sent her many presents?

Margaret Poins was a very large, fair, and credulous

creature, rising twenty. Florid and slow-speaking, she had impulses of daring that covered her broad face with immense blushes. She was dressed in grey linsey-woolsey, and wore a black hood after the manner of the stricter Protestants, but she had round her neck a gilt medallion on a gold chain that Katharine Howard had given her already. She was, it was true, the daughter of a gentleman courtier, but he had been knocked on the head by rebels near Exeter just before her birth, and her mother had died soon after. She had been treated with gloomy austerity by her uncle and with sinister kindness by her grandfather, whom she dreaded. So that, coming from her Bedfordshire aunt, who had a hard cane, to this palace, where she had seen fine dresses and had already been kissed by two lords in the corridors, she was ready to aver that the Lady Katharine had a breath as sweet as the kine, a white skin which the small-pox had left unscarred, hair that reached to her ankles, and a learning and a wit unimaginable. Her own fortune was made, she believed, in serving her. Both the magister and her brother had sworn it, and, living in an age of marvels—dragons, portents from the heavens, and the romances of knight errantry—she was ready to believe it. It was true that the lady's room had proved a cell more bare and darker than her own at home, but Katharine's bright and careless laughter, her fair and radiant height, and her ready kisses and pleasant words, made the girl say with hot loyalty:

'She is more fair than any in the land, and, indeed, she is the apple of the King's eye.' Her voice was gruff with emotion, but, suddenly becoming very aware that she was talking to a strange young gentleman who might scoff, she seemed to choke and put her hand over her mouth.

Brocades for dresses, perfumes, gloves, oranges, and even another netted purse of green silk holding gold had continued to be brought to their chamber ever since Privy Seal had signed the warrant, and, it being about the new year, these ordinary vails and perquisites of a Maid of Honour made a show. Margot believed very sincerely that these things came direct from the King's hands, since they were formally announced as coming of his Highness' great bounty.

She reported to young Pewtress, 'And even now she is with the Lord Privy Seal, who brought her to Court.'

'He will go poaching among our Howards now,' Pewtress said. He stood considering with an air of gloom that the Norfolk servants imitated from their master, along with such sayings as that the times were very evil, and that no true man's neck was safe on his shoulders. 'Pray you, Sweetlips, tell no one this for a day until I have told my master. It may get me some crowns.' He pinched her chin between his thumb and forefinger. 'I will be your sweetheart, pretty.'

'Nay, I am provided with a good one,' Margot said seriously.

'You cannot have too many in this place. Take me for when the other's in gaol and another for when I am hung, as all good men are like to be.' He turned away lightly and loosened one of his jewelled garters, so that his stockings should hang in slovenly folds to prove that he was a man and despised niceness in his dress.

'I would that you be not too cheap to these gentry,' her brother said, with his eyes on Pewtress.

'I did naught,' she answered. 'If a gentleman will kiss one, it is uncourtly to turn away the cheek.'

'There is a way of not lending the lip,' he lectured her. 'I shall school you. A kiss here, a kiss there, I grant you. But consider that you be a gentleman's child, and ask who a man is.'

'He was well enough favoured,' she remonstrated.

'In these changing days many upstarts are come about the Court,' he went on with his lesson. 'Such were not here in the old days. Crummock hath wrought this. Seek advancement; pleasure your mistress, who can advance you; smile upon the magister, who, being advanced, can advance you. Speak courteous and fair words to any great lords that shall observe you. So we can rise in the world.'

'I will observe thy words,' she said submissively, for he seemed to her great and learned; 'but I like not that thou call'st me "you."'

'Why, these be grave matters,' he replied, 'and "you" is graver than "thou." But I love thee well. I will take thee a walk if the sun shine to-morrow.' He tightened his belt and took his pike from the corner. 'As for your lady; those that made these lies are lowsels. I could slay a score of them if they pressed upon you two.'

'I would not be so spoken of,' Margot answered.

'Then you must never rise in the world, as I am minded you shall,' he retorted, 'for, you being in a high place, eyes will be upon you.'

Nevertheless, Katharine Howard heard no evil words shouted after her that day. Pikemen and servitors of Cromwell were too thick upon all the road to the Tower, where the courtiers took barge again. Cromwell made very good order that no insults should reach the ears of such of the Papist nobles as came to his feast; they would make use with the King of evil words if any such were shouted. Thus the more dangerous and the most foul-mouthed of that neighbourhood, when the Court went by, found hands pressed over their mouths or scarves suddenly tightened round their throats by stalwart men that squeezed behind them in the narrow ways, so that not many more than twenty heads on both sides were broken that day; and Margot Poins kept her mouth closed tight with a sort of rustic caution—a shyness of her mistress and a desire to spare her any pain. Thus it was not until long after that Katharine heard of these rumours.

Katharine was in high good spirits. She had no great reason, for Viridus had threatened her; the Queen had rolled her large eyes round when Katharine had made her courtesy, but no words intelligible to a Christian had come from the thick lips; and no lord or lady had noticed her with a word except that, late in the afternoon, her cousin Surrey, a young man with a sleepily insolent air and front teeth that resembled a rabbit's, had suddenly planted himself in front of her as she sat on a stool against the hangings. He had begun to ask her where she was housed, when another young man caught him by the shoulder and pulled him away before he could do more than bid her sit there till he came again. She had been in no mood to do that for her cousin Surrey; besides, she would not be seen to speak much with a Papist henchman in that house. He could seek her if he wanted her company, so she went into another part of the hall, where they were all strangers.

Except for the mere prudence of pretending to obey Viridus until it should be safe to defy him and his master, she troubled little about what was going to happen to her. It was enough that she was away from the home where she had pined and been lonely. She sat on her stool, watched the many figures that passed her, marked fashions of embroidery, and thought that such speeches as she chanced to hear were ill-turned. Her sister Maids of Honour turned their backs upon her. Only the dark girl, Cicely Elliott, who had gibed at her a week ago, helped her to pin her sleeve that had been torn by a sword-hilt of some man who had turned suddenly in a crowd. But Katharine had learnt, as well as the magister, that when one is poor one must accept what the gods send. Besides, she knew that in the Lady Mary's household she was certain to be avoided, for she was regarded still as a spy of old Crummock's. That, most likely, would end some day, and she had no love for women's chatter.

She sat late at night correcting the embroidery of some true-love-knots that Margot had been making for her. A huckster had been there selling ribands from France, and showing a doll dressed as the ladies of the French King's Court were dressing that new year. He had been talking of a monster that had been born to a pig-sty on Cornhill, and lamenting that travel was become a grievous costly thing since the monasteries, with their free hostel, had been done away with. The monster had been much pondered in the city; certainly it portended wars or strange public happenings, since it had the face of a child, greyhound's ears, a sow's forelegs, and a dragon's tail. But the huckster had gone to another room, and Margot was getting her supper with the Lady Mary's serving-maids.

'Save us!' Katharine said to herself over her embroidery-frame, 'here be more drunkards. If I were a Queen I would make a law that any man should be burnt on the tongue that was drunk more than seven times in the week.' But she was already on her feet, making for the door, her frame dropped to the ground. There had been a murmur of voices through the thick oak, and then shouts and objurgations.

Thomas Culpepper stood in the doorway, his sword drawn, his left hand clutching the throat of the serving man who was guarding her room.

'God help us!' Katharine said angrily; 'will you ruin me?'

'Cut throats?' he muttered. 'Aye, I can cut a throat with any man in Christendom or out.' He shook the man backwards and forwards to support himself. 'Kat, this offal would have kept me from thee.'

Katharine said, 'Hush! it is very late.'

At the sound of her voice his face began to smile.

'Oh, Kat,' he stuttered jovially, 'what law should keep me from thee? Thou'rt better than my wife. Heathen to keep man and wife apart, I say, I.'

'Be still. It is very late. You will shame me,' she answered.

'Why, I would not have thee shamed, Kat of the world,' he said. He shook the man again and threw him good humouredly against the wall. 'Bide thou there until I come out,' he muttered, and sought to replace his sword in the scabbard. He missed the hole and scratched his left wrist with the point. 'Well, 'tis good to let blood at times,' he laughed. He wiped his hand upon his breeches.

'God help thee, thou'rt very drunk,' Katharine laughed at him. 'Let me put up thy sword.'

'Nay, no woman's hand shall touch this blade. It was my father's.'

An old knight with a fat belly, a clipped grey beard and roguish, tranquil eyes was ambling along the gallery, swinging a small pair of cheverel gloves. Culpepper made a jovial lunge at the old man's chest and suddenly the sword was whistling through the shadows.

The old fellow planted himself on his sturdy legs. He laughed pleasantly at the pair of them.

'An' you had not been very drunk I could never have done that,' he said to Culpepper, 'for I am passed of sixty, God help me.'

'God help thee for a gay old cock,' Culpepper said. 'You could not have done it without these gloves in your fist.'

'See you, but the gloves are not cut,' the knight answered. He held them flat in his fat hands. 'I learnt that twist forty years ago.'

'Well, get you to the wench the gloves are for,' Culpepper retorted. 'I am not long together of this pleasant mind.' He went into Katharine's room and propped himself against the door post.

The old man winked at Katharine.

'Bid that gallant not draw his sword in these galleries,' he said. 'There is a penalty of losing an eye. I am Rochford of Bosworth Hedge.'

'Get thee to thy wench, for a Rochford,' Culpepper snarled over his shoulder. 'I will have no man speak with my coz. You struck a good blow at Bosworth Hedge. But I go to Paris to cut a better throat than thine ever was, Rochford or no Rochford.'

The old man surveyed him sturdily from his head to his heels and winked once more at Katharine.

'I would I had had such manners as a stripling,' he uttered in a round and friendly voice. 'I might have prospered better in love.' Going sturdily along the corridor he picked up Culpepper's sword and set it against the wall.

Culpepper, leaning against the doorpost, was gazing with ferocious solemnity at the open clothes-press in which some hanging dresses appeared like women standing. He smoothed his red beard and thrust his cap far back on his thatch of yellow hair.

'Mark you,' he addressed the clothes-press harshly, 'that is Rochford of Bosworth Hedge. At the end of that day they found him with seventeen body wounds and the corpses of seventeen Scotsmen round him. He is famous throughout Christendom. Yet in me you see a greater than he. I am sent to cut such a throat. But that's a secret. Only I am a made man.'

Katharine had closed her door. She knew it would take her twenty minutes to get him into the frame of mind that he would go peaceably away.

'Thou art very pleasant to-night,' she said. 'I have seldom seen thee so pleasant.'

'For joy of seeing thee, Kat. I have not seen thee this six days.' He made a hideous grinding sound with his teeth. 'But I have broken some heads that kept me from thee.'

'Be calm,' Katharine answered; 'thou seest me now.'

He passed his hand over his eyes.

'I'll be calm to pleasure thee,' he muttered apologetically. 'You said I was very pleasant, Kat.' He puffed out his chest and strutted to the middle of the room. 'Behold a made man. I could tell you such secrets. I am sent to slay a traitor at Rome, at Ravenna, at Ratisbon— wherever I find him. But he's in Paris, I'll tell thee that.'

Katharine's knees trembled; she sank down into her tall chair.

'Whom shalt thou slay?'

'Aye, and that's a secret. It's all secrets. I have sworn upon the hilt of my knife. But I am bidden to go by an old-young man, a make of no man at all, with lips that minced and mowed. It was he bade the guards pass me to thee this night.'

'I would know whom thou shalt slay,' she asked harshly.

'Nay, I tell no secrets. My soul would burn. But I am sent to slay this traitor—a great enemy to the King's

Highness, from the Bishop of Rome. Thus I shall slay him
as he comes from a Mass.'

He squatted about the room, stabbing at shadows.

'It is a man with a red hat,' he grunted. 'Filthy for an
Englishman to wear a red hat these days!'

'Put up your knife,' Katharine cried, 'I have seen too
much of it.'

'Aye, I am a good man,' he boasted, 'but when I come
back you shall see me a great one. There shall be patents
for farms given me. There shall be gold. There shall be
never such another as I. I will give thee such gowns, Kat.'

She sat still, but smoothed back a lock of her fair hair
that glowed in the firelight.

'When I am a great man,' he babbled on, 'I will not wed
thee, for who art thou to wed with a great man? Thou art
more cheaply won. But I will give thee . . .'

'Thou fool,' she shrieked suddenly at him. 'These men
shall slay thee. Get thee to Paris to murder an thou wilt.
Thou shalt never come back and I shall be well rid of thee.'

He gave her a snarling laugh:

'Toy thou with no man when I am gone,' he said with
sudden ferocity, so that his blue eyes appeared to start
from his head.

'Poor fool, thou shalt never come back,' she answered.

He had an air of cunning and triumph.

'I have settled all this with that man that's no man,
Viridus; thou art here as in a cloister amongst the maids
of the Court. No man shall see thee; thou shalt speak with
none that wears not a petticoat. I have so contracted with
that man.'

'I tell thee they have contrived this to be rid of thee,'
she said.

His tone became patronising.

'Wherefore should they?' he asked. When there came
no answer from her he boasted, 'Aye, thou wouldst not
have me go because thou lovest me too well.'

'Stay here,' she said. 'I will give thee money.' He stood
gazing at her with his jaw fallen. 'Thou art a drunkard

and a foul tongue,' she said, 'but if thou goest to Paris to murder a cardinal thou shalt never come out of that town alive. Be sure thou shalt be rendered up to death.'

He staggered towards her and caught one of her hands.

'Why, it is but cutting of a man's throat,' he said. 'I have cut many throats and have taken no harm. Be not sad! This man is a cardinal. But 'tis all one. It shall make me a great man.'

She muttered, 'Poor fool.'

'I have sworn to go,' he said. 'I am to have great farms and a great man shall watch over thee to keep thee virtuous. They have promised it or I had not gone.'

'Do you believe their promises?' she asked derisively.

'Why, 'tis a good knave, yon Viridus. He promised or ever I asked it.'

He was on his knees before her as she sat, with his arms about her waist.

'Sha't not cry, dear dove,' he mumbled. 'Sha't go with me to Paris.'

She sighed:

'No, no. Bide here,' and passed her hand through his ruffled hair.

'I would slay thee an thou were false to me,' he whispered over her hand. 'Get thee with me.'

She said, 'No, no,' again in a stifled voice.

He cried urgently:

'Come! Come! By all our pacts. By all our secret vows.'

She shook her head, sobbing:

'Poor fool. Poor fool. I am very lonely.'

He clutched her tightly and whispered in a hoarse voice:

'It were merrier at home now. Thou didst vow. At home now. Of a summer's night . . .'

She whispered: 'Peace. Peace.'

'At home now. In June, thou didst . . .'

She said urgently: 'Be still. Wouldst thou woo me again to the grunting of hogs?'

'Aye, would I,' he answered. 'Thou didst . . .'

She moved convulsively in her chair. He grasped her more tightly.

'Thou yieldest, I know thee!' he cried triumphantly. He staggered to his feet, still holding her hand.

'Thou shalt come to Paris. Sha't be lodged like a Princess. Sha't see great sights.'

She sprang up, tearing herself from him.

'Get thee gone from here,' she shivered. 'I am done with starving with thee. I know thy apple orchard wooings. Get thee gone from here. It is late. I shall be shamed if a man be seen to leave my room so late.'

'Why, I would not have thee shamed, Kat,' he muttered, her strenuous tone making him docile as a child.

'Get thee gone,' she answered, panting. 'I will not starve.'

'Wilt not come with me?' he asked ruefully. 'Thou didst yield in my arms.'

'I do bid thee begone,' she answered imperiously. 'Get thee gold if thou would'st have me. I have starved too much with thee.'

'Why, I will go,' he muttered. 'Buss me. For I depart towards Dover to-night, else this springald cardinal will be gone from Paris ere I come.'

IV

'Men shall make us cry, in the end, steel our hearts how we will,' she said to Margot Poins, who found her weeping with her head down upon the table above a piece of paper.

'I would weep for no man,' Margot answered.

Large, florid, fair, and slow speaking, she gave way to one of her impulses of daring that covered her afterwards with immense blushes and left her buried in speechless confusion. 'I could never weep for such an oaf as your cousin. He beats good men.'

'Once he sold a farm to buy me a gown,' Katharine said, 'and he goes to a sure death if I may not stay him.'

'It is even the province of men—to die,' Margot answered. Her voice, gruff with emotion, astonished herself. She covered her mouth with the back of her great white hand as if she wished to wipe the word away.

'Beseech you, spoil not your eyes with sitting to write at this hour for the sake of this roaring boy.'

Katharine sat to the table: a gentle knocking came at the door. 'Let no one come, I have told the serving knave as much.' She sank into a pondering over the wording of her letter to Bishop Gardiner. It was not to be thought of that her cousin should murder a Prince of the Church; therefore the bishop must warn the Catholics in Paris that Cromwell had this in mind. And Bishop Gardiner must stay her cousin on his journey: by a false message if needs were. It would be an easy matter to send him such a message as that she lay dying and must see him, or anything that should delay him until this cardinal had left Paris.

The great maid behind her back was fetching from the clothes-prop a waterglobe upon its stand; she set it down on the table before the rush-light, moving on tiptoe, for to her the writing of a letter was a sort of necromancy, and she was distressed for Katharine's sake. She had heard that to write at night would make a woman blind before thirty. The light grew immense behind the globe; watery rays flickered broad upon the ceiling and on the hangings, and the paper shone with a mellow radiance. The gentle knocking was repeated, and Katharine frowned. For before she was half way through with the humble words of greeting to the bishop it had come to her that this was a very dangerous matter to meddle in, and she had no one by whom to send the letter. Margot could not go, for it was perilous for her maid to be seen near the bishop's quarters with all Cromwell's men spying about.

Behind her was the pleasant and authoritative voice of old Sir Nicholas Rochford talking to Margot Poins. Katharine caught the name of Cicely Elliott, the dark

maid of honour who had flouted her a week ago, and had
pinned up her sleeve that day in Privy Seal's house.

The old man stood, grey and sturdy, his hand upon her
doorpost. His pleasant keen eyes blinked upon her in the
strong light from her globe as if he were before a good fire.

'Why, you are as fair as a saint with a halo, in front of
that jigamaree,' he said. 'I am sent to offer you the friendship of Cicely Elliott.' When he moved, the golden collar
of his knighthood shone upon his chest; his cropped grey
beard glistened on his chin, and he shaded his eyes with
his hand.

'I was writing of a letter,' Katharine said. She turned
her face towards him: the stray rays from the globe outlined her red curved lips, her swelling chest, her low forehead; and it shone like the moon rising over a hill, yellow
and fiery in the hair above her brow. The lines of her face
drooped with her perplexities, and her eyes were large and
shadowed, because she had been shedding many tears.

'Cicely Elliott shall make you a good friend,' he said,
with a modest pride of his property; 'she shall marry me,
therefore I do her such services.'

'You are old for her,' Katharine said.

He laughed.

'Since I have neither chick nor child and am main rich
for a subject.'

'Why, she is happy in her servant,' Katharine said
abstractedly. 'You are a very famous knight.'

'There are ballads of me,' he answered complacently.
'I pray to die in a good tulzie yet.'

'If Cicely Elliott have her scarf in your helmet,'
Katharine said, 'I may not give you mine.' She was considering of her messenger to the bishop. 'Will you do me
a service?'

'Why,' he answered, with a gentle mockery, 'you have
one tricksy swordsman to bear your goodly colours.'

Katharine turned clean about to him and looked at him
with attention, to make out whether he might be such a
man as would carry her letter for her.

He returned her gaze directly, for he was proud of himself and of his fame. He had fought in all the wars that a man might fight in since he had been eighteen, and for fifteen years he had been captain of a troop employed by the Council in keeping back the Scots of the Borders. It was before Flodden Field that he had done his most famous deed, about which there were many ballads. Being fallen upon by a bevy of Scotsmen near a tall hedge, after he had been unhorsed, he had set his back into a thorn bush, and had fought for many hours in the rear of the Scottish troop, alone and with only his sword. The ballad that had been made about him said that seventeen corpses lay in front of the bush after the English won through to him. But since Cromwell had broken up the Northern Councils, and filled them again with his own men of no birth, the old man had come away from the Borders, disdaining to serve at the orders of knaves that had been butchers' sons and worse. He owned much land and was very wealthy, and, having been very abstemious, because he came of an old time when knighthood had still some of the sacredness and austerity of a religion, he was a man very sound in limb and peaceable of disposition. In his day he had been esteemed the most graceful whiffler in the world: now he used only the heavy sword, because he was himself grown heavy.

Katharine answered his gentle sneer at her cousin:

'It is true that I have a servant, but he is gone and may not serve me.' Yet the knight would find it in the books of chivalry that certain occasions or great quests allowed of a knight's doing the errands of more than one lady: but one lady, as for instance the celebrated Dorinda, might have her claims asserted by an illimitable number of knights, and she begged him to do her a service.

'I have heard of these Errantry books,' he said. 'In my day there were none such, and now I have no letters.'

'How, then, do you pass the long days of peace,' Katharine asked, 'if you neither drink nor dice?'

He answered: 'In telling of old tales and teaching their paces to the King's horses.'

He drew himself up a little. He would have her understand that he was not a horse leech: but there was in these four-footed beasts a certain love for him, so that Richmond, the King's favourite gelding, would stand still to be bled if he but laid his hand on the great creature's withers to calm him. These animals he loved, since he grew old and might not follow arguments and disputations of *hic* and *hoc*. 'There were none such in my day. But a good horse is the same from year's end to year's end . . .'

'Will you carry a letter for me?' Katharine asked.

'I would have you let me show you some of his Highness' beasts,' he added. 'I breed them to the manage myself. You shall find none that step more proudly in Christendom or Heathenasse.'

'Why, I believe you,' she answered. Suddenly she asked: 'You have ridden as knight errant?'

He said: 'For three weeks only. Then the Scots came on too thick and fast to waste time.' His dark eyes blinked and his broad lips moved humorously with his beard. 'I swore to do service to any lady; pray you let me serve you.'

'You can do me a service,' she said.

He moved his hand to silence her.

'Pray you take it not amiss. But there is one that hates you.'

She said:

'Perhaps there are a many; but do me a service if you will.'

'Look you,' he said, 'these times are no times of mine. But I know it is prudent to have servitors that love one. I saw yours shake a fist at your door.'

Katharine said:

'A man?' She looked at Margot, who, big, silent and flushed, was devouring the celebrated hero of ballads with adoring eyes. He laughed.

'That maid would kiss your feet. But, in these days, it

is well to make friends with them that keep doors. The fellow at yours would spit upon you if he dared.'

Katharine said carelessly:

'Let him even spit in his imagination, and I shall whip him.'

The old knight looked out of the door. He left it wide open, so that no man might listen.

'Why, he is still gone,' he said. He cleared his throat. 'See you,' he began. 'So I should have said in the old days. These fellows then we could slush open to bathe our feet in their warm blood when we came tired-foot from hunting. Now it is otherwise. Such a loon may be a spy set upon one.'

He turned stiffly and majestically to move back her new hangings that only that day, in her absence at Privy Seal's, had been set in place. He tapped spots in the wall with his broad and gentle fingers, talking all the time with his broad back to her.

'See you, you have had here workmen to hang you a new arras. There be tricks of boring ear-holes through walls in hanging these things. So that if you have a cousin who shall catch a scullion by the throat . . .'

Katharine said hastily:

'He hath heard little to harm me.'

'It is what a man swears he hath heard that shall harm one,' the old knight answered. 'I meddle in no matters of statecraft, but I am sent to you by certain ladies; one shall wed me and I am her servant; one bears my name and wedded a good cousin of mine, now dead for his treasons.'

Katharine said:

'I am beholden to Cicely Elliott and the Lady Rochford . . .'

He silenced her with one of his small gestures of old-fashioned dignity and distinction.

'I meddle in none of these matters,' he said again. 'But these ladies know that you hate one they hate.'

He said suddenly, 'Ah!' a little grunt of satisfaction. His fingers tapping gently made what seemed a stone of the wall quiver and let drop small flakes of plaster. He turned gravely upon Katharine:

'I do not ask what you spoke of with that worshipful swordsman,' he said. 'But your servitor is gone to tell upon you. A stone is gone from here and there is his ear-hole, like a drum of canvas.'

Katharine said swiftly:

'Take, then, a letter for me—to the Bishop of Winchester!'

He started back with a little exaggerated pantomime of horror.

'Must I go into your plots?' he asked, blinking and amused, as if he had expected the errand.

She said urgently:

'I would have you tell me what Englishman now wears a red hat and is like to be in Paris. I am very ignorant in these matters.'

'Then meddle not in them,' he said, 'for that man is even Cardinal Pole; one that the King's Highness would very willingly know to be dead.'

'God forbid that my cousin should murder a Prince of the Church, and be slain in that quarrel,' she answered.

He started back and held his hands over his head.

'Why, God help you, child! Is that your errand?' he said, deep from his chest. 'I meddle not in this matter.'

She answered obstinately:

'Pray you—by your early vows—consent to carry me my letter.'

He shook his head bodingly.

'I thought it had been a matter of a masque at the Bishop of Winchester's; or I had never come nigh you. Cicely Elliott hath copied out the part you should speak. Pray you ask me no more of the other errand.'

She said:

'For a great knight you are a friend only in little matters!'

He uttered reproachfully:

'Child: it is no little matter to act as go-between for the

Bishop of Winchester, even if it be for no more than a masque. How otherwise does he not send to you direct? So much I was ready to do for you, a stranger, who am a man that has no party.'

She uttered maliciously:

'Well, well. I thought you came of the better times before our day.'

'I have shewn myself a good enough man,' he said composedly. He pointed one of his fingers at her.

'Pole is not one that shall be easily slain. He is like to have in his pay the defter spadassins of the two. I have known him since he was a child till when he fled abroad.'

'But my cousin!' Katharine pleaded.

'For the sake of your own little neck, let that gallant be hanged,' he said smartly. 'You have need of many friends; I can see it in your complexion, which is of a hasty loyalty. But I tell you, I had never come near you, so your cousin miscalled me, a man of worth and credit, had these ladies not prayed me to come to you.'

She raised herself to her full height.

'It is not in the books of your knight-errantry,' she cried, 'that one should leave one's friends to the hangman of Paris.'

The large figure of Margot Poins thrust itself upon them.

'A' God's name,' said her gruff voice of great emotion, 'hear the words of this valiant soldier. Your cousin shall ruin you. It is true that he will drive from you all your good friends . . .' She faltered, and her impulse carried her no further. Rochford tapped her flushed cheek gently with his glove, but a light and hushing step in the corridor made them all silent.

The Magister Udal stood before the door blinking his eyes at the light; Katharine addressed him imperiously—

'You will carry a letter for me to save my cousin from death.'

He started, and leered at Margot, who was ready to sink into the ground.

'Why, I had rather carry a bull to the temple of Jupiter, as Macrobius has it,' he said, 'meaning that . . .'

'Yet you have drunk with him,' Katharine interrupted him hotly, 'you have gone hurling through the night with him. You have shamed me together.'

'Yet I cannot forget Tully,' he answered sardonically, 'who warns me that a prudent man should be able to moderate the course of his friendship, even as he reins his horse. *Est prudentis sustinere ut cursum* . . .'

'Mark you that!' the old knight said to Katharine. 'I will get my boy to read to me out of Tully, for that is excellent wisdom.'

'God help me, this is Christendom!' Katharine said, bitterly. 'Shall one abandon one that lay in the same cradle with one?'

'Your ladyship hath borne with him a day too long,' Udal said. 'He beat me like a dog five days since. Have you heard of the city called Ponceropolis, founded by the King Philip? Your good cousin should be ruler of that city, for the Great King peopled it with all the brawlers, cut-throats, and roaring boys of his dominions, to be rid of them.' She became aware that he was very angry, for his whisper shook like the neigh of a horse.

The old knight winked at Margot.

'Why this is a monstrous wise man,' he said, 'who yet speaks some sense.'

'In short,' the magister said, 'If you will stick to this man, you shall lose me. For I have taken beatings and borne no malice—as in the case of men with whose loves or wives I have prospered better than themselves. But that this man should miscall me and beat me for the pure frenzy of his mind, causelessly, and for the love of blows! That is unbearable. To-night I walk for the first time after five days since he did beat me. And I ask you whom you shall here find the better servant?'

His thin figure was suddenly shaking with rage.

'Why, this is conspiracy!' Katharine cried.

'A conspiracy!' Udal's voice rose up into a shriek. 'If

your ladyship were a Queen I would not be a Queen's cousin's whipping post.' His arms jerked with the spasms of his rage like those of a marionette.

'A shame that learned men should be so beaten!' Margot's gruff voice uttered.

Katharine turned upon her.

'That is what made you speak e'ennow. You have been with this flibbertigibbet.'

'This is a free land,' the girl mumbled, her mild eyes sparkling with the contagious anger of her lover.

The old knight stood blinking upon Katharine.

'You are like to lose all your servants in this quarrel,' he said.

Katharine wrung her hands, and then turned her back upon them and drummed upon the table with her fingers. Udal caught Margot's large hand and fumbled it beneath the furs of his robe: the old knight kept his smiling eyes upon Katharine's back. Her voice came at last:

'Why, I will not have Tom killed upon this occasion into which I brought him.'

Rochford shrugged his shoulders up to his ears.

'Oh marvellous infatuation,' he said.

Katharine spoke, still with her back turned and her shoulders heaving:

'A marvellous infatuation!' she said, her voice coming softly and deeply in her chest. 'Why, after his fashion this man loved me. God help us, what other men have I seen here that would strike a straight blow? Here it is moving in the dark, listening at pierced walls, swearing of false treasons——'

She swept round upon the old man, her face moved, her eyes tender and angry. She stretched out her hand, and her voice was pitiful and urgent.

'Sir! Sir! What counsel do you give me, who are a knight of honour? Would you let a man who lay in the cradle with you go to a shameful death in an errand you had made for him?'

She leaned back upon the table with her eyes upon his

face. 'No you would not. How then could you give me such counsel?'

He said: 'Well, well. You are in the right.'

'Nearly I went with him to another place,' she answered, 'but half an hour ago. Would to God I had! for here it is all treacheries.'

'Write your letter, child,' he answered. 'You shall give it to Cicely Elliott to-morrow in the morning. I will have it conveyed, but I will not be seen to handle it, for I am too young to be hanged.'

'Why, God help you, knight,' Udal whispered urgently from the doorway, 'carry no letter in this affair—if you escape, assuredly this mad pupil of mine shall die. For the King——?' Suddenly he raised his voice to a high nasal drawl that rang out like a jackdaw's: 'That is very true; and, in this matter of Death you may read in Socrates' Apology. Nevertheless we may believe that if Death be a transmigration from one place into another, there is certainly amendment in going whither so many great men have already passed, and to be subtracted from the way of so many judges that be iniquitous and corrupt.'

'Why, what a plague . . .' Katharine began.

He interrupted her quickly.

'Here is your serving man back at last if you would rate him for leaving your door unkept.'

The man stood in the doorway, his lanthorn dangling in his hand, his cudgel stuck through his belt, his shock of hair rough like an old thatch, and his eyes upon the ground. He mumbled, feeling at his throat:

'A man must eat. I was gone to my supper.'

'You are like to have the nightmare, friend,' the old knight said pleasantly. 'It is ill to eat when most of the world sleeps.'

V

Cicely Elliott had indeed sent her old knight to Katharine with those overtures of friendship. Careless, dark, and a madcap, she had flown at Katharine because she had believed her a creature of Cromwell's, set to spy upon the Lady Mary's maids. They formed, the seven of them, a little, mutinous, babbling circle. Their lady's cause they adored, for it was that of an Old Faith, such as women will not let die. The Lady Mary treated them with a hard indifference: it was all one to her whether they loved her or not; so they babbled, and told evil tales of the other side. The Lady Rochford could do little to hold them, for, having come very near death when the Queen Anne fell, she had been timid ever since, and Cicely Elliott was their ringleader.

Thus it was to her that one of Gardiner's priests had come begging her to deliver to Katharine a copy of the words she was to speak in the masque, and from the priest Cicely had learnt that Katharine loved the Old Faith and hated Privy Seal as much as any of them. She had been struck with a quick remorse, and had suddenly seen Katharine as one that must be helped and made amends to. Thus she had pinned up her sleeve at Privy Seal's. There, however, it had not been safe to speak with her.

'Dear child,' she said to Katharine next morning, 'we may well be foils one to another, for I am dark and pert, like a pynot. They call me Mag Pie here. You shall be Jenny Dove of the Sun. But I am not afraid of your looks. Men that like the touch of the sloe in me shall never be drawn away by your sweet lips.'

She was, indeed, like a magpie, never still for a minute, fingering Katharine's hair, lifting the medallion upon her chest, poking her dark eyes close to the embroidery on her stomacher. She had a trick of standing with her side face to you, so that her body seemed very long to her hips, and her dark eyes looked at you askance and roguish, whilst her lips puckered to a smile, a little on one side.

'It was not your old knight called me Sweetlips,' Katharine said. 'I miscalled him foully last night.'

Cicely Elliott threw back her head and laughed.

'Why, he is worshipful heavy to send on a message; but you may trust his advice when he gives it.'

'I am come to think the same,' Katharine said; 'yet in this one matter I cannot take it.'

Cicely Elliott had taken to herself the largest and highest of the rooms set apart for these maids. The tapestries, which were her own, were worked in fair reds and greens, like flowers. She had a great silver mirror and many glass vases, in which were set flowers worked in silver and enamel, and a large, thin box carved out of an elephant's tusk, to hold her pins; and all these were presents from the old knight.

'Why,' she said, 'sometimes his advice shall fit a woman's mood; sometimes he goes astray, as in the case of these gloves. Cheverel is a skin that will stretch so that after one wearing you may not tell the thumbs from stocking-feet. Nevertheless, I would be rid of your cousin.'

'Not in this quarrel,' Katharine answered. 'Find him an honourable errand, and he shall go to Kathay.'

Cicely threw the stretched cheverel glove into the fire.

'My knight shall give me a dozen pairs of silk, stitched with gold to stiffen them,' she said. 'You shall have six; but send your cousin in quest of the Islands of the Blest. They lie well out in the Western Ocean. If you can make him mislay his compass he will never come back to you.'

Katharine laughed.

'I think he would come without compass or chart. Nevertheless, I will send me my letter by means of your knight to Bishop Gardiner.'

Cicely Elliott hung her head on her chest.

'I do not ask its contents, but you may give it me.'

Katharine brought it out from the bosom of her dress, and the dark girl passed it up her sleeve.

'This shall no doubt ruin you,' she said. 'But get you to our mistress. I will carry your letter.'

Katharine started back.

'You!' she said. 'It was Sir Nicholas should have it conveyed.'

'That poor, silly old man shall not be hanged in this matter,' Cicely answered. 'It is all one to me. If Crummock would have had my head he could have shortened me by that much a year ago.'

Katharine's eyes dilated proudly.

'Give me my letter,' she said; 'I will have no woman in trouble for me.'

The dark girl laughed at her.

'Your letter is in my sleeve. No hands shall touch it before mine deliver it to him it is written to. Get you to our mistress. I thank you for an errand I may laugh over; laughter here is not over mirthful.'

She stood side face to Katharine, her mouth puckered up into her smile, her eyes roguish, her hands clasped behind her back.

'Why, you see Cicely Elliott,' she said, 'whose folk all died after the Marquis of Exeter's rising, who has neither kith nor kin, nor house nor home. I had a man loved me passing well. He is dead with the rest; so I pass my time in pranks because the hours are heavy. To-day the prank is on thy side; take it as a gift the gods send, for to-morrow I may play thee one, since thou art soft, and fair, and tender. That is why they call me here the Magpie. My old knight will tell you I have tweaked his nose now and again, but I will not have him shortened by the head for thy sake.'

'Why, you are very bitter,' Katharine said.

The girl answered, 'If your head ached as mine does now and again when I remember my men who are dead; if your head ached as mine does . . .' She stopped and gave a peal of laughter. 'Why, child, your face is like a startled moon. You have not stayed days enough here to have met many like me; but if you tarry here for long you will laugh much as I laugh, or you will have grown blind long since with weeping.'

Katharine said, 'Poor child, poor child!'

But the girl cried out, 'Get you gone, I say! In the Lady Mary's room you shall find my old knight babbling with the maidens. Send him to me, for my head aches scurvily, and he shall dip his handkerchief in vinegar and set it upon my forehead.'

'Let me comb thy hair,' Katharine said; 'my hand is sovereign against a headache.'

'No, get you gone,' the girl said harshly; 'I will have men of war to do these errands for me.'

Katharine answered, 'Sit thee down. Thou wilt take my letter; I must ease thy pains.'

'As like as not I shall scratch thy pink face,' Cicely said. 'At these times I cannot bear the touch of a woman. It was a woman made my father run with the Marquis of Exeter.'

'Sweetheart,' Katharine said softly, 'I could hold both thy wrists with my two fingers. I am stronger than most men.'

'Why, no!' the girl cried; 'I may not sit still. Get you gone. I will run upon your errand. If you had knelt to as many men as I have you could not sit still either. And not one of my men was pardoned.'

She ran from the room with a sidelong step like a magpie's, and her laugh rang out discordantly from the corridor.

The Lady Mary sat reading her Plautus in her large painted gallery, with all her maids about her sewing, some at a dress for her, some winding silk for their own uses. The old knight stood holding his sturdy hands apart between a rope of wool that his namesake Lady Rochford was making into balls. Other gentlemen were beside some of the maids, toying with their silks or whispering in their ears. No one much marked Katharine Howard.

She glided to her lady and kissed the dry hand that lay in the lap motionless. Mary raised her eyes from her book, looked for a leisurely time at the girl's face, and then began again to read. Old Rochford winked pleasantly at her, and, after she had saluted his cousin, he begged her to hold the wool in his stead, for his hands, which were used to sword and shield, were very cold, and his legs, inured to the saddle, brooked standing very ill.

'Cicely Elliott hath a headache,' Katharine said; 'she bade me send you to her.'

He waited before her, helping her to adjust the wool on to her white hands, and she uttered, in a low voice:

'She hath taken my letter for me.'

He said, 'Why, what a' the plague's name . . . .' and stood fingering his peaked little beard in a gentle perplexity.

Lady Rochford pulled at her wool and gave a hissing sigh of pain, for the joint of her wrist was swollen.

'It has always been easterly winds in January since the Holy Blood of Hailes was lost,' she sighed. 'In its day I could get me some ease in the wrist by touching the phial that held it.' She shivered with discomfort, and smiled distractedly upon Katharine. Her large and buxom face was mild, and she seemed upon the point of shedding tears.

'Why, if you will put your wool round a stool, I will wind it for you,' Katharine said, because the gentle helplessness of the large woman filled her with compassion, as if this were her old, mild mother.

Lady Rochford shook her head disconsolately.

'Then I must do something else, and my bones would ache more. But I would you would make my cousin Rochford ask the Archbishop where they have hidden the Sacred Blood of Hailes, that I may touch it and be cured.'

The old knight frowned very slightly.

'I have told thee to wrap thy fist in lamb's-wool,' he said. 'A hundred times I have told thee. It is very dangerous to meddle with these old saints and phials that are done away with.'

Lady Rochford sighed gently and hung her head.

'My cousin Anne, that was a sinful Queen, God rest her soul . . . .' she began.

Sir Nicholas listened to her no more.

'See you,' he whispered to Katharine. 'Peradventure it is best that Cicely have gone. Being a madcap, her comings and goings are heeded by no man, and it is true that she resorteth daily to the Bishop of Winchester, to plague his priests.'

'I would not speak so, being a man,' Katharine said.

He smiled at her and patted her shoulder.

'Why, I have struck good blows in my time,' he said.

'And have learned worldly wisdom,' Katharine retorted.

'I would not risk my neck on grounds where I am but ill acquainted,' he answered soberly. He was all will to please her. The King, he said, was coming on the Wednesday, after the Bishop of Winchester's, to see three new stallions walk in their manage-steps. 'I pray that you will come with Cicely Elliott to watch from the little window in the stables. These great creatures are a noble sight. I bred them myself to it.' His mild brown eyes were bright with enthusiasm and cordiality.

Suddenly there was a great silence in the room, and the Lady Mary raised her head. The burly figure of Throckmorton, the spy, was in the doorway. Katharine shuddered at the sight of him, for, in her Lincolnshire house, where he was accounted more hateful than Judas who betrayed the Lord, she had seen him beat the nuns when the convents had been turned out of doors, and he had brought to death his own brother, who had had a small estate near her father's house. The smile upon his face made her feel sick. He stroked his long, golden-brown beard, glanced swiftly round the room, and advanced to the mistress's chair, swinging his great shoulders. He made a leg and pulled off his cap, and at that there was a rustle of astonishment, for it had been held treasonable to cap the Lady Mary. Her eyes regarded him fixedly, with a granite cold and hardness, and he seemed to have at once a grin of power and a shrinking motion of currying favour. He said that Privy Seal begged her leave that her maid Katharine Howard might go to him soon after one o'clock. The Lady Mary neither spoke nor moved, but the old knight shrank away from Katharine, and affected to be talking in the ear of Lady Rochford, who went on winding her wool. Throckmorton turned on his heels and swung away, his eyes on the floor, but with a grin on his evil face.

He left a sudden whisper behind him, and then the silence fell once more. Katharine stood, a tall figure, holding out the hands on which the wool was as if she were praying to some invisible deity or welcoming some invisible lover. Some heads were raised to look at her, but they fell again; the old knight shuffled nearer her to whisper hoarsely from his moustachioed lips:

'Your serving man hath reported. Pray God we come safe out of this!' Then he went out of the room. Lady Rochford sighed deeply, for no apparent reason.

After a time the Lady Mary raised her head and made a minute, cold beckoning to Katharine. Her dry finger pointed to a word in her book of Plautus.

'Tell me what you know of this,' she commanded.

The play was the *Menechmi*, and the phrase ran, '*Nimis autem bene ora commetavi. . . .*' It was difficult for Katharine to bring her mind down to this text, for she had been wondering if indeed her time were at an end before it had begun. She said:

'I have never loved this play very well,' to excuse herself.

'Then you are out of the fashion,' Mary said coldly, 'for this *Menechmi* is prized here above all the rest, and shall be played at Winchester's before his Highness.'

Katharine bowed her head submissively, and read the words again.

'I remember me,' she said, 'I had this play in a manuscript where your *commetavi* read *commentavi*.'

Mary kept her eyes upon the girl's face, and said:

'Signifying?'

'Why, it signifies,' Katharine said, 'that Messenio did well mark a face. If you read *commetavi* it should mean that he scratched it with his nails so that it resembled a harrowed field; if *commentavi*, that he bethumped it with his fist so that bruises came out like the stops on a fair writing.'

'It is true that you are a good Latinist,' Mary said

expressionlessly. 'Bring me my inkhorn to that window. I will write down your *commentavi*.'

Katharine lifted the inkhorn from its hole in the arm of the chair and gracefully followed the stiff and rigid figure into the embrasure of a distant window.

Mary bent her head over the book that she held in her hand, and writing in the margin, she uttered:

'Pity that such an excellent Latinist should meddle in matters that nothing concern her.'

Katharine held the inkhorn carefully, as if it had been a precious vase.

'If you will bid me do naught but serve you, I will do naught else,' she said.

'I will neither bid thee nor aid thee,' Mary answered. 'The Bishop of Winchester claims thy service. Serve him as thou wilt.'

'I would serve my mistress in serving him,' Katharine said. 'He is a man I love little.'

Mary pulled suddenly from her bodice a piece of crumpled parchment that had been torn across. She thrust it into Katharine's free hand.

'Such letters I have had written me by my father's men,' she said. 'If this bishop should come to be my father's man I would take no service from him.'

Katharine read on the crumpled parchment such words as:

'Be you dutiful . . .

I will not protect . . .

You shall be ruined utterly . . .

You had better creep underground . . .

Therefore humble you . . .'

'It was Thomas Cromwell wrote that,' the Lady Mary cried. 'My father's man!'

'But if this brewer's son be brought down?' Katharine pleaded.

'Why, I tore his letter across for it is filthy,' Mary said, 'and I keep the halves of his letter that I may remember.

If he be brought down, who shall bring his master down that let him write so?'

Katharine said:

'If this tempter of the Devil's brood were brought down there should ensue so great an atonement from his sorrowful master whom he deludes. . . .'

Mary uttered a 'Tush!' of scorn and impatience. 'This is the babbling of a child. My father is no holy innocent as you and your like feign to believe.'

'Nevertheless I love you most well,' Katharine pleaded.

Mary snapped her book to. Her cold tone came back over her heat as the grey clouds of a bitter day shut down again upon a dangerous flicker of lightning.

'Do as you will,' she said, 'only if your head fall I will stir no finger to aid you. Or, if by these plottings my father could be got to send me his men upon their knees and bearing crowns, I would turn my back upon them and say no word.'

'Well, my plottings are like to end full soon,' Katharine said. 'Privy Seal hath sent for me upon no pleasant errand.'

Mary said: 'God help you!' with a frigid unconcern, and walked back to her chair.

VI

Cromwell kept as a rule his private courts either in his house at Austin Friars, or in a larger one that he had near the Rolls. But, when the King was as far away from London as Greenwich, or when such ill-wishers as the Duke of Norfolk were in the King's neighbourhood, Cromwell never slept far out of earshot from the King's rooms. It was said indeed that never once since he had become the King's man had he passed a day without seeing his Highness once at least, or writing him a great letter. But he contrived continually to send the nobles that were against him upon errands at a distance—as when Bishop Gardiner was made Ambassador to Paris, or Norfolk sent to put down the North after the Pilgrimage of Grace. Such errands served a double purpose: Gardiner, acting under the pressure of the King, was in Paris forced to make enemies of many of his foreign friends; and the Duke, in his panic-stricken desire to curry favour with Henry, had done more harrying, hanging and burning among the Papists than ever Henry or his minister would have dared to command, for in those northern parts the King's writ did not run freely. Thus, in spite of himself the Duke at York had been forced to hold the country whilst creatures of Privy Seal, men of the lowest birth and of the highest arrogance, had been made Wardens of the Marches and filled the Councils of the Borders. Such men, with others, like the judges and proctors of the Court of Augmentations, which Cromwell had invented to administer the estates of the monasteries and escheated lords' lands, with a burgess or two from the shires in Parliament, many lawyers and some suppliants of rank, filled the anterooms of Privy Seal. There was a matter of two hundred of them, mostly coming not upon any particular business so much as that any enemies they had who should hear of their having been there might tremble the more.

Cromwell himself was in the room that had the King's and Queen's heads on the ceiling and the tapestry of Diana hunting. He was speaking with a great violence to Sir Leonard Ughtred, whose sister-in-law, the widow of Sir Anthony Ughtred, and sister of the Queen Jane, his son Gregory had married two years before. It was a good match, for it made Cromwell's son the uncle of the Prince of Wales, but there had been a trouble about their estates ever since.

'Sir,' Cromwell threatened the knight, 'Gregory my son was ever a fool. If he be content that you have Hyde Farm that am not I. His wife may twist him to consent, but I will not suffer it.'

Ughtred hung his head, which was closely shaved, and fingered his jewelled belt.

'It is plain justice,' he muttered. 'The farm was ceded

to my brother after Hyde Monastery was torn down. It was to my brother, not to my brother's wife, who is now your son's.'

Cromwell turned upon the Chancellor of the Augmentations who stood in the shadow of the tall mantelpiece. He was twisting his fingers in his thin grey beard that wagged tremulously when he spoke.

'Truly,' he bleated piteously, 'it stands in the register of the Augmentations as the worshipful knight says.'

Cromwell cried out, in a studied rage: 'I made thee and I made thy office: I will unmake the one and the other if it and thou know no better law.'

'God help me,' the Chancellor gasped. He shrank again into the shadow of the chimney, and his blinking eyes fell upon Cromwell's back with a look of dread and the hatred of a beast that is threatened at the end of its hole.

'Sir,' Cromwell frowned darkly upon Ughtred, 'the law stands thus if the Augmentation people know it not. This farm and others were given to your late brother upon his marriage, that the sister of the Queen might have a proper state. The Statute of Uses hath here no say. Understand me: It was the King's to give; it is the King's still.' He opened his mouth so wide that he appeared to bellow. 'That farm falleth to the survivor of those two, who is now my son's wife. What judge shall gainsay that?' He swayed his body round on his motionless and sturdily planted legs, veering upon the Chancellor and the knight in turn, as if he challenged them to gainsay him who had been an attorney for ten years after he had been a wool merchant.

Ughtred shrugged his shoulders heavily, and the Chancellor hastened to bleat:

'No judge shall gainsay your lordship. Your lordship hath an excellent knowledge of the law.'

'Why hast thou not as good a one?' Cromwell rated him. 'I made thee since I thought thou hadst.' The Chancellor choked in his throat and waved his hands.

'Thus the law is,' Cromwell said to Ughtred. 'And if it were not so Parliament should pass an Act so to make it.

For it is a scandal that a Queen's sister, an aunt of the Prince that shall be King, should lose her lands upon the death of her husband. It savours of treason that you should ask it. I have known men go to the Tower upon less occasion.'

'Well, I am a broken man,' Sir Leonard muttered.

'Why, God help you,' Cromwell said. 'Get you gone. The law takes no account of whether a man be broken, but seeketh to do honour to the King's Highness and to render justice.'

Viridus and Sadler, who was another of Cromwell's secretaries, had come in whilst Privy Seal had been speaking, and Cromwell turned upon them laughing as the knight went out, his head hanging.

'Here is another broken man,' he said, and they all laughed together.

'Well, he is another very notable swordsman,' Viridus said. 'We might well post him at Milan, lest Pole flee back to Rome that way.'

Cromwell turned upon the Chancellor with a bitter contempt.

'Find thou for this knight some monk's lands in Kent. He shall to Milan with them for a price.'

Viridus laughed.

'Now we shall soon have these broken swordsmen in every town of Italy between France and Rome. Such a net Pole shall not easily break through.'

'It were well he were done with soon,' Cromwell said.

'The King shall love us much the more; and it is time.'

'Why, there will in two days be such a clamour of assassins in Paris that he shall soon bolt from there towards Rome,' Viridus answered. 'It will go hard if he escape all our Italy men. I hold it for certain that Winchester shall have reported to him in Paris that this Culpepper is on the road. Will you speak with this Howard wench?'

Cromwell knitted his brows in uncertainty.

'It was her cousin that should clamour about this murder in Paris,' Viridus reminded him.

'Is she without?' Cromwell asked. 'Have you it for certain that she hath reported to my lord of Winchester?'

'Winchester's priest of the bedchamber hath shewn me a copy of the letter she wrote. I would have your lordship send some reward to that Father Michael. He hath served us in many other matters.'

Cromwell motioned with his hand that Sadler should note down this Father Michael's name.

'Are there many men in my antechambers?' he asked Viridus, and hearing that there were more than one hundred and fifty: 'Why, let this wench stay there a half-hour. It humbles a woman to be alone among so many men, and she shall come here without a sound clout to her back for the crush of them.'

He began talking with Sadler about two globes of the world that he had ordered his agent to buy in Antwerp, one for himself and the other for a present to the King. Sadler answered that the price was very high; a thousand crowns or so, he had forgotten just how many. They had been twelve years in the making, but the agent had been afraid of the greatness of the expense.

Cromwell said:

'Tush; I must have the best of these Flemish furnishings.'

He signed to Viridus to send for Katharine Howard, and went on talking with Sadler about the furnishing of his house in the Austin Friars. He had his agents all over Flanders watching the noted masters of the crafts to see what notable pieces they might turn out; for he loved fine carvings, noble hangings, great worked chests and other signs of wealth, and the money was never thrown away, for the wood and the stuffs and the gold thread remained so long as you kept the moth and the woodlouse from them. To the King too he gave presents every day.

Katharine entered by a door from a corridor at which he had not expected her. She wore a great head-dress of net like the Queen's and her dress was in no disarray, neither were her cheeks flushed by anything more than apprehension. She said that she had been shown that way by a large gentleman with a great beard. She would not bring herself to mention the name of Throckmorton, so much she detested him.

Cromwell answered with a benevolent smile, 'Aye, Throckmorton had ever an eye for beauty. Otherwise you had come scurvily out of that wash.'

He twisted his mouth up as if he were mocking her, and asked her suddenly how the Lady Mary corresponded with her cousin the Emperor, for it was certain she had a means of writing to him?

Katharine flushed all over her face with relief and her heart stilled itself a little. Here at least there was no talk of the Tower at once for her, because she had written a letter to Bishop Gardiner. She answered that that day for the first time she had been in the Lady Mary's service.

He smiled benevolently still, and holding out a hand in a little warning gesture and with an air of pleasant reasonableness, said that she must earn her bread like other folks in his Highness' service.

'Why,' she answered, 'I have been marvellous ill, but I shall be more diligent in serving my mistress.'

He marked a distinction, pointing a fat finger at her heart-place. In the serving of her mistress she should do not enough work to pay for bodkins nor for sewing silk, since the Lady Mary asked nothing of her maids, neither their attendance, their converse, nor yet their needlework. Such a place asked nothing of one so fortunate as to fill it. To atone for it the service of the King demanded her labours.

'Why,' she said again, 'if I must spy in those parts it is a great pity that I ever came there as your woman; for who there shall open their hearts to me?'

He laughed at her comfortably still.

'You may put it about that you hate me,' he said. 'You may mix with them that love me not. In the end you may worm yourself into their secrets.'

Again a heavy flush covered Katharine's face from the

chin to the brow. It was so difficult for her to keep from speaking her mind with her lips that she felt as if her whole face must be telling the truth to him. But he continued to shake his plump sides as if he were uttering inaudible, 'Ho—ho—ho's.'

'That is so easy,' he said. 'A child, I think, could compass it.' He put his hands behind his back and stretched his legs apart. She was very pleasant to look at with her flushings, and it amused him to toy with frightened women. 'It is in this way that you shall earn his Highness' bread.' It was known that Mary had this treasonable correspondence with the Emperor; in the devilish malignancy of her heart she desired that her sacred father should be cast down and slain, and continually she implored her cousin to invade her father's dominions, she sending him maps, plans of the new castles in building and the names of such as were malevolent within the realm. 'Therefore,' he finished, 'if you could discover her channels and those channels could then be stopped up, you would indeed both earn your bread and enter into high favour.'

He began again good-humouredly to give her careful directions as to how she should act; as for instance by offering to make for the printers a fair copy of the Lady Mary's Commentary upon Plautus. By pretending that certain words were obscure to her, she should find opportunities for coming suddenly into the room, and she should afford herself excuses for searching among his mistress's papers without awakening suspicions.

'Why, my face is too ingenuous,' Katharine said. 'I am not made for playing the spy.'

He laughed at her.

'That is so much the better,' he said. 'The best spies are those that have open countenances. It needs but a little schooling.'

'I should get me a hang-dog look very soon,' she answered. She paused for a minute and then spoke earnestly, holding out her hands. 'I would you would set me a nobler task. Very surely it is shameful that a daughter should so hate the father that begat her; and I know the angels weep to see her desire that the great and noble prince should be cast down and slain by his enemies. But, sir, it were the better task to seek to soften her mind. Such knowledge as I have of goodly writers should aid me rather to persuade her heart towards her father; for I know no texts that should make me skilful as a spy, but I can give you a dozen from Plautus alone that do inculcate a sweet and dutiful love from daughter to sire.'

He leered at her pleasantly.

'Why, you speak sweetly, by the book. If the Lady Mary were a man now. . . .'

The hitherto silent men laid back their heads to laugh, and the Chancellor of the Augmentations suddenly rubbed his palms together, hissing like an ostler. But, seeing her look became angry and abashed, Cromwell stopped his sentence and once more held out a finger.

'Why, indeed,' he said, gravely, 'if you could do that you might be the first lady in the land, for neither the King nor I, nor yet all nor many have availed there.'

Katharine said:

'Surely there is a way to touch the heart of this noble lady, and by long seeking I may find.'

'Well, you have spoken many words,' Cromwell said. 'This is a great matter. If you shall achieve it, it shall be accounted to you both here and in heaven. But the other task I enjoin upon you.'

She was making sorrowfully to the door, and he called to her:

'I have found your cousin employment.'

The sudden mention made her stop as if she had been struck in the face, and she held her hand to her side. Her face was distorted with fear as she turned to answer:

'Aye. I knew. He hath told me. But I cannot thank you. I would not that my cousin should murder a prince of the Church.' She knew, from the feeling in her heart and the cruel sound of his voice that he had that knowledge already. If he wished to imprison her it could serve no turn to fence about that matter, and she steadied herself by catching hold of the tapestry with one hand behind her back. The faces of Cromwell's three assistants were upon her, hard, sardonic and grinning.

Viridus said, with an air of parade:

'I had told your lordship this lady had flaws in her loyalty.' And the Chancellor was raising his hands in horror, after the fashion of a Greek Chorus. Cromwell, however, grinned still at her.

'When the Queen Katharine died,' he said slowly, 'it was a great relief to this realm. When the late Arch Devil, Pope Clement, died, the King and I were mad with joy. But if all popes and all hostile queens and princes could be stricken with devils and dead to-morrow, his Highness would rather it were Reginald Pole.'

Katharine understood very well that he was setting before her the enormity of her offence: she stood still with her lips parted. He went on rehearsing the crimes of the cardinal: how he had been educated by the King's high bounty: how the King had offered him the Archbishopric of York: how he had the rather fled to the Bishop of Rome: how he had written a book, accusing the King of such crimes and heresies that all Christendom had cried out upon his Highness. Even then this Pole was in Paris with a bull from the Bishop of Rome calling upon the Emperor and the King of France to fall together upon their lord.

Katharine gasped:

'I would well he were dead. But not by my cousin. They should take my cousin and slay him.'

Cromwell had arranged this scene very carefully: for his power over the King fell away daily, and that day he had had to tell Baumbach, the Saxish ambassador, that there was no longer any hope of the King's allying himself with the Schmalkaldner league. Therefore he was the more hot to discover a new Papist treason. The suggestion of Viridus that Katharine might be made either to discover or to invent one had filled him with satisfaction. There was no one who could be more believed if she could be ground down into swearing away the life of her uncle or any other man of high station. And to grind her down thus needed only many threats. He infused gradually more terror into his narrow eyes, and spoke more gravely:

'Neither do I desire the death of this traitor so hotly as doth his Highness. For there be these foul lies—and have you not heard the ancient fool's prophecy that was made over thirty years ago: "That one with a Red Cap brought up from low degree should rule all the land under the King. (I trow ye know who that was.) And that after much mixing the land should by another Red Cap be reconciled or else brought to utter ruin"?'

'I am new to this place,' Katharine said; 'I never heard that saying. God help me, I wish this man were dead.'

His voice grew the more deep as he saw that she was the more daunted:

'Aye: and whether the land be reconciled to the Bishop of Rome, or be brought to utter ruin, the one and the other signify the downfall of his Highness.'

The Chancellor interrupted piously:

'God save us. Whither should we all flee then!'

'It is not,' Viridus commented dryly, 'that his Highness or my lord here do fear a fool prophecy made by a drunken man. But there being such a prophecy running up and down the land, and such a malignant and devilish Red Cap ranting up and down the world, the hearts of foolish subjects are made to turn.'

'Idiot wench,' the Chancellor suddenly yelped at her, 'ignorant, naughty harlot! You had better have died than have uttered those your pretty words.'

'Why,' Cromwell said gently, 'I am very sure that now you desire that your cousin should slay this traitor.' He paused, licked his lips and held out a hand. 'Upon your life,' he barked, 'tell no soul this secret.'

The faces of all the four men were again upon her, sardonic, leering and amused, and suddenly she felt that this was not the end of the matter: there was something untrue in this parade of threats. Cromwell was acting: they were all acting parts. Their speeches were all too long, too dryly spoken: they had been rehearsed! This was not the end of the matter—and neither her cousin nor Cardinal Pole was here the main point. She wondered for a wild moment if Cromwell, too, like Gardiner, thought that she had a voice with the King. But Cromwell knew as well as she that the King had seen her but once for a minute, and he was not a fool like Gardiner to run his nose into a mare's nest.

'There is no power upon earth could save you from your doom if through you this matter miscarried,' he said, softly: 'therefore, be you very careful: act as I would have you act: seek out that secret that I would know.'

It came irresistibly into Katharine's head:

'These men know already very well that I have written to Bishop Gardiner! This is to hold a halter continuously above my head!' Then, at least, they did not mean to do away with her instantly. She dropped her eyes upon the ground and stood submissively whilst Privy Seal's voice came cruel and level:

'You are a very fair wench, made for love and such stuff. You are an indifferent good Latinist who might offer good counsel. But be you very careful that you come not against me. You should not escape, but may burrow underground sooner than that. Your Aristotle should not help you, nor Lucretius, nor Lucan, nor Silius Italicus. Diodorus Siculus hath no maxim that should help you against me; but, like Diodorus the Dialectician, you should die of shame. Seneca shall help you if you but dally with that fool thought who sayeth: "*Quaeris quo jaceas post obitum loco? Quo non nata jacent.*" Aye, thou shalt die and lie in an unknown grave as thou hadst never been born.'

She went, her knees trembling half with fear and half with rage, for it was impossible to imagine anything more threatening or more arrogant than his soft, cruel voice, that seemed to sound for long after in her ears, saying, 'I have you at my mercy; see you do as I have bidden you.'

Watching the door that closed upon her, Viridus said, with a negligent amusement:

'That fool Udal hath set it all about that your lordship designed her for the recreation of his Highness.'

'Why,' Cromwell answered, with his motionless smile of contempt for his fellow men, 'it is well to offer bribes to fools and threats to knaves.'

The Chancellor bleated, with amazed adulation, 'Marvel that your lordship should give so much care to such a worthless rag!'

'An I had never put my heart into trifles, I had never stood here,' Cromwell snarled at him. 'Would that my knaves would ever come to learn that!' He spoke again to Viridus: 'See that this wench come never near his Highness. I like not her complexion.'

'Well, we may clap her up at any moment,' his man answered.

VII

The King came to the revels at the Bishop of Winchester's, for these too were given in honour of the Queen, and he had altered in his mind to let the Emperor and Francis know that he was inclined to weaken in his new alliances. Besides, there was the newest suitor for the hand of the Lady Mary, the young Duke Philip of Wittelsbach, who must be shown how great were the resources of the land. Young, gay, dark, a famous warrior and a good Catholic, he sat behind the Queen and speaking German of a sort he made her smile at times. The play was the *Menechmi* of Plautus, and Duke Philip interpreted it to her. She seemed at times so nearly human that the King, glancing back over his shoulder to note whether she disgraced him, could settle down into his chair and rest both his back and his misgivings. Seeing the frown leave his brow all the courtiers grew glad behind him; Cromwell talked with animation to Baumbach, the ambassador from the

Schmalkaldner league, since he had not seen the King so gay for many days, and Gardiner in his bishop's robes smiled with a black pleasure because his feast was so much more prosperous than Privy Seal's had been. There was no one there of the Lady Mary's household, because it was not seemly that she should be where her suitor was before he had been presented to her.

The large hall was lit with tapers at dusk and hung with ivy and with holly; dried woodruff, watermint and other sweet herbs were scattered about the floors to give an agreeable odour; the antlers of deer from the bishop's chase in Winchester were like a forest of dead boughs, branching from the walls, some gilded, some silvered, some supporting shields emblazoned with the arms of the See, of the bishop, of the King or of Cleves; an army of wood-pigeons and stock-doves with silver collars about their necks was at one time let fly into the hall, and the swish of their wings and afterwards their cooing among the golden rafters of the high ceiling made pleasing sound and mingled with the voices of sweet singing from the galleries at each end of the hall, near the roof. The players spoke their parts bravely, and, because this play was beloved among all others at the Court, there was a great and general contentment.

For the after scene they had a display of theology. There were three battles of men. In black with red hats, horns branching above them and in the centre a great devil with a triple tiara, who danced holding up an enormous key. These stood on the right. On the left were priests in fustian, holding enormous flagons of Rhenish wine and dancing in a drunken measure with their arms round more drunken doxies dressed like German women. In the centre stood grave and reverend men wearing horsehair beards and the long gowns of English bishops and priests. Before these there knelt an angel in flame-coloured robes with wings like the rainbow. The angel supported a great volume on the back of which might be read in letters of gold, 'Regis Nostri Sapientia.'

The great devil, dancing forward, brandishing his key, roared that these reverend men should kneel to him; he held out a cloven foot and bade them kiss it. But a venerable bishop cried out, 'You be Antichrist. I know you. You be the Arch Devil. But from this book I will confound you. Thank God that we have one that leads us aright.' Coming forward he read in Latin from the book of the King's Wisdom and the great devil fell back fainting into the arms of the men in red hats.

The King called out, 'By God, goodman Bishop, you have spoken well!' and the Court roared.

Then one from the other side danced out, holding his flagon and grasping his fat wife round the waist. He sang in a gross and German way, smacking his lips, that these reverend Englishmen should leave their godly ways and come down among the Lutherans. But the old bishop cried out, 'Ay, Dr Martinus, I know thee; thou despisest the Body of God; thou art a fornicator. God forbid that our English priests should go among women as ye do. Listen to wisdom. For, thank God, we have one to lead us aright!'

These words spread a sudden shiver into the hall, for no man there knew whether the King had commanded them to be uttered. The King sat back in his chair, half frowning; Anne blinked, Philip of Wittelsbach laughed aloud, the Catholic ambassadors, Chapuys and Marillac, who had fidgeted in their seats as if they would leave the hall, now leant forward.

'Aye,' the player bishop called out, 'our goodly Queen cometh from a Court that was never yet joined to your Schmalkaldners, nor to them that go by your name, Dr Martinus, thou lecher. Here in England you shall find no heresies but the pure and purged Word of God.'

Chapuys bent an aged white hand behind his ear to miss no word: his true and smiling face blinked benevolently. Cromwell smiled too, licking his lips dangerously; Baumbach, the Schmalkaldner, understanding nothing, rolled his German blue eyes in his great head like a pink baby's, and tried to catch the attention of Cromwell, who talked over his shoulder to one of his men. But the many Lutherans that there were in the hall scowled at the floor.

The player bishop was reading thunderous words of the King, written many years before, against married priests. Henry sat back in his round chair, grasping the arms with his enormous hands.

'Why, Master Bishop,' he called out. The player stopped his reading and looked at the King, his air of austerity never leaving him. Henry, however, waved his hand and said no more.

This dreadful incident caused a confusion in the players: they faltered: the player Lutheran slunk back to his place with his wife, and all of them stood with their hands hanging down. They consulted among themselves and at last filed out from the room, leaving the stage for some empty minutes bare and menacing. Men held their breath: the King was seen to be frowning. But a quick music was played from the galleries and a door opened behind. There came in many figures in white to symbolify the deities of ancient Greece and Rome, and, in black, with ashes upon her head, there was Ceres lamenting that Persephone had been carried into the realms of Pluto. No green thing should blow nor grow upon this earth, she wailed in a deep and full voice, until again her daughter trod there. The other deities covered their heads with their white skirts.

No one heeded this show very much in the hall, for the whispers over what had gone before never subsided again that day. Men turned their backs upon the stage in order to talk with others behind them, and it was generally agreed that if this refurbishing of old doctrines were no more than a bold stroke of Bishop Gardiner's, Henry at least had not scowled very harshly upon it. So that, for the most part, they thought that the Old Faith might come back again; whilst others suddenly remembered, much more clearly than before, that Cleves was a principality not truly Lutheran, and that the marriage with Anne had not tied them at all to the Schmalkaldner's league.

Therefore this shadow of the old ways caused new un-easiness, for there was hardly any man there that had not some of the monastery lands.

The King was the man least moved in the hall: he listened to the lamentations of Mother Ceres and gazed at a number of naked boys who issued suddenly from the open door. They spread green herbs in a path from the door to the very feet of Anne, who blinked at them in amazement, and they paid no heed to Mother Ceres, who asked indignantly how any green thing could grow upon the earth that she had bidden lie barren till her daughter came again.

Persephone stood framed in the doorway: she was all in white, very slim and tall; in among her hair she had a wreath of green Egyptian stones called feridets, of which many remained in the treasuries of Winchester, because they were soft and of so little value that the visitors of the monasteries had left them there. And she had these green feridets, cut like leaves, worked into the white lawn, over her breasts. In her left arm there lay a cornucopia filled with gold coins, and in her right a silver coronet of olive leaves. She moved in a slow measure to the music, bending her knees to right and to left, and drawing her long dress into white lines and curves, until she stood in the centre of the green path. She smiled patiently and with a rapt ex-pression as if she had come out of a dream. The wreath of olive leaves, she said, the gods sent to their most virtuous, most beauteous Queen, who had brought peace in England; the cornucopia filled with gold was the offering of Plutus to the noble and benevolent King of these parts. Her words could hardly be heard for the voices of the theologians in the hall before her.

Henry suddenly turned back, lifted his hand, and shouted:

'Be silent!'

Persephone's voice became very audible in the midst of the terrified hush of all these people, who feared their enormous King as if he were a wild beast that at one moment you could play with and the next struck you dead.

'—How happy is England among the nations!' The voice rang out clear and fluting like a boy's. 'Her people how free and bold! Her laws how gentle and beneficent, her nobles how courteous and sweet in their communings together for the public weal! How thrice happy that land when peace is upon the earth! Her women how virtuous, her husbandmen how satiated, her cattle how they let down their milk!'—She swayed round to the gods that were uncovering their heads behind her: 'Aye, my masters and fellow godheads: woe is me that we knew never this happy and contented country. Better it had been there to dwell than upon high Olympus: better than in the Cyclades: better than in the Islands of the Blest that hide amid the Bermoothean tempest. Woe is me!' Her expression grew more rapt; she paused as if she had lost the thread of the words and then spoke again, gazing far out over the hall as jugglers do in performing feats of balancing: 'For surely we had been more safe than reigning alone above the clouds had we lived here, the veriest hinds, beneath a King that is five times blessed, in that he is most wealthy and generous of rewards, most noble of courage, most eloquent, most learned in the law of men, and most high interpreter of the law of God!'

Seeing that the King smiled, as though he had received a just panegyric, a great clamour of applause went up in the hall, and swaying beneath the weight of the cornucopia she came to the King over the path of green herbs and boughs. Henry reached out his hands, himself, to take his present, smiling and genial; and that alone was a sign of great favour, for by rights she should have knelt with it, offered it and then receded, giving it into the arms of a serving man. She passed on, and would have crowned the Queen with the silver wreath; but the great hood that Anne wore stood in the way, therefore she laid it in the Queen's lap.

Henry caught at her hanging sleeve.

'That was a gay fine speech,' he said. 'I will have it printed.'

Little ripples of fear and coldness ran over her, for her dress was thin and her arms bared between the loops above. Her eyes roved round upon the people as if, tall and white, she were a Christian virgin in the agonies of martyrdom. She tried to pull her sleeve from between his great fingers, and she whispered in a sort of terror:

'You stay the masque!'

He lay back in his chair, laughing so that his grey beard shook.

'Why, thou art a pert baggage,' he said. 'I could stay their singing for good an I would.'

He looked her up and down, commanding and good-humouredly malicious. She put her hand to her throat as if it throbbed, and uttered with a calmness of desperation:

'That were great pity. They have practised much, and their breaths are passable sweet.'

The godheads with their beards of tow, their lyres and thunderbolts all gilt, stood in an awkward crescent, their music having stopped. Henry laughed at them.

'I know thy face,' he said. 'It would be less than a king to forget it.'

'I am Katharine Howard,' she faltered, stretching out her hands beseechingly. 'Let me go back to my place.'

'Oh, aye!' he answered. 'But thou'st shed thy rags since I saw thee on a mule.' He loosed her sleeve. 'Let the good men sing,'a God's name.'

In her relief to be free she stumbled on the sweet herbs.

*   *   *   *

It was a dark night into which they went out from the bishop's palace. Cressets flared on his river steps, and there were torches down the long garden for those who went away by road. Because there would be a great crowd of embarkers at the bishop's landing place, so that there might be many hours to wait until their barge should come, Katharine, by the office of old Sir Nicholas, had made a

compact with some of the maids of honour of the Lady
Elizabeth; a barge was to wait for them at the Cross
Keys, a common stage some ten minutes down the river.
Katharine, laughing, gay with relief and gladdened with
words of praise, held Margot's hand tight and kept her
fingers on Sir Nicholas' sleeve. It was raining a fine drizzle,
so that the air of the gardens smelt moist even against the
odour of the torches. The old knight pulled the hood of
his gown up over his head, for he was hoarse with a heavy
cold. It was pitch black beyond the gate house; in the open
fields before the wall torches here and there appeared to
burn in mid-air, showing beneath them the heads and the
hoods of their bearers hurrying home, and, where they
turned to the right along a narrow lane, a torch showed
far ahead above a crowd packed thick between dark house-
fronts and gables. They glistened with wet and sent down
from their gutters spouts of water that gleamed, catching
the light of the torch, like threads of opal fire on the pallid
dove colour of the towering house-fronts. The torch went
round a corner, its light withdrew along the walls by long
jumps as its bearer stepped into the distance ahead. Then
it was all black. Walking was difficult over the immense
cobbles of the roadway, but in the pack of the crowd it
was impossible to fall, for people held one another. But it
was also impossible to speak, and, muffling her face in her
hood, Katharine walked smiling and squeezing Margot's
hand out of pure pleasure with the world that was so fair
in the midst of this blackness and this heavy cold.

There was a swishing repeated three times and three
thuds and twists of white on heads and shoulders just
before her. Undistinguishable yells of mockery dwindled
down from high above, and a rushlight shone at an
immense elevation illuminating a faint square of casement
that might have been in the heavens. Three apprentices
had thrown down paper bags of powdered chalk. The men
who had been struck, and several others who had been
maltreated on former nights, or who resented this continual 'prentice scandal, began a frightful outcry at the

door of the house. More bags came bursting down and foul water; the yells and battlecries rolled, in the narrow space under the house-fronts that nearly kissed each other high overhead, and the crowd, brought to a standstill, swayed and pushed against the walls. Katharine lost her hold of the old knight's sleeve, and she could see no single thing. She felt round her in the blackness for his arm, but a heavy man stumbled against her. Suddenly his hand was under her arm, drawing her a little; his voice seemed to say: 'Down this gully is a way about.'

In the passage it was blacker than the mouth of hell, and her eyes still seemed to have in them the dazzle of light and triumph she had just left. There was a frightful stench of garbage; and it appeared to be a vault, because the outcry of the men besieging the door volleyed and echoed the more thunderously. There came the sharp click of a latch and Katharine found herself impelled to descend several steps into a blackness from which came up a breath of closer air and a smell of rotting straw. Fear suddenly seized upon her, and the conviction that another man had taken the place of the old knight during the scuffle. But a heavy pressure of an arm was suddenly round her waist, and she was forced forward. She caught a shriek from Margot; the girl's hand was torn from her own; a door slammed behind, and there was a deep silence in which the heavy breathing of a man became audible.

'If you cry out,' a soft voice said, 'I will let you go. But probably you will lose your life.'

She had not a breath at all in her, but she gasped:

'Will you do a rape?' and fumbled in her pocket for her crucifix. Her voice came back to her, muffled and close, so that she was in a very small cellar.

'When you have seen my face, you may love me,' came to her ears in an inane voice. 'I would you might, for you have a goodly mouth for kisses.'

She breathed heavily; the click of the beads on her cross filled the silence. She fitted the bar of the crucifix to her knuckles and felt her breath come calmer. For, if the man struck a light she could strike him in the face with the metal of her cross, held in the fist; she could blind him if she hit an eye. She stepped back a little and felt behind her the damp stone of a wall. The soft voice uttered more loudly:

'I offer you a present of great price; I can solve your perplexities.' Katharine breathed between her teeth and said nothing. 'But if you draw a knife,' the voice went on, 'I will set you loose; there are as good as Madam Howard.' On the door there came the sound of soft thuds. 'That is your maid, Margot Poins,' the voice said. 'You had better bid her begone. This is a very evil gully; she will be strangled.'

Katharine called:

'Go and fetch some one to break down this door.'

The voice commented:

'In the City she will find none to enter this gully; it is a sanctuary of outlaws.'

There was the faintest glimmer of a casement square, high up before Katharine; violence and carryings off were things familiar to her imagination. A hundred men might have desired her whilst she stood on high in the masque. She said hotly:

'If you will hold me here for a ransom, you will find none to pay it.'

She heard the soft hiss of a laugh, and the voice:

'I would myself pay more than other men, but I would have no man see us together.'

She shrank into herself, and held to the wall for comfort. She heard a click, and in the light of a shower of brilliant sparks was the phantom of a man's beard and dim walls; one tiny red glow remained in the tinder, like an illuminant in a black nothingness. He seemed to hold it about breast-high and to pause.

'You had best be rid of Margot Poins,' the musing voice came out of the thick air. 'Send her back to her mother's people: she gets you no friends.'

Katharine wondered if she might strike about eighteen

inches above the tiny spark: or if in these impenetrable shadows there were a very tall man.

'Your Margot's folk miscall you in shameful terms. I would be your servant; but it is distasteful to a proper man to serve one that hath about her an atmosphere of lewdness.'

Katharine cursed at him to relieve the agony of her fear.

The voice answered composedly:

'One greater than the devil is my master. But it is good hearing that you are loyal to them that serve you: so you shall be loyal to me, for I will serve you well.'

The spark in the tinder moved upwards; the man began to blow on it; in the dim glimmer there appeared red lips, a hairy moustache, a straight nose, gleaming eyes that looked across the flame, a high narrow forehead, and the gleam of a jewel in a black cap. This glowing and dusky face appeared to hang in the air. Katharine shrank with despair and loathing: she had seen enough to know the man. She made a swift step towards it, her arm drawn back; but the glow of the box moved to one side, the ashes faded: there was already nothing before she could strike.

'You see I am Throckmorton: a goodly knight,' the voice said, laughing.

This man came from Lincolnshire, near her own home. He had been the brother of a gentleman who had a very small property, and he had had one sister. God alone knew for what crime his father had cursed Throckmorton and left his patrimony to the monks at Ely—but his sister had hanged herself. Throckmorton had disappeared.

In that black darkness she had seemed to feel his gloating over her helplessness, and his laughing over all the villainies of his hateful past. He was so loathsome to her that merely to be near him had made her tremble when, the day before, he had fawned over her and shown her the side door to Privy Seal's room. Now the sound of his breathing took away all her power to breathe. She panted:

'Infamous dog, I will have you shortened by the head for this rape.'

'It is true I am a fool to play cat and mouse,' he answered. 'But I was ever thus from a child: I have played silly pranks: listen to gravity. I bring you here because I would speak to you where no ear dare come to listen: this is a sanctuary of night robbers.' His voice took on fantastically and grotesquely the nasal tones of Doctors of Logic when they discuss abstract theses: 'I am a bold man to dare come here; but some of these are in my pay. Nevertheless I am a bold man, though indeed the step from life into death is so short and so easily passed that a man is a fool to fear it. Nevertheless some do fear it; therefore, as men go, I am bold; tho', since I set much store in the intervention of the saints on my behalf, may be I am not so bold. Yet I am a good man, or the saints would not protect me. On the other hand, I am fain to do their work for them: so may be, they would protect me whether I were virtuous or no. Maybe they would not, however: for it is a point still disputed as to whether a saint might use an evil tool to do good work. But, in short, I am here to tell you what Privy Seal would have of you.'

'God help the pair of you,' Katharine said. 'Have ye descended to cellar work now?'

'Madam Howard,' the voice came, 'for what manner of man do you take me? I am a very proper man that do love virtue. There are few such philosophers as I since I came out of Italy.'

It was certain to her now that Privy Seal, having seen her thick with the Bishop of Winchester, had delivered her into the hands of this vulture. 'If you have a knife,' she said, 'put it into me soon. God will look kindly on you and I would pardon you half the crime.' She closed her eyes and began to pray.

'Madam Howard,' he answered, in a lofty tone of aggrievement, 'the door is on the latch: the latch is at your hand to be found for a little fumbling: get you gone if you will not trust me.'

'Aye: you have cut-throats without,' Katharine said. She prayed in silence to Mary and the saints to take her into the kingdom of heaven with a short agony here below. Nevertheless, she could not believe that she was to die: for being still young, though death was always round her, she believed herself born to be immortal.

The sweat was cold upon her face; but Throckmorton was upbraiding her in a lofty nasal voice.

'I am an honourable knight,' he cried, in his affected and shocked tones. 'If I have undone men, it was for love of the republic. I have nipped many treasons in the bud. The land is safe for a true man, because of my work.'

'You are a werewolf,' she shuddered; 'you eat your brother.'

'Why, enough of this talk,' he answered. 'I offer you a service, will you take it? I am the son of a gentleman: I love wisdom for that she alone is good. Virtue I love for virtue's sake, and I serve my King. What more goeth to the making of a proper man? You cannot tell me.'

His voice changed suddenly:

'If you do hate a villain, now is the time to prove it. Would you have him down? Then tell your gossip Winchester that the time approaches to strike, and that I am ready to serve him. I have done some good work for the King's Highness through Privy Seal. But my nose is a good one. I begin to smell out that Privy Seal worketh treasonably.'

'You are a mad fool to think to trick me,' Katharine said. 'Neither you nor I, nor any man, believes that Privy Seal would work a treason. You would trick me into some foolish utterances. It needed not a cellar in a cut-throat's gully for that.'

'Madam Spitfire,' his voice answered, 'you are a true woman; I a true man. We may walk well together. Before the Most High God I wish you no ill.'

'Then let me go,' she cried. 'Tell me your lies some other where.'

'The latch is near your hand still,' he said. 'But I will speak to you no other where. It is only here in the abode of murder and evil men that in these evil times a man may speak his mind and fear no listener.'

She felt tremulously for the latch; it gave, and its rattling set her heart on the jump. When she pulled the door ajar she heard voices in the distant street. It rushed through her mind that he was set neither on murder nor unspeakable things. Or, indeed, he had cut-throats waiting to brain her on the top step. She said tremulously:

'Tell me what you will with me in haste!'

'Why, I have bidden your barge fellows wait for you,' he answered. 'Till cock-crow if need were. They shall not leave you. They fear me too much. Shut the door again, for you dread me no more.'

Her knees felt suddenly limp and she clung to the latch for support; she believed that Mary had turned the heart of this villain. He repeated that he smelt treason working in the mind of an evil man, and that he would have her tell the Bishop of Winchester.

'I did bring you here, for it is the quickest way. I came to you for I saw that you were neither craven nor fool: nor high placed so that it would be dangerous to be seen talking with you later, when you understood my good will. And I am drawn towards you since you come from near my home.'

Katharine said hurriedly, between her prayers:

'What will you of me? No man cometh to a woman without seeking something from her.'

'Why, I would have you look favourably upon me,' he answered. 'I am a goodly man.'

'I am meat for your masters,' she answered with bitter contempt. 'You have the blood of my kin on your hands.'

He sighed, half mockingly.

'If you will not give me your favours,' he said in a low, laughing voice, 'I would have you remember me according as my aid is of advantage to you.'

'God help you,' she said; 'I believe now that you have it in mind to betray your master.'

'I am a man that can be very helpful,' he answered, with

his laughing assurance that had always in it the ring of a sneer. 'Tell Bishop Gardiner again, that the hour approaches to strike if these cowards will ever strike.'

Katharine felt her pulses beat more slowly.

'Sir,' she said, 'I tell you very plainly that I will not work for the advancement of the Bishop of Winchester. He turned me loose upon the street to-night after I had served him, with neither guard to my feet nor bit to my mouth. If my side goes up, he may go with it, but I love him not.'

'Why, then, devise with the Duke of Norfolk,' he answered after a pause. 'Gardiner is a black rogue and your uncle a yellow craven; but bid them join hands till the time comes for them to cut each other's throats.'

'You are a foul dog to talk thus of noblemen,' she said. He answered:

'Oh, la! You have little to thank your uncle for. What do you want? Will you play for your own hand? Or will you partner those two against the other?'

'I will never partner with a spy and a villain,' she cried hotly.

He cried lightly:

'Ohé, Goosetherumfoodle! You will say differently before long. If you will fight in a fight you must have tools. Now you have none, and your situation is very parlous.'

'I stand on my legs, and no man can touch me,' she said hotly.

'But two men can hang you to-morrow,' he answered. 'One man you know; the other is the Sieur Gardiner. Cromwell hath contrived that you should write a treasonable letter; Gardiner holdeth that letter's self.'

Katharine braved her own sudden fears with:

'Men are not such villains.'

'They are as occasion makes them,' he answered, with his voice of a philosopher. 'What manner of men these times breed you should know if you be not a fool. It is very certain that Gardiner will hang you, with that letter, if you work not into his goodly hands. See how you stand in need of a counsellor. Now you wish you had done otherwise.'

She said hotly:

'Never. So I would act again to-morrow.'

'Oh fool madam,' he answered. 'Your cousin's province was never to come within a score miles of the cardinal. Being a drunkard and a boaster he was sent to Paris to get drunk and to boast.'

The horror of the blackness, the damp, the foul smell, and all this treachery made her voice faint. She stammered:

'Shew me a light, or let the door be opened. I am sick.'

'Neither,' he answered. 'I am as much as you in peril. With a light men may see in at the casement; with an open door they may come eavesdropping. When you have been in this world as long as I you will love black night as well.'

Her brain swam for a moment.

'My cousin was never in this plot against me,' she uttered faintly.

He answered lightly:

'You may keep your faith in that toppet. Where you are a fool is to have believed that Privy Seal, who is a wise man, or Viridus, who is a philosopher after my heart, would have sent such a sot and babbler on such a tickle errand.'

'He was sent!' protested Katharine.

'Aye, he was sent to blab about it in every tavern in Paris town. He was sent to frighten the Red Cap out of Paris town. He was suffered to blab to you that you might set your neck in a noose and be driven to be a spy.'

His soft chuckle came through the darkness like an obscene applause of a successful villainy; it was as if he were gloating over her folly and the rectitude of her mind.

'Red Cap was working mischief in Paris—but Red Cap is timorous. He will go post haste back to Rome, either because of your letter or because of your cousin's boasting. But there are real and secret murderers waiting for him in every town in Italy on the road to Rome. Some are at

Brescia, some at Rimini: at Padua there is a man with his neck, like yours, in a noose. It is a goodly contrivance.'

'You are a vile pack,' Katharine said, and once more the smooth and unctuous sound came from his invisible throat.

'How shall you decide what is vileness, or where will you find a virtuous man?' he asked. 'Maybe you will find some among the bones of your old Romans. Yet your Seneca, in his day, did play the villain. Or maybe some at the Court of Mahound. I know not, for I was never there. But here is a goodly world, with prizes for them that can take them. Yet virtue may still flourish, for I have done middling well by serving my country. Now I am minded to retire into my lands, to cultivate good letters and to pursue virtue. For here about the Courts there are many distractions. The times are evil times. Yet will I do one good stroke more before I go.'

Katharine said hotly:

'If you go down into Lincolnshire, I will call upon every man there to fall upon you and hang you.'

'Why,' he said, 'that is why I did come to you, since you are from where my lands are. If I serve you, I would have you to smooth my path there. I ask no more, for now I crave rest and a private life. It is very assured that I should never find that here or in few parts of the land—so well I have served my King. Therefore, if I serve you, you and yours shall cast above my retired farms and my honourable leisure the shadow of your protection. I ask no more.' He chuckled almost inaudibly. 'I am set to watch you,' he said. 'Viridus will go to Paris to catch another traitor called Brancetor, for the world is full of traitors. Therefore, in a way, it rests with me to hang you.'

He seemed to be seated upon a cask, for there was a creaking of old wood, and he spoke very leisurely.

Katharine said, 'Good night, and God send you better thoughts.'

'Why, stay, and I will be brief,' he pleaded. 'I dally because it is sweet talking to a fair woman in a black place.'

'You are easily content, for all the sweet words you get from me,' she scorned him.

'See you,' he said earnestly. 'It is true that I am set to watch you. I love you because you are fair; I might bend you, since I hold you in the hollow of my hand. But I am a continent man, and there is here a greater stake to be had than any amorous satisfaction. I would save my country from a man who has been a friend, but is grown a villain. Listen.'

He appeared to pause to collect his words together.

'Baumbach, the Saxish ambassador, is here seeking to tack us to the Schmalkaldner heresies. Yesterday he was with Privy Seal, who loveth the Lutheran alliance. So Privy Seal takes him to his house, and shows him his marvellous armoury, which is such that no prince nor emperor hath elsewhere. So says Privy Seal to Baumbach: "*I love your alliance; but his Highness will naught of it.*" And he fetched a heavy sigh.'

Katharine said:

'What is this hearsay to me?'

'He fetched a heavy sigh,' Throckmorton continued. 'An your uncle or Gardiner knew how heavy a sigh it was their hearts would be very glad.'

'This means that the King's Highness is very far from Privy Seal?' Katharine asked.

'His Highness hateth to do business with small princelings.' Throckmorton seemed to laugh at the King's name. 'His high and princely stomach loveth only to deal with his equals, who are great kings. I have seen the letters that have passed about this Cleves wedding. Not one of them is from his Highness' hand. It is Privy Seal alone that shall bear the weight of the blow when rupture cometh.'

'Well, she is a foul slut,' Katharine said, and her heart was full of sympathy for the heavy King.

'Nay, she is none such,' Throckmorton answered. 'If you look upon her with an unjaundiced eye, she will pass for a Christian to be kissed. It is not her body that his Highness hateth, but her fathering. This is a very old

quarrel betwixt him and Privy Seal. His Highness hath
been wont to see himself the arbiter of the Christian world.
Now Privy Seal hath made of him an ally of German
princelings. His Highness loveth the Old Faith and the
old royal ways. Now Privy Seal doth seek to make him
take up the faith of Schmalkaldners, who are a league of
bakers and unfrocked monks. Madam Howard, I tell you
that if there were but one man that could strike after the
new Parliament is called together . . .'

Katharine cried:

'The very stones that Cromwell hath soaked with blood
will rise to fall upon him when the King's feet no longer
press them down.'

Throckmorton laughed almost inaudibly.

'Norfolk feareth Gardiner for a spy; Gardiner feareth
the ambition of Norfolk; Bonner would sell them both to
Privy Seal for the price of an archbishopric. The King
himself is loth to strike, since no man in the land could
get him together such another truckling Parliament as can
Privy Seal.'

He stopped speaking and let his words soak into her in
the darkness, and after a long pause her voice came back
to her.

'It is true that I have heard no man speak as you do.
. . . I can see that his dear Highness must be hatefully
inclined to this filthy alliance.'

'Why, you are minded to come into my hut with me,'
he chuckled. 'There are few men so clear in the head as I
am. So listen again to me. If you would strike at this man,
it is of no avail to meddle with him at home. It shall in no
way help you to clamour of good monks done to death, of
honest men ruined, of virgins thrown on to dung-heaps.
The King hath had the pence of these good monks, the
lands of these honest men, and the golden neck-collars off
these virgins.'

She called out, 'Keep thy tongue off this sacred King's
name. I will listen to no more lewdness.'

A torch passing outside sent a moving square of light

through the high grating across the floor of the cellar. The damp walls became dimly visible with shining snail-tracks on them, and his great form leaning negligently upon a cask, his hand arrested in the pulling of his long beard, his eyes gleaming upon her, sardonic and amused. The light twisted round abruptly and was gone.

'You are monstrous fair,' he said, and sighed. She shuddered.

'No,' his mocking voice came again, 'speak not to the King—not to whomsoever you shall elect to speak to the King—of this man's work at home. The King shall let him go very unwillingly, since no man can so pack a Parliament to do the King's pleasure. And he hath a nose for treasons that his Highness would give his own nose to possess.'

'Keep thy tongue off the King's name,' she said again.

He laughed, and continued pensively: 'A very pretty treason might be made up of his speech before his armoury to Baumbach. Mark again how it went. Says he: "*Here are such weaponings as no king, nor prince, nor emperor hath in Christendom. And in this country of ours are twenty gentlemen, my friends, have armouries as great or greater.*" Then he sighs heavily, and saith: "*But our King will never join with your Schmalkaldners. Yet I would give my head that he should.*". . . Your madamship marks that this was said to the ambassador from the Lutheran league?'

'You cannot twist that into a treason,' Katharine whispered.

'No doubt,' he said reasonably, 'such words from a minister to an envoy are but a courtesy, as one would say, "*I fain would help you, but my master wills it not.*" '

The voice suddenly grew crafty. 'But these words, spoken before an armoury and the matter of twenty gentlemen with armouries greater. Say that these twenty are creatures of my Lord Cromwell, *implicitur*, for the Lutheran cause. And again, the matter, "*No king hath such an armoury.*". . . *No* king, I would have you observe.'

'Why, this is monstrous foolish pettifogging,' Katharine said. 'No king would believe a treason in such words.'

'I call to mind Gilmaw of Hurstleas, near our homes,' the voice came, reflectively.

'I did know him,' said Katharine. 'You had his head.'

'You never heard how Privy Seal did that,' the voice came back mockingly. 'Goodman Gilmaw had many sheep died of the rot because it rained seven weeks on end. So, coming back from a market-day, with too much ale for prudence and too little for silence, he cried, "*Curse on this rain! The weather was never good since knaves ruled about the King.*" So that came to the ears of Privy Seal, who made a treason of it, and had his sheep, and his house, and his lands, and his head. He was but one in ten thousand that have gone the same road home from market and made speeches as treasonable.'

'Thus poor Gilmaw died?' Katharine asked. 'What a foul world this is!'

'Time it was cleansed,' he answered.

He let his words rankle for a time, then he said softly: 'Privy Seal's words before his armoury were as treasonable as Gilmaw's on the market road.'

Again he paused.

'Privy Seal may call thee to account for such a treason,' he said afterwards. 'He holdeth thee in a hollow of his hand.'

She did not speak.

He said softly: 'It is a folly to be too proud to fight the world with the world's weapons.'

The heavy darkness seemed to thrill with her silence. He could tell neither whether she were pondering his words nor whether she still scorned him. He could not even hear her breathing.

'God help me!' he said at last, in an angry high note, 'I am not such a man as to be played with too long. People fear me.'

She kept silence still, and his voice grew high and shrill: 'Madam Howard, I can bend you to my will. I have the power to make such a report of you as will hang you to-morrow.'

Her voice came to him expressionlessly—without any inflexion. In few words, what would he have of her? She played his own darkness off against him, so that he could tell nothing new of her mood.

He answered swiftly: 'I will that you tell the men you know what I have told you. You are a very little thing; it were no more to me to cut you short than to drown a kitten. But my own neck I prize. What I have told you I would have come to the ears of my lord of Winchester. I may not be seen to speak with him myself. If you will not tell him, another will; but I would rather it were you.'

'Evil dreams make thy nights hideous!' she cried out so suddenly that his voice choked in his throat. 'Thou art such dirt as I would avoid to tread upon; and shall I take thee into my hand?' She was panting with disgust and scorn. 'I have listened to thee; listen thou to me. Thou art so filthy that if thou couldst make me a queen by the touch of a finger, I had rather be a goose-girl and eat grass. If by thy forged tales I could cast down Mahound, I had rather be his slave than thy accomplice! Could I lift my head if I had joined myself to thee? thou Judas to the Fiend. Junius Brutus, when he did lay siege to a town, had a citizen come to him that would play the traitor. He accepted his proffered help, and when the town was taken he did flay the betrayer. But thou art so filthy that thou shouldst make me do better than that noble Roman, for I would flay thee, disdaining to be aided by thee; and upon thy skin I would write a message to thy master saying that thou wouldst have betrayed him!'

His laugh rang out discordant and full of black mirth; for a long time his shoulders seemed to shake. He spoke at last quite calmly.

'You will have a very short course in this world,' he said.

A hoarse and hollow shouting reverberated from the gully; the glow of a torch grew bright in the window-space. Katharine had been upon the point of opening the door, but she paused, fearing to meet some night villains in the gully. Throckmorton was now silent, as if he utterly disdained her, and a frightful blow upon the wood of the door—so certain were they that the torch would pass on—made them spring some yards further into the cellar. The splintering blows were repeated; the sound of them was deafening. Glaring light entered suddenly through a great crack, and the smell of smoke. Then the door fell in half, one board of it across the steps, the other smashing back to the wall upon its hinges. Sparks dripped from the torch, smoke eddied down, and upon the cellar steps were the legs of a man who rested a great axe upon the ground and panted for breath.

'Up the steps!' he grunted. 'If you ever ran, now run. The guard will not enter here.'

Katharine sped up the steps. It was old Rochford's face that greeted hers beneath the torch. He grunted again, 'Run you; I am spent!' and suddenly dashed the torch to the ground.

At the entry of the tunnel some make of creature caught at her sleeve. She screamed and struck at a gleaming eye with the end of her crucifix. Then nothing held her, and she ran to where, at the mouth of the gully, there were a great many men with torches and swords peering into the darkness of the passage.

*   *   *   *

In the barge Margot made an outcry of joy and relief, and the other ladies uttered civil speeches. The old man, whose fur near the neck had been slashed by a knife-thrust as he came away, explained pleasantly that he was able to strike good blows still. But he shook his head nevertheless. It was evil, he said, to have such lovers as this new one. Her cousin was bad, but this rapscallion must be worse indeed to harbour her in such a place. . . . Margot, who knew her London, had caught him at the barge, to which he had hurried.

'Aye,' he said, 'I thought you had played me a trick and gone off with some spark. But when I heard to what place, I fetched the guard along with me. . . . Well for you that it

was I, for they had not come for any other man, and then
you had been stuck in the street. For, see you, whether
you would have had me fetch you away or no it is ten to
one that a gallant who would take you there would mean
that you should never come away alive—and God help you
whilst you lived in that place.'

Katharine said:

'Why, I pray God that you may die on the green grass
yet, with time for a priest to shrive you. I was taken there
against my will.' She told him no more of the truth, for it
was not every man's matter, and already she had made up
her mind that there was but one man to whom to speak. . . .
She went into the dark end of the barge and prayed until
she came to Greenwich, for the fear of the things she had
escaped still made her shudder, and in the company of
Mary and the saints of Lincolnshire alone could she feel
any calmness. She thought they whispered round her in
the night amid the lapping of the water.

VIII

The stables were esteemed the most magnificent that the
King had: three times they had been pulled down and
again set up after designs by Holbein the painter. The
buildings formed three sides of a square: the fourth gave
into a great paddock, part of the park, in which the horses
galloped or the mares ran with their foals. That morning
there was a glint of sun in the opalescent clouds: horse-
boys in grey with double roses worked on their chests were
spreading sand in the great quadrangle, fenced in with
white palings, between the buildings where the chargers
were trained to the manage. Each wing of the buildings
was a quarter of a mile long, of grey stone thatched with
rushwork that came from the great beds all along the river
and rose into curious peaks like bushes along each gable.
On the right were the mares, the riding jennets for the
women and their saddle rooms; on the left the pack

animals, mules for priests and the places for their housings:
in the centre, on each side of a vast barn that held the
provender, were the stables of the coursers and stallions
that the King himself rode or favoured; of these huge
beasts there were two hundred: each in a cage within the
houses—for many were savage tearers both of men and of
each other. On the door of each cage there was written the
name of the horse, as Sir Brian, Sir Bors, or Old Leo —
and the sign of the constellation under which each was
born, the months in which, in consequence, it was propitious or dangerous to ride them, and pentagons that
should prevent witches, warlocks or evil spirits from casting spells upon the great beasts. Their housings and their
stall armour, covered with grease to keep the rust from
them, hung upon pulleys before each stall, and their
polished neck armours branched out from the walls in a
long file, waving over the gateways right into the distance,
the face-pieces with the shining spikes in the foreheads
hanging at the ends, the eyeholes carved out and the
nostril places left vacant, so that they resembled an arcade
of the skeletons of unicorns' heads.

It was quiet and warm in the long and light aisles: there
was a faint smell of stable hartshorn and the sound of
beans being munched leisurely. From time to time there
came a thunder from distant boxes, as two untrained
stallions that Privy Seal the day before had given the King
kicked against the immense balks of the sliding doors in
their cage-stalls.

The old knight was flustered because it was many days
since the King had deigned to come in the morning, and
there were many beasts to show him. In his steel armour,
from which his old head stood out benign and silvery, he
strutted stiffly from cage to cage, talking softly to his
horses and cursing at the harnessers. Cicely Elliott sat on
a high stool from which she could look out of window and
gibed at him as he passed.

'Let me grease your potlids, goodly servant. You creak
like a roasting-jack.' He smiled at her with an engrossed

air, and hurried himself to pull tight the headstrap of a great barb that was fighting with four men.

A tucket of trumpets sounded, silvery and thin through the cold grey air: a page came running with his sallete-helmet.

'Why, I will lace it for him,' Cicely cried, and ran, pushing away the boy. She laced it under the chin and laughed. 'Now you may kiss my cheek so that I know what it is to be kissed by a man in potlids!'

He swung himself, grunting a little, into the high saddle and laughed at her with the air of a man very master of himself. The tucket thrilled again. Katharine Howard pushed the window open, craning out to see the King come: the horse, proud and mincing, appearing in its grey steel as great as an elephant, stepped yet so daintily that all its weight of iron made no more sound than the rhythmic jingling of a sabre, and man and horse passed like a flash of shadow out of the door.

Cicely hopped back on to the stool and shivered.

'We shall see these two old fellows very well without getting such a rheumatism as Lady Rochford's,' and she pulled the window to against Katharine's face and laughed at the vacant and far-away eyes that the girl turned upon her. 'You are thinking of the centaurs of the Isles of Greece,' she jeered, 'not of my knight and his old fashions of ironwork and horse dancing. Yet such another will never be again, so perfect in the old fashions.'

The old knight passed the window to the sound of trumpets towards his invisible master, swaying as easily to the gallop of his enormous steel beast as cupids that you may see in friezes ride upon dolphins down the sides of great billows; but Katharine's eyes were upon the ground.

The window showed only some yards of sand, of grey sky and of whitened railings; trumpet blew after trumpet, and behind her back horse after horse went out, its iron feet ringing on the bricks of the stable to die into thuds and silence once the door was passed.

Cicely Elliott plagued her, tickling her pink ears with

a piece of straw and sending out shrieks of laughter, and
Katharine, motionless as a flower in breathless sunlight,
was inwardly trembling. She imagined that she must be
pale and hollow-eyed enough to excite the compassion of
the black-haired girl, for she had not slept at all for thinking, and her eyes ached and her hands felt weak, resting
upon the brick of the window sill. Horses raced past,
shaking the building, in pairs, in fours, in twelves. They
curvetted together, pawed their way through intricate
figures, arched their great necks, or, reined in suddenly at
the gallop, cast up the sand in showers and great flakes of
white foam.

The old knight came into view, motioning with his lance
to invisible horsemen from the other side of the manage,
and the top notes of his voice reached them thinly as he
shouted the words of direction. But the King was still
invisible.

Suddenly Cicely Elliott cried out:

'Why, the old boy hath dropped his lance! *Quel
malheur!*'—and indeed the lance lay in the sand, the
horse darting wildly aside at the thud of its fall. The old
man shook his iron fist at the sky, and his face was full of
rage and shame in the watery sunlight that penetrated into
his open helmet. 'Poor old sinful man!' Cicely said with
a note of concern deep in her throat. A knave in grey ran
to pick up the lance, but the knight sat, his head hanging
on his chest, like one mortally stricken riding from a
battlefield.

Katharine's heart was in her mouth, and all her limbs
were weak together; a great shoulder in heavy furs, the
back of a great cap, came into the view of the window, an
immense hand grasped the white balustrade of the manage
rails. He was leaning over, a figure all squares, like that on
a court-card, only that the embroidered bonnet raked
abruptly to one side as if it had been thrown on to the
square head. Henry was talking to the old knight across
the sand. The sight went out of her eyes and her throat

uttered indistinguishable words. She heard Cicely Elliott say:

'*What* will you do? My old knight is upon the point of tears,' and Katharine felt herself brushing along the wall of the corridor towards the open door.

The immense horse with his steel-plates spreading out like skirts from its haunches dropped its head motionlessly close to the rail, and the grey, wrinkling steel of the figure on its back caught the reflection of the low clouds in flakes of light and shadow.

The old knight muttered indistinguishable words of shame inside his helmet; the King said: 'Ay, God help us, we all grow old together!' and Katharine heard herself cry out:

'Last night you were about very late because evil men plotted against me. Any man might drop his lance in the morning. . . .'

Henry moved his head leisurely over his shoulder; his eyelids went up, in haughty incredulity, so that the whites showed all round the dark pupils. He could not turn far enough to see her without moving his feet, and appearing to disdain so much trouble he addressed the old man heavily:

'Three times I dropped my pen, writing one letter yesterday,' he said; 'if you had my troubles you might groan of growing old.'

But the old man was too shaken with the disgrace to ride any more, and Henry added testily:

'I came here for distractions, and you have run me up against old cares because the sun shone in your eyes. If you will get tricking it with wenches over night you cannot be fresh in the morning. That is gospel for all of us. Get in and disarm. I have had enough of horses for the morning.'

As if he had dispatched that piece of business he turned, heavily and all of one piece, right round upon Katharine. He set his hands into his side and stood with his square feet wide apart:

'It is well that you remember how to kneel,' he laughed, ironically, motioning her to get up before she had reached her knees. 'You are the pertest baggage I have ever met.'

He had recognised her whilst the words were coming out of his great lips. 'Why, is it you the old fellow should marry? I heard he had found a young filly to frisk it with him.'

Katharine, her face pale and in consternation, stammered that Cicely Elliott was in the stables. He said:

'Bide there, I will go speak with her. The old fellow is very cast down; we must hearten him. It is true that he groweth old and has been a good servant.'

He pulled the dagger that hung from a thin gold chain on his neck into its proper place on his chest, squared his shoulders, and swayed majestically into the door of the stable. Katharine heard his voice raised to laugh and dropping into his gracious but still peremptory ardent tones. She remained alone upon the level square of smooth sand. Not a soul was in sight, for when the King came to seek distraction with his horses he brought no one that could tease him. She was filled with fears.

He beckoned her to him with his head, ducking it right down to his chest and back again, and the glances of his eyes seemed to strike her like hammer-blows when he came out from the door.

'It was you then that composed that fine speech about the Fortunate Isles?' he said. 'I had sent for you this morning. I will have it printed.'

She wanted to hang her head like a pupil before her master, but she needs must look him in the eyes, and her voice came strangely and unearthly to her own ears.

'I could not remember the speech the Bishop of Winchester set me to say. I warned him I have no memory for the Italian, and my fright muddled my wits.'

Internal laughter shook him, and once again he set his feet far apart, as if that aided him to look at her.

'Your fright!' he said.

'I am even now so frightened,' she uttered, 'that it is as if another spoke with my throat.'

His great mouth relaxed as if he accepted as his due a piece of skilful flattery. Suddenly she sank down upon her knees, her dress spreading out beneath her, her hands extended and her red lips parted as the beak of a bird opens with terror. He uttered lightly:

'Why, get up. You should kneel so only to your God,' and he touched his cap, with his habitual heavy gesture, at the sacred name.

'I have somewhat to ask,' she whispered.

He laughed again.

'They are always asking! But get up. I have left my stick in my room. Help me to my door.'

She felt the heavy weight of his arm upon her shoulder as soon as she stood beside him.

He asked her suddenly what she knew of the Fortunate Islands that she had talked of in her speech.

'They lie far in the Western Ocean; I had an Italian would have built me ships to reach them,' he said, and Katharine answered:

'I do take them to be a fable of the ancients, for they had no heaven to pray for.'

When his eyes were not upon her she was not afraid, and the heavy weight of his hand upon her shoulder made her feel firm to bear it. But she groaned inwardly because she had urgent words that must be said, and she imagined that nothing could be calmer in the Fortunate Islands themselves than this to walk and converse about their gracious image that shone down the ages. He said, with a heavy, dull voice:

'I would give no little to be there.'

Suddenly she heard herself say, her heart leaping in her chest:

'I do not like the errand they have sent my cousin upon.'

The blessed Utopia of the lost islands had stirred in the King all sorts of griefs that he would shake off, and all sorts of remembrances of youth, of open fields, and a wide world that shall be conquered—all the hopes and instincts of happiness, ineffable and indestructible, that never die in passionate men. He said dully, his thoughts far away:

'What errand have they sent him upon? Who is your goodly cousin?'

She answered:

'They put it about that he should murder Cardinal Pole,' and she shook so much that he was forced to take his hand from her shoulder.

He leaned upon the manage rail, and halted to rest his leg that pained him.

'It is a good errand enough,' he said.

She was panting like a bird that you hold in your hand, so that all her body shook, and she blurted out:

'I would not that my cousin should murder a Churchman!' and before his eyebrows could go up in an amazed and haughty stare: 'I am like to be hanged between Privy Seal and Winchester.'

He seemed to fall against the white bar of the rail for support, his eyes wide with incredulity.

He said: 'When were women hanged here?'

'Sir,' she said earnestly, 'you are the only one I can speak to. I am in great peril from these men.'

He shook his head at her.

'You have gone mad,' he said gravely. 'What is this fluster?'

'Give me your ear for a minute,' she pleaded. Her fear of him as a man seemed to have died down. As a king she had never feared him. 'These men do seek each other's lives, and many are like to be undone between them.'

His nostrils dilated like those of a high-mettled horse that starts back.

'What maggot is this?' he said imperiously. 'Here there is no disunion.'

He rolled his eyes angrily and breathed short, twisting his hands. It was part of his nature to insist that all the

world should believe in the concord of his people. He had
walked there to talk with a fair woman. He had imagined
that she would pique him with pert speeches.

'Speak quickly,' he said in a peremptory voice, and his
eyes wandered up the path between the rails and the stable
walls. 'You are a pretty piece, but I have no time to waste
in woeful nonsense.'

'Alas,' she said, 'this is the very truth of the truth. Privy
Seal hath tricked me.'

He laughed heavily and incredulously, and he sat right
down upon the rail. She began to tell him her whole story.

All through the night she had been thinking over the
coil into which she had fallen. It was a matter of desperate
haste, for she had imagined that Throckmorton would go
at once or before dawn and make up a tale to Privy Seal
so that she should be put out of the way. To her no
counter-plotting was possible. Gardiner she regarded with
a young disdain: he was a man who walked in plots. And
she did not love him because he had treated her like a
servant after she had walked in his masque. Her uncle
Norfolk was a craven who had left her to sink or swim.
Throckmorton, a werewolf who would defile her if she
entered into any compact with him. He would inform
against her, with the first light of the morning, and she
had trembled in her room at every footstep that passed the
door. She had imagined guards coming with their pikes
down to take her. She had trembled in the very stables.

The King stood above these plots and counter-plots. She
imagined him breathing a calmer air that alone was fit for
her. To one of her house the King was no more than a
man. At home she had regarded him very little. She had
read too many chronicles. He was first among such men as
her men-folk because her men-folk had so willed it: he was
their leader, no more majestic than themselves, and less
sacred than most priests. But in that black palace she felt
that all men trembled before him. It gave her for him a
respect: he was at least a man before whom all these

cravens trembled. And she imagined herself such another being: strong, confident, unafraid.

Therefore to the King alone she could speak. She imagined him sympathising with her on account of the ignoble trick that Cromwell had played upon her, as if he too must recognise her such another as himself. Being young she felt that God and the saints alike fought on her side. She was accustomed to think of herself as so assured and so buoyant that she could bear alike the commands of such men as Cromwell, as Gardiner and as her cousin with a smile of wisdom. She could bide her time.

Throckmorton had shocked her, not because he was a villain who had laid hands upon her, but because he had fooled her so that unless she made haste those other men would prove too many for her. They would hang her.

Therefore she must speak to the King. Lying still, looking at the darkness, listening to the breathing of Margot Poins, who slept across the foot of her bed, she had felt no fear whatsoever of Henry. It was true she had trembled before him at the masque, but she swept that out of her mind. She could hardly believe that she had trembled and forgotten the Italian words that she should have spoken. Yet she had stood there transfixed, without a syllable in her mind. And she had managed to bring out any words at all only by desperately piecing together the idea of Ovid's poem and Aulus Gellius' Eulogy of Marcus Crassus, which was very familiar in her ears because she had always imagined for a hero such a man: munificent, eloquent, noble and learned in the laws. The hall had seemed to blaze before her—it was only because she was so petrified with fright that she had not turned tail or fallen on her knees.

Therefore she must speak to him when he came to see his horses. She must bring him to her side before the tall spy with the eyes and the mouth that grinned as if at the thought of virtue could give Cromwell the signal to undo her.

She spoke vehemently to the King; she was indignant, because it seemed to her she was defiled by these foul men who had grasped at her.

'They have brought me down with a plot,' she said. She stretched out her hand and cried earnestly: 'Sir, believe that what I would have I ask for without any plotting.'

He leant back upon his rail. His round and boding eyes avoided her face.

'You have spoilt my morning betwixt you,' he muttered. First it was old Rochford who failed. Could a man not see his horses gallop without being put in mind of decay and death? Had he need of that? 'Why, I asked you for pleasant converse,' he finished.

She pleaded: 'Sir, I knew not that Pole was a traitor. Before God, I would now that he were caught up. But assuredly a way could be found with the Bishop of Rome....'

'This is a parcel of nonsense,' he shouted suddenly, dismissing her whole story. Would she have him believe it thinkable that a spy should swear away a woman's life? She had far better spend her time composing of fine speeches.

'Sir,' she cried, 'before the Most High God....'

He lifted his hand.

'I am tired of perpetual tears,' he muttered, and looked up the perspective of stable walls and white rails as if he would hurry away.

She said desperately: 'You will meet with tears perpetual so long as this man ...'

He lifted his hand, clenched right over his head.

'By God,' he bayed, 'may I never rest from cat and dog quarrels? I will not hear you. It is to drive a man mad when most he needs solace.'

He jerked himself down from the rail and shot over his shoulder:

'You will break your head if you run against a wall; I will have you in gaol ere night fall.' And he seemed to push her backward with his great hand stretched out.

IX

'Why, sometimes,' Throckmorton said, 'a very perfect folly is like a very perfect wisdom.' He sat upon her table. 'So it is in this case, he did send for me. No happening could have been more fortunate.'

He had sent away the man from her door and had entered without any leave, laughing ironically in his immense fan-shaped beard.

'Your ladyship thought to have stolen a march upon me,' he said. 'You could have done me no better service.'

She was utterly overcome with weariness. She sat motionless in her chair and listened to him.

He folded his arms and crossed his legs.

'So he did send for me,' he said. 'You would have had him belabour me with great words. But his Highness is a politician like some others. He beat about the bush. And be sure I left him openings to come in to my tidings.'

Katharine hung her head and thought bitterly that she had had the boldness; this other man reaped the spoils. He leaned forward and sighed. Then he laughed.

'You might wonder that I love you,' he said. 'But it is in the nature of profound politicians to love women that be simple, as it is the nature of sinners to love them that be virtuous. Do not believe that an evil man loveth evil. He contemns it. Do not believe that a politician loveth guile. He makes use of it to carry him into such a security that he may declare his true nature. Moreover, there is no evil man, since no man believeth himself to be evil. I love you.'

Katharine closed her eyes and let her head fall back in her chair. The dusk was falling slowly, and she shivered.

'You have no warrant to take me away?' she asked, expressionlessly.

He laughed again.

'Thus,' he said, 'devious men love women that be simple. And, for a profound, devious and guileful politician you shall find none to match his Highness.'

He looked at Katharine with scrutinising and malicious eyes. She never moved.

'I would have you listen,' he said.

She had had no one to talk to all that day. There was no single creature with whom she could discuss. She might have asked counsel of old Rochford. But apart from the disorder of his mind he had another trouble. He had a horse for sale, and he had given the refusal of it to a man called Stey who lived in Warwickshire. In the meanwhile two Frenchmen had made him a greater offer, and no answer came from Warwickshire. He was in a fume. Cicely Elliott was watching him and thinking of nothing else, Margot Poins was weeping all day, because the magister had been bidden to go to Paris to turn into Latin the letters of Sir Thomas Wyatt. There was no one around Katharine that was not engrossed in his own affairs. In that beehive of a place she had been utterly alone with horror in her soul. Thus she could hardly piece together Throckmorton's meanings. She thought he had come to gibe at her.

'Why should I listen?' she said.

'Because,' he answered sardonically, 'you have a great journey indicated for you, and I would instruct you as to certain peaks that you may climb.'

She had been using her rosary, and she moved it in her lap.

'Any poor hedge priest would be a better guide on such a journey,' she answered listlessly.

'Why, God help us all,' he laughed, 'that were to carry simplicity into a throne-room. In a stable-yard it served. But you will not always find a king among horse-straws.'

'God send I find the King of Peace on a prison pallet,' she answered.

'Why, we are at cross purposes,' he said lightly. He laughed still more loudly when he heard that the King had threatened her with a gaol.

'Do you not see,' he asked, 'how that implies a great favour towards you?'

'Oh, mock on,' she answered.

He leaned forward and spoke tenderly.

'Why, poor child,' he said. 'If a man be moved because you moved him, it was you who moved him. Now, if you can move such a heavy man that is a certain proof that he is not indifferent to you.'

'He threatened me with a gaol,' Katharine said bitterly.

'Aye,' Throckmorton answered, 'for you were in fault to him. That is ever the weakness of your simple natures. They will go brutally to work upon a man.'

'Tell me, then, in three words, what his Highness will do with me,' she said.

'There you go brutally to work again,' he said. 'I am a poor man that do love you. You ask what another man will do with you that affects you.'

He stood up to his full height, dressed all in black velvet.

'Let us, then, be calm,' he said, though his voice trembled and he paused as if he had forgotten the thread of his argument. 'Why, even so, you were in grievous fault to his Highness that is a prince much troubled. As thus: You were certain of the rightness of your cause.'

'It is that of the dear saints,' Katharine said.... He touched his bonnet with three fingers.

'You are certain,' he repeated. 'Nevertheless, here is a man whose fury is like an agony to him. He looks favourably upon you. But, if a man be formed to fight he must fight, and call the wrong side good.'

'God help you,' Katharine said. 'What can be good that is set in array against the elect of God?'

'These be brave words,' he answered, 'but the days of the Crusades be over. Here is a King that fights with a world that is part good, part evil. In part he fights for the dear saints; in part they that fight against him fight for the elect of God. Then he must call all things well upon his side, if he is not to fail where he is right as well as where he is wrong.'

'I do not take you well,' Katharine said. 'When the Lacedæmonians strove with the Great King...'

'Why, dear heart,' he said, 'those were the days of a black and white world; now we are all grey or piebald.'

'Then tell me what the King will do with me,' she answered.

He made a grimace.

'All your learning will not make of you but a very woman. It is: What will he do? It is: A truce to words. It is: Get to the point. But the point is this...'

'In the name of heaven,' she said, 'shall I go to gaol or no?'

'Then in the name of heaven,' he said, 'you shall—this next month, or next year, or in ten years' time. That is very certain, since you goad a King to fury.'

She opened her mouth, but he silenced her with his hand.

'No, you shall not go to gaol upon this quarrel!' She sank back into her chair. He surveyed her with a sardonic malice.

'But it is very certain,' he said, 'that had there been there ready a clerk with a warrant and a pen, you had not again seen the light of day until you came to a worse place on a hill.'

Katharine shivered.

'Why, get you gone, and leave me to pray,' she said.

He stretched out towards her a quivering hand.

'Aye, there you be again, simple and brutal!' His jaws grinned beneath his beard. 'I love the air you breathe. I go about to tell a tale in a long way that shall take a long time, so that I may stay with you. You cry: "For pity, for pity, come to the point." I have pity. So you cry, having obtained your desire, "Get ye gone, and let me pray!"'

She said wearily:

'I have had too many men besiege me with their suits.'

He shrugged his great shoulders and cried:

'Yet you never had friend better than I, who bring you comfort hoping for none in return.'

'Why,' she answered, 'it is a passing bitter thing that my sole friend must be a man accounted so evil.'

He moved backwards again to the table; set his white hands upon it behind him, and balancing himself upon them swung one of his legs slowly.

'It is a good doctrine of the Holy Church,' he said, 'to call no man evil until he be dead.' He looked down at the ground, and then, suddenly, he seemed to mock at her and at himself. 'Doubtless, had such a white soul as yours led me from my first day, you to-day had counted me as white. It is evident that I was not born with a nature that warped towards sin. For, let us put it that Good is that thing that you wish.' He looked up at her maliciously. 'Let that be Good. Then, very certainly, since I am enlisted heart and soul in the desire that you may have what you wish, you have worked a conversion in me.'

'I will no longer bear with your mocking,' she said. She began to feel herself strong enough to command for him.

'Why,' he answered, 'hear me you shall. And I must mock, since to mock and to desire are my nature. You pay too little heed to men's natures, therefore the day will come to shed tears. That is very certain, for you will knock against the whole world.'

'Why, yes,' she answered. 'I am as God made me.'

'So are all Christians,' he retorted. 'But some of us strive to improve on the pattern.' She made an impatient movement with her hands, and he seemed to force himself to come to a point. 'It may be that you will never hear me speak again,' he said quickly. 'Both for you and for me these times are full of danger. Let me then leave you this legacy of advice. . . . Here is a picture of the King's Highness.'

'I shall never go near his Highness again,' Katharine said.

'Aye, but you will,' he answered, 'for 'tis your nature to meddle; or 'tis your nature to work for the blessed saints. Put it which way you will. But his Highness meditateth to come near you.'

'Why, you are mad,' Katharine said wearily. 'This is that maggot of Magister Udal's.'

He lifted one finger in an affected, philosophic gesture.

'Oh, nay,' he laughed. 'That his Highness meditateth more speech with you I am assured. For he did ask me where you usually resorted.'

'He would know if I be a traitor.'

'Aye, but from your own word of mouth he would know it.' He grinned once more at her. 'Do you think that I would forbear to court you if I were not afraid of another than you?'

She shrugged her shoulders up to her ears, and he sniggered, stroking his beard.

'You may take that as a proof very certain,' he said. 'None of your hatred should have prevented me, for I am a very likeworthy man. Ladies that have hated afore now, I have won to love me. With you, too, I would essay the adventure. You are most fair, most virtuous, most simple— aye, and most lovable. But for the moment I am afraid. From now on, for many months, I shall not be seen to frequent you. For I have known such matters of old. A great net is cast: many fish—smaller than I be, who am a proper man—are taken up.'

'It is good hearing that you will no more frequent me,' Katharine said.

He nodded his great head.

'Why, I speak of what is in my mind,' he answered. 'Think upon it, and it will grow clear when it is too late. But here I will draw you a picture of the King.'

'I have seen his Highness with mine own eyes,' she caught him up.

'But your eyes are so clear,' he sighed. 'They see the black and the white of a man. The grey they miss. And you are slow to learn. Nevertheless, already you have learned that here we have no yea-nay world of evil and good. . . .'

'No,' she said, 'that I have not learned, nor never shall.'

'Oh, aye,' he mocked at her. 'You have learned that the

Bishop of Winchester, who is on the side of your hosts of heaven, is a knave and a fool. You have learned that I, whom you have accounted a villain, am for you, and a very wise man. You have learned that Privy Seal, for whose fall you have prayed these ten years, is, his deeds apart, the only good man in this quaking place.'

'His acts are most hateful,' Katharine said stoutly.

'But these are not the days of Plutarch,' he answered. 'And I doubt the days of Plutarch never were. For already you have learned that a man may act most evilly, even as Privy Seal, and yet be the best man in the world. And . . . .' he ducked his great head sardonically at her, 'you have learned that a man may be most evil and yet act passing well for your good. So I will draw the picture of the King for you. . . .'

Something seductive in his voice, and the good humour with which he called himself villain, made Katharine say no more than:

'Why, you are an incorrigible babbler!'

Whilst he had talked she had grown assured that the King meditated no imprisoning of her. The conviction had come so gradually that it had merely changed her terrified weariness into a soft languor. She lay back in her chair and felt a comfortable limpness in all her limbs.

'His Highness,' Throckmorton said, 'God preserve him and send him good fortune—is a great and formidable club. His Highness is a most great and most majestic bull. He is a thunderbolt and a glorious light; he is a storm of hail and a beneficent sun. There are few men more certain than he when he is certain. There is no one so full of doubts when he doubteth. There is no wind so mighty as he when he is inspired to blow; but God alone, who directeth the wind in its flight, knoweth when he will storm through the world. His Highness is a balance of a pair of scales. Now he is up, now down. Those who have ruled him have taken account of this. If you had known the Sieur Cromwell as I have, you would have known this very well. The excellent the Privy Seal hath been beknaved by the hour, and hath borne it with a great composure. For, well he knew that the King, standing in midst of a world of doubts, would, in the next hour, the next week, or the next month, come in the midst of doubts to be of Privy Seal's mind. Then Privy Seal hath pushed him to action. Now his Highness is a good lover, and being himself a great doubter, he loveth a simple and convinced nature. Therefore he hath loved Privy Seal . . .'

'In the name of the saints,' Katharine laughed, 'call you Privy Seal's a simple nature?'

He answered imperturbably:

'Call you Cato's a complex one? He who for days and days and years and years said always one thing alone: "Carthage must be destroyed!"''

'But this man is no noble Roman,' Katharine cried indignantly.

'There was never a nature more Roman,' Throckmorton mocked at her. 'For if Cato cried for years: *Delenda est Carthago*, Cromwell hath contrived for years: *Floreat rex meus*. Cato stuck at no means. Privy Seal hath stuck at none. Madam Howard: Privy Seal wrote to the King in his first letter, when he was but a simple servant of the Cardinal, "I, Thomas Cromwell, if you will give ear to me, will make your Grace the richest and most puissant king ever there was." So he wrote ten years agone; so he hath said and written daily for all those years. This it is to have a simple nature . . .'

'But the vile deeds!' Katharine said.

'Madam Howard,' Throckmorton laughed, 'I would ask you how many broken treaties, how many deeds of treachery, went to the making of the Roman state, since Sinon a traitor brought about the fall of Troy, since Aeneas betrayed Queen Dido and brought the Romans into Italy, until Sylla played false with Marius, Cæsar with the friends of Sylla, Brutus with Cæsar, Antony with Brutus, Octavius with Antony—aye, and until the Blessed Constantine played false to Rome herself.'

'Foul man, ye blaspheme,' Katharine cried.

'God keep me from that sin,' he answered gravely.

'—And of all these traitors,' she continued, 'not one but fell.'

'Aye, by another traitor,' he caught her up. 'It was then as now. Men fell, but treachery prospered—aye, and Rome prospered. So may this realm of England prosper exceedingly. For it is very certain that Cromwell hath brought it to a great pitch, yet Cromwell made himself by betraying the great Cardinal.'

Katharine protested too ardently to let him continue. The land was brought to a low and vile estate. And it was known that Cromwell had been, before all things, and to his own peril, faithful to the great Cardinal's cause.

Throckmorton shrugged his shoulders.

'Without doubt you know these histories better than I,' he answered. 'But judge them how you will, it is very certain that the King, who loveth simple natures, loveth Privy Seal.'

'Yet you have said that he lay under a great shadow,' Katharine convicted him.

'Well,' he said composedly, 'the balance is down against him. This league with Cleves hath brought him into disfavour. But well he knoweth that, and it will be but a short time ere he will work again, and many years shall pass ere again he shall misjudge. Such mistakes hath he made before this. But there hath never been one to strike at him in the right way and at the right time. Here then is an opening.'

Katharine regarded him with a curiosity that was friendly and awakened: he caught her expression and laughed.

'Why, you begin to learn,' he said.

'When you speak clearly I can take your meaning,' she answered.

'Then believe me,' he said earnestly. 'Tell all with whom you may come together. And you may come to your uncle very easily. Tell him that if he may find France and Spain embroiled within this five months, Privy Seal and Cleves may fall together. But, if he delay till Privy Seal hath shaken him clear of Cleves, Cromwell shall be our over-king for twenty years.'

He paused and then continued:

'Believe me again. Every word that is spoken against Privy Seal shall tell its tale—until he hath shaken himself clear of this Cleves coil. His Highness shall rave, but the words will rankle. His Highness shall threaten you—but he shall not strike—for he will doubt. It is by his doubts that you may take him.'

'God help me,' Katharine said. 'What is this of "you" to me?'

He did not heed her, but continued:

'You may speak what you will against Privy Seal—but speak never a word against the glory of the land. It is when you do call this realm the Fortunate Land that at once you make his Highness incline towards you—and doubt. "Island of the Blest," say you. This his Highness rejoices, saying to himself: "My governing appeareth Fortunate to the World." But his Highness knoweth full well the flaws that be in his Fortunate Island. And specially will he set himself to redress wrongs, assuage tears, set up chantries, and make his peace with God. But if you come to him saying: "This land is torn with dissent. Here heresies breed and despair stalks abroad"; if you say all is not well, his Highness getteth enraged. "All is well," he will swear. "All is well, for I made it"—and he would throw his cap into the face of Almighty God rather than change one jot of his work. In short, if you will praise him you make him humble, for at bottom the man is humble; if you will blame him you will render him rigid as steel and more proud than the lightning. For, before the world's eyes, this man must be proud, else he would die.'

Katharine had her hand upon her cheek. She said musingly:

'His Highness did threaten me with a gaol. But you say he will not strike. If I should pray him to restore the Church of God, would he not strike then?'

'Child,' Throckmorton answered, 'it will lie with the way you ask it. If you say: "This land is heathen, your Grace hath so made it," his Highness will be more than terrible. But if you say: "This land prospereth exceedingly and is beloved of the Mother of God," his Highness will begin to doubt that he hath done little to pleasure God's Mother—or to pleasure you who love that Heavenly Rose. Say how all good people rejoice that his Highness hath given them a faith pure and acceptable. And very shortly his Highness will begin to wonder of his Faith.'

'But that were an ignoble flattery,' Katharine said.

He answered quietly:

'No! no! For indeed his Highness hath given all he could give. It is the hard world that hath pushed him against you and against his good will. Believe me, his Highness loveth good doctrine better than you, I, or the Bishop of Rome. So that . . .'

He paused, and concluded:

'This Lord Cromwell moves in the shadow of a little thing that casts hardly any shadow. You have seen it?'

She shook her head negligently, and he laughed:

'Why, you will see it yet. A small, square thing upon a green hill. The noblest of our land kneel before it, by his Highness' orders. Yet the worship of idols is contemned now.' He let his malicious eyes wander over her relaxed, utterly resting figure.

'I would ye would suffer me to kiss you on the mouth,' he sighed.

'Why, get you gone,' she said, without anger.

'Oh, aye,' he said, with some feeling. 'It is pleasant to be desired as I desire you. But it is true that ye be meat for my masters.'

'I will take help from none of your lies.' She returned to her main position.

He removed his bonnet, and bowed so low to her that his great and shining beard hung far away from his chest.

'Madam Howard,' he mocked, 'my lies will help you well when the time comes.'

PART THREE

THE KING MOVES

I

MARCH was a month of great storms of rain in that year, and the river-walls of the Thames were much weakened. April opened fine enough for men to get about the land, so that, on a day towards the middle of the month, there was a meeting of seven Protestant men from Kent and Essex, of two German servants of the Count of Oberstein, and of two other German men in the living-room of Eadge, the printer, in Austin Friars. It happened that the tide was high at four in the afternoon, and, after a morning of glints of sun, great rain fell. Thus, when the Lord Oberstein's men set out into the weather, they must needs turn back, because the water was all out between Austin Friars and the river. They came again into the house, not very unwillingly, to resume their arguments about Justification by Faith, about the estate of the Queen Anne, about the King's mind towards her, and about the price of wool in Flanders.

The printer himself was gloomy and abstracted; arguments about Justification interested him little, and when the talk fell upon the price of wool, he remained standing, absolutely lost in gloomy dreams. It grew a little dark in the room, the sky being so overcast, and suddenly, all the voices having fallen, there was a gurgle of water by the threshold, and a little flood, coming in between sill and floor, reached as it were, a tiny finger of witness towards his great feet. He looked down at it uninterestedly, and said:

'Talk how you will, I can measure this thing by words

and by print. Here hath this Queen been with us a matter of four months. Now in my chronicle the pageants that have been made in her honour fill but five pages.' Whereas the chronicling of the jousts, pageants, merry-nights, masques and hawkings that had been given in the first four months of the Queen Jane had occupied sixteen pages, and for the Queen Anne Boleyn sixty and four. 'What sort of honour is it, then, that the King's Highness showeth the Queen?' He shook his head gloomily.

'Why, goodman,' a woolstapler from the Tower Hamlets cried at him, 'when they shot off the great guns against her coming to Westminster in February all my windows were broken by the shrinking of the earth. Such ordnance was never yet shot off in a Queen's honour.'

The printer remained gloomily silent for a minute; the wind howled in the chimney-place, and the embers of the fire spat and rustled.

'Even as ye are held here by the storm, so is the faith of God in these lands,' he said. 'This is the rainy season.' More water came in beneath the door, and he added, 'Pray God we be not all drowned in our holes.'

A motionless German, who had no English, shifted his feet from the wet floor to the cross-bar of his chair. Gloom, dispiritude, and dampness brooded in the low, dark room. But a young man from Kent, who, being used to ill weather, was not to be cast down by gloomy skies, cried out in his own dialect that they had arms to use and leaders to lead them.

'Aye, and we have racks to be stretched on and hang-men to stretch them,' the printer answered. 'Is it with the sound of ordnance that a Queen is best welcomed? When she came to Westminster, what welcome had she? Sirs, I tell you the Mayor of London brought only barges and pennons and targets to her honour. The King's Highness ordered no better state; therefore the King's Highness honoureth not this Queen.'

A scrivener who had copied chronicles for another printer answered him:

'Master Printer John Badge, ye are too much in love with velvet; ye are too avid of gold. Earlier records of this realm told of blows struck, of ships setting sail, of godly ways of life and of towns in France taken by storm. But in your books of the new reign we read all day of cloths of estate, of cloth of gold, of blue silk full of eyes of gold, of garlands of laurels set with brims of gold, of gilt bars, of crystal corals, of black velvet set with stones, and of how the King and his men do shift their suits six times in one day. The fifth Harry never shifted his harness for fourteen days in the field.'

The printer shrugged his enormous shoulders.

'Oh, ignorant!' he said. 'A hundred years ago kings made war with blows. Now it is done with black velvets or the lack of black velvets. And I love laurel with brims of gold if such garlands crown a Queen of our faith. And I lament their lack if by it the King's Highness maketh war upon our faith. And Privy Seal shall dine with the Bishop of Winchester, and righteousness kiss with the whoredom of abomination.'

'An my Lord Cromwell knew how many armed men he had to his beck he had never made peace with Winchester,' the man from Kent cried. He rose from his bench and went to stand near the fire.

A door-latch clicked, and in the dark corner of the room appeared something pale and shining—the face of old Badge, who held open the stair-door and grinned at the assembly, leaning down from a high step.

'Weather-bound all,' he quavered maliciously. 'I will tell you why.'

He slipped down the step, pulling behind him the large figure of his grandchild Margot.

'Get you gone back,' the printer snarled at her.

'That will I not,' her gruff voice came. 'See where my back is wet with the drippings through the roof.'

She and her grandfather had been sitting on a bed in the upper room, but the rain was trickling now through

the thatch. The printer made a nervous stride to his printing stick, and, brandishing it in the air, poured out these
words:

'Whores and harlots shall not stand in the sight of the
godly.'

Margot shrank back upon the stair-place and remained
there, holding the bolt of the door in her hand, ready to
shut off access to the upper house.

'I will take no beating, uncle,' she panted; 'this is my
grandfather's abode and dwelling.'

The old man was sniggering towards the window. He
had gathered up his gown about his knees and picked his
way between the pools of water on the floor and the
Lutherans on their chairs towards the window. He
mounted upon an oak chest that stood beneath the casement and, peering out, chuckled at what he saw.

'A mill race and a dam,' he muttered. 'This floor will be
a duck pond in an hour.'

'Harlot and servant of a harlot,' the printer called to his
niece. The Lutherans, who came from houses where father
quarrelled with son and mother with daughter, hardly
troubled more than to echo the printer's words of abuse.
But one of them, a grizzled man in a blue cloak, who had
been an ancient friend of the household, broke out:

'Naughty wench, thou wast at the ordeal of Dr Barnes.'

Margot, drawing her knees up to her chin where she sat
on the stairs, answered nothing. Had she not feared her
uncle's stick, she was minded to have taken a mop to the
floor and to have put a clout in the doorway.

'Abominable naughty wench,' the grizzled man went on.
'How had ye the heart to aid in that grim scene? Knew ye
no duty to your elders?'

Margot closed the skirts round her ankles to keep away
the upward draught and answered reasonably:

'Why, Neighbour Ned, my mistress made me go with
her to see a heretic swinged. And, so dull is it in our service, that I would go to a puppet show far less fine and
thank thee for the chance.'

The printer spat upon the floor when she mentioned her mistress.

'I will catechize,' he muttered. 'Answer me as I charge thee.'

The old man, standing on the chest, tapped one of the Germans on the shoulder.

'See you that wall, friend?' he laughed. 'Is it not a noble dam to stay the flood back into our house? Now the Lord Cromwell . . .'

The Lanzknecht rolled his eyes round, because he understood no English. The old man went on talking, but no one there, not even Margot Poins, heeded him. She looked at her uncle reasonably, and said:

'Why, an thou wilt set down thy stick I will even consider thee, uncle.' He threw the stick into the corner and immediately she went to fetch a mop from the cooking closet, where there lived a mumbling old housekeeper. The printer followed her with gloomy eyes.

'Is not thy mistress a naughty woman?' he asked, as a judge talks to a prisoner condemned.

She answered, 'Nay,' as if she had hardly attended to him.

'Is she not a Papist?'

She answered, 'Aye,' in the same tone and mopped the floor beneath a man's chair.

Her grandfather, standing high on the oak chest, so that his bonnet brushed the beams of the dark ceiling, quavered at her:

'Would she not bring down this Crummock, whose wall hath formed a dam so that my land-space is now a stream and my house-floor a frog pond?'

She answered, 'Aye, grandfer,' and went on with her mopping.

'Did she not go with a man to a cellar of the Rogues' Sanctuary after Winchester's feast?' Neighbour Ned barked at her. 'Such are they that would bring down our Lord!'

'Did she not even so with her cousin before he went to Calais?' her uncle asked.

Margot answered seriously:

'Nay, uncle, no night but what she hath slept in these arms of mine that you see.'

'Aye, you are her creature,' Neighbour Ned groaned.

'Foul thing,' the printer shouted. 'Eyes are upon thee and upon her. It was the worst day's work that ever she did when she took thee to her arms. For I swear to God that her name shall be accursed in the land. I swear to God . . .'

He choked in his throat. His companions muttered Harlot; Strumpet; Spouse of the Fiend. And suddenly the printer shouted:

'See you; Udal is her go-between with the King, and he shall receive thee as his price. He conveyeth her to his Highness, she hath paid him with thy virtue. Foul wench, be these words not true?'

She leaned upon her mop handle and said:

'Why, uncle, it is a foul bird that 'files his own nest.'

He shook his immense fist in her face.

'Shame shall out in the communion of the godly, be it whose kin it will.'

'Why, I wish the communion of the godly joy in its hot tales,' she answered. 'As for me, speak you with the magister when he comes from France. As for my mistress, three times she hath seen the King since Winchester's feast was three months agone. She in no wise affected his Highness till she had heard his Highness confute the errors of Dr Barnes in the small closet. When she came away therefrom she said that his Highness was like a god for his knowledge of God's law. If you want better tales than that go to a wench from the stairs to make them for you.'

'Aye,' said their neighbour, 'three times hath she been with the King. And the price of the first time was the warrant that took thee to pay Udal for his connivance. And the price of the second was that the King's Highness should confute our sacred Barnes in the conclave. And the price of the third was that the Lord Cromwell should dine with the Bishop of Winchester and righteousness sit with its head in ashes.'

'Why, have it as thou wilt, Neighbour Ned,' she answered. 'In my life of twenty years thou hast brought me twenty sugar cates. God forbid that I should stay thy willing lips over a sweet morsel.'

In the gloomy and spiritless silence that fell upon them all—since no man there much believed the things that were alleged, but all very thoroughly believed that evil days were stored up against them—the bursting open of the door made so great a sound that the speechless German tilted backward with his chair and lay on the ground, before any of them knew what was the cause. The black figure of a boy shut out the grey light and the torrents of rain. His head was bare, his frieze clothes dripped and sagged upon his skin: he waved his clenched fist half at the sky and half at Margot's face and screamed:

'I ha' carried letters for thee, 'twixt thy mistress and the King! I ha' carried letters. I . . . ha' . . . been gaoled for it.'

'O fool,' Margot's deep voice uttered, unmoved, 'the letters went not between those two. And thou art free; come in from the rain.'

He staggered across the prostrate German.

'I ha' lost my advancement,' he sobbed. 'Where shall I go? Twenty hours I have hidden in the reeds by the riverside. I shall be taken again.'

'There is no hot pursuit for thee then,' Margot said, 'for in all the twenty hours no man hath sought thee here.' She had the heavy immobility of an elemental force. No fright could move her till she saw the cause for fright. 'I will fetch thee a dram of strong waters.'

He passed his hand across his wet forehead.

'Thy mistress is taken,' he cried. 'I saw Privy Seal's pikes go to her doorway.'

'Now God be praised,' the printer cried out, and caught

at the boy's wrist. 'Tell your tale!' and he shook him on his legs.

'Me, too, Privy Seal had taken—but I 'scaped free,' he gasped. 'These twain had promised me advancement for braving their screeds. And I ha' lost it.'

'Gossips all,' the Neighbour Ned barked out, 'to your feet and let us sing: "A fortress fast is God the Lord." The harlot of the world is down.'

II

During the time that had ensued between January and that month of March, it had been proved to Katharine Howard how well Throckmorton, the spy, voiced the men folk of their day. He had left her alone, but she seemed to feel his presence in all the air. He passed her in corridors, and she knew from his very silence that he was carrying on a fumbling game with her uncle Norfolk, and with Gardiner of Winchester. He had not induced her to play his game—but he seemed to have made her see that every man else in the world was playing a game like his. It was not, precisely, any more a world of black and white that she saw, but a world of men who did one thing in order that something very different might happen a long time afterwards.

The main Court had moved from Greenwich to Hampton towards the end of January, but the Lady Mary, with her ladies, came to a manor house at Isleworth; and shut in as she was with a grim mistress—who assuredly was all white or black—Katharine found herself like one with ears strained to catch sounds from a distance, listening for the smallest rumours that could come from the other great house up stream.

The other ladies each had their men, as Cicely Elliott had the old knight. One of them had even six, who one day fought a *mêlée* for her favours on an eyot before the manor windows. These men came by barge in the evenings, or rode over the flats with a spare horse to take their mistresses a-hawking after the herons in the swampy places. So that each of them had her channel by which true gossip might reach her. But Katharine had none. Till the opening of March the magister came to whisper with Margot Poins— then he was sent again to Paris to set his pen at the service of Sir Thomas Wyatt, who had so many letters to write. Thus she heard much women's tattle, but knew nothing of what passed. Only it seemed certain that Gardiner of Winchester was seeing fit—God knows why—to be hot in favour of the Old Faith. It was certain, from six several accounts, that at Paul's Cross he had preached a sermon full of a very violent and acceptable doctrine. She wondered what move in the game this was: it was assuredly not for the love of God. No doubt it was part of Throckmorton's plan. The Lutherans were to be stirred to outrages in order to prove to the King how insolent were they upon whom Privy Seal relied.

It gratified her to see how acute her prescience had been when Dr Barnes made his furious reply to the bishop. For Dr Barnes was one of Privy Seal's most noted men: an insolent fool whom he had taken out of the gutter to send ambassador to the Schmalkaldners. And it was on the day when Gardiner made his complaint to the King about Dr Barnes, that her uncle Norfolk sent to her to come to him at Hampton.

He awaited her, grim and jaundiced, in the centre of a great, empty room, where, shivering with cold, he did not let his voice exceed a croaking whisper though there was panelling and no arras on the dim walls. But, to his queries, she answered clearly:

'Nay, I serve the Lady Mary with her Latin. I hear no tales and I bear none to any man.' And again:

'Three times I have spoken with the King's Highness, the Lady Mary being by. And once it was of the Islands of the Blest, and once of the Latin books I read, and once of indifferent matters—such as of how apple trees may be planted against a wall in Lincolnshire.'

Her uncle gazed at her: his dark eyes were motionless and malignant by habit; he opened his lips to speak; closed them again without a word spoken. He looked at a rose, carved in a far corner of the ceiling, looked at her again, and muttered:

'The French are making great works at Ardres.'

'Oh, aye,' she answered, 'my cousin Tom wrote me as much. He is commanded to stay at Calais.'

'Tell me,' he said, 'will they go against Calais town in good earnest?'

'If I knew that,' she answered, 'I should have had it in private words from my lady whom I serve. And, if I had it in private words I would tell it neither to you nor to any man.'

He scowled patiently and muttered:

'Then tell in private words back again this: That if the French King or the Emperor do war upon us now Privy Seal will sit upon the King's back for ever.'

'Ah, I know who hath talked with you,' she answered. 'Uncle, give me your hand to kiss, for I must back to my mistress.'

He put his thin hand grimly behind his back.

'Ye spy, then, for others,' he said. 'Go kiss their feet.'

She laughed in a nettled voice:

'If the others get no more from me than your Grace of Norfolk. . . .'

He frowned ominously, pivoted stiffly round on his heels, and said over his shoulder:

'Then I will have thy cousin clapped up the first time he is found in a drunken brawl at Calais.'

She was after him beseechingly, with her hands held out:

'Oh no, uncle,' and 'Oh, dear uncle. Let poor fool Tom be drunken when drunken brawls work no manner of ill.'

'Then get you sent to the King of France, through the channel that you wot of, the message I have given you to convey.' He kept his back to her and spoke as if to the distant door.

'Why must I mull in these matters?' she asked him piteously, 'or why must poor Tom? God help him, he found me bread when you had left me to starve.' It came to her as pitiful that her cousin, swaggering and unconscious, at a great distance, should be undone because these men quarrelled near her. He moved stiffly round again—he was so bolstered over with clothes against the cold.

'It is not you that must meddle here,' he said. 'It is your mistress. Only she will be believed by those you wot of.'

'Speak you yourself,' she said.

He scowled hatefully.

'Who of the French would believe *me*,' he snarled. He had been so made a tool of by Privy Seal in times past that he had lost all hope of credence.

'If I may come to it, I will do it,' she said suddenly.

After all, it seemed to her, this action might bring about the downfall of Privy Seal—and she desired his downfall. It would be a folly to refuse her aid merely because her uncle was a craven man or Throckmorton a knave. It was a true thing that she was to ask the Lady Mary to say— that if France and Spain should molest England together the Cleves alliance must stand for good—and with it Privy Seal.

'But, a' God's name, let poor Tom be,' she added.

He stood perfectly motionless for a moment, shrugged his shoulders straight up and down, stood motionless for another moment, and then held out his hand. She touched it with her lips.

There was a certain cate, or small cake, made of a paste sweetened with honey and flavoured with cinnamon, that Katharine Howard very much loved. She had never tasted them till one day the King had come to visit his daughter, bearing with his own hands a great box of them. He had had the receipt from Thomas Cromwell, who had had it of a Jew in Italy. Mary so much disaffected her father that, taking them from his hands with one knee nearly upon the ground, she had said that her birth ill-fitted her to eat these princely viands, and she had placed them on a ledge of her writing-pulpit. Heaving a heavy sigh, he glanced at her book and said that he would not have her spoil her eyes with too much of study; let her bid Lady Katharine to read and write for her.

'She will have greater need of her eyes than ever I of mine,' Mary answered with her passionless voice.

'I will not have you spoil your eyes,' he said heavily, and she gave him back the reply:

'My eyes are your Highness'.'

He made with his shoulders a slow movement of exasperation, and, turning to Katharine Howard, he began once more to talk of the Islands of the Blest. He was dressed all in black furs that day, so that his face appeared less pallid than when he had worn scarlet, and it seemed to her suddenly that he was a very pitiful man—a man who could do nothing; and one who, as Throckmorton had said, was nothing but a doubt. There beside him, between the two of them, stood his daughter—pale, straight, silent, her hands clasped before her. And her father had come to placate her. He had brought her cates to eat, or he would have beaten her into loving him. Yet Mary of England stood as rigid as a knife-blade; you could move her neither by love nor by threats. This man had sinned against this daughter; here he was brought up against an implacability. He was omnipotent in everything else; this was his Pillars of Hercules. So she exerted herself to be pleasant with him, and at one moment of the afternoon he stretched out a great hand to the cinnamon cakes and placed one in his own mouth. He sat still, and, his great jaws moving slowly, he said that he scarcely doubted that, if he himself could set sail with a great armada and many men, he should find a calm region of tranquil husbandry and a pure faith.

'It might be found,' he said; then he sighed heavily, and, looking earnestly at her, brushed the crumbs from the furs about his neck.

'One day, doubtless, your Highness shall find them,'

Katharine answered, 'if your Highness shall apply yourself to the task.' She was impatient with him for his sighs. Let him, if he would, abandon his kingdom and his daughter to set out upon a quest, or let him stay where he was and set to work at any other task.

'But whether your Highness shall find them beyond the Western Isles or hidden in this realm of England . . .'

He shrugged his great shoulders right up till the furs on them were brushed by the feathers that fell from his bonnet.

'God, wench!' he said gloomily, 'that is a question you are main happy to have time to dally with. I have wife and child, and kith and kin, and a plaguey basket of rotten apples to make cider from.'

He pulled himself out of his chair with both hands on the arms, stretched his legs as if they were cramped, and rolled towards the door.

'Why, read of this matter in old books,' he said, 'and if you find the place you shall take me there.' Then he spoke bitterly to the Lady Mary, who had never moved.

'Since your eyes are mine, I bid you not spoil them,' he said. 'Let this lady aid you. She has ten times more of learning than you have.' But, taking his jewelled walking-stick from beside the door, he added, 'God, wench! you are my child. I have read your commentary, and I, a man who have as much of good letters as any man in Christendom, am well content to father you.'

'Did your Highness mark—this book being my child— which side of the paper it was written on?' his daughter asked.

Katharine Howard sighed, for it was the Lady Mary's bitter jest that she wrote on the rough side of the paper, having been born on the wrong side of the blanket.

'Madam Howard,' she said to Katharine with a cold sneer, as of a very aged woman, 'my father, who has taken many things from me to give to other women, takes now my commentary to give to you. Pray you finish it, and I will save mine eyes.'

As the King closed the door behind him she moved across to the chair and sat herself down to gaze at the coals. Katharine knelt at her feet and stretched out her hands. She was, she said, her mistress's woman. But the Lady Mary turned obdurately the side of her face to her suppliant; only her fingers picked at her black dress.

'I am your woman,' Katharine said. 'Before God and St Anthony, the King is naught to me! Before God and the Mother of God, no man is aught to me! I swear that I am your woman. I swear that I will speak as you bid me speak, or be silent. May God do so to me if in aught I act other than may be of service to you!'

'Then you may sit motionless till the green mould is over your cheeks,' Mary answered.

But two days later, in the afternoon, Katharine Howard came upon her mistress with her jaws moving voraciously. Half of the cinnamon cates were eaten from the box on the writing-pulpit. A convulsion of rage passed over the girl's dark figure; her eyes dilated and appeared to blaze with a hot and threatening fury.

'If I could have thy head, before God I would shorten thee by the neck!' she said. 'Stay now; go not. Take thy hand from the door-latch.'

Sudden sobs shook her, and tears dropped down her furrowed and pallid cheeks. She was tormented always by a gnawing and terrible hunger that no meat and no bread might satisfy, so that, being alone with the cakes in the cold spring afternoon, she had, in spite of the donor, been forced always nearer and nearer to them.

'God help me!' she said at last. 'Udal is gone, and the scullion that supplied me in secret has the small-pox. How may I get me things to eat?'

'To have stayed to ask me!' Katharine cried. 'What a folly was here!' For, as a daughter of the King, the Lady Mary was little more than herself; but because she was daughter to a queen that was at once a saint and martyr, Katharine was ready to spend her life in her service.

'I would stay to ask a service of any man or woman,'

Mary answered, 'save only that I have this great hunger.'
She clutched angrily at her skirt, and so calmed herself.

'How may you help me?' she asked grimly. 'There are
many that would put poison in my food. My mother was
poisoned.'

'I would eat myself of all the food that I bring you,' said
Katharine.

'And if thou wast poisoned, I must get me another, and
yet another after that. You know who it is that would have
me away.'

At that hint of the presence of Cromwell, Katharine
grew more serious.

'I will save of my own food,' she answered simply.

'Till your bones stick through your skin!' Mary sneered.
'See you, do you know one man you could trust?'

The shadow fell the more deeply upon Katharine, because her cousin—as she remembered every day—the one
man that she could trust, was in Calais town.

'I know of two women,' she said; 'my maid Margot and
Cicely Elliott.'

Mary of England reflected for a long time. Her eyes sunk
deep in her head, grey and baleful, had the look of her
father's.

'Cicely Elliott is too well known for my woman,' she
said. 'Thy maid Margot is a great lump, too. Hath she no
lover?'

The magister was in Paris.

'But a brother she hath,' Katharine said; 'one set upon
advancement.'

Mary said moodily:

'Advancement, then, may be in this. God knoweth his
own good time. But you might tell him; or it were better
you should bid her tell him. . . . In short words, and fur . . .
wait.'

She had a certain snake-like eagerness and vehemence
in her motions. She opened swiftly an aumbry in which
there stood a tankard of milk. She took a clean pen, and
then turned upon Katharine.

'Before thou goest upon this errand,' she said, 'I would have thee know that, for thee, there may be a traitor's death in this—and some glory in Heaven.'

'You write to the Empress,' Katharine cried.

'I write to a man,' the Lady Mary said. 'Might you speak with clear eyes to my father if you knew more than that?'

'I do not believe that you would bring your father down,' Katharine said.

'Why, you have a very comfortable habit of belief,' Mary sneered at her. 'In two words! Will you carry this treasonable letter or no?'

'God help me,' Katharine cried.

'Well, God help you,' her mistress jeered. 'Two nights agone you swore to be my woman and no other man's. Here you are in a taking. Think upon it.'

She dipped her white pen in the milk and began to write upon a great sheet of paper, holding her head aslant to see the shine of the fluid.

Katharine fought a battle within herself. Here was treason to the King—but that was a little thing to her. Yet the King was a father whom she would bring back to this daughter, and the traitor was a daughter whom she was sworn to serve and pledged to bring back to this father. If then she conveyed this letter....

'Tell me,' she asked of the intent figure above the paper, 'when, if ever, this plot shall burst?'

'Madam Howard,' the other answered, 'I heard thee not.'

'I say I will convey your Highness' letter if the plot shall not burst for many days. If it be to come soon I will forswear myself and be no longer your woman.'

'Why, what a pax is here?' her mistress faced round on her. 'What muddles thy clear head? I doubt, knowing the craven kings that are of my party, no plot shall burst for ten years. And so?'

'Before then thou mayest be brought back to thy father,' Katharine said.

Mary of England burst into a hoarse laughter.

'As God's my life,' she cried, 'that may well be. And you may find a chaste whore before either.'

Whilst she was finishing her letter, Katharine Howard prayed that Mary the Mother of Mercy might soften the hatred of this daughter, even as, of old times, she had turned the heart of Lucius the Syracusan. Then there should be an end to plotting and this letter might work no ill.

Having waved the sheet of paper in the air to dry it, Mary crumpled it into a ball.

'See you,' she said, 'if this miscarry I run a scant risk. For, if this be a treason, this treason is well enough known already to them you wot of. They might have had my head this six years on one shift or another had they so dared. So to me it matters little.—But for thee—and for thy maid Margot and this maid's brother and his house and his father and his leman—death may fall on ye all if this ball of paper miscarry.'

Katharine made no answer and her mistress spoke on.

'Take now this paper ball, give it to thy maid Margot, bid thy maid Margot bear it to her brother Ned.' Her brother Ned should place it in his sleeve and walk with it to Herring Lane at Hampton. There, over against the house of the Sieur Chapuys, who was the Emperor's ambassador to this Christian nation—over against that house there was a cookshop to which resorted the servants of the ambassador. Passing it by, Katharine's maid's brother should thrust his hand in at the door and cry 'a pox on all stinking Kaiserliks and Papists,'—and he should cast the paper at that cook's head. Then out would come master cook to his door and claim reparation. And for reparation Margot's brother Ned should buy such viands as the cook should offer him. These viands he was to bring, as a good brother should, to his hungry sister, and these viands his sister should take to her room—which was Katharine's room. 'And, of an evening,' she finished, 'I shall come to thy room to commune with thee of the writers that be dead and yet beloved. Hast thou the lesson by heart? I will say it again.'

III

It was in that way, however sorely against her liking, that Katharine Howard came into a plot. It subdued her, it seemed to age her, it was as if she had parted with some virtue. When again she spoke with the King, who came to loll in his daughter's armed chair one day out of every week, it troubled her to find that she could speak to him with her old tranquillity. She was ashamed at feeling no shame, since all the while these letters were passing behind his back. Once even he had been talking to her of how they nailed pear trees against the walls in her Lincolnshire home.

'Our garden man would say. . . .' she began a sentence. Her eye fell upon one of these very crumpled balls of paper. It lay upon the table and it confused her to think that it appeared like an apple. 'Would say . . . would say . . .' she faltered.

He looked at her with enquiring eyes, round in his great head.

'It is too late,' she finished.

'Even too late for what?' he asked.

'Too late in the year to set the trees back,' she answered and her fit of nervousness had passed. 'For there is a fluid in trees that runneth upward in the spring of the year to greet the blessed sun.'

'Why, what a wise lady is this!' he said, half earnest. 'I would I had such an adviser as thou hast,' he continued to his daughter.

He frowned for a moment, remembering that, being who he was, he should stand in need of no advice.

'See you,' he said to Katharine. 'You have spoken of many things and wisely, after a woman's fashion of book-learning. Now I am minded that you should hear me speak upon the Word of God which is a man's matter and a King's. This day sennight I am to have brought to my closet a heretic, Dr Barnes. If ye will ye may hear me confound him with goodly doctrines.'

He raised both his eyebrows heavily and looked first at the Lady Mary.

'You, I am minded, shall hear a word of true doctrine.'

And to Katharine, 'I would hear how you think that I can manage a disputation. For the fellow is the sturdiest rogue with a yard of tongue to wag.'

Katharine maintained a duteous silence; the Lady Mary stood with her hands clasped before her. Upon Katharine he smiled suddenly and heavily.

'I grow too old to be a match for thee in the learning of this world. Thy tongue has outstripped me since I am become stale. . . . But hear me in the other make of talk.'

'I ask no better,' Katharine said.

'Therefore,' he finished, 'I am minded that you, Mog, and your ladies all, do move your residences from here to my house at Hampton. This is an old and dark place; there you shall be better honoured.'

He lay back in his chair and was pleased with the care that he took of his daughter. Katharine glided intently across the smooth bare floor and took the ball of paper in her hand. His eyes followed her and he moved his head round after her movements, heavily, and without any motion of his great body. He was in a comfortable mood, having slept well the night before, and having conversed agreeably in the bosom of a family where pleasant conversation was a rare thing. For the Lady Mary had forborne to utter biting speeches, since her eyes too had been upon that ball of paper. The King did not stay for many minutes after Katharine had gone.

She was excited, troubled and amused—and, indeed, the passing of those letters held her thoughts in those few days. Thus it was easy to give the paper to her maid Margot, and easy to give Margot the directions. But she knew very well by what shift Margot persuaded her scarlet-clothed springald of a brother to take the ball and to throw it into the cookshop. For the young Poins was set upon advancement, and Margot, buxom, substantial and honest-faced, stood before him and said: 'Here is your chance for advancement made . . .' if he could carry these missives very secretly.

'For, brother Poins,' she said, 'thou knowest these great folks reward greatly—and these things pass between folks very great. If I tell thee no names it is because thou canst see more through a stone wall than common folk.'

So the young Poins cocked his bonnet more jauntily, and, setting out up river to Hampton, changed his scarlet clothes for a grey coat and puritan hose, and in the dark did his errand very well. He carried a large poke in which he put the larded capons and the round loaves that the cook sold to him. Later, following a reed path along the river, he came swiftly down to Isleworth with his bag on a cord and, in the darkness from beneath the walls, he slung bag and cord in at Katharine Howard's open window. For several times this happened before the Lady Mary's court was moved to Hampton. At first, Katharine had her tremors to put up with—and it was only when, each evening, with a thump and swish, the bag, sweeping out of the darkness, sped across her floor—it was only then that Katharine's heart ceased from pulsing with a flutter. All the while the letters were out of her own hands she moved on tip-toe, as if she were a hunter intent on surprising a coy quarry. Nevertheless, it was impossible for her to believe that this was a dangerous game; it was impossible to believe that the heavy, unsuspicious and benevolent man who tried clumsily to gain his daughter's love with bribes of cakes and kerchiefs—that this man could be roused to order her to her death because she conveyed from one place to another a ball of paper. It was more like a game of passing a ring from hand to hand behind the players' backs, for kisses for forfeits if the ring were caught. Nevertheless, this was treason-felony; yet it was furthering the dear cause of the saints.

It was on the day on which her uncle Norfolk had sent for her that the King had his interview with the heretical Dr Barnes—nicknamed Antoninus Anglicanus.

The Lady Mary and Katharine Howard and her maid, Margot, were set in a tiny closet in which there was, in a hole in the wall, a niche for the King's confessor. The King's own chamber was empty when they passed through, and they left the door between ajar. There came a burst of voices, and swiftly the Bishop of Winchester himself entered their closet. He lifted his black eyebrows at sight of them, and rubbed his thin hands with satisfaction.

'Now we shall hear one of Crummock's henchmen swinged,' he whispered. He raised a finger for them to lend ear and gazed through the crack of the door. They heard a harsh voice, like a dog's bay, utter clearly:

'Now goodly goodman Doctor, thou hast spoken certain words at Paul's Cross. They touched on Justification; thou shalt justify them to me now.' There came a sound of a man who cleared his throat—and then again the heavy voice:

'Why, be not cast down; we spoke as doctor to doctor. Without a doubt thou art learned. Show then thy learning. Wast brave at Paul's Cross. Justify now!'

Gardiner, turning from gazing through the door-crack, grinned at the three women.

'He rated *me* at Paul's Cross!' he said. 'He thumped me as I had been a thrashing floor.' They missed the Doctor's voice—but the King's came again.

'Why, this is a folly. I am Supreme Head, but I bid thee to speak.'

There was a long pause till they caught the words.

'Your Highness, I do surrender my learning to your Highness'.' Then, indeed, there was a great roar:

'Unworthy knave; surrender thyself to none but God. He is above me as above thee. To none but God.'

There was another long silence, and then the King's voice again:

'Why, get thee gone. Shalt to gaol for a craven . . .' And

then came a hissing sound of vexation, a dull thud, and other noises.

The King's bonnet lay on the floor, and the King himself alone was padding down the room when they opened their door. His face was red with rage.

'Why, what a clever fiend is this Cromwell!' the Lady Mary said; but the Bishop of Winchester was laughing. He pushed Margot Poins from the closet, but caught Katharine Howard tightly by the arm.

'Thou shalt write what thy uncle asked of thee!' he commanded in a low voice, 'an thou do it not, thy cousin shall to gaol! I have a letter thou didst write me.'

A black despair settled for a moment upon Katharine, but the King was standing before her. He had walked with inaudible swiftness up from the other end of the room.

'Didst not hear me argue!' he said, with the vexation of a great child. 'That poxy knave out-marched me!'

'Why,' the Lady Mary sniggered at him, 'thy brewer's son is too many for your Highness.'

Henry snarled round at her; but she folded her hands before her and uttered:

'The brewer's son made your Highness Supreme Head of the Church. Therefore, the brewer's son hath tied your Highness' tongue. For who may argue with your Highness?'

He looked at her for a moment with a bemused face.

'Very well,' he said.

'The brewer's son should have made your Highness the lowest suppliant at the Church doors. Then, if, for the astounding of certain beholders, your Highness were minded to argue, your Highness should find adversaries.'

The bitter irony of her words made Katharine Howard angry. This poor, heavy man had other matters for misgiving than to be badgered by a woman. But the irony was lost upon the King. He said very simply:

'Why, that is true. If I be the Head, the Tail shall fear to bandy words with me.' He addressed himself again to Katharine: 'I am sorry that you did not hear me argue. I am main good at these arguments.' He looked reflectively at Gardiner and said: 'Friend Winchester, one day I will cast a main at arguments with thee, and Kat Howard shall hear. But I doubt thou art little skilled with thy tongue.'

'Why, I will make a better shift with my tongue than Privy Seal's men dare,' the bishop said. He glanced under his brows at Henry, as if he were measuring the ground for a leap.

'The Lady Mary is in the right,' he ventured.

The King, who was thinking out a speech to Katharine, said, 'Anan?' and Gardiner ventured further:

'I hold it for true that this man held his peace, because Cromwell so commanded it. He is Cromwell's creature, and Cromwell is minded to escape from the business with a whole skin.'

The King bent him an attentive ear.

'It is to me, in the end, that Privy Seal owes amends,' Gardiner said rancorously. 'Since it was at me that this man, by Cromwell's orders, did hurl his foul words at Paul's Cross.'

The King said:

'Why, it is true that thou art more sound in doctrine than is Privy Seal. What wouldst thou have?'

Gardiner made an immense gesture, as if he would have embraced the whole world.

Katharine Howard trembled. Here they were, all the three of them Cromwell's enemies. They were all alone with the King in a favouring mood, and she was on the point of crying out:

'Give us Privy Seal's head.'

But, in this very moment of his opportunity, Gardiner faltered. Even the blackness of his hatred could not make him bold.

'That he should make me amends in public for the foul words that knave uttered. That they should both sue to me for pardon: that it should be showed to the world what manner of man it is that they have dared to flout.'

'Why, goodman Bishop, it shall be done,' the King said,

and Katharine groaned aloud. A clock with two quarter boys beside the large fire-place chimed the hour of four.

'Aye!' the King commented to Katharine. 'I thought to have had a pleasanter hour of it. Now you see what manner of life is mine: I must go to a plaguing council!'

'An I were your Highness,' Katharine cried, 'I would be avenged on them that marred my pleasures.'

He touched her benevolently upon the cheek.

'Sweetheart,' he said, 'an thou wert me thou'dst do great things.' He rolled towards the door, heavy and mountainous: with the latch in his hand, he cried over his shoulder: 'But thou shalt yet hear me argue!'

'What a morning you have made of this!' Katharine threw at the bishop. The Lady Mary shrugged her shoulders to her ears and turned away. Gardiner said:

'Anan?'

'Oh, well your Holiness knows,' Katharine said. 'You might have come within an ace of having Cromwell down.'

His eyes flashed, and he swallowed with a bitter delight.

'I have him at my feet,' he said. 'He shall do public reparation to me. You have heard the King say so.'

There were tears of vexation in Katharine's eyes.

'Well I know how it is that this brewer's son has king'd it so long!' she said. 'An I had been a man it had been his head or mine.'

Gardiner shook himself like a dog that is newly out of the water.

'Madam Howard,' he said, 'you are mighty high. I have observed how the King spoke all his words for your ear. His passions are beyond words and beyond shame.'

The Lady Mary was almost out of the room, and he came close enough to speak in Katharine's ears.

'But be you certain that his Highness' passions are not beyond the reverse of passion, which is jealousy. You have a cousin at Calais. . . .'

Katharine moved away from him.

'Why, God help you, priest,' she said. 'Do you think you are the only man that knows that?'

He laughed melodiously, with a great anger.

'But I am the man that knoweth best how to use my knowledge. Therefore you shall do my will.'

Katharine Howard laughed back at him:

'Where your lordship's will marches with mine I will do it,' she said. 'But I am main weary of your lordship's threats. You know the words of Artemidorus?'

Gardiner contained his rage.

'You will write the letter we have asked you to write?'

She laughed again, and faced him, radiant, fair and flushed in the cheeks.

'In so far as you beg me to write a letter praying the King of France and the Emperor to abstain from war upon this land, I will write the letter. But, in so far as that helps forward the plotting of you and a knave called Throck-morton, I am main sorry that I must write it.'

The bishop drew back, and uttered:

'Madam Howard, ye are forward.'

'Why, God help your lordship,' she said. 'Where I see little course for respect I show little. You see I am friends with the King—therefore leave you my cousin be. Because I am friends with the King, who is a man among wolves, I will pray my mistress to indite a letter that shall save this King some troubles. But, if you threaten me with my cousin, or my cousin with me, I will use my friendship with the King as well against you as against any other.'

Gardiner swallowed in his throat, winked his eyes, and muttered:

'Why, so you do what we will, it matters little in what spirit you shall do it.'

'So you and my uncle and Throckmorton keep your feet from my paths, you may have my leavings,' she said. 'And they will be the larger part, since I ask little for myself.'

He gave her his episcopal blessing as she followed the Lady Mary to her rooms.

Her mind was made up—and she knew that it had been made up hastily, but she was never one to give much time to doubting. She wished these men to leave her out of their plots—but four men are stronger than one woman. Yet, as her philosophy had it, you may make a woman your tool, but she will bend in your hand and strike where she will, for all that. Therefore she must plot, but not with them.

As soon as she could she found the Lady Mary alone, and, setting her valour up against the other's dark and rigid figure, she spoke rapidly:

She would have her lady write to her friends across the sea that, if Cromwell were ever to fall, they must now stay their hands against the King: they must diminish their bands, discontinue their fortifyings and feign even to quarrel amongst themselves. Otherwise the King must rest firm in his alliance with Cleves, to counterbalance them.

The Lady Mary raised her eyebrows with a show of insolent astonishment that was for all the world like the King's.

'You affect my father!' she said. 'Is it not a dainty plan?'

Katharine brushed past her words with:

'It matters little who affects what thing. The main is that Privy Seal must be cast down.'

'Carthage must be destroyed, O Cato,' the Lady Mary sneered. 'Ye are peremptory.'

'I am as God made me,' Katharine answered. 'I am for God's Church. . . .' She had a sharp spasm of impatience. 'Here is a thing to do, and the one and the other snarl like dogs, each for his separate ends.'

'Oh, la, la,' the Lady Mary laughed.

'A Howard is as good as any man,' Katharine said. Her ingenuous face flushed, and she moved her hand to her throat. 'God help me: it is true that I swore to be your woman. But it is the true province of your woman to lead you to work for justice and the truth.'

A black malignancy settled upon the face of the princess.

'I have been called bastard,' she said. 'My mother was done to death.'

'No true man believes you misbegotten,' Katharine answered hotly.

'Well, it is proclaimed treason, to speak thus,' the Lady Mary sneered.

'Neither can you give your sainted mother her life again.' Katharine ignored her words. 'But these actions were not your father's. It was an ill man forced him to them. The saints be good to you; is it not time to forgive a sad man that would make amends? I would have you to write this letter.'

The Lady Mary's lips moved into the curves of a tormenting smile.

'You plead your lover's cause main well,' she uttered.

Katharine had another motion of impatience.

'Your cause I plead main better,' she said. 'It is certain that, this man once down, your bastardy should be reversed.'

'I do not ask it,' the Lady Mary said.

'But I ask that you give us peace here, so that the King may make amends to many that he hath sorely wronged. Do you not see that the King inclineth to the Church of God? Do you not see. . . .'

'I see very plainly that I needs must thank you for better housing,' Mary answered. 'It is certain that my father had never brought me from that well at Isleworth, had it not been that he desireth converse with thee at his ease.'

Katharine's lips parted with a hot anger, but before she could speak the bitter girl said calmly:

'Oh, I have not said thou art his leman. I know my father. His blood is not hot—but his ears crave tickling. Tickle them whilst thou mayest. Have I stayed thee? Have I sent thee from my room when he did come?'

Katharine cast back the purple hood from over her forehead, she brushed her hand across her brow, and made herself calm.

'This is a trifling folly,' she said. 'In two words: will your Highness write me this letter?'

'Then, in four words,' Mary answered, 'my Highness cares not.'

The mobile brows above Katharine's blue eyes made a hard straight line.

'An you will not,' she brought out, 'I will leave your Highness' service. I will get me away to Calais, where my father is.'

'Why, you will never do that,' the Lady Mary said; 'you have tasted blood here.'

Katharine hung her head and meditated for a space.

'No, before God,' she said earnestly, 'I think you judge me wrong. I think I am not as you think me. I think that I do seek no ends of my own.'

The Lady Mary raised her eyebrows and snickered ironically.

'But of this I am very certain,' Katharine said. She spoke more earnestly, seeming to plead: 'If I thought that I were grown a self-seeker, by Mars who changed Alectryon to a cock, and by Pallas Athene who changed Arachne to a spider—if I were so changed, I would get me gone from this place. But here is a thing that I may do. If you will aid me to do it I will stay. If you will not I will get me gone.'

'Good wench,' Mary answered, 'let us say for the sake of peace that thou art honest. . . . Yet I have sworn by other gods than thine that never will I do aught that shall be of aid, comfort or succour to my father's cause.'

'Take back your oaths!' Katharine cried.

'For thee!' Mary said. 'Wench, thou hast brought me food: thou hast served me in the matter of letters. I might only with great trouble get another so to serve me. But, by Mars and Pallas and all the constellation of the deities, thou mightest get thee to Hell's flames or ever I would take back an oath.'

'Oh, madness,' Katharine cried out. 'Oh, mad frenzy of one whom the gods would destroy.' Three times before she had reined in her anger: now she stretched out her hands with her habitual gesture of pitiful despair. Her eyes looked straight before her, and, as she inclined her knees, the folds of her grey dress bent round her on the floor.

'Here I have pleaded with you, and you have gibed me with the love of the King. Here I have been earnest with you, and you have mocked. God help me!' she sobbed, with a catch in her throat. 'Here is rest, peace and the blessing of God offered to this land. Here is a province that is offered back to the Mother of God and the dear hosts of heaven. Here might we bring an erring King back to the right way, a sinful man back unto his God. But you, for a parcel of wrongs of your own. . . .'

'Now hold thy peace,' Mary said, between anger and irony. 'Here is a matter of a farthing or two. Be the letter written, and kiss upon it.'

Katharine stayed herself in the tremor of her emotions, and the Lady Mary said drily:

'Be the letter written. But thou shalt write it. I have sworn that I will do nothing to give this King ease.'

'But my writing . . .' Katharine began.

'Thou shalt write,' Mary interrupted her harshly. 'If thou wilt have this King at peace for a space that Cromwell may fall, why I am at one with thee. For this King is such a palterer that without this knave at his back I might have had him down ten years ago. Therefore, thou shalt write, and I will countersign the words.'

'That were to write thyself,' Katharine said.

'Good wench,' the Lady Mary said. 'I am thy slave: but take what thou canst get.'

Towards six of the next day young Poins clambered in at Katharine Howard's window and stood, pale, dripping with rain and his teeth chattering, between Cicely Elliott and her old knight.

'The letter,' he said. 'They have taken thy letter. My advancement is at an end!' And he fell upon the floor.

Going jauntily along the Hampton Street, he had been filled, that afternoon, with visions of advancement. Drifts of rain hid the osiers across the river and made the mud ooze in over the laces of his shoes. The tall white and black house, where the Emperor's ambassador had his lodgings, leaned in all its newness over the path, and the water from its gutters fell right into the river, making a bridge above a passer's head. The little cookshop, with its feet, as it were, in the water, made a small hut nestling down beneath the shadow of the great house. It was much used by Chapuys' grooms, trencher boys and javelin men, because the cook was a Fleming, and had a comfortable hand in stewing eels.

Ned Poins must pass the ambassador's house in his walk, but in under the dark archway there stood four men sheltering, in grey cloaks that reached to their feet. Stepping gingerly on the brick causeway that led down to the barge-steps, they came and stood before the young man, three being in a line together and one a little to the side. He hardly looked at them because he was thinking: 'This afternoon I will say to my sister Margot: "Fifteen letters I have carried for thy great persons. I have carried them with secrecy and speed. Now, by Cock, I will be advanced to ancient." ' He had imagined his sister pleading with him to be patient, and himself stamping with his foot and swearing that he would be advanced instantly.

The solitary one of the four men barred his way, and said:

'No further! You go back with us!'

Poins swung his cape back and touched his sword-hilt.

'You will have your neck stretched if you stay me,' he said.

The other loosened his cloak which had covered him up to the nose. He showed a mocking mouth, a long red beard that blew aside in a wild gust of the weather, and displayed on his breast the lion badge of the Lord Privy Seal.

'An you will not come you shall be carried!' he said.

'Nick Throckmorton,' Poins answered, 'I will slit thy weazand! I am on a greater errand than thine.'

It was strong in his mind that he was bearing a letter for the King's Highness. The other three laid hands swiftly upon him, and a wet cloak flapped over his head. They had his elbows bound together behind his back before his eyes again had the river and the muddy path to look upon. Throckmorton grinned sardonically, and they forced him along in the mud. The rain fell down; his cloak was gone. And then a great dread entered into his simple mind. It kept running through his head:

'I was carrying a letter for the King—I was carrying a letter for the King!' but his addled brains would bear his thoughts no further until he was cast loose in the very room of Privy Seal himself. They had used him very roughly, and he staggered back against the wall, gasping for breath and weeping with rage and fear.

Privy Seal stood before the fire; his eyes lifted a little but he said nothing at all. Throckmorton took a dagger from the chain round his neck, and cut the bag from the boy's girdle. Still smiling sardonically, he placed it in Privy Seal's fat hands.

'Here is the great secret,' he said. 'I took it even in the gates of Chapuys.'

Privy Seal started a little and cried, 'Ah!' The boy would have spoken, but he feared even to cry out; his eyes were starting from his head, and his breath came in great gusts that shook him. Privy Seal sat down in a large chair by the fire and considered for a moment. Then he slowly drew out the crumpled ball of paper. Here at last he held the Lady Mary utterly in his power; here at last, at the eleventh hour, he had a new opportunity to show to the King his vigilance, his power, and how necessary he was to the safety of the realm. He had been beginning to despair; Winchester was to confess the King that night. Now he held them. . . .

'I have been diligent,' Throckmorton said. 'I had had the Lady Mary set in the room that has a spy-hole beside a rose in the ceiling. So I saw the writing of this letter.'

Cromwell said, 'Ah!' He had pulled the paper apart, smoothed it across his knee, and looked at it attentively.

Then he held it close to the fire, for no blank paper could trouble the Privy Seal. This was a child's trick at best.

In the warmth faint lines became visible on the paper; they darkened and darkened beneath his intent eyes. Behind his back Throckmorton, with his immense beard and sardonic eyes, rubbed his hands and smiled. Privy Seal's fingers trembled, but he gave no further sign.

Suddenly he cried, 'What!' and then, 'Both women! both . . .'

He fell back in the chair, and the sudden quaver of his face, the deep breath that he drew, showed his immense joy.

'God of my heart! Both women!' he said again.

The rain hurled itself with a great rustling against the casement. Though it was so early, it was already nearly dark. Cromwell sat up suddenly and pointed at the boy.

'Take that rat away!' he said. 'Set him in irons, and come back here.'

Throckmorton caught the quivering boy by the ear and led him out at the door. He took him down a small stair that opened behind a curtain. At the stair-foot he pulled open a small, heavy door. He still held his dagger, and he cut the ropes that tied Poins' elbows. With a sudden alacrity and a grin of malice he kicked him violently.

'Get you gone to your mistress,' he said.

Poins stood for a moment, wavering on his feet. He slipped miserably in the mud of the park, and suddenly he ran. His grey, straining form disappeared round the end of the dark buildings, and then Throckmorton waved a hand at the grey sky and laughed noiselessly. Thomas Cromwell was making notes in his tablets when his spy re-entered the room, with the rain-drops glistening in his beard.

'Here are some notes for you,' Cromwell said. He rose to his feet with a swift and intense energy. 'I have given you five farms. Now I go to the King.'

Throckmorton spoke gently.

'You are over-eager,' he said. 'It is early to go to the King's Highness. We may find much more yet.'

'It is already late,' Cromwell said.

'Sir,' Throckmorton urged, 'consider that the King is much affected to this lady. Consider that this letter contains nothing that is treasonable; rather it urges peace upon the King's enemies.'

'Aye,' said Cromwell; 'but it is written covertly to the King's enemies.'

'That, it is true, is a treason,' Throckmorton said; 'but it is very certain that the Lady Mary hath written letters very much more hateful. By questioning this boy that we have in gaol, by gaoling this Lady Katharine— why, we shall put her to the thumbscrews!—by gaol and by thumbscrew, we shall gar her to set her hand to another make of confession. Then you may go to the King's Highness.'

'Nick Throckmorton,' Cromwell said, 'Winchester hath to-night the King's ear. . . .'

'Sir,' Throckmorton answered, and a tremble in his calm voice showed his eagerness, 'I beseech you to give my words your thoughts. Winchester hath the King's ear for the moment; but I will get you letters wherein these ladies shall reveal Winchester for the traitor that we know him to be. Listen to me. . . .' He paused and let his crafty eyes run over his master's face. 'Let this matter be for an hour. See you, you shall make a warrant to take this Lady Katharine.'

He paused and appeared to reflect.

'In an hour she shall be here. Give me leave to use my thumbscrews. . . .'

'Aye, but Winchester,' Cromwell said.

'Why,' Throckmorton answered confidently, 'in an hour, too, Winchester shall be with the King in the King's Privy Chapel. There will be a make of prayers; ten minutes to that. There shall be Gardiner talking to the King against your lordship; ten minutes to that. And, Winchester being craven, it shall cost him twice ten minutes to come to begging your lordship's head of the King, if ever he dare to beg it. But he never shall.'

Cromwell said, 'Well, well!'

'There we have forty minutes,' Throckmorton said. He licked his lips and held his long beard in his hand carefully, as if it had been a bird. 'But give me ten minutes to do my will upon this lady's body, and ten to write down what she shall confess. Then, if it take your lordship ten minutes to dress yourself finely, you shall have still ten in which you shall show the King how his Winchester is traitor to him.'

Cromwell considered for a minute; his lips twitched cautiously the one above the other.

'This is a great matter,' he said. He paused again. 'If this lady should not confess! And it is very certain that the King affects her.'

'Give me ten minutes of her company,' the spy answered.

Cromwell considered again.

'You are very certain,' he said; and then:

'Wilt thou stake thy head upon it?'

Throckmorton wagged his beard slowly up and down.

'Thy head and beard!' Cromwell repeated. He struck his hands briskly together. 'It is thine own asking. God help thee if thou failest!'

'I will lay nothing to your lordship's door,' Throckmorton said eagerly.

'God knows!' Cromwell said. 'No man that hath served me have I deserted. So it is that no one hath betrayed me. But thou shalt take this lady without warrant from my hand.'

Throckmorton nodded.

'If thou shalt wring avowal from her thou shalt be the wealthiest commoner of England,' Cromwell said. 'But I will not be here. Nay, thou shalt take her to thine own rooms. I will not be seen in this matter. And if thou fail . . .'

'Sir, I stand more sure of my succeeding than ever your lordship stood,' Throckmorton answered him.

'It is not I that shall betray thee if thou fail,' Cromwell answered. 'Get thee gone swiftly . . .' He took the jewelled badge from his cap that lay on the table. 'Thou hast served me well,' he said; 'take this in case I never see thy face again.'

'Oh, you shall see my triumph!' Throckmorton answered.

He bent himself nearly double as he passed through the door.

Cromwell sat down in his great chair, and his eyes gazed at nothing through the tapestry of his room.

IV

In Katharine Howard's room they had the form of the boy, wet, grey, and mud-draggled, lying on the ground between them. Cicely Elliott rose in her chair: it was not any part of her nature to succour fainting knaves, and she let him stay where he was. Old Rochford raised his hands, and cried out to Katharine:

'You have been sending letters again!'

Katharine stood absolutely still. They had taken her letters!

She neither spoke nor stirred. Slowly, as she remembered that this was indeed a treason, that here without doubt was death, that she was outwitted, that she was now the chattel of whosoever held her letters—as point after point came into her mind, the blood fled from her face. Cicely Elliott sat down in her chair again, and whilst the two sat watching her in the falling dusk they seemed to withdraw themselves from her world of friendship and to become spectators. Ten minutes before she would have laughed at this nightmare: it had seemed to her impossible that her letters could have been taken. So many had got in safety to their bourne. Now . . .

'Who has my letter?' she cried.

How did she know what was to arise: who was to strike the blow: whence it would come: what could she still do to palliate its effects? The boy lay motionless upon the floor, his face sideways upon the boards.

'Who? Who? Who?' she cried. She wrung her hands, and kneeling, with a swift violence shook him by the coat near his neck. His head struck the boards and he fell back, motionless still, and like a dead man.

Cicely Elliott looked around her in the darkening room: beside the ambry there hung a brush of feathers such as they used for the dusting of their indoor clothes. She glided and hopped to the brush and back to the hearth: thrust the feathers into the coals and stood again, the brush hissing and spluttering, before Katharine on her knees.

'Dust the springald's face,' she tittered.

At the touch of the hot feathers and the acrid perfume in his nostrils, the boy sneezed, stirred and opened his eyes.

'Who has my letter?' Katharine cried.

The lids opened wide in amazement, he saw her face and suddenly closed his eyes, and lay down with his face to the floor. A spasm of despair brought his knees up to his chin, his cropped yellow head went backwards and forwards upon the boards.

'I have lost my advancement,' he sobbed. 'I have lost my advancement.' A smell of strong liquors diffused itself from him.

'Oh beast,' Katharine cried from her knees, 'who hath my letter?'

'I have lost my advancement,' he moaned.

She sprang from her feet to the fireplace and caught the iron tongs with which they were wont to place pieces of wood upon the fire. She struck him a hard blow upon the arm between the shoulder and elbow.

'Sot!' she cried. 'Tell me! Tell me!'

He rose to his seat and held his arms to protect his head and eyes. When he stuttered:

'Nick Throckmorton had it!' her hand fell powerless to

her side; but when he added: 'He gave it to Privy Seal!'
she cast the tongs into the brands to save herself from
cleaving open his head.

'God!' she said drily, 'you have lost your advancement.
And I mine!... And I mine.'

She wavered to her chair by the hearth-place, and
covered her face with her white hands.

The boy got to his knees, then to his feet; he staggered
backwards into the arras beside the door.

'God's curse on you!' he said. 'Where is Margot? That
I may beat her! That I may beat her as you have beaten
me.' He waved his hand with a tipsy ferocity and staggered
through the door.

'Was it for this I did play the ―― for thee?' he
menaced her. 'By Cock! I will swinge that harlot!'

The old knight got to his feet. He laid his hand heavily
upon Cicely Elliott's shoulder.

'Best begone from here,' he said, 'this is no quarrel of
mine or thine.'

'Why, get thee gone, old boy,' she laughed over her
shoulder. 'Seven of my men have been done to death in
such like marlocks. I would not have thee die as they did.'

'Come with me,' he said in her ear. 'I have dropped my
lance. Never shall I ride to horse again. I would not lose
thee; art all I have.'

'Why, get thee gone for a brave old boy,' she said. 'I
will come ere the last pynot has chattered its last chatter.'

'It is no light matter,' he answered. 'I am Rochford of
Bosworth Hedge. But I have lost lance and horse and manhood. I will not lose my dandery thing too.'

Katharine Howard sat, a dark figure in the twilight, with
the fire shining upon her hands that covered her face.
Cicely Elliott looked at her and stirred.

'Why,' she said, 'I have lost father and mother and men-
folk and sister. But my itch to know I will not lose, if I pay
my head for the price. I would give a silken gown to know
this tale.'

Katharine Howard uncovered her face; it shewed white

even in the rays of the fire. One finger raised itself to a level with her temple.

'Listen!' she uttered. They heard through the closed door a dull thud, metallic and hard—and another after four great beats of their hearts.

'Pikestaves!' the old knight groaned. His mouth fell open. Katharine Howard shrieked; she sprang to the clothes press, to the window—and then to the shadows beside the fireplace where she cowered and sobbed. The door swung back: a great man stood in the half light and cried out:

'The Lady Katharine Howard.'

The old knight raised his hands above his head—but Cicely Elliott turned her back to the fire.

'What would you with me?' she asked. Her face was all in shadows.

'I have a warrant to take the Lady Katharine.'

Cicely Elliott screamed out:

'Me! Me! Ah God! ah God!'

She shrank back; she waved her hands, then suddenly she caught at the coif above her head and pulled forward the tail of her hood till, like a veil, it covered her face.

'Let me not be seen!' she uttered hoarsely.

The old knight's impatient desires burst through his terror.

'Nick Throckmorton,' he bleated, 'yon mad wench of mine...'

But the large man cut in on his words with a harsh and peremptory vehemence.

'It is very dark. You cannot see who I be. Thank your God I cannot see whether you be a man who fought by a hedge or no. There shall be reports written of this. Hold your peace.'

Nevertheless the old man made a spluttering noise of one about to speak.

'Hold your peace,' Throckmorton said roughly, again, 'I cannot see your face. Can you walk, madam, and very fast?'

He caught her roughly by the wrist and they passed out, twin blots of darkness, at the doorway. The clank of the pikestaves sounded on the boards without, and old Rochford was tearing at his white hairs in the little light from the fire.

Katharine Howard ran swiftly from the shadow of the fireplace.

'Give me time, till they have passed the stairhead,' she whispered. 'For pity! for pity.'

'For pity,' he muttered. 'This is to stake one's last years upon woman.' He turned upon her, and his white face and pale blue eyes glinted at her hatefully.

'What pity had Cicely Elliott upon me then?'

'Till they are out of the gate,' she pleaded, 'that I may get me gone.'

At her back she was cut off from the night and the rain by a black range of corridors. She had never been through them because they led to rooms of men that she did not know. But, down the passage and down the stairway was the only exit to the rest of the palace and the air. She threw open her press so that the hinges cracked. She caught her cloak and she caught her hood. She had nowhither to run —but there she was at the end of a large trap. Their footsteps as they receded echoed and whispered up the stairway from below.

'For pity!' she pleaded. 'For pity! I will go miles away before it is morning.'

He had been wavering on his feet, torn backwards and forwards literally and visibly, between desire and fear, but at the sound of her voice he shook with rage.

'Curses on you that ever you came here,' he said. 'If you go free I shall lose my dandling thing.'

He made as if to catch her by the wrist; but changing his purpose, ran from the room, shouting:

'Ho la!... Throck...morton...That...is not...' His voice was lost in reverberations and echoes.

In the darkness she stood desolately still. She thought of how Romans would have awaited their captors: the ideal of a still and worthy surrender was part of her blood. Here was the end of her cord; she must fold her hands. She folded her hands. After all, she thought, what was death?

'It is to pass from the hardly known to the hardly unknown.' She quoted Lucretius. It was very dark all around her: the noises of distant outcries reached her dimly.

'*Vix ignotum*,' she repeated mechanically, and then the words: 'Surely it were better to pass from the world of unjust judges to sit with the mighty. . . .'

A great burst of sound roamed, vivid and alive, from the distant stairhead. She started and cried out. Then there came the sound of feet hastily stepping the stair treads, coming upwards. A man was coming to lay hands upon her!

Then, suddenly she was running, breathing hard, filled with the fear of a man's touch. At last, in front of her was a pale, leaded window; she turned to the right; she was in a long corridor; she ran; it seemed that she ran for miles. She was gasping, 'For pity! for pity!' to the saints of heaven. She stayed to listen; there was a silence, then a voice in the distance. She listened and listened. The feet began to run again, the sole of one shoe struck the ground hard, the other scarcely sounded. She could not tell whether they came towards her or no. Then she began to run again, for it was certain now that they came towards her. As if at the sound of her own feet the footfalls came faster. Desperately, she lifted one foot and tore her shoe off, then the other. She half overbalanced, and catching at the arras to save herself, it fell with a rustling sound. She craved for darkness; when she ran there was a pale shimmer of night—but the aperture of an arch tempted her. She ran and sprang, upwards, in a very black, narrow stairway.

At the top there was—light! and the passage ended in a window. A great way off, a pine torch was stuck in a wall, a knave in armour sat on the floor beneath it—the heavy breathing was coming up the stairway. She crept on tiptoe across the passage to the curtains beside the casement.

Then a man was within touch of her hand, panting hard, and he stood still as if he were out of breath. His voice called in gasps to the knave at the end of the gallery:

'Ho . . . There . . . Simon! . . . Peter! . . . Hath one passed that way?'

The voice came back:

'No one! The King comes!'

He moved a step down the corridor and, as he was lifting the arras a little way away, she moved to peep through a crack in the curtain.

It was Throckmorton! The distant light glinted along his beard. At the slight movement she made he was agog to listen, so that his ears appeared to be pricked up. He moved swiftly back to cover the stairhead. In the distance, beneath the light, the groom was laying cards upon the floor between his parted legs.

Throckmorton whispered suddenly:

'I can hear thee breathe. Art near! Listen!'

She leant back against the wall and trembled.

'This seems like a treachery,' he whispered. 'It is none. Listen? There is little time! Do you hear me?'

She kept her peace.

'Do you hear me?' he asked. 'Before God, I am true to you.'

When still she did not speak he hissed with vexation and raised one hand above his head. He sank his forehead in swift meditation.

'Listen,' he said again. 'To take you I have only to tear down this arras. Do you hear?'

He bared his head once more and said aloud to himself, 'But perhaps she is even in the chapel.'

He stepped across the corridor, lifted a latch and looked in at double doors that were just beside her. Then, swiftly, he moved back once more to cover the stairhead.

'God! God! God!' she heard him mutter between his teeth.

'Listen!' he said again. 'Listen! listen! listen!' The

words seemed to form part of an eager, hissed refrain. He was trembling with haste.

He began to press the arras, along the wall towards her, with his finger tips. Her breast sank with a sickening fall. Then, suddenly, he started back again; she could not understand why he did not come further—then she noticed that he was afraid, still, to leave the stairhead.

But why did he not call his men to him? He had a whole army at his back.

He was peering into the shadows—and something familiar in the poise of his head, his intent gaze, the line of his shoulders, as you may see a cat's outlined against a lighted doorway, filled her with an intense lust for revenge. This man had wormed himself into her presence: he was a traitor over and over again. And he had fooled her! He had made her believe that he was lover to her. He had made her believe, and he had fooled her. He had shown her letter to Privy Seal.

After the night in the cellar she had had the end of her crucifix sharpened till it was needle-pointed. She trembled with eagerness. This foul carrion beast had fooled her that he might get her more utterly in his power. For this he had brought her down. He would have her to himself—in some dungeon of Privy Seal's. Her fair hopes ended in this filth . . .

He was muttering:

'Listen if you be there! Before God, Katharine Howard, I am true to you. Listen! Listen!'

His hand shivered, turned against the light. He was hearkening to some distant sound. He was looking away.

She tore the arras aside and sprang at him with her hand on high. But, at the sharp sound of the tearing cloth, he started to one side and the needle point that should have pierced his face struck softly in at his shoulder or there-abouts. He gave a sharp hiss of pain. . . .

She was wrestling with him then. One of his hands was hot across her mouth, the other held her throat.

'Oh fool!' his voice sounded. 'Bide you still.' He snorted

with fury and held her to him. The embroidery on his chest scraped her knuckles as she tried to strike upwards at his face. Her crucifix had fallen. He strove to muffle her with his elbows, but with a blind rage of struggle she freed her wrists and, in the darkness, struck where she thought his mouth would be.

Then his hand over her mouth loosened and set free her great scream. It rang down the corridor and seemed to petrify his grasp upon her. His fingers loosened—and again she was running, bent forward, crying out, in a vast thirst for mere flight.

As she ran, a red patch before her eyes, distant and clear beneath the torch, took the form of the King. Her cries were still loud, but they died in her throat. . . .

He was standing still with his fingers in his ears.

'Dear God,' she cried, 'they have laid hands upon me. They have laid hands upon me.' And she pressed her fingers hard across her throat as if to wipe away the stain of Throckmorton's touch.

The King lifted his fingers from his ears.

'Bones of Jago,' he cried, 'what new whimsy is this?'

'They have laid hands upon me,' she cried and fell upon her knees.

'Why,' he said, 'here is a day nightmare. I know all your tale of a letter. Come now, pretty one. Up, pretty soul.' He bent over benevolently and stroked her hand.

'These dark passages are frightening to maids. Up now, pretty. I was thinking of thee.

'Who the devil shall harm thee?' he muttered again. 'This is mine own house. Come, pray with me. Prayer is a very soothing thing. I was bound to pray. I pray ever at nightfall. Up now. Come—pray, pray, pray!'

His heavy benevolence for a moment shed a calmness upon the place. She rose, and pressing back the hair from her forehead, saw the long, still corridor, the guard beneath the torch, the doors of the chapel.

She said to herself pitifully: 'What comes next?' She was too wearied to move again.

Suddenly the King said:

'Child, you did well to come to me, when you came in the stables.'

She leaned against the tapestry upon the wall to listen to him.

'It is true,' he admitted, 'that you have men that hate you and your house. The Bishop of Winchester did show me a letter you wrote. I do pardon it in you. It was well written.'

'Ah,' she uttered wearily, 'so you say now. But you shall change your mind ere morning.'

'Body of God, no,' he answered. 'My mind is made up concerning you. Let us call a truce to these things. It is my hour for prayer. Let us go to pray.'

Knowing how this King's mind would change from hour to hour, she had little hope in his words. Nevertheless slowly it came into her mind that if she were ever to act, now that he was in the mood was the very hour. But she knew nothing of the coil in which she now was. Yet without the King she could do nothing; she was in the hands of other men: of Throckmorton, of Privy Seal, of God knew whom.

'Sir,' she said, 'at the end of this passage stood a man.'

The King looked past her into the gloom.

'He stands there still,' he said. 'He is tying his arm with a kerchief. He looks like one Throckmorton.'

'Then, if he have not run,' she said. 'Call him here. He has had my knife in his arm. He holds a letter of mine.'

His neck stiffened suddenly.

'You have been writing amorous epistles?' he muttered.

'God knows there was naught of love,' she answered. 'Do you bid him unpouch it.' She closed her eyes; she was done with this matter.

Henry called:

'Ho, you, approach!' and as through the shadows Throckmorton's shoes clattered on the boards he held out a thickly gloved hand. Throckmorton made no motion to put anything into it, and the King needs must speak.

'This lady's letter,' he muttered.

Throckmorton bowed his head.

'Privy Seal holdeth it,' he answered.

'You are all of a make,' the King said gloomily. 'Can no woman write a letter but what you will be of it?'

'Sir,' Throckmorton said, 'this lady would have Privy Seal down.'

'Well, she shall have him down,' the King threatened him. 'And thee! and all of thy train!'

'I do lose much blood,' Throckmorton answered. 'Pray you let me finish the binding of my arm.'

He took between his teeth one end of his kerchief and the other in his right hand, and pulled and knotted with his head bent.

'Make haste!' the King grumbled. 'Here! Lend room.' And himself he took one end of the knot and pulled it tight, breathing heavily.

'Now speak,' he said. 'I am not one made for the healing of cripples.'

Throckmorton brushed the black blood from the furs on his sleeve, using his gloves.

'Sir,' he said, 'I am in pain and my knees tremble, because I have lost much blood. I were more minded to take to my pallet. Nevertheless, I am a man that do bear no grudge, being rather a very proper man, and one intent to do well to my country and its Lord.'

'Sir,' the King said, 'if you are minded to speak ill of this lady you had best had no mouth.'

Throckmorton fell upon one knee.

'Grant me the boon to be her advocate,' he said. 'And let me speak swiftly, for Privy Seal shall come soon and the Bishop of Winchester.'

'Ass that you are,' the King said, 'fetch me a stool from the chapel, that I may not stand all the day.'

Throckmorton ran swiftly to the folding doors.

'—Winchester comes,' he said hurriedly, when he returned.

The King sat himself gingerly down upon the

three-legged stool, balancing himself with his legs wide
apart. A dark face peered from the folding doors: a
priest's shape came out from them.

'Cousin of Winchester,' the King called, 'bide where
you be.'

He had the air of a man hardly intent on what the spy
could say. He had already made up his mind as to what he
himself was to say to Katharine.

'Sir,' Throckmorton said, 'this lady loves you well, and
most well she loveth your Highness' daughter. Most well,
therefore, doth she hate Privy Seal. I, as your Highness
knoweth, have for long well loved Privy Seal. Now I
love others better—the common weal and your great and
beneficent Highness. As I have told your Highness, this
Lady Katharine hath laboured very heartily to bring the
Lady Mary to love you. But that might not be. Now, your
Highness being minded to give to these your happy realms
a lasting peace, was intent that the Lady Mary should
write a letter, very urgently, to your Highness' foes urging
them to make a truce with this realm, so that your Highness might cast out certain evil men and then better purge
this realm of certain false doctrines.'

Amazement, that was almost a horror, made Katharine
open wide the two hands that hung at her side.

'You!' she cried to the King. '*You* would have that letter
written?'

He looked at her with a heavy astonishment.

'Wherefore not?' he asked.

'My God! my God!' she said. 'And I have suffered!'

Her first feeling of horror at this endless plot hardly
gave way to relief. She had been used as a tool; she had
done the work. But she had been betrayed.

'Aye, would I have the letter written,' the King said.
'What could better serve my turn? Would I not have mine
enemies stay their arming against me?'

'Then I have written your letter,' she said bitterly.
'That is why I should be gaoled.'

The King's look of heavy astonishment did not leave him.

'Why, sweetheart, shalt be made a countess,' he said. 'Y' have done more in this than I or any man could do with my daughter.'

'Wherefore, then, should this man have gaoled me?' Katharine asked.

The King turned his heavy gaze upon Throckmorton. The big man's eyes had a sunny and devious smile.

'Sir,' he said, 'this is a subtle conceit of mine, since I am a subtle man. If I am set a task I do it ever in mine own way. Here there was a task. . . .

'Pray you let me sit upon the floor!' he craved. 'My legs begin to fail.'

The King made a small motion with his hand, and the great man, letting himself down by one hand against the arras, leaned back his head and stretched his long legs half across the corridor.

'In ten minutes Privy Seal shall be here with the letter,' he said. 'My head swims, but I will be brief.'

He closed his eyes and passed his hand across his fore-head.

'I do a task ever in mine own way,' he began again. 'Here am I. Here is Privy Seal. Your Highness is minded to know what passes in the mind of Privy Seal. Well: I am Privy Seal's servant. Now, if I am to come at the mind of Privy Seal, I must serve him well. In this thing I might seem to serve him main well. Listen . . .'

He cleared his throat and then spoke again.

'Your Highness would have this letter written by the Lady Mary. That, with the help of this fair dame, was a thing passing easy. But neither your Highness nor Privy Seal knew the channel through which these letters passed. Yet I discovered it. Now, think I to myself: here is a secret for which Privy Seal would give his head. Therefore, how better may I ingratiate myself with Privy Seal than by telling him this same fine secret?'

'Oh, devil!' Katharine Howard called out. 'Who was Judas to thee?'

Throckmorton raised his head, and winked upwards at her.

'It was a fine device?' he asked. 'Why, I am a subtle man. . . . Do you not see?' he said. 'The King's Highness would have me keep the confidence of Privy Seal that I may learn out his secrets. How better should I keep that confidence than by seeming to betray your secret to Privy Seal?

'It was very certain,' he added, 'that Privy Seal should give a warrant to gaol your la'ship. But it was still more certain that the King's Highness should pardon you. Therefore no bones should have been broken. And I did come myself to take you to a safe place, and to enlighten you as to the comedy.'

'Oh, Judas, Judas,' she cried.

'Could you but have trusted me,' he said reproachfully, 'you had spared yourself a mad canter and me a maimed arm.'

'Why, you have done well,' the King said heavily. 'But you speak this lady too saucily.'

He was in a high and ponderous good humour, but he stayed to reflect for a moment, with his head on one side, to see what he had gained.

'This letter is written,' he said. 'But Cromwell holdeth it. How, then, has it profited me?'

'Why,' Throckmorton said, 'Privy Seal shall come to bring the letter to your Highness; your Highness shall deliver it to me; I to the cook; the cook to the ambassador; the ambassador to the kings. And so the kings shall be prayed, by your daughter, whom they heed, to stay all unfriendly hands against your Highness.'

'You are a shrewd fellow,' the King said.

'I have a shrewd ache in the head,' the spy answered. 'If you would give me a boon, let me begone.'

The King got stiffly up from his stool, and, bracing his

feet firmly, gave the spy one hand. The tall man shook upon his legs.

'Why, I have done well!' he said, smiling. 'Now Privy Seal shall take me for his very bedfellow, until it shall please your Highness to deal with him for good and all.'

He went, waveringly, along the corridor, brushing the hangings with his shoulder.

Katharine stood out before the King.

'Now I will get me gone,' she said. 'This is no place for me.'

He surveyed her amiably, resting his hands on his red-clothed thighs as he sat his legs akimbo on his stool.

'Why, it is main cold here,' he said. 'But bide a short space.'

'I am not made for courts,' she answered.

'We will go pray anon,' he quieted her, with his hand stretched out. 'Give me a space for meditation, I am not yet in the mood for prayer.'

She pleaded, 'Let me begone.'

'Body of God,' he said good-humouredly. 'It is fitting that at this time that you do pray. You have escaped a great peril. But I am wont to drive away earthly passions ere I come before the Throne of grace.'

'Sir,' she pleaded more urgently, 'the night draws near. Before morning I would be upon my road to Calais.'

He looked at her interestedly, and questioned in a peremptory voice:

'Upon what errand? I have heard of no journeying of yours.'

'I am not made for courts,' she repeated.

He said: 'Anan?' with a sudden, half-comprehending anger, and she quailed.

'I will get me gone to Calais,' she uttered. 'And then to a nunnery. I am not for this world.'

He uttered a tremendous: 'Body of God,' and repeated it four times.

He sprang to his feet and she shrank against the wall. His eyes rolled in his great head, and suddenly he shouted:

'Ungrateful child. Ungrateful!' Then he lost words; his swollen brow moved up and down. She was afraid to speak again.

Then, suddenly, with a light and brushing step, the Lord Privy Seal was coming towards them. His sagacious eyes looked from one to the other, his lips moved with their sideways motion.

'Fiend,' the King uttered. 'Give me the letter and get thee out of earshot.' And whilst Cromwell was bending before his person, he continued: 'I have pardoned this lady. I would have you both clasp hands.'

Cromwell's mouth fell open for a minute.

'Your Highness knoweth the contents?' he asked. And by then he appeared as calm as when he asked a question about the price of chalk at Calais.

'My Highness knoweth!' Henry said friendlily. He crumpled the letter in his hand, and then, remembering its use, moved to put it in his own pouch. 'This lady has done very well to speak to me who am the fountain-head of power.'

'Get thee out of earshot,' he repeated. 'I have things as to which I would admonish this lady.'

'Your Highness knoweth . . .' Privy Seal began again, then his eye fell upon Winchester, who still stayed by the chapel door at the far end of the corridor. He threw up his hands.

'Sir,' he said. 'Traitors have come to you!'

Gardiner, indeed, was gliding towards them, drawn, in spite of all prudence, by his invincible hatred.

The King watched the pair of them with his crafty eyes, deep seated in his head.

'It is certain that no traitors have come to me,' he uttered gently; and to Cromwell: 'You have a nose for them.'

He appeared placable and was very quiet.

Winchester, his black eyes glaring with desire, was almost upon them in the shadows.

'Here is enough of wrangling,' Henry said. He appeared to meditate, and then uttered: 'As well here as elsewhere.'

'Sir,' Gardiner said, 'if Privy Seal misleads me, I have somewhat to say of Privy Seal.'

'Cousin of Winchester,' Henry answered. 'Stretch out your hand, I would have you end your tulzies in this place.'

Winchester, bringing out his words with a snake's coldness, seemed to whisper:

'Your Highness did promise that Privy Seal should make me amends.'

'Why, Privy Seal shall make amends,' the King answered. 'It was his man that did miscall thee. Therefore, Privy Seal shall come to dine with thee, and shall, in the presence of all men, hold out to thee his hand.'

'Let him come, then, with great state,' the bishop stuck to his note.

'Aye, with a great state,' the King answered. 'I will have an end to these quarrels.'

He set his hand cordially upon Privy Seal's shoulder.

'For thee,' he said, 'I would have thee think between now and the assembling of the Parliaments of what title thou wilt have to an earldom.'

Cromwell fell upon one knee, and, in Latin, made three words of a speech of thanks.

'Why, good man,' the King said, 'art a man very valuable to me.' His eyes rested upon Katharine for a moment. 'I am well watched for by one and the other of you,' he went on. 'Each of you by now has brought me a letter of this lady's.'

Katharine cried out at Gardiner:

'You too!'

His eyes sought the ground, and then looked defiantly into hers.

'You did threaten me!' he said doggedly. 'I was minded to be betimes.'

'Why, end it all, now and here,' the King said. 'Here is a folly with a silly wench in it.'

'Here was a treason that I would show your Highness,' the Bishop said doggedly.

'Sirs,' the King said. He touched his bonnet: 'God in His great mercy has seen fit much to trouble me. But here are troubles that I may end.   Now I have ended them all. If this lady would not have her cousin to murder a cardinal, God, she would not. There are a plenty others to do that work.'

He pressed one hand on Cromwell's chest and pushed him backwards gently.

'Get thee gone, now,' he said, 'out of earshot. I shall speak with thee soon.—And you!' he added to Winchester.

'Body of God, Body of God,' he muttered beneath his breath, as they went, 'very soon now I can rid me of these knaves,' and then, suddenly, he blared upon Katharine:

'Thou seest how I am plagued and would'st leave me. Before the Most High God, I swear thou shalt not.'

She fell upon her knees.

'With each that speaks, I find a new traitor to me,' she said. 'Let me begone.'

He threatened her with one hand.

'Wench,' he said, 'I have had better converse with thee than with man or child this several years. Thinkest thou I will let thee go?'

She began to sob:

'What rest may I have? What rest?'

He mocked her:

'What rest may I have? What rest? My nights are full of evil dreams! God help me. Have I offered thee foul usage? Have I pursued thee with amorous suits?'

She said pitifully:

'You had better have done that than set me amongst these plotters.'

'I have never seen a woman so goodly to look upon as thou art,' he answered.

She covered her face with her hands, but he pulled them apart and gazed at it.

'Child,' he said, 'I will cherish thee as I would a young

lamb. Shalt have Cromwell's head; shalt have Winchester in what gaol thou wilt when I have used them.'

She put her fingers in her ears.

'For pity,' she whispered. 'Let me begone.'

'Why,' he reasoned with her, 'I cannot let thee have Cromwell down before he has called this Parliament. There is no man like him for calling of truckling Parliaments. And, rest assured,' he uttered solemnly, 'that that man dies that comes between thee and me from this day on.'

'Let me begone,' she said wearily. 'Let me begone. I am afraid to look upon these happenings.'

'Look then upon nothing,' he answered. 'Stay you by my daughter's side. Even yet you shall win for me her obedience. If you shall earn the love of the dear saints, I will much honour you and set you on high before all the land.'

She said:

'For pity, for pity. Here is a too great danger for my soul.'

'Never, never,' he answered. 'You shall live closed in. No man shall speak with you but only I. You shall be as you were in a cloister. An you will, you shall have great wealth. Your house shall be advanced; your father close his eyes in honour and estate. None shall walk before you in the land.'

She said: 'No. No.'

'See you,' he said. 'This world goes very wearily with me. I am upon a make of husbandry that bringeth little joy. I have no rest, no music, no corner to hide in save in thy converse and the regard of thy countenance.'

He paused to search her face with his narrow eyes.

'God knows that the Queen there is is no wife of mine,' he said slowly. 'If thou wilt wait till the accomplished time. . . .'

She said:

'No, no!' and her voice had an urgent sharpness.

She stretched out both her hands, being still upon her knees. Her fair face worked convulsively, her lips moved, and her hood, falling away from her brows, showed her hair that had golden glints.

'For pity let me go,' she moaned. 'For pity.'

He answered:

'When I renounce my kingdom and my life!'

From opposite ends of the gallery Winchester and Cromwell watched them with intent and winking eyes.

'Let us go pray,' the King said. 'For now I am in the mood.'

She got upon her legs wearily, and, for a moment, took his hand to steady herself.

PRIVY SEAL

His Last Venture

"Ille potens . . . et lætus cui licet in diem
Dixisse : Vixi ! . . ."

To
Frau Laura Schmedding

who has so often combated
my prejudices and corrected
my assertions
this with affection

PART ONE

THE RISING SUN

I

THE Magister Udal sat in the room of his inn in Paris, where customarily the King of France lodged such envoys as came at his expense. He had been sent there to Latinise the letters that passed between Sir Thomas Wyatt and the King's Ministers of France, for he was esteemed the most learned man in these islands. He had groaned much at being sent there, for he must leave in England so many loves—the great, blonde Margot Poins, that was maid to Katharine Howard; the tall, swaying Katharine Howard herself; Judge Cantre's wife that had fed him well; and two other women, with all of whom he had succeeded easily or succeeded in no wise at all. But the mission was so well paid—with as many crowns the day as he had had groats for teaching the Lady Mary of England—that fain he had been to go. Moreover, it was by way of being a favour of Privy Seal's. The magister had written for him a play in English; the rich post was the reward—and it was an ill thing, a thing the magister dreaded, to refuse the favours of Privy Seal. He consoled himself with the thought that the writing of letters in Latin might wash from his mouth the savour of the play he had written in the vulgar tongue.

But his work in Paris was ended—for with the flight of Cardinal Pole, who had left Paris precipitately upon news that the King of England had sent a drunken roisterer to assassinate him, it was imagined that soon now more concord between Francis and England might ensue, and the magister sat in his room planning his voyage back to Dover.

The room was great in size, panelled mostly in wood, lit with lampwicks that floated in oil dishes and heated with a sea-coal fire, for though it was April the magister was of a cold disposition of the hands and shins. The inn—of the Golden Astrolabe—was kept by an Englishwoman, a masterful widow with a broad face and a great mouth that smiled. She stood beside him there. Forty-seven she might have been, and she called herself the Widow Annot.

The magister sat over his fire with his gown parted from his legs to warm his shins, but his hands waved angrily and his face was crestfallen.

'Oh, keeper of a tavern,' he said. 'It is set down in holy writ that it is not good for a man to be alone.'

'That a hostess shall keep her tavern clean is writ in the books of the provost of Paris town,' the Widow Annot answered, and the shadow of her great white hood, which she wore in the older English fashion, danced over the brown wooden beams of the ceiling.

'Nay, nay,' he answered, 'it is written there that it is the enjoined devoir of every hotelier to provide things fitting for the sojourners' ease, pleasure and recreation.'

'The maid is locked in another house,' the hostess answered, 'and should have been this three week.' She swung her keys on a black riband and gazed at him masterfully. 'Will your magistership eat capon or young goat?'

'Capon will have a savour like sawdust, and young goat like the dust of the road,' the magister moaned. 'Give me the girl to wait upon me again.'

'No maid will wait upon thee,' she answered.

'Even thou thyself?' he asked. He glanced across his shoulder and his eyes measured her, hers him. She had large shoulders, a high, full stomacher, and her cheeks were an apple-red. 'The maiden was a fair piece,' he tittered.

'Therefore you must spoil the ring of the coin,' she answered.

He sighed: 'Then eat you with me. "*Soli cantare periti Arcades*." But it is cold here alone of nights.'

They ate goat and green leeks sweetened with honey,

and wood thrushes pickled in wine, and salt fish from the mouth of the Beauce. And because this gave the magister a great thirst he drank much of a warmed wine from Burgundy that the hostess brought herself. They sat, byside, on cushions on a couch before the warm fire.

'*Filia pulchra mater pulchrior!*' the magister muttered, and he cast his arms about her soft and plump waist. 'The maid was a fair skewer, the hostess is a plumper roasting bit.' She took his kisses on her fire-warmed cheeks, but in the end she thrust him mightily from her with a large elbow.

He gasped with the strength of her thrust, and she said:

'Greedy dogs getten them hard cuffs,' and rearranged her neckercher. When he tried to come nearer her she laughed and thrust him aback.

'You have tried and tasted,' she said. 'A fuller meal you must pay for.'

He stood before her, lean and lank, his gown flapping about his calves, his eyes smiling humorously, his lips twitching.

'Oh soft and warm woman,' he cried, 'payment shall be yours'; and whilst he fumbled furiously in his clothes-press, he quoted from Tully: '*Haec civitas mulieri re-dimiculum praebuit.*' He pulled out one small bag: '*Haec in collum.*' She took another. '*Haec in crines!*' and he added a third, saying: 'Here is all I have,' and cast the three into her lap. Whilst she counted the coins composedly on the table before her he added: 'Leave me nevertheless the price to come to England with.'

'Sir Magister,' she said, turning her large face to him. 'This is nòt one-tenth enough. You have tasted an en-sample. Will you have the whole meal?'

'Oh, unconscionable,' he cried. 'More I have not!' He began to wave his hands. 'Consider what you do do,' he uttered. 'Think of what a pest is love. How many have died of it. Pyramus, Thisbe, Dido, Medea, Croesus, Callirhoe, Theagines the philosopher ... Consider what writes Gordonius: "*Prognosticatio est talis: si non*

succuratur iis aut in maniam cadunt: aut moriuntur."
Unless lovers be succoured either they fall into a madness,
either they die or grow mad. And Fabian Montaltus: "If
this passion be not assuaged, the inflammation cometh to
the brain. It drieth up the blood. Then followeth madness
or men make themselves away." I would have you ponder
of what saith Parthenium and what Plutarch in his tales of
lovers.'

Her face appeared comely and smooth in his eyes, but
she shook her head at him.

'These be woeful and pretty stories,' she said. 'I would
have you to tell me many of them.'

'All through the night,' he said eagerly, and made to
clasp her in his arms. But she pushed him back again with
her hand on his chest.

'All through the night an you will,' she said. 'But first
you shall tell a prettier tale before a man in a frock.'

He sprang full four feet back at one spring.

'I have wedded no woman, yet,' he said.

'Then it is time you wed one now,' she answered.

'Oh widow, bethink you,' he pleaded. 'Would you spoil
so pretty a tale? Would you humble so goodly a man's
pride?'

'Why, it were a pity,' she said. 'But I am minded to take
a husband.'

'You have done well this ten years without one,' he cried
out.

Her face seemed to set like adamant as she turned her
cheek to him.

'Call it a woman's mad freak,' she said.

'Six and twenty pupils in the fair game of love I have
had,' he said. 'You shall be the seven and twentieth.
Twenty and seven are seven and two. Seven and two are
nine. Now nine is the luckiest of numbers. Be you that
one.'

'Nay,' she answered. 'It is time you learned husbandry
who have taught so many and earned so little.'

He slipped himself softly into the cushions beside her.

'Would you spoil so fair a tale?' he said. 'Would you have me to break so many vows? I have promised a mort of women marriage, and so long as I be not wed I may keep faith with any one of them.'

She held her face away from him and laughed.

'That is as it may be,' she said. 'But when you wed with me to-night you will keep faith with one woman.'

'Woman,' he pleaded. 'I am a great scholar.'

'Ay,' she answered, 'and great scholars have climbed to great estates.'

She continued to count the coins that came from his little money-bags; the shadow of her hood upon the great beams grew more portentous.

'It is thought that your magistership may rise to be Chancellor of the Realm of England,' she added.

He clutched his forehead.

'Eheu!' he said. 'If you have heard men say that, you know that wedded to thee I could never climb.'

'Then I shall very comfortably keep my inn here in Paris town,' she answered. 'You have here fourteen pounds and eleven shillings.'

He stretched forth his lean hands:

'Why, I will marry thee in the morning,' he said, and he moistened his lips with the tip of his tongue. Outside the door there was a shuffling of several feet.

'I knew not other guests were in the house,' he uttered, and fell again to kissing her.

'Knew you not an envoy was come from Cleves?' she whispered.

Her head fell back and he supported it with one trembling hand. He shook like a leaf when her voice rang out:

'*Au secours! Au secours!*'

There was a great jangle, light fell into the dusky room through the doorhole, and he found himself beneath the eyes of many scullions with spits, cooks with carving forks, and kitchenmaids with sharpened distaffs of steel.

'Now I will be wed this night,' she laughed.

He moved to the end of the couch and blinked at her in the strong light.

'I will be wed this night,' she said again, and rearranged her head-dress, revealing, as her sleeves fell open, her white, plump arms.

'Why, no!' he answered irresolutely.

She said in French to her aids:

'Come near him with the spits!'

They moved towards him, a white-clad body with their pointed things glittering in the light of torches. He sprang behind the great table against the window and seized the heavy-leaden sandarach. The French scullions knew, tho' he had no French, that he would cleave one of their skulls, and they stood, a knot of seven—four men and three maids —in blue hoods, in the centre of the room.

'By Mars and by Apollo!' he said, 'I was minded to wed with thee if I could no other way. But now, like Phaeton, I will cast myself from the window and die, or like the wretches thrown from the rock, called Tarpeian. I was minded to a folly: now I am minded rather for death.'

'How nobly thy tongue doth wag, husband,' she said, and cried in French for the rogues to be gone. When the door closed upon the lights she said in the comfortable gloom: 'I dote upon thy words. My first was tongue-tied.' She beckoned him to her and folded her arms. 'Let us discourse upon this matter,' she said comfortably. 'Thus I will put it: you wed with me or spring from the window.'

'I am even trapped?' he asked.

'So it comes to all foxes that too long seek for capons,' she answered.

'But consider,' he said. He sat himself by the fireside upon a stool, being minded to avoid temptation.

'I would have your magistership forget the rogues that be without,' she said.

'They were a nightmare's tale,' he said.

'Yet forget them not too utterly,' she answered. 'For I am of some birth. My father had seven horses and never followed the plough.'

'Oh buxom one!' he answered. 'Of a comfortable birth
and girth thou art. Yet with thee around my neck I might
not easily climb.'

'Magister,' she said, 'whilst thou climbest in London
town thy wife will bide in Paris.'

'Consider!' he said. 'There is in London town a fair,
large maid called Margot Poins.'

'Is she more fair than I?' she asked. 'I will swear she is.'
He tilted his stool forward.

'No; no, I swear it,' he said eagerly.

'Then I will swear she is more large.'

'No; not one half so bounteous is her form,' he answered,
and moved across to the couch.

'Then if you can bear her weight up you can bear mine,'
she said, and moved away from him.

'Nay,' he answered. 'She would help me on,' and he
fumbled in the shadows for her hand. She drew herself
together into a small space.

'You affect her more than me,' she said, with a swift
motion simulating jealousy.

'By the breasts of Venus, no!' he answered.

'Oh, once more use such words,' she murmured, and
surrendered to him her soft hand. He rubbed it between
both of his cold ones and uttered:

'By the Paphian Queen: by her teams of doves and
sparrows! By the bower of Phyllis and the girdle of
Egypt's self! I love thee!'

She gurgled 'oh's' of pleasure.

'But this Margot Poins is tirewoman to the Lady
Katharine Howard.'

'I am tirewoman to mine own self alone,' she said.
'Therefore you love her better.'

'Nay, oh nay,' he said gently. 'But this Lady Katharine
Howard is mistress to the King's self.'

'And I have been mistress to no married man save my
husbands,' she answered. 'Therefore you love this Margot
Poins better.'

He fingered her soft palm and rubbed it across his own neck.

'Nay, nay,' he said. 'But I must wed with Margot Poins.'

'Why with her more than with me or any other of your score and seven?' she said softly.

'Since the Lady Katharine will be Queen,' he answered, and once again he was close against her side. She sighed softly.

'Thus if you wed with me you will never be Chancellor,' she said.

'I would not anger the Queen,' he answered. She nestled bountifully and warmly against him.

'Swear even again that you like me more than the fair, large wench in London town,' she whispered against his ear.

'Even as Jove prized Danaë above the Queen of Heaven, even as Narcissus prized his shadow above all the nymphs, even as Hercules placed Omphale above his strength, or even as David the King of the Jews Bathsheba above . . .'

She murmured 'Oh, oh,' and placed her arms around his shoulders.

'How I love thy brave words!'

'And being Chancellor,' he swore, 'I will come back to thee, oh woman of the sweet smiles, honey of Hymettus, Cypriote wine . . .'

She moved herself a little from him in the darkness.

'And if you do not wed with Margot Poins . . .'

'I pray a plague may fall upon her, but I must wed with her,' he answered. 'Come now; come now!'

'Else the Lady Katharine shall be displeased with your magistership?'

He sought to draw her to him, but she stiffened herself a little.

'And this Lady Katharine is mistress to the King of England's realm?'

His hands moved tremblingly towards her in the darkness.

'And this Lady Katharine shall be Queen?'

A hiss of exasperation came upon his lips, for she had slipped from beneath his hands into the darkness.

'Why, then, I will not stay your climbing,' she said. 'Good-night,' and in the darkness he heard her sob.

The couch fell backwards as he swore and sprang towards her voice.

'Magister!' she said. 'Hands off! Unwed thou shalt not have me, for I have sworn it.'

'I have sworn to wed seven and twenty women,' he said, 'and have wedded with none.'

'Nay, nay,' she sobbed. 'Hands off. Henceforth I will make no vows—but no one but thee shall wed me.'

'Then wed me, in God's name!' he cried, and, screaming:

'*Ho là! Apportez le prestre!*' she softened herself in his arms.

The magister confronted the lights, the leering scullions and the grinning maids with their great mantles; his brown, woodpecker-like face was alike crestfallen and thirsty with desire. A lean Dominican, with his brown cowl back and spectacles of horn, gabbled over his missal and took a crown's fee—then asked another by way of penitence for the sin with the maid locked up in another house. When they brought the bride favours of pink to pin into her gorget she said:

'I long had loved thee for thy great words, husband. Therefore all these I had in readiness.'

With that knot fast upon him, the magister, clasping his gown upon his shins, looked askance at the floor. Whilst they made ready the bride, with great lights and laughter, she said:

'I was minded to have a comfortable husband. And a comfortable husband is a husband much absent. What more comfortable than me in Paris town and thee in London city? I keep my inn here, thou mindest thy book there. Thou shalt here find a goodly capon upon occasion, and when thou hast a better house in London I will come share it.'

'Trapped! Trapped!' the magister muttered to himself. 'Even as was Sir Launcelot!'

He considered of the fair and resentful Margot Poins whom it was incumbent indeed that he should wed: that Katharine Howard loved her well and was in these matters strait-laced. When his eyes measured his wife he licked his lips; when his eyes were on the floor his jaw fell. At best the new Mistress Udal would be in Paris. He looked at the rope tied round the thin middle of the brown priest, and suddenly he leered and cast off his cloak.

'Let me remember to keep an equal mind in these hard matters,' he quoted, and fell to laughing.

For he remembered that in England no marriage by a friar or monk held good in those years. Therefore he was the winner. And the long, square room, with the cave bed behind its shutter in the hollow of the wall, the light-coloured, square beams, and the foaming basin of bride-ale that a fat-armed girl in a blue kerseymere gown served out to scullion after scullion; the open windows from which a little knave was casting bride-pennies to some screaming beggars and women in the street; the blind hornman whose unseeing eyes glanced along the reed of his bassoon that he played before the open door; the two saucy maids striving to wrest the bride's stockings one from the other—all these things appeared friendly and jovial in his eyes. So that, when one of the maids, wresting the stocking, fell hard against him, he clasped her in his arms and kissed her till she struggled from him to drink a mug of bride-ale.

'*Hodie mihi: mihi atque cras!*' he said. For it was in his mind a goodly thing to pay a usuress with base coins.

II

It was three days later, in the morning, that his captress said to the Magister Udal:

'Husband, it is time that I gave thee the bridal gift.'

The magister, happy with a bellyful of carp, bread and breakfast ale, muttered 'Anan?' from above his copy of Lucretius. He sat in the window-seat of the great stone kitchen. Upon one long iron spit before the fire fourteen trussed capons turned in unison; the wooden shoes of the basting-maid clattered industriously; and from the chimney came the clank of the invisible smoke-vanes and the be-sooted chains. The magister, who loved above all things warmth, a full stomach, a comfortable woman and a good book, had all these things; he was well minded to stay in Paris town for fourteen days, when they were to slay a brown pig from the Ardennes, against whose death he had written an elegy in Sapphics.

'For,' said his better half, standing before him with a great loaf clasped to her bosom, 'if you turn a horse from the stable between full and half full, like as not he will return of fair will to the crib.'

'Oh Venus and Hebe in one body,' the magister said, 'I am minded to end here my scholarly days.'

'I am minded that ye shall travel far erstwhile,' she answered.

He laid down his book upon a clean chopping-board.

'I know a good harbourage,' he said.

She sat down beside him in the window and fingered the fur on his long gown, saying that, in this light, it showed ill-favouredly worm-eaten; and he answered that he never had wishes nor money for gowning himself, who cultivated the muses upon short commons. She turned rightway to the front the medal upon his chest, and folded her arms.

'Whilst ye have no better house to harbour us,' she said, 'this shall serve. Let us talk of the to-come.'

He groaned a little.

'Let us love to-day that's here,' he said. 'I will read thee a verse from Lucretius, and you shall tell me the history of that fourth capon'—he pointed to a browned carcase that, upon the spit, whirled its elbows a full third longer than any of the line.

'That is the master roasting-piece,' she said, 'so he browns there not too far, nor too close, for the envoy's own eating.'

He considered the chicken with his head to one side.

'It is the place of a wife to be subject to her lord,' he said.

'It is the place of a husband that he fendeth for 's wife,' she answered him. She tapped her fingers determinedly upon her elbows.

'So it is,' she continued. 'To-morrow you shall set out for London city to make road towards becoming Sir Chancellor.' Whilst he groaned she laid down for him her law. He was to go to England, he was to strive for great posts: if he gained, she would come share them; if he failed, he might at odd moments come back to her fireside. 'Have done with groaning now,' she said, stilling his lamentations. 'Keep them even for the next wench that you shall sue to—of me you have had all you asked.'

He considered for five seconds, his elbow upon his crossed knees and his wrist supporting his lean brown face.

'It is in the essence of it a good bargain,' he said. 'You put against the chance of being, you a chancellor's madam, mine of having for certain a capon in Paris town.'

He tapped his long nose. 'Nevertheless, for your stake you have cast down a very little: three nights of bed and board against the chaining me up.'

'Husband,' she answered. 'More than that you shall have.'

He wriggled a little beneath his furs.

'Husband is an ill name,' he commented. 'It smarts.'

'But it fills the belly.'

'Aye,' he said. 'Therefore I am minded to bide here and take with the sourness the sweet of it.'

She laughed a little, and, with a great knife, cut a large manchet from the loaf between them.

'Nay,' she said, 'to-morrow my army with their spits and forks shall drive thee from the door.'

He grinned with his lips. She was fair and fat beneath

her hood, but she was resolute. 'I have it in me greatly to advance you,' she said.

A boy brought her a trencher filled with chopped things, and a man in a blue jerkin came to her side bearing a middling pig, seared to a pale clear pinkness. The boy held the slit stomach carefully apart, and she lined it with slices of bread, dropping into the hollow chives, nutmegs, lumps of salt, the buds of bergamot, and marigold seeds with their acrid perfume, and balls of honied suet. She bound round it a fair linen cloth that she stitched with a great bone needle.

'Oh ingenuous countenance,' the magister mused above the pig's mild face. 'Is it not even the spit of the Cleves envoy's? And the Cleves envoy shall eat this adorable monster. Oh, cruel anthropophagist!'

She resigned her burden to the spit and gave the loaf to the boy, wiped her fingers upon her apron, and said:

'That pig shall help thee far upon thy road.'

'Goes it into my wallet?' he asked joyfully.

She answered: 'Nay; into the Cleves envoy's weam.'

'You speak in hard riddles,' he uttered.

'Nay,' she laughed, 'a baby could unriddle it.' She looked at him for a moment to enjoy her triumph of mystery. 'Husband mine, a pig thus stuffed is good eating for Cleves men. I have not kept a hostel for twelve years for envoys and secretaries without learning what each eats with pleasure. And long have I thought that if I wed a man it should be such a man as could thrive by learning of envoys' secrets.'

He leaned towards her earnestly.

'You know wherefore the man from Cleves is come?'

'You are, even as I have heard it said, a spy of Thomas Cromwell?' she asked in return.

He looked suddenly abashed, but she held to her question.

'I pass for Privy Seal's man,' he answered at last.

'But you have played him false,' she said. He grew pale, glanced over his shoulder, and put his finger on his lips.

'I'll wager it was for a woman,' she accused him. She wiped her lips with her apron and dropped her hands upon her lap.

'Why, keep troth to Cromwell if you can,' she said.

'I do think his sun sets,' he whispered.

'Why, I am sorry for it,' she answered. 'I have always loved him for a brewer's son. My father was a brewer.'

'Cromwell was begotten even by the devil,' Udal answered. 'He made me write a comedy in the vulgar tongue.'

'Be it as you will,' she answered. 'You shall know on which side to bite your cake better than I.'

He was still a little shaken at the thought of Privy Seal.

'If you know wherefore cometh Cleves' envoy, much it shall help me to share the knowledge,' he said at last, 'for by that I may know whether Cromwell or we do rise or fall.'

'If you have made a pact with a woman, have very great cares,' she answered dispassionately. 'Doubtless you know how the dog wags its tail; but you are always a fool with a woman.'

'This woman shall be Queen if Cromwell fall,' the magister said, 'and I shall rise with her.'

'But is no woman from Cleves' Queen there now?' she asked.

'Cicely,' he answered highly, 'you know much of capons and beeves, but there are queens that are none and do not queen it, and queans that are no queens and queen it.'

'And so 'twill be whilst men are men,' she retorted. 'But neither my first nor my second had his doxies ruling within my house, do what they might beyond the door.'

He tried to impart to her some of the adoration he had for Katharine Howard—her learning, her faith, her tallness, her wit, and the deserved empiry that she had over King Henry VIII; but she only answered:

'Why, kiss the wench all you will, but do not come to tell me how she smells!'—and to his new protests: 'Aye, you may well be right and she may well be Queen—for I

know you will sacrifice your ease for no wench that shall
not help you somewhere forwards.'

The magister held his hands above his head in shocked
negation of this injustice—but there came from the street
the thin wail of a trumpet; another joined it, and a third;
the three sounds executed a triple convolution and died
away one by one. Holding his thin hand out for silence and
better hearing, he muttered:

'Norfolk's tucket! Then it is true that Norfolk comes to
Paris.'

His wife slipped down from her seat.

'Gave I you not the ostler's gossip from Calais three
days since?' she said, and went towards her roastings.

'But wherefore comes the yellow dog to Paris?' Udal
persisted.

'That you may go seek,' she answered. 'But believe
always what an innkeeper says of who are on the road.'

Udal too slipped down from the window-seat; he buttoned his gown down to his shins, pulled his hat over his
ears and hurried through the galleried courtyard into the
comfortless shadows of the street. There was no doubt that
Norfolk was coming; round the tiny crack that, two houses
away, served for all the space that the road had between
the towering housefronts, two men in scarlet and yellow,
with leopards and lions and fleurs-de-lis on their chests,
walked between two in white, tabarded with the great lilies
of France. They crushed round the corner, for there was
scarce space for four men abreast; behind them squeezed
men in purple with the Howard knot, bearing pikes, and
men in mustard yellow with the eagle's wing and ship
badge of the Provost of Paris. In the broader space before the arch of Udal's courtyard they stayed to wait for
the horsemen to disentangle themselves from the alley;
the Englishmen looked glumly at the tall housefronts; the
French loosened the mouthplates of their helmets to
breathe the air for a minute. Hostlers, packmen and
pedlars began to fill the space behind Udal, and he heard

his wife's voice calling shrilly to a cook who had run across the yard.

The crowd a little shielded him from the draught which came through the arch, and he waited with more contentment. Undoubtedly there was Norfolk upon a great yellow horse, so high that it made his bonnet almost touch the overhanging storey of the third house; behind him the white and gold litter of the provost, who, having three weeks before broken his leg at tennis-play, was still unable to sit in a saddle. The duke rode as if implacably rigid, his yellow, long face set, listening as if with a sour deafness to something that the provost from below called to him with a great, laughing voice.

The provost's litter, too, came up alongside the duke's horse in the open space, then they all moved forward at the slow processional: three steps and a halt for the trumpets to blow a tucket; three more and another tucket; the great yellow horse stepping high and casting up his head, from which flew many flakes of white foam. With its slow, regularly interrupted gait, dominated by the impassive yellow face of Norfolk, the whole band had an air of performing a solemn dance, and Udal shivered for a long time, till amidst the train of mules bearing leathern sacks, cupboards, chests and commodes, he saw come riding a familiar figure in a scholar's gown—the young pedagogue and companion of the Earl of Surrey. He was a fair, bearded youth with blue eyes, riding a restless colt that embroiled itself and plunged amongst the mules' legs. The young man leaned forward in the saddle and craned to avoid a clothes chest.

The magister called to him:

'Ho, Longstaffe!' and having caught his pleased eyes: *'Ecce quis sto in arce plenitatis. Veni atque bibe! Magister sum. Udal sum. Longstaffe ave.'*

Longstaffe slipped from his horse, which he left to be rescued by whom it might from amongst the hard-angled cases.

'Assuredly,' he said, 'there is no love between that beast

and me as there was betwixt his lord and Bucephalus,' and
he followed Udal into the galleried courtyard, where their
two gowned figures alone sought shelter from the March
showers.

'News from overseas there is none,' he said. 'Privy Seal
ruleth still about the King; the German astronomers have
put forth a tract *De Quadratura Circuli*; the lost continent
of Atlantis is a lost continent still—and my bones ache.'

'But your mission?' Udal asked.

The doctor, his hard blue eyes spinning with sardonic
humour beneath his black beretta, said that his mission,
even as Udal's had been, was to gain some crowns by
setting into the learned language letters that should pass
between his ambassador and the King's men of France.
Udal grinned disconcertedly.

'Be certified in your mind,' he said, 'that I am not here
a spy or informer of Privy Seal's.'

'Forbid it, God,' Doctor Longstaffe answered good-
humouredly. None the less his jaw hardened beneath his
fair beard and he answered, 'I have as yet written no
letters—*litteras nullas scripsi: argal nihil scio.*'

'Why, ye shall drink a warmed draught and eat a
drippinged soppet,' Udal said, 'and you shall tell me what
in England is said of this mission.'

He led the fair doctor into the great kitchen, and felt a
great stab of dislike when the young man set his arm round
the hostess's waist and kissed her on the red cheeks. The
young man laughed:

'Aye indeed; I am *mancipium paucae lectionis* set beside
so learned a man as the magister.'

The hostess received him with a bridling favour, rubbing
her cheek pleasantly, whilst Udal was seeking to persuade
himself that, since the woman was in law no wife of his,
he had no need to fear. Nevertheless rage tore him when
the doctor, leaning his back against the window-side, talked
to the woman. She stood between them holding a pewter
flagon of mulled hypocras upon a salver of burnished
pewter.

'Who I be,' he said, gazing complacently at her, 'is a poor student of good letters; how I be here is as one of the amanuenses of the Duke of Norfolk. Origen, Eusebius telleth, had seven, given him by Ambrosius to do his behest. The duke hath but two, given him by the grace of God and of the King's high mercy.'

'I make no doubt,' she answered, 'ye be as learned as the seven were.'

'I be twice as hungry,' he laughed; 'but with me it has always been "*Quid scribam non quemadmodum,*" wherein I follow Seneca.'

'Doctor,' the magister uttered, quivering, 'you shall tell me why this mission—which is a very special embassy—at this time cometh to this town of Paris.'

'Magister,' the doctor answered, wagging his beard upon his poor collar to signify that he desired to keep his neck where it was, 'I know not.'

'Injurious man,' Udal fulminated, 'I be no spy.'

The doctor surveyed his perturbation with cross-legged calmness.

'An ye were,' he said—'and it is renowned that ye are— ye could get no knowledge from where none is.'

'Why, tell me of a woman,' the hostess said. 'Who is Kat Howard?'

The doctor's blue eyes shot a hard glance at her, and he let his head sink down.

'I have copied to her eyes a sonnet or twain,' he said, 'and they were writ by my master, Surrey, the Duke o' Norfolk's son.'

'Then these rave upon her as doth the magister?' she asked.

'Why, an ye be jealous of the magister here,' the doctor clipped his words precisely, 'cast him away and take me who am a proper sweetheart.'

'I be wed,' she answered pleasantly.

'What matters that,' he said, 'when husbands are not near?'

The magister, torn between his unaccustomed gust of

jealousy and the desire to hide his marriage from a disastrous discovery in England, clutched with straining fingers at his gown.

'Tell wherefore cometh your mission,' he said.

'We spoke of a fair woman,' the doctor answered. 'Shame it were before Apollo and Priapus that men's missions should come before kings' mistresses.'

'It is true, then, that she shall be queen?' Udal's wife asked.

The fall of a great dish in the rear of the tall kitchen gave the scholar time to collect his suspicions—for he took it for an easy thing that this woman, if she were Udal's leman, might be, she too, a spy in the service of Privy Seal.

'Forbid it, God,' he said, 'that ye take my words as other than allegorical. The lady Katharine may be spoken of as a king's mistress since in truth she were a fit mistress for a king, being fair, devout, learned, courteous, tall and sweet-voiced. But that she hath been kind to the King, God forbid that I should say it.'

'Aye,' Udal said, 'but if she hath sent this mission?'

Panic rose in the heart of the doctor; he beheld himself there, in what seemed a spy's kitchen, asked disastrous questions by a man and woman and pinned into a window-seat. For there was no doubt that the rumour ran in England that this mission had been sent by the King because Katharine Howard so wished it sent. In that age of spies and treacheries no man's head was safe on his shoulders—and here were Cromwell's spies asking news of Cromwell's chief enemy.

He stretched out a calm hand and spoke slowly:

'Madam hostess,' he said, 'if ye be jealous of the magister ye may well be jealous, for great beauty and worship hath this lady.' Yet she need be little jealous, for this lady was nowadays prized so high that she might marry any man in the land—and learned men were little prized. Any man in the land of England she might wed—saving only such as were wed, amongst whom was their lord the King, who was happily wed to the gracious lady whom my Lord Privy Seal did bring from Cleves to be their very virtuous Queen.

Here, it seemed to him, he had cleared himself very handsomely of suspicion of ill will to Privy Seal or of wishing ill to Anne of Cleves.

'For the rest,' he said, sighing with relief to be away from dangerous grounds, 'your magister is safe from the toils of marriage with the Lady Katharine.' Still it might be held that jealousy is aroused by the loving and not by the returning of that love; for it was very certain that the magister much had loved this lady. Many did hold it a treachery in him, till now, to the Privy Seal whom he served. But now he might love her duteously, since our lord the King had commanded the Lady Katharine to join hands with Privy Seal, and Privy Seal to cement a friendly edifice in his heart towards the lady. Thus it was no treason to Privy Seal in him to love her. But to her it was a treason great and not to be comprehended.

He ogled Udal's wife in the gallant manner and prayed her to prepare a bed for him in that hostelry. He had been minded to lodge with a Frenchman named Clement; but having seen her . . .

'Learned sir,' she answered, 'a good bed I have for you.' But if he sought to go beyond her lips she had a body-guard of spitmen that the magister's self had seen.

The doctor kissed her agreeably and, with a great sigh of relief, hurried from the door.

'May Bacchus who maketh mad, and the Furies that pursued Orestes, defile the day when I cross this step again,' he muttered as he swung under the arch and ran to follow the mule train.

For the magister, by playing with his reputation of being Cromwell's spy, had so effectually caused terror of himself to pervade those who supported the old faith that he had much ado at times to find company even amongst the lovers of good letters.

III

In the kitchen the spits had ceased turning, the dishes had been borne upstairs to the envoy from Cleves, the scullions were wiping knives, the maids were rubbing pieces of bread in the dripping pans and licking their fingers after the succulent morsels. The magister stood, a long crimson blot in the window-way; the hostess was setting flagons carefully into the great armoury.

'Madam wife,' the magister said to her at last, when she came near, 'ye see how weighty it is that I bide here.'

'Husband,' she said, 'I see how weighty it is that ye hasten to London.'

His rage broke—he whirled his arms above his head.

'Naughty woman!' he screamed harshly. 'Shalt be beaten.' He strode across to the basting range and gripped a great ladle, his brown eyes glinting, and stood caressing his thin chin passionately.

She folded her arms complacently.

'Husband,' she said, 'it is well that wives be beaten when they have merited it. But, till I have, I have seven cooks and five knaves to bear my part.'

Udal's hand fell suddenly and dispiritedly to his side. What indeed could he do? He could not beat this woman unless she would be beaten—and she stood there, square, buxom, solid and composed. He had indeed that sense that all scholars must have in presence of assured wives, that she was the better man. Moreover, the rage that had filled him in presence of Doctor Longstaffe had cooled down to nothing in Longstaffe's absence.

He folded his arms and tried impatiently to think where, in this pickle, his feet had landed him. His wife turned once more to place flagons in the armoury.

'Woman,' he said at last, in a tone half of majesty, half of appeal, 'see ye not how weighty it is that I bide here?'

'Husband,' she answered with her tranquil nonchalance,

'see ye not how weighty it is that ye waste here no more days?'

'But very well you know,' and he stretched out to her a thin hand, 'that here be two embassies of mystery: you have had, these three days, the Cleves envoy in the house. You have seen that the Duke of Norfolk comes here as ambassador.'

She took a stool and sat near his feet to listen to him.

'Now,' he began again, 'if I be in truth a spy for Thomas Cromwell, Lord Privy Seal, where can I spy better for him than here? For the Cleves people are befriended with Privy Seal; then why come they to France, where bide only Privy Seal's enemies? Now Norfolk is the chiefest enemy of Privy Seal; then wherefore cometh Norfolk to this land, where abide only these foes of Privy Seal?'

She set her elbows on her knees and her knuckles below her chin, and gazed up at him like a child.

'Tell me, husband,' she said; 'be ye a true spy for Thomas Cromwell?'

He glanced round him with terror—but no man stood nearer than the meat boards across the kitchen, so far out of earshot that they could not hear feet upon the bricks.

'Nay, ye may tell me the very truth of the very truth,' she said. 'These be false days—but my kitchen gear is thine, and nothing doth so bind folks together.'

'But other listeners—' he said.

'Hosts and hostesses are listeners,' she answered. ' 'Tis their trade. And their trade it is, too, to fend from them all other listeners. Here you may speak. Tell me then, if I may serve you, very truly whether ye be a true spy for Thomas Cromwell or against him.'

Her round face, beneath the great white hood, had a childish earnestness.

'Why, you are a fair doxy,' he said. He hung his head for some more minutes, then he spoke again.

'It is a folly to speak of me as Privy Seal's spy, though I have so spoken of myself. For why? It gaineth me wor-

ship, maketh men to fear me and women to be dazzled by
my power. But in truth, I have little power.'

'That is the very truth?' she asked.

He nodded nonchalantly and waited again to find very
clear words for her understanding.

'But, though it be true that I am no spy of Cromwell's,
true it is also that I am a very poor man who craves very
much for money. For I love good books that cost much
gold; comely women that cost far more; succulent meats,
sweet wines, high piled fires and warm furs.'

He smacked his lips thinking of these same things.

'I am, in short, no stoic,' he said, 'the stoics being
ancient curmudgeons that were low-stomached.' Now, he
continued, the Old Faith he loved well, but not over well;
the Protestants he called busy knaves, but the New Learning he loved beyond life. Cromwell thwacked the Old
Faith; he loved him not for that. Cromwell upheld in a
sort the Protestants; he little loved him for that. 'But the
New Learning he loveth, and, oh fair sharer of my dreams
o' nights, Cromwell holdeth the strings of the money-bags.'

She scratched her cheek meditatively, and then unfolded
her arms.

'How then ha' ye come by his broad pieces?'

'It is three years since,' he answered, 'that Privy Seal
sent for me. I had been cast out of my mastership at Eton
College, for they said—foul liars said—that I had stolen
the silver salt-cellars.' He had been teaching, for his sins,
in the house of the Lord Edmund Howard, where he had
had his best pupil, but no more salary than what his belly
could hold of poor mutton. 'So Privy Seal did send for
me——'

'Kat Howard was thy best pupil?' his wife asked meditatively.

'By the shrine of Saint Eloi—' he commenced to swear.

'Nay, lie not,' she cut him short. 'You love Kat Howard
and six other wenches. I know it well. What said Privy
Seal?'

He meditated again to protest that he loved not Katharine, but her quiet stolidity set him to change his mind.

'It was that the Lady Mary of England needed a preceptor, an amanuensis, an aid for her studies in the learned language.' For the King's Highness' daughter had a great learning and was agate of writing a commentary of Plautus his plays. But the Lady Mary hated also virulently—and with what cause all men know—the King her father. And for years long, since the death of the Queen her mother—whom God preserve in Paradise!—for years long the Lady Mary had maintained a treasonable correspondence with the King's enemies, with the Emperor, with the Bishop of Rome——

'Our Holy Father the Pope,' his wife said, and crossed herself.

'And with this King here of France,' Udal continued, whilst he too crossed himself with graceful waves of his brown hand. He continued to report that the way in which the Lady Mary sent her letters abroad had never been found; that Cromwell had appointed three tutors in succession to be aid to the Lady Mary in her studies. Each of these three she had broken and cast out from her doors, she being by far the more learned, so that, though Privy Seal in his might had seven thousand spies throughout the realm of England, he had among them no man learned enough to take this place and to spy out the things that he would learn.

'Therefore Privy Seal did send for thee, who art accounted the most learned doctor in Christendom.' His wife's eyes glowed and her face became ruddy with pride in her husband's fame.

The magister waved his hand pleasantly.

'Therefore he did send for me.' Privy Seal had promised him seven hundred pounds, farms with sixty pounds by the year, or the headship of New College if the magister could discover how the Lady Mary wrote her letters abroad.

'So I have stayed three years with the Lady Mary,' Udal said. 'But before God,' he asseverated, 'though I have known these twenty-nine months that she sent away her letters in the crusts of pudding pies, never hath cur Crummock had word of it.'

'A fool he, to set thee to spy upon a petticoat,' she answered pleasantly.

'Woman,' he answered hotly, 'crowns I have made by making reports to Privy Seal. I have set his men to watch doors and windows where none came in or entered; I have reported treasons of men whose heads had already fallen by the axe; I have told him of words uttered by maids of honour whom he knew full well already miscalled him. Sometimes I have had a crown or two from him, sometimes more; but no good man hath been hurt by my spying.'

'Husband,' she uttered, with her face set expressionlessly, 'knew ye that the Frenchman's cook that made the pudding pies had been taken and cast into the Tower gaol?'

Udal's arms flew above his head; his eyes started from their sockets; his tongue came forth from his pale mouth to lick his dry lips, and his legs failed him so that he sat himself down, wavering from side to side in the window-seat.

'Then the commentary of Plautus shall never be written,' he wailed. He wrung his hands. 'Whom have they taken else?' he said. 'How knew ye these things when I nothing knew? What make of house is this where such things be known?'

'Husband,' she answered, 'this house is even an inn. Where many travellers pass through, many secrets are known. I know of this cook's fate since the fate of cooks is much spoken of in kitchens, and this was the cook of a Frenchman, and this is France.'

'Save us, oh pitiful saints!' the magister whispered. 'Who else is taken? What more do ye know? Many others have aided. I too. And there be friends I love.'

'Husband,' she answered, 'I know no more than this: three days ago the cook stood where now you stand——'

He clasped his hair so that his cap fell to the ground.

'Here!' he said. 'But he was in the Tower!'

'He was in the Tower, but stood here free,' she answered. Udal groaned.

'Then he hath blabbed. We are lost.'

She answered:

'That may be the truth. But I think it is not. For so the matter is that the cook told me.' He was taken and set in the Tower by the men of Privy Seal. Yet within ten hours came the men of the King; these took him aboard a cogger, the cogger took them to Calais, and at the gate of Calais town the King's men kicked him into the country of France, he having sworn on oath never more to tread on English soil.

Udal groaned.

'Aye! But what others were taken? What others shall be?'

She shook her head.

The report ran: a boy called Poins, a lady called Elliott, and a lady called Howard. Yet all three drank the free air before that day at nightfall.

Udal, huddled against the wall, took these blows of fate with a quiver for each. In the back of the kitchen the servers, come down from the meal of the Cleves envoy, made a great clatter with their dishes of pewter and alloy. The hostess, working with her comfortable sway of the hips, drove them gently through the door to let a silence fall; but gradually Udal's jaw closed, his eyes grew smaller, he started suddenly and the muscles of his knees regained their tension. The hostess, swishing her many petticoats beneath her, sat down again on the stool.

'*Insipiens et infacetus quin sum!*' the magister mused. 'Fool that I am! Wherefore see I no clue?' He hung his head; frowned; then started anew with his hand on his side.

'Wherefore shall I not read pure joy in this?' he said,

'save that Austin waileth: *"Inter delicias semper aliquid saevi nos strangulat."* I would be joyful—but that I fear.'

Norfolk had come upon an embassy here; then assuredly Cromwell's power waned, or never had this foe of his been sent in this office of honour. The cook was cast in the Tower, but set free by the King's men; young Poins was cast too, but set free—the Lady Elliott—and the Lady Howard. What then? What then?

'Husband,' she said, 'have you naught forgotten?'

Udal, musing with his hand upon his chin, shook his head negligently.

'I keep more track of the King's leman than thou, then,' she said. 'What was it Longstaffe said of her?'

'Nay,' Udal answered, 'so turned my bowels were with jealousy that little I noted.'

'Why, you are a fine spy,' she said. And she repeated to him that Longstaffe had reported the King's commanding Katharine and Privy Seal to join hands and be friends. Udal shook his head gloomily.

'I would not have my best pupil friends with Cromwell,' he said.

'Oh, magister,' she retorted, with a first touch of scorn in her voice; 'have you, who have had so much truck with women, yet to learn that you may command a woman to be friends with a man, yet no power on earth shall make her love him. Nevertheless, well might Cromwell seek to win her love, and thence these pardons.'

Udal started forward upon his tiptoes.

'I must to London!' he cried. She smiled at him as at a child.

'You are come to be of my advice,' she said.

Udal gazed at her with a wondering patronage.

'Why, what a wench it is,' he said, and he crooked his arm around her ample waist. His face shone with pleasure. 'Angel!' he uttered; 'for Angelos is the Greek for messenger, and signifieth more especially one that bringeth good tidings.' Out of all this holus bolus of envoys, ambassadors, cooks and prisoners one thing appeared plain to view: that, for the first time, *a solis ortus cardine*, Cromwell had loosened his grip of some that he held. 'And if Crummock looseneth grip, Crummock's power in the land waneth.'

She looked up at him with a coy pleasure.

'Hatest Cromwell then full fell-ly?' she asked.

He put his hands upon her shoulders and solemnly regarded her.

'Woman,' he said; 'this man rideth England with seven thousand spies; these three years I have lived in terror of my life. I have had no bliss that fear hath not entered into—in very truth *inter delicias semper aliquid saevi nos strangulavit.*' His lugubrious tones grew higher with hatred; he raised one hand above his head and one gripped tight her fat shoulder. 'Terror hath bestridden our realm of England; no man dares to whisper his hate even to the rushes. Me! Me! Me!' he reached a pitch of high-voiced fury. 'Me! *Virum doctissimum!* Me, the first learned man in Britain, he did force to write a play in the vulgar tongue. Me, a master of Latin, to write in English! I had pardoned him my terror. I had pardoned him the heads of the good men he hath struck off. For that princes should inspire terror is just, and that the great ones of the earth should prey one upon the other is a thing all history giveth precedent for since the days when Sylla hunted to death Marius that sat amidst the ruins of Carthage. But that the learned should be put to shame! that good letters should be cast into the mire! History showeth no ensample of a man so vile since the Emperor Alexander removed his shadow from before the tub of Diogenes.'

'In truth,' she said, blenching a little before his fury, 'I was ever one that loved the rolling sound of your Greek and your Roman.'

'Give me my journey money,' he said, 'let me begone to England. For, if indeed the Lady Katharine hath the King's ear, much may I aid her with my counsels.'

She began to fumble in beneath her apron, and then, as

if she suddenly remembered herself, she placed her finger upon her lips.

'Husband,' she said, 'I have for you a gift. How it shall value itself to you I little know, but I have before been much besought and offered high payment for that which now I offer thee. Come.'

The finger still upon her plump lips, she led him to a small door behind the chimney stack. They climbed up through cobwebs, ham, flitches of smoked beef, and darkness, and the reek of wood-smoke, until they came, high up, to a store-room in the slope of a mansard roof. Light filtered dimly between the tiles, and many bales and sacks lay upon the raftered floor like huge monsters in a huge, dim cave.

'Hearken! make no sound,' she whispered, and in the intense gloom they heard a sullen, stertorous, intermittent rumble.

'The envoy sleeps,' she said. She set her eye to a knot-hole in the planked wall. ' 'A sleeps!' she whispered. 'My pigling made a great thirst in him. Much wine he drank. Set your eye to the knot-hole.'

With his face glued against the rough wood, the magister could see in the large room a great fair man, in a great blue chair behind a littered table. His head hung forward, shewed only a pink bald spot in the thin hair, and brilliant red ears. A slow rumble of snoring came for a long minute, then ceased for as long.

From behind Udal's back came a crash, and he started back to see the large woman, who had overturned a chest.

'That is to test how he sleeps,' she said. 'See if he have moved.' The man, plain to see through the knot-hole, had stirred no muscle; again the heavy rumble of the snore came to them. She spoke quite loudly now. 'Why, naught shall wake him these five hours. 'A hath bolted the door; thus his secretaries shall not come to him. See now.'

She slid back a board in the wall, and Udal could see into what appeared to be a cupboard filled with a litter of papers and of parchments. Udal's heart began to beat so that he noted it there; his eyes searched hers with a glittering excitement—nevertheless a half fear of awakening the envoy kept him from speaking.

'Take them! Take them!' she nudged him with her elbow. 'Six hours ye have to read and to copy.'

'What papers are these?' he muttered, his voice thick betwixt incredulous joy and fear.

'They be the envoy's papers,' she said; 'doubtless these be his letters to the king of this land.... What there may be I know not else.'

Udal's hands were in at the hole with the swift clutch of a miser visiting his treasure-chest. The woman surveyed him with pleasure and with pride in her achievement, and with the calmness of routine she fitted a bar across the door of the cupboard where it opened into the envoy's room. Udal was fumbling already with the strings of a packet, his eyes searching the superscription in the gloom.

'Six hours ye have to read and to copy,' she said happily, 'for, for six hours the poppy seed in his wine that he drank shall surely keep him snoring.' And, whilst they went again down the stairway, the papers secreted beneath the magister's gown, she explained with her pride and happiness. The aumbry was so contrived that any envoy or secretary sleeping in her best room must needs put his papers therein, since there was in the room no other chest that locked. And the King of France's chancellors allotted to all envoys her hostelry for a lodging; and once there, she made them heavy with wine and poppy seed after a receipt she had from an Egyptian, and at the appointed time the King of France's men came to read through the papers and to pay her much money and many kisses.

*　　*　　*　　*

It was six hours later that the magister stood in his own room crushing a fillet of papers into the breast of his brown jerkin. The hostess, walking always calmly as if disorder of the mind were a thing she were a stranger to, had reclimbed the narrow stairway, replaced the papers in the envoy's cupboard and returned to her husband. She sought, mutely, for commendations, and he gave her them.

'Y'have made me the man that holds the secret of England's future,' he said. 'All England that groans beneath Cromwell awaiteth to hear how the cat jumps in Cleves. Now I know how the cat jumps in Cleves.'

She wiped the dust from her hands upon her apron.

'See that ye make good use of the knowledge,' she said. She considered for a moment whilst he ferreted amongst his clothes in the great black press beside the great white bed. 'I have long thought,' she said, 'that greatly might I be of service to a man of laws and of policies. But I have long known that to serve a man is to have little reward unless a woman tie him up in fast bands——' He made one of his broad gestures of negation, but she cut in upon his words: 'Aye, so it is. A gossip may serve a man how she will, but once his occasion is past he shall leave her in the ditch for the first fairer face. So I made resolve to make such a man my husband, that his being advanced might advance me. For, for sure this shall not be the last spying service I shall do thee. Many envoys more shall be lodged in this house and many more secrets ye shall learn.'

'Oh beloved Pandora!' he cried; 'opener of all secret places, caskets, aumbries, caves of the winds, thrice blessed Sibyl of the keyhole!' She nodded her head with grave contentment.

'I chose thee for thy resounding speeches,' she said. Her tranquillity and her buxom pleasantness overcame him with sudden affection. He was minded to tell her—because indeed she had made his fortunes for him—that her marriage to him did not hold good since a friar had read the rites.

'I chose thee for thy resounding speeches,' she said, 'and because art so ill-clothed i' the ribs. Give me a thin man of policies to move my bowels of compassion, say I.' For with her secret closets she might make him stand well among the princes, and with her goodly capons set grease upon his ribs, poor soul!

'Oh Guenevere!' he said; 'for was it not the queen of Arthur that made bag-puddings for his starving knights?'

'Aye,' she said; 'great learning you possess.' A little moisture bedewed her blue eyes. 'It grieves me that you must begone. I love to hear thy broad o's and a's!'

'Then by all that is fattest in the land hight Cokaigne I will stay here, thy dutiful goodman,' he said, and tears filled his own eyes.

'Oh nay,' she answered; 'you shall get yourself into the Chancellery, and merry will we feast and devise beneath the gilded roofs.' Her eyes sought the brown beams that ceiled the long room. 'I have heard that chancellors have always gilded roofs.'

Again the tenderness overcame him for the touch of simple pride in her voice. And the confession slipped from his lips:

'Poor befooled soul! Shalt never be a chancellor's dame.' She was sobbing a little.

'Oh aye,' she said; 'thou shalt yet be chancellor, and I will baste thy cooks' ribs an they baste not thy meat full well.' Such a man as he would find favour with princes for his glosing tongue—aye, and with queens too. At that she covered her face with her apron, and from beneath it her voice came forth:

'If this Kat Howard come to be queen, shall not the old faith be restored?'

The recollection of this particular certainty affected the magister like a stab, for, if the old faith came back, then assuredly marriages by friars should again be acknowledged. He cursed himself beneath his breath: he was loath to leave the woman in the ditch, her trusting face and pleasing ways stirred the strings of his heart. But he was more than loath that the wedding should hold a wedding. He shook his perplexity from him with starting towards the door.

'Time to be gone!' he said, and added, 'Be certain and take care that no Englishman heareth of wedding betwixt thee and me.' It must in England work his sure undoing.

She removed her apron and nodded gravely.

'Aye,' she said, 'that is certain enow with Court ladies, such as they be to-day.' But she asked that when he went among women she should hear nothing of it. For she had had three husbands and several courtiers to prove it upon, that it is better to be lied to than to know truth.

'There is in the world no woman like to thee!' he said with a great sincerity. Once more she nodded.

'Aye, that is the lie that I would hear,' she said. On his part, he started suddenly with pain.

'But thee!' he uttered.

'Aye,' she cried again, 'that too is needed. But be very certain of this, that not easily will I plant upon thy brow that which most husbands wear!' She paused, and once more rubbed her hands. Courteous she must be, since her calling called therefor. But assuredly, having had three husbands, she had had embraces enow to crave little for men. And, if she did that which few good women have a need to—save very piteous women in ballads—she would suffer him to belabour her;—she nodded again—'And that to a man is a great solace.'

He fled with precipitancy from the thought of this solace, brushing through the narrow passages, stalking across the great guest-chamber and the greater kitchen where, in the falling dusk, the fires glowed red upon the maids' faces and the cooks' aprons, the smoke rose unctuously upward tended with rich smells of meat, and the windjacks clanked in the chimneys. She trotted behind him, weeping in the gloaming.

'If you come to be chancellor in five years,' she whimpered, 'I shall come across the seas to ye. If ye fail, this shall be your plenteous house.'

Whilst she hung round his neck in the shadowy court-yard and he had already one foot in the stirrup, she begged for one more great speech.

'Before Jupiter!' he said, 'I can think of none for crying!'

The big black horse, with its bags before and behind

the saddle, stirred, so that, standing upon one foot, he fell
away from her. But he swung astride the saddle, his cloak
flying, his long legs clasping round the belly. It reared and
pawed the twilight mists, but he smote it over one ear with
his palm, and it stood trembling.

'This is a fine beast y'have given me,' he said, pleasure
thrilling his limbs.

'I have given it a fine rider!' she cried. He wheeled it
near her and stooped right down to kiss her face. He was
very sure in his saddle, having learned the trick of the
stirrup from old Rowfant, that had taught the King.

'Wife,' he said, 'I have bethought me of this: *Post
equitem sedet*——' He faltered—'*sedet—Behind the rider
sitteth*—But for the life of me I know not whether it be
atra cura or no.'

And, as he left Paris gates behind him and speeded
towards the black hills, bending low to face the cold wind
of night, for the life of him he knew not whether black
care sat behind him or no. Only, as night came down and
he sped forward, he knew that he was speeding for England
with the great news that the Duke of Cleves was seeking
to make his peace with the Emperor and the Pope through
the mediancy of the king of that land and, on the soft road,
the hoofs of the horse seemed to beat out the rhythm
of the words:

'Crummock is down: Cromwell is down. Crummock is
down: Cromwell is down.'

He rode all through the night thinking of these things,
for, because he carried letters from the English ambassador
to the King of England, the gates of no small town could
stay his passing through.

IV

Five men talked in the long gallery overlooking the River
Thames. It was in the Lord Cromwell's house, upon which
the April showers fell like handsful of peas, with a sifting

sound, between showers of sunshine that fell themselves like rain, so that at times all the long empty gallery was gilded with light and at times it was all saddened and frosty. They were talking all, and all with earnestness and concern, as all the Court and the city were talking now, of Katharine Howard whom the King loved.

The Archbishop leant against one side of a window, close beside him his spy Lascelles; the Archbishop's face was round but worn, his large eyes bore the trace of sleeplessness, his plump hands were a little tremulous within his lawn sleeves.

'Sir,' he said, 'we must bow to the breeze. In time to come we may stand straight enow.' His eyes seemed to plead with Privy Seal, who paced the gallery in short, pursy strides, his plump hands hidden in the furs behind his back. Lascelles, the Archbishop's spy, nodded his head sagaciously; his yellow hair came from high on his crown and was brushed forward towards his brows. He did not speak, being in such high company, but looking at him, the Archbishop gained confidence from the support of his nod.

'If we needs must go with the Lady Katharine towards Rome,' he pleaded again, 'consider that it is but for a short time.' Cromwell passed him in his pacing and, unsure of having caught his ear, Cranmer addressed himself to Throckmorton and Wriothesley, the two men of forty who stood gravely, side by side, fingering their long beards. 'For sure,' Cranmer appealed to the three silent men, 'what we must avoid is crossing the King's Highness. For his Highness, crossed, hath a swift and sudden habit of action.' Wriothesley nodded, and: 'Very sudden,' Lascelles allowed himself utterance, in a low voice. Throckmorton's eyes alone danced and span; he neither nodded nor spoke, and, because he was thought to have a great say in the councils of Privy Seal, it was to him that Cranmer once more addressed himself urgently:

'Full-bodied men who are come upon failing years are very prone to women. 'Tis a condition of the body, a humour, a malady that passeth. But, while it lasteth, it must be bowed to.'

Cromwell, with his deaf face, passed once more before them. He addressed himself in brief, sharp tones to Wriothesley:

'You say, in Paris an envoy from Cleves was come a week agone?' and passed on.

'It must be bowed to,' Cranmer continued his speech. 'I do maintain it. There is no way but to divorce the Queen.' Again Lascelles nodded; it was Wriothesley this time who spoke.

'It is a lamentable thing!' and there was a heavy sincerity in his utterance, his pose, with his foot weightily upon the ground, being that of an honest man. 'But I do think you have the right of it. We, and the new faith with us, are between Scylla and Charybdis. For certain, our two paths do lie between divorcing the Queen and seeing you, great lords, who so well defend us, cast down.'

Coming up behind him, Cromwell placed a hand upon his shoulder.

'Goodly knight,' he said, 'let us hear thy thoughts. His Grace's of Canterbury we do know very well. He is for keeping a whole skin!'

Cranmer threw up his hands, and Lascelles looked at the ground. Throckmorton's eyes were filled with admiration of this master of his that he was betraying now. He muttered in his long, golden beard.

'Pity we must have thy head.'

Wriothesley cleared his throat, and having considered, spoke earnestly.

'It is before all things expedient and necessary,' he said, 'that we do keep you, my Lord Privy Seal, and you, my Lord of Canterbury, at the head of the State.' That was above all necessary. For assuredly this land, though these two had brought it to a great pitch of wealth, clean living, true faith and prosperity, this land needed my Lord Privy Seal before all men to shield it from the treason of the old faith. There were many lands now, bringing wealth and commodity to the republic, that should soon again revert towards and pay all their fruits to Rome; there were many cleaned and whitened churches that should again hear the old nasty songs and again be tricked with gewgaws of the idolaters. Therefore, before all things, my Lord Privy Seal must retain the love of the King's Highness—— Cromwell, who had resumed his pacing, stayed for a moment to listen.

'Wherefore brought ye not news of why Cleves' envoy came to Paris town?' he said pleasantly. 'All the door turneth upon that hinge.'

Wriothesley stuttered and reddened.

'What gold could purchase, I purchased of news,' he said. 'But this envoy would not speak; his knaves took my gold and had no news. The King of France's men——'

'Oh aye,' Cromwell continued; 'speak on about the other matter.'

Wriothesley turned his slow mind from his vexation in Paris, whence he had come a special journey to report of the envoy from Cleves. He spoke again swiftly, turning right round to Cromwell.

'Sir,' he said, 'study above all to please the King. For unless you guide us we are lost indeed.'

Cromwell worked his lips one upon another and moved a hand.

'Aye,' Wriothesley continued; 'it can be done only by bringing the King's Highness and the Lady Katharine to a marriage.'

'Only by that?' Cromwell asked enigmatically.

Throckmorton spoke at last:

'Your lordship jests,' he said; 'since the King is not a man, but a high and beneficent prince with a noble stomach.'

Cromwell tapped him upon the cheek.

'That you do see through a millstone I know,' he said. 'But I was minded to hear how these men do think. You and I do think alike.'

'Aye, my lord,' Throckmorton answered boldly. 'But in

ten minutes I must be with the Lady Katharine, and I am minded to hear the upshot of this conference.'

Cromwell laughed at him sunnily:

'Go and do your message with the lady. An you hasten, you may return ere ever this conference ends, since slow wits like ours need a store of words to speak their minds with.'

Lascelles, the silent spy of the archbishop, devoured with envious eyes Throckmorton's great back and golden beard. For his life he dared not speak three words unbidden in this company. But Throckmorton being gone the discussion renewed itself, Wriothesley speaking again.

He voiced always the same ideas, for the same motives: Cromwell must maintain his place at the cost of all things, for the sake of all these men who leaned upon him. And it was certain that the King loved this lady. If he had sent her few gifts and given her no titles nor farms, it was because—either of nature or to enhance the King's appetite—she shewed a prudish disposition. But day by day and week in week out the King went with his little son in his times of ease to the rooms of the Lady Mary. And there he went, assuredly, not to see the glum face of the daughter that hated him, but to converse in Latin with his daughter's waiting-maid of honour. All the Court knew this. Who there had not seen how the King smiled when he came new from the Lady Mary's rooms? He was heavy enow at all other times. This fair woman that hated alike the new faith and all its ways had utterly bewitched and enslaved the King's eyes, ears and understanding. If the King would have Katharine Howard his wife the King must have her. Anne of Cleves must be sent back to Germany; Cromwell must sue for peace with the Howard wench; a way must be found to bribe her till the King tired of her; then Katharine must go in her turn, once more Cromwell would have his own, and the Protestants be reinstated. Cromwell retained his silence; at the last he uttered his unfailing words with which he closed all these discussions:

'Well, it is a great matter.'

The gusts of rain and showers of sun pursued each other down the river; the lights and shadows succeeded upon the cloaked and capped shapes of the men who huddled their figures together in the tall window. At last the Archbishop lost his patience and cried out:

'What will you *do*? What will you *do*?'

Cromwell swung his figure round before him.

'I will discover what Cleves will do in this matter,' he said. 'All dependeth therefrom.'

'Nay; make a peace with Rome,' Cranmer uttered suddenly. 'I am weary of these strivings.'

But Wriothesley clenched his fist.

'Before ye shall do that I will die, and twenty thousand others!'

Cranmer quailed.

'Sir,' he temporised. 'We will give back to the Bishop of Rome nothing that we have taken of property. But the Bishop of Rome may have Peter's Pence and the deciding of doctrines.'

'Canterbury,' Wriothesley said, 'I had rather Antichrist had his old goods and gear in this realm than the handling of our faith.'

Cromwell drew in the air through his nostrils, and still smiled.

'Be sure the Bishop of Rome shall have no more gear and no more guidance of this realm than his Highness and I need give,' he said. 'No stranger shall have any say in the councils of this realm.' He smiled noiselessly again. 'Still and still, all turneth upon Cleves.'

For the first time Lascelles spoke:

'All turneth upon Cleves,' he said.

Cromwell surveyed him, narrowing his eyes.

'Speak you now of your wisdom,' he uttered with neither friendliness nor contempt. Lascelles caressed his shaven chin and spoke:

'The King's Highness I have observed to be a man for women—a man who will give all his goods and all his gear to a woman. Assuredly he will not take this woman to his leman; his princely stomach revolteth against an easy won mastership. He will pay dear, he will pay his crown to win her. Yet the King would not give his policies. Neither would he retrace his steps for a woman's sake unless Fate too cried out that he must.'

Cromwell nodded his head. It pleased him that this young man set a virtue sufficiently high upon his prince.

'Sirs,' he said, 'daily have I seen this King in ten years, and I do tell ye no man knoweth how the King loves king-craft as I know.' He nodded again to Lascelles, whose small stature seemed to gain bulk, whose thin voice seemed to gain volume from this approval and from his 'Speak on. About Cleves.'

'Sirs,' Lascelles spoke again, 'whiles there remains the shade of a chance that Cleves' Duke shall lead the princes of Germany against the Emperor and France, assuredly the King shall stay his longing for the Lady Katharine. He shall stay firm in his marriage with the Queen.' Again Cromwell nodded. 'Till then it booteth little to move to-wards a divorce; but if that day should come, then our Lord Privy Seal must bethink himself. That is in our lord's mind.'

'By Bacchus!' Cromwell said, 'your Grace of Canter-bury hath a jewel in your crony and helper. And again I say, we must wait upon Cleves.' He seemed to pursue the sunbeams along the gallery, then returned to say:

'I know ye know I love little to speak my mind. What I think or how I will act I keep to myself. But this I will tell you:' Cleves might have two minds in sending to France an envoy. On the one hand, he might be minded to abandon Henry and make submission to the Emperor and to Rome. For, in the end, was not the Duke of Cleves a vassal of the Emperor? It might be that. Or it might be that he was sending merely to ask the King of France to intercede betwixt him and his offended lord. The Emperor was preparing to wage war upon Cleves. That was known. And doubtless Cleves, desiring to retain his friendship with Henry, might have it in mind to keep friends with both. There the matter hinged, Cromwell repeated. For, if Cleves remained loyal to the King of England, Henry would hear nothing of divorcing Cleves' sister, and would master his desire for Katharine.

'Believe me when I speak,' Cromwell added earnestly. 'Ye do wrong to think of this King as a lecher after the common report. He is a man very continent for a king. His kingcraft cometh before all women. If the Duke of Cleves be firm friend to him, firm friend he will be to the Duke's sister. The Lady Howard will be his friend, but the Lady Howard will be neither his leman nor his guide to Rome. He will please her if he may. But his kingcraft. Never!' He broke off and laughed noiselessly at the Archbishop's face of dismay. 'Your Grace would make a pact with Rome?' he asked.

'Why, these are very evil times,' Cranmer answered. 'And if the Bishop of Rome will give way to us, why may we not give pence to the Bishop of Rome?'

'Goodman,' Cromwell answered, 'these are evil times because we men are evil.' He pulled a paper from his belt. 'Sirs,' he said, 'will ye know what manner of woman this Katharine Howard is?' and to their murmurs of assent: 'This lady hath asked to speak with me. Will ye hear her speak? Then bide ye here. Throckmorton is gone to seek her.'

V

Katharine Howard sat in her own room; it had in it little of sumptuousness, for all the King so much affected her. It was the room she had first had at Hampton after coming to be maid to the King's daughter, and it had the old, green hangings that had always been round the walls, the long oak table, the box-bed set in the wall, the high chair and the three stools round the fire. The only thing she had taken of the King was a curtain in red cloth to hang on a rod before the door where was a great draught, the leading of the windows being rotted. She had lived so poor a life,

her father having been a very poor lord with many children—she was so attuned to flaws of the wind, ill-feeding
and harsh clothes, that such a tall room as she there had
seemed goodly enough for her. Barely three months ago
she had come to the palace of Greenwich riding upon a
mule. Now accident, or maybe the design of the dear
saints, had set her so high in the King's esteem that she
might well try a fall with Privy Seal.

She sat there dressed, awaiting the summons to go to
him. She wore a long dress of red velvet, worked around
the breast-lines with little silver anchors and hearts, and
her hood was of black lawn and fell near to her hips
behind. And she had read and learned by heart passages
from Plutarch, from Tacitus, from Diodorus Siculus, from
Seneca and from Tully, each one inculcating how salutary
a thing in a man was the love of justice. Therefore she felt
herself well prepared to try a fall with the chief enemy of
her faith, and awaited with impatience his summons to
speak with him. For she was anxious, now at last, to speak
out her mind, and Privy Seal's agents had worked upon
the religious of a poor little convent near her father's house
a wrong so baleful that she could no longer contain herself. Either Privy Seal must redress or she must go to the
King for justice to these poor women that had taught her
the very elements of virtue and lay now in gaol.

So she spoke to her two chief friends, her that had been
Cicely Elliott and her old husband Rochford, the knight of
Bosworth Hedge. They happened in upon her just after
she was attired and had sent her maid to fetch her dinner
from the buttery.

'Three months agone,' she said, 'the King's Highness
did bid me cease from crying out upon Privy Seal; and not
the King's Highness' self can say that in that time I have
spoken word against the Lord Cromwell.'

Cicely Elliott, who dressed, in spite of her new wedding,
all in black for the sake of some dead men, laughed round
at her from her little stool by the fire.

'God help you! that must have been hard, to keep thy tongue from the flail of all Papists.'

The old knight, who was habited like Katharine, all in red, because at that season the King favoured that colour, pulled nervously at his little goat's beard, for all conversations that savoured of politics and religion were to him very fearful. He stood back against the green hangings and fidgeted with his feet.

But Katharine, who for the love of the King had been silent, was now set to speak her mind.

'It is Seneca,' she said, 'who tells us to have a check upon our tongues, but only till the moment approaches to speak.'

'Aye, goodman Seneca!' Cicely laughed round at her. Katharine smoothed her hair, but her eyes gleamed deeply.

'The moment approaches,' she said; 'I do like my King, but better I like my Church.' She swallowed in her throat. 'I had thought,' she said, 'that Privy Seal would stay his harryings of the goodly nuns in this land.' But now she had a petition, come that day from Lincoln gaol. Cromwell's servants were more bitter still than ever against the religious. Here was a false accusation of treason against her foster-mother's self. 'I will soon end it or mend it, or lose mine own head,' Katharine ended.

'Aye, pull down Cur Crummock,' Cicely said. 'I think the King shall not long stay away from thy desires.'

The old knight burst in:

'I take it ill that ye speak of these things. I take it ill. I will not have 'ee lose thy head in these quarrels.'

'Husband,' Cicely laughed round at him, 'three years ago Cur Crummock had the heads of all my menfolk, having sworn they were traitors.'

'The more reason that he have not mine and thine now,' the old knight answered grimly. 'I am not for these meddlings in things that concern neither me nor thee.'

Cicely Elliott set her elbows upon her knees and her chin upon her knuckles. She gazed into the fire and grew moody, as was her wont when she had chanced to think of her menfolk that Cromwell had executed.

'He might have had my head any day this four years,' she said. 'And had you lost my head and me you might have had any other maid any day that se'nnight.'

'Nay, I grow too old,' the knight answered. 'A week ago I dropped my lance.'

Cicely continued to gaze at nothings in the fire.

'For thee,' she said scornfully to Katharine, 'it were better thou hadst never been born than have meddled between kings and ministers and faiths and nuns. You are not made for this world. You talk too much. Get you across the seas to a nunnery.'

Katharine looked at her pitifully.

'Child,' she said, 'it was not I that spoke of thy menfolk.'

'Get thyself mewed up,' Cicely repeated more hotly; 'thou wilt set all this world by the ears. This is no place for virtues learned from learned books. This is an ill world where only evil men flourish.'

The old knight still fidgeted to be gone.

'Nay,' Katharine said seriously, 'ye think I will work mine own advantage with the King. But I do swear to thee I have it not in my mind.'

'Oh, swear not,' Cicely mumbled, 'all the world knoweth thee to be that make of fool.'

'I would well to get me made a nun—but first I will bring nunneries back from across the seas to this dear land.'

Cicely laughed again—for a long and strident while.

'You will come to no nunnery if you wait till then,' she said. 'Nuns without their heads have no vocation.'

'When Cromwell is down, no woman again shall lose her head,' Katharine answered hotly.

Cicely only laughed.

'No woman again!' Katharine repeated.

'Blood was tasted when first a queen fell on Tower Hill.' Cicely pointed her little finger at her. 'And the taste of blood, even as the taste of wine, ensureth a certain oblivion.'

'You miscall your King,' Katharine said.

Cicely laughed and answered: 'I speak of my world.'

Katharine's blood came hot to her cheeks.

'It is a new world from now on,' she answered proudly.

'Till a new queen's blood seal it an old one,' Cicely mocked her earnestness. 'Hadst best get thee to a nunnery across the seas.'

'The King did bid me bide here.' Katharine faltered in the least.

'You have spoken of it with him?' Cicely said. 'Why, God help you!'

Katharine sat quietly, her fair hair gilded by the pale light of the gusty day, her lips parted a little, her eyelids drooping. It behoved her to move little, for her scarlet dress was very nice in its equipoise, and fain she was to seem fine in Privy Seal's eyes.

'This King hath a wife to his tail,' Cicely mocked her.

The old knight had recovered his quiet; he had his hand upon his haunch, and spoke with his air of wisdom:

'I would have you to cease these talkings of dangerous things,' he said. 'I am Rochford of Bosworth Hedge. I have kept my head and my lands, and my legs from chains—and how but by leaving to talk of dangerous things?'

Katharine moved suddenly in her chair. This speech, though she had heard it a hundred times before, struck her now as so craven that she forgot alike her desire to keep fine and her friendship for the old man's new wife.

'Aye, you have been a coward all your life,' she said: for were not her dear nuns in Lincoln gaol, and this was a knight that should have redressed wrongs!

Old Rochford smiled with his air of tranquil wisdom and corpulent age.

'I have struck good blows,' he said. 'There have been thirteen ballads writ of me.'

'You have kept so close a tongue,' Katharine said to him hotly, 'that I know not what you love. Be you for the old faith, or for this Church of devils that Cromwell hath set up in the land? Did you love Queen Katharine or Queen

Anne Boleyn? Were you glad when More died, or did you weep? Are you for the Statute of Users, or would you end it? Are you for having the Lady Mary called bastard—God pardon me the word!—or would you defend her with your life?—I do not know. I have spoken with you many times —but I do not know.'

Old Rochford smiled contentedly.

'I have saved my head and my lands in these perilous times by letting no man know,' he said.

'Aye,' Katharine met his words with scorn and appeal. 'You have kept your head on your shoulders and the rent from your lands in your poke. But oh, sir, it is certain that, being a man, you love either the new ways or the old; it is certain that, being a spurred knight, you should love the old ways. Sir, bethink you and take heed of this: that the angels of God weep above England, that the Mother of God weeps above England; that the saints of God do weep—and you, a spurred knight, do wield a good sword. Sir, when you stand before the gates of Heaven, what shall you answer the warders thereof?'

'Please God,' the old knight answered, 'that I have struck some good blows.'

'Aye; you have struck blows against the Scots,' Katharine said. 'But the beasts of the field strike as well against the foes of their kind—the bull of the herd against lions; the Hyrcanian tiger against the troglodytes; the basilisk against many beasts. It is the province of a man to smite not only against the foes of his kind but—and how much the more? —against the foes of his God.'

In the full flow of her speaking there came in the great, blonde Margot Poins, her body-maid. She led by the hand the Magister Udal, and behind them followed, with his foxy eyes and long, smooth beard, the spy Throckmorton, vivid in his coat of green and scarlet stockings. And, at the antipathy of his approach, Katharine's emotions grew the more harrowing—as if she were determined to shew this evil supporter of her cause how a pure fight should be waged. They moved on tiptoe and stood against the hangings at the back.

She stretched out her hands to the old knight.

'Here you be in a pitiful and afflicted land from which the saints have been driven out; have you struck one blow for the saints of God? Nay, you have held your peace. Here you be where good men have been sent to the block: have you decried their fates? You have seen noble and beloved women, holy priests, blessed nuns defiled and martyred; you have seen the poor despoiled; you have seen that knaves ruled by aid of the devil about a goodly king. Have you struck one blow? Have you whispered one word?'

The colour rushed into Margot Poins' huge cheeks. She kept her mouth open to drink in her mistress's words, and Throckmorton waved his hands in applause. Only Udal shuffled in his broken-toed shoes, and old Rochford smiled benignly and tapped his chest above the chains.

'I have struck good blows in the quarrels that were mine,' he answered.

Katharine wrung her hands.

'Sir, I have read it in books of chivalry, the province of a knight is to succour the Church of God, to defend the body of God, to set his lance in rest for the Mother of God; to defend noble men cast down, and noble women; to aid holy priests and blessed nuns; to succour the despoiled poor.'

'Nay, I have read no books of chivalry,' the old man answered; 'I cannot read.'

'Ah, there be pitiful things in this world,' Katharine said, and her chest was troubled.

'You should quote Hesiodus,' Cicely mocked her suddenly from her stool. 'I marked this text when all my menfolk were slain: πλείη μὲν γὰρ γαῖα, πλείη δέ θάλασσα so I have laughed ever since.'

Upon her, too, Katharine turned.

'You also,' she said; 'you also.'

'No, before God, I am no coward,' Cicely Elliott said.

'When all my menfolk were slain by the headsman something broke in my head, and ever since I have laughed. But before God, in my way I have tried to plague Cromwell. If he would have had my head he might have.'

'Yet what hast thou done for the Church of God?' Katharine said.

Cicely Elliott sprang to the floor and raised her hands with such violence that Throckmorton moved swiftly forward.

'What did the Church of God for me?' she cried. 'Guard your face from my nails ere you ask me that again. I had a father; I had two brothers; I had two men I loved passing well. They all died upon one day upon the one block. Did the saints of God save them? Go see their heads upon the gates of York?'

'But if they died for God His pitiful sake,' Katharine said—'if they did die in the quarrel of God's wounds——'

Cicely Elliott screamed, with her hands above her head. 'Is that not enow? Is that not enow?'

'Then it is I, not thou, that love them,' Katharine said; 'for I, not thou, shall carry on the work for which they died.'

'Oh gaping, pink-faced fool!' Cicely Elliott sneered at her.

She began to laugh, holding her black sides in, her face thrown back. Then she closed her mouth and stood smiling.

'You were made for a preacher, coney,' she said. 'Fine to hear thee belabouring my old, good knight with doughty words.'

'Gibe as thou wilt; scream as thou wilt——' Katharine began. Cicely Elliott tossed in on her words:

'My head ached so. I had the right of it to scream. I cannot be minded of my menfolk but my head will ache. But I love thy fine preaching. Preach on.'

Katharine raised herself from her chair.

'Words there must be that will move thee,' she said, 'if God will give them to me.'

'God hath withdrawn Himself from this world,' Cicely answered. 'All mankind goeth a-mumming.'

'It was another thing that Polycrates said.' Katharine, in spite of her emotion, was quick to catch the misquotation.

'Coney,' Cicely Elliott answered, 'all men wear masks; all men lie; all men desire the goods of all men and seek how they may get them.'

'But Cromwell being down, these things shall change,' Katharine answered. '*Res, aetas, usus, semper aliquid apportent novi.*'

Cicely Elliott fell back into her chair and laughed.

'What are we amongst that multitude?' she said. 'Listen to me: When my menfolk were cast to die, I flew to Gardiner to save them. Gardiner would not speak. Now is he Bishop of Winchester—for he had goods of my father's, and greased with them the way to his bishop's throne. Fanshawe is a goodly Papist; but Cromwell hath let him have goods of the Abbey of Bright. Will Fanshawe help thee to bring back the Church? Then he must give up his lands. Will Cranmer help thee? Will Miners? Coney, I loved Federan, a true man: Miners hath his land to-day, and Federan's mother starves. Will Miners help thee to gar the King do right? Then the mother of my love Federan must have Miners' land and the rents for seven years. Will Cranmer serve thee to bring back the Bishop of Rome? Why, Cranmer would burn.'

'But the poorer sort——' Katharine said.

'There is no man will help thee whose help will avail,' Cicely mocked at her. 'For hear me: No man now is up in the land that hath not goods of the Church; fields of the abbeys; spoons made of the parcel gilt from the shrines. There is no rich man now but is rich with stolen riches; there is no man now up that was not so set up. And the men that be down have lost their heads. Go dig in graves to find men that shall help thee.'

'Cromwell shall fall ere May goeth out,' Katharine said.

'Well, the King dotes upon thy sweet face. But Cromwell being down, there will remain the men he hath set up.

Be they lovers of the old faith, or thee? Now, thy pranks
will ruin all alike.'

'The King is minded to right these wrongs,' Katharine
protested hotly.

'The King! The King!' Cicely laughed. 'Thou lovest
the King ... Nay an thou lovest the King ... But to be
enamoured of the King ... And the King enamoured of
thee ... why, this pair of lovers cast adrift upon the
land——'

Katharine said:

'Belike I am enamoured of the King: belike the King of
me, I do not know. But this I know: he and I are minded
to right the wrongs of God.'

Cicely Elliott opened her eyes wide.

'Why, thou art a very infectious fanatic!' she said. 'You
may well do these things. But you must shed much blood.
You must widow many men's wives. Body of God! I
believe thou wouldst.'

'God forbid it!' Katharine said. 'But if He so willeth it,
fiat voluntas.'

'Why, spare no man,' Cicely answered. 'Thou shalt not
very easily escape.'

It was at this point that the magister was moved to keep
no longer silence.

'Now, by all the gods of high Olympus!' he cried out,
'such things shall not be alleged against me. For I do swear,
before Venus and all the saints, that I am your man.'

Nevertheless, it was Margot Poins, wavering between
her love for her magister and her love for her mistress, that
most truly was carried away by Katharine's eloquence.

'Mistress,' she said, and she indicated both the magister
and his tall and bearded companion, 'these two have made
up a pretty plot upon the stairs. There are in it papers
from Cleves and a matter of deceiving Privy Seal and thou
shouldst be kept in ignorance asking to—to——'

Her gruff voice failed and her blushes overcame her, so
that she wanted for a word. But upon the mention of
papers and Privy Seal the old knight fidgeted and faltered:

'Why, let us begone.' Cicely Elliott glanced from one to the other of them with a malicious glee, and Throckmorton's eyes blinked sardonically above his beard.

* * * *

It had been actually upon the stairs that he had come upon the magister, newly down from his horse, and both stiff and bruised, with Margot Poins hanging about his neck and begging him to spare her a moment. Throckmorton crept up the dark stairway with his shoes soled with velvet. The magister was seeking to disengage himself from the girl with the words that he had a treaty form of the Duke of Cleves in his bosom and must hasten on the minute to give it to her mistress.

'Before God!' Throckmorton had said behind his back, 'ye will do no such thing,' and Udal had shrieked out like a rabbit caught by a ferret in its bury. For here he had seemed to find himself caught by the chief spy of Privy Seal upon a direct treason against Privy Seal's self.

But, dragging alike the terrified magister and the heavy, blonde girl who clung to him out from the dark stairhead into the corridor, where, since no one could come upon them unseen or unheard, it was the safest place in the palace to speak, Throckmorton had whispered into his ear a long, swift speech in which he minced no matters at all.

The time, he said, was ripe to bring down Privy Seal. He himself—Throckmorton himself—loved Kat Howard with a love compared to which the magister's was a rushlight such as you bought fifty for a halfpenny. Privy Seal was ravening for a report of that treaty. They must, before all things, bring him a report that was false. For, for sure, upon that report Privy Seal would act, and, if they brought him a false report, Privy Seal would act falsely.

Udal stood perfectly still, looking at nothing, his thin brown hand clasped round his thin brown chin.

'But, above all,' Throckmorton had concluded, 'show ye no papers to Kat Howard. For it is very certain that she will have no falsehoods employed to bring down Privy

Seal, though she hate him as the Assyrian cockatrice hateth the symbol of the Cross.'

'Sir Throckmorton,' Margot Poins had uttered, 'though ye be a paid spy, ye speak true words there.'

He pulled his beard and blinked at her.

'I am minded to reform,' he said. 'Your mistress hath worked a miracle of conversion in me.'

She shrugged her great fair shoulders at this, and spoke to the magister:

'It is very true,' she said, 'that this spying knight affects my mistress. But whether it be for the love of virtue, or for the love of her body, or because the cat jumps that way and there he observeth fortune to rise, I leave to God who reads all hearts.'

'There speaks a wench brought up and taught by Protestants,' Throckmorton gibed pleasantly at her; 'or ye have caught the trick of Kat Howard, who, though she be a Papist as good as I, yet prates virtue like a Lutheran.'

'Ye lie!' Margot said; 'my mistress getteth her virtue from good letters.'

Throckmorton smiled at her again.

'Wench,' he said, 'in all save doctrine, this Kat Howard and her learning are nearer Lutheran than of the old faith.'

With his malice he set himself to bewilder Margot. They made a little, shadowy knot in the long corridor. For he wished to give Udal, who in his long gown stood deaf-faced, like a statue of contemplation, the time to come to a conclusion.

'Why, you are a very mean wag,' Margot said. 'I have heard my uncle—who is, as ye wot, a Protestant and a printer—I have heard him speak of Luther and of Bucer and of the word of God and suchlike canting books, but never once of Seneca and Tully, that my mistress loves.'

'Why, ye are learning the trick of tongues,' Throckmorton mocked. 'Please God, when your mistress cometh to be Queen—may He send it soon!—there shall be such a fashion and contagion of talking——'

Having his eyes on Udal, he broke off suddenly, and said with a harsh sharpness:

'I have given you time to make a resolution. Speak quickly. Will you come into our boat with us that will bring down Privy Seal?'

Udal winced, but Throckmorton held him by the wrist.

'Then unpouch quickly thy Cleves papers,' he said; 'we have but a little time to turn them round.'

Udal's thin hand sought nervously the opening of his jerkin beneath his gown: he drew it back, moved it forward again, and stood quivering with doubt.

Throckmorton stood vaingloriously back upon his feet and combed his great beard with his white fingers.

'Magister,' he uttered triumphantly, 'well you wot that such a man as you cannot plot for himself alone; you will make naught of your treasure trove save a cleft neck!'

And, furtively, cringing back into the dark hangings, a bent, broken figure like a miser unpouching his gold, Udal undid his breast lacings.

*   *   *   *

It was hot from this colloquy that Margot Poins had led the two men in upon her mistress in her large dim room. Because she hated the great spy, since he loved Kat Howard and had undone many good men with false tales, she had not been able to keep her tongue from seeking to wound him.

'Ye are too true to mix in plots,' she brought out gruffly.

Cicely Rochford came close to Katharine and measured her neck with the span of her small hand.

'There is room!' she said. 'Hast a long and a straight neck.'

Her husband muttered that he liked not these talkings. By diligent avoidance of such, he had kept his own hair and neck uncut in troublesome times.

'I will take thee to another place,' Cicely threw at him over her shoulder. 'Shalt kiss me in a dark room. It is very certain maids' talk is no fit hearing for thy jolly old ears.'

She took him delicately at the end of his short white beard between her long finger and thumb, and, with her high and mincing step, led him through the door.

'God save this room, where all the virtues bide!' she cried out, and drew her overskirt closer to her as she passed near the great, bearded spy.

Katharine turned and faced Throckmorton.

'It is even as the maid saith,' she uttered. 'I am too true to mix in plots.'

'Neither will ye give us to death!' Throckmorton faced her back so that she paused for breath, and the pause lasted a full minute.

'Sir,' she said, 'I do give you a fair and a full warning that, if you do plot against Privy Seal, and if knowledge of your plotting cometh to mine ears—though I ask not to know of them—I will tell of your plottings——'

'Oh, before God!' Udal cried out, 'I have suckled you with learned writers; I have carried letters for you; will you give me to die?' and Margot wailed from a deep chest: 'The magister so well hath loved thee. Give him not into the hands of Cur Crummock!—would I had never told thee that they plotted!'

'Fool!' Throckmorton said; 'it is to the King she will go with her tales.' He sat down upon her yellow-wood table and swung one crimson leg before the other, laughing gleefully at Katharine's astonished face.

'Sir,' she said at last; 'it is true that I will go, not to my lord Privy Seal, but to the King.'

Throckmorton held up one of his white hands to the light and, with the other, smoothed down its little finger.

'See you?' he gibed softly at Margot. 'How better I guess this thing, mistress, than thou. For I do know her better.'

Katharine looked at him with a soft glance and said pitifully:

'Nevertheless, what shall it profit thee if I take a tale of thy treasons to the King's Highness?'

Throckmorton sprang from the table and clapped his
heels together on the floor.

'It shall get me made an earl,' he said. 'The King will
do that much for the man that shall rid him of his
minister.' He reflected foxily and for a quick moment.
'Before God!' he said, 'take this tale to the King, for it is
the true tale: That the Duke of Cleves seeks, in France, to
have done with his alliance. He will no more cleave to his
brother-in-law, but will make submission to the Emperor
and to Rome!'

He paused, and then finished:

'For that news the King shall love you much more than
before. But God help me! it takes thee the more out of
my reach!'

As they left the room to go to the audience with Cromwell, Katharine, squaring the frills of her hood behind her
back, could hear Margot Poins grumbling to the magister:

'After these long days ye ha' time for five minutes to
hold my hand,' and the magister, perturbed and fumbling
in his bosom, muttered:

'Nay, I have no minutes now. I must write much in
Latin ere thy mistress return.'

VI

'By God,' Wriothesley said when she entered the long
gallery where the men were. 'This is a fair woman!'

She had command of her features, and her eyes were
upon the ground; it was a part of a woman's upbringing
to walk well, and her masters had so taught her when she
had lived with her grandmother, the old duchess. Not the
tips of her shoes shewed beneath the zigzag folds of her
russet-brown underskirt; the tips of her scarlet sleeves
netted with gold touched the waxed wood of the floor; her
hood fell behind to the ground, and her fair hair was
golden where the sunlight fell on it with a last, watery ray.

Upon Privy Seal she raised her eyes; she bent her knees

so that her gown spread out all around her when she
curtsied, and, having arranged it with a slow hand, she
came to her height again, rustling as if she rose from a
wave.

'Sir,' she said, 'I come to pray you to right a great wrong
done by your servants.'

'By God!' Wriothesley said, 'she speaks high words.'

'Madam Howard,' Cromwell answered—and his eyes
graciously dwelt upon her tall form. She had clasped her
hands before her lap and looked into his face. 'Madam
Howard, you are more learned in the better letters than I;
but I would have you call to memory one Pancrates, of
whom telleth Lucian. Being in a desert or elsewhere, this
magician could turn sticks, stocks and stakes into servants
that did his will. Mark you, they did his will—no more
and no less.'

'Sir,' Katharine said, 'ye have better servants than ever
had Pancrates. They do more than your behests.'

Cromwell bent his back, stretched aside his white hand
and smiled still.

'Ye trow truth,' he said. 'Yet ye do me wrong; for had
I the servants of Pancrates, assuredly he should hear no
groans of injustice from men of good will.'

'It is too good hearing,' Katharine said gravely. 'This is
my tale——'

Once before she had trembled in this man's presence,
and still she had a catching in the throat as her eyes
measured his face. She was mad to do right and to right
wrongs, yet in his presence the doing of the right, the
righting of wrongs, seemed less easy than when she stood
before any other man. 'Sir,' she uttered, 'I have thought
ye have done ill afore now. I am nowise certain that ye
thought your ill-doing an evil. I beseech you for a patient
hearing.'

But, though she told her story well—and it was an old
story that she had learned by heart—she could not be rid
of the feeling that this was a less easy matter than it had
seemed to her, to call Cromwell accursed. She had a

moving tale of wrongs done by Cromwell's servant, Dr Barnes, a visitor of a church in Lincolnshire near where her home had been. For the lands had been taken from a little priory upon an excuse that the nuns lived a lewd life; and so well had she known the nuns, going in and out of the convent every week-day, that well she knew the falseness of Cromwell's servant's tale.

'Sir,' she said to Cromwell, 'mine own foster-sister had the veil there; mine own mother's sister was there the abbess.' She stretched out a hand. 'Sir, they dwelled there simply and godly, withdrawn from the world; succouring the poor; weaving of fine linens, for much flax grew upon those lands by there; and praying God and the saints that blessings fall upon this land.'

Wriothesley spoke to her slowly and heavily:

'Such little abbeys ate up the substance of this land in the old days. Well have we prospered since they were done away who ate up the fatness of this realm. Now husbandmen till their idle soil and cattle are in their buildings.'

'Gentleman whose name I know not,' she turned upon him, 'more wealth and prosperity God granted us in answer to their prayers than could be won by all the husbandmen of Arcadia and all the kine of Cacus. God standeth above all men's labours.' But Cromwell's servants had sworn away the lands of the small abbey, and now the abbess and her nuns lay in gaol accused—and falsely—of having secreted an image of Saint Hugh to pray against the King's fortunes.

'Before God,' she said, 'and as Christ is my Saviour, I saw and make deposition that these poor simple women did no such thing but loved the King as he had been their good father. I have seen them at their prayers. Before God, I say to you that they were as folk astonished and dismayed; knowing so little of the world that ne one ne other knew whence came the word that had bared them to the skies. I have seen them—I.'

'Where went they?' Wriothesley said; 'what worked they?'

'Gentleman,' she answered; 'being cast out of their houses and their veils, they knew nowhither to go; homes they had none; they lived with their own hinds in hovels, like frightened lambs, the saints their pastors being driven from their folds.'

'Aye,' Wriothesley said grimly, 'they cumbered the ground; they did meet in knots for mutinies.'

'God had appointed them the duty of prayer,' Katharine answered him. 'They met and prayed in sheds and lodges of the house that had been theirs, poor ghosts revisiting and bewailing their earthly homes. I have prayed with them.'

'Ye have done a treason in that day,' Wriothesley answered.

'I have done the best that ever I did for this land,' she met him fully. 'I prayed naught against the King and the republic. I have prayed you and your like might be cast down. So do I still. I stand here to avow it. But they never did, and they do lie in gaol.' She turned again upon Cromwell and spoke piteously from her full throat. 'My lord,' she cried. 'Soften your heart and let the wax in your ears melt so that ye hear. Your servants swore falsely when they said these women lived lewdly; your men swore falsely when they said that these women prayed treasonably. For the one count they took their lands and houses; for the other they lay them in the gaols. Sir, my lord, your servants go up and down this land; sir, my lord, they ride rich men with boots of steel and do strangle the poor with gloves of iron. I do think ye know they do it; I do pray ye know not. But, sir, if ye will right this wrong I will kiss your hands; if you will set up again these homes of prayer I will take a veil, and in one of them spend my days praying that good befall you and yours.' She paused in her speaking and then began again: 'Before I came here I had made me a fair speech. I have forgot it, and words come haltingly to me. Sirs, ye think I seek mine own aggrandisement; ye think I do wish ye cast down. Before God, I wish ye were cast down if ye continue in these ways; but I have prayed to God who sent the Pentecostal fires, to give me the gift of tongues that shall soften your hearts——'

Cromwell interrupted her, smiling that Venus, who made her so fair, gave her no need of a gift of tongues, and Minerva, who made her so learned, gave her no need of fairness. For the sake of the one and the other, he would very diligently enquire into these women's courses. If they ha been guiltless, they should be richly repaid; if they ha been guilty, they should be pardoned.

Katharine flushed with a hot anger.

'Ye are a very craven lord,' she said. 'If you may find them guilty, you shall have my head. But if you do find them innocent and shield them not, I swear I will strive to have thine.' Anger made her blue eyes dilate. 'Have you no bowels of compassion for the right? Ye treat me as a fair woman—but I speak as a messenger of the King's, that is God's, to men who too long have hardened their hearts.'

Throckmorton laid back his head and laughed suddenly at the ceiling; Cranmer crossed himself; Wriothesley beat his heel upon the floor and shrugged his shoulders bitterly —but Lascelles, the Archbishop's spy, kept his eyes upon Throckmorton's face with a puzzled scrutiny.

'Why now does that man laugh?' he asked himself. For it seemed to him that by laughing Throckmorton applauded Katharine Howard. And indeed, Throckmorton applauded Katharine Howard. As policy her speech was neither here nor there, but as voicing a spirit, infectious and winning to men's hearts, he saw that such speaking should carry her very far. And, if it should embroil her more than ever with Cromwell, it would the further serve his adventures. He was already conspiring to betray Cromwell, and he knew that, very soon now, Cromwell must pierce his mask of loyalty; and the more Katharine should have cast down her glove to Cromwell, the more he could shelter behind her; and the more men she could have made her friends with her beauty and her fine speeches, the more friends he too should have to his back when the day of discovery came. In the meantime he had in his sleeve a trick that he would speedily play upon Cromwell, the most dangerous of any that he had played. For below the stairs he had Udal, with his news of the envoy from Cleves to France, and with his copies of the envoy's letters. But, in her turn, Katharine played him, unwittingly enough, a trick that puzzled him.

'Bones of St Nairn!' he said; 'she has him to herself. What mad prank will she play now?'

Katharine had drawn Cromwell to the very end of the gallery.

'As I pray that Christ will listen to my pleas when at the last I come to Him for pardon and comfort,' she said, 'I swear that I will speak true words to you.'

He surveyed her, plump, alert, his lips moving one upon the other. He brought one white soft hand from behind his back to play with the furs upon his chest.

'Why, I believe you are a very earnest woman,' he said.

'Then, sir,' she said, 'understand that your sun is near its setting. We rise, we wane; our little days do run their course. But I do believe you love your King his cause more than most men.'

'Madam Howard,' he said, 'you have been my foremost foe.'

'Till five minutes agone I was,' she said.

He wondered for a moment if she were minded to beg him to aid her in growing to be Queen; and he wondered too how that might serve his turn. But she spoke again:

'You have very well served the King,' she said. 'You have made him rich and potent. I believe ye have none other desire so great as that desire to make him potent and high in this world's gear.'

'Madam Howard,' he said calmly, 'I desire that—and next to found for myself a great house that always shall serve the throne as well as I.'

She gave him the right to that with a lowering of her eyebrows.

'I too would see him a most high prince,' she said. 'I

would see him shed lustre upon his friends, terror upon his foes, and a great light upon this realm and age.'

She paused to touch him earnestly with one long hand, and to brush back a strand of her hair. Down the gallery she saw Lascelles moving to speak with Throckmorton and Wriothesley holding the Archbishop earnestly by the sleeve.

'See,' she said, 'you are surrounded now by traitors that will bring you down. In foreign lands your cause wavers. I tell you, five minutes agone I wished you swept away.'

Cromwell raised his eyebrows.

'Why, I knew that this was difficult fighting,' he said. 'But I know not what giveth me your good wishes.'

'My lord,' she answered, 'it came to me in my mind: What man is there in the land save Privy Seal that so loveth his master's cause?'

Cromwell laughed.

'How well do you love this King,' he said.

'I love this King; I love this land,' she said, 'as Cato loved Rome or Leonidas his realm of Sparta.'

Cromwell pondered, looking down at his foot; his lips moved furtively, he folded his hand inside his sleeves; and he shook his head when again she made to speak. He desired another minute for thought.

'This I perceive to be the pact you have it in your mind to make,' he said at last, 'that if you come to sway the King towards Rome I shall still stay his man and yours?'

She looked at him, her lips parted with a slight surprise that he should so well have voiced thoughts that she had hardly put into words. Then her faith rose in her again and moved her to pitiful earnestness.

'My lord,' she uttered, and stretched out one hand. 'Come over to us. 'Tis such great pity else—'tis such pity else.'

She looked again at Throckmorton, who, in the distance, was surveying the Archbishop's spy with a sardonic amusement, and a great mournfulness went through her. For there was the traitor and here before her was the betrayed.

Throckmorton had told her enough to know that he was conspiring against his master, and Cromwell trusted Throckmorton before any man in the land; and it was as if she saw one man with a dagger hovering behind another. With her woman's instinct she felt that the man about to die was the better man, though he were her foe. She was minded—she was filled with a great desire to say: 'Believe no word that Throckmorton shall tell you. The Duke of Cleves is now abandoning your cause.' That much she had learnt from Udal five minutes before. But she could not bring herself to betray Throckmorton, who was a traitor for the sake of her cause. ' 'Tis such pity,' she repeated again.

'Good wench,' Cromwell said, 'you are indifferent honest; but never while I am the King's man shall the Bishop of Rome take toll again in the King's land.'

She threw up her hands.

'Alack!' she said; 'shall not God and His Son our Saviour have their part of the King's glory?'

'God is above us all,' he answered. 'But there is no room for two heads of a State, and in a State is room but for one army. I will have my King so strong that ne Pope ne priest ne noble ne people shall here have speech or power. So it is now; I have so made it, the King helping me. Before I came this was a distracted State; the King's writ ran not in the east, not in the west, not in the north, and hardly in the south parts. Now no lord nor no bishop nor no Pope raises head against him here. And, God willing, in all the world no prince shall stand but by grace of this King's Highness. This land shall have the wealth of all the world; this King shall guide this land. There shall be rich husbandmen paying no toll to priests, but to the King alone; there shall be wealthy merchants paying no tax to any prince nor emperor, but only to this King. The King's court shall redress all wrongs; the King's voice shall be omnipotent in the council of the princes.'

'Ye speak no word of God,' she said pitifully.

'God is very far away,' he answered.

'Sir, my lord,' she cried, and brushed again the tress from her forehead. 'Ye have made this King rich with gear of the Church: if ye will be friends with me ye shall make this King a pauper to repay; ye have made this King stiffen his neck against God's Vicegerent: if you and I shall work together ye shall make him re-humble himself. Christ the King of all the world was a pauper; Christ the Saviour of all mankind humbled Himself before God that was His Saviour.'

Cromwell said 'Amen.'

'Sir,' she said again; 'ye have made this King rich, but I will give to him again his power to sleep at night; ye have made this realm subject to this King, but, by the help of God, I will make it subject again to God. You have set up here a great State, but oh, the children of God do weep since ye came. Where is a town where lamentation is not heard? where is a town where no orphan or widow bewails the day that saw your birth?' She had sobs in her voice and she wrung her hands. 'Sir,' she cried, 'I say you are as a dead man already—your day of pride is past, whether ye aid us or no. Set yourself then to redress as heartily as ye have set yourself in the past to make sad. That land is blest whose people are happy; that State is aggrandised whence there arise songs praising God for His blessings. You have built up a great city of groans; set yourself now to build a kingdom where "Praise God" shall be sung. It is a contented people that makes a State great; it is the love of God that maketh a people rich.'

Cromwell laughed mirthlessly:

'There are forty thousand men like Wriothesley in England,' he said. 'God help you if you come against them; there are forty times forty thousand and forty times that that pray you not again to set disorder loose in this land. I have broken all stiff necks in this realm. See you that you come not against some yet.' He stopped, and added: 'Your greatest foes should be your own friends if I be a dead man as you say.' And he smiled at her bewilderment when he had added: 'I am your bulwark and your safeguard.'

... 'For, listen to me,' he took up again his parable. 'Whilst I be here I bear the rancour of your friends' hatred. When I am gone you shall inherit it.'

'Sir,' she said, 'I am not here to hear riddles, but here I am to pray you seek the right.'

'Wench,' he said pleasantly, 'there are in this world many rights—you have yours; I mine. But mine can never be yours nor yours mine. I am not yet so dead as ye say; but if I be dead, I wish you so well that I will send you a phial of poison ere I send to take you to the stake. For it is certain that if you have not my head I shall have yours.'

She looked at him seriously, though the tears ran down her cheeks.

'Sir,' she uttered, 'I do take you to be a man of your word. Swear to me, then, that if upon the fatal hill I do save you your life and your estates, you will nowise work the undoing of the Church in time to come.'

'Madam Queen that shall be,' he said, 'an ye gave me my life this day, to-morrow I would work as I worked yesterday. If ye have faith of your cause I have the like of mine.'

She hung her head, and said at last:

'Sir, an ye have a little door here at the gallery end I will go out by it'; for she would not again face the men who made the little knot before the window. He moved the hangings aside and stood before the aperture smiling.

'Ye came to ask a boon of me,' he said. 'Is it your will still that I grant it?'

'Sir,' she answered, 'I asked a boon of you that I thought you would not grant, so that I might go to the King and shew him your evil dealings with his lieges.'

'I knew it well,' he said. 'But the King will not cast me down till the King hath had full use of me.'

'You have a very great sight into men's minds,' she uttered, and he laughed noiselessly once again.

'I am as God made me,' he said. Then he spoke once

more. 'I will read your mind if you will. Ye came to me in this crisis, thinking with yourself: *Liars go unto the King saying, "This Cromwell is a traitor; cast him down, for he seeks your ill." I will go unto the King saying, "This Cromwell grindeth the faces of the poor and beareth false witness. Cast him down, though he serve you well, since he maketh your name to stink to heaven."* So I read my fellow-men.'

'Sir,' she said, 'it is very true that I will not be linked with liars. And it is very true that men do so speak of you to the King's Highness.'

'Why,' he answered her debonairly, 'the King shall listen neither to them nor to you till the day be come. Then he will act in his own good way—upon the pretext that I be a traitor, or upon the pretext that I have borne false witness, or upon no pretext at all.'

'Nevertheless will I speak for the truth that shall prevail,' she answered.

'Why, God help you!' was his rejoinder.

*   *   *   *

Going back to his friends in the window Cromwell meditated that it was possible to imagine a woman that thought so simply; yet it was impossible to imagine one that should be able to act with so great a simplicity. On the one hand, if she stayed about the King she should be his safeguard, for it was very certain that she should not tell the King that he was a traitor. And that above all was what Cromwell had to fear. He had, for his own purposes, so filled the King with the belief that treachery overran his land, that the King saw treachery in every man. And Cromwell was aware, well enough, that such of his adherents as were Protestant—such men as Wriothesley—had indeed boasted that they were twenty thousand swords ready to fall upon even the King if he set against the reforming religion in England. This was the greatest danger that he had—that an enemy of his should tell the King that

Privy Seal had behind his back twenty thousand swords. For that side of the matter Katharine Howard was even a safeguard, since with her love of truth she would assuredly combat these liars with the King.

But, on the other hand, the King had his superstitious fears; only that night, pale, red-eyed and heavy, and being unable to sleep, he had sent to rouse Cromwell and had furiously rated him, calling him knave and shaking him by the shoulder, telling him for the twentieth time to find a way to make a peace with the Bishop of Rome. These were only night-fears—but, if Cleves should desert Henry and Protestantism, if all Europe should stand solid for the Pope, Henry's night-fears might eat up his day as well. Then indeed Katharine would be dangerous. So that she was indeed half foe, half friend.

It hinged all upon Cleves; for if Cleves stood friend to Protestantism the King would fear no treason; if Cleves sued for pardon to the Emperor and Rome, Henry must swing towards Katharine. Therefore, if Cleves stood firm to Protestantism and defied the Emperor, it would be safe to work at destroying Katharine; if not, he must leave her by the King to defend his very loyalty.

The Archbishop challenged him with uplifted questioning eyebrows, and he answered his gaze with:

'God help ye, goodman Bishop; it were easier for thee to deal with this maid than for me. She would take thee to her friend if thou wouldst curry with Rome.'

'Aye,' Cranmer answered. 'But would Rome have truck with me?' and he shook his head bitterly. He had been made Archbishop with no sanction from Rome.

Cromwell turned upon Wriothesley; the debonair smile was gone from his face; the friendly contempt that he had for the Archbishop was gone too; his eyes were hard, cruel and red, his lips hardened.

'Ye have done me a very evil turn,' he said. 'Ye spoke stiffnecked folly to this lady. Ye shall learn, Protestants that ye are, that if I be the flail of the monks I may be a hail, a lightning, a bolt from heaven upon Lutherans that cross the King.'

The hard malice of his glance made Wriothesley quail and flush heavily.

'I thought ye had been our friend,' he said.

'Wriothesley,' Cromwell answered, 'I tell thee, silly knave, that I be friend only to them that love the order and peace I have made, under the King's Highness, in this realm. If it be the King's will to stablish again the old faith, a hammer of iron will I be upon such as do raise their heads against it. It were better ye had never been born, it were better ye were dead and asleep, than that ye raised your heads against me.' He turned, then he swung back with the sharpness of a viper's spring.

'What help have I had of thee and thy friends? I have bolstered up Cleves and his Lutherans for ye. What have he and ye done for me and my King? Your friend the Duke of Cleves has an envoy in Paris. Have ye found for why he comes there? Ye could not. Ye have botched your errand to Paris; ye have spoken naughtily in my house to a friend of the King's that came friendlily to me.' He shook a fat finger an inch from Wriothesley's eyes. 'Have a care! I did send my visitors to smell out treason among the convents and abbeys. Wait ye till I send them to your conventicles! Ye shall not scape. Body of God! ye shall not scape.'

He placed a heavy hand upon Throckmorton's shoulder.

'I would I had sent thee to Paris,' he said. 'No envoy had come there whose papers ye had not seen. I warrant thou wouldst have ferreted them through.'

Throckmorton's eyes never moved; his mouth opened and he spoke with neither triumph nor malice:

'In very truth, Privy Seal,' he said, 'I have ferreted through enow of them to know why the envoy came to Paris.'

Cromwell kept his hands still firm upon his spy's shoulder whilst the swift thoughts ran through his mind. He scowled still upon Wriothesley.

'Sir,' he said, 'ye see how I be served. What ye could not find in Paris my man found for me in London town.' He moved his face round towards the great golden beard of his spy. 'Ye shall have the farms ye asked me for in Suffolk,' he said. 'Tell me now wherefore came the Cleves envoy to France. Will Cleves stay our ally, or will he send like a coward to his Emperor?'

'Privy Seal,' Throckmorton answered expressionlessly— he fingered his beard for a moment and felt at the medal depending upon his chest—'Cleves will stay your friend and the King's ally.'

A great sigh went up from his three hearers at Throckmorton's lie; and impassive as he was, Throckmorton sighed too, imperceptibly beneath the mantle of his beard. He had burned his boats. But for the others the sigh was of a great contentment. With Cleves to lead the German Protestant confederation, the King felt himself strong enough to make headway against the Pope, the Emperor and France. So long as the Duke of Cleves remained a rebel against his lord the Emperor, the King would hold over Protestantism the mantle of his protection.

Cromwell broke in upon their thoughts with his swift speech.

'Sirs,' he uttered, 'then what ye will shall come to pass. Wriothesley, I pardon thee; get thee back to Paris to thy mission. Archbishop, I trow thou shalt have the head of that wench. Her cousin shall be brought here again from France.'

Lascelles, the Archbishop's spy, who kept his gaze upon Throckmorton's, saw the large man's eyes shift suddenly from one board of the floor to another.

'That man is not true,' he said to himself, and fell into a train of musing. But from the others Cromwell had secured the meed of wonder that he desired. He had closed the interview with a dramatic speech; he had given them something to talk of.

VII

He held Throckmorton in the small room that contained upon its high stand the Privy Seal of England in an embroidered purse. All red and gold, this symbol of power held the eye away from the dark-green tapestry and from the pigeon-holes filled with parchment scrolls wherefrom there depended so many seals each like a gout of blood. The room was so high that it appeared small, but there was room for Cromwell to pace about, and here, walking from wall to wall, he evolved those schemes that so fast held down the realm. He paced always, his hands behind his back, his lips moving one upon the other as if he ruminated—(His foes said that he talked thus with his familiar fiend that had the form of a bee)—and his black cap with ear-flaps always upon his head, for he suffered much with the earache.

He walked now, up and down and up and down, saying nothing, whilst from time to time Throckmorton spoke a word or two. Throckmorton himself had his doubts— doubts as to how the time when it would be safe to let it be known that he had betrayed his master might be found to fit in with the time when his master must find that he had betrayed him. He had, as he saw it, to gain time for Katharine Howard so she might finally enslave the King's desires. That there was one weak spot in her armour he thought he knew, and that was her cousin that was said to be her lover. That Cromwell knew of her weak spot he knew too; that Cromwell through that would strike at her he knew too. All depended upon whether he could gain time so that Cromwell should be down before he could use his knowledge.

For that reason he had devised the scheme of making Cromwell feel a safety about the affairs of Cleves. Udal fortunately wrote a very swift Latin. Thus, when going to fetch Katharine to her interview with Privy Seal he had found Udal bursting with news of the Cleves embassy and

with the letters of the Duke of Cleves actually copied on
papers in his poke, Throckmorton had very swiftly advised
with himself how to act. He had set Udal very earnestly to
writing a false letter from Cleves to France—such a letter
as Cleves might have written—and this false letter, in the
magister's Latin, he had placed now in his master's hands,
and, pacing up and down, Cromwell read from time to
time from the scrap of paper.

What Cleves had written was that he was fain to make
submission to the Emperor, and leave the King's alliance.
What Cromwell read was this: That the high and mighty
Prince, the Duke of Cleves, was firmly minded to adhere
in his allegiance with the King of England: that he feared
the wrath of the Emperor Charles, who was his very good
suzerain and over-lord: that if by taxes and tributes he
might keep away from his territory the armies of the
Emperor he would be well content to pay a store of gold:
that he begged his friend and uncle, King of France, to
intercede betwixt himself and the Emperor to the end that
the Emperor might take these taxes and tributes; for that,
if the Emperor would none of this, come peace, come war,
he, the high and mighty Prince, Duke of Cleves, Elector
of the Empire, was minded to protect in Germany the
Protestant confession and to raise against the Emperor the
Princes and Electors of Almain, being Protestants. With
the aid of his brother-in-law the King of England he would
drive the Emperor Charles from the German lands together with the heresies of the Romish Bishop and all
things that pertained to the Emperor Charles and his
religion.

Cromwell had listened to the reading of this letter in
silence; in silence he re-perused it himself, pacing up and
down, and in between phrases of his thoughts he read
passages from it and nodded his head.

That this was a very dangerous enterprise Throckmorton was assured; it was the first overt act of his that
Privy Seal could discover in him as a treachery. In a month
or six weeks he must know the truth; but in a month or

six weeks Katharine must have so enslaved the King that all danger from Cromwell would be past. And he trusted that the security that Cromwell must feel would gar him delay striking at Katharine by means of her cousin.

Cromwell said suddenly:

'How got the magister these papers?' and Throckmorton answered that it was through the widow that kept the tavern. Cromwell said negligently:

'Let the magister be rewarded with ten crowns a quarter to his fees. Set it down in my tables'; and then like lightning came the query:

'Do ye believe of her cousin and the Lady Katharine?'

Craving a respite for thought and daring to take none for fear Cromwell should read him, Throckmorton answered:

'Ye know I think yes.'

'I have said I think no,' Cromwell answered in turn, but dispassionately as though it were a matter of the courses of stars; 'though it is very certain that her cousin is so mad with love for her that we had much ado to send him from her to Paris.' He paced three times from wall to wall and then spoke again:

'Men enow have said she was too fond with her cousin?'

With despair in his heart Throckmorton answered:

'It is the common talk in Lincolnshire where her home is. I have seen a cub in a cowherd's that was said to be her child by him.'

It was useless to speak otherwise to Privy Seal; if he did not report these things, twenty others would. But, beneath his impassive face and his great beard, despair filled him. He might swear treason against Cromwell to the King; but the King would not hear him alone, and without the King and Katharine he was a sparrow in Cromwell's hawk's talons.

'Why,' Cromwell said, 'since Cleves is true to us we will have this woman down. An he had played us false I would have kept her near the King.'

This saying, that ran so counter to Throckmorton's schemes, caused him such dismay that he cried out:

'God forgive us, why?'

Cromwell smiled at him as one who smiles from a great height, and pointed a finger.

'This is a hard fight,' he said; 'we are in some straits. I trow ye would have voiced it otherwise.' And then he voiced his own idea—that so long as Cleves was friends with him Katharine was an enemy; if Cleves fell away she was none the less an enemy, but she would, from her love of justice, bear witness to the King that Cromwell was no traitor. 'And ye shall be very certain,' he added pleasantly, 'that once men see the King so inclined, they will go to the King saying I be a traitor, with Protestants like Wriothesley ready to rise and aid me. In that pass the Lady Katharine should stay by me, in the King's ear.'

A deep and intolerable dejection overcame Throckmorton and forced from his lips the words:

'Ye reason most justly.' And again he cursed himself, for he had forced Cromwell to this reasoning and action. Yet he dared not say that his news of the Cleves embassy was false, that Cleves indeed was minded to turn traitor, and that it most would serve Privy Seal's turn to stay Katharine Howard up. He dared not say the words, yet he saw his safety crumbling, and he saw Privy Seal set to ruin both himself and Katharine Howard. For in his heart he could not believe that the woman was virtuous, since he believed that no woman was virtuous who had been given the opportunity for joyment. As a spy, he had gone nosing about in Lincolnshire where Katharine's home had been near her cousin's. He had heard many tales against her such as rustics will tell against the daughters of poor lords like Katharine's father. And these tales, before ever he had come to love her, he had set down in Privy Seal's private registers. Now they were like to undo him and her. And in truth, according to his premonitions, Cromwell spoke:

'We shall bring very quickly Thomas Culpepper, her cousin, back from France. We shall inflame his mind with jealousy of the King. We shall find a place where he shall

burst upon the King and her together. We shall bring
witnesses enow from Lincolnshire to swear against her.'

He crossed his hands behind his back.

'This work of fetching her cousin from Paris I will put
into the hands of Viridus,' he said. 'I believe her to be
virtuous, therefore do you bring many witnesses, and some
that shall swear to have seen her in the act. That shall be
your employment. For I tell you she hath so great a power
of pleading that, being innocent, she will with difficulty be
proved unchaste.'

Throckmorton's head hung upon his shoulders.

'Remember,' Privy Seal said again, 'you and Viridus
shall send to find her cousin in France. Fill him with tales
that his cousin plays the leman with the King. He shall
burst here like a bolt from heaven. You will find him
betwixt Calais and Paris town, dallying in evil places without a doubt. We sent him thither to frighten Cardinal Pole.'

'Aye,' Throckmorton said, his mind filled with other and
bitter thoughts. 'He hath frightened the Cardinal from
Paris by the mere renown of his violence.'

'Then let him do some frighting in our goodly town of
London,' Cromwell said.

PART TWO

THE DISTANT CLOUD

I

THE young Poins, once an ensign of the King's guard,
habited now in grey, stood awaiting Thomas Culpepper,
Katharine Howard's cousin, beneath the new gateway towards the east of Calais. Four days he had waited already
and never had he dared to stir, save when the gates were
closed for the night. But it had chanced that one of the
gatewardens was a man from Lincolnshire—a man, once
a follower of the plough, whose father had held a farm in
the having of Culpepper himself.

'——But he sold 'un,' Nicholas Hogben said, 'sold 'un
clear away.' He made a wry face, winked one eye, and
drawing up the right corner of his mouth, displayed square,
huge teeth. The young Poins making no question, he repeated twice: 'Clear away. Right clear away.'

Poins, however, could hold but one thing of a time in
his head. And, by that striving, dangerous servant of Lord
Privy Seal, Throckmorton, it had been firmly enjoined
upon him that he must not fail to meet Thomas Culpepper
and stay him upon his road to England. Throckmorton,
with his great beard and cruel snake's eyes, had said: 'I
hold thy head in fee. If ye would save it, meet Thomas
Culpepper in Calais and give him this letter.' The letter
he had in his poke. It carried with it a deed making
Culpepper lieutenant of the stone barges in Calais. But he
had it too, by word of mouth, that if Thomas Culpepper
would not be stayed by the letter, he, Hal Poins, must stay
him—with the sword, with a stab in the back, or by being

311

stabbed himself and calling in the guard to lay Thomas
Culpepper's self by the heels.

'You will enjoin upon him,' Throckmorton had said,
'how goodly a thing is the lieutenancy of stone lighters that
in this letter is proffered him. You will tell him that, if a
barge of stone go astray, it is yet a fair way to London,
and stone fetches good money from townsmen building in
Calais. If he will gainsay this you will pick a quarrel with
him, as by saying he gives you the lie. In short,' Throckmorton had finished, earnestly and with a sinuous grace of
gesture in his long and narrow hands, 'you will stay him.'

It was a desperate measure, yet it was the best he could
compass. If Culpepper came to London, if he came to the
King, Katharine's fortunes were not worth a rushlight such
as were sold at twenty for a farthing. He knew, too, that
Viridus had Cromwell's earnest injunctions to send a messenger that should hasten Culpepper's return; and, though
he had seven hundred of Cromwell's spies that he could
trust to do Privy Seal's errand, he had not one that he
could trust to do his own. There was no one of them that
he could trust. If he took a spy and said: 'At all costs
stay Culpepper, but observe very strict secrecy from Privy
Seal's men all,' the spy would very certainly let the news
come to Privy Seal.

It was in this pass that the thought of the young Poins
had come to him. Here was a fellow absolutely stupid. He
was a brother of Katharine Howard's tiring maid who had
already come near to losing his head in a former intrigue
in the Court. He had, at the instigation of his sister, carried
two Papist letters of Katharine Howard. And, if it was the
King who pardoned him, it was Throckmorton who first
had taken him prisoner; it was Throckmorton who had
advised him to lie hidden in his grandfather's house for a
month or two. At the time Throckmorton had had no
immediate reason to give the boy this counsel. Poins had
been so small a tool in the past embroilment of Katharine's
letter that, had he gone straight back to his post in the
yeomanry of the King's guard, no man would have noticed

him. But it had always been part of the devious and great
bearded man's policy—it had been part of his very nature
—to play upon people's fears, to trouble them with appre-
hensions. It was part of the tradition that Cromwell had
given all his men. He ruled England by such fears.

Thus Throckmorton had sent Poins trembling to hide
in the old printer's his grandfather's house in the wilds of
Austin Friars. And Throckmorton had impressed upon
him that he alone had really saved him. It was in his grandfather's mean house that Poins had remained for a brace
of months, grumbled at by his Protestant uncle and
sneered at by his malicious Papist grandfather. And it was
here that Throckmorton had found him, dressed in grey,
humbled from his pride and raging for things to do.

The boy would be of little service—yet he was all that
Throckmorton had. If he could hardly be expected to trick
Culpepper with his tongue, he might wound him with his
sword; if he could not kill him he might at least scotch
him, cause a brawl in Calais town, where, because the place
was an outpost, brawling was treason, and Culpepper
might be had by the heels for long enough to let Cromwell
fall. Therefore, in the low room with the black presses, in
the very shadow of Cromwell's own walls, Throckmorton
—who was given the privacy of the place by the Lutheran
printer because he was Cromwell's man—large, golden-
bearded and speaking in meaning whispers, with lifting of
his eyebrows, had held a long conference with the lad.

*   *   *   *

His dangerous and terrifying presence seemed to
dominate, for the young Poins, even the dusty archway of
the Calais gate—and, even though he saw the flat, green
and sunny levels of the French marshland, with the town
of Ardres rising grey and turreted six miles away, the
young Poins felt that he was still beneath the eyes of
Throckmorton, the spy who had sought him out in his
grandfather's house in Austin Friars to send him here
across the seas to Calais. Up above in the archway the

stonemasons who came from Lydd sang their Kentish songs as hammers clinked on chisels and the fine dust filtered through the scaffold boards. But the young Poins kept his eyes upon the dusty and winding road that threaded the dykes from Ardres, and thought only that when Thomas Culpepper came he must be stayed. He had oiled his sword that had been his father's so that it would slip smoothly from the scabbard; he had filed his dagger so that it would pierce through thin coat of mail. It was well to be armed, though he could not see why Thomas Culpepper should not stay willingly at Calais to be lieutenant of the stone lighters and steal stone to fill his pockets, since such were the privileges of the post that Throckmorton offered him.

'Mayhap, if I stay him, it will get me advancement,' he grumbled between his teeth. He was enraged in his slow, fierce way. For Throckmorton had promised him only to save his neck if he succeeded. There had been no hint of further rewards. He did not speculate upon why Thomas Culpepper was to be held in Calais; he did not speculate upon why he should wish to come to England; but again and again he muttered between his teeth, 'A curst business! a curst business!'

In the mysterious embroilment in which formerly he had taken part, his sister had told him that he was carrying letters between the King and Kat Howard. Yes; his large, slow sister had promised him great advancement for carrying certain letters. And still, in spite of the fact that he had been told it was a treason, he believed that the letters he had carried for Kat Howard were love letters to the King. Nevertheless, for his services he had received no advancement; he had, on the contrary, been bidden to leave his comrades of the guard and to hide himself. Throckmorton had bidden him do this. And instead of advancement, he had received kicks, curses, cords on his wrists, an interview with the Lord Privy Seal that still in the remembrance set him shivering, and this chance, offered him by Throck-

morton, that if he stayed Thomas Culpepper he might save
his neck.

'Why, then,' he grumbled to himself, 'is it treason to
carry the King's letters to a wench? Helping the King is
no treason. I should be advanced, not threatened with a
halter. Letters between the King and Kat Howard!' He
even attempted to himself a clumsy joke, polishing it and
repolishing it till it came out: 'A King may write to a Kat.
A Kat may write to a King. But my neck's in danger!'

Beside him, whitened by the dust that fell from above,
the gatewarden wandered in speech round *his* grievance.

'You ask me, young lad, if I know Tom Culpepper. Well
I know Tom Culpepper. Y' ask me if he have passed this
way going for England. Well I know he have not. For if
Tom Culpepper, squire that was of Durford and Maintree
and Sallowford that was my father's farm—if so be Tom
Culpepper had passed this way, I had spat in the dust
behind him as he passed.'

He made his wry face, winked his eye and showed his
teeth once more. 'Spat in the dust—I should ha' spat in
the dust,' he remarked again. 'Or maybe I'd have cast my
hat on high wi' "Huzzay, Squahre Tom!" according as the
mood I was in,' he said. He winked again and waited.

'For sure,' he affirmed after a pause, 'that will move 'ee
to ask why I du spit in the dust or for why—the thing
being contrary—I'd ha' cast up my cap.'

The young Poins pulled an onion from his poke.

'If you are so main sure he have not passed the gate,' he
said, 'I may take my ease.' He sat him down against the
gate wall where the April sun fell warm through the arch
of shadows. He stripped the outer peel from the onion and
bit into it. 'Good, warming eating,' he said, 'when your
stomach's astir from the sea.'

'Young lad,' the gatewarden said, 'I'm as fain to swear
my mother bore me—though God forbid I should swear
who my father was, woman being woman—as that Thomas
Culpepper have not passed this way. For why: I'd have
cast my hat on high or spat on the ground. And such

things done mark other things that have passed in the mind of a man. And I have done no such thing.'

But because the young Poins sat always silent with his eyes on the road to Ardres and slept—being privileged because he was yeoman of the King's guard—always in the little stone guard cell of the gateway at nights; because, in fact, the young man's whole faculties were set upon seeing that Thomas Culpepper did not pass unseen through the gate, it was four days before the gatewarden contrived to get himself asked why he would have spat in the dust or cast his hat on high. It was, as it were, a point of honour that he should be asked for all the information that he gave; and he thirsted to tell his tale.

His tale had it that he had been ruined by a wench who had thrown her shoe over the mill and married a horse-smith, after having many times tickled the rough chin of Nicholas Hogben. Therefore, he had it that all women were to be humbled and held down—for all women were traitors, praters, liars, worms and vermin. (He made a great play of words between wermen, meaning worms, and wermin and wummin.) He had been ruined by this woman who had tickled him under the chin—that being an in-gratiating act, fit to bewitch and muddle a man, like as if she had promised him marriage. And then she had married a horse-smith! So he was ready and willing, and prayed every night that God would send him the chance, to ruin and hold down every woman who walked the earth or lay in a bed.

But he had been ruined, too, by Thomas Culpepper, who had sold Durford and Maintree and Sallowford—which last was Hogben's father's farm. For why? Selling the farm had let in a Lincoln lawyer, and the Lincoln lawyer had set the farm to sheep, which last had turned old Hogben, the father, out from his furrows to die in a ditch—there being no room for farmers and for sheep upon one land. It had sent old Hogben, the father, to die in a ditch; it had sent his daughters to the stews and his sons to the road for sturdy beggars. So that, but for

Wallop's band passing that way when Hogben was grinning through the rope beneath Lincoln town tree—but for the fact that men were needed for Wallop's work in Calais, by the holy blood of Hailes! Hogben would have been rating the angel's head in Paradise.

But there had been great call for men to man the walls there in Calais, so Wallop's ancient had written his name down on the list, beneath the gallows tree, and had taken him away from the Sheriff of Lincoln's man.

'So here a be,' he drawled, 'cutting little holes in my pikehead.'

' 'Tis a folly,' the young Poins said.

'Sir,' the Lincolnshire man answered, 'you say 'tis a folly to make small holes in a pikehead. But for me 'tis the greatest of ornaments. Give you, it weakens the pikehead; but 'tis a gradely ornament.'

'Ornaments be folly,' the young Poins reiterated.

'Sir,' the Lincolnshire man answered again, 'there is the goodliest folly that ever was. For if I weaken my eyes and tire my wrists with small tappers and little files, and if I weaken the steel with small holes, each hole represents a woman I have known undone and cast down in her pride by a man. Here be sixty-and-four holes round and firm in a pattern. Sixty-and-four women I have known undone.'

He paused and surveyed, winking and moving the scroll that the little holes made in the tough steel of his axehead. Where a perforation was not quite round, he touched it with his file.

'Hum! ha!' he gloated. 'In the centre of the head is the master hole of all, planned out for being cut. But not yet cut! Mark you, 'tis not yet cut. That is for the woman I hate most of all women. She is not yet cast down that I have heard tell on, though some have said "Aye," some "Nay." Tell me, have you heard yet of a Kat Howard in the stews?'

'There is a Kat Howard is like to be——' the young Poins began. But his slow cunning was aroused before he had the sentence out. Who could tell what trick was this?

'Like to be what?' the Lincolnshire man badgered him. 'Like to be what? To be what?'

'Nay, I know not,' Poins answered.

'Like to be what?' Hogben persisted.

'I know no Kat Howard,' Poins muttered sulkily. For he knew well that the Lady Katharine's name was up in the taverns along of Thomas Culpepper. And this Lincolnshire cow-dog was a knave too of Thomas's; therefore the one Kat Howard who was like to be the King's wench and the other Kat Howard known to Hogben might well be one and the same.

'Nay; if you will not, neither even will I,' Hogben said. 'You shall have no more of my tale.'

Poins kept his blue eyes along the road. Far away, with an odd leap, waving its arms abroad and coming by fits and starts, as a hare gambols along a path—a figure was tiny to see, coming from Ardres way towards Calais. It passed a load of hay on an ox-cart, and Poins could see the peasants beside it scatter, leap the dyke and fly to stand panting in the fields. The figure was clenching its fists; then it fell to kicking the oxen; when they had overset the cart into the dyke, it came dancing along with the same hare's gait.

'That is too like the repute of Thomas Culpepper to be other than Thomas Culpepper,' the young Poins said. 'I will go meet him.'

He started to his feet, loosed the sword in its scabbard; but the Lincolnshire man had his halberd across the gateway.

'Pass! Shew thy pass!' he said vindictively.

'I go but to meet him,' Poins snarled.

'A good lie; thou goest not,' Hogben answered. 'No Englishman goes into the French lands without a pass from the lord controller. An thou keepest a shut head I can e'en keep a shut gate.'

None the less he must needs talk or stifle.

'Thee, with thy Kat Howard,' he snarled. 'Would 'ee

have me think thy Kat was my kitten whose name stunk in our nostrils?'

He shook his finger in Poins' face.

'Here be three of us know Kat Howard,' he said. 'For I know her, since for her I must leave home and take the road. And *he* knoweth her over well or over ill, since, to buy her a gown, he sold the three farms, Maintree, Durford and Sallowford—which last was my father's farm. And *thee* knowest her. Thee knowest her. To no good, I'se awarned. For thou stoppedst in thy speech like a colt before a wood snake. God bring down all women, I pray!'

He went on to tell, as if it had been a rosary, the names of the ruined women that the holes in his pikehead represented. There was one left by the wayside with her child; there was one hung for stealing cloth to cover her; there was one whipped for her naughty ways. He reached the square mark in the centre as the figure on the road reached the gateway.

'Huzzay, Squahre Tom! Here bay three kennath Kat Howard. Let us three tak part to kick her down.'

Thomas Culpepper like a green cat flew at his throat, clutched him above the steel breastplate, and shook three times, the gatewarden's uncovered, dun-coloured head swaying back and forward as if it were a loose bundle of clouts on a mop. When they parted company, because he could no longer keep his fingers clenched, Hogben fell back; he fell back, and they lay with their heels touching each other and their arms stretched out in the dust.

II

Nicholas Hogben was the first to rise. He felt at his neck, swallowed as though a piece of apple were stuck in his throat, brushed his leather breeches, and picked up his pike.

'Why,' he said, 'you may hold it for main and certain that he have not had Kat Howard down. For, having had her down, a would never have thrown a man by the throat for miscalling of her. Therefore Kat Howard is up for all of he, and I may loosen my feelings.'

He spat gravely at Culpepper's feet. Culpepper lay in the dust, his arms stretched out to form a cross, his face dead white and his beard of brilliant red pointing at the keystone of the arch of Calais gate. Poins lifted his hand, but the pulse still beat, and he dropped it moodily in the dust.

'Not dead,' he muttered.

'Dead!' Hogben laughed at him. 'Hath been in a boosing ken. There they drug the wine with simples, and the women—may pox fall on all women—perfume themselves so that a man goeth stark raving. I warrant he had silver buttons to his Lincoln green, but they be torn off. I warrant he had gold buckles to his shoen, but they be gone. His sword is away, the leather hangers being cut.'

'Wilt not stick him with thy pike, having, as he hath, so mishandled thee?'

'O aye,' the Lincolnshire man shewed his strong teeth. 'Thee wouldst have Kat Howard from him. But he may live for me, being more like to bring her to dismay than ever thee wilt be!'

He looked into the narrow street of the town that the dawn pierced into through the gateway. Two skinny men in jerkins drawn tight with belts were yawning in a hovel's low doorway. Under his eyes, still stretching their arms abroad, they made to slink between the mud walls of the next alley.

'Oh, hi! *Arrestez. Vesnez!*' he hailed. '*Cestui à comforter!*' The thin men made to break away, halted, hesitated, and then with dragging feet made through the pools and filth to the gateway.

'*Tombé! Voleurs! Secourez!*' Hogben pointed at the prostrate figure in green. They rubbed their shins on their thin calves and appeared bewildered and uncertain.

'*Portez à lous maisons!*' Hogben commanded.

They stood one on each side and bent down, extending skinny arms to lift him. Thomas Culpepper sat up and spat in their faces—they fled like scared wolves, noiselessly, gazing behind them in trepidation.

'Stay them; thieves ho! Stay them!' Culpepper panted. He scrambled to his feet, and stood reeling, his face like death, when he tried to make after them.

'God!' he said. 'Give me to drink.'

The young Poins mused under his breath because the man had neither sword nor dagger. Therefore it would be impossible to have sword play with him. He had, the young man, no ferocity—but he was set there to stay Thomas Culpepper's going on to England; he was to stay him by word or by deed. Deeds came so much easier than words.

'Squahre Tom!' the Lincolnshire man grunted. 'Reckon you have no money. Without groats and more ye shall get nowt to drink in Calais town, save water. Water you may have in plenty.'

With a sigh the young Poins unbuckled his belt to get his papers.

'Money I have for you,' he said. 'A main of money.' He was engaged now to pass words with this man—and he sighed again.

But Thomas Culpepper disregarded his words and his sigh. He was more in the mood to talk Lincolnshire than Kent, for his fever had given him a touch of homesickness and the young Poins to him was a very foreigner. He shut his eyes to let the Lincolnshire gatewarden's words go down to his brain; then with sudden violence he spat out:

'Give me water! What do ah ask but water! Pig! brood of a sow! gi'e me water and choke!'

Nicholas Hogben fetched a leather bottle as long as his leg, dusty and dinted, but nevertheless bedight with the arms of England, from the stone recess where the guard sheltered at nights. He fitted it on to the crook of his pike by the handle, and, craning over the drawbridge, first smoothed away the leaf-green duck-weed on the moat and then sank the bottle in the black water.

'I have money: a main of money for ye,' the young Poins said to Thomas Culpepper; but the man, with his red beard and white face, swayed on his legs and had ears only for the gurgling and gulping of the water as it entered the bottle neck. The black jack swayed and jumped below the bridge like a glistening water-beast.

He had little green spangles of duckweed in his orange beard when he took the bottle away, empty, from his mouth. He drew deep gasps of breath, and suddenly sat down upon a squared block of stone that the masons above were waiting to hoist into place over the archway.

'Good water!' he grunted to Hogben—grunting as all the Lincolnshire men did, in those days, like a two-year hog.

'Bean't but that good in all Calais town!' Hogben grunted back to him. 'Curses on the two wurmen that sent me here.' And indeed, to Lincolnshire men the water tasted good, since it reminded them of their dyke water, tasting of marshweed and smelling of eggs.

'Tü wurmen!' Culpepper said lazily. 'Hast thou been jigging with *tü* puticotties to wunst? One is enow to undo seven men. Who be 'hee?'

The young Poins, with a sulky sense of his importance, uttered:

'I have money for thee—a main of money!'

Culpepper looked at him with sleepy blue eyes.

'Thrice y' ha' told me that,' he said. 'And money is a goodly thing in its place—but not to a man with a bellyful of water. Y' shall feel my fist when I be rested. Meanwhile wait and, being a cub, hear how *men* talk.' He slapped his chest and repeated to Hogben: 'Who be 'ee?'

Hogben, delighted to be asked at last a question, shewed his formidable teeth and beneath his familiar contortion of the eyelids brought out the words that one of the women who had brought him down was her that had brought Squahre Culpepper to sit on a squared stone before Calais gate.

'Why, I am a made man, for all you see me sit here,' Culpepper answered indolently. 'I ha' done a piece of work for which I am to be seised of seven farms in Kent land.

See yo'—they send me messengers with money to Calais gate.' He pointed his thumb at the young Poins.

The boy, to prove that he was no common messenger, drew his right leg up and said:

'Nay, goodman Squire; an ye had slain the Cardinal the farms should have been yours. As it lies, ye are no more than lieutenant of Calais stone barges.'

'Thou liest,' Culpepper answered negligently, not turning his gaze from the gatewarden to whom he addressed a friendly question of, Who was the woman that had brought the two of them down.

'Now, Squahre!' the Lincolnshire man grinned delightedly; 'thu hast askëd me tü questions. Answer me one: Did *thee* lie upon her when thee put her name up in the township of Stamford?'

'Stamford in Lincolnshire was thy townplace?' Culpepper asked. 'But who was thy woman? I ha' had so many women and lied about so many more that I never had!'

The Lincolnshire man threw his leather cap to the keystone of the archway, caught it again and set it upon his thatch of hair, having the solemnity of one who performs his rituals.

'Goodly squahre that thee art!' he said; 'thou has harmed a many wenches in truth and in lies.'

Culpepper spied a down feather on his knee.

'Curse the mattress that I lay upon this night,' he said amiably.

He set his head back and blew the feather high into the air so that it floated out towards the tranquil and sunny pasture fields of France.

'Cub!' he said to Hal Poins, 'take this as a lesson of the death that lies about the pilgrim's path. For why am I not a pilgrim? I was sent to rid Paris of a Cardinal Pole, who, being in league with the devil, hath a magic tongue. Mark this story well, cub, who art sent me with money and gifts from the King in his glory to me that sit upon a stone. Now mark—' He extended his white hand. 'This hand, o' yestereen, had a ring with a great green stone. Now no ring is here. It was given me by my seventeenth leman, who had two eyes that looked not together. No twelve robbers had taken it from me by force, since I had made a pact with the devil that these wall eyes should never look across my face whilst that ring was there. Now, God knows, I may find her in Calais. So mark well——' He had been sent to Paris to rid France of the Cardinal Pole; for the Cardinal Pole, being a succubus of the fiend, had a magical tongue and had been inducing the French King to levy arms, in the name of that arch-devil, the Bishop of Rome, against their goodly King Henry, upon whom God shed His peace. Culpepper raised his bonnet at the Deity's name, stuck it far back on his red head, and continued: Therefore the mouth of Cardinal Pole was to be stayed in Paris town.

Culpepper smote his breast ferociously and with a black pride.

'And I have stayed it!' he peacocked. 'I and no other. I—T. Culpepper—a made man!'

'Not so,' Poins answered stubbornly. 'Thou wast sent to Paris to slay, and thou hast not slain!'

'Thou liest!' Culpepper asseverated. 'I was sent to purge Paris town, and I ha' purged un. No pothicary had done it better nor Hercules that was a stall groom and cleaned stables in antick days.' For, at the first breath of news that Culpepper was in the town, at the first rumour that the king's assassin was in Paris, Cardinal Pole had gathered his purple skirts about his knees; at the second sound he had cast them off altogether and, arrayed as a woman or a barber's leech, had fled hot foot to Brescia and thence to Rome.

'That was a nothing!' Culpepper asseverated. 'Though I ha' heard said that Hercules was made a god for cleaning stables that he found no easy task. But I will grant that it was no task for me to cleanse a whole town. For I needed no besoms, nor even no dagger, but the mere shadow of my beard upon the cobbly stones of Paris sufficed. I say nothing of that which befel in the day's journey; but mark this! mark what follows!' He had set out from Paris upon a high horse, with a high heart; he had frighted off all robbers and all sturdy rogues upon the road; he had slept at good inns as became a made man, and had bought himself a goodly pair of embroidered gloves which he could well pay for out of his superfluity. Being in haste to reach England, where he had that that called for him, he had ridden through the town of Ardres at nightfall, being minded to ride his horse dead, reach Calais gates in the hour, and beat down the gate if the warder would not suffer him to enter, it being dark. But outside the town of Ardres upon a make of no man's ground, being neither French nor English, he had espied a hut, and in the dark hut a lighted window hole that sparkled bravely, and, within, a big, fair woman drinking wine between candles with the light in her hair and a white tablecloth. And, feeling goodly, and Calais gate being shut, whether he broke it down one hour or three hours later was all one to him. He had gone into the hut to take by force or for payment a glass of wine from the black jacks, a kiss from the woman's mouth, and what else of ease the place afforded.

'Now I will have you mark, cub,' he said—'cub that shall have to learn many wiles if thy throat be not cut by me within the next two hours. Mark this, cub: these were no Egyptians!' They were not Bohemians, not swearers, not subtle cozeners, not even black a-vised, or he would have been on his guard against them; but they were plain, fair folks of Normandy. So he had drunk his wine, and cast a main or two at dice with the woman and two men, losing no more and no less than was decent. And he had drunk more wine and had taken his kisses—since it was all one whether he came three hours or four hours later to Calais gate. And there had been candles on the table and stuffs upon the wall, and a crock on the fire for mulling the wine, and a sheet upon the feather bed. But when he awoke in the morning he had lain upon the hard earth, between the bare walls. And all that was his was gone that was worth the taking.

'Now mark, cub,' he said. 'It was a simple thing this flitting with the hangings and the clothes and the pot rolled in bales and hung upon my horse. Upon my horse! But what is not simple is that simple folk of Normandy should have learned the arts of subtlety and drugging of wines. Mark that!' He pointed a finger at Poins.

'Had God been good to you you might have been as good a warring boy as Thomas Culpepper, who with the shadow of his hand held back the galleons of France and France's knights from the goodly realm of England. For this I have done by frighting from Paris, Cardinal Pole that was moving the French King to war on us. Had God been good to you you might have been as brave. But marvel and consider and humble you in the dust to think that a man with my brain pan and all it holds could have been so cozened. For sure, a dolt like you would have been stripped more clean till you had neither nails to your toes nor hair to your eyebrows.'

Hal Poins snarled that Culpepper would have been shaved too but that red hair stunk in the nostrils even of cozeners and thieves.

Culpepper wagged his head from side to side.

'This is a main soft stone,' he said; 'I am main weary. When the stone grows hard, which is a sign that I shall no longer be minded to rest, I will break thy back with a cudgel.'

Poins stamped his foot with rage and tears filled his eyes.

'An thou had a sword!' he said. 'An only thou had a sword!'

'A year-old carrot to baste thee with!' Culpepper answered. 'Swords are for men!' He turned to Hogben, who was sitting on the ground furbishing his pike-head. 'Heard you the like of my tale?' he asked lazily.

'Oh aye!' the Lincolnshire man answered. 'The simple folk of Normandy are simple only because they have no suitors. But they ha' learned that marlock from the sailors of Rye town. For in Rye town, which is the sinkhole of Sussex, you will meet every morning ten travellers travelling to France in the livery of Father Adam. Normans can learn,' he added sententiously, 'as the beasts of the field can learn from a man. My father had a ewe lamb that danced a pavane to my pipe on the farm of Sallowford that you sold to buy a woman the third part of a gown.'

'Why! Art Nick Hogben?' Culpepper said.

'Hast that question answered,' Hogben said. 'Now answer me one. Liedst thou when saidst what thou saidst of that wurman?'

Culpepper on the stone swung his legs vain-gloriously: 'I sold three farms to buy her a gown,' he said.

'Aye!' Nick Hogben answered. 'So thou saidst in Stamford town three years gone by. And thou saidst more and the manner of it. But betwixt the buying the gowns and the more of it lie many things. As this: Did she take the gown of thee? Or as this: Having taken the gown of thee, did she pay thee in the kind payment should be made in?'

Culpepper looked up at him with a sharp snarl.

'For—' and Nick Hogben shook his head sagaciously, 'Stamford town believed the more and the manner of it, and Kat Howard's name is up in the town of Stamford. But I have not yet chiselled out the great piece that shall come from my pike when certain sure I am that Kat Howard is down under a man's foot.'

Culpepper rose suddenly to his feet and wagged a finger at Hogben.

'Now I am minded to wed Kat Howard!' he said. 'Therefore I will say I lied then. But as for what you shall think, consider that I had her alone many days and nights; consider that though she be over learned in the Latin tongues that set a woman against joyment, I have a proper person and a strong wrist, a pleasant tongue but a hot and virulent purpose. Consider that she welly starved in her father, the Lord Edmund's, house and I had pies and gowns for her. Consider these things and make a hole or no hole as thou wilt——'

Nicholas Hogben considered with his eyes on the ground; he scratched his head with a black finger.

'I can make nowt out,' he said. 'But I will curse thee for a lily-livered hoggit an thou marry Kat Howard.'

'Why, I am minded to marry her,' Culpepper answered, 'over here in France,' and he stretched a hand towards the long white road where in the distance the French peasants were driving lean beasts for a true Englishman's provender in Calais. 'Over here in France. Body of God!—Body of God!——' He wavered, being still fevered. 'In England it had been otherwise. But here, shivering across plains and seas—why, I will wed with her.'

'Talkest like a Blind God Boy,' Hogben said sarcastically. 'How knowest she be thine to take?' He pointed at the young Poins. 'Here be another hath had doings with a Kat Howard, though I cannot well discern if she be thine or whose.'

Culpepper sprang, a flash of green, straight at the callow boy. But Poins had sprung too, back and to the left, and his oiled sword was from its scabbard and warring in the air.

'Holy Sepulchre! I will spit thee—Holy Sepulchre! I will spit thee!' he cried.

'Ass!' Culpepper answered. 'In God's time I will break thy back across my knee. But God's time is not yet.'

He poured out a flood of questions about the Kat Howard Poins had seen.

'Squahre Thomas,' Nicholas Hogben interrupted him maliciously, 'that young man of Kent saith e'ennow: "Kat Howard is like to——" and then he chokes upon his words. Now even what make of thing is it that Kat Howard is like to do or be done by?'

With his sword whiffling before him the young Poins could think rapidly—nay, upon any matter that concerned his advancement he could think rapidly always.

'Goodman Thomas Culpepper,' he said in a high voice, 'the mistress Katharine Howard I spoke of is thin and dark and small, and married to Edward Howard of Biggleswade. She is like to die of a quinsy.'

For well he knew that his advancement depended on his keeping Thomas Culpepper on the hither side of the water; and if it muddled his brain to have been so usefully mishandled for carrying letters betwixt the King's Grace and the Lady Katharine Howard, he knew enough of a jealous man to know that that was no news to keep Thomas Culpepper in Calais.

Culpepper's animation dropped like the light of a torch that is dowsed.

'Put up thy pot skewer,' he said; 'my Kat is tall and fairish and unwed. Ha' ye not seen her with the Lady Mary of England's women?'

The young Poins, zealous to be rid of the matter, answered fervently:

'Never. She is not talked of in the Court.'

'That is the best hearing,' Thomas Culpepper said. 'I do absolve thee of five kicks for being the messenger of that.'

III

They were a-walking in the little garden below the windows of the late Cardinal's house at Hampton; the April sun shone, for May came on apace, and in that sheltered spot the light lay warm and no breezes came. They took great pleasure there beneath the windows. One girl kept three golden balls flying in the air, whilst three others and two lords sought to distract her by inducing her little hound to bark shrilly below her hands up at the flying balls that caught in them the light of the sun, the blue of the sky, and the red and grey of the warm palace walls. Down the nut walk, where the trees that the dead Cardinal had set were already fifteen years old and dark with young green leaves as bright as little flowers, they had set up archery targets. Cicely Elliott, in black and white, flashing like a magpie in the alleys, ran races with the Earl of

Surrey beneath the blinking eyes of her old knight; the Lady Mary, herself habited all in black, moved like a dark shadow upon a dial between the little beds upon paths of red brick between box hedges as high as your ankles. She spoke to none save once when she asked the name of a flower. But laughter went up, and it seemed as if, in this first day out of doors, all the Court opened its lungs to drink the new air; and they were making plans for May Day already.

They asked, too, a riddle: 'An a nutshell from Candlemas loved a merry bud in March, how should it come to pleasure and content?' and men who had the answer looked wise and shook their sides at guessing faces.

In a bower at the south end of the small garden Katharine Howard sat to play cat's-cradle with the old lady of Rochford. This foolish game and this foolish old woman, with her unceasing tales of the Queen Anne Boleyn—who had been her cousin—gave to Katharine a great feeling of ease. With her troubled eyes and weary expression, her occasional groans as the rheumatism gnawed at her joints, the old lady minded her of the mother she had so seldom seen. She had always been somewhere away, all through Katharine's young years, planning and helping her father to advancement that never came, and hopeless to control her wild children. Thus Katharine had come to love this poor old woman and consorted much with her, for she was utterly bewildered to control the Lady Mary's maids that were beneath her care.

Katharine held out her hands, parallel, as if she were praying, with the strand of blue wool and silver cord crisscross and diagonal betwixt her fingers. The old lady bent above them, silent and puzzled, to get the key to the strings. Twice she protruded her gouty fingers, with swollen ends; and twice she drew them back to stroke her brows.

'I mind,' she said suddenly, 'that I played cat's-cradle with my cousin Anne, that was a sinful queen.' She bent again and puzzled about the strings. 'In those days I had a great skill, I mind. We revised it to the eleventh change many times before her death.' Again she leant forward and again back. 'I did come near my death, too,' she added.

Katharine's eyes had been gazing past her; suddenly she asked:

'Was Anne Boleyn loved after she grew to be Queen?'

The old woman's face took on a palsied and haunted look.

'God help you!' she said; 'do you ask that?' and she glanced round her furtively in an agony of apprehension. Something had drawn all the gay gowns and embroidered stomachers towards the higher terrace. They were all alone in the arbour.

'Why,' Katharine said, 'so many innocent creatures have been done to death since Cromwell came, that, though she was lewd before and a heretic all her days, I think doubts may be.'

The old lady pressed her hand upon her bosom where her heart beat.

'Madam Howard,' she said, 'for my life I know not the truth of the matter. There was much trickery; God knoweth the truth.'

Katharine mused for a moment above the cat's-cradle on her fingers. Near the joint at the end of the little one there was a small mole.

'Take you the fifth and third strings,' she said. 'The king string holds your wrist,' and whilst the old face was still intent upon the problem she said:

'I think that if a woman come to be Queen it is odds that she will live chastely, how lewd soever she ha' been aforetime.'

Lady Rochford set her fingers in between Katharine's, but when she drew them back with the strings upon them, they wavered, lost their straightness, knotted and then resolved themselves into a single loop as in a swift wind a cloud dies away beneath the eyes of the beholder.

'Why, 'tis pity,' Katharine said.

All the lords and all the ladies were now upon the terrace above. The old lady had the string in her broad lap. Suddenly she bent forward, her eyes opened.

'She was the enemy of your Church,' she said. 'But this I will tell you: upon occasions when men swore she had been with other men o' nights, the Queen was in my bed with me!'

Katharine nodded silently.

'Who was I that I dare speak?' the old woman sobbed; and Katharine nodded again.

Lady Rochford rubbed together her fat hands as she were ringing them.

'Before God,' she moaned, 'and by the blessed blood of Hailes that cured ever my pains, if a soul know a soul I knew Anne. If she was a woman like other women before she wedded the King, she was minded to be chaste after. Madam Howard,'—and she rocked her fat body to and fro upon the seat—'they came to me from both sides, your Papists and her heretics; they threatened me to keep silence of what I knew. I was to keep silence. I name no names. But they came o' both sides, Papists and heretics; though she was middling true to the heretics they could not be true to her.'

Katharine answered her own thoughts with:

'Ay; but my cause is the good cause. Men shall be true to it.'

The old lady leaned forward and stroked her hands.

'Dearie,' she said, 'dandling piece, sweet bit, there are no true men.' She had an entreaty in her tone, and her large blue eyes gazed fixedly. 'Say that my cousin Anne was a heretic. I know naught of it save that my bones have ached always since the holy blood of Hailes was done away with that was wont to cure me. But the Queen Anne was hard driven because of a plotting; and no man stood her friend.' With her large and tear-filled eyes she gazed at the palace, where the pear trees upon the walls shewed new, pale leaves in the sunlight. 'The great Cardinal was hard driven because of a plot, and no man was true to him.

There is no true man. Hope not for one. Hope not for any one. The great Cardinal builded those walls and that palace —and where is he?'

'Yet,' Katharine said, 'Privy Seal that is was true to him and profited exceedingly.'

Lady Rochford shook her head.

'For a little while truth may help you,' she said; 'but your name in the end shall be but a stink.'

'Ay,' Katharine answered her; 'but ye shall gain at the end of all. For I hold it for certain that because, to the uttermost dregs of his cup, Cromwell was true to his master Wolsey, before the throne of God much shall be pardoned him.'

The old woman answered bitterly:

'The throne of God is a long way from here.'

'Please it Mary and the saints,' Katharine said, 'the ten years to come shall bring Heaven a thousand leagues nearer to this land.' But her words died away because the Lady Rochford's mouth fell open.

From the terrace a great square man led down a tiny, small man, giving the child his finger to help him down the steps. It clung to him, the little, squared replica of himself, sturdily and with a blonde, small face laughing up into his father's that laughed down past a huge shoulder. Henry was dressed all in black, and his son too; the boy's callow head shone in the sunshine, and they came dallying down the little path, many faces and shoulders peering over the terrace wall at them. Once the child stumbled, loosed his hold of his father's finger and came down upon all fours. He crawled to the pathside, filled his little hands with leaves, and held them up towards his sire; and they could hear the King say:

'Who-hoop, Ned! Princes walk not like quadrumanes,' as he bent to take the leaves. The child twisted himself, gripping his little fingers into Henry's garter, and, catching again at his finger, pulled his father towards their bower.

The Lady Rochford rose, but Katharine sat where she was to smile upon the child and brush his head with a pink tassel of her sleeve. The little prince hid his face in the voluminous velvet of his father's vast thighs. The King, diffusing a great and embracing pride, laughed to Lady Rochford.

'Ye played cat's-cradle,' he said. 'I warrant ye brought it not beyond seven changes. Time was when I have done fourteen with a lady if her hands were white enough.'

He threw away the green leaves of the clove pinks that his son had given him, and took the blue and silver loop from the old woman's hands. He sat himself heavily on the bench facing Katharine, and crying, 'See you, silly Ned,' held his son's hands apart and fitted the cord over the little wrists.

Suddenly he bent clumsily forward and picked up again the carnation leaves that lay in green strands upon the floor of the arbour, grunting a little with the effort.

'This is the first offering my son ever made me,' he said, and he drew a pocket purse from his breast to lay them in. 'Please God he shall yet lay at my feet a province or two of our heritage of France.' He touched his cap at the Deity's name, and called gruffly at his son: 'See you, forget not ever that we be Kings of France too, you and I,' and the little boy with his cropped head uttered:

'*Rex Angliae, Galliae, Franciae et Hiberniae!*'

'Aye, I ha' learned ye that,' the King said, and roared with laughter. Of a sudden he turned his head, without moving his body, towards Katharine.

'I ha' news from Norfolk in France,' he said, and, as the Lady Rochford made to move, he uttered good-naturedly: 'Aye, avoid. But ye may buss my son.'

He stretched back his head, laid an arm along the back of his seat, put out his feet and pushed at the child, who played with his shoe-tags.

'The boy grows,' he said, and motioned for Katharine to sit beside him. Then his face shewed a quick dissatisfaction. 'A brave boy, but a should be braver,' and looking down, 'see you not blue lines about 's gills?' He caught at her hand with a masterful grip.

'Here we're a picture,' he said: 'a lusty husbandman, his lusty son, his lusty wife, resting all beneath his goodly vine.' His face clouded again. 'I—I am not lusty; my son, he is not lusty.' He touched her cheek. 'Thou art lusty enow—hast such pink cheeks.'

'Aye, we were always lusty at home when we had enow to eat,' Katharine said. She took the child upon her knee and blew lightly in his face. 'I will wager you I will guess his weight within a pound,' she added, and began to play a game with the tiny fingers. 'Wherefore do ye habit little children in black?'

'Why,' the King answered, 'I know not if I myself appear less monstrous in black or red, and my son shall be habited as I be. 'Tis to make the trial.'

'Aye,' Katharine said, 'ye think first of yourself. But dress the child in white and go in white yourself. And set up a chantry of priests to pray the child grow sturdy. It was thus my cousin Surrey's life was saved that was erst a weakling.'

'Be Queen,' he said suddenly. 'Marry me. I came here to ask it.'

Her lips parted; she left her hand in his. The expected words had come.

'I have thought on it,' she said. 'I knew ye could not long hold to child and sire as ye sware ye would.'

'Kat,' he said, 'ye shall do my will. I ha' news from France. Ye gave me good rede. I ha' news from Cleves: the Cleves woman shall no more be queen of mine. Thee I will have.'

She raised herself from the bench and turned in the entrance of the arbour to look at him.

'Give me leave to walk on the path,' she said. 'I have thought on this—for I was sure I gave you good advice, and well I knew Cleves would sever from ye.' She faltered: 'I ha' thought on it. But 'tis different to think on it and to ha' the thing in your face.'

He uttered, 'Make haste,' and she walked down the path. He saw her, tall, fair, swaying a little in the wind, raise her face to the skies; her long fingers made the sign of the cross, her hood fell back. Her lips moved; the fringes of her lashes came down over her blue eyes, and she seemed to wrestle with her hands.

'Aye,' he muttered to himself half earnest, half sardonic, 'prayer is better than thoughts. God strike with palsy them that made me afraid to pray.... Aye, pray on, pray on,' he said again. 'But by God and His wounds! ye shall be my queen.'

By the time she came back he laughed at her tempestuously, and pushing the little prince tenderly with his huge foot, watched him roll on the floor catching at the air.

'Why,' he said to her, 'what's the whimsy now? Shalt be the queen. 'Tis the sole way. 'Tis the way to the light.' He leant forward. 'Cleves has gone to the bastard called Charles to sue for mercy. Ye led me so well to set Francis against Charles that I may snap my fingers against both. None but thee could ha' forged that bolt. Child, I will make a league with the Pope against Charles or Francis, with Francis or Charles. Anne may go hang herself.' He rose to his feet and stretched out both his hands, his eyes glowing beneath his deep brows. 'Body o' God! thou art a very fair woman; and now I will be such a king as never was, and take France for mine own and set up Holy Church again, and say good prayers and sleep in a warm bed. Body o' God! Body o' God!'

'God and the saints save the issue!' she said. 'I am thy servant and slave.'

But her tone made him recoil.

'What whimsy's here?' he muttered heavily, and his eyes became suffused with red. 'Speak, wench!' He pulled at the stuff round his throat. 'I will have peace,' he said. 'I will at last have peace.'

'God send you have it,' she said, and trembled a little, half in fear, half in sheer pity at the thought of thwarting him.

'Speak thy fool whimsy,' he muttered huskily. 'Speak!'

'My lord,' she said, 'where is the Queen that is?'

He flared suddenly at her as if she had reproved him.

'At Windsor. 'Tis a better palace than this of mine here.' He shook his finger heavily and uttered with a boastful defiance: 'Shalt not say I shower no gifts on her. Shalt not say she has no state. I ha' sent her seven jennets this day. I shall go bring her golden apples on the morrow. Scents she has had o' me; French gowns, Southern fruits. No man nor wench shall say I be not princely——' His boasting bluster died away before her silence. To please a mute desire in her, he had showered more gifts on Anne of Cleves than on any other woman he had ever seen; and thinking that she used him ill not to praise him for this, he could not hold his tongue: 'What is't to thee what she hath? What she hath thou losest. 'Tis a folly.'

'My lord,' she said, 'I will myself to see the Queen that is.'

'And whysomever?' he voiced his astonishment.

'My lord,' she said, 'I have a tickly conscience in divorces. I will ask her mine own self.'

He roared out suddenly indistinguishable words, stamped his feet, waved his hands at the skies, and lost his voice altogether.

'Aye,' she said, catching at some of his speech, 'I ha' read your Highness' depositions. I ha' read depositions of the Archbishop's. But I will be satisfied of her own mouth that she be not your wife.'

And when he swore that Anne would lie:

'Nay,' she answered; 'if she will lie to keep her queen-ship, keep it she shall. I am upon the point of honour.'

'Before God!'—and his voice had a sneering haughti-ness—'ye will not be long of this world if ye steer by the point of honour.'

'Sir,' she cried out and stretched forth her hands; 'for the love of Mary who guides the starry counsels and of the saints who sit in conclave, speak not in that wise.'

He shrugged his shoulders and said, with a touch of angry shame:

'God send the world were another world; I would it were other. But I am a prince in this one.'

'My lord,' she said; 'if the world so is, kings and princes are here to be above the world. In your greatness ye shall change it; with your justice ye shall purify it; with your clemencies ye should it chasten and amerce. Ye ask me to be a queen. Shall I be a queen and not such a queen? No, I tell you; if a woman may swear a great oath, I swear by Leonidas that saved Sparta and by Christ Jesus that saved this world, so will I come by my queenship and so act in it that, if God give me strength the whole world never shall find speck upon mine honour—or upon thine if I may sway thee.'

'Why,' he said, 'thy voice is like little flutes.'

He considered, patting his square, soft-shod feet upon the bricks of the arbour floor.

'By Guy! I will have thee,' he said; 'though ye twist my senses as never woman twisted them—and it is not good for a man to be swayed by his women.'

'My lord,' she said, 'in naught would I sway a man save in where my conscience pricks and impels me.' She rubbed her hand across her eyes. 'It is difficult to see the right in these matters. The only way is to be firm for God and for the cause of the saints.' She looked down at her feet. 'I will be ceaseless in my entreaties to you for them,' she uttered. Suddenly again she stretched forth both her hands that had sunk to her sides:

'Dear lord,' and her voice was full of pity for herself and for entreaty; 'let me go to a convent to pray unceasing for thee.'

He shook his head.

'Dear lord,' she repeated; 'use me as thou wilt and I will stay beside thee and urge thee to the cause of God.'

Again he shook his head.

'The saints would pardon me it,' she whispered; 'or if I even be damned to save England, it were a good burnt-offering.'

'Wench,' he said; 'I was never a man to go a-whoring.

I ha' done it, but had no savour with it.' His boastfulness returned to the heavy voice. 'I am a king that will give. I will give a crown, a realm, jewels, honours, monies. All I have I will give; but thou shalt wed me.' He threw out his chest and gazed down at her. 'I was ever thus,' he said.

'And I ever thus,' she answered him swiftly. 'Mary hath put this thing in my mind; and though ye scourge me, ye shall not have it otherwise.'

'Even how?' he said.

'My lord,' she answered; 'if the Queen, so it be true, will say she be no wife of thine, I will wed thee. If the Queen, seeing that it is for the good of this suffering realm, will give to me her crown, I will wed with thee. I wot ye may get for yourself another woman with another gear of conscience to bear t'ee children. All the ills of this realm came with a divorce of a queen. I do hate the word as I hate Judas, and will have no truck with the deed.'

'Ye speak me hard,' he said; 'but no man shall say I could not bear with the truth at odd moments.'

A great and hasty eagerness came into her voice.

'Ye say that it is truth?' she cried. 'God hath softened thy heart.'

'God or thee,' he said, and muttered, 'I do not make this avowal to the world.' Suddenly he smote his thigh. 'Body o' God!' he called out; 'the day shall soon come. Cleves falls away, France and Spain are sundering. I will sue for peace with the Pope, and set up a chapel to Kat's memory.' He breathed as if a weight had fallen from his chest, and suddenly laughed: 'But ye must wed me to keep me in the right way.'

He changed his tone again.

'Why, go to Anne,' he said; 'she is such a fool she will not lie to thee; and, before God, she is no wife of mine.'

'God send ye speak the truth,' she answered; 'but I think few men be found that will speak truth in these matters.'

IV

But it was with Throckmorton that the real pull of the rope came. Henry was by then so full of love for her that, save when she crossed his purpose, he would have given her her way to the bitter end of things. But Throckmorton bewailed her lack of loyalty. He came to her on the morning of the next day, having heard that, if the rain held off, a cavalcade of seventeen lords, twelve ladies and their bodyguards were commanded to ride with her in one train to Windsor, where the Queen was.

'I am main sure 'tis for Madam Howard that this cavalcade is ordered,' he said; 'for there is none other person in Court to whom his Highness would work this honour. And I am main sure that if Madam Howard goeth, she goeth with some mad maggot of a purpose.'

His foxy, laughing eyes surveyed her, and he stroked his great beard deliberately.

'I ha' not been near ye this two month,' he said, 'but God knows that I ha' worked for ye.'

Save to take her to Privy Seal the day before, when Privy Seal had sent him, he had in truth not spoken with her for many weeks. He had deemed it wise to keep from her.

'Nevertheless,' he said earnestly, 'I know well that thy cause is my cause, and that thou wilt spread upon me the mantle of thy favour and protection.'

They were in her old room with the green hangings, the high fireplace, and before the door the red curtain worked with gold that the King had sent her, and Cromwell had given orders that the spy outside should be removed, for he was useless. Thus Throckmorton could speak with a measure of freedom.

'Madam Howard,' he said; 'ye use me not well in this. Ye are not so stable nor so safe in your place as that ye may, without counsel or guidance, risk all our necks with these mad pranks.'

'Goodman,' she said, 'I asked ye not to come into my barque. If ye hang to the gunwale, is it my fault an ye be drowned in my foundering if I founder?'

'Tell me why ye go to Windsor,' he urged.

'Goodman,' she answered, 'to ask the Queen if she be the King's wife.'

'Oh, folly!' he cried out, and added softly, 'Madam Howard, ye be monstrous fair. I do think ye be the fairest woman in the world. I cannot sleep for thinking on thee.'

'Poor soul!' she mocked him.

'But, bethink you,' he said; 'the Queen is a woman, not a man. All your fairness shall not help you with her. Neither yet your sweet tongue nor your specious reasons. Nor yet your faith, for she is half a Protestant.'

'If she be the King's wife,' Katharine said, 'I will not be Queen. If she care enow for her queenship to lie over it, I will not be Queen either. For I will not be in any quarrel where lies are—either of my side or of another's.'

'God help us all!' Throckmorton mocked her. 'Here is my neck engaged on your quarrel—and by now a dozen others. Udal hath lied for you in the Cleves matter; so have I. If ye be not Queen to save us ere Cromwell's teeth be drawn, our days are over and past.'

He spoke with so much earnestness that Katharine was moved to consider her speaking.

'Knight,' she said at last, 'I never asked ye to lie to Cromwell over the Cleves matter. I never asked Udal. God knows, I had the rather be dead than ye had done it. I flush and grow hot each time I think this was done for me. I never asked ye to be of my quarrel—nay, I take shame that I have not ere this sent to Privy Seal to say that ye have lied, and Cleves is false to him.' She pointed an accusing finger at him: 'I take shame; ye have shamed me.'

He laughed a little, but he bent a leg to her.

'Some man must save thee from thy folly's fruits,' he said. 'For some men love thee. And I love thee so my head aches.'

She smiled upon him faintly.

'For that, I believe, I have saved thy neck,' she said. 'My conscience cried: "Tell Privy Seal the truth"; my heart uttered: "Hast few men that love thee and do not pursue thee." '

Suddenly he knelt at her feet and clutched at her hand.

'Leave all this,' he said. 'Ye know not how dangerous a place this is.' He began to whisper softly and passionately. 'Come away from here. Well ye know that I love 'ee better than any man in land. Well ye know. Well ye know. And well ye know no man could so well fend for ye or jump nimbly to thy thoughts. The men here be boars and bulls. Leave all these dangers; here is a straight issue. Ye shall not sway the wild boar king for ever. Come with me.'

As she did not at once find words to stop his speech, he whispered on:

'I have gold enow to buy me a baron's fee in Almain. I have been there: in castles in the thick woods, silken bowers may be built——'

But suddenly again he rose to his feet and laughed:

'Why,' he said, 'I hunger for thee: at times 'tis a madness. But 'tis past.'

His eyes twinkled again and he waved a hand.

'Mayhap 'tis well that ye go to the Queen,' he said drily. 'If the Queen say, "Yea," ye ha' gained all; if "Nay" ye ha' lost naught, for ye may alway change your mind. And a true and steadfast cause, a large and godly innocence is a thing that gaineth men's hearts and voices.' He paused for a moment. 'Ye ha' need o' man's good words,' he said drily; then he laughed again. 'Aye: *Nolo episcopari* was always a good cry,' he said.

Katharine looked at him tenderly.

'Ye know my aims are other,' she said, 'or else you would not love me. I think ye love me better than any man ever did—though I ha' had a store of lovers.'

'Aye,' he nodded at her gravely, 'it is pleasant to be loved.'

She was sitting by her table and leant her hand upon her cheek; she had been sewing a white band with pearls and silken roses in red and leaves in green, and it fell now to her feet from her lap. Suddenly he said:

'Answer me one question of three?'

She did not move, for a feeling of languor that often overcame her in Throckmorton's presence made her feel lazy and apt to listen. She itched to be Queen—on the morrow or next day; she desired to have the King for her own, to wear fair gowns and a crown; to be beloved of the poor people and beloved of the saints. But her fate lay upon the knees of the gods then: on the morrow the Queen would speak—betwixt then and now there was naught for it but to rest. And to hearken to Throckmorton was to be surprised as if she listened at a comedy.

'One question of three may be answered,' she said.

'On the forfeit of a kiss,' he added. 'I pray God ye answer none.'

He pondered for a moment, and leaning back against the chimney-piece crossed one silk-stockinged, thin, red leg. He spoke very swiftly, so that his words were like lightning.

'And the first is: An ye had never come here but elsewhere seen me, had ye it in you to ha' loved me? And the second: How ye love the King's person? And the third: Were ye your cousin's leman?'

Leaning against the table she seemed slowly to grow stiff in her pose; her eyes dilated; the colour left her cheeks. She spoke no word.

'Privy Seal hath sent a man to hasten thy cousin back to here,' he said at last, after his eyes had steadily surveyed her face. She sat back in her chair, and the strip of sewing fell to wreathe, white and red and green, round her skirts on the floor.

'I have sent a botcher to stay his coming,' he said slowly. 'Thy maid Margot's brother.'

'I had forgotten Tom,' she said with long pauses between her words. She had forgotten her cousin and playmate. She had given no single thought to him since a day that she no longer remembered.

Reading the expression of her face and interpreting her slow words, Throckmorton was satisfied in his mind that she had been her cousin's.

'He hath passed from Calais to Dover, but I swear to you that he shall never come to you,' he said. 'I have others here.' He had none, but he was set to comfort her.

'Poor Tom!' she uttered again almost in a whisper.

'Thus,' he uttered slowly, 'you have a great danger.'

She was silent, thinking of her Lincolnshire past, and he began again:

'Therefore ye have need of help from me as I from thee.'

'Aye,' he said, 'you shall advise with me. For at least, if I may not have the pleasure of thy body, I will have the enjoyment of thy converse.' His voice became husky for a moment. 'Mayhap it is a madness in me to cling to thee; I do set in jeopardy my earthly riches and my hope of profit. But it is Macchiavelli who says: "*If ye hoard gold and at the end have not pleasure in what gold may pay, ye had better have loitered in pleasing meadows and hearkened to the madrigals of sweet singing fowls.*" ' He waved his hand: 'Ye see I be still somewhat of a philosopher, though at times madness takes me.'

She was still silent—shaken into thinking of the past she had had with her cousin when she had been very poor in Lincolnshire; she had had leisure to read good letters there, and the time to think of them. Now she had not held a book for four days on end.

'You are in a very great danger of your cousin,' Throckmorton was repeating. 'Yet I will stay his coming.'

'Knight,' she said, 'this is a folly. If guards be needed to keep me from his knife, the King shall give me guards.'

'His knife!' Throckmorton raised his hands in mock surprise. 'His knife is a very little thing.'

'Ye would not say it an ye had come anear him when he was crossed,' she said. 'I, who am passing brave, fear his knife more than aught else in this world.'

'Oh, incorrigible woman,' he cried, 'thinking ever of straight things and clear doings. It is not the knife of your cousin, but the devious policy of Privy Seal that calleth for fear.'

'Why, or ever Privy Seal bind Tom to his policy he shall bind iron bars to make a coil.'

He looked at her with lifted eyebrows, and then scratched with his finger nail a tiny speck of mud from his shoe-point, balancing himself back against the chimney piece and crossing his red legs above the knees.

'Madam Howard,' he said, 'Privy Seal is minded to use thy cousin for a battering-ram.' She was hardly minded to listen to him, and he uttered stealthily, as if he were sure of moving her: 'Thy cousin shall breach a way to the ears of the King—for thy ill fame to enter in.'

She leaned forward a little.

'Tell me of my ill fame,' she said; and at that moment Margot Poins, her handmaid, placid still, large, fair and florid, came in to bring her mistress an embroidery frame of oak wood painted with red stripes. At Throckmorton's glance askance at the cow-like girl, Katharine said: 'Ye may speak afore Margot Poins. I ha' heard tales of her bringing.'

Margot kneeled at Katharine's feet to stretch a white linen cloth over the frame on the floor.

'Privy Seal planneth thus,' Throckmorton answered Katharine's challenge. He spoke low and level, hoping to see her twinge at every new phrase. 'The King hath put from him every tale of thee; it is not easy to bring him tales of those he loves, but very dangerous. But Cromwell planneth to bring hither thy cousin and to keep him privily till one day cometh the King to be alone with thee in thy bower or his. Then, having removed all lets, shall Cromwell gird this cousin to spring in upon thee and the King, screaming out and with his sword drawn.' Still Katharine did not move, but leaned along her table of yellow wood. 'It is not the sword ye shall fear,' he said slowly, 'but what cometh after. For, for sure, Privy Seal holdeth, then shall be the time to bring witnesses against thee to the hearing of the King. And Privy Seal hath witnesses.'

'He would have witnesses,' Katharine answered.

'There be those that will swear——'

'Aye,' she caught him up, speaking very calmly. 'There be those that will swear they ha' seen me with a dozen men. With my cousin, with Nick Ardham, with one and another of the hinds. Why, he will bring a hind to swear I ha' loved him. And he will bring a bastard child or twain——' She paused, and he paused too.

At last he said: 'Anan?'

'Ye might do it against Godiva of Coventry, against the blessed Katharine or against Caesar's helpmeet in those days,' Katharine said. 'Margot here can match all thy witnesses from the city of London—men that never were in Lincolnshire.'

Margot's face flushed with a tide of exasperation, and, sitting motionless, she uttered deeply:

'My uncle the printer hath a man will swear he saw ye walk with a fiend having horns and a tail.' And indeed these things were believed among the Lutherans that flocked still to Margot's uncle's printing room. 'My uncle hath printed this,' she muttered, and fumbled hotly in her bosom. She drew out a sheet with coarse black letters upon it and cast it across the floor with a flushed disdain at Throckmorton's feet. It bore the heading: '*Newes from Lincoln*.' Throckmorton kicked with his toe the white scroll and scrutinised Katharine's face dispassionately with his foxy eyes that jumped between his lids like little beetles of blue. He thrust his cap back upon his head and laughed.

'Before God!' he said; 'ye are the joyfullest play that ever I heard. And how will Madam Howard act when the King heareth these things?'

Katharine opened her lips with surprise.

'For a subtile man ye are strangely blinded,' she said; 'there is one plain way.'

'To deny it and call the saints to witness!' he laughed.

'Even that,' she answered. 'I pray the saints to give me the place and time.'

'Ha' ye seen the King in a jealous rage?' he asked.

'Subtile man,' she answered, 'the King knows his world.'

'Aye,' he answered, 'knoweth that women be never chaste.'

Katharine bent to pick up her sewing.

'Sir,' she said, 'if the King will not have faith in me I will wed no King.'

His jaw fell. 'Ye have so much madness?' he asked.

She stretched towards him the hand that held her sewing now.

'I swear to you,' she said—'and ye know me well—I seek a way to bring these rumours to the King's ears.'

He said nothing, revolving these things in his mind.

'Goodly servant,' she began, and he knew from the round and silvery sound she drew from her throat that she was minded to make one of the long speeches that appalled and delighted him with their childish logic and wild honour. 'If it were not that my cousin would run his head into danger I would will that he came to the King. Sir, ye are a wise man, can ye not see this wisdom? There is no good walking but upon sure ground, and I will not walk where the walking is not good. Shall I wed this King and have these lies to fear all my life? Shall I wed this King and do him this wrong? Neither wisdom nor honour counsel me to it. Since I have heard these lies were abroad I have at frequent moments thought how I shall bring them before the King.'

He thrust his hands into his pockets, stretched his legs out, and leaned back as though he were supporting the chimney-piece with his back.

'The King knoweth how men will lie about a woman,' she began again. 'The King knoweth how ye may buy false witness as ye may buy herrings in the market-place at so much a score. An the King were such a man as not to know these things, I would not wed with him. An the King were such a man as not to trust in me, I would not wed with him. I could have no peace. I could have no rest. I am not one that ask little, but much.'

'Why, you ask much of them that do support your cause,' he laughed from his private thinking.

'I do ask this oath of you,' she answered: 'that neither with sword nor stiletto, nor with provoked quarrel, nor staves, nor clubs, nor assassins, ye do seek to stay my cousin's coming.'

He cut across her purpose with asking again: 'Ha' ye seen the King rage jealously?'

'Knight,' she said, 'I will have your oath.' And, as he paused in thought, she said: 'Before God! if ye swear it not, I will make the King to send for him hither guarded and set around with an hundred men.'

'Ye will not have him harmed?' he asked craftily. 'Ye do love him better than another?'

She rose to her feet, her lips parted. 'Swear!' she cried.

His fingers felt around his waist, then he raised his hand and uttered:

'I do swear that ne with sword ne stiletto, ne with staves nor with clubs, ne with any quarrels nor violence so never will I seek thy goodly cousin's life.'

He shook his head slowly at her.

'All the men ye have known have prayed ye to be rid of him,' he said; 'ye will live to rue.'

'Sir,' she answered him, 'I had rather live to rue the injury my cousin should do me than live to rue the having injured him.' She paused to think for a moment. 'When I am Queen,' she said, 'I will have the King set him in a command of ships to sail westward over the seas. He shall have the seeking for the Hesperides or the city of Atalanta, where still the golden age remains to be a model and en-sample for us.' Her eyes looked past Throckmorton. 'My cousin hath a steadfast nature to be gone on such pil-grimages. And I would the discovery were made, this King being King and I his Queen; rather that than the regaining of France; more good should come to Christendom.'

'Madam Howard,' Throckmorton grinned at her, 'if men of our day and kin do come upon any city where yet re-maineth the golden age, very soon shall be shewn the miracle of the corruptibility of gold. The rod of our corruption no golden state shall defy.'

She smiled friendlily at him.

'There we part company,' she said. 'For I do believe God made this world to be bettered. I think, and answer your question, I could never ha' loved you. For you be a child of the new Italians and I a disciple of the older holders of that land, who wrote, Cato voicing it for them, "Virtue spreadeth even as leaven leaveneth bread; a little lump in your flour in the end shall redeem all the loaf of the Republic."'

He smiled for a moment noiselessly, his mouth open but no sound coming out. Then he coaxed her:

'Answer my two other questions.'

'Knight,' she answered; 'for the truth of the last, ask, with thumbscrews, the witnesses ye found in Lincolnshire, and believe them as ye list. Or ask at the mouth of a drawwell if fishes be below in the water before ye ask a woman if she be chaste. For the other, consider of my actions hereafter if I do love the King's person.'

'Why, then, I shall never have kiss from mouth of thine,' he said, and pulled his cap down over his eyes to depart.

'When the sun shall set in the east,' she retorted, and gave him her hand to kiss.

Margot Poins raised her large, fair head from her stitching after he was gone, and asked:

'Tell me truly how ye love the King's person. Often I ha' thought of it; for I could love only a man more thin.'

'Child,' Katharine answered, 'his Highness distilleth from his person a make of majesty; there is no other such a man in Christendom. His Highness culleth from one's heart a make of pity—for, for sure, there is not in Christendom a man more tried or more calling to be led Godwards. The Greek writers had a myth, that the two wings of Love were made of Awe and Pity. Flaws I may find in him; but hot anger rises in my heart if I hear him miscalled. I will not perjure myself at his bidding; but being with him, I will kneel to him unbidden. I will not, to be his queen, have word in a divorce, for I have no truck with divorces; but I will humble myself to his Queen that is to pray her give me ease and him if the marriage be not consummated. For, so I love him that I will humble mine own self in the dust; but so I love love and its nobleness that, though I must live and die a cookmaid, I will not stoop in evil ways.'

'There is no man worth that guise of love,' Margot answered, her voice coming gruff and heavy, 'not the magister himself. I ha' smote one kitchenmaid i' the face this noon for making eyes at him.'

V

'My mad nephew,' Master Printer Badge said to Throckmorton, 'shall travel down from his chamber anon. When ye shall see the pickle he is in ye shall understand wherefore it needeth ten minutes to his downcoming.' To Throckmorton's query he shook his dark, bearded head and muttered: 'Nay; ye used him for your own purposes. Ye should know better than I what is like to have befallen him.'

Throckmorton swallowed his haste and leant back against the edge of a press that was not at work. Of these presses there were four there in the middle of the room: tall, black, compounded of iron and wood, the square inwards of each rose and fell rhythmically above the flutter of the printed leaves that the journeymen withdrew as they rose, and replaced, white, unsullied and damp as they came together again. Along the walls the apprentice setters stood before the black formes and with abstruse, deliberate or hesitating expressions, made swift snatches at the little leaden dice. The sifting sound of the leads going home and the creak of the presses with the heavy wheeze of one printer, huge and grizzled like a walrus, pulling the press-lever back and bending forward to run his eyes across the type—wheeze, creak and click—made a level and monotonous sound.

'Ye drill well your men,' Throckmorton said lazily, and smoothed his white fingers, holding them up against the light, as if they of all things most concerned him.

He had received that day at Hampton a letter from the printer here in Austin Friars, sent hastening by the hands of the pressman whose idle machine he now leant against. 'Sir,' the letter said, 'my nephew saith urgently that T.C. is landed at Greenwich. He might not stay him. What this importeth best is yknown to your worshipful self. By the swaying of the sea which late he overpassed, being tempestive, and by other things, my nephew is rendered incoherent. That God may save you and guide your counsels and those of your master to the more advantaging of the Protestant religion that now, praised be God! standeth higher in the realm than ever it did, is the prayer of Jno. Badge the Younger.'

Throckmorton had hastened there to the hedges of Austin Friars at the fastest of his bargemen's oars. The printer had told him that, but that the business was the Lord Privy Seal's and, as he understood, went to the advantaging of Protestantism and the casting down of Popery, never would he ha' sent with the letter his own printer journeyman, busied as they were with printing of his great Bible in English.

'Here is an idle press,' he said, pointing at the mute and lugubrious instrument of black, 'and I doubt I ha' done wrong.' His moody brow beneath the black, dishevelled hair became overcast so that it wrinkled into great furrows like crowns. 'I doubt whether I have done wrong,' and he folded his immense bare arms, on which the hair was like a black boar's, and pondered. 'If I thought I had done wrong, I might not sleep seven nights.'

A printer yawned at his loom, and the great dark man shouted at him:

'Foul knave, ye show indolence! Wot ye that ye be printing the Word of God to send abroad in this land?

Wot ye that for this ye shall stand with the elect in Heaven?' He turned upon Throckmorton. 'Sir,' he said, 'your master Cromwell advanceth the cause, therefore I ha' served him in this matter of the letter. But, sir, I am doubtful that, by losing one moment from the printing of the pure Word of God, I have not lost more time than a year's work of thy master.'

Throckmorton rubbed gently the long hand that he still held against the light.

'Ye fall away from Privy Seal?' he asked.

The printer gazed at him with glowering and suffused eyes, choking in his throat. He raised an enormous hand before Throckmorton's face.

'Courtier,' he cried, 'with this hand I ha' stopped an ox, smiting it between the eyes. Wo befal the man, traitor to Privy Seal, that I do meet and betwixt whose eyes this hand doth fall.' The hand quivered in the air with fury. 'I can raise a thousand 'prentices and a thousand journeymen to save Privy Seal from any peril; I can raise ten thousand citizens, and ten thousand to-morrow again from the shires by pamphlets of my printing; I can raise a mighty army thus to shield him from Papists and the devil's foul contrivances. An I were a Papist, I would pray to him, were he dead, as he were a saint.' Throckmorton moved his face a line or two backwards from the gesticulating ham of a hand, and blinked his eyes. 'My gold were Privy Seal's an he needed it; my blood were his and my prayers. Nevertheless,' and his voice took a more exalted note, 'one letter of the Word of God, God aiding it, is of more avail than Privy Seal, or I, and all those I can love, or he. With his laws and his nose for treason he hath smitten the Amalekites above the belt; but a letter of the Word of God can smite them hip and thigh, God helping.' He seemed again to choke in his throat, and said more quietly: 'But ye shall not think a man in land better loveth this godly flail of the monks.'

'Why, I do think ye would stand up against the King's self,' Throckmorton said, 'and I am glad to hear it.'

'Against all printers and temporal powers,' the printer answered. Amongst the apprentices and journeymen a murmur arose of acclamation or of denial, some being of opinion that the King was divine in origin and inspiration, but for the most part they supported their master, and Throckmorton's blue eyes travelled from one to the other.

But the printer heaved a sigh of satisfaction.

'God be thanked,' he said, 'that keepeth the hearts of princes and guideth with His breath all temporal occurrences.' Throckmorton was about to touch his cap at the name of Omnipotence, but remembering that he was among Protestants changed the direction of his hand and scratched his cheek among the little hairs of his beard; 'the signs are favourable that our good King's Highness shall still incline to our cause and Privy Seal's.'

Throckmorton said: 'Anan?'

'Aye,' the printer said heavily, 'good news is come of Cleves.'

'Ye ha' news from Cleves?' Throckmorton asked swiftly.

'From Cleves not,' the printer answered; 'but from the Court by way of Paris and thence from Cleves.' And to the interested spy he related, accurately enough, that a make of mouthing, mowing, magister of the Latin tongues had come from Paris, having stolen copies of the Cleves envoy's letters in that town, and that these letters said that Cleves was fast inclined to the true Schmalkaldner league of Lutherans and would pay tribute truly, but no more than that do fealty to the accursed leaguer of the Pope called Charles the Emperor.

Throckmorton inclined his cap at an angle to the floor.

'How had ye that news that was so secret?' he asked.

The printer shook his dark beard with an air of heavy pleasure.

'Ye have a great organisation of spies,' he said, 'but better is the whisper of God among the faithful.'

'Why,' Throckmorton answered, 'the magister Udal hath to his sweetheart thy niece Margot Poins.'

At her name the printer's eyes filled with a sudden and violent heat.

'Seek another channel,' he cried, and waved his arms at the low ceiling. 'Before the face of Almighty God I swear that I ha' no truck with Margot my niece. Since she has been sib with the whore of the devil called Kat Howard, never hath she told me a secret through her paramour or elsewise. A shut head the heavy logget keepeth—let her not come within reach of my hand.' He swayed back upon his feet. 'Let her not come,' he said. He bent his brows upon Throckmorton. 'I marvel,' he uttered, 'that ye who are so faithful a servant o' Privy Seal's can have truck with the brother of my niece Margot.'

'Printer,' Throckmorton answered him, 'ye know well that when the leaven of Protestantism hath entered in there, houses are divided against themselves. A wench may be a foul Papist and serve, if ye will, Kat Howard; but her brother shall yet be an indifferent good servant for me.'

The printer, who had tolerated that his men should hear his panegyric of the Bible and Privy Seal, scowled at them now so that again the arms swung to and fro with the levers, the leads clicked. He put his great head nearer Throckmorton's and muttered:

'Are ye certain my nephew serveth ye well? He was never wont to favour our cause, and, before ye sent him on this errand, he was wont to cry out in his cups that he was disgraced for having carried letters betwixt Kat Howard and the King. If this were true he was no friend of ours.'

'Why, it was true,' Throckmorton uttered negligently.

The printer caught at the spy's wrist, and the measure of his earnestness showed the extent of his passion for Privy Seal's cause.

'Use him no more,' he said. 'Both children of my sister were ever indifferents. They shall not serve thee well.'

'It was ever Privy Seal's motto and habit to use for his servitors those that had their necks in his noose. Such men serve him ever the best.'

The printer shook his head gloomily.

'I wager my nephew will yet play the traitor to Privy Seal.'

'I will do it myself ere that,' and Throckmorton yawned, throwing his head back.

'The scaldhead is there,' the printer said; and in the doorway there stood, supporting himself by the lintel, the young Poins. His face was greenish white; a plaster was upon his shaven head; he held up one foot as if it pained him to set it to the floor. Through the house-place where sat the aged grandfather with his cap pulled over his brows, pallid, ironical and seeming indescribably ancient, the printer led the spy. The boy hobbled after them, neglecting the old man's words:

'Ha' no truck with men of Privy Seal's. Privy Seal hath stolen my ground.' In the long shed where they ate all, printer, grandfather, apprentices and journeymen, the printer thrust open the door with a heavy gesture, entering first and surveying the long trestles.

'Ye can speak here,' he said, and motioned away an aged woman. She bent above a sea coal fire on the hearth where boiled, hung from a hook, a great pot. The old thing, in short petticoats and a linsey woolsey bodice that had been purple and green, protested shrilly. Her crock was on the boil; she was not there to be driven away; she had work like other folk, and had been with the printer's mother eight years before he was born. His voice, raised to its height, was useless to drown her words. She could not hear him; and shrugging his shoulders, he said to Throckmorton that she heard less than the walls, and that was the best place he had for them to talk in. He slammed the door behind him.

Throckmorton set his foot upon the bench that ran between table and wall. He scowled fell-ly at the boy, so that his brows came down below his nose-top. 'Ye ha' not stayed him,' he said.

The boy burst forth in a torrent of rage and despair.

He cursed Throckmorton to his face for having sent him upon this errand.

'I ha' been beaten by a gatewarden! by a knave! by a ploughman's son from Lincolnshire!' he cried. 'A' cracked my skull with a pikestave and kicked me about the ribs when I lay on the ship's floor, sick like a pig. God curse the day you sent me to Calais, a gentleman's son, to be beat by a boor!' He broke off and began again. 'God curse you and the day I saw you! God curse Kat Howard and the day I carried her letter! God curse my sister Margot and the day she gar'd me carry the letters! And may a swift death of the pox take off Kat Howard's cousin—may he rot and stink through the earth above his grave. He would not fight with me, but aboard a ship when I was sick set a Lincolnshire logget to beat me, a gentleman's son!'

'Why, thy gentility shall survive it,' Throckmorton said. 'But an it will not have more beating to its back, ye shall tell me where ye left T. Culpepper.'

'At Greenwich,' said the young Poins, and vomited forth curses. The old woman came from her pots to peer at the plasters on his skull, and then returned to the fire gibbering and wailing that she was not in that house plasters for to make.

'Knave,' Throckmorton said, 'an ye will not tell me your tale swiftly ye shall right now to the Tower. It is life and death to a leaden counter an I find not Culpepper ere nightfall.'

The young Poins stretched forth his arm and groaned.

'Part is bruises and part is sickness of the waves,' he muttered; 'but if I make not shift to slit his weazand ere nightfall, pox take all my advancement for ever. I will tell my weary tale.'

Throckmorton paused, held his head down, fingered his beard, and said:

'When left ye him at Greenwich?'

'This day at dawn,' Poins answered, and cursed again.

'Drunk or sober?'

'Drunk as a channel codfish.'

The old woman came, a sheaf of jack-knives in her arms, muttering along the table.

'Get you to bed,' she croaked. 'I will not ha' warmed new sheets for thee, and thee not use them. Get thee to bed.'

Throckmorton pushed her back, and caught the boy by the jacket near the throat.

'Ye shall tell me the tale as we go,' he said, and punctuated his words by shakes. 'But, oaf that I trusted to do a man's work, ye swing beneath a tree this night an we find not the man ye failed to stay.'

The young Poins—he panted out the story as he trotted, wofully keeping pace to Throckmorton's great strides between the hedges—had stuck to Culpepper as to his shadow, in Calais town. At each turn he had showed the warrant to be master of the lighters; he had handed over the gold that Throckmorton had given him. But Culpepper had turned a deaf ear to him, and, setting up a violent friendship with the Lincolnshire gatewarden over pots of beer in a brewhouse, had insisted on buying Hogben out of his company and taking him over the sea to be witness of his wedding with Katharine Howard. Dogged, and thrusting his word and his papers in at every turn, the young Poins had pursued them aboard a ship bound for the Thames.

This story came out in jerks and with divagations, but it was evident to Throckmorton that the young man had stuck to his task with a dogged obtuseness enough to have given offence to a dozen Culpeppers. He had begged him, in the inn, to take the lieutenancy of the Calais lighters; he had trotted at Culpepper's elbow in the winding streets; he had stood in his very path on the gangway to the ship that was to take them to Greenwich. At every step he had pulled out of his poke the commission for the lieutenancy —so that Throckmorton had in his mind, by the time they sat in the stern of the swift barge, the image of Culpepper as a savage bulldog pursued along streets and up ship-sides by a gambolling bear cub that pulled at his ears and danced before him. And he could credit Culpepper only with a saturnine and drunken good humour at having very successfully driven Cardinal Pole out of Paris. That was the only way in which he could account for the fact that Culpepper had not spitted the boy at the first onslaught. But for the sheer ill-luck of his sword's having been stolen, he might have done it, and been laid by the heels for six months in Calais. For Calais being a frontier town of the English realm, it was an offence very serious there for English to draw sword upon English, however molested.

It was that upon which Throckmorton had counted; and he cursed the day when Culpepper had entered the thieves' hut outside Ardres. But for that Culpepper must have drawn upon the boy; he must have been lying then in irons in Calais holdfast. As it was, there was this long chase. God knew whether they would find him in Greenwich; God knew where they would find him. He had gone to Greenwich, doubtless, because when he had left England the Court had been in Greenwich, and he expected there to find his cousin Kat. He would fly to Hampton as soon as he knew she was at Hampton; but how soon would he know it? By Poins' account, he was too drunk to stand, and had been carried ashore on the back of his Lincolnshire henchman. Therefore he might be lying in the streets of Greenwich—and Greenwich was a small place. But different men carried their liquor so differently, and Culpepper might go ashore too drunk to stand and yet reach Hampton sober enow to be like a raging bear by eventide.

That above all things Throckmorton dreaded. For that evening Katharine would be come back from the interview with Anne of Cleves at Windsor; and whether she had succeeded or not with her quest, the King was certain to be with her in her room—to rejoice on the one hand, or violently to plead his cause on the other. And Throckmorton knew his King well enough—he knew, that is to say, his private image of his King well enough—to be assured that a meeting between the King then and Culpepper there, must lead Katharine to her death. He considered the blind, immense body of jealousy that the King was. And, at Hampton, Privy Seal would have all avenues open for Culpepper to come to his cousin. Privy Seal had detailed Viridus, who had had the matter all the while in hand, to inflame Culpepper's mind with jealousy so that he should run shouting through the Court with a monstrous outcry.

It was because of this that Throckmorton dreaded to await Culpepper at Hampton; there he was sure enow to find him, sooner or later, but there would be the many spies of Privy Seal's around all the avenues to the palace. He might himself send away the spies, but it was too dangerous; for, say what he would, if he held Culpepper from Katharine Howard, Cromwell would visit it mercilessly upon him.

He turned the nose of his barge down the broadening, shining grey stream towards Greenwich. The wind blew freshly up from the sea; the tide ran down, and Throckmorton pulled his bonnet over his eyes to shade them from sea and breeze, and the wind that the rowers made. For it was the swiftest barge of the kingdom: long, black, and narrow, with eight watermen rowing, eight to relieve them, and always eight held in reserve at all landing stages for that barge's crew. So well Privy Seal had organised even the mutinous men of the river that his service might be swift and sudden. Throckmorton had set down the bower at the stern, that the wind might have less hold.

Nevertheless it blew cold, and he borrowed a cloak and a pottle of sack to warm the young Poins, who had run with him capless and without a coat. For, listening to the boy's disjointed tale out in the broad reaches below London, Throckmorton recognised that if the young man were incredibly a fool he was incredibly steadfast too, and a steadfast fool is a good tool to retain for simple work. He had, too—the boy—a valuable hatred for Culpepper that he allowed to transfer itself to Katharine herself: a brooding hatred that hung in his blue eyes as he gazed downwards at the barge floor or spat at the planks of the side. Its ferocity was augmented by the patches of plaster that stretched over his skull and dropped over one blonde eyebrow.

'Cod!' he ejaculated. 'Cod! Cod! Cod!' and waved a fist ferociously at the rushes that spiked the waters of the river in their new green. 'They waited till I was too sick of the sickness of the sea, too sick to stand—more mortal sick than ever man was. I hung to a rope and might not let go. And Cod! Cod! Cod! Culpepper lay under the sterncastle in a hole and set his Lincolnshire beast to baste my ribs.'

He spat again with gloomy quiescence into the bottom of the boat.

'In the mid of the sea,' he said, 'where the ship pointed at heaven and then at the fiend his home, I hung to a rope and was basted! And that whore's son lay in his hole and laughed. For I was a cub, says he, and not fit for a man's converse or striking.'

Throckmorton's eyes glimmered a little.

'You have been used as befits no gentleman's son,' he said. 'I will see to the righting of your wrongs.'

Poins swore with an amazing obscenity.

'Shall right 'em myself,' he said, 'so I meet T. Culpepper in this flesh as a man.'

Throckmorton leaned gently forward and touched his arm.

'I will right thy wrongs,' he said, 'and see to thine advancement; for if in this service you ha' failed, yet ha' you been persistent and feal.' He dabbled one white hand in the water. 'Nevertheless,' he said slowly, 'I would have you consider that your service in this ends here.' He spoke still more slowly: 'I would have you to understand this. Aforetime I gave you certain instructions as to using your sword upon this Culpepper if you might not otherwise stay him.' He held up one finger. 'Now mark; your commission is ceased. You shall no longer for my service draw sword, knife or dagger, stave nor club, upon this man.'

Poins looked at him with gloomy surprise that was changing swiftly to hot rage.

'I am under oath to a certain one to use no violence upon this man,' Throckmorton said, 'and to encourage no other to do violence.'

Poins thrust his round, brick-red brow out like a turkey cock's from the boat cloak into Throckmorton's face.

'I am under no oath of yourn!' he shouted. Throckmorton shrugged his shoulders and wagged one finger at him. 'No oath o' yourn!' the boy repeated. 'God knows who ye be or why it is so. But I ha' heard ye ha' my neck in a noose; I ha' heard ye be dangerous. Yet, before God, I swear in your teeth that if I meet this man to his face, or come upon his filthy back, drunk, awake, asleep, I will run him through the belly and send his soul to hell. He had me, a gentleman's son, basted by a hind!'

This long speech exhausted his breath, and he fell back panting.

'I had as soon ye had my head as not,' he muttered desperately, 'since I have been basted.'

'Why,' Throckmorton answered, 'for your private troubles, I know naught of them. There may be some that will thank ye or advance ye for spitting of this gallant. But I am not one of them. Nevertheless will I be your friend, whom ye would have served better an ye could.'

He smiled in his inward manner and went to polishing of his nails. A little later he felt the bruises on the boy's arms, and stayed the barge for a moment the stage where, swiftly, eight oarsmen took the places of the eight that had rowed two shifts out of three—stayed the barge for time enough to purchase for the boy a ham, a little ginger, some raw eggs and sack.

The barge rushed forward, with the jar of oars and the sound, like satin tearing, of the water at the bows, across the ruffled reaches of the broad waters. The gilded roofs, the gabled fronts of the palace at Greenwich called Placentia, winked in the fresh sunlight. Throckmorton had a great fever of excitement, but having sworn to let his oarsmen be scourged with leathern thongs if they made no more efforts, he lay back upon the purple cushions and toyed with the strings of the yellow ensign that floated behind them. It was his purpose to put heart in the boy and to feed his rage, so that alternately he promised to give him the warding of the Queen's door—a notable advancement—or assented to the lad's gloom when he said that he was fit only for the stables, having been beaten by a groom. So that at the quay the boy sprang forth mightily, swaying the boat behind him. The trace of his sea-sickness had left him; he swore to tear Culpepper's throat apart as if it had been capon flesh.

Throckmorton swiftly quartered the gardens, sending, in his passage beneath the tall palace arch, a dozen men to search all the paths for any drunkards that might there lie hidden. He sent the young Poins to search the three ale-houses of the village where seamen new landed sat to drink. But, having found the sergeant of void palaces asleep in a small cell at the house end, he learned that two men, speaking Lincolnshire, had been there two hours agone, questing for Master Viridus and swearing that they had rid France of the devil and were to be made great lords for it. The sergeant, an old, corpulent Spaniard who had been in England forty years, having come with the dead Queen Katharine and been given this honourable post because the queen had loved him, folded his fat hands across his round stomach as he sat on the floor, his legs stretched out, his head against the hangings.

'I might not make out if they were lords or what manner of cavaliers,' he said. 'They sought some woman whom they would not name, and ran through a score of empty rooms. God knows whither they went.'

He pulled his nightcap further over his head, nodded at Throckmorton, and resumed his meditations.

There was no finding them in the still and empty corridors of the palace; but at the gateway he heard that the two men had clamoured to know where they might purchase raw shinbone of beef, and had been directed to the

house of a widow Emden. There Throckmorton found
their tracks, for the sacking that covered the window-holes
was burst outwards, beef-bones lay on the road before the
door, and, within, the widow, black, begrimed and very
drunk, lay inverted on the clay of the floor, her head
beneath the three legs of the chopping block, so that she
was as if in a pillory, but too fuddled to do more than wave
her legs. A prentice who crouched, with a broken head, in
a corner of the filthy room, said that a man from Lincolnshire, all in Lincoln green, with a red beard, had wrought
this ruin of beef-bones that he had cast through the windows, and had then comforted the screaming widow with
much strong drink from a black bottle. They had wanted
raw beef to make them valiant against some wedding, and
they threw the beef-bones through the sacking because
they said the place stunk villainously. They seemed, these
two, to have visited every hovel in the damp and squalid
village that lay before the palace gates. They had kicked
beds of straw over the floors, thrown crocks at the pigs,
melted pewter plates in the fires.

For pure joy at being afoot and ashore in England again,
they had cast coins into all the houses and hovels of mud;
they had brought out cans and casks from the alehouses,
and cast pies into the streets, and caused the dismal ward
to cry out: 'God save free Englishmen!' 'Curse the sea!'
and 'A plague of Frenchmen that be devils!'

And the after effects of their carnival menaced Throckmorton, for from the miserable huts, where ragged women
were rearranging the scattered straws and wiping egg-yolk
from the broken benches, there issued a ragged crowd of
men with tangled and muddy hair and boys unclothed save
for sacks that whistled about their lean hips. The liquor
that Culpepper and Hogben had distributed had rendered
them curious or full of mutiny and discontent, and they
surrounded Throckmorton's brilliant figure in its purple
velvet, with the gold neck-chains and the jewelled hat, and
some of them asked for money, and some called him

'Frenchman,' and some knew him for a spy, and some caught up stones and jawbones furtively to cast at him.

But, arrogant and with his head set high, he borrowed a whip from a packman that shouldered his way through the street, and lashed at their legs and ragged heads. The crowd slunk, one by one, back under the darkness that was beneath the roofs of reeds, and the idea of a good day that for a moment had risen in their minds at Culpepper's legendary approach, sank down and flickered out once more in their hungry bellies and fever-dimned minds.

'God!' he said, 'we will have hangmen here,' and pursued his search. He met the young Poins at the head of the village street, and learned from him that Culpepper and his supporter had hired horses to ride to Hampton and had galloped away three hours before, holding legs of mutton by the feet and using them for cudgels to beat their horses.

'Before God!' the boy said, 'an I had money to hire horses I would overtake them, if I overtook not the devil erstwhile.'

Throckmorton pulled out his purple purse that was embroidered with silk crosses. He extracted from it four crowns of gold.

'Lad,' he said, 'I do not give thee gold to follow Kat Howard's cousin with. This is thy wage for the service thou hast done aforetime.' He reflected for a moment. 'If thou wilt have a horse—but I urge it not—to go to Hampton where thy fellows of the guard are—for, having served well ye may once more and without danger rejoin your mates—if ye will have such a horse, go to the horseward of the palace and say I sent you. Withouten doubt ye are mad to hasten back to your mates, a commendable desire. And the King's horses shall hasten faster than any hired horse—so that ye may easily overtake a man that hath but two hours' start towards Hampton.'

Whilst Poins was already hastening towards the gateway, Throckmorton cried to him at a distance:

'Ask at each cross-road guard-house and at all ferries and bridges if some have passed that way; and at the landing-stage if perchance caballeros have altered their desires and had it in their minds to take to boats.'

He sped through the wind to the riverside, set again his oars in motion and swept up the tide. It had turned and they made good progress.

VI

The Queen sat in her painted gallery at Richmond, and all around her her maids sewed and span. The gallery was long; along the panels that faced the windows were angels painted in red and blue and gold, and in the three centre squares St George, whose face was the face of the King's Highness, in one issued from a yellow city upon a green plain; in one with a cherry-coloured lance slew a green dragon from whose mouth issued orange-coloured flames; and in one carried away, that he might wed her in a rose-coloured tower on a hillside, a princess in a black gown with hair painted of real gold.

Whilst the maids sewed in silence the Queen sat still upon a stool. Light-skinned, not very stout, with a smooth oval face, she had laid her folded hands on the gold and pearl embroidery of her lap and gazed away into the distance, thinking. She sat so still that not even the lawn tips of her wide hood with its invisible, minute sewings of white, quivered. Her gown was of cloth of gold, but since her being in England she had learned to wear a train, and in its folds on the ground slept a small Italian greyhound. About her neck she had a partelet set with green jewels and with pearls. Her maids sewed; the spinning-wheels ate away the braided flax from the spindles, and the sunlight poured down through the high windows. She was a very fair woman then, and many that had seen her there sit had marvelled of the King's disfavour for her; but she was accounted wondrous still, sitting thus by the hour with the little hounds in the folds of her dress. Only her eyes with their half-closed lids gave to her lost gaze the appearance of a humour and irony that she never was heard to voice.

They turned to the opening door, a flush came into her face, spread slowly down her white neck and was lost in the white opening of her shoulder-pieces, and she greeted Katharine Howard, kneeling at her feet, with an inclination of the head so tiny that you could not see the motion. Her eyes remained motionlessly upon the girl's face; only the lids moved suddenly when Katharine spoke to her in German.

'You speak my tongue?' the Queen asked, motionless still and speaking very low. Katharine remained upon her knees.

'I learned to read books in German when I was a child,' Katharine said; 'and since you came I have spoken an hour a day with a German astronomer that I might give you pleasure if so be it chanced.'

'So it is well,' the Queen said. 'Not many have so done.'

'God has endowed me with an ease of tongues,' Katharine answered; 'many others would have ventured it for your Grace's pleasure. But your tongue is a hard tongue.'

'I have needed to learn hard sentences in yours,' the Queen said, 'and have had many masters many hours of the day. I will have you stand up upon your feet.'

Katharine remained upon her knees.

'I will have you stand up upon your feet,' the Queen repeated.

'I have a prayer to make,' Katharine answered.

The Queen looked for a minute straight before her, then slowly turned her head to one side. When her gaze rested upon her women they rose and, with a clatter of their feet and a rustle of garments, carrying their white sewings and their spinning-wheels stilled, went away down the gallery. The German lord of Overstein, bearded and immense in the then German fashion, came from behind the retreating women to stand before the Queen signifying that he would offer his interpretership. She dismissed him without speaking, letting her eyes rest upon him. She was the most silent woman in the world, but all people said that no queen had women and men servers that needed fewer words or so discreetly did their devoirs.

The silence and the bright light of the sun swathed these two women's figures, so that Katharine seemed to hear the flutter against the window-glass of a brown butterfly that, having sheltered in the hall all winter, now sought to take a part in the new brightness of the world. Katharine kept her knees, her eyes upon the floor; the Queen, motionless and soft, let her eyes rest upon Katharine's hood. From time to time they travelled to her face, to the medallion that hung from her neck, and to her dark green skirt of velvet that lay around her upon the floor. The butterfly sought another window; the Queen spoke at last.

'You seek my queenship'; and in her still voice there was neither passion, nor pity, nor question, nor resignation.

Katharine raised her eyes: they saw the imprisoned butterfly, but she found no words.

'You have more courage than I,' the Queen said.

Suddenly she made a single gesture with her hands, as if she swept something from her lap: some invisible dust— and that was all. Still Katharine did not move nor speak; she had prepared speeches—speeches against the Queen's being disdainful, enraged, or dissolved in tears. She had read in books all night from Aulus Gellius to Cicero to get wisdom. But here there were no speeches called for; no speeches could be made. The significance of the Queen's gesture of sweeping dust from her lap slowly overwhelmed her.

'You have more courage than I,' the Queen repeated, as though slowly she were making a catalogue of Katharine's qualities to set dispassionately against her own; and again her eyes moved over Katharine. With her first swift gesture she drew from the stool-top a pamphlet of writing, upon which she had sat. Her face grew slowly red.

'It did not need this long writing against my person,' she said. 'I take it grievously.'

Katharine moved upon her knees as if she had been stung by an intolerable accusation.

'Before God!——' she began to say.

'Well, I believe you had no part in the writing,' the Queen interrupted her. 'Yet the more I say you have courage: to wed a man that will write lies of another woman's body and powers.'

Katharine sat still; the Queen's slow anger faded slowly away.

'I do not see why this King thinks you more fair than I be,' she said dispassionately; 'but what draweth the love of man to woman is not yet known.'

Again she repeated:

'There was no need of this writing against me. The King has never played the husband's part to me; I would have you tell him, if I go in danger from him, that, for me, he may go his ways. I have no mind to stay him, nor to be a queen in this country. Here, it is said, they slay queens.'

'If I will be Queen, it is that God may bless this realm and King with the old faith again,' Katharine said. Anne's eyelids narrowed.

'It is best known to yourself why you will be Queen,' she said. 'It is best known to God what faith he will have in this your realm. I know not what faith he liketh best, nor yet what side of a queen's functions most commendeth itself unto you.'

She seemed to withdraw herself more and more from any struggle, as if she were a novice that took an invisible veil—and she uttered only requests as to the world into which she would withdraw from this one.

'I am not minded to go back to Cleves,' she stipulated; for she had thought much and long in her stillnesses of what she would have; 'the Duke, my brother, is to blame for having brought me to this pass. Moreover, he is not able to defend his lands; so that if, with a proper establishing and revenue, I go back to Cleves, the Emperor Charles, who hath a tooth for gold, may too easily undo me. I would have a castle here in England; for England is an island, and well defended in all its avenues, and its King a man of honour and his word to such as never cross him, as never will I.'

She spoke slowly, as if in her mind she were ticking off little notes pencilled on her tablets; for since she could not read she had a memory that she could trust to. 'I will have a castle built me not strong enough to withstand the King's forces, since those I make no call to withstand, but strong enough to guard me against robber bands and the insurrections that are ordinary. Upon a slope that shall take the sun in winter, with trees about beneath which I may sit in the heat of summer-time. I will have a good show of servants, because I am a princess of noble lineage; I will have most of them Germans that I may speak easily with them, but some English, understanding German, so that the King may be advised I work no treasons against him. From time to time I will have the King to visit and to talk with me courteously and fairly as well he can: this in order to counterpart and destroy the report that I smell foul and am so ill to see that it makes a man ill——'

Her eyes, resting upon Katharine, closed slightly again with a tiny malice.

'I will have you not to fear that, upon such visits, I will use wiles to entrap the King. I do not favour him. I am not content to be queen of this country. It is as fair as my own country. In summer it is more cool, in the winter time more temperate. Meats here are good; cooks are better than with us. What a woman and a princess in this world would have is here all at the best, save only its men, and the most dangerous of all its men is the King.'

Katharine's ready anger rose at her words, though before the Queen's speeches had flowed above her head and left her speechless and ashamed.

'The King is known throughout Christendom,' she said, 'for the royallest prince, the noblest speaker, the most princely horseman, the most munificent and the most learned in the law.'

'That he may be,' the Queen smiled faintly, 'to them

that have never crossed him. It has been my ill-destiny so to do.'

'Madam,' Katharine cried out, 'never man was so crossed, ill-served, evilly-led, or betrayed. Ye may not mislike him if at times he be petulant. I do the more praise him for it.'

'Why, you do love him,' the Queen said. 'I have no cause so to do.'

Katharine caught at one of her hands.

'Your Grace,' she said, 'Queen and high potentate, this realm calleth out that some one person do lead the King aright. Before God, I think I do not seek powers or temporal crowns. Maybe it is sweet to sit in a painted gallery and be a queen, but I have very little considered it; only, here is a King that crieth for the peace of God, a people that clamoureth aloud to be led back to the ways of God, a land parched for rain, swept by gales of wind and pestilences, bewailing the lost favour of God, and the Holy Church devastated that standeth between God and the realm.' The Queen listened to her as if, having made her stipulations, she had no more personal interest in the matter and were listening to the tale of a journey. 'Before God!' Katharine said, 'if you were not a virgin for the King, or if the King have coerced you to forswearing yourself in this matter, I would not be the King's wife, but his concubine. Only, sore is his need of me; he hath sworn it many times, and I do believe it, that I best, if anyone may, may give him rest with my converse and lead him to peace. He hath sworn that never woman save I made him so clearly to see his path to goodness; and never woman save I, at convenient seasons, have made him so forget his many cares.'

'Why, you have still more courage than I had thought,' the Queen said, 'to take a man so dangerous upon so little assurance.' She moved the hand that Katharine touched in her lap neither forward nor away; but at last she said:

'I am neither of your country nor for it; neither of your faith nor against it. But, being here, here I do sojourn. I came not here of mine own will. Men have handled me as they would, as if I had been a doll. But, if I may have as much of the sun as shines, and as much of comfort as the realm affords its better sort, being a princess, and to be treated with some reverence, I care not if ye take King, crown, and commonalty, so ye leave me the ruling of my house and the freedom to wash my face how I will. I had as soon see England linked again with the Papists as the Schmalkaldners; I had as lief see the King married to you as another; I had as lief all men do what they will so they leave me to go my ways and feed me well.'

She looked again upon Katharine, and for the first time spoke as if she were addressing her:

'I make out that you are a woman with an itch to meddle at the righting of the world. There have been more men than women at the task, but such an one was I never. The King was never man of mine, nor should have been had I any say in the matter.' She half closed her eyes again. 'Doubtless had it been otherwise the King would have constrained me by threats and tortures to forswear myself. I am as I was when I came to Dover. As the King saw me so he left me. Yet do I maintain and avow it was rather because he feared alliance with my brother's party than for any foulness of my person.'

Katharine passed her hands over her eyes.

'I do feel myself a thief and a cozener,' she said.

'Ye be none,' the Queen said; 'ye take no more than what I least prize of this world. Had it not been thee it might have been a worse; for assuredly I was not made to foot it with this King.'

'Nevertheless—— ' Katharine began. But the Queen was no more content to listen to her.

'Ye are as some I have known,' she said; 'they scruple to take what they very much crave, though it hang ready to drop into their hands; because they much crave it, therefore they scruple.' She had a small golden bullet beneath her clasped hands, and she cast it into a basin of silver that stood on a tripod beside her skirts. At the silvery clash and roll of the ball's running sound on the metal, doors opened along the gallery, and servitors came in bearing Rhenish wine in glass flagons and, upon great salvers, cakes in the forms of hearts or twisted into true-love-knots of pastry.

Katharine noted these things as being worthy of imitation.

'It is no more to me,' the Queen said, 'to lose the other things to you than to lose to you the wine that you shall drink or a pile of cakes.' Nevertheless she left Katharine upon her knees till she had taken her cup, for it pleased her that her servitors should see her treated with due worship.

VII

It was noon of that day when Katharine Howard set out again from Richmond to ride back to Hampton Court; and at noon of that day Throckmorton's barge shot dangerously beneath London Bridge, hastening to Hampton Court. At noon Thomas Culpepper passed over London Bridge, because a great crowd pressed across it from the south going to see a burning at Smithfield; at noon, too, or five minutes later, the young Poins galloped furiously past the end of the bridge and did not cross over, but sped through Southwark towards Hampton Court. And at noon or thereabouts the King, dressed in green as a husbandman, sat on a log to await a gun-fire, in the forest that was near to Richmond river path opposite Isleworth. He had given to Katharine a paper that she was to deliver to the master gunner of Richmond Palace in case the Queen Anne did satisfy her that the marriage was no marriage. So that, when among the green glades where the great trees let down their branches near the sward and shewed little tips of tender green leaves, he heard three thuds come echoing, he sprang to his feet, and, smiting his great, green-clothed thigh, he cried out: 'Ha! I be young again!' He pulled to his lips the mouth of the English horn that was girdled across his shoulder and under his arm; he set his feet wide apart, filled his lungs with air, and blew a thin, clear call. At once there issued from brakes, thickets and glades the figures of men, dressed like the King in yeoman's green, bearing bows over their shoulders, horns at their elbows, or having straining dogs in their leashes.

'Ho!' the King said to his chief verderer, a man of sixty with a grey beard, but so that all others could hear; 'be it well understood that I will have you shew some ladies what make of thing it is to rule over jolly Englishmen.' He directed them how he would have them drive the deer at the end of the glade; he saw to the setting up of white wands of peeled willows and, taking from his yeoman-companion, that was the Earl of Surrey, his great bow, he shot a mighty shaft along the glade, to shew how far away he would have the deer to pass like swift ghosts between the aisles of the trees.

But the palace of Hampton lay deserted and given up to scullions, who lay in the sunlight and took their rare ease. For a great many lords that could shoot well with the bow were gone to play the yeoman with the King; and a great many that had sumptuous and gallant apparel were gone to join the ladies riding back from Richmond; and the King's whole council, together with many lords that were awful or reverend in their appearance, were gone to sit in the scaffold to see the burning of the friar that had denied the King's supremacy of the Church and the burnings of the six Protestants that had denied the presence of Christ's body in the Sacrament. Only Privy Seal, who had ordered these things, was still walking in his gallery where he so often had walked of late.

He had with him Wriothesley, whose face was utterly downcast and abashed; he walked turning more swiftly than had been his wont ever before. Wriothesley hung down his great bearded, honest head and sighed three times.

'Sir,' he said at last, 'I see before us nothing but that ye make to divorce the Queen Anne.' And the words seemed to come from him as if they cost him his heart's blood.

Cromwell paused before him, his hands behind his back, his feet apart.

'The weighty question,' he said, 'is this: Who hath betrayed me: of Udal; of the alewife that he should have had the papers of; or Throckmorton?'

He had that morning received from Cleves, in the letter of his agent there, the certain proof that the Duke had written to the Emperor Charles making an utter submission to save his land from ruin, and as utterly abjuring his alliance with the King his brother-in-law and with the Schmalkaldner league and its Protestant princes. Cromwell had immediately called to him Wriothesley that was that day ordering the horses to take him back to Paris town. He had given him this news, which, if it were secret then, must in a month be made known to all the world. To Wriothesley the Protestant this blow was the falling in of the world; here was Protestantism at an end and dead. There remained nothing but to save the necks of some to carry on the faith to distant days. Therefore he had brought out his reluctant words to urge Privy Seal to the divorce of Anne of Cleves. There was no other way; there was no other issue. Privy Seal must abjure Cleves' Queen, and the very savour of a desire for a Protestant league.

But for Privy Seal the problem was not what to do, a thing he might settle in a minute's swift thought, but the discovery of who had betrayed him—for his whole life had been given to bringing together his machine of service. You might determine an alliance or a divorce between breath and breath; but the training of your instruments, the weeding out of them that had flaws in their fidelities; the exhibiting of a swift and awful vengeance upon mutineers —these were the things that called for thinking and long furrowing of brows. He considered of this point whilst Wriothesley spoke long and earnestly.

It was expedient before all things that Privy Seal keep the helm of the State; it was very certain that the King should not long keep to his marriage with the lady from Cleves; lamentable it was that Cleves had fallen away from

Protestantism and from the league that so goodly had promised for truth in religion. But so, alas that the day had come! so it was. The King was a man brave and royal in his degree, but unstable, so that to keep him to Protestantism and good government a firm man was earnestly needed. There was none other man than Privy Seal. Let him consider earnestly that if it tasted ill with his conscience to move this divorce, yet elsewise such great ills should strike the kingdom, that far better it were to deaden his conscience than to sacrifice for a queen of doubtful faith the best hope that they had then, all of them, in the world. He spoke for many minutes in this strain, for twice the clock struck the half-hour from the tower above the gallery.

Finally, long-bearded, solemn, and richly attired as he was, Wriothesley went down upon one knee, and, laying his bonnet on the ground, stretched out a long hand.

'My lord,' he said, 'I do beseech you that you stay with us and succour us. We are a small band, but zealous and well-caparisoned. Bethink you that you put this land in peril if by maintaining this Queen ye do endanger your precious neck. For I were loath to take arms against the King's Majesty, and we are loyal and faithful subjects all; yet sooner than ye should fall——'

Cromwell stood over him, looking at him dispassionately, his hands still behind his back.

'Well, it is a great matter,' he uttered elusively. He moved as if to walk off, then suddenly turned upon his heel again. 'Ye do me more ill by speaking in that guise than ever Cleves or Gardiner or all my enemies have done. For assuredly if rumours of your words should reach the King when he was ill-affected, it should go hardly with me.'

He paused, and then spoke gently.

'And assuredly ye do me more wrong than ill,' he said. 'For this I swear to you, ye have heard evil enow of me to have believed some. But there is no man dare call me traitor in his heart of them that do know me. And this I

tell you: I had rather die a thousand deaths than that ye
should prop me up against the majesty and awe of government. By so doing ye might, at a hazard, save my life, but
for certain ye would imperil that for which I have given
my life.'

Again he paused and paced, and again came back in his
traces to where Wriothesley knelt.

'Some danger there is for me,' he said, 'but I think it a
very little one. The King knoweth too well how good a
servant and how profitable I have been to him. I do think
he will not cast me away to please a woman. Yet this is a
very notable woman—ye wot of whom I speak; but I hope
very soon to have one to my hand that shall utterly cast
down and soil her in the eyes of the King's Highness.'

'Ye do think her unchaste?' Wriothesley asked. 'I have
heard you say——'

'Knight,' Cromwell answered; 'what I think will not be
revealed to-day nor to-morrow, but only at the Day of
Judgment. Nevertheless, so do I love my master's cause
that—if it peril mine own upon that awful occasion—I so
will strive to tear this woman down.'

Wriothesley rose, stiff and angular.

'God keep the issue!' he said.

'Why, get you gone,' Cromwell said. 'But this I pray you
gently: that ye restrain your fellows' tongues from speaking
treason and heresy. Three of your friends, as you know, I
must burn this day for such speakings; you, too—you yourself, too—I must burn if it come to that pass, or you shall
die by the block. For I will have this land purged.' His
cold eyes flamed dangerously for a minute. 'Fool!' he
thundered, 'I will have this land purged of treasons and
schisms. Get you gone before I advise further with myself
of your haughty and stiff-necked speeches. For learn this:
that before all creeds, and before all desires, and before all
women, and before all men, standeth the good of this
commonwealth, and state, and King, whose servant I be.
Get you gone and report my words ere I come terribly
among ye.'

Making his desultory pacings from end to end of the gallery, Cromwell considered that in that speech he had done a good morning's work, for assuredly these men put him in peril. More than one of these dangerous proclaimings of loyalty to him rather than to the King had come to his ears. They must be put an end to.

But this issue faded from his mind. Left to himself, he let his hands twitch as feverishly as they would. Cleves and its Duke had played him false! His sheet anchor was gone! There remained only, then, the device of proving to the King that Katharine Howard was a monster of unchastity. For so strong was the witness that he had gathered against her that he could not but try his Fate once more—to give the King, as so often he had done, proof of how diligently his minister fended for him and how requisite he was, as a man who had eyes in every corner of this realm.

To do that it was necessary that he should find her cousin; he had all the others under lock and key already in that palace. But her cousin—he must come soon or he would come too late!

Privy Seal was a man of immense labours, that carried him to burning his lamp into hours when all other men in land slept in their beds. And, at that date, he had a many letters to indite, because the choosing of burgesses for the Parliament was going forward, and he had ado in some burghs to make the citizens choose the men that he bade them have. He gave to each shire and burgh long thought and minute commands. He knew the mayor of each town, and had note-books telling him the opinions and deeds of every man that had freedom to elect all over England. And into each man he had instilled the terror of his vengeance. This needed anxious labours, and it was the measure of his concern that he stayed now from this work to meditate a full ten minutes upon this matter of bringing Thomas Culpepper before the King.

Thus, when, after he had for many hours been busy with his papers, Lascelles, the gentleman informer of the Archbishop's, came to tell him that he had seen Thomas

Culpepper at Greenwich that dawn and had followed him to the burning at Smithfield, whence he had hastened to Hampton, the Lord Privy Seal took from his neck his own golden collar of knighthood and cast it over Lascelles' neck. In part this was because he had never before been so glad in his life, and in part because it was his policy to reward very richly them that did him a chance service.

'Sir,' he said, 'I grudge that ye be the Archbishop's man and not mine, so your judgment jumps with mine.'

And indeed Lascelles' judgment had jumped with Privy Seal's. He was the Archbishop's confidential gentleman; he swayed in many things the Archbishop's judgments. Yet in this one thing Cranmer had been too afraid to jump with him.

'To me,' Lascelles said, 'it appeared that the sole thing to be done was to strike at the esteem of the King for Kat Howard, and the sole method to strike at her was through her dealings with her cousin.'

'Sir,' Cromwell interrupted him, 'in this ye have hit upon mine own secret judgment that I had told to no man save my private servants.'

Lascelles bent his knee to acknowledge this great praise.

'Very gracious lord,' he said, 'his Grace of Canterbury opines rather that this woman must be propitiated. He hath sent her books to please her tickle fancy of erudition; he hath sent her Latin chronicles and Saxon to prove to her, if he may, that the English priesthood is older than that of Rome. He is minded to convince her if he may, or, if he may not, he plans to make submission to her, to commend her learning and in all things to flatter her—for she is very approachable by these channels, more than by any other.'

In short, as Lascelles made it appear to Cromwell's attentive brain, the Archbishop was, as always, anxious to run with the hare and hunt with the hounds. He was a schismatic bishop, appointed by the King and the King's creature, not the Bishop of Rome's. So that if with his high pen and his great gift of penning weighty sentences, he might bring Kat Howard to acknowledging him bishop and archbishop, he was ready so to do. If he must make submission to her judgment, he was ready so to do.

'Yet,' Lascelles concluded, 'I have urged him against these courses; or yet not against these courses, but to this other end in any case.' For it was certain that Kat Howard would have no truck with Cranmer. She would make him go on his knees to Rome and then she would burn him; or if she did not burn him she would make him end his days with a hair shirt in the cell of an anchorite. 'I hold it manifested,' Lascelles said, 'that this lady is such an one as will listen to no reason nor policy, neither will she palter, for whatever device, with them that have not lifelong paid lip-service to the arch-devil whose seat is in Rome.'

Cromwell nodded his head once more to commend the Archbishop's gentleman with a perfect acquiescence.

It had chanced that that morning Lascelles had gone to Greenwich to fetch for the Archbishop some books and tractates. The Archbishop was minded to lend them to the Bishop Hugh Latimer of Worcester; that day he was to dispute publicly with the friar Forest that was cast to be burned. And, coming to Greenwich, still thinking much upon Katharine Howard and her cousin, at the dawn, Lascelles had seen the tall, drunken, red-bearded man in green, with his squat, broad gossip in grey, come staggering up from the ship at the public quay.

'I did leave my burthen of books,' he said; 'for what be Bishop Hugh Latimer's arguments from a pulpit to a burning priest to the pulling down of this woman?' He had dogged Thomas Culpepper and his crony; he had seen him burst open windows, cast meat about in the mud and feed the populace of the Greenwich hamlet.

'And for sure,' he said, 'if the King's Highness should see this man's filthiness and foul demeanour, he will not be fain to feed after such a make of hound.'

Coming to Smithfield, where Culpepper stayed to cheer on the business, Lascelles had very swiftly begged the Archbishop, where, behind Hugh Latimer's pulpit, he sat to see Friar Forest corrected—had very swiftly begged the Archbishop to give him leave to come to Hampton.

'Sir,' Lascelles said, 'with a great sigh he gave me leave; for much he fears to have a hand in this matter.'

'Why, he shall have no hand,' Cromwell said. He clapped his hands, and told the blonde page-boy that appeared to send him very quickly Viridus, that had had this matter in his care.

Lascelles recounted shortly how he had set four men to watch Thomas Culpepper till he came to Hampton, and very swiftly to send word of when he came. Then the spy dropped his voice and pulled out a parchment from his bosom.

'Sir,' he said, 'whilst Culpepper was in the palace of Greenwich I made haste to go on board the ship that had brought him from Calais, being minded if I could to discover what was discoverable concerning his coming.'

He dropped his voice still further.

'Sir,' he began again, 'there be those in this realm, and maybe very close to your own person, that would have stayed his coming. For upon that ship lay a boy, sore sick of the sea and very beaten, by name Harry Poins. Wherefore, or at whose commands, he had done this I had no occasion to discover, since he lay like a sick dog and might not see nor hear nor speak; but this it was told me he had done: in every way he sought to let and hinder T. Culpepper's coming to England with so marked an importunity that at last Culpepper did set his crony to beat this boy.' He paused again. 'And this too I discovered, taking it from the boy's person, for in my avocations and service to his Grace, whom God preserve and honour! I have much practised these abstractions.'

Lascelles held the parchment, from which fell a seal like a drop of blood.

'Sir,' he said, 'this agreement is sealed with your own seal; it is from one Throckmorton in your service. It maketh this T. Culpepper lieutenant of barges and lighters in the town and port of Calais. It enjoineth upon him to stay diligently there and zealously to persevere in these duties.'

Cromwell neither started nor moved; he stood looking down at the floor for a minute space; then he held out his hand for the parchment, considered the seal and the subscription, let his eyes course over the lines of Throckmorton's handwriting that made a black patch on the surface soiled with sea-water and sweat, and uttered composedly:

'Why, it is well; it is monstrous well that you have saved this parchment from coming to evil hands.'

He rolled it neatly, placed it in his belt, and four times stamped his foot on the floor.

There came in at this signal, Viridus, the one of his secretaries that had first instructed Katharine Howard as to her demeanour. Since then, he had had among his duties the watching over Thomas Culpepper. Calm, furtive, with his thin hands clasped before him, the Sieur Viridus answered the swift, hard questions of his master. He was more attached and did more services to the Chancellor of the Augmentations, whom he kept mostly mindful of such farms and fields as Privy Seal intended should be given to benefit his particular friends and servants; for he had a mind that would hold many details of figures and directions.

Thus, he had sent two men to Calais and the road Paris-ward with injunctions to meet Thomas Culpepper and tell him tales of Katharine Howard's lewdness in the King's Court; to tell him, too, that the farms in Kent, promised him as a guerdon for ridding Paris of the Cardinal Pole, were deeded and signed to him, but that evil men sought to have them away.

'Ye sent no boy to stay him at Calais with lieutenancy of barges?' Cromwell asked, swiftly and hard in voice.

'No boy ne no man,' Viridus answered.

He had acted by the card of Privy Seal's injunctions; men were posted at Calais, at Dover, at Ashford, at Maidstone, at Sandwich, at Rochester, at Greenwich, at all the

landing places of London. Each several one was instructed
to tell Thomas Culpepper some new story that, if Culpepper were not already hastening to Hampton, should
make him mend his paces. If he were hastening to Hampton they were to leave him be. All these things were done
as Privy Seal had directed.

'What witnesses have ye here from Lincolnshire?'
Cromwell asked.

In his monotonous sing-song Viridus named these
people: Under lock and key in the King's cellary house,
five from Stamford that had heard Culpepper swear Kat
Howard was his leman—these had really heard this thing,
and called for no priming; under instruction in the Well
Ward gate chamber, four that should swear a certain boy
was her child—these needed to have their tales evened as
to the night the child was born, and how it had been
brought from the Lord Edmund's house wrapped in a
napkin. In his own pantry, Viridus had three under guard
and admonition of his own—these should swear that
whenas they served the Lord Edmund they had seen at
several times Culpepper with her in thickets, or climbing
to her window in the night, or at dawn coming away from
her chamber door. These needed to be instructed as to all
these things.

Cromwell listened with little nods, marking each item
of these instructions.

'Listen now to me,' he said; 'give attentive ear.' Viridus
dropped his eyes to the floor, as one who lends all his
faculties to be subservient to his hearing. 'At six or there-
abouts T. Culpepper shall reach this Court. Ye shall have
men ready to bring him straightway to thee. At seven or
thereabouts shall come the Lady Katharine to her room;
with her shall come the King's Highness, habited as a
yeoman. Be attentive. Next Katharine Howard's door is
the door of the Lady Deedes. Her I have this day sent to
other quarters. Having T. Culpepper with you, you shall
go to this room of the Lady Deedes. You shall sit at the
table with the door a little opened, so that ye may see when

the King's Highness cometh. But you shall sit opposite
T. Culpepper that he may not see.' Viridus remained like
a statue carved of wood, motionless, his head inclined to
the ground. Lascelles had his head forward, his mouth a
little open. 'Whilst you wait you shall have with you the
deeds giving to T. Culpepper his farms in Kent. These ye
shall display to him. Ye shall dilate upon the goodness of
the fields, upon the commodity in barns and oasthouses,
upon the sweetness of the water wells, upon the goodliness
of the air. But when the King shall be entered into the
Lady Katharine's room you shall give T. Culpepper to
drink of a certain flagon of wine that I shall give to you.
When he hath drunk you shall begin to hint that all is ill
with the lady he would wed; as thus you shall say: "Aye,
your nest is well lined, but how of the bird?" And you
shall talk of her having consorted much with a large yeoman. And when you shall observe him to be much heated
with the subtle drug and your hintings, you shall say to
him, "Lo, next this door is the door of the Lady Katharine.
Go see if perchance she have not even now this yeoman
with her." '

Viridus nodded his head once up and down; Lascelles
clapped his hands twice for joy at this contrivance. Cromwell added further injunctions: that Viridus should have
in the corner of the gallery a man that should come hastening to him, the Lord Privy Seal, where he walked in the
gallery; another who, at his own signal, should hastily
bring the witnesses prepared against Kat Howard; another
who should bring the engrossment of a command to be-
head T. Culpepper that night in the King's Tower House,
and yet another who should bring up guards and captains.
All these, in their separate companies, should be set in the
great room abovestairs next the King's chapel, so that they
might swiftly and without hindrance or accident come
down the little stair to the Lady Katharine's room. Again
Viridus once bowed his head, moving his lips the while
repeating these commands in words as they were uttered.

Cromwell paused again to think, then he added:

'I will set this gentleman, Lascelles, to bring T. Culpepper to you. And because I will make very certain that this man shall not touch the person of the King, I will have this gentleman to stay with you in the room where you be, to follow with you T. Culpepper into the Lady Katharine's room. He shall run with you betwixt T. Culpepper and the King; but if T. Culpepper be minded to fall upon the Lady Katharine, ye shall not either of you stay him. It were best if he might stab her dead. Doubtless he shall.'

'Before God!' Lascelles cried out, 'would I were a king to have so masterful and devising a minister as Privy Seal!'

'Get you gone,' Privy Seal said to Viridus. 'I ha' no need to tell you that if ye do faithfully and to a good issue carry out this play, you shall be greatly rewarded so that few shall hold their heads higher than you in the land. Ye know how I befriend my friends. But know too this: that if this scheme miscarry, either of your fault or another's, either through inattention or ill chance, either through treason or dullness of the brain of man, down to the least pin of it, ye shall not this night sleep in your bed, nor ever more shall you be seen in daylight above the earth.' He pointed suddenly from the window to the low sun. 'Have a care that ye so act as ye shall see that disc again!'

Viridus spoke no word, but having waited a minute to hear if Privy Seal had more to enjoin, noiselessly and with his hands folded before him as they had been when he came, moved away over the shining floor. He went to tell the old, shivering Chancellor of the Augmentations that he must absent himself upon their common master's errands. 'I misdoubt some heads will fall to-night,' he added as he went; 'our lord's nose for treasons is sharpened again.' And that creature of Privy Seal's shook beneath the furs that he wore, though it was already April; for the Chancellor had his private reasons to dread Privy Seal's outbursts of suspicion.

In the gallery, Privy Seal still spoke earnestly with Lascelles.

'I give this part of honour and privilege to thee,' he said; 'for though I was well prepared in all things, I trow I may trust thee better than another person.'

Lascelles was to watch for Culpepper, to hasten to Viridus, to attend upon the pair of them as the pilot-fish attendeth upon the ghostly and silent shark, not to leave them till the work was accomplished, or, upon the least sign of treason in Viridus or another, to come hastening as never man hastened, to Privy Seal.

'For,' Cromwell ended, 'ye have felt like me how, if this realm is to be saved, saved it shall be by this thing alone.'

Lascelles, who had had no opening to speak, opened now his lips. Great ferreter as he was, he had discovered former servants of the Duchess of Norfolk, that were ready, for consideration of threats, to swear that they had seen the Lady Katharine when a child in her grand-mother's house to be over familiar with one Francis Dearham. He himself had these witnesses earmarked and attainable, and he was upon the point of offering them to Privy Seal. But he recollected that Privy Seal had witnesses enow of his own. To-morrow was also a day; and the King, if he would not now listen to tales against Kat Howard, might be brought to give ear to those and others added in a year's time, or when he began to tire of his woman as all men tire of women. Therefore he once more closed his lips. And Cromwell spoke as if his thoughts of a truth jumped together with Lascelles'.

'Sir,' he said, 'I would willingly bribe you from the service of his Grace of Canterbury to come into mine. But it may be that I shall not long outlive these days. Therefore I enjoin upon you these things: Serve well your master; guide him, for he needeth guidance, subtly as to-day ye would have guided him. I will not take you from him for this cause, that there is little need in one house of two that think alike. One sufficeth. For two houses with like minds are stronger than one that is bicephalous. Therefore serve you well Cranmer as in my day I served well the great Cardinal; so at his death, even as I at Wolsey's, ye may rise very high.'

He went swiftly into his little cabinet, and returning, had in his hand a little book.

'Read well in this,' he said, 'where much I have read. You shall see in it mine own annotations. This is "*Il Principe*" of Macchiavelli; there is none other book like it in the world. Study of it well: read it upon your walks. I am a simple man, yet hath it made me.'

Shadows were falling into the gallery, for the descending sun had come behind the dark, tall elms beyond the river.

'Upon my faith,' Cromwell said, 'and as I hope to enter into Paradise by the aid of Christ the King that commended faithful servants, I tell you I had great joy when you told me this woman's cousin had come into these parts. But greater joy than any were mine could I discern in this land a disciple that could carry on my work. As yet I have seen none; yet ponder well upon this book. God may work in thee, as in me, great changes by its study . . . Get you gone.'

He continued long to pace the gallery, his hands behind his back, his cap pulled over his narrow eyes; it grew dusk so that his figure could scarce be seen where it was at the further end. He looked from the casement up into the moon, small and tenuous in the pale western skies. He had been going over in his mind the details of how he had commanded Culpepper to be brought before the King. And at the last when he considered again that Culpepper might well strike his cousin dead at his feet, and that then she would have no tongue to stand against calumnies withal, he uttered the words:

'I think I hold them.'

And, pondering upon the wonderful destiny that had brought him up from a trooper in Italy to these high places, he saluted the moon with his crooked forefinger— for the moon was the president at his birth.

'Why,' he uttered aloud, 'I have survived four queens' days.'

For Katharine of Aragon he had seen die; and Anne Boleyn had died on the scaffold; and Jane Seymour was dead in childbed; and now, with the news from Cleves, Anne's reign was over and done with.

'Four queens,' he repeated.

And, turning swiftly to the door, he commanded that Throckmorton be sent him at once when he came to the archway.

PART THREE

THE SUNBURST

I

In the great place of Smithfield, towards noon, Thomas Culpepper sat his horse on the outskirts of the crowd. By his side Hogben, the gatewarden, had much ado to hold his pikestaff across his horse's crupper in the thick of the people.

The pavement of heads filled the place—bare some of them, some of them covered, according as their owners had cast their caps on high for joy at the Bishop of Worcester's words against the Papist that was to be burned, or as they pressed their thumbs harder down in disfavour and waited to shew their joy at the hanging of the three Protestants that should follow. In the centre towered on high a great gallows from which depended a chain; and at the end of the chain, half-hidden by the people, but shewing his shoulders and his head, a man in a friar's cowl. And, towering as high as the gallows, painted green as to its coat and limbs, but gilt in the helmet and brandishing a great spear, was the image called David Darvel Gatheren that the Papist Welsh adored. This image had been brought there that, in its burning, it might consume the friar Forest. It gazed, red-cheeked and wooden, across the sunlight space at the pulpit of the Bishop of Worcester in his white cassock and black hat, waving his white arms and exhorting the man in the gallows to repent at the last moment. Some words of Latimer might now and again be heard; the chained friar stood upon the rungs of a ladder set against the gallows post; he hung down his head and shook it, but no word could be heard to come from his lips.

'Damnable heretic and foul traitor!' Latimer's urgings came across the sea of heads. 'Here sitteth his Majesty's council——' At these words went up a little buzz of question, but sufficient from all that great crowd to send as it were a wind that blew away the Bishop's words. For the style 'his Majesty' was so new to the land that people were questioning what new council this might be, or what lord's whose style they did not know. Latimer waved his arm behind him, half turning, to indicate the King's men. These ministers, bravely bonneted so that the jewels sparkled, habited in brown so that the red cloth covering their tiers of seats shewed between their arms and shoulders, sat, like a gay bank of flowers above the lake of heads, surrounded by many other lords and ladies in shining colours. They sat there ready to sign the pardon that was prepared if the friar would be moved by fear or by the Bishop's argument to hang his head and recant.

The friar, truly, hung his head, clung to the rungs of the ladder, trembled so that all men might see, and once caught furiously at the iron chain and shook it; but no word came from his lips. Culpepper was bursting with pride and satisfaction because he was a made man and would have all the world to know it. He swung his green bonnet round his red head and called for huzzays when the friar shewed fear. Hogben called for huzzays for Squahre Tom of Lincoln, and many men cheered. But the silence dropped again, and the Bishop's words, raised now very high, dominated the sunlight and eddied around the tall faces of the house fronts behind.

'Here have sat the nobles of the realm and the King's Majesty's most honourable council only to have granted pardon to you, wretched creature, if but some spark of repentance would have happened in ye.' Hanging his cowled poll beneath the beam that reached gigantic and black across the crowd, the friar shook his head slowly. 'Declared to you your errors I have,' cried Latimer.

'Openly and manifestly by the scriptures of God, with many and godly exhortations have I moved you to repentance. Yet will you neither hear nor speak——'

'Bones of St Nairn!' Culpepper cried; 'here is too much speaking and no work. Huzzay! e caitiffs. Burn. Burn. Burn. For the honour of England.' And, starting from his figure at the verge of the crowd, cries went up of 'Huzzay!' of 'Burn!' and 'St George for London!' and unquiet rumours and struggles and waving in the crowd of heads, so that the Bishop's voice was not heard any more that day.

But through the crowd a silence fell as the image slowly and totteringly moved forward, ankle deep only in the crowd. Ropes from the figure's neck ran out and tightened —some among the crowd began to sing the song against Welsh Papists that ran—

> 'David Darvel Gatheren
> As sayeth the Welshmen
> Fetched outlaws out of hell!'

and the burden of it rose so loud that the image swayed over and fell unheard. At that too a silence fell, and presently there came the sound of axes chopping. The friar, swaying on his ladder, looked down and then made a great sign of the cross. The Bishop in his pulpit, raising his white arms in horror and imprecation, seemed to be giving the signal for new uproars.

Whilst he shouted with delight, Culpepper felt a man catch at his leg. He kicked his foot loose, but his hand on the bridle was clutched. There was a fair man at his horse's shoulder that bore Privy Seal's lion badge upon his chest. His face was upturned, and in the clamour he spoke indistinguishable words. Culpepper struck towards the mouth with his fist; the man shrank back, but stood, nevertheless, close still in the crowd. When the silence fell again, Culpepper could hear amongst the swift chopping of the axes the words—

'I rede ye ride swiftly to Hampton. I am the Lord Cromwell's man.'

Culpepper brought his excited mind from the thought of the burning and the joy of the day, with its crowd and its odour of men, and sunshine and tumult.

'Ye say? Swine,' he shouted. 'Come aside!' He caught at the man's collar and kicked his horse and pulled at its jaws till it drew them out of the thin crowd to a street's opening.

'Sir,' the man said—he had a goodly cloth suit of dark green that spoke to his being of weight in some household—'ye are like to lose your farms at Bromley an ye hasten not to Master Viridus, who holdeth the deedings to you.'

Culpepper uttered an inarticulate roar and smote his patient horse on the side of the head for two minutes of fierce blows, digging with his heels into the girthings.

'Sir,' the man said again, 'some lord will have these lands an ye come not to Hampton ere six of the clock. I know not the way of it that be a servant. But Master Viridus sent me with this message.'

Already a thin swirl of blue smoke was ascending past the friar's figure to the bright sky; it caressed the beam of the gallows and Culpepper's bloodshot eye pursued it upwards.

'Before God!' he muttered, 'I was set to see this burning. Ye have seen many; I never a one.' A new spasm of rage caught him: he dragged at his horse's head, and shouting, 'Gallop! gallop!' set off into the dark streets, his crony behind his back.

In the Poultry he knocked over a man in a red coat that had a gold chain about his neck; on the Chepe he jumped his horse across a pigman's booth—it brought down Hogben, horse and pike; three drunken men were fighting in Paternoster Street—Culpepper charged above their bodies; but very shortly he came through Temple Bar and was in the marshes and fields. Well out between the hedgerows he was aware that one galloped behind him. He drew a violent rein where the Cow Brook crossed the deep muddied road and looked back.

'Sir,' he called, 'this night I will hold a mouse on a chain above a coal fire. So I will see a burning, and my cousin Kat shall see it with me.' He spurred on again.

By the time he was come to Brentford four men, habited like the first, rode behind him. When he stayed to let his horse drink from the river opposite Richmond Hill, he was aware that across the stream a pageant with sweet music marched a little beyond the further bank. He could see the tops of pikes and pennons amid the tree trunks.

He muttered that such a pageant he would very soon make for himself; for, filled with the elation of his new magnificence, since Privy Seal was his friend and Viridus was earnest to do him favour, he imagined that no captain nor lord in that land soon should overpass him. For that any lord should desire his new lands troubled him little; only he hastened to cut that lord's throat and to kiss his cousin Kat.

It was a quarter before six when he drew rein in the green yard that lay before the King's arch in Hampton. There befel the strangest scuffle there; flaring for a moment and gone out like the gunpowder they sometimes lit in saucers for sport. A man called Lascelles came slowly from under the arch to meet him, and then, running over the green grass from the little side door, came the young Poins in red breeches, pulling off a red coat that he had had but half the time to don and tugging at his sword whose hilt was caught in the sleeve hole. Even as he issued, Lascelles, walking slowly, began to run and to call. Four other men of Privy Seal's ran from under the arch, and the four men that had followed behind him so far, closed their horses round his. The boy had his sword out and his coat gave as he ran. Lascelles closed near him on the grass, stretched out a foot to trip, and the boy lay sprawling, his hands stretched out, his sword three yards before him. The four men that had run from the arch had him up upon his feet and held his arms when Culpepper had ridden the hundred yards from the gate to them.

'Why,' said Culpepper, gazing upon the boy's face, 'it was thee wouldst have my farms.' He spat in the boy's face and rode complacently under the archway where were many men of Privy Seal's in the side chambers and on the steps that ran steeply to the King's new hall.

'I do conceive now,' Culpepper, in descending from his horse, spoke to Lascelles, 'wherefore that knave would have had me stay in Calais and be warder of barges. 'A would have my lands here.'

Word was given him that he must without delay go to the Sieur Viridus, and in a high good humour he followed the lead of Lascelles through the rabbit warren of small and new passages of the palace. In them it was already nearly dark.

It was in that way that, landing at the barge stage, a little stiff with the cold of his barge journey, Throckmorton came upon the young Poins in his scarlet breeches, his face cut and bleeding in his contact with the earth, his sword gone. Privy Seal's men that had fallen upon him had kicked him out of the palace gates. They had no warrant yet to take him; the quarrel was none of theirs. The boy was of the King's Guard, it was true, but his company lay then at the Tower.

Throckmorton cursed at him when he heard his news; and when he heard that Culpepper was then in the palace where window lights already shone before him, he ran to the archway. He had no time for reflection save as he ran. Word was given him in the archway itself that Privy Seal would see him instantly and with great haste and urgency. He asked only for news where Thomas Culpepper was, and ran, upon the disastrous hearing that Viridus had taken him up the privy stairway. And, in that darkness, thoughts ran in his head. Disaster was here. But what? Privy Seal called for him. He had no time for Privy Seal. Culpepper was gone to Kat Howard's room. Viridus there had taken him. There was no other room up the winding staircase to which he could go. Here was disaster! For whether he stayed Culpepper or no, Privy Seal must know that he had betrayed him. As he ran swiftly the desperate alternative coursed in his mind. Rich, the Chancellor of the Augmentations, and he had their tale pat, that Privy Seal was secretly raising the realm against the King. He himself had got good matter that morning listening to the treasonable talking of the printer Badge.

Several men in the stair angle would have stopped him when at last he was at foot of the winding stairs. He whispered:

'I be Throckmorton upon my master's business,' and was through and in the darkness of the stairway.

Why was there no cresset? Why were there these men? It came into his mind that already the King had heard Culpepper. Already Katharine was arrested. He groaned as he mounted the stairs. For in that case, with those men behind him, he was in a gaol already. He paused to go back; then it came to him that, if he could win forward and find the King, who alone, by giving ear, could save him, he would yet not know first how Katharine had fared. He had a great stabbing at his heart with that thought, and once more mounted.

From the door next hers there streamed a light. Hers was closed. He ran to it and knocked, leaning his head against the panels to listen. There was no sound, no sound at all when he knocked again. It was intolerable. He thrust the door open. No woman was there and no man. He went in. He thought: 'If the room be in disorder——'

He made out in the twilight that the room stood as always; the chair loomed where it should; there was a spark on the hearth; the books were ordered on the table; no stool was overturned. He stood amid these things, his heart beating tumultuously, his ears pricked up, stilling his breathing to listen, in the blue twilight, like a wild beast.

A voice said:

'Body o' God! Throckmorton!' beneath its breath, the light of the next door grew large and smaller again; he caught from there the words: 'It is Throckmorton.' And at the sound Throckmorton loosened his dagger in its sheath. Some glimmering of the plan reached him; they were awaiting Katharine's coming, and a great load fell from his mind. She was not yet taken.

He paused to stroke his beard for fear it was disordered, pulled from over his shoulder the medallion on the chain; it had flown there as he ran. He pushed ajar the next door a minute later, having thought many thoughts and appearing stately and calm.

He replaced the door at its exact angle and gazed at the three silent men. Thomas Culpepper, his brows knotted, his lips moving, was holding his head askew to see the measurements upon a map of his farm at Bromley. That Lascelles had gone out and come back saying that one Throckmorton was in the next room was nothing to him. The next room was nothing to him; he was there to hear of his farms.

Viridus, silent, dark and enigmatic, gazed at a spot upon the table; Lascelles, his mouth a little open, his eyes dilated, had his hands upon it.

Without speaking, Throckmorton noted that the room was empty save for the table and benches; the hangings had been taken down; all the furnishings were gone. That morning the room had been well filled, warm, and in the occupancy of the Lady Deedes. Therefore Cromwell had worked this change. No other had this power. They waited, then, those three, for the coming of Katharine Howard or the King. Lascelles shewed fear and surprise at his being there; therefore Lascelles was deeply concerned in this matter. Lascelles was in the service of Cranmer that morning; now he sat there. Thus he, too, for certain, was in this plan; he was a new servant to Privy Seal—and new servants are zealous. With Viridus he had had some talk of events. Therefore Lascelles was the greatest danger.

Throckmorton moved slowly behind Culpepper and sat down beside him; in his left hand he had his small dagger, its blue blade protruding from the ham; Culpepper beside him was at his right. He said very softly in Italian to Lascelles:

'Both your hands are upon the table; if you move one my dagger pierces your eye to the brain. So also if you speak in the English language.'

Lascelles muttered: 'Judas! *Traditore!*' Viridus sat motionless, and Culpepper moved his finger across the plan of the farm.

'Here is the mixen,' he appealed to Viridus, who nodded.

It was as if Throckmorton, with his slow manner and low voice, was a friend who had come in to speak to Lascelles about the weather or the burnings. He was no concern of Culpepper's, nor was Lascelles who had spoken no word at all.

Throckmorton kept his head turned towards Lascelles as if he were still addressing him, and spoke in the same level voice, still in Italian.

'Viridus, to thee I speak. This is a very great matter.' Unconsciously he used the set form of words of Privy Seal. 'Consider well these things. The day of our master is nigh at an end. Rich, Chancellor of the Augmentations, thy crony and master, and my ally, hath made a plan to go with me to the King this night with witnesses and papers accusing Privy Seal of raising the land against his Highness. Will you join with us, or will you be lost with Privy Seal?'

Viridus kept his eyes upon the same spot of the table.

'Tell me more,' he said. 'This matter is very weighty.' His tone was level, monotonous and still. He too might have been saying that the sunshine that day had been long.

'A fad to talk Latin of ye courtiers,' Culpepper said with uninterested scorn. 'Ye will forget God's language of English.' He slapped Throckmorton on the sleeve. 'See, what a fine farm I have for my deserts,' he said.

'Ye shall have better,' Throckmorton said. 'I have moved the King in your behalf.' But he kept his eyes on Lascelles.

Culpepper cast back his cap from his eyes and leant away the better to slap Throckmorton on the back.

'Ye ha' heard o' my deeds,' he said.

'All England rings with them,' Throckmorton said. He interjected, 'Still! hound!' to Lascelles in Italian, and went on to Culpepper: 'I ha' moved the King to come this night to thy cousin's room hard by for I knew ye would go to her. The King is hot to speak with thee. Comport thyself as I do bid thee and art a made man indeed.'

Culpepper laughed with hysterical delight.

'By Cock!' he shouted. 'Master Viridus, thou art naught to this. Three farms shall not content me nor yet ten.'

Throckmorton's eyes shot a glance at Viridus and back again to Lascelles' face.

'If you speak I slay you,' he said. Lascelles' eyes started from his head, his mouth worked, and on the table his hands jerked convulsively. But Throckmorton had seen that Viridus still sat motionless.

'By Cock!' Culpepper cried. 'By Guy and Cock! let me kiss thee.'

'Sir,' Throckmorton said, 'I pray you speak no more words, not at all till I bid you speak. I am a very great lord here; you shall observe gravity and decorum or never will I bring you to the King. You are not made for Courts.'

'Oh, I kiss your hands,' Culpepper answered him. 'But wherefore have you a dagger?'

'Sir,' Throckmorton said again, 'I will have you silent, for if the King should pass the door he will be offended by your babble.' He interjected to Viridus, speaking in Italian, 'Speak thou to this fool and engage him to think. I can give you no more grounds, but you must quickly decide either to go with Rich the Chancellor and myself or to remain the liege of the Privy Seal.'

Never once did he take his eyes from Lascelles, and the sweat stood upon his forehead. Once when Lascelles moved he slid the dagger along the table with a sharp motion and a gasping of breath, as a pincer pressed to the death will make a faint. Yet his voice neither raised itself nor fell one shade.

'And if I will aid you in this, what reward do I get?' Viridus asked. He too spoke low and unmovedly, keeping his eyes upon the table.

'The one-half of my enrichments for five years, the one-half of those of the Chancellor, and my voice for you with the King and with the new Queen.'

'And if I will not go with you?'

'Then when the King passeth this door I do cry out "Treason! treason!" and you, I, and this man, and this shall to-night sleep in the King's prison, not in Privy Seal's. And I will have you think that I am sib and rib with Kat Howard who shall sway the King if her cousin be induced not to play the beast.'

Viridus spoke no word; but when Culpepper, idle and gaping, reached out his hand to take the black flagon of wine that was between them under the candles on the table, Viridus stretched forth his hand and clasped the bottle.

'It is not expedient that you drink,' he said.

'Why somever then?' Culpepper asked.

'That neither do you make a beast of yourself if you come before the King's great majesty this night,' Viridus said in his cold and minatory voice, 'not yet smell beastly of liquors when you kiss the King his hand.'

Culpepper said:

'By Cock! I had forgot the King's highness.'

'See that you kneel before him and speak not; see that you raise your eyes not from the floor nor breathe loudly; see that when the King's high and awful majesty dismisses you you go quietly.' Throckmorton spoke. 'See that you speak not with nor of your cousin. For so dreadful is a king, and this King more than others; and so terrible his wrath and desire of worship—and this King's more than others—that if ye speak above a whisper's sound, if ye act other than as a babe before its preceptor's rod, you are cast out utterly and undone. You shall never more have farms nor lands; you shall never more have joyance nor gladness; you shall rot forgotten in a hole as you had never done brave things for the King's grace.'

'By Cock!' Culpepper said, 'it seems it is easier to talk of a king than with one.'

'See that you remember it,' Throckmorton said, 'for with great trouble have I brought this King so far to talk with you!'

He moved his dagger yet nearer to Lascelles' form and held his finger to his lip. Viridus had never once moved; he stayed now as still as ever. Culpepper crammed his hand over his lips.

For from without there came the sound of voices and, in that dead silence, the rustle of a woman's gown, swishing and soft. A deep voice uttered heavily:

'Aye, I know your feelings. I have had my sadness.' It paused for a moment, and mouthed on: 'I can cap your Lucretius too with "*Usque adeo res humanas vis abdita——*" ' It seemed that for a moment the speaker stayed before the door where all three held their breaths. 'I have read more of the Fathers, of late days, than of the writers profane.'

They heard the breathing of a heavy man who had mounted stairs. The voice sounded more faintly:

'Now you have naught further to think of than the goodly words of Ecclesiastes: "*Et cognovi quod non esset melius, nisi laetare et....*" ' The voice died dead away with the closing of the door. And as a torch passed, Throckmorton knew that the King had waited there whilst light was being made in Katharine's room. He said softly to Viridus:

'Whilst I go unto them you shall hold this dagger against this fool's throat. We gain as many hours as we may hold him from blabbing to Privy Seal. And consider that we must bring to the King Rich and Udal and many other witnesses this night.'

'Throckmorton,' Viridus said, 'before thou goest thou shalt satisfy me of many things. I have not yet given myself into thy hands.'

II

A weary sadness had beset Katharine Howard ever since she had knelt before Anne of Cleves at Richmond, and it was of this the King had spoken outside the door whilst they had waited for light to be made.

All Anne's protesting that willingly she rendered up a distasteful crown could not make Katharine hugely glad with the manner of her own taking it. And, when a messenger, dressed as a yeoman in green, had come into the bright gallery to beg the Queen and that fair lady the Lady Katharine Howard to come a-riding side by side and witness the sports that certain poor yeomen made in the woods upon Thames-side, she felt a sinking in her heart that no Rhenish of the Queen's could relieve. She desired to be alone and to pray—or to be alone with Henry and speak out her heart and devise how they might atone to the Queen. But she must ride at the Queen's right hand with the Duke of Suffolk at her left. It was so between their captives that the Cæsars had ridden into Rome after the taking of barbaric kings. But she had waged no war.

She did not, in her heart, call shame upon the King; she knew him to be a heavy man with bitter sorrows who must in these violentnesses and brave shows find refuge and surcease; it was her province to endure and to find excuse for him. But to herself she quoted that phrase of Lucretius that the King again repeated: there was a hidden destiny that tamed the shows of the great; and she was the mutest of that throng that upon white horses, all with little flags flying and horns blowing, cantered to see the yeomen shoot. For the ladies and knights, avid of these things, loved above all good bowmanry and wagered with out-stretched hands for the marksmen that most they deemed to have skill or that usually seemed to enjoy the fortunate favours of chance and the winds.

But, being alone with the King—(for when the Queen rode back to Richmond the notable bowman in green walked, holding Katharine's stirrup, back to Hampton at her saddle-bow)—she could not stay herself from venting her griefs.

'*Et cognovi quod non esset melius nisi laetari et facere bene in vita sua*'—Henry finished his quotation when they were within her room. He sat himself down in her chair and stretched his legs apart; being tired with his long walk at her saddle bow, the more boisterous part of his great pleasure had left him. He was no more minded to slap his thigh, but he felt, as it was his favourite image of blessed- ness to desire, like a husbandman who sat beneath his vine and knew his harvesting prosper.

'Body of God!' he said, 'this is the best day of my life. There doth no cloud remain. Here is the sunburst. For Cleves hath cut himself adrift; I need have no more truck with Anne; you have no more cause nor power to bend yourself from me; to-morrow the Parliament meets, such a Parliament to do my will as never before met in a Republic; therefore I have no more need of Cromwell.' He snapped his thumb and finger as if he were throwing away a pinch of dust, and when she fell to her knees before his chair, placed his hand upon her head and, smiling, huge and indulgent, spoke on.

'This is such a day as seldom I have known since I was a child.' He leaned forward to stroke her dusky and golden hair and laid his hand upon her shoulder, his fingers touch- ing her flushed cheek.

'On other days I have said with Horace, who is more to my taste than your Lucretius: "*That man is great and happy who at day's end may say: To-day I have lived, what of storms or black clouds on the morrow betide.*" ' . . .

He crossed his great legs encased in green, set his heavy head to one side and, though he could see she was minded to pray to him, continued to speak like a man uttering of his memories.

'Such days as that of Horace I have known. But never yet such a day as to-day, which, good in itself, leadeth on to goodness and fair prospects for a certain morrow.' He smiled again. 'Why, I am no more an old man as I had thought to be. I have walked that far path beside thy horse.' It pleased him for two things: because he had walked with little fatigue and because he had been enabled to show her great and prodigal honour by so serving her for groom. 'This too I set to thy account as my good omen. And that thou art. No woman shall have such honours as thou in this land, save only the Mother of God.' And, after touching his green and jewelled bonnet, he cast it from his head on to the table.

'Sir,' she cried out, and clasping her hands uttered her words in anguish and haste. 'Great kings and lords upon their affiancing day have ever had the habit of granting their brides a boon or twain—as the conferring of the revenues of a province, or the pardoning of criminals.'

'Why, an thou come not to me to pardon Privy Seal——' he began.

'Sir,' she cut in on his words, 'I crave no pardon for Privy Seal; but let me speak my mind.'

He said tenderly:

'Art in the mood to talk! Talk on! for I know no way to hinder thee.'

'Sir,' she said, 'I ask thee no pardon for Privy Seal, neither his goods ne his life. I maintain this man hath well served thee and is no traitor; but since that he hath ground the faces of the poor, hath made thee to be hated by bringing of false witness, hath made the thirsty earth shrink from drinking of blood, hath cast down the Church—since that this man in this way hath brought peril upon the republic and upon the souls of poor and witless folk, this man hath wrought worse treasons than any that I wot of. If ye will adjudge him to die, I am no fool to say: No!'

Henry wrinkled his brows and said:

'Grinding the faces of the poor is in law no treason. Yet I may not slay him save upon the occasion of treason. I would a man would come to me that could prove him traitor.'

Kneeling before the King she grasped each of his knees with one of her hands.

'Sir,' she said, 'this is your occasion, none of mine. I would ye would reconcile it to your conscience so to act to him as I would have you, for his injustice to the poor and for his cogged oaths. But yet grant me this: to cog oaths for the downfall of Privy Seal upon the occasion of treason ye must have many other innocents implicated with him; such men as have had no idea, no suspicion, no breath of treason in their hearts. Grant me their lives. Sir, let me tell you a tale that I read in Seneca.' She moved her body nearer to him upon the floor, set her hands upon his two arms and gazed, beseeching and piteous, up into his face.

'Sir,' she said, 'you may read it in Seneca for yourself that upon the occasion of Cinna's treachery being made known to the Emperor Augustus, the Emperor lay at night debating this matter in his mind. For on the one side, says he in words like this: "*Shall I pardon this man after that he hath assailed my life, my life that I have preserved in so many battles by sea and by land, after I have stablished one single peace throughout the globe into all the corners thereof? Shall he go free who has considered with himself not only to slay me but to slay me when I offered sacrifice, ere its consummation, so that I may be damned as well as slain? Shall I pardon this man?*" And, upon the other side, the Emperor Augustus, lying in the black of the night, being a prince, even as thou art, prone to leniency, said such words as these: "*Why dost thou, Augustus, live, if it is of import to so many people that thou diest? Shall there never be an end to thy vengeance and thy punishments? Is thy single life of such worth that so much ruin shall for ever be wrought to preserve it?*" '

'Why, I have had these thoughts,' Henry said. 'Speak on. What did this Emperor that thought like me?'

'Sir,' Katharine continued, and now she had her hands upon his shoulders, 'the Empress Livia his wife lay beside him and was aware of these his night sweats and his anguishes. "*And the counsels of a woman; shall these be listened to?*" she spoke to him. "*Do thou in this what the Physicians follow when their accustomed recipes are of no avail to cure. They do try the contrary drugs. By severity thou hast never, sire, profited from the beginning to this very hour that is; Lepidus has followed to death Savidienus; Murena, Lepidus; Caepio followed Murena; Eynatius, Caepio. Commence to essay at this pass how clemency shall act in cure. Cinna is convicted: pardon him. Further to harm thee he hath no power, and it shall for ever redound to thy glory.*" '

She leaned upon him with all her weight, having her arms about his neck.

'Sir,' she said, 'the Emperor Augustus listened to his wife, and the days that followed are styled the Golden Age of Rome, he and the Empress having great glory.'

Henry scratched his head, holding his beard back from her face that lay upon his chest; she drew herself from him and once more laid her hands upon his knees. Her fair face was piteous and afraid; her lips trembled.

'Dear lord,' she began tremulously, 'I live in this world, and, great pity 'tis! I cannot but have seen how many have died by the block and faggots. Yet is there no end to this. Even to-day they have burnt upon the one part and the other. I do know thy occasions, thy trials, thy troubles. But think, sir, upon the Empress Livia. Cromwell being dead, find then a Cinna to pardon. Thou hast with thy great and princely endeavourings given a Roman peace to the world. Let now a Golden Age begin in this dear land.'

She rose to her feet and stretched out both her hands.

'These be the glories that I crave,' she said. 'I would have the glory of advising thee to this. Before God I would escape from being thy Queen if escape I might. I would live as the Sibyls that gave good counsel and lived in rocky cells in sackcloth. So would I fainer. But if you will have me, upon your oaths to me of this our affiancing, I beseech you to give me no jewels, neither the revenue of provinces for my dower. But grant it to me that in after ages men may conceive of me as of such a noble woman of Rome.'

Henry leaned forward and stroked first one knee and then the other.

'Why, I will pardon some,' he said. 'It had not need of so many words of thine. I am sick of slaughterings when you speak.' A haughty and challenging frown came into his face; his brows wrinkled furiously; he gazed at the opening door that moved half imperceptibly, slowly, in the half light, after the accustomed manner, so that one within might have time to cry out if a visitor was not welcome. For, for the most part, in those days, ladies set bolts across their doors.

Throckmorton stood there, blinking his eyes in the candle-light, and, slowly, he fell upon his knees.

'Majesty,' he said, 'I knew not.'

The King maintained a forbidding silence, his green bulk inert and dangerous.

'This lady's cousin,' Throckmorton pronounced his words slowly, 'is new come from France whence he hath driven out from Paris town the Cardinal Pole.'

The King lifted one hand from his thigh, and, heavily, let it fall again.

Throckmorton felt his way still further.

'This lady's cousin would speak with this lady in cousin-ship. He was set in my care by my lord Privy Seal. I have brought him thus far in safety. For some have made attacks upon him with swords.'

Katharine's hand went to her throat where she stood, tall and half turning from the King to Throckmorton. The word 'Wherefore?' came from her lips.

'Wherefore, I know not,' Throckmorton answered her steadily. His eyes shifted for a moment from the King and rested upon her face. 'But this I know, that I have him in my safe keeping.'

'Belike,' the King said, 'these swordsmen were friends of Pole.'

'Belike,' Throckmorton answered.

He fingered nonchalantly the rim of his cap that lay beside his knees.

'For his sake,' he said, 'it were well if your Grace, having rewarded him princely for this deed, should send him to a distant part, or to Edinbro' in the Kingdom of Scots, where need for men is to lie and observe.'

'Belike,' the King said. 'Get you gone.' But Throckmorton stayed there on his knees and the King uttered: 'Anan?'

'Majesty,' Throckmorton said, 'I would ye would see this man who is a poor, simple swordsman. He being ill made for courts I would have you reward him and send him from hence ere worse befal him.'

The King raised his brows.

'Ye love this man well,' he said.

'Here is too much beating about the bush,' burst from Katharine's lips. She stood, tall, winding her hands together, swaying a little and pale in the half light of the two candles. 'This cousin of mine loves me well or over well. This gentleman feareth that this cousin of mine shall cause disorders—for indeed he is of disordered intervals. Therefore, he will have you send him from this Court to a far land.'

'Why, this is a monstrous sensible gentleman,' Henry said. 'Let us see this yokel.' He had indeed a certain satisfaction at the interrupting, for with Katharine in her begging moods he was never certain that he must not grant her his shirt and go a penance to St Thomas' shrine.

Katharine stayed with her hand upon her heart, but when her cousin came his green figure in the doorway was stiff; he trembled to pass the sill, and looking never at her but at the King's shoes, he knelt him down in the centre of the floor. The words coming to her in the midst of anguishes and hot emotions, she said:

'Sire, this is my much-loved cousin, who hath bought

me food and dress in my days of poverty, selling his very farms.'

Culpepper grunted over his shoulder:

'Hold thy tongue, cousin Kat. Ye know not that ye shall observe silence in the awful presence of kings.'

Henry threw his head back and laughed, whilst the chair creaked for a minute's space.

'Silence!' he said. 'Before God, silence! Have ye ever heard this lady's tongue?' He grew still and dreadful at the end of his mirth.

'Ye have done well,' he said. 'Give me your sword. I will knight you. I hear you are a poor man. I give you a knight's fee farm of a hundred pounds by the year. I hear you are a rough honest man. I had rather ye were about my nephew's courts than mine. Get you to Edinbro'.' He waved his hand to Throckmorton. 'See him disposed,' he said.

Culpepper uttered a sound of remonstrance. The King leaned forward in his seat and thundered:

'Get you gone. Be you this night thirty miles towards the Northland. I ha' heard ye ha' made brawls and broils here. See you be gone. By God, I am Harry of Windsor!'

He laid the heavy flat of the sword like a blow upon the green shoulders below him.

'Rise up, Sir Thomas Culpepper,' he said. 'Get you gone!'

Dazed and trembling still a little, Culpepper stuttered his way to the door. When he came by her Katharine cast her arms about his shoulder.

'Poor Tom,' she cried. 'Best it is for thee and me that thou goest. Here thou hast no place.' He shook his head like a man in a daze and was gone.

'Art too patient with the springald,' the King said.

He thundered 'Body of God!' again when he saw Throckmorton once more fall to his knees.

'Sire,' he said—and for the first time he faltered in his level tones—'a very great treason has come to my ken this day!'

'Holy altar fires!' the King growled, 'let your treasons
wait. Here hath this lady been talking to me very reasonably of a golden age.'

'Sire,' Throckmorton said, and he leant one hand on the
floor to support him. 'This is a very great treason of men
arming to sustain Privy Seal against thee! I have seen it;
with mine own eyes I have seen it in thy town of London.'

Katharine cried out, 'Ah!'

The King leapt to his feet.

'Ho, I will arm,' he said, and grew pale. For, with a
sword in his hand or where fighting was, this King had
middling little fear. But, even as the lion dreads a little
mouse, so he feared secret rebellions.

'Sire,' Throckmorton said, and his face was towards
Katharine as if he challenged her:

'This is the very truth of the very truth, I call upon
what man will to gainsay me. This day I heard in the city
of London, at the house of the printer, John Badge——'
and he repeated the speech of the saturnine man—'that
*"he would raise a thousand prentices and a thousand
journeymen to shield Privy Seal from peril; that he could
raise ten thousand citizens and ten thousand tenned again
from the shires!"* '

Katharine kept her eyes upon Throckmorton who,
knowing her power to sway the King, nodded gravely and
looked into her eyes to assure her that these words were
true.

But the King, upon his feet, marched towards the door.

'Let us arm my guard,' he said. 'I will play Nero to
London town.'

Nevertheless Throckmorton kept his knees.

'Majesty,' he said, 'I have this man in my keeping.' And
indeed, at his passing London Bridge he had sent men to
take the printer and bring him to Hampton. 'I pray your
pardon that I took him lacking your warrant, and Privy
Seal's I dare not ask.'

The King stayed in his pacing.

'Thou art a jewel of a man,' he said. 'By Cock, I would

I had many like thee.' And at the news that the head of
this confederacy was taken his sudden fear fell. 'I will see
this man. Bring him to me.'

'Sire,' Katharine said, 'we spoke even now of Cinna.
Remember him!'

'Madam,' Throckmorton dared to speak. 'This is the
man that hath printed broadsides against you. No man
more hateth you in land or hath uttered more lewdnesses
of your chastity.'

'The more I will have him pardoned,' Katharine said,
'that his Highness and all people may see how little I fear
his lyings.'

Throckmorton shrugged his shoulders right up to his
ears to signify that this was a very madness of Roman
pardoning.

'God send you never rue it,' he said. 'Majesty,' he continued to the King, 'give me some safe conduct that for
half-an-hour I may go about this palace unletted by men
of Privy Seal's. For Privy Seal hath a mighty army of men
to do his bidding and I am one man unaided. Give me
half-an-hour's space and I will bring to you this captain of
rebellion to your cabinet. And I will bring to you them
that shall mightily and to the hilt against all countervail
and denial prove that Privy Seal is a false and damnable
traitor to thee and this goodly realm. So I swear: Throckmorton who am a trusty knight.'

He was not minded to utter before Katharine Howard
the names of his other witnesses. For one of them was the
Chancellor of the Augmentations, who was ready to swear
that Cromwell, upon the barge when they went in the
night from Rochester to Greenwich, had said that he would
have the King down if he would not wed with Anne of
Cleves. And he had Viridus to swear that Cromwell had
said, before his armoury, to the Ambassador of the
Schmalkaldners, that ne King, ne Emperor had such
another armoury, yet were there twenty score great houses
in England that had better, all ready to arm to defend the
Protestant faith and Privy Seal. These things he was

minded to lay before the King; but before Kat Howard he would not speak them. For, with her mad fury for truth and the letter of Truth that she had gained from reading Seneca till, he thought, her brains were turned, she would begin a wrangle with him. And he had no time to lose; for his ears were pricked up, even as he spoke, to catch any breaking of the silence from the next room where Viridus held Lascelles at the point of his dagger.

The King said:

'Go thou. If any man stay thee in going whithersoever thou wilt, say that thou beest upon my business; and woe betide them that stay thee if thou be not in my cabinet in the half of an hour with them ye speak of.'

Throckmorton rose stiffly to his feet; at the door he staggered for a moment, and closed his eyes. His cause was won; but he leant against the door-post and gazed at Katharine with a piteous and passionate glance, moving his fingers in his beard, as if he appealed to her in silence as with the eyes of a faithful hound, neither to judge him harshly nor to plead against him. This was the day of the most strain that ever was in his life.

And gazing back at him, Katharine's eyes were filled with pity, so sick he appeared to be.

'Body of God!' the King said in the silence that fell upon them. 'Now I hold Cromwell.'

Katharine cried out, 'Let me go; let me go; this is no world for me!'

He caught her masterfully in his arms.

'This is a golden world, and thou a golden Queen,' he said.

She held her head back from his lips, and struggled from him.

'I may not find any straightness here. I can see no clear way. Let me go.'

He took her again to him, and again she tore herself free.

'Listen to me,' she cried, 'listen to me! There have been broadsides printed against the truth of my body; there have been witnesses prepared against me. I will have you swear that you will read of these broadsides, and consider of these witnesses.'

'Before God,' he said, 'I will hang the printers, and slay the witnesses with my fist. I know how these things be made.' He shook his fist. 'I love thee so that were they true, and wert thou the woman of Sodom, I would have thee to my Queen!'

She cried out 'Ah!'

'Child,' he calmed himself, 'I will keep my hands from thee. But I would fain have the kisses of thy mouth.'

She went to lean upon her table, for her knees trembled.

'Let me speak,' she said.

'Why, none hinders,' he answered her kindly.

'I swear I do love thee, so that thy voice is as the blows of hammers upon iron to me,' she said. 'I may have little rest, save when I speak with thee, for that sustaineth thy servant. But I fear these days and ways. This is a very crooked riddle. So much I desire thee that I am tremulous to take thee. If it be a madness call it a madness, but grant me this!'

She looked at him distractedly, brushing her hands across her eyes.

'It feels within my heart that I must do a penance,' she said. 'I have been wishful to feel upon my brow the pressure of the great crown. Therefore, grant me this: that I may not feel it. And be this the penance!'

'Child,' he said, 'how may you be a Queen, and not crowned with pomp and state?'

'Majesty,' she faltered, 'to prepare myself against that high office I have been reading in chronicles of the lives of them that have been Queens of England. It was his Grace of Canterbury that sent me these books for another purpose. But there ye shall read—in Asser and the Saxon Chronicles—how that the old Queens of Saxondom, when that they were humble or were wives coming after the first, sat not upon the throne to be crowned and sacred, but— so it was with Judith that was stepmother to King Alfred, and with some others whose names in this hurry I may not discover nor remember in my mind—they were, upon some holidays, shewn to the people as being the King's wife.'

She hung her head.

'For that I am humble in truth before the world and before my mother Mary in Heaven, and for that I am not thy first Queen, but even thy fifth; so I would be shewn and never crowned.'

She leaned back against the table, supporting herself with her hands against its edges; her eyes piteously devoured his face.

'Why, child,' he said, 'so thou wilt be that fifth Queen; whether thou wilt be a Queen crowned or a Queen shewn, what care I?'

She no longer refused herself to his arms, for she had no more strength.

'Mary be judge between me and them that speak against me,' she said, 'I can no more hold out against my joy or longings.'

'Sha't wear a hair shirt,' he said tenderly. 'Sha't go in sackcloth. Sha't have enow to do praying for me and thee. But hast no need of prayers.' He lulled her in his arms, swaying on his feet. 'Hast a great tongue. Speakest many words. But art a very child. God send thee all the joy I purpose thee. And, an thou hast sins, weight me further down in hell therewith.'

The light of the candles threw their locked shadows along the wall and up the ceilings. Her head fell back, her eyes closed, so that she seemed to be dead and her listless hands were open in her skirts.

THE
FIFTH QUEEN
CROWNED

A Romance

" Da habt Ihr schon das End vom Lied "

To
Arthur Marwood

PART ONE

THE MAJOR CHORD

I

'THE Bishop of Rome——'

Thomas Cranmer began a hesitating speech. In the pause after the words the King himself hesitated, as if he poised between a heavy rage and a sardonic humour. He deemed, however, that the humour could the more terrify the Archbishop—and, indeed, he was so much upon the joyous side in those summer days that he had forgotten how to browbeat.

'Our holy father,' he corrected the Archbishop. 'Or I will say my holy father, since thou art a heretic——'

Cranmer's eyes had always the expression of a man's who looked at approaching calamity, but at the King's words his whole face, his closed lips, his brows, the lines from his round nose, all drooped suddenly downwards.

'Your Grace will have me write a letter to the—to his—to him——'

The downward lines fixed themselves, and from amongst them the panic-stricken eyes made a dumb appeal to the griffins and crowns of his dark green hangings, for they were afraid to turn to the King. Henry retained his heavy look of jocularity: he jumped at a weighty gibe—

'My Grace will have thy Grace write a letter to his Holiness.'

He dropped into a heavy impassivity, rolled his eyes, fluttered his swollen fingers on the red and gilded table, and then said clearly, 'My. Thy. His.'

When he was in that mood he spoke with a singular distinctness that came up from his husky and ordinary

419

joviality like something dire and terrible—like that something that upon a clear smooth day will suggest to you suddenly the cruelty that lies always hidden in the limpid sea.

'To Cæsar—egomet, I mineself—that which is Cæsar's: to him—that is to say to his Holiness, our lord of Rome— the things which are of God! But to thee, Archbishop, I know not what belongs.'

He paused and then struck his hand upon the table: 'Cold porridge is thy portion! Cold porridge!' he laughed; 'for they say: Cold porridge to the devil! And, since thou art neither God's nor the King's, what may I call thee but the devil's self's man?'

A heavy and minatory silence seemed to descend upon him; the Archbishop's thin hands opened suddenly as if he were letting something fall to the ground. The King scowled heavily, but rather as if he were remembering past heavinesses than for any present griefs.

'Why,' he said, 'I am growing an old man. It is time I redded up my house.'

It was as if he thought he could take his time, for his heavily pursed eyes looked down at the square tips of his fingers where they drummed on the table. He was such a weighty man that the old chair in which he sat creaked at the movement of his limbs. It was his affectation of courtesy that he would not sit in the Archbishop's own new gilded and great chair that had been brought from Lambeth on a mule's back along with the hangings. But the other furnishings of that Castle of Pontefract were as old as the days of Edward IV—even the scarlet wood of the table had upon it the arms of Edward IV's Queen Elizabeth, side by side with that King's. Henry noted it and said—

'It is time these arms were changed. See that you have here fairly painted the arms of my Queen and me—Howard and Tudor—in token that we have passed this way and sojourned in this Castle of Pontefract.'

He was dallying with time as if it were a luxury to dally: he looked curiously round the room.

'Why, they have not housed you very well,' he said, and, as the Archbishop shivered suddenly, he added, 'there should be glass in the windows. This is a foul old kennel.'

'I have made a complaint to the Earl Marshal,' Cranmer said dismally, 'but 'a said there was overmuch room needed above ground.'

This room was indeed below ground and very old, strong, and damp. The Archbishop's own hangings covered the walls, but the windows shot upwards through the stones to the light; there was upon the ground of stone not a carpet but only rushes; being early in the year, no provision was made for firing, and the soot of the chimney back was damp, and sparkled with the track of a snail that had lived there undisturbed for many years, and neither increasing, because it had no mate, nor dying, because it was well fed by the ferns that, behind the present hangings, grew in the joints of the stones. In that low-ceiled and dark place the Archbishop was aware that above his head were fair and sunlit rooms, newly painted and hung, with the bosses on the ceilings fresh silvered or gilt, all these fair places having been given over to kinsmen of the yellow Earl Marshal from the Norfolk Queen downwards. And the temporal and material neglect angered him and filled him with a querulous bitterness that gnawed up even through his dread of a future—still shadowy—fall and ruin.

The King looked sardonically at the line of the ceiling. He had known that Norfolk, who was the Earl Marshal, had the mean mind to make him set these indignities upon the Archbishop, and loftily he considered this result as if the Archbishop were a cat mauled by his own dog whose nature it was to maul cats.

The Archbishop had been standing with one hand on the arm of his heavy chair, about to haul it back from the table to sit himself down. He had been standing thus when the King had entered with the brusque words—

'Make you ready to write a letter to Rome.'

And he still stood there, the cold feet among the damp rushes, the cold hand still upon the arm of the chair, the cap pulled forward over his eyes, the long black gown hanging motionless to the boot tops that were furred around the ankles.

'I have made a plaint to the Earl Marshal,' he said; 'it is not fitting that a lord of the Church should be so housed.'

Henry eyed him sardonically.

'Sir,' he said, 'I am being brought round to think that ye are only a false lord of the Church. And I am minded to think that ye are being brought round to trow even the like to mine own self.'

His eyes rested, little and twinkling like a pig's, upon the opening of the Archbishop's cloak above his breastbone, and the Archbishop's right hand nervously sought that spot.

'I was always of the thought,' he said, 'that the prohibition of the wearing of crucifixes was against your Highness' will and the teachings of the Church.'

A great crucifix of silver, the Man of Sorrows depending dolorously from its arms and backed up by a plaque of silver so that it resembled a porter's badge, depended over the black buttons of his undercoat. He had put it on upon the day when secretly he had married Henry to the papist Lady Katharine Howard. On the same day he had put on a hair shirt, and he had never since removed either the one or the other. He had known very well that this news would reach the Queen's ears, as also that he had fasted thrice weekly and had taken a Benedictine sub-prior out of chains in the tower to be his second chaplain.

'Holy Church! Holy Church!' the King muttered amusedly into the stiff hair of his chin and lips. The Archbishop was driven into one of his fits of panic-stricken boldness.

'Your Grace,' he said, 'if ye write a letter to Rome you will—for I see not how ye may avoid it—reverse all your acts of this last twenty years.'

'Your Grace,' the King mocked him, 'by your setting on

of chains, crucifixes, phylacteries, and by your aping of monkish ways, ye have reversed—well ye know it—all my and thy acts of a long time gone.'

He cast himself back from the table into the leathern shoulder-straps of the chair.

'And if,' he continued with sardonic good-humour, 'my fellow and servant may reverse my acts—videlicet, the King's—wherefore shall not I—videlicet, the King—reverse what acts I will? It is to set me below my servants!'

'I am minded to redd up my house!' he repeated after a moment.

'Please it, your Grace——' the Archbishop muttered. His eyes were upon the door.

The King said, 'Anan?' He could not turn his bulky head, he would not move his bulky body.

'My gentleman!' the Archbishop whispered.

The King looked at the opposite wall and cried out—

'Come in, Lascelles. I am about cleaning out some stables of mine.'

The door moved noiselessly and heavily back, taking the hangings with it; as if with the furtive eyes and feathery grace of a blonde fox Cranmer's spy came round the great boards.

'Ay! I am doing some cleansing,' the King said again. 'Come hither and mend thy pen to write.'

Against the King's huge bulk—Henry was wearing purple and black upon that day—and against the Archbishop's black and pillar-like form, Lascelles, in his scarlet, with his blonde and tender beard had an air of being quill-like. The bones of his knees through his tight and thin silken stockings showed almost as those of a skeleton; where the King had great chains of gilt and green jewels round his neck, and where the Archbishop had a heavy chain of silver, he had a thin chain of fine gold and a tiny badge of silver-gilt. He dragged one of his legs a little when he walked. That was the fashion of that day, because the King himself dragged his right leg, though the ulcer in it had been cured.

Sitting askew in his chair at the table, the King did not look at this gentleman, but moved the fingers of his outstretched hand in token that his crook of the leg was kneeling enough for him.

'Take your tablets and write,' Henry said; 'nay, take a great sheet of parchment and write——'

'Your Grace,' he added to the Archbishop, 'ye are the greatest penner of solemn sentences that I have in my realm. What I shall say roughly to Lascelles you shall ponder upon and set down nobly, at first in the vulgar tongue and then in fine Latin.' He paused and added—

'Nay; ye shall write it in the vulgar tongue, and the Magister Udal shall set it into Latin. He is the best Latinist we have—better than myself, for I have no time——'

Lascelles was going between a great cabinet with iron hinges and the table. He fetched an inkhorn set into a tripod, a sandarach, and a roll of clean parchment that was tied around with a green ribbon.

Upon the gold and red of the table he stretched out the parchment as if it had been a map. He mended his pen with a little knife and kneeled down upon the rushes beside the table, his chin level with the edge. His whole mind appeared to be upon keeping the yellowish sheet straight and true upon the red and gold, and he raised his eyes neither to the Archbishop's white face nor yet to the King's red one.

Henry stroked the short hairs of his neck below the square grey beard. He was reflecting that very soon all the people in that castle, and very soon after, most of the people in that land would know what he was about to say.

'Write now,' he said. ' "Henry—by the grace of God— Defender of the Faith—King, Lord Paramount." ' He stirred in his chair.

'Set down all my styles and titles: "Duke Palatine— Earl—Baron—Knight"—leave out nothing, for I will show how mighty I am.' He hummed, considered, set his head on one side and then began to speak swiftly—

'Set it down thus: "We, Henry, and the rest, being a very mighty King, such as few have been, are become a very humble man. A man broken by years, having suffered much. A man humbled to the dust, crawling to kiss the wounds of his Redeemer. A Lord of many miles both of sea and land." Why, say—

' "Guide and Leader of many legions, yet comes he to thee for guidance." Say, too, "He who was proud cometh to thee to regain his pride. He who was proud in things temporal cometh to thee that he may once more have the pride of a champion in Christendom——" '

He had been speaking as if with a malicious glee, for his words seemed to strike, each one, into the face of the pallid figure, darkly standing before him. And he was aware that each word increased the stiff and watchful constraint of the figure that knelt beside the table to write. But suddenly his glee left him; he scowled at the Archbishop as if Cranmer had caused him to sin. He pulled at the collar around his throat.

'No,' he cried out, 'write down in simple words that I am a very sinful man. Set it down that I grow old! That I am filled with fears for my poor soul! That I have sinned much! That I recall all that I have done! An old man, I come to my Saviour's Regent upon earth. A man aware of error, I will make restitution tenfold! Say I am broken and aged and afraid! I kneel down on the ground——'

He cast his inert mass suddenly a little forward as if indeed he were about to come on to his knees in the rushes.

'Say——' he muttered—'say——'

But his face and his eyes became suffused with blood.

'It is a very difficult thing,' he uttered huskily, 'to meddle in these sacred matters.'

He fell heavily back into his chair-straps once more.

'I do not know what I will have you to say,' he said.

He looked broodingly at the floor.

'I do not know,' he muttered.

He rolled his eyes, first to the face of the Archbishop, then to Lascelles—

'Body of God—what carved turnips!' he said, for in the one face there was only panic, and in the other nothing at all. He rolled on to his feet, catching at the table to steady himself.

'Write what you will,' he called, 'to these intents and purposes. Or stay to write—I will send you a letter much more good from the upper rooms.'

Cranmer suddenly stretched out, with a timid pitiful-ness, his white hands. But, rolling his huge shoulders, like a hastening bear, the King went over the rushes. He pulled the heavy door to with such a vast force that the latch came again out of the hasp, and the door, falling slowly back and quivering as if with passion, showed them his huge legs mounting the little staircase.

A long silence fell in that dim room. The Archbishop's lips moved silently, the spy's glance went, level, along his parchment. Suddenly he grinned mirthlessly and as if at a shameless thought.

'The Queen will write the letter his Grace shall send us,' he said.

Then their eyes met. The one glance, panic-stricken, seeing no issue, hopeless and without resource, met the other—crafty, alert, fox-like, with a dance in it. The glances transfused and mingled. Lascelles remained upon his knees as if, stretching out his right knee behind him, he were taking a long rest.

II

It was almost within earshot of these two men in their dim cell that the Queen walked from the sunlight into shadow and out again. This great terrace looked to the north and west, and, from the little hillock, dominating miles of gently rising ground, she had a great view over rolling and very green country. The original builders of the Castle of Pontefract had meant this terrace to be flagged with stone:

but the work had never been carried so far forward. There was only a path of stone along the bowshot and a half of stone balustrade; the rest had once been gravel, but the grass had grown over it; that had been scythed, and nearly the whole space was covered with many carpets of blue and red and other very bright colours. In the left corner when you faced inwards there was a great pavilion of black cloth, embroidered very closely with gold and held up by ropes of red and white. Though forty people could sit in it round the table, it appeared very small, the walls of the castle towered up so high. They towered up so high, so square, and so straight that from the terrace below you could hardly hear the flutter of the huge banner of St George, all red and white against the blue sky, though sometimes in a gust it cracked like a huge whip, and its shadow, where it fell upon the terrace, was sufficient to cover four men.

To take away from the grimness of the flat walls many little banners had been suspended from loopholes and beneath windows. Swallow-tailed, long, or square, they hung motionless in the shelter, or, since the dying away of the great gale three days before, had looped themselves over their staffs. These were all painted green, because that was the Queen's favourite colour, being the emblem of Hope.

A little pavilion, all of green silk, at the very edge of the platform, had all its green curtains looped up, so that only the green roof showed; and, within, two chairs, a great leathern one for the King, a little one of red and white wood for the Queen, stood side by side as if they conversed with each other. At the top of it was a golden image of a lion, and above the peak of the entrance another, golden too, of the Goddess Flora, carrying a cornucopia of flowers, to symbolise that this tent was a summer abode for pleasantness.

Here the King and Queen, for the four days that they had been in the castle, had delighted much to sit, resting after their long ride up from the south country. For it pleased Henry to let his eyes rest upon a great view of this realm that was his, and to think nothing; and it pleased

Katharine Howard to think that now she swayed this land, and that soon she would alter its face.

They looked out, over the tops of the elm trees that grew right up against the terrace wall; but the land itself was too green, the fields too empty of dwellings. There was no one but sheep between all the hedgerows: there was, in all the wide view, but one church tower, and where, in place and place, there stood clusters of trees as if to shelter home-steads—nearly always the homesteads had fallen to ruin beneath the boughs. Upon one ridge one could see the long walls of an unroofed abbey. But, to the keenest eye no men were visible, save now and then a shepherd leaning on his crook. There was no ploughland at all. Now and then companies of men in helmets and armour rode up to or away from the castle. Once she had seen the courtyard within the keep filled with cattle that lowed uneasily. But these, she had learned, had been taken from cattle thieves by the men of the Council of the Northern Borders. They were destined for the provisioning of that castle during her stay there, they being forfeit, whether Scotch or English.

'Ah,' she said, 'whilst his Grace rides north to meet the King's Scots I will ride east and west and south each day.'

At that moment, whilst the King had left Cranmer and his spy and, to regain his composure, was walking up and down in her chamber, she was standing beside the Duke of Norfolk about midway between the end of the terrace and the little green pavilion.

She was all in a dark purple dress, to please the King whose mood that colour suited; and the Duke's yellow face looked out above a suit all of black. He wore that to please the King too, for the King was of opinion that no gather-ing looked gay in its colours that had not many men in black amongst the number.

He said—

'You do not ride north with his Grace?'

He leaned upon his two staves, one long and of silver, the other shorter and gilt; his gown fell down to his ankles, his dark and half-closed eyes looked out at a tree that, struck lately by lightning, stretched up half its boughs all naked from a little hillock beside a pond a mile away.

'So it is settled between his Grace and me,' she said. She did not much like her uncle, for she had little cause. But, the King being away, she walked with him rather than with another man.

'I ask, perforce,' he said, 'for I have much work in the ordering of your progresses.'

'We meant that you should have that news this day,' she said.

He shot one glance at her face, then turned his eyes again upon the stricken tree. Her face was absolutely calm and without expression, as it had been always when she had directed him what she would have done. He could trace no dejection in it: on the other hand, he gave her credit for a great command over her features. That he had himself. And, in the niece's eyes, as they moved from the backs of a flock of sheep to the dismantled abbey on the ridge, there was something of the enigmatic self-containment that was in the uncle's steady glance. He could observe no dejection, and at that he humbled himself a little more.

'Ay,' he said, 'the ordering of your progresses is a heavy burden. I would have you commend what I have done here.'

She looked at him, at that, as if with a swift jealousy. His eyes were roving upon the gay carpets, the pavilions, and the flags against the grim walls, depending in motionless streaks of colour.

'The King's Grace's self,' she said, 'did tell me that all these things he ordered and thought out for my pleasuring.

Norfolk dropped his eyes to the ground.

'Aye,' he said, 'his Grace ordered them and their placing. There is no man to equal his Grace for such things; but I had the work of setting them where they are. I would have your favour for that.'

She appeared appeased and gave him her hand to kiss. There was a little dark mole upon the third finger.

'The last niece that I had for Queen,' he said, 'would not suffer me to kiss her hand.'

She looked at him a little absently, for, because since she had been Queen—and before—she had been a lonely woman, she was given to thinking her own thoughts whilst others talked.

She was troubled by the condition of her chief maid Margot Poins. Margot Poins was usually tranquil, modest, submissive in a cheerful manner and ready to converse. But of late she had been moody, and sunk in a dull silence. And that morning she had suddenly burst out into a smouldering, heavy passion, and had torn Katharine's hair whilst she dressed it.

'Ay,' Margot had said, 'you are Queen: you can do what you will. It is well to be Queen. But we who are dirt underfoot, we cannot do one single thing.'

And, because she was lonely, with only Lady Rochford, who was foolish, and this girl to talk to, it had grieved the Queen to find this girl growing so lumpish and dull. At that time, whilst her hair was being dressed, she had answered only—

'Yea; it is good to be a Queen. But you will find it in Seneca——' and she had translated for Margot the passage which says that eagles are as much tied by weighty ropes as are finches caught in tiny fillets.

'Oh, your Latin,' Margot had said. 'I would I had never heard the sound of it, but had stuck to clean English.'

Katharine imagined then that it was some new flame of the Magister Udal's that was troubling the girl, and this troubled her too, for she did not like that her maids should be played with by men, and she loved Margot for her past loyalties, readiness, and companionship.

She came out of her thoughts to say to her uncle, remembering his speech about her hands—

'Aye; I have heard that Anne Boleyn had six fingers upon her right hand.'

'She had six upon each, but she concealed it,' he answered. 'It was her greatest grief.'

Katharine realised that his sardonic tone, his bitter yellow face, the croak in his voice, and his stiff gait—all these things were signs of his hostility to her. And his mention of Anne Boleyn, who had been Queen, much as she was, and of her bitter fate, this mention, if it could not be a threat, was, at least, a reminder meant to give her fears and misgiving. When she had been a child—and afterwards, until the very day when she had been shown for Queen —her uncle had always treated her with a black disdain, as he treated all the rest of the world. When he had—and it was rarely enough—come to visit her grandmother, the old Duchess of Norfolk, he had always been like that. Through the old woman's huge, lonely, and ugly halls he had always stridden, halting a little over the rushes, and all creatures must keep out of his way. Once he had kicked her little dog, once he had pushed her aside; but probably, then, when she had been no more than a child, he had not known who she was, for she had lived with the servants and played with the servants' children, much like one of them, and her grandmother had known little of the household or its ways.

She answered him sharply—

'I have heard that you were no good friend to your niece, Anne Boleyn, when she was in her troubles.'

He swallowed in his throat and gazed impassively at the distant oak tree, nevertheless his knee trembled with fury. And Katharine knew very well that if, more than another, he took pleasure in giving pain with his words, he bore the pain of other's words less well than most men.

'The Queen Anne,' he said, 'was a heretic. No better was she than a Protestant. She battened upon the goods of our Church. Why should I defend her?'

'Uncle,' she said, 'where got you the jewel in your bonnet?'

He started a little back at that, and the small veins in his
yellow eye-whites grew inflamed with blood.

'Queen——' he brought out between rage and astonishment that she should dare the taunt.

'I think it came from the great chalice of the Abbey of
Rising,' she said. 'We are valiant defenders of the Church,
who wear its spoils upon our very brows.'

It was as if she had thrown down a glove to him and to
a great many that were behind him.

She knew very well where she stood, and she knew very
well what her uncle and his friends awaited for her, for
Margot, her maid, brought her alike the gossip of the
Court and the loudly voiced threats and aspirations of the
city. For the Protestants—she knew them and cared little
for them. She did not believe there were very many in the
King's and her realm, and mostly they were foreign merchants and poor men who cared little as long as their
stomachs were filled. If these had their farms again they
would surely return to the old faith, and she was minded
to do away with the sheep. For it was the sheep that had
brought discontent to England. To make way for these
fleeces the ploughmen had been dispossessed.

It was natural that Protestants should hate her; but with
Norfolk and his like it was different. She knew very well
that Norfolk came there that day and waited every day,
watching anxiously for the first sign that the King's love
for her should cool. She knew very well that they said in
the Court that with the King it was only possession and
then satiety. And she knew very well that when Norfolk's
eyes searched her face it was for signs of dismay and of
discouragement. And when Norfolk had said that he himself had placed the banners, the tents, the pavilions and
carpets that made gay all that grim terrace of the air, he
was essaying to make her think that the King was abandoning the task of doing her honour. This had made her angry,
for it was such folly. Her uncle should have known that
the King had discussed all these things with her, asking her
what she liked, and that all these bright colours and these

plaisaunces were what her man had gallantly thought out for her. She carried her challenge still further.

'It ill becomes us Howards and all like us,' she said, 'to talk of how we will defend the Church of God——'

'I am a swordsman only,' he said. 'Give me that——'

She was not minded to listen to him.

'It becomes us ill,' she said; 'and I take shame in it. For, a very few years agone we Howards were very poor. Now we are very rich—though it is true that my father is still a very poor man, and your stepmother, my grandmother, has known hard shifts. But we Howards, through you who are our head, became amongst the richest in the land. And how?'

'I have done services——' the Duke began.

'Why, there has been no new wealth made in this realm,' she said; 'it came from the Church. Consider what you have had of this Abbey of Risings that I speak of, because I knew it well as a child, and saw many times then, sparkling in that which held the blood of my Saviour, the jewel that is now in your cap.'

The Abbey of Risings, after the visitors had been to it and the monks had been driven out, had fallen to the Duke of Norfolk. And his men had stripped the lead from the roofs, the glass from the windows, the very tiles from the floor. And this little abbey was only one of many, large and small, that had fallen to the Duke, so that it was true enough that, through him, the Howards had become a very rich family.

Norfolk burst into a sudden speech—

'I hold these things only as a trust,' he said. 'I am ready to restore.'

'Why, that is very well,' Katharine said; 'and I have hopes that soon you will be called to make that restoration to your God.'

Norfolk looked at the square toes of his shoes for a long time.

'Will you have *all* things to be given back?' he said at last after he had thought much.

'The King will have all things be as they were before the Queen Katharine, my namesake of Aragon, was undone,' Katharine answered. 'And me he will have to take her place so that all things shall be as before they were.'

The Duke, leaning on his silver and gold staves, shrugged his shoulders very slowly.

'This will make a very great confusion,' he said.

'Ay,' Katharine answered, 'there will a very many be confounded, and a great number of hundreds be much annoyed.

She broke in again upon his slow meditations—

'Sir,' she said, 'this is a very pitiful thing! Privy Seal that is dead and done with worked with a very great cunning. Well he knew that for most men the heart resideth in the pocket. Therefore, though ye said all that he rode this land with a bridle of iron, he was very careful to stop all your mouths alike with pieces of gold. It was not only to his friends that he gave what had been taken from God, but he was very careful that much also should fall into the greedy mouths of those that cried out. If he had not done this, do you think that he would have remained so long above the earth that he made weary? No. But since he made all rich alike with this plunder, so there was no man, either Catholic or Lutheran, very anxious to have him away. And, now that he is dead he worketh still. For who among you lords that do call yourselves sons of the Church, but holdeth of the Church's goods? Oh, bethink you! bethink you! The moment is at hand when ye may work restoration. See that ye do it willingly and with good hearts, smoothing and making plain the way by which the bruised feet of our Saviour shall come across this, His land.'

Norfolk kept his eyes upon the ground.

'Why, for me,' he said, 'I am very willing. This day I will send to set clerks at work discovering that which is mine and that which came from the Church; but I think you will find some that will not do it so eagerly.'

She believed him very little; and she said—

'Why, if you will do this thing I think there will not many be behindhand.'

He did what he could to conceal his wincing, and her voice changed its tone.

'Sir,' she said, and she was eager and pleading, 'you have many men that take counsel with you, for I trow that you and my Lord of Winchester do lead such lords as be Catholic in this realm. I know very well that you and my Lord Bishop of Winchester and such Catholic lords would have me to be your puppet and so work as you would have me, giving back to the Church such things as have fallen to Protestants or to men that ye mislike. But that may not be, for, since I owe mine advancement not to you, nor to mine own efforts, but to God alone, so to God alone do I owe fealty.'

She stretched out towards him the hand that he had kissed. The tail of her coif fell almost to her feet; her body in the fresh sunlight was all cased in purple velvet, only the lawn of her undershirt showed, white and tremulous at her wrists and her neck; and, fair and contrasted with the gold of her hair, her face came out of its abstraction, to take on a pitiful and mournful earnestness.

'Sir,' she said, 'if you shall speak for God in the councils that you will hold, believe that your rewards shall be very great. I think that you have been a man of a very troubled mind, for you have thought only or mostly of the affairs of this world. But do now this one good stroke for God His piteous sake, and such a peace shall descend upon you as you have never yet known. You shall have no more griefs; you shall have no more fears. And that is better than the jewels of chalices, and than much lead from the roofs of abbeys. Speak you thus in these councils that you shall hold, give you such advice to them that come to you seeking it, and this I promise you —for it is too little a thing to promise you the love of a Queen and a King's favour, though that too ye shall not lack —but this I promise you, that there shall descend upon your heart that most blessed miracle and precious wealth, the peace of God.'

III

When Henry was calmed by his pacing in her chamber he came out to her in the sunlight, rolling and bear-like, and so huge that the terrace seemed to grow smaller.

'Chuck,' he said to her, 'I ha' done a thing to pleasure thee.' He moved two fingers upwards to save the Duke of Norfolk from falling to his knees, caught Katharine by the elbow, and, turning upon himself as on a huge pivot, swung her round him so that they faced the pavilion. 'Sha't not talk with a citron-faced uncle,' he said; 'sha't save sweet words for me. I will tell thee what I ha' done to pleasure thee.'

'Save it a while and do another ere ye tell me,' she said.

'Now, what is your reasoning about that, wise one?' he asked.

She laughed at him, for she took pleasure in his society and, except when she was earnest to beg things of him, she was mostly gay at his side.

'It takes a woman to teach kings,' she said.

He answered that it took a Queen to teach him.

'Why,' she said, 'listen! I know that each day ye do things to pleasure me, things prodigal or such little things as giving me pouncet boxes. But you will find—and a woman, quean or queen, knows it well—that to take the full pleasure of her lover's surprises well, she must have an easy mind. And to have an easy mind she must have granted her the little, little boons she asketh.'

He reflected ponderously upon this point and at last, with a sort of peasant's gravity, nodded his head.

'For,' she said, 'if a woman is to take pleasure she must guess at what you men have done for her. And if she be to guess pleasurably, she must have a clear mind. And if I am to have a clear mind I must have a maiden consoled with a husband.'

Henry seated himself carefully in the great chair of the small pavilion. He spread out his knees, blinked at the view and when, having cast a look round to see that Norfolk was gone—for it did not suit her that he should see on what terms she was with the King—she seated herself on a little foot-pillow at his feet, he set a great hand upon her head. She leaned her arms across over his knees, and looked up at him appealingly.

'I do take it,' he said, 'that I must make some man rich to wed some poor maid.'

'Oh, Solomon!' she said.

'And I do take it,' he continued with gravity, 'that this maid is thy maid Margot.'

'How know you that?' she said.

'I have observed her,' he maintained gravely.

'Why, you could not well miss her,' she answered. 'She is as big as a plough-ox.'

'I have observed,' he said—and he blinked his little eyes as if, pleasurably, she were, with her words, whispering around his head. 'I have observed that ye affected her.'

'Why, she likes me well. She is a good wench—and to-day she tore my hair.'

'Then that is along of a man?' he asked. 'Didst not stick thy needle in her arm? Or wilto be quit of her?'

She rubbed her chin.

'Why, if she wed, I mun be quit of her,' she said, as if she had never thought of that thing.

He answered—

'Assuredly; for ye may not part man and lawful wife were you seven times Queen.'

'Why,' she said, 'I have little pleasure in Margot as she is.'

'Then let her go,' he answered.

'But I am a very lonely Queen,' she said, 'for you are much absent.'

He reflected pleasurably.

'Thee wouldst have about thee a little company of well-wishers?'

'So that they be those thou lovest well,' she said.

'Why, thy maid contents me,' he answered. He reflected

slowly. 'We must give her man a post about thee,' he uttered triumphantly.

'Why, trust thee to pleasure me,' she said. 'You will find out a way always.'

He scrubbed her nose gently with his heavy finger.

'Who is the man?' he said. 'What ruffler?'

'I think it is the Magister Udal,' she answered.

Henry said—

'Oh ho! oh ho!' And after a moment he slapped his thigh and laughed like a child. She laughed with him, silverly upon a little sound between 'ah' and 'e.' He stopped his laugh to listen to hers, and then he said gravely—

'I think your laugh is the prettiest sound I ever heard. I would give thy maid Margot a score of husbands to make thee laugh.'

'One is enough to make her weep,' she said; 'and I may laugh at thee.'

He said—

'Let us finish this business within the hour. Sit you upon your chair that I may call one to send this ruffler here.'

She rose, with one sinuous motion that pleased him well, half to her feet and, feeling behind her with one hand for the chair, aided herself with the other upon his shoulder because she knew that it gave him joy to be her prop.

'Call the maid, too,' she said, 'for I would come to the secret soon.'

That pleased him too, and, having shouted for a knave he once more shook with laughter.

'Oh ho,' he said, 'you will net this old fox, will you?'

And, having sent his messenger off to summon the Magister from the Lady Mary's room, and the maid from the Queen's, he continued for a while to soliloquise as to Udal's predicament. For he had heard the Magister rail against matrimony in Latin hexameters and doggerel Greek. He knew that the Magister was an incorrigible fumbler after petticoats. And now, he said, this old fox was to be bagged and tied up.

He said—

'Well, well, well; well, well!'

For, if a Queen commanded a marriage, a marriage there must be; there was no more hope for the Magister than for any slave of Cato's. He was cabined, ginned, trapped, shut in from the herd of bachelors. It pleased the King very well.

The King grasped the gilded arms of his great chair, Katharine sat beside him, her hands laid one within another upon her lap. She did not say one single word during the King's interview with Magister Udal.

The Magister fell upon his knees before them and, seeing the laughing wrinkles round the King's little eyes, made sure that he was sent for—as had often been the case—to turn into Latin some jest the King had made. His gown fell about his kneeling shins, his cap was at his side, his lean, brown, and sly face, with the long nose and crafty eyes, was like a woodpecker's.

'Goodman Magister,' Henry said. 'Stand up. We have sent for thee to advance thee.' Without moving his head he rolled his eyes to one side. He loved his dramatic effects and wished to await the coming of the Queen's maid, Margot, before he gave the weight of his message.

Udal picked up his cap and came up to his feet before them; he had beneath his gown a little book, and one long finger between its leaves to keep his place where he had been reading. For he had forgotten a saying of Thales, and was reading through Cæsar's Commentaries to find it.

'As Seneca said,' he uttered in his throat, 'advancement is doubly sweet to them that deserve it not.'

'Why,' the King said, 'we advance thee on the deserts of one that finds thee sweet, and is sweet to one doubly sweet to us, Henry of Windsor that speak sweet words to thee.'

The lines on Udal's face drooped all a little downwards.

'Y'are reader in Latin to the Lady Mary,' the King said.

'I have little deserved in that office,' Udal answered; 'the lady reads Latin better than even I.'

'Why, you lie in that,' Henry said, ' 'a readeth well for she's my daughter; but not so well as thee.'

Udal ducked his head; he was not minded to carry modesty further than in reason.

'The Lady Mary—the Lady Mary of England——' the King said weightily—and these last two words of his had a weight all their own, so that he added, 'of England' again, and then, 'will have little longer need of thee. She shall wed with a puissant Prince.'

'I hail, I felicitate, I bless the day I hear those words,' the Magister said.

'Therefore,' the King said—and his ears had caught the rustle of Margot's grey gown—'we will let thee no more be reader to that my daughter.'

Margot came round the green silk curtains that were looped on the corner posts of the pavilion. When she saw the Magister her great, fair face became slowly of a fiery red; slowly and silently she fell, with motions as if bovine, to her knees at the Queen's side. Her gown was all grey, but it had roses of red and white silk round the upper edges of the square neck-place, and white lawn showed beneath her grey cap.

'We advance thee,' Henry said, 'to be Chancellier de la Royne, with an hundred pounds by the year from my purse. Do homage for thine office.'

Udal fell upon one knee before Katharine, and dropping both cap and book, took her hand to raise to his lips. But Margot caught her hand when he had done with it and set upon it a huge pressure.

'But, Sir Chancellor,' the King said, 'it is evident that so grave an office must have a grave fulfiller. And, to ballast thee the better, the Queen of her graciousness hath found thee a weighty helpmeet. So that, before you shall touch the duties and emoluments of this charge you shall, and that even to-night, wed this Madam Margot that here kneels.'

Udal's face had been of a coppery green pallor ever since he had heard the title of Chancellor.

'Eheu!' he said, 'this is the torture of Tantalus that might never drink.'

In its turn the face of Margot Poins grew pale, pushed forward towards him; but her eyes appeared to blaze, for all they were a mild blue, and the Queen felt the pressure upon her hand grow so hard that it pained her.

The King uttered the one word, 'Magister!'

Udal's fingers picked at the fur of his moth-eaten gown.

'God be favourable to me,' he said. 'If it were anything but Chancellor!'

The King grew more rigid.

'Body of God,' he said, 'will you wed with this maid?'

'Ahí!' the Magister wailed; and his perturbation had in it something comic and scarecrowlike, as if a wind shook him from within. 'If you will make me anything but a Chancellor, I will. But a Chancellor, I dare not.'

The King cast himself back in his chair. The suggested gibe rose furiously to his lips; the Magister quailed and bent before him, throwing out his hands.

'Sire,' he said, 'if—which God forbid—this were a Protestant realm I might do it. But oh, pardon and give ear. Pardon and give ear——'

He waved one hand furiously at the silken canopy above them.

'It is agreed with one of mine in Paris that she shall come hither—God forgive me, I must make avowal, though God knows I would not—she shall come hither to me if she do hear that I have risen to be a Chancellor.'

The King said, 'Body of God!' as if it were an earthquake.

'If it were anything else but Chancellor she might not come, and I would wed Margot Poins more willingly than any other. But—God knows I do not willingly make this avowal, but am in a corner, *sicut vulpis in lucubris*, like a fox in the coils—this Paris woman is my wife.'

Henry gave a great shout of laughter, but slowly Margot Poins fell across the Queen's knees. She uttered no sound, but lay there motionless. The sight affected Udal to an epileptic fury.

'Jove be propitious to me!' he stuttered out. 'I know not

what I can do.' He began to tear the fur of his cloak and toss it over the battlements. 'The woman is my wife—wed by a friar. If this were a Protestant realm now—or if I pleaded pre-contract—and God knows I ha' promised marriage to twenty women before I, in an evil day, married one—eheu!—to this one——'

He began to sob and to wring his thin hands.

'*Quod faciam? Me miser! Utinam. Utinam*——'

He recovered a little coherence.

'If this were a Protestant land ye might say this wedding was no wedding, for that a friar did it; but I know ye will not suffer that——' His eyes appealed piteously to the Queen.

'Why, then,' he said, 'it is not upon my head that I do not wed this wench. You be my witness that I would wed; it gores my heart to see her look so pale. It tears my vitals to see any woman look pale. As Lucretius says, "Better the sunshine of smiles——" '

A little outputting of impatient breath from Katharine made him stop.

'It is you, your Grace,' he said, 'that make me thus tied. If you would let us be Protestant, or, again, if I could plead pre-contract to void this Paris marriage it would let me wed with this wench—eheu—eheu. Her brother will break my bones——'

He began to cry out so lamentably, invoking Pluto to bear him to the underworld, that the King roared out upon him—

'Why, get you gone, fool.'

The Magister threw himself suddenly upon his knees, his hands clasped, his gown drooping over them down to his wrists. He turned his face to the Queen.

'Before God,' he said, 'before high and omnipotent Jove, I swear that when I made this marriage I thought it was no marriage!' He reflected for a breath and added, at the recollection of the cook's spits that had been turned against him when he had by woman's guile been forced into marriage with the widow in Paris, 'I was driven into it by force, with sharp points at my throat. Is that not enow to void a marriage? Is that not enow? Is that not enow?'

Katharine looked out over the great levels of the view. Her face was rigid, and she swallowed in her throat, her eye being glazed and hard. The King took his cue from a glance at her face.

'Get you gone, Goodman Rogue Magister,' he said, and he adopted a canonical tone that went heavily with his rustic pose. 'A marriage made and consummated and properly blessed by holy friar there is no undoing. You are learned enough to know that. Rogue that you be, I am very glad that you are trapped by this marriage. Well I know that you have dangled too much with petticoats, to the great scandal of this my Court. Now you have lost your preferment, and I am glad of it. Another and a better than thou shall be the Queen's Chancellor, for another and a better than thou shall wed this wench. We will get her such a goodly husband——'

A low, melancholy wail from Margot Poins' agonised face—a sound such as might have been made by an ox in pain—brought him to a stop. It wrung the Magister, who could not bear to see a woman pained, up to a pitch of ecstatic courage.

'*Quid fecit Cæsar*,' he stuttered; 'what Cæsar hath done, Cæsar can do again. It was not till very lately since this canon of wedding and consummating and blessing by a holy friar hath been derided and contemned in this realm. And so it might be again——'

Katharine Howard cried out, 'Ah!' Her features grew rigid and as ashen as cold steel. And, at her cry, the King—who could less bear than Udal to hear a woman in pain—the King sprang up from his chair. It was as amazing to all them as to hunters it is to see a great wild bull charge with a monstrous velocity. Udal was rigid with fear, and the King had him by the throat. He shook him backwards and forwards so that his book fell upon the Queen's feet, bursting out of his ragged gown, and his cap, flying from his opened hand, fell down over the battlement into an elm top. The King guttered out unintelligible sounds of fury from his vast chest and, planted on his huge feet, he swung the Magister round him till, backwards and staggering, the eyes growing fixed in his brown and rigid face, he was pushed, jerking at each step of the King, out of sight behind the green silk curtains.

The Queen sat motionless in her purple velvet. She twisted one hand into the chain of the medallion about her throat, and one hand lay open and pale by her side. Margot Poins knelt at her side, her face hidden in the Queen's lap, her two arms stretched out beyond her grey coifed head. For a minute she was silent. Then great sobs shook her so that Katharine swayed upon her seat. From her hidden face there came muffled and indistinguishable words, and at last Katharine said dully—

'What, child? What, child?'

Margot moved her face sideways so that her mouth was towards Katharine.

'You can unmake it! You can unmake the marriage,' she brought out in huge sobs.

Katharine said—

'No! No!'

'You unmade a King's marriage,' Margot wailed.

Katharine said—

'No! No!' She started and uttered the words loudly; she added pitifully, 'You do not understand! You do not understand!'

It was the more pitiful in that Margot understood very well. She hid her face again and only sobbed heavily and at long intervals, and then with many sobs at once. The Queen laid her white hand upon the girl's head. Her other still played with the chain.

'Christ be piteous to me,' she said. 'I think it had been better if I had never married the King.'

Margot uttered an indistinguishable sound.

'I think it had been better,' the Queen said; 'though I had jeoparded my immortal part.'

Margot moved her head up to cry out in her turn—

'No! No! You may not say it!'

Then she dropped her face again. When she heard the King coming back and breathing heavily, she stood up, and with huge tears on her red and crumpled face she looked out upon the fields as if she had never seen them before. An immense sob shook her. The King stamped his foot with rage, and then, because he was soft-hearted to them that he saw in sorrow, he put his hand upon her shoulder.

'Sha't have a better mate,' he uttered. 'Sha't be a knight's dame! There! there!' and he fondled her great back with his hand. Her eyes screwed tightly up, she opened her mouth wide, but no words came out, and suddenly she shook her head as if she had been an enraged child. Her loud cries, shaken out of her with her tears, died away as she went across the terrace, a loud one and then a little echo, a loud one and then two more.

'Before God!' the King said, 'that knave shall eat ten years of prison bread.'

His wife looked still over the wooded enclosures, the little stone walls, and the copses. A small cloud had come before the sun, and its shadow was moving leisurely across the ridge where stood the roofless abbey.

'The maid shall have the best man I can give her,' the King said.

'Why, no good man would wed her!' Katharine answered dully.

Henry said—

'Anan?' Then he fingered the dagger on the chain before his chest.

'Why,' he added slowly, 'then the Magister shall die by the rope. It is an offence that can be quitted with death. It is time such a thing were done.'

Katharine's dull silence spurred him; he shrugged his shoulders and heaved a deep breath out.

'Why,' he said, 'a man can be found to wed the wench.'

She moved one hand and uttered—

'I would not wed her to such a man!' as if it were a matter that was not much in her thoughts.

'Then she may go into a nunnery,' the King said; 'for before three months are out we will have many nunneries in this realm.'

She looked upon him a little absently, but she smiled at him to give him pleasure. She was thinking that she wished she had not wedded him; but she smiled because, things being as they were, she thought that she had all the authorities of the noble Greeks and Romans to bid her do what a good wife should.

He laughed at her griefs, thinking that they were all about Margot Poins. He uttered jolly grossnesses; he said that she little knew the way of courts if she thought that a man, and a very good man, might not be found to wed the wench.

She was troubled that he could not better read what was upon her mind, for she was thinking that her having consented to his making null his marriage with the Princess of Cleves that he might wed her would render her work always the more difficult. It would render her more the target for evil tongues, it would set a sterner and a more stubborn opposition against her task of restoring the Kingdom of God within that realm.

Henry said—

'Ye hannot guessed what my secret was? What have I done for thee this day?'

She still looked away over the lands. She made her face smile—

'Nay, I know not. Ha' ye brought me the musk I love well?'

He shook his head.

'It is more than that!' he said.

She still smiled—

'Ha' ye—ha' ye—made make for me a new crown?'

She feared a little that that was what he had done. For he had been urgent with her, many months, to be crowned. It was his way to love these things. And her heart was a little gladder when he shook his head once again and uttered—

'It is more than that!'

She dreaded his having made ready in secret a great pageant in her honour, for she was afraid of all aggrandisements, and thought still it had been better that she had remained his sweet friend ever and not the Queen. For in that way she would have had as much empire over him, and there would have been much less clamour against her —much less clamour against the Church of her Saviour.

She forced her mind to run upon all the things that she could wish for. When she said it must be that he had ordered for her enough French taffetas to make twelve gowns, he laughed and said that he had said that it was more than a crown. When she guessed that he had made ready such a huge cavalcade that she might with great comfort and safety ride with him into Scotland, he laughed, contented that she should think of going with him upon that long journey. He stood looking at her, his little eyes blinking, his face full of pride and joy, and suddenly he uttered—

'The Church of God is come back again.' He touched his cap at the sacred name. 'I ha' made submission to the Pope.'

He looked her full in the face to get all the delight he might from her looks and her movements.

Her blue eyes grew large; she leaned forward in her chair; her mouth opened a little; her sleeves fell down to the ground. 'Now am I indeed crowned!' she said, and closed her eyes. '*Benedicta sit mater dei!*' she uttered, and her hand went over her heart place; '*deo clamavi nocte atque dië.*'

She was silent again, and she leaned more forward.

'*Sit benedicta dies haec; sit benedicta hora haec bene-dictaque, saeculum saeculûm, castra haec.*'

She looked out upon the great view: she aspired the air.

'*Ad colles,*' she breathed, '*levavi oculos meos; unde venit salvatio nostra!*'

'Body of God,' Henry said, 'all things grow plain. All things grow plain. This is the best day that ever I knew.'

IV

The Lady Mary of England sat alone in a fair room with little arched windows that gave high up on to the terrace. It was the best room that ever she had had since her mother, the Queen Katharine of Aragon, had been divorced.

Dressed in black she sat writing at a large table before one window. Her paper was fitted on to a wooden pulpit that rose before her; one book stood open upon it, three others lay open too upon the red and blue and green pattern of the Saracen rug that covered her table. At her right hand was a three-tiered inkstand of pewter, set about with the white feathers of pens; and the snakelike pattern of the table-rug serpentined in and out beneath seals of parcel gilt, a platter of bread, a sandarach of pewter, books bound in wooden covers and locked with chains, books in red velvet covers, sewn with silver wire and tied with ribbons. It ran beneath a huge globe of the world, blue and pink, that had a golden pin in it to mark the city of Rome. There were little wooden racks stuck full with written papers and parchments along the wainscoting between the arched windows, but all the hangings of the other walls were of tinted and dyed silks, not any with dark colours, because Katharine Howard had deemed that that room with its deep windows in the thick walls would be otherwise dark. The room was ten paces deep by twenty long, and the wood of the floor was polished. Against the wall, behind the Lady Mary's back, there stood a high chair upon a platform. Upon the platform a carpet began that ran up the wall and, overhead, depended from the gilded rafters of the ceiling so that it formed a dais and a canopy.

The Lady Mary sat grimly amongst all these things as if none of them belonged to her. She looked in her book, she made a note upon her paper, she stretched out her hand and took a piece of bread, putting it in her mouth, swallowing it quickly, writing again, and then once more eating, for the great and ceaseless hunger that afflicted her gnawed always at her vitals.

A little boy with a fair poll was reaching on tiptoe to smell at a pink that depended from a vase of very thin glass standing in the deep window. The shield of the coloured pane cast a little patch of red and purple on to his callow head. He was dressed all in purple, very square, and with little chains and medallions, and a little dagger with a golden sheath was about his neck. In one hand he had a piece of paper, in the other a pencil. The Lady Mary wrote; the child moved on tiptoe, with a sedulous expression of silence about his lips, near to her elbow. He watched her writing for a long time with attentive eyes.

Once he said, 'Sister, I——' but she paid him no heed.

After a time she looked coldly at his face and then he moved along the table, fingered the globe very gently, touched the books and returned to her side. He stood with his little legs wide apart. Then he sighed, then he said—

'Sister, the Queen did bid me ask you a question.'

She looked round upon him.

'This was the Queen's question,' he said bravely: ' "*Cur*—why—*nunquam*—never—*rides*—dost thou smile—*cum*—when—*ego, frater tuus*—I, thy little brother—*ludo*—play—*in camerâ tuâ*—in thy chamber?" '

'Little Prince,' she said, 'art not afeared of me?'

'Aye, am I,' he answered.

'Say then to the Queen,' she said, ' "*Domina Maria*—the Lady Mary—*ridet nunquam*—smileth never—*quod*—because—*timoris ratio*—the reason of my fear—*bona et satis*—is good and sufficient." '

He held his little head upon one side.

'The Queen did bid me say,' he uttered with his brave little voice, ' "Holy Writ hath it: *Ecce quam bonum et dignum est fratres—fratres*——" ' He faltered without embarrassment and added, 'I ha' forgot the words.'

'Aye!' she said, 'they ha' been long forgotten in these places; I deem it is overlate to call them to mind.'

She looked upon him coldly for a long time. Then she stretched out her hand for his paper.

'Your Highness, I will set you a copy.'

She took his paper and wrote—

'Malo malo malâ.'

He held it in his chubby fist, his head on one side.

'I cannot conster it,' he said.

'Why, think upon it,' she answered. 'When I was thy age I knew it already two years. But I was better beaten than thou.'

He rubbed his little arm.

'I am beaten enow,' he said.

'Knowest not what a swingeing is,' she answered.

'Then thou hadst a bitter childhood,' he brought out.

'I had a good mother,' she cut him short.

She turned her face to her writing again; it was bitter and set. The little prince climbed slowly into the chair on the dais. He moved sturdily and curled himself up on the cushion, studying the words on the paper all the while with a little frown upon his brows. Then, shrugging his shoulders, he set the paper upon his knee and began to write.

At that date the Lady Mary was still called a bastard, though most men thought that that hardship would soon be reversed. It was said that great honours had been shown her, and that was apparent in the furnishing of her rooms, the fineness of her gear, the increase in the number of the women that waited on her, and the store of sweet things that was provided for her to eat. A great many men noted the chair with a dais that was set up always where she might be, in her principal room, and though her ladies said that she never sat in it, most men believed that she had made a pact with the King to do him honour and so to be reinstated in the estate in which she held her own. It was considered, too, that she no longer plotted with the King's enemies inside or out of the realm; it was at least certain that she no longer had men set to spy upon her, though it was noted that the Archbishop's gentleman, Lascelles, nosed about her quarters and her maids. But he was always spying somewhere and, as the Archbishop's days were thought to be numbered, he was accounted of little weight. Indeed, since the fall of Thomas Cromwell there seemed to be few spies about the Court, or almost none at all. It was known that gentlemen wrote accounts of what passed to Gardiner, the Bishop of Winchester. But Gardiner was gone back into his see and appeared to have little favour, though it was claimed for him that he had done much to advance the new Queen. So that, upon the whole, men breathed much more freely—and women too—than in the days before the fall of Privy Seal. The Queen had made little change, and seemed to have it in mind to make little more. Her relatives had, nearly none of them, been advanced. There were few Protestants oppressed, though many Catholics had been loosed from the gaols, most notably him whom the Archbishop Cranmer had taken to be his chaplain and confessor, and others that other lords had taken out of prison to be about them.

All in all the months that had passed since Cromwell's fall had gone quietly. The King and Queen had gone very often to mass since Katharine had been shown for Queen in the gardens at Hampton Court, and saints' days and the feasts of the life of our Lady had been very carefully observed, along with fasts such as had used to be observed. The King, however, was mightily fond with his new Queen, and those that knew her well, or knew her servants well, expected great changes. Some were much encouraged, some feared very much, but nearly all were heartily glad of that summer of breathing space; and the weather was mostly good, so that the corn ripened well and there was little plague or ague abroad.

Thus most men had been heartily glad to see the new Queen upon her journey there to the north parts. She had ridden upon a white horse with the King at her side; she had asked the names of several that had come to see her;

she had been fair to look at; and the King had pardoned many felons, so that men's wives and mothers had been made glad; and most old men said that the good times were come again, with the price of malt fallen and twenty-six to the score of herrings. It was reported, too, that a cider press in Herefordshire had let down a dozen firkins of cider without any apples being set in it, and this was accounted an omen of great plenty, whilst many sheep had died, so that men who had set their fields down in grass talked of giving them to the plough again, and upon St Swithin's Day no rain had fallen. All these things gave a great contentment, and many that in the hard days had thought to become Lutheran in search of betterment, now looked in byres and hidden valleys to find priests of the old faith. For if a man could plough he might eat, and if he might eat he could praise God after his father's manner as well as in a new way.

Thus, around the Lady Mary, whilst she wrote, the people of the land breathed more peace. And even she could not but be conscious of a new softness, if it was only in the warmth that came from having her window-leads properly mended. She had hardly ever before known what it was to have warm hands when she wrote, and in most days of the year she had worn fur next her skin, indoors as well as out. But now the sun beat on her new windows, and in that warmth she could wear fine lawn, so that, in spite of herself, she took pleasure and was softened, though, since she spoke to no man save the Magister Udal, and to him only about the works of Plautus or the game of cards that they played together, few knew of any change in her.

Nevertheless, on that day she had one of her more ill moods and, presently, having written a little more, she rang a small silver bell that was shaped like a Dutch woman with wide skirts.

'The Prince annoys me,' she said to her woman; 'send for his lady governess.'

The woman, dressed all in black, like her mistress, and with a little frill of white cambric over her temples as if she were a nun, stood in the open doorway that was just level with the Lady Mary's chair, so that the stone wall of the passage caught the light from the window. She folded her hands before her.

'Alack, Madam,' she said, 'your Madamship knows that at this hour his Highness' lady governess taketh ever the air.'

The little boy in the chair looked over his paper at his sister.

'Send for his physician then,' Mary said.

'Alack, sister,' the little Prince said before the woman could move, 'my physician is ill. *Jacet*—He lieth—*in cubiculo*—in his bed.'

The Lady Mary would not look round on him.

'Get thee, then,' she uttered coldly, 'to thine own apartments, Prince.'

'Alack, sister,' he answered, 'thou knowest that I may not walk along the corridors alone for fear some slay me. Nor yet may I be anywhere save with the Queen, or thee, or with my uncles, or my lady governess, or my physicians, for fear some poison me.'

He spoke with a clear and shrill voice, and the woman cast down her eyes, trembling a little, partly to hear such a small, weary child speak such a long speech as if by wizardry—for it was reported among the serving maids that he had been overlooked—and partly for fear of the black humour that she perceived to be upon her mistress.

'Send me then my Magister to lay out cards with me,' the Lady Mary said. 'I cannot make my studies with this Prince in my rooms.'

'Alack, Madam,' the girl said. She was high coloured and with dark eyes, but when she faltered then the colour died from her cheeks. The Lady Mary surveyed her coldly, for she was in the mood to give pain. She uttered no words.

'Alack, alack——' the maid whimpered. She was full of fear lest the Lady Mary should order her to receive short rations or many stripes; she was filled with consternation and grief since her sweetheart, a server, had told her that he must leave her. For it was rumoured that the Magister had been cast into gaol for sweethearting, and that the King had said that all sweethearts should be gaoled from thenceforth. 'The Magister is gaoled,' she said.

'Wherefore?' the Lady uttered the one expressionless word.

'I do not know,' the maid wailed; 'I do not know.'

The form of the Archbishop's gentleman glided noiselessly behind her back. His eyes shot one sharp, sideways glance in at the door, and, like a russet fox, he was gone. He was so like a fox that the Lady Mary, when she spoke, used the words—

'Catch me that gentleman.'

He was brought to the doorsill by the panting maid, for he had walked away very fast. He stood there, blinking his eyes and stroking his fox-coloured beard. When the Lady Mary beckoned him into the room he pulled off his cap and fell to his thin knees. He expected her to bid him rise, but she left him there.

'Wherefore is my secretary gaoled?' she asked cruelly.

He ran his finger round the rim of his cap where it lay on the floor beside him.

'That he is gaoled, I know,' he said; 'but the wherefore of it, not.'

He looked down at the floor and she down at his drooped eyelids.

'God help you,' she uttered scornfully. 'You are a spy and yet know no more than a Queen's daughter.'

'God help me,' he repeated gravely and touched his eyelid with one finger. 'What passed, passed between the King and him. I know no more than common report.'

'Common report?' she said. 'I warrant thee thou wast slinking around the terrace. I warrant thee thou heardst words of the King's mouth. I warrant thee thou followedst here to hear at my doorhole how I might take this adventure.'

One of his eyelids moved delicately, but he said no word.

The Lady Mary turned her back on him and he expected her order to be gone. But she turned again—

'Common report?' she uttered once more. 'I do bid you give me the common report upon this, that the Queen sends to me every day this little Prince to be alone with me two hours.'

He winced with his eyebrows again.

'Out with the common report,' she said.

'Madam,' he uttered, 'it is usually commended that the Queen should seek to bring sister and Prince-brother together.'

She shrugged her stiff shoulders up to her ears.

'What a poor liar for a spy,' she said. 'It is more usually reported'—and she turned upon the little Prince—'that the Queen sends thee here that I may work thee a mischief so that thou die and her child reign after the King thy father.'

The little Prince looked at her with pensive eyes. At that moment Katharine Howard came to the room door and looked in.

'Body of God,' the Lady Mary said; 'here you spy out a spy committing treason. For it is still treason to kneel to me. I am of illegal birth and not of the blood royal.'

Katharine essayed her smile upon the black-avised girl.

'Give me leave,' she said.

'Your Grace's poor room,' Mary said, 'is open ever to your Grace's entry. *Ubi venis ibi tibi.*'

The Queen bade her waiting women go. She entered the room and looked at Lascelles.

'I think I know thy face,' she said.

'I am the Archbishop's poor gentleman,' he answered. 'I think you have seen me.'

'No. It is not that,' she said. 'It was long ago.'

She crossed the room to smell at the pinks in the window.

'How late the flowers grow,' she said. 'It is August, yet here are still vernal perfumes.'

She was unwilling to bid the gentleman rise and go, because this was the Lady Mary's room.

'Where your Grace is, there the spring abideth,' Mary said sardonically. '*Ecce miraculum sicut erat, Joshuâ rege.*'

The little Prince came timidly down to beg a flower from the Queen and they all had their backs upon the spy. He ran his hands down his beard and considered the Queen's words. Then swiftly he was on his feet and through the door. He was more ready to brave the Lady Mary's after-wrath than let the Queen see him upon his knees. For actually it was a treason to kneel to the Lady Mary. It had been proclaimed so in the old days when the King's daughter was always subject to new debasements. And who knew whether now the penalty of treason might not still be enacted? It was certain that the Queen had no liking for the Archbishop. Then, what use might she not make of the fact that the Archbishop's man knelt, seeming to curry favour, though in these days all men knelt to her, even when the King was by? He cursed himself as he hastened away.

The Queen looked over her shoulder and caught the glint of his red heel as it went past the doorpost.

'In our north parts,' she said, and she was glad that Lascelles had fled, 'the seasons come ever tardily.'

'Well, your Grace has not delayed to blossom,' Mary said.

It was part of her humour when she was in a taunting mood to call the Queen always 'your Grace' or 'your Majesty' at every turn of the phrase.

Katharine looked at the pink intently. Her face had no expression, she was determined at once to have a cheerful patience and not to show it in her face.

The little Prince stole his hand into hers.

'Wherefore did my father—*rex pater meus*—pummel the man in the long cloak?' he asked.

'You knew it then?' Katharine asked of her stepdaughter.

'I knew it not,' the Lady Mary answered.

'I saw it from this window, but my sister would not look,' the Prince said.

The Queen was going to shut, with her own hand, the door, the little boy trotting behind her, but, purple-clothed and huge, the King was there.

'Well, I will not be shut out in mine own castle,' he said pleasantly.

In those, the quiet days of his realm when most things were going well, his face beneath his beard had taken a rounder and a smoother outline. He moved with motions less hasty than those he had had two years before, and when he had cast a task off it was done with and went out of his mind, so that he appeared a very busy man with, between whiles, the leisure to saunter.

'In a half hour,' he said, 'I go north to meet the King o' Scots. I would I had not the long journey to make but could stay with ye. It is pleasant here; the air is livening.' He caught his little son by the armpits and hoisted him on to his purple shoulders. 'Hey, princekin,' he said, 'what news ha' you o' the day?'

The little Edward pulled his father's bonnet off that he might the better see the huge brows and the little eyes.

'I told my sister that you did pummel a man in a long gown. What is even "long gown" in the learned tongue?' He played daintily and languidly with the hair of the King's temples, and when the King had said that he might call it '*doctorum toga*,' he added, 'But my sister would not come to look.'

'Well, thy sister is a monstrous learned wench,' the King said with a heavy benignity. 'She could not leave her book.'

The Lady Mary stood rigid, with a mock humility. She had her hands clasped before her, the folds of her black skirt fell stiffly just to the ground. She pursed her lips and strove with herself to speak, for she was minded to exhibit disdain, but her black mood was too strong for her.

'I did not read in my book, because I could not,' she said numbly. 'Your son disturbed my reading. But I did not come to look, because I would not.'

With one arm round the boy's little waist as he sat on high, and one hand on the little feet, the King looked at his daughter in a sudden hot rage; for to speak contemptuously of his son was a thing that filled him with anger and surprise. He opened his mouth to shout. Katharine Howard was gently turning a brass sphere with the constellations upon it that stood upon the table. She moved her fair face round towards the King and set her finger upon her lips. He shrugged his shoulders, prince and all moving up together, and his face took on the expression, half abashed and half resigned, of a man who is reminded by his womankind that he is near to a passionate folly.

Katharine by that time had schooled him how to act when Mary was in that humour, and he let out no word.

'I do not like that this Prince should play in my room,' the Lady Mary pursued him relentlessly, and he was so well lessoned that he answered only—

'Ye must fight that cock with Kat. It is Kat that sends him, not I.'

Nevertheless he was too masterful a man to keep his silence altogether; he was, besides, so content upon the whole that he was sure he could hold his temper in check, and the better to take breath for a long speech, he took the little boy from his shoulder and planted his feet abroad on the carpet.

'See now, Moll,' he said, 'make friends!' and he stretched out a large hand. She shrugged her shoulders half invisibly.

'I will kneel down to the King of this country and to the Supreme Head of the Church as it is here set up by law. What more would you have of me?'

'See now, Moll!' he said.

He fingered the medal upon his chest and cast about for words.

'Let us have peace in this realm,' he said. 'We are very near it.'

She raised her eyelids with a tiny contempt.

'It hangs much around you,' he went on. 'Listen! I will tell ye the whole matter.'

Slowly and sagaciously he disentangled all his coil of policies. His letter to the Holy Father was all drafted and ready to be put into fine words. But, before he sent it, he must be sure of peace abroad. It was like this—

'Ye know,' he said, 'though great wrangles have been in the past betwixt him and thee and mine own self, how my heart has ever been well inclined to my nephew, thy cousin the Emperor. There are in Christendom now only he and France that are anyways strong to stand against me or to invade me. But France I ha' never loved, and him much.'

'Ye are grown gentle then,' Mary said, 'and forgiving in your old age, for ye know I ha' plotted against you with my cousin and my cousin with me.'

'It is a very ancient tale,' the King said. 'Forget it, as do I and he.'

'Why, you live in the sun where the dial face moves. I in the shadow where Time stays still. To me it is every day a new tale,' the Lady Mary answered.

His face took on an expression of patience and resignation that angered her, for she knew that when her father looked so it was always very difficult to move him.

'Why, all the world forgets,' he said.

'Save only I,' she answered. 'I had only one parent—a mother. She is dead: she was done to death.'

'I have pardoned your cousin that he plotted against me,' he stuck to his tale, 'and he me what I did against your mother.'

'Well, he was ever a popinjay,' the Lady Mary said.

'Lately,' Henry continued, 'as ye wiz he had grown very thick with Francis of France. He went across the French country into the Netherlands, so strict was their alliance. It is more than I would do to trust myself to France's word. All Holland marvelled.'

'What is this to me?' the Lady Mary said. 'Will you send me across France to the Netherlands?'

He left her gibe alone.

'But in these latter months,' he said, 'Kat and I ha' weakened with true messages and loyal conceits this unholy alliance.'

'Why, I ha' heard,' Mary said, 'ye did send the Duke of Norfolk to tell the King o' France that my cousin had said in private that he was the greater King of the twain. These be princely princes!'

'An unholy alliance it was,' Henry went on his way, 'for the Emperor is a very good Christian and a loyal son of the Church. But Francis worships the devil—I have heard it said and I believe it—or, at least, he believes not in God and our Saviour; and he pays allegiance to the Church only when it serves his turn, now holding on, now letting go. I am glad this alliance is dissolving.'

'Why, I am glad to hear you speak like this,' Mary said bitterly. 'You are a goodly son to Mother Church.'

The King took her scorn with a shrug of the shoulders.

'I am glad this alliance is dissolved or dissolving,' he said, 'for when it is fully dissolved I will make my peace with Rome. And I long for that day, for I am weary of errors.'

'Well, this is a very goodly tale,' Mary said. 'I am glad you are minded to escape hell-flame. What is it all to me?'

'The burden of it rests with thee,' he answered, 'for thou alone canst make thy cousin believe in my true mind.'

'God help me,' Mary said.

'See you, Moll,' the King broke in on her eagerly, 'if you will marry the Infant of Spain——'

'God's sakes,' she said lightly, 'my cousin's son will wed no bastard as I be.'

He brushed her jest aside with one hand.

'See you,' he said, 'now I ride to the north to meet the King o' Scots. That nephew of mine has always been too thick with Francis. But I will be so friendly with him. And see you, with the Scots cut away and the Emperor unloyal, the teeth of Francis are drawn. I might not send my letter to the Pope with all Christendom arrayed together against me. But when they are set by the ears I am strong enow.'

'Oh, good!' the Lady Mary said. 'Strong enow to be humble!'

Her eyes sparkled so much and her bosom so heaved, that Katharine moved solicitously and swiftly to come between them.

'See you, Moll,' the King said, 'forgive the ill I wrought thee, and so shall golden days come again. Once more there shall be a deep peace with contented husbandmen and the spreading of the vines abroad upon the stakes. And once more *venite creator spiritus* shall be sung in this land. And once more you shall be much honoured; nay, you shall be as one that saved this realm——'

She screamed out—

'Stay your tongue!' with such a shrill voice that the King's words were drowned. Katharine Howard ran in between them, but she pushed her aside, speaking over her shoulder.

'Before God,' she said, 'you gar me forget that you are the King that begot me illegally.'

Katharine turned upon the King and sought to move him from the room. But he was still of opinion that he could convince his daughter and stood his ground, looking over her shoulder as Mary had done.

'Body of God!' Mary said. 'Body of God! That a man could deem me so base!' She looked, convulsed, into Henry's eyes. 'Can you bring my mother alive by the truckling and cajoling and setting lying prince against lying prince? You slew my mother by lies, or your man slew her by poison. It is all one. And will you come to me that you have decreed misbegotten, to help you save your soul!'

There was such a violent hatred in her tone that the King could bring no word out, and she swept on—

'Could even a man be such a dull villain? To creep into heaven by bribing his daughter! To creep into heaven by strengthening himself with lies about one prince to another till he be strong enow to be humble! This is a king! This is even a man! I would be ashamed of such manhood!'

She took a deep breath.

'What can you bribe me with? a marriage with my cousin's son? Why, he has deserted my mother's cause. I had rather wed a falconer than that prince. You will have me no longer called bastard? Why, I had rather be called bastard than the acknowledged child of such a royal King. You will cover me with brocades and set me on high? By God, the sun in the heaven has looked upon such basenesses that I seek only a patch of shade. God help me; you will recall the decree that said my mother was not a Queen! God help us! God help us all! You will ennoble my mother's memory. With a decree! Can all the decrees you can make render my mother more sacred? When you decreed her not a Queen, did a soul believe it? If now you decree that a Queen she was, who will believe you? I think I had rather you left it alone, it is such a foul thing to have been thy wife!'

The saying of these things had pleased her so much that she gained control of her tongue.

'You cannot bribe me,' she said calmly. 'You have naught to give that I have need of.'

But the King was so used to his daughter's speeches that, though he had seldom seen her so mutinous, he could still ignore them.

'Well,' he said, 'I think you are angered with me for having set the Magister in gaol——'

'And in addition,' the Lady Mary pursued her own speech, for she deemed that she had thought of a thing to pain both him and the Queen, 'how might I with a good conscience tell my cousin that you have a true inclination to him? I do believe you have; it is this lady that has given it you. But how much longer will this lady sway you? No doubt the King o' Scots hath a new lady for you—and she will be on the French side, for the King o' Scots is the French King's man.'

The King opened his mouth convulsively, but Katharine Howard laid her hand right across it.

'You must be riding soon,' she said. 'I have had a collation set in my chamber.' She was so used by now to the violent humours of these Tudors. 'You have still to direct me,' she added, 'what is to be done with these rived cattle.'

As they went through the door, the little Prince holding his father's hand and she moving him gently by the shoulder, the child said—

'I thought ye wad ha' little profit speaking to my sister in her then mood.'

The King, in the gallery, looked with a gentle apprehension at his wife.

'I trow ye think I ha' done wrong,' he said.

She answered—

'Oh nay; she must come to know one day what your Grace had to tell her. Now it is over. But I would not have had you heated. For it is ill to start riding in a sweat. You shall not go for an hour yet.'

That pleased him, for it made him think she was unwilling he should go.

In her own room the Lady Mary sat back in her chair and smiled grimly at the ceiling.

'Body of God,' she said, 'I wish he had married this wench or ever he saw my mother.' Nevertheless, upon reflection, she got pleasure from the thought that her mother, with her Aragonia pride, had given the King some ill hours before he had put her away to her death. Katharine of Aragon had been no Katharine Howard to study her lord's ways and twist him about her finger; and Mary took her rosary from a nail beside her and told her beads for a quarter hour to calm herself.

V

There fell upon the castle a deep peace when the King and most of the men were gone. The Queen had the ordering of all things in the castle and of most in the realm. Beneath her she had the Archbishop and some few of the lords of the council who met most days round a long table in the largest hall, and afterwards brought her many papers to sign or to approve. But they were mostly papers of accounts for the castles that were then building, and some few letters from the King's envoys in foreign courts. Upon the whole, there was little stirring, though the Emperor Charles V was then about harrying the Protestant Princes of Almain and Germany. That was good enough news, and though the great castle had well-nigh seven hundred souls, for the most part women, in it, yet it appeared to be empty. High up upon the upper battlements the guards kept a lazy watch. Sometimes the Queen rode a-hawking with her ladies and several lords; when it rained she held readings from the learned writers amongst her ladies, to teach them Latin better. For she had set a fashion of good learning among women that did not for many years die out of the land. In that pursuit she missed the Magister Udal, for the ladies listened to him more willingly than to another. They were reading the *True History of Lucian*, which had been translated into Latin from the Greek about that time.

What occupied her most was the writing of the King's letter to the Pope. Down in their cellar the Archbishop and Lascelles wrought many days at this very long piece of writing. But they made it too humble to suit her, for she would not have her lord to crawl, as if in the dust upon his belly, so she told the Archbishop. Henry was to show contrition and repentance, desire for pardon and the promise of amendment. But he was a very great King and had wrought greatly. And, having got the draft of it in the vulgar tongue, she set about herself to turn it into Latin, for she esteemed herself the best Latinist that they had there.

But in that again she missed the Magister at last, and in the end she sent for him up from his prison to her antechamber where it pleased her to sit. It was a tall, narrow room, with much such a chair and dais as were in the room of the Lady Mary. It gave on to her bedchamber that was larger, and it had little, bright, deep windows in the thick walls. From them there could be seen nothing but the blue sky, it was so high up. Here she sat, most often with the Lady Rochford, upon a little stool writing, with the parchments upon her knee or setting a maid to sew. The King had lately made her a gift of twenty-four satin quilts. Most of her maids sat in her painted gallery, carding and spinning wool, but usually she did not sit with them, since she was of opinion that they spoke more freely and took more pleasure when she was not there. She had brought many maids with her into Yorkshire for this spinning, for she believed that this northern wool was the best that could be had. Margot Poins sat always with these maids to keep them to their tasks, and her brother had been advanced to keep the Queen's door when she was in her private rooms, being always without the chamber in which she sat.

When the Magister came to her, she had with her in the little room the Lady Rochford and the Lady Cicely Rochford that had married the old knight when she was Cicely Elliott. Udal had light chains on his wrists and on his ankles, and the Queen sent her guards to await him at her outer door. The Lady Cicely set back her head and laughed at the ceiling.

'Why, here are the bonds of holy matrimony!' she said to his chains. 'I ha' never seen them so plain before.'

The Magister had straws on his cloak, and he limped a little, being stiff with the damp of his cell.

'*Ave, Regina!*' he said. '*Moriturus te saluto!*' He sought to kneel, but he could not bend his joints; he smiled with a humorous and rueful countenance at his own plight.

The Queen said she had brought him there to read the Latin of her letter. He ducked his brown, lean head.

'*Ha,*' he said, '*sine cane pastor*—without his dog, as Lucretius hath it, the shepherd watches in vain. Wolves—videlicet, errors—shall creep into your marshalled words.'

Katharine kept to him a cold face and, a little abashed, he muttered under his breath—

'I ha' played with many maids, but this is the worst pickle that ever I was in.'

He took her parchment and read, but, because she was

the Queen, he would not say aloud that he found solecisms in her words.

'Give me,' he said, 'your best pen, and let me sit upon a stool!'

He sat down upon the stool, set the writing on his knee, and groaned with his stiffness. He took up his task, but when those ladies began to talk—the Lady Cicely principally about a hawk that her old knight had training for the Queen, a white sea hawk from Norway—he winced and hissed a little because they disturbed him.

'Misery!' he said; 'I remember the days when no mouse dared creak if I sat to my task in the learned tongues.'

The Queen then remembered very well how she had been a little girl with the Magister for tutor in her father's great and bare house. It was after Udal had been turned out of his mastership at Eton. He had been in vile humour in most of those days, and had beaten her very often and fiercely with his bundle of twigs. It was only afterwards that he had called her his best pupil.

Remembering these things, she dropped her voice and sat still, thinking. Cicely Elliott, who could not keep still, blew a feather into the air and caught it again and again. The old Lady Rochford, her joints swollen with rheumatism, played with her beads in her lap. From time to time she sighed heavily and, whilst the Magister wrote, he sighed after her. Katharine would not send her ladies away, because she would not be alone with him to have him plague her with entreaties. She would not go herself, because it would have been to show him too much honour then, though a few days before she would have gone willingly because his vocation and his knowledge of the learned tongues made him a man that it was right to respect.

But when she read what he had written for her, his lean, brown face turning eagerly and with a ferreting motion from place to place on the parchment, she was filled with pity and with admiration for the man's talent. It was as if

Seneca were writing to his master, or Pliny to the Emperor Trajan. And, being a very tender woman at bottom—

'Magister,' she said, 'though you have wrought me the greatest grief I think ye could, by so injuring one I like well, yet this is to me so great a service that I will entreat the King to remit some of your pains.'

He stumbled up from his stool and this time managed to kneel.

'Oh, Queen,' he said, '*Doctissima fuisti;* you were the best pupil that ever I had——' She tried to silence him with a motion of her hand. But he twined his lean hands together with the little chains hanging from them. 'I call this to your pitiful mind,' he brought out, 'not because I would have you grateful, but to make you mindful of what I suffer—*non quia grata sed ut clemens sis.* For, for advancement I have no stomach, since by advancing me you will advance my wife from Paris, and for liberty I have no use since you may never make me free of her. Leave me to rot in my cell, but, if it be but the tractate of Diodorus Siculus, a very dull piece, let me be given some book in a learned tongue. I faint, I starve, I die for lack of good letters. I that no day in my life have passed—*nulla die sine*—no day without reading five hours in goodly books since I was six and breeched. Bethink you, you that love learning——'

'Now tell me,' Cicely Elliott cried out, 'which would you rather in your cell—the Letters of Cicero or a kitchen wench?'

The Queen bade her hold her peace, and to the Magister she uttered—

'Books I will have sent you, for I think it well that you should be so well employed. And, for your future, I will have you set down in a monastery where there shall be for you much learning and none of my sex. You have done harm enow! Now, get you gone!'

He sighed that she had grown so stern, and she was glad to be rid of him. But he had not been gone a minute into the other room when there arose such a clamour of harsh voices and shrieks and laughter that she threw her door open, coming to it herself before the other ladies could close their mouths, which had opened in amazement.

The young Poins was beating the Magister, so that the fur gown made a greyish whirl about his scarlet suit in the midst of a tangle of spun wool; spinning wheels were overset, Margot Poins crashed around upon them, wailing; the girls with their distaffs were crouching against the window-places and in corners, crying out each one of them.

The Queen had a single little gesture of the hand with which she dismissed all her waiting-women. She stood alone in the inner doorway with the Lady Cicely and the Lady Rochford behind her. The Lady Rochford wrung her gouty hands; the Lady Cicely set back her head and laughed.

The Queen spoke no word, but in the new silence it was as if the Magister fell out of the boy's hands. He staggered amidst the trails of wool, nearly fell, and then made stiff zigzags towards the open outer door, where his prison guards awaited him, since they had no warrant to enter the antechamber. He dragged after him a little trail of fragments of spinning wheels and spindles.

'Well, there's a fine roister-doister!' the Lady Cicely laughed behind the Queen's back. The Queen stood very still and frowned. To her the disturbance was monstrous and distasteful, for she was minded to have things very orderly and quiet. The boy, in his scarlet, pulled off his bonnet and panted, but he was not still more than a second, and suddenly he called out to the Queen—

'Make that pynot to marry my sister!'

Margot Poins hung round him and cried out—

'Oh no! Oh no!'

He shook her roughly loose.

'An' you do not wed with him how shall I get advancement?' he said. ' 'A promised me that when 'a should come to be Chancellor 'a would advance me.'

He pushed her from him again with his elbow when she came near.

'Y've grown over familiar,' the Queen said, 'with being too much near me. Y'are grown over familiar. For seven days you shall no longer keep my door.'

Margot Poins raised her arms over her head, then she leant against a window-pane and sobbed into the crook of her elbow. The boy's slender face was convulsed with rage; his blue eyes started from his head; his callow hair was crushed up.

'Shall a man——' he began to protest.

'I say nothing against that you did beat this Magister,' the Queen said. 'Such passions cannot be controlled, and I pass it by.'

'But will ye not make this man to wed with my sister?' the boy said harshly.

'I cannot. He hath a wedded wife!'

He dropped his hands to his side.

'Alack; then my father's house is down,' he cried out.

'Gentleman Guard,' Katharine said, 'get you for seven days away from my door. I will have another sentry whilst you bethink you of a worthier way to advancement.'

He gazed at her stupidly.

'You will not make this wedding?' he asked.

'Gentleman Guard,' Katharine said, 'you have your answer. Get you gone.'

A sudden rage came into his eyes; he swallowed in his throat and made a gesture of despair with his hand. The Queen turned back into her room and busied herself with her task, which was the writing into a little vellum book of seven prayers to the Virgin that the Lady Elizabeth, Queen Anne Boleyn's daughter, a child then in London, was to turn each one into seven languages, written fair in the volume as a gift, against Christmas, for the King.

'I would not have that boy to guard my door,' the Lady Cicely said to the Queen.

'Why, 'tis a good boy,' Katharine answered; 'and his sister loves me very well.'

'Get your Highness another,' the Lady Cicely persisted. 'I do not like his looks.'

The Queen gazed up from her writing to where the dark girl, her figure raked very much back in her stiff bodice, played daintily with the tassels of the curtain next the window.

'My Lady,' Katharine said, 'my Highness must get me a new maid in place of Margot Poins, that shall away into a nunnery. Is not that grief enough for poor Margot? Shall she think in truth that she has undone her father's house?'

'Then advance the springald to some post away from you,' the Lady Cicely said.

'Nay,' the Queen answered; 'he hath done nothing to merit advancement.'

She continued, with her head bent down over the writing on her knee, her lips moving a little as, sedulously, she drew large and plain letters with her pen.

'By Heaven,' the Lady Cicely said, 'you have too tickle a conscience to be a Queen of this world and day. In the time of Cæsar you might have lived more easily.'

The Queen looked up at her from her writing; her clear eyes were untroubled.

'Aye,' she said. '*Lucio Domitio, Appio Claudio consulibus*——'

Cicely Rochford set back her head and laughed at the ceiling.

'Aye, your Highness is a Roman,' she tittered like a magpie.

'In the day of Cæsar it was simple to do well,' the Queen said.

'Why, I do not believe it,' Cicely answered her.

'Cousin! Cousin!' The old Lady Rochford warned her that this was the Queen, not her old playmate.

'But now,' the Queen said, 'with such a coming together and a concourse of peoples about us; with such holes and corners in a great Court——' She paused and sighed.

'Well, if I may not speak my mind,' Cicely Rochford said to the old lady, 'what good am I?'

'I did even what I might to keep this lamb Margot from the teeth of that wolf Magister,' the Queen said. 'I take shame to myself that I did no more. I will do a penance for it. But still I think that these be degenerate days.'

'Oh, Queen of dreams and fancies,' Cicely Rochford said. 'I am very certain that in the days of your noble Romans it was as it is now. Tell me, if you can, that in all your readings of hic and hoc you lit not upon such basenesses? You will not lay your hand upon your heart and say that never a man of Rome bartered his sister for the hope of advancement, or that never a learned doctor was a corrupter of youth? I have seen the like in the plays of Plautus that here have been played at Court.'

'Why,' the Queen said, 'the days of Plautus were days degenerated and fallen already from the ancient nobleness.'

'You should have Queened it before Goodman Adam fell,' Cicely Rochford mocked her. 'If you go back before Plautus, go back all the way.'

She shrugged her shoulders up to her ears and uttered a little sound like '*Pfui!*' Then she said quickly—

'Give me leave to be gone, your Highness, that I may not grow over familiar like the boy with the pikestaff, for if it do not gall you it shall wring the withers of this my old husband's cousin!'

The old Lady Rochford, who was always thinking of what had been said two speeches ago, because she was so slow-witted, raised her gouty hands in the air and opened her mouth. But the Queen smiled faintly at Cicely.

'When I ask you to mince matters in my little room you shall do it. It was Lucius the Praetor that went always accompanied by a carping Stoic to keep him from being puffed up, and it was a good custom.'

'Before Heaven,' Cicely Rochford said in the midst of her curtsey at the door, 'shall I have the office of such a one as Diogenes who derided Alexander the Emperor? Then must my old husband live with me in a tub!'

'Pray you,' the Queen said after her through the door, 'look you around and spy me out a maid to be my tiringwoman and ward my spinsters. For nowadays I see few maids to choose from.'

When she was gone the old Lady Rochford timorously berated the Queen. She would have her be more distant with knights' wives and the like. For it was fitting for a Queen to be feared and deemed awful.

'I had rather be loved and deemed pitiful,' Katharine answered. 'For I was once such a one—no more—than she or thou, or very little more. Before the people I bear myself proudly for my lord his high honour. But I do lead a very cloistered life, and have leisure to reflect upon for what a little space authority endureth, and how that friendship and true love between friends are things that bear the weather better.' She did not say her Latin text, for the old lady had no Latin.

VI

In the underground cell, above the red and gold table that afternoon, Lascelles wrought at a fair copy of the King's letter to the Pope, amended as it had been by Udal's hand. The Archbishop had come into the room reading a book as he came from his prayers, and sate him down in his chair at the tablehead without glancing at his gentleman.

'Prithee, your Grace,' Lascelles said, 'suffer me to carry this letter mine own self to the Queen.'

The Archbishop looked up at him; his mournful eyes started wide; he leaned forward.

'Art thou Lascelles?' he asked.

'Aye, Lascelles I am,' the gentleman answered; 'but I have cut off my beard.'

The Archbishop was very weak and startled; he fell into an anger.

'Is this a time for vanities?' he said. 'Will you be after the wenches? You look a foolish boy! I do not like this prank.'

Lascelles put up his hand to stroke his vanished beard. His risible lips writhed in a foxy smile; his chin was fuller than you would have expected, round and sensuous with a dimple in the peak of it.

'Please it, your Grace,' he said, 'this is no vanity, but a scheme that I will try.'

'What scheme? What scheme?' the Archbishop said. 'Here have been too many schemes.' He was very shaken and afraid, because this world was beyond his control.

'Please it, your Grace,' Lascelles answered, 'ask me not what this scheme is.'

The Archbishop shook his head and pursed his lips feebly.

'Please it, your Grace,' Lascelles urged, 'if this scheme miscarry, your Grace shall hear no more of it. If this scheme succeed I trow it shall help some things forward that your Grace would much have forwarded. Please it, your Grace, to ask me no more, and to send me with this letter to the Queen's Highness.'

The Archbishop opened his nerveless hands before him; they were pale and wrinkled as if they had been much soddened in water. Since the King had bidden him compose that letter to the Pope of Rome, his hands had grown so. Lascelles wrote on at the new draft of the letter, his lips following the motions of his pen. Still writing, and with his eyes down, he said—

'The Queen's Highness will put from her her tire-woman in a week from now.'

The Archbishop moved his fingers as who should say—

'What is that to me!' His eyes gazed into the space above his book that lay before him on the table.

'This Margot Poins is a niece of the master-printer Badge, a Lutheran, of the Austin Friars.' Lascelles pursued his writing for a line further. Then he added—

'This putting away and the occasion of it shall make a great noise in the town of London. It will be said amongst the Lutherans that the Queen is answerable therefor. It will be said that the Queen hath a very lewd Court and companionship.'

The Archbishop muttered wearily—

'It hath been said already.'

'But not,' Lascelles said, 'since she came to be Queen.'

The Archbishop directed upon him his hang-dog eyes, and his voice was the voice of a man that would not be disturbed from woeful musings.

'What use?' he said bitterly; and then again, 'What use?'

Lascelles wrote on sedulously. He used his sandarach to the end of the page, blew off the sand, eyed the sheet sideways, laid it down, and set another on his writing-board.

'Why,' he brought out quietly, 'it may be brought to the King's Highness' ears.'

'What way?' the Archbishop said heavily, as if the thing were impossible. His gentleman answered—

'This way and that!' The King's Highness had a trick of wandering about among his faithful lieges unbeknown; foreign ambassadors wrote abroad such rumours which might be re-reported from the foreign by the King's servants.

'Such a report,' Lascelles said, 'hath gone up already to London town by a swift carrier.'

The Archbishop brought out wearily and distastefully—

'How know you? Was it you that wrote it?'

'Please it, your Grace,' his gentleman answered him, 'it was in this wise. As I was passing by the Queen's chamber wall I heard a great outcry——'

He laid down his pen beside his writing-board the more leisurely to speak.

He had seen Udal, beaten and shaking, stagger out from the Queen's door to where his guards waited to set him back in prison. From Udal he had learned of this new draft of the letter; of Udal's trouble he knew before. Udal gone, he had waited a little, hearing the Queen's voice and what she said very plainly, for the castle was very great and quiet. Then out had come the young Poins, breathing like a volcano through his nostrils, and like to be stricken with palsy, boy though he was. Him Lascelles had followed at a convenient distance, where he staggered and snorted. And, coming upon the boy in an empty guard-room near the great gate, he had found him aflame with passion against the Queen's Highness.

'I,' the boy had cried out, 'I that by my carrying of letters set this Howard where she sits! I!—and this is my advancement. My sister cast down, and I cast out, and another maid to take my sister's place.'

And Lascelles, in the guard-chamber, had shown him sympathy and reminded him that there was gospel for saying that princes had short memories.

'But I did not calm him!' Lascelles said.

On the contrary, upon Lascelles' suggestion that the boy had but to hold his tongue and pocket his wrongs, the young Poins had burst out that he would shout it all abroad at every street corner. And suddenly it had come into his head to write such a letter to his Uncle Badge the printer as, printed in a broadside, would make the Queen's name to stink, until the last generation was of men, in men's nostrils.

Lascelles rubbed his hands gently and sinuously together. He cast one sly glance at the Archbishop.

'Well, the letter was written,' he said. 'Be sure the broadside shall be printed.'

Cranmer's head was sunk over his book.

'This lad,' Lascelles said softly, 'who in seven days' time again shall keep the Queen's door (for it is not true that the Queen's Highness is an ingrate, well sure am I), this lad shall be a very useful confidant; a very serviceable guide to help us to a knowledge of who goes in to the Queen and who cometh out.'

The Archbishop did not appear to be listening to his gentleman's soft voice and, resuming his pen, Lascelles finished his tale with—

'For I have made this lad my friend. It shall cost me some money, but I do not doubt that your Grace shall repay.'

The Archbishop raised his head.

'No, before God in heaven on His throne!' he said. His voice was shrill and high; he agitated his hands in their fine, tied sleeves. 'I will have no part in these Cromwell tricks. All is lost; let it be lost. I must say my prayers.'

'Has it been by saying of your Grace's prayers that your Grace has lived through these months?' Lascelles asked softly.

'Aye,' the Archbishop wrung his hands; 'you girded me and moved me when Cromwell lay at death, to write a letter to the King's Highness. To write such a letter as should appear brave and faithful and true to Privy Seal's cause.'

'Such a letter your Grace wrote,' Lascelles said; 'and it was the best writing that ever your Grace made.'

The Archbishop gazed at the table.

'How do I know that?' he said in a whisper. 'You say so, who bade me write it.'

'For that your Grace lives yet,' Lascelles said softly; 'though in those days a warrant was written for your capture. For, sure it is, and your Grace has heard it from the King's lips, that that your letter sounded so faithful and piteous and true to him your late leader, that the King could not but believe that you, so loyal in such a time to a man disgraced and cast down beyond hope, could not but be faithful and loyal in the future to him, the King, with so many bounties to bestow.'

'Aye,' the Archbishop said, 'but how do I know what of a truth was in the King's mind who casteth down to-day one, to-morrow another, till none are left?'

And again Cranmer dropped his anguished eyes to the table.

In those days still—and he slept still worse since the King had bidden him write this letter to Rome—the Archbishop could not sleep on any night without startings and sweats and cryings out in his sleep. And he gave orders that, when he so cried out, the page at his bedside should wake him.

For then he was seeing the dreadful face of his great master, Privy Seal, when the day of his ruin had come. Cromwell had been standing in a window of the council chamber at Westminster looking out upon a courtyard. In behind him had come the other lords of the council, Norfolk with his yellow face, the High Admiral, and many others; and each, seating himself at the table, had kept his bonnet on his head. So Cromwell, turning, had seen them and had asked with his hard insolence and embittered eyes of hatred, how they dared be covered before he who was their president sat down. Then, up against him in the window-place there had sprung Norfolk at the chain of the George round his neck, and Suffolk at the Garter on his knee; and Norfolk had cried out that Thomas Cromwell was no longer Privy Seal of that kingdom, nor president of that council, but a traitor that must die. Then such rage and despair had come into Thomas Cromwell's terrible face that Cranmer's senses had reeled. He had seen Norfolk and the Admiral fall back before this passion; he had seen Thomas Cromwell tear off his cap and cast it on the floor; he had heard him bark and snarl out certain words into the face of the yellow dog of Norfolk.

'*Upon your life you dare not call me traitor!*' and Norfolk had fallen back abashed.

Then the chamber had seemed to fill with an awful gloom and darkness; men showed only like shadows against the window lights; the constable of the Tower had come in with the warrants, and in that gloom the earth had appeared to tremble and quake beneath the Archbishop's feet.

He crossed himself at the recollection, and, coming out of his stupor, saw that Lascelles was finishing his writings. And he was glad that he was here now and not there then.

'Prithee, your Grace,' the gentleman's soft voice said, 'let me bear, myself, this letter to the Queen.'

The Archbishop shivered frostily in his robes.

'I will have no more Cromwell tricks,' he said. 'I have said it'; and he affected an obdurate tone.

'Then, indeed, all is lost,' Lascelles answered; 'for this Queen is very resolved.'

The Archbishop cast his eyes up to the cold stone ceiling above him. He crossed himself.

'You are a very devil,' he said, and panic came into his eyes, so that he turned them all round him as if he sought an issue at which to run out.

'The Papist lords in this castle met on Saturday night,' Lascelles said; 'their meeting was very secret, and Norfolk was their head. But I have heard it said that not one of them was for the Queen.'

The Archbishop shrank within himself.

'I am not minded to hear this,' he said.

'Not one of them was for the Queen altogether; for she will render all lands and goods back to the Church, and there is no one of them but is rich with the lands and goods of the Church. That they that followed Cromwell are not for the Queen well your Grace knoweth,' his gentleman continued.

'I will not hear this; this is treason,' the Archbishop muttered.

'So that who standeth for the Queen?' Lascelles whispered. 'Only a few of the baser sort that have no lands to lose.'

'The King,' the Archbishop cried out in a terrible voice; 'the King standeth for her!'

He sprang up in his chair and then sank down again, covering his mouth with his hands, as if he would have intercepted the uttered words. For who knew who listened at what doors in these days. He whispered horribly—

'What a folly is this. Who shall move the King? Will reports of his ambassadors that Cleves, or Charles, or Francis miscall the Queen? You know they will not, for the King is aware of how these princes batten on carrion. Will broad sheets of the Lutheran? You know they will not, for the King is aware of how those coggers come by their tales. Will the King go abroad among the people any more to hear what they say? You know he will not. For he is grown too old, and his fireside is made too sweet——'

He wavered, and he could not work himself up with a longer show of anger.

'Prithee,' Lascelles said, 'let me bear this letter myself to the Queen.' His voice was patient and calm.

The Archbishop lay back, impotent, in his chair. His arms were along the arms of it: he had dropped his book upon the table. His long gown was draped all over him down to his feet; his head remained motionless; his eyes did not wink, and gazed at despair; his hands drooped, open and impotent.

Suddenly he moved one of them a very little.

VII

It was the Queen's habit to go every night, when the business of the day was done, to pray, along with the Lady Mary, in the small chapel that was in the roof of the castle. To vespers she went with all the Court to the big chapel in the courtyard that the King had builded especially for her. But to this little chapel, that was of Edward IV's time, small and round-arched, all stone and dark and bare, she went with the Lady Mary alone. Her ladies and her door-guards they left at the stair foot, on a level with the sleeping rooms of the poorer sort, but up the little stairway they climbed by themselves, in darkness, to pray privately for the conversion of England. For this little place was so small and so forgotten that it had never been desecrated by Privy Seal's men. It had had no vessels worth the taking, and only very old vestments and a few ill-painted pictures on the stone walls that were half hidden in the dust.

Katharine had found this little place when, on her first day at Pontefract, she had gone a-wandering over the castle with the King. For she was curious to know how men had lived in the old times; to see their rooms and to mark what old things were there still in use. And she had climbed thus high because she was minded to gaze upon the huge expanse of country and of moors that from the upper leads of the castle was to be seen. But this little chapel had seemed to her to be all the more sacred because it had been undesecrated and forgotten. She thought that you could not find such another in the King's realm at that time; she was very assured that not one was to be found in any house of the King's and hers.

And, making inquiries, she had found that there was also an old priest there served the chapel, doing it rather secretly for the well-disposed of the castle's own guards. This old man had fled, at the approach of the King's many, into the hidden valleys of that countryside, where still the faith lingered and lingers now. For, so barbarous and remote those north parts were, that a great many people had never heard that the King was married again, and fewer still, or none, knew that he and his wife were well inclined again towards Rome.

This old priest she had had brought to her. And he was so well loved that along with him came a cluster of weather-battered moorsmen, right with him into her presence. They kneeled down, being clothed with skins, and several of them having bows of a great size, to beg her not to harm this old man, for he was reputed a saint. The Queen could not understand their jargon but, when their suit was interpreted to her by the Lord Dacre of the North, and when she had had a little converse with the old priest, she answered that, so touched was her heart by his simplicity and gentleness, that she would pray the good King, her lord and master, to let this priest be made her confessor whilst there they stayed. And afterwards, if it were convenient, in reward for his faithfulness, he should be made a prior or a bishop in those parts. So the moorsmen, blessing her uncouthly for her fairness and kind words, went back with their furs and bows into their fastnesses. One of them was a great lord of that countryside, and each day he sent into the castle bucks and moor fowl, and once or twice a wolf. His name was Sir John Peel, and Sir John Peel, too, the priest was called.

So the priest served that little altar, and of a night, when the Queen was minded next day to partake of the host, he heard her confession. On other nights he left them there alone to say their prayers. It was always very dark with the little red light burning before the altar and two tapers that they lit beneath a statue of the Virgin, old and black and ill-carved by antique hands centuries before. And, in that blackness, they knelt, invisible almost, and still in the black gowns that they put on for prayers, beside a low pillar that gloomed out at their sides and vanished up into the darkness of the roof.

Having done their prayers, sometimes they stayed to converse and to meditate, for there they could be very private. On the night when the letter to Rome was re-drafted, the Queen prayed much longer than the Lady Mary, who sat back upon a stool, silently, to await her finishing—for it seemed that the Queen was more zealous for the converting of those realms again to the old faith than was ever the Lady Mary. The tapers burned with a steady, invisible glow in the little side chapel behind the pillar; the altar gleamed duskily before them, and it was so still that through the unglassed windows they could hear, from far below in the black countryside, a tenuous bleating of late-dropped lambs. Katharine Howard's beads clicked and her dress rustled as she came up from her knees.

'It rests more with thee than with any other in this land,' her voice reverberated amongst the distant shadows. A bat that had been drawn in by the light flittered invisibly near them.

'Even what?' the Lady Mary asked.

'Well you know,' the Queen answered; 'and may the God to whom you have prayed, that softened the heart of Paul, soften thine in this hour!'

The Lady Mary maintained a long silence. The bat flittered, with a leathern rustle, invisible, between their very faces. At last Mary uttered, and her voice was taunting and malicious—

'If you will soften my heart much you must beseech me.'

'Why, I will kneel to you,' the Queen said.

'Aye, you shall,' Mary answered. 'Tell me what you would have of me.'

'Well you know!' Katharine said again.

In the darkness the lady's voice maintained its bitter mirth, as it were the broken laughter of a soul in anguish.

'I will have you tell me, for it is a shameful tale that will shame you in the telling.'

The Queen paused to consider of her words.

'First, you shall be reconciled with, and speak pleasantly with, the King your father and my lord.'

'And is it not a shameful thing you bid me do, to bid me speak pleasant words to him that slew my mother and called me bastard?'

The Queen answered that she asked it in the name of Christ, His pitiful sake, and for the good of this suffering land.

'None the less, Queen, thou askest it in the darkness that thy face may not be seen. And what more askest thou?'

'That when the Duke of Orleans his ambassadors come asking your hand in marriage, you do show them a pleasant and acquiescent countenance.'

The sacredness of that dark place kept Mary from laughing aloud.

'That, too, you dare not ask in the light of day, Queen,' she said. 'Ask on!'

'That when the Emperor's ambassadors shall ask for your hand you shall profess yourself glad indeed.'

'Well, here is more shame, that I should be prayed to feign this gladness. I think the angels do laugh that hear you. Ask even more.'

Katharine said patiently—

'That, having in reward of these favours, been set again on high, having honours shown you and a Court appointed round you, you shall gladly play the part of a princess royal to these realms, never gibing, nor sneering upon this

King your father, nor calling upon the memory of the
wronged Queen your mother.'

'Queen,' the Lady Mary said, 'I had thought that even
in the darkness you had not dared to ask me this.'

'I will ask it you again,' the Queen said, 'in your room
where the light of the candles shines upon my face.'

'Why, you shall,' the Lady Mary said. 'Let us presently
go there.'

They went down the dark and winding stair. At the foot
the procession of the *coucher de la royne* awaited them,
first being two trumpeters in black and gold, then four
pikemen with lanthorns, then the marshal of the Queen's
household and five or seven lords, then the Queen's ladies,
the Lady Rochford that slept with her, the Lady Cicely
Rochford; the Queen's tiring-women, leaving a space between them for the Queen and the Lady Mary to walk in,
then four young pages in scarlet and with the Queen's
favours in their caps, and then the guard of the Queen's
door, and four pikemen with torches whose light, falling
from behind, illumined the path for the Queen's steps.
The trumpeters blew four shrill blasts and then four with
their fists in the trumpet mouths to muffle them. The
brazen cries wound down the dark corridors, fathoms and
fathoms down, to let men know that the Queen had done
her prayers and was going to her bed. This great state was
especially devised by the King to do honour to the new
Queen that he loved better than any he had had. The purpose of it was to let all men know what she did that she
might be the more imitated.

But the Queen bade them guide her to the Lady Mary's
door, and in the doorway she dismissed them all, save only
her women and her door guard and pikemen who awaited
her without, some on stools and some against the wall,
ladies and men alike.

The Lady Mary looked into the Queen's face very close
and laughed at her when they were in the fair room and
the light of the candles.

'Now you shall say your litany over again,' she sneered; 'I will sit me down and listen.' And in her chair at the table, with her face averted, she dug with little stabs into the covering rug the stiletto with which she was wont to mend her pens.

Standing by her, her face fully lit by the many candles that were upon the mantel, the Queen, dressed all in black and with the tail of her hood falling down behind to her feet, went patiently through the list of her prayers—that the Lady Mary should be reconciled with her father, that she should show at first favour to the ambassadors that sued for her hand for the Duke of Orleans, and afterwards give a glad consent to her marriage with the Prince Philip, the Emperor's son; and then, having been reinstated as a princess of the royal house of England, she should bear herself as such, and no more cry out upon the memory of Katharine of Aragon that had been put away from the King's side.

The Queen spoke these words with a serious patience and a level voice; but when she came to the end of them she stretched out her hand and her voice grew full.

'And oh,' she said, her face being set and earnest in entreaty towards the girl's back, 'if you have any love for the green and fertile land that gave birth both to you and to me——'

'But to me a bastard,' the Lady Mary said.

'If you would have the dishoused saints to return home to their loved pastures; if you would have the Mother of God and of us all to rejoice again in her dowry; if you would see a great multitude of souls, gentle and simple reconducted again towards Heaven——'

'Well, well!' the Lady Mary said; 'grovel! grovel! I had thought you would have been shamed thus to crawl upon your belly before me.'

'I would crawl in the dust,' Katharine said. 'I would kiss the mire from the shoon of the vilest man there is if in that way I might win for the Church of God——'

'Well, well!' the Lady Mary said.

'You will not let me finish my speech about our Saviour and His mother,' the Queen said. 'You are afraid I should move you.'

The Lady Mary turned suddenly round upon her in her chair. Her face was pallid, the skin upon her hollowed temples trembled—

'Queen,' she called out, 'ye blaspheme when ye say that a few paltry speeches of yours about God and souls will make me fail my mother's memory and the remembrances of the shames I have had.'

She closed her eyes; she swallowed in her throat and then, starting up, she overset her chair.

'To save souls!' she said. 'To save a few craven English souls! What are they to me? Let them burn in the eternal fires! Who among them raised a hand or struck a blow for my mother or me? Let them go shivering to hell.'

'Lady,' the Queen said, 'ye know well how many have gone to the stake over conspiracies for you in this realm.'

'Then they are dead and wear the martyr's crown,' the Lady Mary said. 'Let the rest that never aided me, nor struck blow for my mother, go rot in their heresies.'

'But the Church of God!' the Queen said. 'The King's Highness has promised me that upon the hour when you shall swear to do these things he will send the letter that ye wot of to our Father in Rome.'

The Lady Mary laughed aloud—

'Here is a fine woman,' she said. 'This is ever the woman's part to gloss over crimes of their men folk. What say you to the death of Lady Salisbury that died by the block a little since?'

She bent her body and poked her head forward into the Queen's very face. Katharine stood still before her.

'God knows,' she said. 'I might not stay it. There was much false witness—or some of it true—against her. I pray that the King my Lord may atone for it in the peace that shall come.'

'The peace that shall come!' the Lady Mary laughed. 'Oh, God, what things we women are when a man rules us.

The peace that shall come? By what means shall it have been brought on?'

'I will tell you,' she pursued after a moment. 'All this is cogging and lying and feigning and chicaning. And you who are so upright will crawl before me to bring it about. Listen!'

And she closed her eyes the better to calm herself and to collect her thoughts, for she hated to appear moved.

'I am to feign a friendship to my father. That is a lie that you ask me to do, for I hate him as he were the devil. And why must I do this? To feign a smooth face to the world that his pride may not be humbled. I am to feign to receive the ambassadors of the Duke of Orleans. That is cogging that you ask of me. For it is not intended that ever I shall wed with a prince of the French house. But I must lead them on and on till the Emperor be affrighted lest your King make alliance with the French. What a foul tale! And you lend it your countenance!'

'I would well——' Katharine began.

'Oh, I know, I know,' Mary snickered. 'Ye would well be chaste but that it must needs be other with you. It was the thief's wife said that.

'Listen again,' she pursued, 'anon there shall come the Emperor's men, and there shall be more cogging and chicaning, and honours shall be given me that I may be bought dear, and petitioning that I should be set in the succession to make them eager. And then, perhaps, it shall all be cried off and a Schmalkaldner prince shall send ambassadors——'

'No, before God,' Katharine said.

'Oh, I know my father,' Mary laughed at her. 'You will keep him tied to Rome if you can. But you could not save the venerable Lady of Salisbury, nor you shall not save him from trafficking with Schmalkaldners and Lutherans if it shall serve his monstrous passions and his vanities. And if he do not this yet he will do other villainies. And you will cosset him in them—to save his hoggish dignity and buttress up his heavy pride. All this you stand there and ask.'

'In the name of God I ask it,' Katharine said. 'There is no other way.'

'Well then,' the Lady Mary said, 'you shall ask it many times. I will have you shamed.'

'Day and night I will ask it,' Katharine said.

The Lady Mary sniffed.

'It is very well,' she said. 'You are a proud and virtuous piece. I will humble you. It were nothing to my father to crawl on his belly and humble himself and slaver. He would do it with joy, weeping with a feigned penitence, making huge promises, foaming at the mouth with oaths that he repented, calling me his ever loved child——'

She stayed and then added—

'That would cost him nothing. But that you that are his pride, that you should do it who are in yourself proud— that is somewhat to pay oneself with for shamed nights and days despised. If you will have this thing you shall do some praying for it.'

'Even as Jacob served so will I,' Katharine said.

'Seven years!' the Lady Mary mocked at her. 'God forbid that I should suffer you for so long. I will get me gone with an Orleans, a Kaiserlik, or a Schmalkaldner leaguer before that. So much comfort I will give you.' She stopped, lifted her head and said, 'One knocks!'

They said from the door that a gentleman was come from the Archbishop with a letter to the Queen's Grace.

VIII

There came in the shaven Lascelles and fell upon his knees, holding up the sheets of the letter he had copied.

The Queen took them from him and laid them upon the great table, being minded later to read them to the Lady Mary, in proof that the King very truly would make his submission to Rome, supposing only that his daughter would make submission to her.

When she turned, Lascelles was still kneeling before the doorway, his eyes upon the ground.

'Why, I thank you,' she said. 'Gentleman, you may get you gone back to the Archbishop.'

She was thinking of returning to her duel of patience with the Lady Mary. But looking upon his blond and agreeable features she stayed for a minute.

'I know your face,' she said. 'Where have I seen you?'

He looked up at her; his eyes were blue and noticeable, because at times of emotion he was so wide-lidded that the whites showed round the pupils of them.

'Certainly I have seen you,' the Queen said.

'It is a royal gift,' he said, 'the memory of faces. I am the Archbishop's poor gentleman, Lascelles.'

The Queen said—

'Lascelles? Lascelles?' and searched her memory.

'I have a sister, the spit and twin of me,' he answered; 'and her name is Mary.'

The Queen said—

'Ah! ah!' and then, 'Your sister was my bed-fellow in the maid's room at my grandmother's.'

He answered gravely—

'Even so!'

And she—

'Stand up and tell me how your sister fares. I had some kindnesses of her when I was a child. I remember when I had cold feet she would heat a brick in the fire to lay to them, and such tricks. How fares she? Will you not stand up?'

'Because she fares very ill I will not stand upon my feet,' he answered.

'Well, you will beg a boon of me,' she said. 'If it is for your sister I will do what I may with a good conscience.'

He answered, remaining kneeling, that he would fain see his sister. But she was very poor, having married an esquire called Hall of these parts, and he was dead, leaving her but one little farm where, too, his old father and mother dwelt.

'I will pay for her visit here,' she said; 'and she shall have lodging.'

'Safe-conduct she must have too,' he answered; 'for none cometh within seven miles of this court without your permit and approval.'

'Well, I will send horses of my own, and men to safeguard her,' the Queen said. 'For, sure, I am beholden to her in many little things. I think she sewed the first round gown that ever I had.'

He remained kneeling, his eyes still upon the floor.

'We are your very good servants, my sister and I,' he said. 'For she did marry one—that Esquire Hall—that was done to death upon the gallows for the old faith's sake. And it was I that wrote the English of most of this letter to his Holiness, the Archbishop being ill and keeping his bed.'

'Well, you have served me very well, it is true,' the Queen answered. 'What would you have of me?'

'Your Highness,' he answered, 'I do well love my sister and she me. I would have her given a place here at the Court. I do not ask a great one; not one so high as about your person. For I am sure that you are well attended, and places few there are to spare about you.'

And then, even as he willed it, she bethought her that Margot Poins was to go to a nunnery. That afternoon she had decided that Mary Trelyon, who was her second maid, should become her first, and others be moved up in a rote.

'Why,' she said, 'it may be that I shall find her an occupation. I will not have it said—nor yet do it—that I have ever recompensed them that did me favours in the old times, for there are a many that have served well in the Court that then I was outside of, and those it is fitting first to reward. Yet, since, as you say you have writ the English of this letter, that is a very great service to the Republic, and if by rewarding her I may recompense thee, I will think how I may come to do it.'

He stood up upon his feet.

'It may be,' he said, 'that my sister is rustic and un-suited. I have not seen her in many years. Therefore, I will not pray too high a place for her, but only that she and I may be near, the one to the other, upon occasions, and that she be housed and fed and clothed.'

'Why, that is very well said,' the Queen answered him. 'I will bid my men to make inquiries into her demeanour and behaviour in the place where she bides, and if she is well fitted and modest, she shall have a place about me. If she be too rustic she shall have another place. Get you gone, gentleman, and a good-night to ye.'

He bent himself half double, in the then newest courtly way, and still bent, pivoted through the door. The Queen stayed a little while musing.

'Why,' she said, 'when I was a little child I fared very ill, if now I think of it; but then it seemed a little thing.'

'Y'had best forget it,' the Lady Mary answered.

'Nay,' the Queen said. 'I have known too well what it was to go supperless to my bed to forget it. A great shadowy place—all shadows, where the night airs crept in under the rafters.'

She was thinking of the maids' dormitory at her grand-mother's, the old Duchess.

'I am climbed very high,' she said; 'but to think——'

She was such a poor man's child and held of only the littlest account, herding with the maids and the serving-men's children. At eight by the clock her grandmother locked her and all the maids—at times there were but ten, at times as many as a score—into that great dormitory that was, in fact, nothing but one long attic or grange beneath the bare roof. And sometimes the maids told tales or slept soon, and sometimes their gallants, grooms and others, came climbing through the windows with rope ladders. They would bring pasties and wines and lights, and coarsely they would revel.

'Why,' she said, 'I had a gallant myself. He was a musician, but I have forgot his name. Aye, and then there was another, Dearham, I think; but I have heard he is since dead. He may have been my cousin; we were so many in family, I have a little forgot.'

She stood still, searching her memory, with her eyes distant. The Lady Mary surveyed her face with a curious irony.

'Why, what a simple Queen you are!' she said. 'This is something rustic.'

The Queen joined her hands together before her, as if she caught at a clue.

'I do remember me,' she said. 'It was a make of a comedy. This Dearham, calling himself my cousin, beat this music musician for calling himself my gallant. Then goes the musicker to my grandam, bidding the old Duchess rise up again one hour after she had sought her bed. So comes my grandam and turns the key in the padlock and looketh in over all the gallimaufrey of lights and pasties and revels.

'Why,' she continued. 'I think I was beaten upon that occasion, but I could not well tell why. And I was put to sleep in another room. And later came my father home from some war. And he was angry that I had consorted so with false minions, and had me away to his own poor house. And there I had Udal for my Magister and evil fare and many beatings. But this Mary Lascelles was my bed-fellow.'

'Why, forget it,' the Lady Mary said again.

'Other teachers would bid me remember it that I might remain humble,' Katharine answered.

'Y'are humble enow and to spare,' the Lady Mary said. 'And these are not good memories for such a place as this. Y'had best keep this Mary Lascelles at a great distance.'

Katharine said—

'No; for I have passed my word.'

'Then reward her very fully,' the Lady Mary commended, and the Queen answered—

'No, for that is against my conscience. What have I to fear now that I be Queen?'

Mary shrugged her squared shoulders.

'Where is your Latin,' she said, 'with its *nulla dies felix* —call no day fortunate till it be ended.'

'I will set another text against that,' she said, 'and that from holy sayings—that *justus ab aestimatione non timebit.*'

'Well,' Mary answered, 'you will make your bed how you will. But I think you would better have learned of these maids how to steer a course than of your Magister and the Signor Plutarchus.'

The Queen did not answer her, save by begging her to read the King's letter to his Holiness.

'And surely,' she said, 'if I had never read in the noble Romans I had never had the trick of tongue to gar the King do so much of what I will.'

'Why, God help you,' her step-daughter said. 'Pray you may never come to repent it.'

PART TWO

THE THREATENED RIFT

I

IN these summer days there was much faring abroad in the broad lands to north and to south of the Pontefract Castle. The sunlight lay across moors and uplands. The King was come with all his many to Newcastle; but no Scots King was there to meet him. So he went farther to northwards. His butchers drove before him herds of cattle that they slew some of each night: their hooves made a broad and beaten way before the King's horses. Behind came an army of tent men: cooks, servers, and sutlers. For, since they went where new castles were few, at times they must sleep on moorsides, and they had tents all of gold cloth and black, with gilded tent-poles and cords of silk and silver wire. The lords and principal men of those parts came out to meet him with green boughs, and music, and slain deer, and fair wooden kegs filled with milk. But when he was come near to Berwick there was still no Scots King to meet him, and it became manifest that the King's nephew would fail that tryst. Henry, riding among his people, swore a mighty oath that he would take way even into Edinburgh town and there act as he listed, for he had with him nigh on seven thousand men of all arms and some cannon which he had been minded to display for the instruction of his nephew. But he had, in real truth, little stomach for this feat. For, if he would go into Scotland armed, he must wait till he got together all the men that the Council of the North had under arms. These were scattered over the whole of the Border country, and it must be many days before he had them all there together. And already the summer was well advanced, and if he delayed much longer his return, the after progress from Pontefract to London must draw them to late in the winter. And he was little minded that either Katharine or his son should bear the winter travel. Indeed, he sent a messenger back to Pontefract with orders that the Prince should be sent forthwith with a great guard to Hampton Court, so that he should reach that place before the nights grew cold.

And, having stayed in camp four days near the Scots border—for he loved well to live in a tent, since it re-awoke in him the ardour of his youth and made him think himself not so old a man —he delivered over to the Earl Marshal forty Scots borderers and cattle thieves that had been taken that summer. These men he had meant to have handed, pardoned, to the Scots King when he met him. But the Earl Marshal set up, along the road into Scotland, from where the stone marks the border, a row of forty gallows, all high, but some higher than others; for some of the prisoners were men of condition. And, within sight of a waiting crowd of Scots that had come down to the boundaries of their land to view the King of England, Norfolk hanged on these trees the forty men.

And, laughing over their shoulders at this fine harvest of fruit, gibbering and dangling against the heavens on high, the King and his host rode back into the Border country. It was pleasant to ride in the summer weather, and they hunted and rendered justice by the way, and heard tales of battle that there had been before in the north country.

But there was one man, Thomas Culpepper, in the town of Edinburgh to whom this return was grievous. He had been in these outlandish parts now for more than nineteen months. The Scots were odious to him, the town was odious; he had no stomach for his food, and such clothes as he had were ragged, for he would wear nothing that had there been woven. He was even a sort of prisoner. For he had been appointed to wait on the King's Ambassador to the King of Scots, and the last thing that Throckmorton, the notable spy, had done before he had left the Court had been to write to Edinburgh that T. Culpepper, the Queen's cousin, who was a dangerous man, was to be kept very close and given no leave of absence.

And one thing very much had aided this: for, upon receiving news, or the rumour of news, that his cousin Katharine Howard—he was her mother's brother's son—had wedded the King, or had been shown for Queen at Hampton Court, he had suddenly become seized with such a rage that, incontinently, he had run his sword through an old fishwife in the fishmarket where he was who had given him the news, newly come by sea, thinking that because he was an Englishman this marriage of his King might gladden him. The fishwife died among her fish, and Culpepper with his sword fell upon all that were near him in the market, till, his heel slipping upon a haddock, he fell, and was fallen upon by a great many men.

He must stay in jail for this till he had compounded with the old woman's heirs and had paid for a great many cuts and bruises. And Sir Nicholas Hoby, happening to be in Edinburgh at that time, understood well what ailed Thomas Culpepper, and that he was mad for love of the Queen his cousin—for was it not this Culpepper that had brought her to the court, and, as it was said, had aforetime sold farms to buy her food and gowns when, her father being a poor man, she was well-nigh starving? Therefore Sir Nicholas begged alike the Ambassador and the King of Scots that they would keep this madman clapped up till they were very certain that the fit was off him. And, what with the charges of blood ransom and jailing for nine months, Culpepper had no money at all when at last he was enlarged, but must eat his meals at the Ambassador's table, so that he could not in any way come away into England till he had written for more money and had earned a further salary. And that again was a matter of many months, and later he spent more in drinking and with Scots women till he persuaded himself that he had forgotten his cousin that was now a Queen. Moreover, it was made clear to him by those about him that it was death to leave his post unpermitted.

But, with the coming of the Court up into the north parts, his impatience grew again, so that he could no longer eat but only drink and fight. It was rumoured that the Queen was riding with the King, and he swore a mighty oath that he would beg of her or of the King leave at last to be gone from that hateful city; and the nearer came the King the more his ardour grew. So that, when the news came that the King was turned back, Culpepper could no longer compound it with himself. He had then a plenty of money, having kept his room for seven days, and the night before that he had won half a barony at dice from a Scots archer. But he had no passport into England; therefore, because he was afraid to ask for one, being certain of a refusal, he blacked his face and hands with coal and then took refuge on a coble, leaving the port of Leith for Durham. He had well bribed the master of this ship to take him as one of his crew. In Durham he stayed neither to wash nor to eat, but, having bought himself a horse, he rode after the King's progress that was then two days' journey to the south, and came up with them. He had no wits left more than to ask of the sutlers at the tail of the host where the Queen was. They laughed at this apparition upon a haggard horse, and one of them that was a notable cutpurse took all the gold that he had, only giving him in exchange the news that the Queen was at Pontefract, from which place she had never stirred. With a little silver that he had in another bag he bought himself a provision of food, a store of drink, and a poor Kern to guide him, running at his saddle-bow.

He saw neither hills nor valleys, neither heather nor ling: he had no thoughts but only that of finding the Queen his cousin. At times the tears ran down his begrimed face, at times he waved his sword in the air and, spurring his horse he swore great oaths. How he fared, where he rested, by what roads he went over the hills, that he never knew. Without a doubt the Kern guided him faithfully.

For the Queen, having news that the King was nearly come within a day's journey, rode out towards the north to meet him. And as she went along the road, she saw, upon a hillside not very far away, a man that sat upon a dead horse, beating it and tugging at its bridle. Beside him stood a countryman, in a garment of furs and pelts, with rawhide boots. She had a great many men and ladies riding behind her, and she had come as far as she was minded to go. So she reined in her horse and sent two prickers to ask who these men were.

And when she heard that this was a traveller, robbed of all his money and insensate, and his poor guide who knew nothing of who he might be, she turned her cavalcade back and commanded that the traveller should be borne to the castle on a litter of boughs and there attended to and comforted until again he could take the road. And she made occasion upon this to comment how ill it was for travellers that the old monasteries were done away with. For in the old time there were seven monasteries between there and Durham, wherein poor travellers might lodge. Then, if a merchant were robbed upon the highways, he could be housed at convenient stages on his road home, and might afterwards send recompense to the good fathers or not as he pleased or was able. Now, there was no harbourage left on all that long road, and, but for the grace of God, that pitiful traveller might have lain there till the ravens picked out his eyes.

And some commended the Queen's words and actions, and some few, behind their hands, laughed at her for her soft heart. And the more Lutheran sort said that it was God's mercy that the old monasteries were gone; for they had, they said, been the nests for lowsels, idle wayfarers, palmers, pilgrims, and the like. And, praise God, since that clearance fourteen thousand of these had been hanged by the waysides for sturdy rogues, to the great purging of the land.

II

In the part of Lincolnshire that is a little to the north-eastward of Stamford was a tract of country that had been granted to the monks of St Radigund's at Dover by William the Conqueror. These monks had drained this land many centuries before, leaving the superintendence of the work at first to priors by them appointed, and after-wards, when the dykes, ditches, and flood walls were all made, to knights and poor gentlemen, their tenants, who farmed the land and kept up the defences against inunda-tions, paying scot and lot to a bailiff and water-wardens and jurats, just as was done on the Romney marshes by the bailiff and jurats of that level.

And one of these tenants, holding two hundred acres in a simple fee from St Radigund's for a hundred and fifty years back, had been always a man of the name of Hall. It was an Edward Hall that Mary Lascelles had married when she was a maid at the Duchess of Norfolk's. This Edward Hall was then a squire, a little above the condition of a groom, in the Duchess's service. His parents dwelled still on the farm which was called Neot's End, because it was in the angle of the great dyke called St Neot's and the little sewer where St Radigund's land had its boundary stone.

But in the troublesome days of the late Privy Seal, Edward Hall had informed Throckmorton the spy of a conspiracy and rising that was hatching amongst the Radi-gund's men a little before the Pilgrimage of Grace, when all the north parts rose. For the Radigund's men cried out and murmured amongst themselves that if the Priory was done away with there would be an end of their easy and comfortable tenancy. Their rents had been estimated and appointed a great number of years before, when all goods and the produce of the earth were very low priced. And the tenants said that if now the King took their lands to himself or gave them to some great lord, very heavy burdens would be laid upon them and exacted; whereas in some years under easy priors the monks forgot their distant territory, and in bad seasons they took no rents at all. And even under hard and exacting priors the monks could take no more than their rentals, which were so small. They said, too, that the King and Thomas Cromwell would make them into heathen Greeks and turn their children to be Saracens. So these Radigund's men meditated a rising and conspiracy.

But, because Edward Hall informed Throckmorton of what was agate, a posse was sent into that country, and most of the men were hanged and their lands all taken from them. Those that survived from the jailing betook themselves to the road, and became sturdy beggars, so that many of them too came to the gallows tree.

Most of the land was granted to the Sieur Throckmorton with the abbey's buildings and tithe barns. But the Halls' farm and another of near three hundred acres were granted to Edward Hall. Then it was that Edward Hall could marry and take his wife, Mary Lascelles, down into Lincolnshire to Neot's End. But when the Pilgrimage of Grace came, and the great risings all over Lincolnshire, very early the rioters came to Neot's End, and they burned the farm and the byres, they killed all the beasts or drove them off, they trampled down the corn and laid waste the flax fields. And, between two willow trees along the great dyke, they set a pole, and from it they hanged Edward Hall over the waters, so that he dried and was cured like a ham in the smoke from his own stacks.

Then Mary Lascelles' case was a very miserable one; for she had to fend for the aged father and bedridden mother of Edward Hall, and there were no beasts left but only a few geese and ducks that the rebels could not lay their hands on. And the only home that they had was the farmhouse that was upon Edward Hall's other farm, and that they had let fall nearly into ruin. And for a long time no men would work for her.

But at last, after the rebellion was pitifully ended, a few

hinds came to her, and she made a shift. And it was better still after Privy Seal fell, for then came Throckmorton the spy into his lands, and he brought with him carpenters and masons and joiners to make his house fair, and some of these men he lent to Mary Hall. But it had been prophesied by a wise woman in those parts that no land that had been taken from the monks would prosper. And, because all the jurats, bailiffs, and water-wardens had been hanged either on the one part or the other and no more had been appointed, at about that time the sewers began to clog up, the lands to swamp, murrain and fluke to strike the beasts and the sheep, and night mists to blight the grain and the fruit blossoms. So that even Throckmorton had little good of his wealth and lands.

Thus one morning to Mary Hall, who stood before her door feeding her geese and ducks, there came a little boy running to say that men-at-arms stood on the other side of the dyke that was very swollen and grey and broad. And they shouted that they came from the Queen's Highness, and would have a boat sent to ferry them over.

The colour came into Mary Hall's pale face, for even there she had heard that her former bedfellow was come to be Queen. And at times even she had thought to write to the Queen to help her in her misery. But always she had been afraid, because she thought that the Queen might re-member her only as one that had wronged her childish innocence. For she remembered that the maids' dormitory at the old Duchess's had been no cloister of pure nuns. So that, at best, she was afraid, and she sent her yard-worker and a shepherd a great way round to fetch the larger boat of two to ferry over the Queen's men. Then she went indoors to redd up the houseplace and to attire herself.

To the old farmstead, that was made of wood hung over here and there with tilework with a base of bricks, she had added a houseplace for the old folk to sit all day. It was built of wattles that had had clay cast over them, and was whitened on the outside and thatched nearly down to the ground like any squatter's hut; it had cupboards of wood nearly all round it, and beneath the cupboards were lockers worn smooth with men sitting upon them, after the Dutch fashion—for there in Lincolnshire they had much traffic with the Dutch. There was a great table made of one slab of a huge oak from near Boston. Here they all ate. And above the ingle was another slab of oak from the same tree. Her little old step-mother sat in a stuff chair covered with a sheep-skin; she sat there night and day, shivering with the shaking palsy. At times she let out of her an eldritch shriek, very like the call of a hedgehog; but she never spoke, and she was fed with a spoon by a little misbegotten son of Edward Hall's. The old step-father sat always opposite her; he had no use of his legs, and his head was always stiffly screwed round towards the door as if he were peering, but that was the rheumatism. To atone for his wife's dumbness, he chattered incessantly whenever anyone was on that floor; but because he spoke always in Lincolnshire, Mary Hall could scarce understand him, and indeed she had long ceased to listen. He spoke of forgotten floods and ploughings, ancient fairs, the boundaries of fields long since flooded over, of a visit to Boston that King Edward IV had made, and of how he, for his fair speech and old lineage, had been chosen of all the Radigund's men to present into the King's hands three silver horseshoes. Behind his back was a great dresser with railed shelves, having upon them a little pewter ware and many wooden bowls for the hinds' feeding. A door on the right side, painted black, went down into the cellar beneath the old house. Another door, of bars of iron with huge locks from the old monastery, went into the old house where slept the maids and the hinds. This was always open by day but locked in the dark hours. For the hinds were accounted brutish lumps that went savage at night, like wild beasts, so that, if they spared the master's throat, which was unlikely, it was certain that they would little spare the salted meat, the dried fish, the mead, metheglin, and cyder that their poor cellar afforded. The floor was of stamped clay, wet and sweating but covered with rushes, so that the place had a mouldering smell. Behind the heavy door there were huge bolts and crossbars against robbers: the raftered ceiling was so low that it touched her hair when she walked across the floor. The windows had no glass but were filled with a thin reddish sheep-skin like parchment. Before the stairway was a wicket gate to keep the dogs—of whom there were many, large and fierce, to protect them alike from robbers and the hinds—to keep the dogs from going into the upper room.

Each time that Mary Hall came into this home of hers her heart sank lower; for each day the corner posts gave sideways a little more, the cupboard bulged, the doors were loth to close or open. And more and more the fields outside were inundated, the lands grew sour, the sheep would not eat or died of the fluke.

'And surely,' she would cry out at times, 'God created me for other guesswork than this!'

At nights she was afraid, and shivered at the thought of the fens and the black and trackless worlds all round her; and the ravens croaked, night-hawks screamed, the dog-foxes cried out, and the flames danced over the swampy grounds. Her mirror was broken on the night that they hanged her husband: she had never had another but the water in her buckets, so that she could not tell whether she had much aged or whether she were still brown-haired and pink-cheeked, and she had forgotten how to laugh, and was sure that there were crow's-feet about her eyelids.

Her best gown was all damp and mouldy in the attic that was her bower. She made it meet as best she could, and indeed she had had so little fat living, sitting at the head of her table with a whip for unruly hinds and louts before her—so little fat living that she could well get into her wedding-gown of yellow cramosyn. She smoothed her hair back into her cord hood that for so long had not come out of its press. She washed her face in a bucket of water: that and the press and her bed with grey woollen curtains were all the furnishing her room had. The straw of the roof caught in her hood when she moved, and she heard

her old father-in-law cackling to the serving-maids through
the cracks of the floor.

When she came down there were approaching, across
the field before the door, six men in scarlet and one in
black, having all the six halberds and swords, and one a
little banner, but the man in black had a sword only. Their
horses were tethered in a clump on the farther side of the
dyke. Within the room the serving-maids were throwing
knives and pewter dishes with a great din on to the table
slab. They dropped drinking-horns and the salt-cellar itself
all of a heap into the rushes. The grandfather was cackling
from his chair; a hen and its chickens ran screaming between the maids' feet. Then Lascelles came in at the
doorway.

III

The Sieur Lascelles looked round him in that dim cave.

'Ho!' he said, 'this place stinks,' and he pulled from his
pocket a dried and shrivelled orange-peel purse stuffed
with cloves and ginger. 'Ho!' he said to the cornet that
was come behind him with the Queen's horsemen. 'Come
not in here. This will breed a plague amongst your men!'
and he added—

'Did I not tell you my sister was ill-housed?'

'Well, I was not prepared against this,' the cornet said.
He was a man with a grizzling beard that had little
patience away from the Court, where he had a bottle that
he loved and a crony or two that he played all day at
chequers with, except when the Queen rode out; then he
was of her train. He did not come over the sill, but spoke
sharply to his men.

'Ungird not here,' he said. 'We will go farther.' For
some of them were for setting their pikes against the mud
wall and casting their swords and heavy bottle-belts on to
the table before the door. The old man in the armchair
began suddenly to prattle to them all—of a horse-thief that
had been dismembered and then hanged in pieces thirty

years before. The cornet looked at him for a moment and
said—

'Sir, you are this woman's father-in-law, I do think.
Have you aught to report against her?' He bent in at the
door, holding his nose. The old man babbled of one Pease-
Cod Noll that had no history to speak of but a swivel eye.

'Well,' the grizzled cornet said, 'I shall get little sense
here.' He turned upon Mary Hall.

'Mistress,' he said, 'I have a letter here from the Queen's
High Grace,' and, whilst he fumbled in his belt to find a
little wallet that held the letter, he spoke on: 'But I misdoubt you cannot read. Therefore I shall tell you the
Queen's High Grace commandeth you to come into her
service—or not, as the report of your character shall be.
But at any rate you shall come to the castle.'

Mary Hall could find no words for men of condition, so
long she had been out of the places where such are found.
She swallowed in her throat and held her breast over her
heart.

'Where is the village here?' the cornet said, 'or what
justice is there that can write you a character under his
seal?'

She made out to say that there was no village, all the
neighbourhood having been hanged. A half-mile from
there there was the house of Sir Nicholas Throckmorton,
a justice. From the house-end he might see it, or he might
have a hind to guide him. But he would have no guide; he
would have no man nor maid nor child to go from there
to the justice's house. He set one soldier to guard the back
door and one the front, that none came out nor went beyond the dyke-end.

'Neither shall you go, Sir Lascelles,' he said.

'Well, give me leave with my sister to walk this knoll,'
Lascelles said good-humouredly. 'We shall not corrupt the
grass blades to bear false witness of my sister's chastity.'

'Ay, you may walk upon this mound,' the cornet answered. Having got out the packet of the Queen's letter,
he girded up his belt again.

'You will get you ready to ride with me,' he said to Mary Hall. 'For I will not be in these marshes after nightfall, but will sleep at Shrimpton Inn.'

He looked around him and added—

'I will have three of your geese to take with us,' he said. 'Kill me them presently.'

Lascelles looked after him as he strode away round the house with the long paces of a stiff horseman.

'Before God,' he laughed, 'that is one way to have information about a quean. Now are we prisoners whilst he inquires after your character.'

'Oh, alack!' Mary Hall said, and she cast up her hands.

'Well, we are prisoners till he come again,' her brother said good-humouredly. 'But this is a foul hole. Come out into the sunlight.'

She said—

'If you are with them, they cannot come to take me prisoner.'

He looked her full in the eyes with his own that twinkled inscrutably. He said very slowly—

'Were your mar-locks and prinking-prankings so very evil at the old Duchess's?'

She grew white: she shrank away as if he had threatened her with his fist.

'The Queen's Highness was such a child,' she said. 'She cannot remember. I have lived very godly since.'

'I will do what I can to save you,' he said. 'Let me hear about it, as, being prisoners, we may never come off.'

'You!' she cried out. 'You who stole my wedding portion!'

He laughed deviously.

'Why, I have laid it up so well for you that you may wed a knight now if you do my bidding. I was ever against your wedding Hall.'

'You lie!' she said. 'You gar'd me do it.'

The maids were peeping out of the cellar, whither they had fled.

'Come upon the grass,' he said. 'I will not be heard to

say more than this: that you and I stand and fall together like good sister and goodly brother.'

Their faces differed only in that hers was afraid and his smiling as he thought of new lies to tell her. Her face in her hood, pale beneath its weathering, approached the colour of his that shewed the pink and white of indoors. She came very slowly near him, for she was dazed. But when she was almost at the sill he caught her hand and drew it beneath his elbow.

'Tell me truly,' she said, 'shall I see the Court or a prison?... But you cannot speak truth, nor ever could when we were tiny twins. God help me: last Sunday I had the mind to wed my yard-man. I would become such a liar as thou to come away from here.'

'Sister,' he said, 'this I tell you most truly: that this shall fall out according as you obey me and inform me'; and, because he was a little the taller, he leaned over her as they walked away together.

On the fourth day from then they were come to the great wood that is to south and east of the castle of Pontefract. Here Lascelles, who had ridden much with his sister, forsook her and went ahead of the slow and heavy horses of that troop of men. The road was broadened out to forty yards of green turf between the trees, for this was a precaution against ambushes of robbers. Across the road, after he had ridden alone for an hour and a half, there was a guard of four men placed. And here, whilst he searched for his pass to come within the limits of the Court, he asked what news, and where the King was.

It was told him that the King lay still at the Fivefold Vents, two days' progress from the castle, and as it chanced that a verderer's pricker came out of the wood where he had been to mark where the deer lay for to-morrow's killing, Lascelles bade this man come along with him for a guide.

'Sir, ye cannot miss the way,' the pricker said surlily. 'I have my deer to watch.'

'I will have you to guide me,' Lascelles said, 'for I little know these parts.'

'Well,' the pricker answered him, 'it is true that I have not often seen you ride a-hawking.'

Whilst they went along the straight road, Lascelles, who unloosened the woodman's tongue with a great drink of sherry-sack, learned that it was said that only very unwillingly did the King lie so long at the Fivefold Vents. For on the morrow there was to be driven by, up there, a great herd of moor stags and maybe a wolf or two. The King would be home with his wife, it was reported, but the younger lords had been so importunate with him to stay and abide this gallant chase and great slaughter that, they having ridden loyally with him, he had yielded to their prayers and stayed there—twenty-four hours, it was said.

'Why, you know a great deal,' Lascelles answered.

'We who stand and wait had needs have knowledge,' the woodman said, 'for we have little else.'

'Aye, 'tis a hard service,' Lascelles said. 'Did you see the Queen's Highness o' Thursday week borrow a handkerchief of Sir Roger Pelham to lure her falcon back?'

'That did not I,' the woodman answered, 'for o' Thursday week it was a frost and the Queen rode not out.'

'Well, it was o' Saturday,' Lascelles said.

'Nor was it yet o' Saturday,' the woodman cried; 'I will swear it. For o' Saturday the Queen's Highness shot with the bow, and Sir Roger Pelham, as all men know, fell with his horse on Friday, and lies up still.'

'Then it was Sir Nicholas Rochford,' Lascelles persisted.

'Sir,' the woodman said, 'you have a very wrong tale, and patent it is that little you ride a-hunting.'

'Well, I mind my book,' Lascelles said. 'But wherefore?'

'Sir,' the woodman answered, 'it is thus: The Queen when she rides a-hawking has always behind her her page Toussaint, a little boy. And this little boy holdeth ever the separate lures for each hawk that the Queen setteth up. And the falcon or hawk or genette or tiercel having stooped, the Queen will call upon that eyass for the lure appropriated to each bird as it chances. And very carefully the Queen's Highness observeth the laws of the chase, of venery and hawking. For the which I honour her.'

Lascelles said, 'Well, well!'

'As for the borrowing of a handkerchief,' the woodman pursued, 'that is a very idle tale. For, let me tell you, a lady might borrow a jewelled feather or a scarlet pouch or what not that is bright and shall take a bird's eye—a little mirror upon a cord were a good thing. But a handkerchief! Why, Sir Bookman, that a lady can only do if she will signify to all the world: "This knight is my servant and I his mistress." Those very words it signifieth—and that the better for it showeth that that lady is minded to let her hawk go, luring the gentleman to her with that favour of his.'

'Well, well,' Lascelles said, 'I am not so ignorant that I did not know that. Therefore I asked you, for it seemed a very strange thing.'

'It is a very foolish tale and very evil,' the man answered. 'For this I will swear: that the Queen's Highness—and I and her honour for it—observeth very jealously the laws of wood and moorland and chase.'

'So I have heard,' Lascelles said. 'But I see the castle. I will not take you farther, but will let you go back to the goodly deer.'

'Pray God they be not wandered fore,' the woodman said. 'You could have found this way without me.'

There was but one road into the castle, and that from the south, up a steep green bank. Up the roadway Lascelles must ride his horse past four men that bore a litter made of two pikes wattled with green boughs and covered with a horse-cloth. As Lascelles passed by the very head of it, the man that lay there sprang off it to his feet, and cried out—

'I be the Queen's cousin and servant. I brought her to the Court.' Lascelles' horse sprang sideways, a great bound up the bank. He galloped ten paces ahead before the rider could stay him and turn round. The man, all rags and with a black face, had fallen into the dust of the road, and still cried out outrageously. The bearers set down the litter, wiped their brows, and then, falling all four upon Culpepper, made to carry him by his legs and arms, for they were weary of laying him upon the litter from which incessantly he sprang.

But before them upon his horse was Lascelles and impeded their way. Culpepper drew in and pushed out his legs and arms, so that they all four staggered, and—

'For God's sake, master,' one of them grunted out, 'stand aside that we may pass. We have toil enow in bearing him.'

'Why, set the poor gentleman down upon the litter,' Lascelles said, 'and let us talk a little.'

The men set Culpepper on the horse-cloth, and one of them knelt down to hold him there.

'If you will lend us your horse to lay him across, we may come more easily up,' one said. In these days the position and trade of a spy was so little esteemed—it had been far other with the great informers of Privy Seal's day—that these men, being of the Queen's guard, would talk roughly to Lascelles, who was a mere poor gentleman of the Archbishop's if his other vocation could be neglected. Lascelles sat, his hand upon his chin.

'You use him very roughly if this be the Queen's cousin,' he said.

The bearer set back his beard and laughed at the sky.

'This is a coif—a poor rag of a merchant,' he cried out. 'If this were the Queen's cousin should we bear him thus on a clout?'

'I am the Queen's cousin, T. Culpepper,' Culpepper shouted at the sky. 'Who be you that stay me from her?'

'Why, you may hear plainly,' the bearer said. 'He is mazed, doited, starved, thirsted, and a seer of visions.'

Lascelles pondered, his elbow upon his saddle-peak, his chin caught in his hand.

'How came ye by him?' he asked.

One with another they told him the tale, how, the Queen

being ridden towards the north parts, at the extreme end of her ride had seen the man, at a distance, among the heather, flogging a dead horse with a moorland kern beside him. He was a robbed, parched, fevered, and amazed traveller. The Queen's Highness, compassionating, had bidden bear him to the castle and comfort and cure him, not having looked upon his face or heard his tongue. For, for sure then, she had let him die where he was; since, no sooner were these four, his new bearers, nearly come up among the knee-deep heather, than this man had started up, his eyes upon the Queen's cavalcade and many at a distance. And, with his sword drawn and screaming, he had cried out that, if that was the Queen, he was the Queen's cousin. They had tripped up his heels in a bed of ling and quieted him with a clout on the poll from an axe end.

'But now we have him here,' the eldest said; 'where we shall bestow him we know not.'

Lascelles had his eyes upon the sick man's face as if it fascinated him, and, slowly, he got down from his horse. Culpepper then lay very still with his eyes closed, but his breast heaved as though against tight and strong ropes that bound him.

'I think I do know this gentleman for one John Robb,' he said. 'Are you very certain the Queen's Highness did not know his face?'

'Why, she came not ever within a quarter mile of him,' the bearer said.

'Then it is a great charity of the Queen to show mercy to a man she hath never seen,' Lascelles answered absently. He was closely casting his eyes over Culpepper. Culpepper lay very still, his begrimed face to the sky, his hands abroad above his head. But when Lascelles bent over him it was as if he shuddered, and then he wept.

Lascelles bent down, his hands upon his knees. He was afraid—he was very afraid. Thomas Culpepper, the Queen's cousin, he had never seen in his life. But he had heard it reported that he had red hair and beard, and went always dressed in green with stockings of red. And this man's hair was red, and his beard, beneath coal grime, was a curly red, and his coat, beneath a crust of black filth, was Lincoln green and of a good cloth. And, beneath the black, his stockings were of red silk. He reflected slowly, whilst the bearers laughed amongst themselves at this Queen's kinsman in rags and filth.

Lascelles gave them his bottle of sack to drink empty among them, that he might have the longer time to think.

If this were indeed the Queen's cousin, come unknown to the Queen and mazed and muddled in himself to Ponte-fract, what might not Lascelles make of him? For all the world knew that he loved her with a mad love—he had sold farms to buy her gowns. It was he that had brought her to Court, upon an ass, at Greenwich, when her mule—as all men knew—had stumbled upon the threshold. Once before, it was said, Culpepper had burst in with his sword drawn upon the King and Kate Howard when they sat together. And Lascelles trembled with eagerness at the thought of what use he might not make of this mad and insolent lover of the Queen's!

But did he dare?

Culpepper had been sent into Scotland to secure him up, away at the farthest limits of the realm. Then, if he was come back? This grime was the grime of a sea-coal ship! He knew that men without passports, outlaws and the like, escaped from Scotland on the Durham ships that went to Leith with coal. And this man came on the Durham road. Then . . .

If it were Culpepper he had come unpermitted. He was an outlaw. Dare Lascelles have trade with—dare he har-bour—an outlaw? It would be unbeknown to the Queen's Highness! He kicked his heels with impatience to come to a resolution.

He reflected swiftly:

What hitherto he had were: some tales spread abroad about the Queen's lewd Court—tales in London Town. He had, too, the keeper of the Queen's door bribed and talked into his service and interest. And he had his sister . . .

His sister would, with threatening, tell tales of the Queen before marriage. And she would find him other maids and grooms, some no doubt more willing still than Mary Hall. But the keeper of the Queen's door! And, in addition, the Queen's cousin mad of love for her! What might he not do with these two?

The prickly sweat came to his forehead. Four horsemen were issuing from the gate of the castle above. He must come to a decision. His fingers trembled as if they were a pickpocket's near a purse of gold.

He straightened his back and stood erect.

'Yes,' he said very calmly, 'this is my friend John Robb.'

He added that this man had been in Edinburgh where the Queen's cousin was. He had had letters from him that told how they were sib and rib. Thus this fancy had doubtless come into his brain at sight of the Queen in his madness.

He breathed calmly, having got out these words, for now the doubt was ended. He would have both the Queen's door-keeper and the Queen's mad lover.

He bade the bearers set Culpepper upon his horse and, supporting him, lead him to a room that he would hire of the Archbishop's chamberlain, near his own in the dark entrails of the castle. And there John Robb should live at his expenses.

And when the men protested that, though this was very Christian of Lascelles, yet they would have recompense of the Queen for their toils, he said that he himself would give them a crown apiece, and they might get in addition what recompense from the Queen's steward that they could. He asked them each their names and wrote them down, pretending that it was that he might send each man his crown piece.

So, when the four horsemen were ridden past, the men hoisted Culpepper into Lascelles' horse and went all together up into the castle.

But, that night, when Culpepper lay in a stupor, Lascelles went to the Archbishop's chamberlain and begged that four men, whose names he had written down, might be chosen to go in the Archbishop's paritor's guard that went next dawn to Ireland over the sea to bring back tithes from Dublin. And, next day, he had Culpepper moved to another room; and, in three days' time, he set it about in the castle that the Queen's cousin was come from Scotland. By that time most of the liquor had come down out of Culpepper's brain, but he was still muddled and raved at times.

IV

On that third night the Queen was with the Lady Mary, once more in her chamber, having come down as before, from the chapel in the roof, to pray her submit to her father's will. Mary had withstood her with a more good-humoured irony; and, whilst she was in the midst of her pleadings, a letter marked most pressing was brought to her. The Queen opened it, and raised her eyebrows; she looked down at the subscription and frowned. Then she cast it upon the table.

'Shall there never be an end of old things?' she said.

'Even what old things?' the Lady Mary asked.

The Queen shrugged her shoulders.

'It was not they I came to talk of,' she said. 'I would sleep early, for the King comes to-morrow and I have much to plead with you.'

'I am weary of your pleadings,' the Lady Mary said. 'You have pleaded enow. If you would be fresh for the King, be first fresh for me. Start a new hare.'

The Queen would have gainsaid her.

'I have said you have pleaded enow,' the Lady Mary said. 'And you have pleaded enow. This no more amuses me. I will wager I guess from whom your letter was.'

Reluctantly the Queen held her peace; that day she had read in many ancient books, as well profane as of the

Fathers of the Church, and she had many things to say, and they were near her lips and warm in her heart. She was much minded to have good news to give the King against his coming on the morrow; the great good news that should set up in that realm once more abbeys and chapters and the love of God. But she could not press these sayings upon the girl, though she pleaded still with her blue eyes.

'Your letter is from Sir Nicholas Throckmorton,' the Lady Mary said. 'Even let me read it.'

'You did know that that knight was come to Court again?' the Queen said.

'Aye; and that you would not see him, but like a fool did bid him depart again.'

'You will ever be calling me a fool,' Katharine retorted, 'for giving ear to my conscience and hating spies and the suborners of false evidence.'

'Why,' the Lady Mary answered, 'I do call it a folly to refuse to give ear to the tale of a man who has ridden far and fast, and at the risk of a penalty to tell it you.'

'Why,' Katharine said, 'if I did forbid his coming to the Court under a penalty, it was because I would not have him here.'

'Yet he much loved you, and did you some service.'

'He did me a service of lies,' the Queen said, and she was angry. 'I would not have had him serve me. By his false witness Cromwell was cast down to make way for me. But I had rather have cast down Cromwell by the truth which is from God. Or I had rather he had never been cast down. And that I swear.'

'Well, you are a fool,' the Lady Mary said. 'Let me look upon this knight's letter.'

'I have not read it,' Katharine said.

'Then will I,' the Lady Mary answered. She made across the room to where the paper lay upon the table beside the great globe of the earth. She came back; she turned her round to the Queen; she made her a deep reverence, so that her black gown spread out stiffly around her, and, keeping her eyes ironically on Katharine's face, she mounted backward up to the chair that was beneath the dais.

Katharine put her hand over her heart.

'What mean you?' she said. 'You have never sat there before.'

'That is not true,' the Lady Mary said harshly. 'For this last three days I have practised how, thus backward, I might climb to this chair and, thus seemly, sit in it.'

'Even then?' Katharine asked.

'Even then I will be asked no more questions,' her step-daughter answered. 'This signifieth that I ha' heard enow o' thy voice, Queen.'

Katharine did not dare to speak, for she knew well this girl's tyrannous and capricious nature. But she was nearly faint with emotion and reached sideways for the chair at the table; there she sat and gazed at the girl beneath the dais, her lips parted, her body leaning forward.

Mary spread out the great sheet of Throckmorton's parchment letter upon her black knees. She bent forward so that the light from the mantel at the room-end might fall upon the writing.

'It seemeth,' she said ironically, 'that one descrieth better at the humble end of the room than here on high '—and she read whilst the Queen panted.

At last she raised her eyes and bent them darkly upon the Queen's face.

'Will you do what this knight asks?' she uttered. 'For what he asks seemeth prudent.'

'A' God's name,' Katharine said, 'let me not now hear of this man.'

'Why,' the Lady Mary answered coolly, 'if I am to be of the Queen's alliance I must be of the Queen's council and my voice have a weight.'

'But will you? Will you?' Katharine brought out.

'Will you listen to my voice?' Mary said. 'I will not listen to yours. Hear now what this goodly knight saith. For, if

I am to be your well-wisher, I must call him goodly that so well wishes to you.'

Katharine wrung her hands.

'Ye torture me,' she said.

'Well, I have been tortured,' Mary answered, 'and I have come through it and live.'

She swallowed in her throat, and thus, with her eyes upon the writing, brought out the words—

'This knight bids you beware of one Mary Lascelles or Hall, and her brother, Edward Lascelles, that is of the Archbishop's service.'

'I will not hear what Throckmorton says,' Katharine answered.

'Ay, but you shall,' Mary said, 'or I come down from this chair. I am not minded to be allied to a Queen that shall be undone. That is not prudence.'

'God help me!' the Queen said.

'God helps most willingly them that take counsel with themselves and prudence,' her step-daughter answered; 'and these are the words of the knight.' She held up the parchment and read out:

' "Therefore I—and you know how much your well-wisher I be—upon my bended knees do pray you do one of two things: either to put out both these twain from your courts and presence, or if that you cannot or will not do, so richly to reward them as that you shall win them to your service. For a little rotten fruit will spread a great stink; a small ferment shall pollute a whole well. And these twain, I am advised, assured, convinced, and have convicted them, will spread such a rotten fog and mist about your reputation and so turn even your good and gracious actions to evil seeming that—I swear and vow, O most high Sovereign, for whom I have risked, as you wot, life, limb and the fell rack——" '

The Lady Mary looked up at the Queen's face.

'Will you not listen to the pleadings of this man?' she said.

'I will so reward Lascelles and his sister as they have

merited,' the Queen said. 'So much and no more. And not all the pleadings of this knight shall move me to listen to any witness that he brings against any man nor maid. So help me, God; for I do know how he served his master Cromwell.'

'For love of thee!' the Lady Mary said.

The Queen wrung her hands as if she would wash a stain from them.

'God help me!' she said. 'I prayed the King for the life of Privy Seal that was!'

'He would not hear thee,' the Lady Mary said. She looked long upon the Queen's face with unmoved and searching eyes.

'It is a new thing to me,' she said, 'to hear that you prayed for Privy Seal's life.'

'Well, I prayed,' Katharine said, 'for I did not think he worked treason against the King.'

The Lady Mary straightened her back where she sat.

'I think I will not show myself less queenly than you,' she said. 'For I be of a royal race. But hear this knight.'

And again she read:

' "I have it from the lips of the cornet that came with this Lascelles to fetch this Mary Lascelles or Hall: I, Throckmorton, a knight, swear that I heard with mine own ears, how for ever as they rode, this Lascelles plied this cornet with questions about your high self. As thus: 'Did you favour any gentleman when you rode out, the cornet being of your guard?' or, 'Had he heard a tale of one Pelham, a knight, of whom you should have taken a kerchief?'—and this, that and the other, for ever, till the cornet spewed at the hearing of him. Now, gracious and most high Sovereign Consort, what is it that this man seeketh?" '

Again the Lady Mary paused to look at the Queen.

'Why,' Katharine said, 'so mine enemies will talk of me. I had been the fool you styled me if I had not awaited it. But——' and she drew up her body highly. 'My life is such and such shall be that none such arrow shall pierce my corslet.'

'God help you,' the Lady Mary said. 'What has your life to do with it, if you will not cut out the tongues of slanderers?'

She laughed mirthlessly, and added—

'Now this knight concludes—and it is as if he writhed his hands and knelt and whined and kissed your feet—he concludeth with a prayer that you will let him come again to the Court. "For," says he, "I will clean your vessels, serve you at table, scrape the sweat off your horse, or do all that is vilest. But suffer me to come that I may know and report to you what there is whispered in these jail places." '

Katharine Howard said—

'I had rather borrow Pelham's kerchief.'

The Lady Mary dropped the parchment on to the floor at her side.

'I rede you do as this knight wills,' she said; 'for, amidst the little sticklers of spies that are here, this knight, this emperor of spies, moves as a pillow of shadow. He stalks amongst them as, in the night, the dread and awful lion of Numidia. He shall be to you more a corslet of proof than all the virtue that your life may borrow from the precepts of Diana. We, that are royal and sit in high places, have our feet in such mire.'

'Now before God on His throne,' Katharine Howard said, 'if you be of royal blood, I will teach you a lesson. For hear me——'

'No, I will hear thee no more,' the Lady Mary answered; 'I will teach thee. For thou art not the only one in this land to be proud. I will show thee such a pride as shall make thee blush.'

She stood up and came slowly down the steps of the dais. She squared back her shoulders and folded her hands before her; she erected her head, and her eyes were dark. When she was come to where the Queen sat, she kneeled down.

'I acknowledge thee to be my mother,' she said, 'that have married the King, my father. I pray you that you do take me by the hand and set me in that seat that you did raise for me. I pray you that you do style me a princess, royal again in this land. And I pray you to lesson me and teach me that which you would have me do as well as that which it befits me to do. Take me by the hand.'

'Nay, it is my lord that should do this,' the Queen whispered. Before that she had started to her feet; her face had a flush of joy; her eyes shone with her transparent faith. She brushed back a strand of hair from her brow; she folded her hands on her breasts and raised her glance upwards to seek the dwelling-place of Almighty God and the saints in their glorious array.

'It is my lord should do this!' she said again.

'Speak no more words,' the Lady Mary said. 'I have heard enow of thy pleadings. You have heard me say that.'

She continued upon her knees.

'It is thou or none!' she said. 'It is thou or none shall witness this my humiliation and my pride. Take me by the hand. My patience will not last for ever.'

The Queen set her hand between the girl's. She raised her to her feet.

When the Lady Mary stood high and shadowy, in black, with her white face beneath that dais, she looked down upon the Queen.

'Now, hear me!' she said. 'In this I have been humble to you; but I have been most proud. For I have in my veins a greater blood than thine or the King's, my father's. For, inasmuch as Tudor blood is above Howard's, so my mother's, that was royal of Spain, is above Tudor's. And this it is to be royal——

'I have had you, a Queen, kneel before me. It is royal to receive petitions—more royal still it is to grant them. And in this, further, I am more proud. For, hearing you say that you had prayed the King for Cromwell's life, I thought, this is a virtue-mad Queen. She shall most likely fall!— Prudence biddeth me not to be of her party. But shall I,

who am royal, be prudent? Shall I, who am of the house
of Aragon, be more afraid than thou, a Howard?

'I tell you—No! If you will be undone for the sake of
virtue, blindly, and like a fool, unknowing the consequences, I, Mary of Aragon and England, will make
alliance with thee, knowing that the alliance is dangerous.
And, since it is more valiant to go to a doom knowingly
than blindfold, so I do show myself more valiant than thou.
For well I know—since I saw my mother die—that virtue
is a thing profitless, and impracticable in this world. But
you—you think it shall set up temporal monarchies and
rule peoples. Therefore, what you do you do for profit. I
do it for none.'

'Now, by the Mother of God,' Katharine Howard said,
'this is the gladdest day of my life.'

'Pray you,' Mary said, 'get you gone from my sight and
hearing, for I endure ill the appearance and sound of joy.
And, Queen, again I bid you beware of calling any day
fortunate till its close. For, before midnight you may be
ruined utterly. I have known more Queens than thou.
Thou art the fifth I have known.'

She added—

'For the rest, what you will I will do: submission to the
King and such cozening as he will ask of me. God keep
you, for you stand in need of it.'

At supper that night there sat all such knights and
lordlings as ate at the King's expense in the great hall that
was in the midmost of the castle, looking on to the courtyard. There were not such a many of them, maybe forty;
from the keeper of the Queen's records, the Lord d'Espahn,
who sat at the table head, down to the lowest of all, the
young Poins, who sat far below the salt-cellar. The greater
lords of the Queen's household, like the Lord Dacre of the
North, did not eat at this common table, or only when the
Queen herself there ate, which she did at midday when
there was a feast.

Nevertheless, this eating was conducted with gravity,

the Lord d'Espahn keeping a vigilant eye down the table, which was laid with a fair white cloth. It cost a man a fine to be drunk before the white meats were eaten—unless, indeed, a man came drunk to the board—and the salt-cellar of state stood a-midmost of the cloth. It was of silver from Holland, and represented a globe of the earth, opened at the top, and supported by knights' bannerets.

The hall was all of stone, with creamy walls, only marked above the iron torch-holds with brandons of soot. A scutcheon of the King's arms was above one end-door, with the Queen's above the other. Over each window were notable deers' antlers, and over each side-door, that let in the servers from the courtyard, was a scutcheon with the arms of a king deceased that had visited the castle. The roof was all gilded and coloured, and showed knaves' faces leering and winking, so that when a man was in drink, and looked upwards with his head on his chair back, these appeared to have life. The hall was called the Dacre Hall, because the Lords Dacre of the North had built it to be an offering to various kings that died whilst it was a-building.

Such knights as had pages had them behind their chairs, holding napkins and ready to fill the horns with wine or beer. From kitchens or from buttery-hatches the servers ran continually across the courtyard and across the tiled floor, for the table was set back against the farther wall, all the knights being on the wall side, since there were not so many, and thus it was easier to come to them. There was a great clatter with the knives going and the feet on the tiles, but little conversing, for in that keen air eating was the principal thing, and in five minutes a boar or a sheep's head would be stripped till the skull alone was shown.

It was in this manner that Thomas Culpepper came into the hall when they were all well set to, without having many eyes upon him. But the Lord d'Espahn was aware, suddenly, of one that stood beside him.

'Gentleman, will you have a seat?' he said. 'Tell me your name and estate, that I may appoint you one.' He was a grave lord, with a pointed nose, dented at the end, a grey, square beard, and fresh colours on his face. He wore his bonnet because he was the highest there, and because there were currents of air at the openings of the doors.

Thomas Culpepper's face was of a chalky white. Somewhere Lascelles had found for him a suit of green and red stockings. His red beard framed his face, but his lips were pursed.

'Your seat I will have,' he said, 'for I am the Queen's cousin, T. Culpepper.'

The Lord d'Espahn looked down upon his platter.

'You may not have my seat,' he said. 'But you shall have this seat at my right hand that is empty. It is a very honourable seat, but mine you may not have for it is the Queen's own that I hold, being her vicar here.'

'Your seat I will have,' Culpepper said.

The Lord d'Espahn was set upon keeping order and quiet in that place more than on any other thing. He looked again down upon his platter, and then he was aware of a voice that whispered in his ear—

'A' God's name, humour him, for he is very mad,' and, turning his eyes a little, he saw that it was Lascelles above his chair head.

'Your seat I will have,' Culpepper said again. 'And this fellow, that tells me he is the most potent lord there is here, shall serve behind my chair.'

The Lord d'Espahn took up his knife and fork in one hand and his manchet of bread in the other. He made as if to bow to Culpepper, who pushed him by the shoulder away. Some lordlings saw this and wondered, but in the noise none heard their words. At the foot of the table the squires said that the Lord d'Espahn must have been found out in a treason. Only the young Poins said that that was the Queen's cousin, come from Scotland, withouten leave, for love of the Queen through whom he was sick in the wits. This news ran through the castle by means of servers, cooks, undercooks, scullions, maids, tiring-maids, and maids of honour, more swiftly than it progressed up the table where men had the meats to keep their minds upon.

Culpepper sat, flung back in his chair, his eyes, lack-lustre and open, upon the cloth where his hands sprawled out. He said few words—only when the Lord d'Espahn's server carved boar's head for him, he took one piece in his mouth and then threw the plate full into the server's face. This caused great offence amongst the serving-men, for this server was a portly fellow that had served the Lord d'Espahn many years, and had a face like a ram's, so grave it was. Having drunk a little of his wine, Culpepper turned out the rest upon the cloth; his salt he brushed off his plate with his sleeve. That was remembered for long afterwards by many men and women. And it was as if he could not swallow, for he put down neither meat nor drink, but sat, deadly and pale, so that some said that he was rabid. Once he turned his head to ask the Lord d'Espahn—

'If a quean prove forsworn, and turn to a Queen, what should her true love do?'

The Lord d'Espahn never made any answer, but wagged his beard from side to side, and Culpepper repeated his question three separate times. Finally, the platters were raised, and the Lord d'Espahn went away to the sound of trumpets. Many of the lords there came peering round Culpepper to see what sport he might yield. Lascelles went away, following the scarlet figure of the young Poins, work-ing his hand into the boy's arm and whispering to him. The servers and disservers went to their work of clearing the board.

But Culpepper sat there without word or motion, so that none of those lords had any sport out of him. Some of them went away to roast pippins at the Widow Amnot's, some to speak with the alchemist that, on the roof, watched the stars. So one and the other left the room; the torches burned out, most of them, and, save for two lords of the Archbishop's following, who said boldly that they would watch and care for this man, because he was the Queen's cousin, and there might be advancement in it, Culpepper was left alone.

His sword he had not with him, but he had his dagger,

and, just as he drew it, appearing about to stab himself in the heart, there ran across the hall the black figure of Lascelles, so that he appeared to have been watching through a window, and the two lords threw themselves upon Culpepper's arm. And all three began to tell him that there was better work for him to do than that of stabbing himself; and Lascelles brought with him a flagon of *aqua vitæ* from Holland, and poured out a little for Culpepper to drink. And one of the lords said that his room was up in the gallery near the Queen's, and, if Culpepper would go with him there, they might make good cheer. Only he must be silent in the going thither; afterwards it would not so much matter, for they would be past the guards. So, linking their arms in his, they wound up and across the courtyard, where the torchmen that waited on their company of diners to light them, blessed God that the sitting was over, and beat their torches out against the ground.

In the shadow of the high walls, and some in the moonlight, the serving-men held their parliament. They discoursed of these things, and some said that it was a great pity that T. Culpepper was come to Court. For he was an idle braggart, and where he was disorder grew, and that was a pity, since the Queen had made the Court orderly, and servants were little beaten. But some said that like sire was like child, and that great disorders there were in the Court, but quiet ones, and the Queen the centre. But these were mostly the cleaners of dishes and the women that swept rooms and spread new rushes. Upon the whole, the cooks blessed the Queen, along with all them that had to do with feeding and the kitchens. They thanked God for her because she had brought back the old fasts. For, as they argued, your fast brings honours to cooks, since, after a meagre day, your lord cometh to his trencher with a better appetite, and then is your cook commended. The Archbishop's cooks were the hottest in this contention, for they had the most reason to know. The stablemen, palfreniers, and falconers' mates were, most part of them, politicians more than the others, and these wondered to have seen, through their peep-holes and door-cracks, the Queen's cousin go away with these lords that were of the contrary party. Some said that T. Culpepper was her emissary to win them over to her interests, and some, that always cousins, uncles, and kin were the bitterest foes a Queen had, as witness the case of Queen Anne Boleyn and the Yellow Dog of Norfolk who had worked to ruin her. And some said it was marvellous that there they could sit or stand and talk of such things—for a year or so ago all the Court was spies, so that the haymen mistrusted them that forked down the straw, and meat-servers them with the wine. But now each man could talk as he would, and it made greatly for fellowship when a man could sit against a wall, unbutton in the warm nights, and say what he listed.

The light of the great fires grew dull in the line of kitchen windows; sweethearting couples came in through the great gateway from the grass-slopes beneath the castle walls. There was a little bustle when four horsemen rode in to say that the King's Highness was but nine miles from the castle, and torchmen must be there to light him in towards midnight. But the Queen should not be told for her greater pleasure and surprise. Then all these serving-men stood up and shook themselves, and said—'To bed.' For, on the morrow, with the King back, there would surely be great doings and hard work. And to mews and kennels and huts, in the straw and beds of rushes, these men betook themselves. The young lords came back laughing from Widow Amnot's at the castle foot; there was not any light to be seen save one in all that courtyard full of windows. The King's torchmen slumbered in the guard-room where they awaited his approach. Darkness, silence, and deep shadow lay everywhere, though overhead the sky was pale with moonlight, and, from high in the air, the thin and silvery tones of the watchman's horn on the roof filtered down at the quarter hours. A drowsy bell marked the hours, and the cries and drillings of the night birds vibrated from very high.

V

Coming very late to her bedroom the Queen found awaiting her her tiring-maid, Mary Trelyon, whom she had advanced into the post that Margot Poins had held, and the old Lady Rochford.

'Why,' she said to her maid, 'when you have unlaced me you may go, or you will not love my service that keeps you so late.'

Mary Trelyon cast her eyes on the ground, and said that it was such pleasure to attend her mistress, that not willingly would she give up that discoiffing, undoing of hair, and all the rest, for long she had desired to have the handling of these precious things and costly garments.

'No, you shall get you gone,' the Queen said, 'for I will not have you, sweetheart, be red-lidded in the morning with this long watching, for to-morrow the King comes, and I will have him see my women comely and fair, though in your love you will not care for yourselves.'

Standing before her mirror, where there burned in silver dishes four tall candles with perfumed wicks, Katharine offered her back to the loosening fingers of this girl.

'I would not have you to think,' she said, 'that I am always thus late and a gadabout. But this day'—the Queen's eyes sparkled, and her cheeks were red with exaltation —'this day and this night are one that shall be marked with red stones in the calendar of England, and late have I travailed so to make them be.'

The girl was very black-avised, and her face beneath her grey hood—for the Queen's maids were all in grey, with crowned roses, the device that the King had given her at their wedding, worked in red silk on each shoulder—her face beneath her grey hood was the clear shape of the thin end of an egg. She worked at the unlacing of the Queen's gown, so that she at last must kneel down to it.

Having finished, she remained upon her knees, but she

twisted her fingers in her skirt as if she were bashful, yet her face was perturbed with red flushes on the dark cheeks.

The Queen, feeling that she knelt there upon her loosened gown and did not get her gone, said—

'Anan?'

'Please you let me stay,' the girl said; but Katharine answered—

'I would commune with my own thoughts.'

'Please you hear me,' the girl said, and she was very earnest; but the Queen answered—

'Why, no! If you have any boon to ask of me, you know very well that to-morrow at eleven is the hour for asking. Now, I will sit still with the silence. Bring me my chair to the table. The Lady Rochford shall put out my lights when I be abed.'

The girl stood up and rolled, with a trick of appeal, her eyes to the old Lady Rochford. This lady, all in grey too, but with a great white hood because she was a widow, sat back upon the foot of the great bed. Her face was perturbed, but it had been always perturbed since her cousin, the Queen Anne Boleyn, had fallen by the axe. She put a gouty and swollen finger to her lips, and the girl shrugged her shoulders with a passion of despair, for she was very hot-tempered, and it was as if mutinously that she fetched the Queen her chair and set it behind her where she stood before the mirror taking off her breast jewel from its chain. And again the girl shrugged her shoulders. Then she went to the little wall-door that corkscrewed down into the courtyard through the thick of the wall. Immediately after she was gone they heard the lockguard that awaited her without set on the great padlock without the door. Then his feet clanked down the stairway, he being heavily loaded with weighty keys. It was the doors along the corridor that the young Poins guarded, and these were never opened once the Queen was in her room, save by the King. The Lady Rochford slept in the anteroom upon a truckle-bed, and the great withdrawing-room was empty.

It was very still in the Queen's room and most shadowy,

except before the mirror where the candle flames streamed upwards. The pillars of the great bed were twisted out of dark wood; the hangings of bed and walls were all of a dark blue arras, and the bedspread was of a dark red velvet worked in gold with pomegranates and pomegranate leaves. Only the pillows and the turnover of the sheets were of white linen-lawn, and the bed curtains nearly hid them with shadows. Where the Queen sat there was light like that of an altar in a dim chapel, for the room was so huge.

She sat before her glass, silently taking off her golden things. She took the jewel off the chain round her neck and laid it in a casket of gold and ivory. She took the rings off her fingers and hung them on the lance of a little knight in silver. She took off her waist where it hung to a brooch of feridets, her pomander of enamel and gold; she opened it and marked the time by the watch studded with sable diamonds that it held.

'Past eleven,' she said, 'if my watch goes right.'

'Indeed it is past eleven,' the Lady Rochford sighed behind her.

The Queen sat forward in her chair, looking deep into the shadows of her mirror. A great relaxation was in all her limbs, for she was very tired, so that though she was minded to let down her hair she did not begin to undo her coif, and though she desired to think, she had no thoughts. From far away there came a muffled sound as if a door had been roughly closed, and the Lady Rochford shot out a little sound between a scream and a sigh.

'Why, you are very affrighted,' the Queen said. 'One would think you feared robbers; but my guards are too good.'

She began to unloosen from her hood her jewel, which was a rose fashioned out of pink shell work set with huge dewdrops of diamonds and crowned with a little crown of gold.

'God knows,' she said, 'I ha' trinkets enow for robbers. It takes me too long to undo them. I would the King did not so load me.'

'Your Highness is too humble for a Queen,' the old
Lady Rochford grumbled. 'Let me aid you, since the maid
is gone. I would not have you speak your maids so humbly.
My Cousin Anne that was the Queen——'

She came stiffly and heavily forward from the bed with
her hands out to discoif her lady; but the Queen turned
her head, caught at her fat hand, put it against her cheek
and fondled it.

'I would have your Highness feared by all,' the old lady
said.

'I would have myself by all beloved,' Katharine answered. 'What, am I to play the Queen and Highness to
such serving-maids as I was once the fellow and companion to?'

'Your Highness should not have sent the wench away,'
the old woman said.

'Well, you have taken on a very sour voice,' the Queen
said. 'I will study to pleasure you more. Get you now back
and rest you, for I know you stand uneasily, and you shall
not uncoif me.'

She began to unpin her coif, laying the golden pins in
the silver candle-dishes. When her hair was thus set free
of a covering, though it was smoothly braided and parted
over her forehead, yet it was lightly rebellious, so that little
mists of it caught the light, golden and rejoiceful. Her face
was serious, her nose a little peaked, her lips rested lightly
together, and her blue eyes steadily challenged their
counterparts in the mirror with an assured and gentle
glance.

'Why,' she said, 'I believe you have the right of it—but
for a queen I must be the same make of queen that I am
as a woman. A queen gracious rather than a queen regnant;
a queen to grant petitions rather than one to brush aside
the petitioners.'

She stopped and mused.

'Yet,' she said, 'you will do me the justice to say that in
the open and in the light of day, when men are by or the
King's presence demands it, I do ape as well as I may the

painted queens of galleries and the stately ladies that are to be seen in pictured books.'

'I would not have had you send away the maid,' the old Lady Rochford said.

'God help me,' the Queen answered. 'I stayed her petition till the morrow. Is that not queening it enough?'

The Lady Rochford suddenly wrung her hands.

'I had rather,' she said, 'you had heard her and let her stay. Here there are not people enough to guard you. You should have many scores of people. This is a dreary place.'

'Heaven help me,' the Queen said. 'If I were such a queen as to be affrighted, you would affright me. Tell me of your cousin that was a sinful queen.'

The Lady Rochford raised her hands lamentably and bleated out—

'Ah God, not to-night!'

'You have been ready enough on other nights,' the Queen said. And, indeed, it was so much the practice of this lady to talk always of her cousin, whose death had affrighted her, that often the Queen had begged her to cease. But to-night she was willing to hear, for she felt afraid of no omens, and, being joyful, was full of pity for the dead unfortunate. She began with slow, long motions to withdraw the great pins from her hair. The deep silence settled down again, and she hummed the melancholy and stately tune that goes with the words—

> 'When all the little hills are hid in snow,
> And all the small brown birds by frost are slain,
> And sad and slow
> The silly sheep do go,
> All seeking shelter to and fro—
> Come once again
> To these familiar, silent, misty lands——'

And—

'Aye,' she said; 'to these ancient and familiar lands of the dear saints, please God, when the winter snows are upon them, once again shall come the feet of God's messenger, for this is the joyfullest day this land hath known since my namesake was cast down and died.'

Suddenly there were muffled cries from beyond the thick door in the corridor, and on the door itself resounding blows. The Lady Rochford gave out great shrieks, more than her feeble body could have been deemed to hold.

'Body of God!' the Queen said, 'what is this?'

'Your cousin!' the Lady Rochford cried out. She came running to the Queen, who, in standing up, had overset her heavy chair, and, falling to her knees, she babbled out—'Your cousin! Oh, let it not all come again. Call your guard. Let it not all come again'; and she clawed into the Queen's skirt, uttering incomprehensible clamours.

'What? What? What?' Katharine said.

'He was with the Archbishop. Your cousin with the Archbishop. I heard it. I sent to stay him if it were so'; and the old woman's teeth crackled within her jaws. 'O God, it is come again!' she cried.

The door flung open heavily, but slowly, because it was so heavy. And, in the archway, whilst a great scream from the old woman wailed out down the corridors, Katharine was aware of a man in scarlet, locked in a struggle with a raging swirl of green manhood. The man in scarlet fell back, and then, crying out, ran away. The man in green, his bonnet off, his red hair sticking all up, his face pallid, and his eyes staring like those of a sleep-walker, entered the room. In his right hand he had a dagger. He walked very slowly.

The Queen thought fast: the old Lady Rochford had her mouth open; her eyes were upon the dagger in Culpepper's hand.

'I seek the Queen,' he said, but his eyes were lacklustre; they fell upon Katharine's face as if they had no recognition, or could not see. She turned her body round to the old Lady Rochford, bending from the hips so as not to move her feet. She set her fingers upon her lips.

'I seek—I seek——' he said, and always he came closer to her. His eyes were upon her face, and the lids moved.

'I seek the Queen,' he said, and beneath his husky voice there were bass notes of quivering anger, as if, just as he had been by chance calmed by throwing down the guard, so by chance his anger might arise again.

The Queen never moved, but stood up full and fair; one strand of her hair, loosened, fell low over her left ear. When he was so close to her that his protruded hips touched her skirt, she stole her hand slowly round him till it closed upon his wrist above the dagger. His mouth opened, his eyes distended.

'I seek——' he said, and then—'Kat!'. as if the touch of her cool and firm fingers rather than the sight of her had told to his bruised senses who she was.

'Get you gone!' she said. 'Give me your dagger.' She uttered each word roundly and fully as if she were pondering the next move over a chequer-board.

'Well, I will kill the Queen,' he said. 'How may I do it without my knife?'

'Get you gone!' she said again. 'I will direct you to the Queen.'

He passed the back of his left hand wearily over his brow.

'Well, I have found thee, Kat!' he said.

She answered: 'Aye!' and her fingers twined round his on the hilt of the dagger, so that his were loosening.

Then the old Lady Rochford screamed out—

'Ha! God's mercy! Guards, swords, come!' The furious blood came into Culpepper's face at the sound. His hand he tore from Katharine's, and with the dagger raised on high he ran back from her and then forward towards the Lady Rochford. With an old trick of fence, that she had learned when she was a child, Katharine Howard set out her foot before him, and, with the speed of his momentum, he pitched over forward. He fell upon his face so that his forehead was upon the Lady Rochford's right foot. His dagger he still grasped, but he lay prone with the drink and the fever.

'Now, by God in His mercy,' Katharine said to her, 'as I am the Queen I charge you——'

'Take his knife and stab him to the heart!' the Lady Rochford cried out. 'This will slay us two.'

'I charge you that you listen to me,' the Queen said, 'or, by God, I will have you in chains!'

'I will call your many,' the Lady Rochford cried out, for terror had stopped up the way from her ears to her brain, and she made towards the door. But Katharine set her hand to the old woman's shoulder.

'Call no man,' she commanded. 'This is a device of mine enemies to have men see this of me.'

'I will not stay here to be slain,' the old woman said.

'Then mine own self will slay you,' the Queen answered. Culpepper moved in his stupor. 'Before Heaven,' the Queen said, 'stay you there, and he shall not again stand up.'

'I will go call——' the old woman besought her, and again Culpepper moved. The Queen stood right up against her; her breast heaved, her face was rigid. Suddenly she turned and ran to the door. That key she wrenched round and out, and then to the other door beside it, and that key too she wrenched round and out.

'I will not stay alone with my cousin,' she said, 'for that is what mine enemies would have. And this I vow, that if again you squeak I will have you tried as being an abettor of this treason.' She went and knelt down at her cousin's head; she moved his face round till it was upon her lap.

'Poor Tom,' she said; he opened his eyes and muttered stupid words.

She looked again at Lady Rochford.

'All this is nothing,' she said, 'if you will hide in the shadow of the bed and keep still. I have seen my cousin a hundred times thus muddied with drink, and do not fear him. He shall not stand up till he is ready to go through the door; but I will not be alone with him and tend him.'

The Lady Rochford waddled and quaked like a jelly to the shadow of the bed curtains. She pulled back the curtain over the window, and, as if the contact with the world without would help her, threw back the casement. Below, in the black night, a row of torches shook and trembled, like little planets, in the distance.

Katharine Howard held her cousin's head upon her knees. She had seen him thus a hundred times and had no fear of him. For thus in his cups, and fevered as he was with ague that he had had since a child, he was always amenable to her voice though all else in the world enraged him. So that, if she could keep the Lady Rochford still, she might well win him out through the door at which he came in.

And, first, when he moved to come to his knees, she whispered—

'Lie down, lie down,' and he set one elbow on to the carpet and lay over on his side, then on his back. She took his head again on to her lap, and with soft motions reached to take the dagger from his hand. He yielded it up and gazed upwards into her face.

'Kat!' he said, and she answered—

'Aye!'

There came from very far the sound of a horn.

'When you can stand,' she said, 'you must get you gone.'

'I have sold farms to get you gowns,' he answered.

'And then we came to Court,' she said, 'to grow great.'

He passed his left hand once more over his eyes with a gesture of ineffable weariness, but his other arm that was extended, she knelt upon.

'Now we are great,' she said.

He muttered, 'I wooed thee in an apple orchard. Let us go back to Lincolnshire.'

'Why, we will talk of it in the morning,' she said. 'It is very late.'

Her brain throbbed with the pulsing blood. She was set to get him gone before the young Poins could call men to her door. It was maddeningly strange to think that none hitherto had come. Maybe Culpepper had struck him dead with his knife, or he lay without fainting. This black

enigma, calling for haste that she dare not show, filled all
the shadows of that shadowy room.

'It is very late,' she said, 'you must get you gone. It was
compacted between us that ever you would get you gone
early.'

'Aye, I would not have thee shamed,' he said. He
spoke upwards, slowly and luxuriously, his head so softly
pillowed, his eyes gazing at the ceiling. He had never been
so easy in two years past. 'I remember that was the occasion
of our pact. I did wooe thee in an apple orchard to the
grunting of hogs.'

'Get you gone,' she said; 'buy me a favour against the
morning.'

'Why,' he said, 'I am a very rich lord. I have lands in
Kent now. I will buy thee such a gown . . . such a gown . . .
The hogs grunted. . . . There is a song about it. . . . Let me
go to buy thy gown. Aye, now, presently. I remember a
great many things. As thus . . . there is a song of a lady
loved a swine. Honey, said she, and hunc, said he.'

Whilst she listened a great many thoughts came into her
mind—of their youth at home, where indeed, to the grunting of hogs, he had wooed her when she came out from
conning her Plautus with the Magister. And at the same
time it troubled her to consider where the young Poins
had bestowed himself. Maybe he was dead; maybe he lay
in a faint.

'It was in our pact,' she said to Culpepper, 'that you
should get you gone ever when I would have it.'

'Aye, sure, it was in our pact,' he said.

He closed his eyes as if he would fall asleep, being very
weary and come to his desired haven. Above his closed
eyes Katharine threw the key of her antechamber on to the
bed. She pointed with her hand to that door that the Lady
Rochford should undo. If she could get her cousin through
that door—and now he was in the mood—if she could but
get him through there and out at the door beyond the Big
Room into the corridor, before her guard came back. . .

But the Lady Rochford was leaning far out beyond the window-sill and did not see her gesture.

Culpepper muttered—

'Ah; well; aye; even so——' And from the window came a scream that tore the air—

'The King! the King!'

And immediately it was as if the life of a demon had possessed Culpepper in all his limbs.

'Merciful God!' the Queen cried out. 'I am patient.'

Culpepper had writhed from her till he sat up, but she hollowed her hand around his throat. His head she forced back till she held it upon the floor, and whilst he writhed with his legs she knelt upon his chest with one knee. He screamed out words like: 'Bawd,' and 'Ilcock,' and 'Hecate,' and the Lady Rochford screamed—

'The King comes! the King comes!'

Then Katharine said within herself—

'Is it this to be a Queen?'

She set both her hands upon his neck and pressed down the whole weight of her frame, till the voice died in his throat. His body stirred beneath her knee, convulsively, so that it was as if she rode a horse. His eyes, as slowly he strangled, glared hideously at the ceiling, from which the carven face of a Queen looked down into them. At last he lay still, and Katharine Howard rose up.

She ran at the old woman—

'God forgive me if I have killed my cousin,' she said. 'I am certain that now He will forgive me if I slay thee.' And she had Culpepper's dagger in her hand.

'For,' she said, 'I stand for Christ His cause: I will not be undone by meddlers. Hold thy peace!'

The Lady Rochford opened her mouth to speak.

'Hold thy peace!' the Queen said again, and she lifted up the dagger. 'Speak not. Do as I bid thee. Answer me when I ask. For this I swear as I am the Queen that, since I have the power to slay whom I will and none question it, I will slay thee if thou do not my bidding.'

The old woman trembled lamentably.

'Where is the King come to?' the Queen said.

'Even to the great gate; he is out of sight,' was her answer.

'Come now,' the Queen commanded. 'Let us drag my cousin behind my table.'

'Shall he be hidden there?' the Lady Rochford cried out. 'Let us cast him from the window.'

'Hold your peace,' the Queen cried out. 'Speak you never one word more. But come!'

She took her cousin by the arm, the Lady Rochford took him by the other and they dragged him, inert and senseless, into the shadow of the Queen's mirror table.

'Pray God the King comes soon,' the Queen said. She stood above her cousin and looked down upon him. A great pitifulness came into her face.

'Loosen his shirt,' she said. 'Feel if his heart beats!'

The Lady Rochford had a face full of fear and repulsion.

'Loosen his shirt. Feel if his heart beats,' the Queen said. 'And oh!' she added, 'woe shall fall upon thee if he be dead.'

She reflected a moment to think upon how long it should be ere the King came to her door. Then she raised her chair, and sat down at her mirror. For one minute she set her face into her hands; then she began to straighten herself, and with her hands behind her to tighten the laces of her dress.

'For,' she continued to Lady Rochford, 'I do hold thee more guilty of his death than himself. He is but a drunkard in his cups, thou a palterer in sobriety.'

She set her cap upon her head and smoothed the hair beneath it. In all her movements there was a great swiftness and decision. She set the jewel in her cap, the pomander at her side, the chain around her neck, the jewel at her breast.

'His heart beats,' the Lady Rochford said, from her knees at Culpepper's side.

'Then thank the saints,' Katharine answered, 'and do up again his shirt.'

She hurried in her attiring, and uttered engrossed commands.

'Kneel thou there by his side. If he stir or mutter before the King be in and the door closed, put thy hand across his mouth.'

'But the King——' the Lady Rochford said. 'And——'

'Merciful God!' Katharine cried out again. 'I am the Queen. Kneel there.'

The Lady Rochford trembled down upon her knees; she was in fear for her life by the axe if the King came in.

'I thank God that the King is come,' the Queen said. 'If he had not, this man must have gone from hence in the sight of other men. So I will pardon thee for having cried out if now thou hold him silent till the King be in.'

There came from very near a blare of trumpets. Katharine rose up, and went again to gaze upon her cousin. The dagger she laid upon her table.

'He may hold still yet,' she said. 'But I charge you that you muzzle him if he move or squeak.'

There came great blows upon the door, and through the heavy wood, the Ha-ha of many voices. Slowly the Queen moved to the bed, and from it took the key where she had thrown it. There came again the heavy knocking, and she unlocked the door, slowly still.

In the corridor there were many torches, and beneath them the figure of the King in scarlet. Behind him was Norfolk all in black and with his yellow face, and Cranmer in black and with his anxious eyes, and behind them many other lords. The King came in, and, slow and stately, the Queen went down on her knees to greet him. The torch-light shone upon her jewels and her garments; her fair face was immobile, and her eyes upon the ground. The King raised her up, bent his knee to her, and kissed her on the hands, and so, turning to the men without, he uttered, roundly and fully, and his cheeks were ruddy with joy, and his eyes smiled—

'My lords, I am beholden to the King o' Scots. For had

he met me I had not yet been here. Get you to your beds;
I could wish ye had such wives——'

'The King! the King!' a voice muttered.

Henry said—

'Ha, who spoke?'

There was a faint squeak, a dull rustle.

'My cousin Kat——' the voice said.

The King said—

'Ha!' again, and incredulous and haughty he raised his
brows.

Above the mirror, in the great light of the candles, there
showed the pale face, the fishy, wide-open and bewildered
eyes of Culpepper. His hair was dishevelled in points; his
mouth was open in amazement. He uttered—

'The King!' as if that were the most astonishing thing,
and, standing behind the table, staggered and clutched the
arras to sustain himself.

Henry said—

'Ha! Treason!'

But Katharine whispered at his ear—

'No; this my cousin is distraught. Speak on to the lords.'

In the King's long pause several lords said aloud—

'The King cried "Treason!" Draw your swords!'

Then the King cast his cap upon the ground.

'By God!' he said. 'What marlocking is this? Is it
general joy that emboldens ye to this license? God help
me!' he said, and he stamped his foot upon the ground—
'Body of God!' And many other oaths he uttered. Then,
with a sudden clutching at his throat, he called out—

'Well! well! I pardon ye. For no doubt to some that be
young—and to some that be old too—it is an occasion for
mummeries and japes when a good man cometh home to
his dame.'

He looked round upon Culpepper. The Queen's cousin
stood, his jaw still hanging wide, and his body crumpled
back against the arras. He was hidden from them all by
wall and door, but Henry could not judge how long he
would there remain. Riding through the night he had

conned a speech that he would have said at the Queen's door, and at the times of joy and graciousness he loved to deliver great speeches. But there he said only—

'Why, God keep you. I thank such of you as were with me upon the campaign and journey. Now this campaign and journey is ended—I dissolve you each to his housing and bed. Farewell. Be as content as I be!'

And, with his great hand he swung to the heavy door.

PART THREE

THE DWINDLING MELODY

I

THE Lady Rochford lay back upon the floor in a great faint.

'Heaven help me!' the Queen said. 'I had rather she had played the villain than been such a palterer.' She glided to the table and picked up the dagger that shone there beneath Culpepper's nose. 'Take even this,' she said to the King. 'It is an ill thing to bestow. Sword he hath none.'

Having had such an estimation of his good wife's wit that, since he would not have her think him a dullard, he passed over the first question that he would have asked, such as, 'I think this be thy cousin and how came he here?'

'Would he have slain me?' he asked instead, as if it were a little thing.

'I do not think so,' Katharine said. 'Maybe it was me he would have slain.'

'Body of God!' the King said sardonically. 'He cometh for no cheap goods.'

He had so often questioned his wife of this cousin of hers that he had his measure indifferent well.

'Why,' the Queen said, 'I do not know that he would have slain me. Maybe it was to save me from dragons that he came with his knife. He was, I think, with the Archbishop's men and came here very drunk. I would pray your Highness' Grace to punish him not over much for he is my mother's nephew and the only friend I had when I was very poor and a young child.'

The King hung his head on his chest, and his rustic eyes surveyed the ground.

541

'I would have you to think,' she said, 'that he has been among evil men that advised and prompted him thus to assault my door. They would ruin and undo him and me.'

'Well I know it,' Henry said. He rubbed his hand up his left side, opened it and dropped it again—a trick he had when he thought deeply.

'The Archbishop,' he said, 'babbled somewhat—I know not what—of a cousin of thine that was come from the Scots, he thought, without leave or license.'

'But how to get him hence, that my foes triumph not?' the Queen said, 'for I would not have them triumph.'

'I do think upon it,' the King said.

'You are better at it than I,' she answered.

Culpepper stood there at gaze, as if he were a corpse about which they talked. But the speaking of the Queen to another man excited him to gurgle and snarl in his throat like an ape. Then another mood coming into the channels of his brain—

'It was the King my cousin Kate did marry. This then is the Queen; I had pacted with myself to forget this Queen.' He spoke straight out before him with the echo of thoughts that he had had during his exile.

'Ho!' the King said and smote his thigh. 'It is plain what to do,' and in spite of his scarlet and his bulk he had the air of a heavy but very cunning peasant. He reflected for a little more.

'It fits very well,' he brought out. 'This man must be richly rewarded.'

'Why,' Katharine said; 'I had nigh strangled him. It makes me tremble to think how nigh I had strangled him. I would well he were rewarded.'

The King considered his wife's cousin.

'Sirrah,' he said, 'we believe that thou canst not kneel, or kneeling, couldst not well again arise.'

Culpepper regarded him with wide, blue, and uncomprehending eyes.

'So, thou standing as thou makest shift to do, we do make thee the keeper of this our Queen's ante-room.'

He spoke with a pleasant and ironical glee, since it joyed him thus to gibe at one that had loved his wife. He—with his own prowess—had carried her off.

'Master Culpepper,' he said—'or Sir Thomas—for I remember to have knighted you—if you can walk, now walk.'

Culpepper muttered—

'The King! Why the King did wed my cousin Kat!'

And again—

'I must be circumspect. Oh aye, I must be circumspect or all is lost.' For that was one of the things which in Scotland he had again and again impressed upon himself. 'But in Lincoln, in bygone times, of a summer's night——'

'Poor Tom!' the Queen said; 'once this fellow did wooe me.'

Great tears gathered in Culpepper's eyes. They overflowed and rolled down his cheeks.

'In the apple-orchard,' he said, 'to the grunting of hogs ... for the hogs were below the orchard wall...'

The King was pleased to think that it had been in his power to raise this lady an infinite distance above the wooing of this poor lout. It gave him an interlude of comedy. But though he set his hands on his hips and chuckled, he was a man too ready for action to leave much time for enjoyment.

'Why weep?' he said to Culpepper. 'We have advanced thee to the Queen's ante-chamber. Come up thither.'

He approached to Culpepper behind the mirror table and caught him by the arm. The poor drunkard, his face pallid, shrank away from this great bulk of shining scarlet. His eyes moved lamentably round the chamber and rested first upon Katharine, then upon the King.

'Which of us was it you would ha' killed?' the King said, to show the Queen how brave he was in thus handling a madman. And, being very strong, he dragged the swaying drunkard, who held back and whose head wagged on his shoulders, towards the door.

'Guard ho!' he called out, and before the door there stood three of his own men in scarlet and with pikes.

'Ho, where is the Queen's door-ward?' he called with a great voice. Before him, from the door side, there came the young Poins; his face was like chalk; he had a bruise above his eyes; his knees trembled beneath him.

'Ho thou!' the King said, 'who art thou that would hinder my messenger from coming to the Queen?'

He stood back upon his feet; he clutched the drunkard in his great fist; his eyes started dreadfully.

The young Poins' lips moved, but no sound came out.

'This was my messenger,' the King said, 'and you hindered him. Body of God! Body of God!' and he made his voice to tremble as if with rage, whilst he told this lie to save his wife's fair fame. 'Where have you been? Where have you tarried? What treason is this? For either you knew this was my messenger—as well I would have you know that he is—and it was treason and death to stay him. Or, if because he was drunk and speechless—as well he might be having travelled far and with expedition—ye did not know he was my messenger; then wherefore did ye not run to raise all the castle for succour?'

The young Poins pointed to the wound above his eye and then to the ground of the corridor. He would signify that Culpepper had struck him, and that there, on the ground, he had lain senseless.

'Ho!' the King said, for he was willing to know how many men in that castle had wind of this mischance. 'You lay not there all this while. When I came here along, you stood here by the door in your place.'

The young Poins fell upon his knees. He shook more violently than a naked man on a frosty day. For here indeed was the centre of his treason, since Lascelles had bidden him stay there, once Culpepper was in the Queen's room, and to say later that there the Queen had bidden him stay whilst she had her lover. And now, before the King's tremendous presence, he had the fear at his heart that the King knew this.

'Wherefore! wherefore!' the King thundered, 'wherefore didst not cry out—cry out—"Treason, Raise the watch!"? Hail out aloud?'

He waited, silent for a long time. The three pikemen leaned upon their pikes; and now Culpepper had fallen against the door-post, where the King held him up. And behind his back the Queen marvelled at the King's ready wit. This was the best stroke that ever she had known him do. And the Lady Rochford lay where she had feigned to faint, straining her ears.

With all these ears listening for his words the young Poins knelt, his teeth chattering like burning wood that crackles.

'Wherefore? wherefore?' the King cried again.

Half inaudibly, his eyes upon the ground, the boy mumbled, 'It was to save the Queen from scandal!'

The King let his jaw fall, in a fine aping of amazement. Then, with the huge swiftness of a bull, he threw Culpepper towards one of the guards, and, leaning over, had the kneeling boy by the throat.

'Scandal!' he said. 'Body of God! Scandal!' And the boy screamed out, and raised his hands to hide the King's intolerable great face that blazed down over his eyes.

The huge man cast him from him, so that he fell over backwards, and lay upon his side.

'Scandal!' the King cried out to his guards. 'Here is a pretty scandal! That a King may not send a messenger to his wife withouten scandal! God help me . . .'

He stood suddenly again over the boy as if he would trample him to a shapeless pulp. But, trembling there, he stepped back.

'Up, bastard!' he called out. 'Run as ye never ran. Fetch hither the Lord d'Espahn and His Grace of Canterbury, that should have ordered these matters.'

The boy stumbled to his knees, and then, a flash of scarlet, ran, his head down, as if eagles were tearing at his hair.

The King turned upon his guard.

'Ho!' he said, 'you, Jenkins, stay here with this my

knight cousin. You, Cale and Richards, run to fetch a launderer that shall set a mattress in the ante-chamber for this my cousin to lie on. For this my cousin is the Queen's chamber-ward, and shall there lie when I am here, if so be I have occasion for a messenger at night.'

The two guards ran off, striking upon the ground before them as they ran the heavy staves of their pikes. This noise was intended to warn all to make way for his Highness' errand-bearers.

'Why,' the King said pleasantly to Jenkins, a guard with a blond and shaven face whom he liked well, 'let us set this gentleman against the wall in the ante-room till his bed be come. He hath earned gentle usage, since he hasted much, bringing my message from Scotland to the Queen, and is very ill.'

So, helping his guard gently to conduct the drunkard into his wife's dark ante-room, the King came out again to his wife.

'Is it well done?' he asked.

'Marvellous well done,' she answered.

'I am the man for these difficult times!' he answered, and was glad.

The Queen sighed a little. For if she admired and wondered at her lord's power skilfully to have his way, it made her sad to think—as she must think—that so devious was man's work.

'I would,' she said, 'that it was not to such an occasion that I spurred thee.'

Her eyes, being cast downwards, fell upon the Lady Rochford, by the table.

'Ho, get up,' she cried. 'You have feigned fainting long enough. But for you all this had been more easy. I would have you relieve mine eyes of the sight of your face.' She moved to aid the old woman to rise, but before she was upon her knees there stood without the door both the Lord d'Espahn and the Archbishop. They had waited just beyond the corridor-end with a great many of the other lords, all afraid of mysteries they knew not what, and thus it was that they came so soon upon the young Poins' summoning.

II

The King thought fit to change his mood, so that it was with uplifted brows and a quizzing smile at the corners of his mouth that for a minute he greeted these frightened lords in the doorway. They stood there silent, the Archbishop very dejected, the Lord d'Espahn, with his grey beard, very erect and ruddy featured.

'Why, God help me,' the King said, 'what make of Court is this of mine where a King may not send a messenger to his wife?'

The Archbishop swallowed in his throat; the Lord d'Espahn did not speak but gazed before him.

'You shall tell me what befell, for I am ignorant,' the King said; 'but first I will tell you what I do know.

'Why, come out with me into the corridor, wife,' he cried over his shoulder. 'For it is not fitting that these lords come into thy apartment. I will walk with them and talk.'

He took the Archbishop by the elbow and the Lord d'Espahn by the upper arm, and, leaning upon them, propelled them gently before him.

'Thus it was,' he said; 'this cousin of my wife's was in the King o' Scots' good town of Edinboro'. And, being there, he was much upon my conscience—for I would not have a cousin of my wife's be there in exile, he being one that formerly much fended for her . . .'

He spoke out his words and repeated these things for his own purposes, the Queen following behind. When they were come to the corridor-end, there he found, as he had thought, a knot of lords and gentlemen, babbling with their ears pricked up.

'Nay, stay,' he said, 'this is a matter that all may hear.'

There were there the Duke of Norfolk and his son, young Surrey with the vacant mouth, Sir Henry Wriothesley with the great yellow beard, the Lord Dacre of the North, the old knight Sir N. Rochford, Sir Henry Peel of these parts, with a many of their servants, amongst them Lascelles. Most of them were in scarlet or purple, but many were in black. The Earl of Surrey had the Queen's favour of a crowned rose in his bonnet, for he was of her party. The gallery opened out there till it was as big as a large room, broad and low-ceiled, and lit with torches in irons at the angles of it. On rainy days the Queen's maids were here accustomed to play at stool-ball.

'This is a matter that all may hear,' the King said, 'and some shall render account.' He let the Lord d'Espahn and the Archbishop go, so that they faced him. The Queen looked over his shoulder.

'As thus . . .' he said.

And he repeated how it had lain upon his conscience and near his heart that the Queen's good cousin languished in the town of Edinburgh.

'And how near we came to Edinboro' those of ye that were with me can make account.'

And, lying there, he had taken occasion to send a messenger with others that went to the King o' Scots—to send a messenger with letters unto this T. Culpepper. One letter was to bid him hasten home unto the Queen, and one was a letter that he should bear.

'For,' said the King, 'we thought thus—as ye wist—that the King o' Scots would come obedient to our summoning and that there we should lie some days awaiting and entertaining him. Thus did I wish to send my Queen swift message of our faring, and I was willing that this, her cousin and mine, should be my postman and messenger. For he should—I bade him—set sail in a swift ship for these coasts and so come quicker than ever a man might by land.'

He paused to observe the effect of his words, but no lord spoke though some whispered amongst themselves.

'Now,' he said, 'what stood within my letter to the Queen was this, after salutations, that she should reward this her cousin that in the aforetime had much fended for her when she was a child. For I was aware how, out of a great delicacy and fear of nepotism, such as was shown by certain of the Popes now dead, she raised up none of her relations and blood, nor none that before had aided her when she was a child and poor. But I was willing that this should be otherwise, and they be much helped that before had helped her since now she helpeth me and assuageth my many and fell labours.'

He paused and went a step back that he might stand beside the Queen, and there, before them all, Katharine was most glad that she had again set on all her jewels and was queen-like. She had composed her features, and gazed before her over their heads, her hands being folded in the lap of her gown.

'Now,' the King said, 'this letter of mine was a little thing—but great maybe, since it bore my will. Yet'—and he made his voice minatory—'in these evil and tickle times well it might have been that that letter held delicate news. Then all my plots had gone to ruin. How came it that some of ye—I know not whom!—thus letted and hindered my messenger?'

He had raised his voice very high. He stayed it suddenly, and some there shivered.

He uttered balefully, 'Anan!'

'As Christ is my Saviour,' the Lord d'Espahn said, 'I, since I am the Queen's Marshal, am answerable in this, as well I know. Yet never saw I this man till to-night at supper. He would have my seat then, and I gave it him. Ne let ne hindrance had he of me, but went his way where and when he would.'

'You did very well,' the King said. 'Who else speaks?'

The Archbishop looked over his shoulder, and with a dry mouth uttered, 'Lascelles!'

Lascelles, deft and blond and gay, shouldered his way through that unwilling crowd, and fell upon his knees.

'Of this I know something,' he said; 'and if any have offended, doubtless it is I, though with good will.'

'Well, speak!' the King said.

Lascelles recounted how the Queen, riding out, had seen afar this gentleman lying amid the heather.

'And if she should not know him who was her cousin, how should we who are servants?' he said. But, having heard that the Queen would have this poor, robbed way-farer tended and comforted, he, Lascelles, out of the love and loyalty he owed her Grace, had so tended and so comforted him that he had given up to him his own bed and board. But it was not till that day that, Culpepper being washed and apparelled—not till that day a little before supper, had he known him for Culpepper, the Queen's cousin. So he had gone with him that night to the banquet-hall, and there had served him, and, after, had attended him with some lords and gentles. But, at the last, Cul-pepper had shaken them off and bidden them leave him.

'And who were we, what warrants had we, to restrain the Queen's noble cousin?' he finished. 'And, as for letters, I never saw one, though all his apparel, in rags, was in my hands. I think he must have lost this letter amongst the robbers he fell in with. But what I could do, I did for love of the Queen's Grace, who much hath favoured me.'

The King studied his words. He looked at the Queen's face and then at those of the lords before him.

'Why, this tale hath a better shewing,' he said. 'Herein appeareth that none, save the Queen's door-ward, came ever against this good knight and cousin of mine. And, since this knight was in liquor, and not overwise sensible—as well he might be after supping in moors and deserts—maybe that door-ward had his reasonable reasonings.'

He paused again, and looking upon the Queen's face for a sign:

'If it be thus, it is well,' he said, 'I will pardon and assoil you all, if later it shall appear that this is the true truth.'

Lascelles whispered in the Archbishop's ear, and Cran-mer uttered—

'The witnesses be here to prove it, if your Highness will.'

'Why,' the King said, 'it is late enough,' and he leered at

Cranmer, for whom he had an affection. He looked again upon the Queen to see how fair she was and how bravely she bore herself, upright and without emotion. 'This wife of mine,' he said, 'is ever of the pardoning side. If ye had so injured me I had been among ye with fines and amercements. But she, I perceive, will not have it so, and I am too glad to be smiled upon now to cross her will. So, get you gone and sleep well. But, before you go, I will have you listen to some words . . .'

He cleared his throat, and in his left hand took the Queen's.

'Know ye,' he said, 'that I am as proud of this my Queen as was ever mother of her first-born child. For lo, even as the Latin poet saith, that, upon bearing a child, many evil women are led to repentance and right paths, so have I, your King, been led towards righteousness by wedding of this lady. For I tell you that, but for certain small hindrances—and mostly this treacherous disloyalty of the King o' Scots that thus with his craven marrow hath featorously dallied to look upon my face—but for that and other small things there had gone forth this night through the dark to the Bishop of Rome certain tidings that, please God, had made you and me and all this land the gladdest that be in Christendom. And this I tell you, too, that though by this misadventure and fear of the King o' Scots, these tidings have been delayed, yet is it only for a little space and, full surely, that day cometh. And for this you shall give thanks first to God and then to this royal lady here. For she, before all things, having the love of God in her heart, hath brought about this desired consummation. And this I say, to her greater praise, here in the midmost of you all, that it be noised unto the utmost corners of the world how good a Queen the King hath taken to wife.'

The Queen had stood very motionless in the bright illuminations and dancings of the torches. But at the news of delay, through the King of Scots, a spasm of pain and concern came into her face. So that, if her features did not again move they had in them a savour of anguish, her eye-brows drooping, and the corners of her mouth.

'And now, good-night!' the King pursued with raised tones. 'If ever ye slept well since these troublous times began, now ye may sleep well in the drowsy night. For now, in this my reign, are come the shortening years like autumn days. Now I will have such peace in land as cometh to the husbandman. He hath ingarnered his grain; he hath barned his fodder and straw; his sheep are in the byres and in the stalls his oxen. So, sitteth he by his fire-side with wife and child, and hath no fear of winter. Such a man am I, your King, who in the years to come shall rest in peace.'

The lords and gentlemen made their reverences, bows and knees; they swept round in their coloured assembly, and the Queen stood very tall and straight, watching their departure with saddened eyes.

The King was very gay and caught her by the waist.

'God help me, it is very late,' he said. 'Hearken!'

From above the corridor there came the drowsy sound of the clock.

'Thy daughter hath made her submission,' the Queen said. 'I had thought this was the gladdest day in my life.'

'Why, so it is,' he said, 'as now day passeth to day.' The clock ceased. 'Every day shall be glad,' he said, 'and gladder than the rest.'

At her chamber door he made a bustle. He would have the Queen's women come to untire her, a leech to see to Culpepper's recovery. He was willing to drink mulled wine before he slept. He was afraid to talk with his wife of delaying his letter to Rome. That was why he had told the news before her to his lords.

He fell upon the Lady Rochford that stood, not daring to go, within the Queen's room. He bade her sit all night by the bedside of T. Culpepper; he reviled her for a craven coward that had discountenanced the Queen. She should pay for it by watching all night, and woe betide her if any had speech with T. Culpepper before the King rose.

III

Down in the lower castle, the Archbishop was accustomed, when he undressed, to have with him neither priest nor page, but only, when he desired to converse of public matters—as now he did—his gentleman, Lascelles. He knelt above his kneeling-stool of black wood; he was telling his beads before a great crucifix with an ivory Son of God upon it. His chamber had bare white walls, his bed no curtains, and all the other furnishing of the room was a great black lectern whereto there was chained a huge Book of the Holy Writ that had his Preface. The tears were in his eyes as he muttered his prayers; he glanced upwards at the face of his Saviour, who looked down with a pallid, uncoloured face of ivory, the features shewing a great agony so that the mouth was opened. It was said that this image, that came from Italy, had had a face serene, before the Queen Katharine of Aragon had been put away. Then it had cried out once, and so remained ever lachrymose and in agony.

'God help me, I cannot well pray,' the Archbishop said. 'The peril that we have been in stays with me still.'

'Why, thank God that we are come out of it very well,' Lascelles said. 'You may pray and then sleep more calm than ever you have done this sennight.'

He leant back against the reading-pulpit, and had his arm across the Bible as if it had been the shoulder of a friend.

'Why,' the Archbishop said, 'this is the worst day ever I have been through since Cromwell fell.'

'Please it your Grace,' his confidant said, 'it shall yet turn out the best.'

The Archbishop faced round upon his knees; he had taken off the jewel from before his breast, and, with his chain of Chaplain of the George, it dangled across the corner of the fald-stool. His coat was unbuttoned at the neck, his robe open, and it was manifest that his sleeves of lawn were but sleeves, for in the opening was visible, harsh and grey, the shirt of hair that night and day he wore.

'I am weary of this talk of the world,' he said. 'Pray you begone and leave me to my prayers.'

'Please it your Grace to let me stay and hearten you,' Lascelles said, and he was aware that the Archbishop was afraid to be alone with the white Christ. 'All your other gentry are in bed. I shall watch your sleep, to wake you if you cry out.'

And in his fear of Cromwell's ghost that came to him in his dreams, the Archbishop sighed—

'Why stay, but speak not. Y'are over bold.'

He turned again to the wall; his beads clicked; he sighed and remained still for a long time, a black shadow, huddled together in a black gown, sighing before the white and lamenting image that hung above him.

'God help me,' he said at last. 'Tell me why you say this is *dies felix*?'

Lascelles, who smiled for ever and without mirth, said—

'For two things: firstly, because this letter and its sending are put off. And secondly, because the Queen is—patently and to all people—proved lewd.'

The Archbishop swung his head round upon his shoulders.

'You dare not say it!' he said.

'Why, the late Queen Katharine from Aragon was accounted a model of piety, yet all men know she was over fond with her confessor,' Lascelles smiled.

'It is an approved lie and slander,' the Archbishop said.

'It served mightily well in pulling down that Katharine,' his confidant answered.

'One day'—the Archbishop shivered within his robes—'the account and retribution for these lies shall be to be paid. For well we know, you, I, and all of us, that these be falsities and cozenings.'

'Marry,' Lascelles said, 'of this Queen it is now sufficiently proved true.'

The Archbishop made as if he washed his hands.

'Why,' Lascelles said, 'what man shall believe it was by chance and accident that she met her cousin on these moors? She is not a compass that pointeth, of miraculous power, true North.'

'No good man shall believe what you do say,' the Archbishop cried out.

'But a multitude of indifferent will,' Lascelles answered.

'God help me,' the Archbishop said, 'what a devil you are that thus hold out and hold out for ever hopes.'

'Why,' Lascelles said, 'I think you were well helped that day that I came into your service. It was the Great Privy Seal that bade me serve you and commended me.'

The Archbishop shivered at that name.

'What an end had Thomas Cromwell!' he said.

'Why, such an end shall not be yours whilst this King lives, so well he loves you,' Lascelles answered.

The Archbishop stood upon his feet; he raised his hands above his head.

'Begone! Begone!' he cried. 'I will not be of your evil schemes.'

'Your Grace shall not,' Lascelles said very softly, 'if they miscarry. But when it is proven to the hilt that this Queen is a very lewd woman—and proven it shall be—your Grace may carry an accusation to the King——'

Cranmer said—

'Never! never! Shall I come between the lion and his food?'

'It were better if your Grace would carry the accusation,' Lascelles uttered nonchalantly, 'for the King will better hearken to you than to any other. But another man will do it too.'

'I will not be of this plotting,' the Archbishop cried out. 'It is a very wicked thing!' He looked round at the white Christ that, upon the dark cross, bent anguished brows upon him. 'Give me strength,' he said.

'Why, your Grace shall not be of it,' Lascelles answered, 'until it is proven in the eyes of your Grace—ay, and in the eyes of some of the Papist Lords—as, for instance, her very uncle—that this Queen was evil in her life before the King took her, and that she hath acted very suspicious in the aftertime.'

'You shall not prove it to the Papist Lords,' Cranmer said. 'It is a folly.'

He added vehemently—

'It is a wicked plot. It is a folly too. I will not be of it.'

'This is a very fortunate day,' Lascelles said. 'I think it is proven to all discerning men that that letter to him of Rome shall never be sent.'

'Why, it is as plain as the truths of the Six Articles,' Cranmer remonstrated, 'that it shall be sent to-morrow or the next day. Get you gone! This King hath but the will of the Queen to guide him, and all her will turns upon that letter. Get you gone!'

'Please it your Grace,' the spy said, 'it is very manifest that with the Queen so it is. But with the King it is otherwise. He will pleasure the Queen if he may. But—mark me well—for this is a subtle matter——'

'I will not mark you,' the Archbishop said. 'Get you gone and find another master. I will not hear you. This is the very end.'

Lascelles moved his arm from the Bible. He bent his form to a bow—he moved till his hand was on the latch of the door.

'Why, continue,' the Archbishop said. 'If you have awakened my fears, you shall slake them if you can—for this night I shall not sleep.'

And so, very lengthily, Lascelles unfolded his view of the King's nature. For, said he, if this alliance with the Pope should come, it must be an alliance with the Pope and the Emperor Charles. For the King of France was an atheist, as all men knew. And an alliance with the Pope and the Emperor must be an alliance against France. But the King o' Scots was the closest ally that Francis had, and never should the King dare to wage war upon Francis till the King o' Scots was placated or wooed by treachery to be a prisoner, as the King would have made him if James had come into England to the meeting. Well would the King, to save his soul, placate and cosset his wife. But that he never dare do whilst James was potent at his back.

And again, Lascelles said, well knew the Archbishop that the Duke of Norfolk and his following were the ancient friends of France. If the Queen should force the King to this Imperial League, it must turn Norfolk and the Bishop of Winchester for ever to her bitter foes in that land. And along with them all the Protestant nobles and all the Papists too that had lands of the Church.

The Archbishop had been marking his words very eagerly. But suddenly he cried out—

'But the King! The King! What shall it boot if all these be against her so the King be but for her?'

'Why,' Lascelles said, 'this King is not a very stable man. Still, man he is, a man very jealous and afraid of fleers and flouts. If we can show him—I do accede to it that after what he hath done to-night it shall not be easy, but we may accomplish it—if before this letter is sent we may show him that all his land cries out at him and mocks him with a great laughter because of his wife's evil ways—why then, though in his heart he may believe her as innocent as you or I do now, it shall not be long before he shall put her away from him. Maybe he shall send her to the block.'

'God help me,' Cranmer said. 'What a hellish scheme is this.'

He pondered for a while, standing upright and fraily thrusting his hand into his bosom.

'You shall never get the King so to believe,' he said; 'this is an idle invention. I will none of it.'

'Why, it may be done, I do believe,' Lascelles said, 'and greatly it shall help us.'

'No, I will none of it,' the Archbishop said. 'It is a foul scheme. Besides, you must have many witnesses.'

'I have some already,' Lascelles said, 'and when we come to London Town I shall have many more. It was not for nothing that the Great Privy Seal commended me.'

'But to make the King,' Cranmer uttered, as if he were aghast and amazed, 'to make the King—this King who knoweth that his wife hath done no wrong—who knoweth it so well as to-night he hath proven—to make *him*, him, to put her away . . . why, the tiger is not so fell, nor the Egyptian worm preyeth not on its kind. This is an imagination so horrible——'

'Please it your Grace,' Lascelles said softly, 'what beast or brute hath your Grace ever seen to betray its kind as man will betray brother, son, father, or consort?'

The Archbishop raised his hands above his head.

'What lesser bull of the herd, or lesser ram, ever so played traitor to his leader as Brutus played to Cæsar Julius? And these be times less noble.'

PART FOUR

THE END OF THE SONG

I

THE Queen was at Hampton, and it was the late autumn. She had been sad since they came from Pontefract, for it had seemed more than ever apparent that the King's letter to Rome must be ever delayed in the sending. Daily, at night, the King swore with great oaths that the letter must be sent and his soul saved. He trembled to think that if then he died in his bed he must be eternally damned, and she added her persuasions, such as that each soul that died in his realms before that letter was sent went before the Throne of Mercy unshriven and unhouselled, so that their burden of souls grew very great. And in the midnights, the King would start up and cry that all was lost and himself accursed.

And it appeared that he and his house were accursed in these days, for when they were come back to Hampton, they found the small Prince Edward was very ill. He was swollen all over his little body, so that the doctors said it was a dropsy. But how, the King cried, could it be a dropsy in so young a child and one so grave and so nurtured and tended? Assuredly it must be some marvel wrought by the saints to punish him, or by the Fiend to tempt him. And so he would rave, and cast tremulous hands above his head. And he would say that God, to punish him, would have of him his dearest and best.

And when the Queen urged him, therefore, to make his peace with God, he would cry out that it was too late. God would make no peace with him. For if God were minded to have him at peace, wherefore would He not smoothe the

way to this reconciliation with His vicegerent that sat at
Rome in Peter's chair? There was no smoothing of that
way—for every day there arose new difficulties and
torments.

The King o' Scots would come into no alliance with
him; the King of France would make no bid for the hand
of his daughter Mary; it went ill with the Emperor in his
fighting with the Princes of Almain and the Schmalkaldners, so that the Emperor would be of the less use as
an ally against France and the Scots.

'Why!' he would cry to the Queen, 'if God in His
Heaven would have me make a peace with Rome, wherefore will He not give victory over a parcel of Lutheran
knaves and swine? Wherefore will He not deliver into my
hands these beggarly Scots and these atheists of France?'

At night the Queen would bring him round to vowing
that first he would make peace with God and trust in His
great mercy for a prosperous issue. But each morning he
would be afraid for his sovereignty; a new letter would
come from Norfolk, who had gone on an embassy to his
French friends, believing fully that the King was minded
to marry to one of them his daughter. But the French King
was not ready to believe this. And the King's eyes grew
red and enraged; he looked no man in the face, not even
the Queen, but glanced aside into corners, uttered blas-
phemies, and said that he—he!—was the head of the
Church and would have no overlord.

The Bishop Gardiner came up from his See in Winchester. But though he was the head of the Papist party in
the realm, the Queen had little comfort in him. For he was
a dark and masterful prelate, and never ceased to urge her
to cast out Cranmer from his archbishopric and to give it
to him. And with him the Lady Mary sided, for she would
have Cranmer's head before all things, since Cranmer it
was that most had injured her mother. Moreover, he was
so incessant in his urging the King to make an alliance
with the Catholic Emperor that at last, about the time that
Norfolk came back from France, the King was mightily

enraged, so that he struck the Bishop of Winchester in the face, and swore that his friend the Kaiser was a rotten plank, since he could not rid himself of a few small knaves of Lutheran princes.

Thus for long the Queen was sad; the little Prince very sick; and the King ate no food, but sat gazing at the victuals, though the Queen cooked some messes for him with her own hand.

One Sunday after evensong, at which Cranmer himself had read prayers, the King came nearly merrily to his supper.

'Ho, chuck,' he said, 'you have your enemies. Here hath been Cranmer weeping to me with a parcel of tales writ on paper.'

He offered it to her to read, but she would not; for, she said, she knew well that she had many enemies, only, very safely she could trust her fame in her Lord's hands.

'Why, you may,' he said, and sat him down at the table to eat, with the paper stuck in his belt. 'Body o' God!' he said. 'If it had been any but Cranmer he had eaten bread in Hell this night. 'A wept and trembled! Body o' God! Body o' God!'

And that night he was more merry before the fire than he had been for many weeks. He had in the music to play a song of his own writing, and afterwards he swore that next day he would ride to London, and then at his council send that which she would have sent to Rome.

'For, for sure,' he said, 'there is no peace in this world for me save when I hear you pray. And how shall you pray well for me save in the old form and fashion?'

He lolled back in his chair and gazed at her.

'Why,' he said, 'it is a proof of the great mercy of the Saviour that He sent you on earth in so fair a guise. For if you had not been so fair, assuredly I had not noticed you. Then would my soul have gone straightway to Hell.'

And he called that the letter to Rome might be brought to him, and read it over in the firelight. He set it in his

belt alongside the other paper, that next day when he came
to London he might lay it in the hands of Sir Thomas
Carter, that should carry it to Rome.

The Queen said: 'Praise God!'

For though she was not set to believe that next day that
letter would be sent, or for many days more, yet it seemed
to her that by little and little she was winning him to her
will.

II

Gardiner, Bishop of Winchester, had builded him a new
tennis court in where his stables had been before poverty
had caused him to sell the major part of his horseflesh. He
called to him the Duke of Norfolk, who was of the Papist
cause, and Sir Henry Wriothesley who was always betwixt
and between, according as the cat jumped, to see this new
building of his that was made of a roofed-in quadrangle
where the stable doors were bricked up or barred to make
the grille.

But though Norfolk and Wriothesley came very early
in the afternoon, while it was yet light, to his house, they
wasted most of the daylight hours in talking of things indifferent before they went to their inspection of this court.
They stood talking in a long gallery beneath very high
windows, and there were several chaplains and young
priests and young gentlemen with them, and most of the
talk was of a bear-baiting that there should be in Smithfield come Saturday. Sir Henry Wriothesley matched seven
of his dogs against the seven best of the Duke's, that they
should the longer hold to the bear once they were on him,
and most of the young gentlemen wagered for Sir Henry's
dogs that he had bred from a mastiff out of Portugal.

But when this talk had mostly died down, and when
already twilight had long fallen, the Bishop said—

'Come, let us visit this new tennis place of mine. I think
I shall show you somewhat that you have not before seen.'

He bade, however, his gentlemen and priests to stay

where they were, for they had all many times seen the court or building. When he led the way, prelatical and black, for the Duke and Wriothesley, into the lower corridors of his house, the priests and young gentlemen bowed behind his back, one at the other.

In the courtyard there were four hounds of a heavy and stocky breed that came bounding and baying all round them, so that it was only by vigilance that Gardiner could save Wriothesley's shins, for he was a man that all dogs and children hated.

'Sirs,' the Bishop said, 'these dogs that ye see and hear will let no man but me—not even my grooms or stablemen—pass this yard. I have bred them to that so I may be secret when I will.'

He set the key in the door that was in the bottom wall of the court.

'There is no other door here save that which goes into the stable where the grille is. There I have a door to enter and fetch out the balls that pass there.'

In the court itself it was absolute blackness.

'I trow we may talk very well without lights,' he said. 'Come into this far corner.'

Yet, though there was no fear of being overheard, each of these three stole almost on tiptoe and held his breath, and in the dark and shadowy place they made a more dark and more shadowy patch with their heads all close together.

Suddenly it was as if the Bishop dropped the veil that covered his passions.

'I may well build tennis courts,' he said, and his voice had a ring of wild and malignant passion. 'I may well build courts for tennis play. Nothing else is left for me to do.'

In the blackness no word came from his listeners.

'You too may do the like,' the Bishop said. 'But I would you do it quickly, for soon neither the one nor the other of you but will be stripped so bare that you shall not have enough to buy balls with.'

The Duke made an impatient sound like a drawing in of his breath, but still he spoke no word.

'I tell you, both of you,' the Bishop's voice came, 'that all of us have been fooled. Who was it that helped to set on high this one that now presses us down? I did! I!...

'It was I that called the masque at my house where first the King did see her. It was I that advised her how to bear herself. And what gratitude has been shown me? I have been sent to sequester myself in my see; I have been set to gnaw my fingers as they had been old bones thrown to a dog. Truly, no juicy meats have been my share. Yet it was I set this woman where she sits....'

'I too have my griefs,' the Duke of Norfolk's voice came.

'And I, God wot,' came Wriothesley's.

'Why, you have been fooled,' Gardiner's voice; 'and well you know it. For who was it that sent you both, one after the other, into France thinking that you might make a match between the Lady Royal and the Duke of Orleans? —Who but the Queen?—For well she knew that ye loved the French and their King as they had been your brothers. And well we know now that never in the mind of her, nor in that of the King whom she bewitches and enslaves, was there any thought save that the Lady Royal should be wedded to Spain. So ye are fooled.'

He let his voice sink low; then he raised it again—

'Fooled! Fooled! Fooled! You two and I. For who of your friends the French shall ever believe again word that you utter. And all your goods and lands this Queen will have for the Church, so that she may have utter power with a parcel of new shavelings, that will not withstand her. So all the land will come in to her leash.... We are fooled and ruined, ye and I alike.'

'Well, we know this,' the Duke's voice said distastefully. 'You have no need to rehearse griefs that too well we feel. There is no lord, either of our part or of the other, that would not have her down.'

'But what will ye do?' Gardiner said.

'Nothing may we do!' the voice of Wriothesley with its dismal terror came to their ears. 'The King is too firmly her Highness's man.'

'Her "Highness," ' the Bishop mocked him with a bitter scorn. 'I believe you would yet curry favour with this Queen of straw.'

'It is a man's province to be favourable in the eyes of his Prince,' the buried voice came again. 'If I could win her favour I would. But well ye know there is no way.'

'Ye ha' mingled too much with Lutheran swine,' the Bishop said. 'Now it is too late for you.'

'So it is,' Wriothesley said. 'I think you, Bishop, would have done it too had you been able to make your account of it.'

The Bishop snarled invisibly.

But the voice of Norfolk came malignantly upon them.

'This is all of a piece with your silly schemings. Did I come here to hear ye wrangle? It is peril enow to come here. What will ye do?'

'I will make a pact with him of the other side?' the Bishop said.

'Misery!' the Duke said; 'did I come here to hear this madness? You and Cranmer have sought each other's heads this ten years. Will you seek his aid now? What may he do? He is as rotten a reed as thou or Wriothesley.'

The Bishop cried suddenly with a loud voice—

'Ho, there! Come you out!'

Norfolk set his hand to his sword and so did Wriothesley. It was in both their minds, as it were one thought, that if this was a treason of the Bishop's he should there die.

From the blackness of the wall sides where the grille was there came the sound of a terroring lock and a creaking door.

'God!' Norfolk said; 'who is this?'

There came the sound of breathing of one man who walked with noiseless shoes.

'Have you heard enow to make you believe that these lords' hearts are true to the endeavour of casting the Queen down?'

'I have heard enow,' a smooth voice said. 'I never thought it had been otherwise.'

'Who is this?' Wriothesley said. 'I will know who this is that has heard us.'

'You fool,' Gardiner said; 'this man is of the other side.'

'They have come to you!' Norfolk said.

'To whom else should we come,' the voice answered.

A subtler silence of agitation and thought was between these two men. At last Gardiner said—

'Tell these lords what you would have of us?'

'We would have these promises,' the voice said; 'first, of you, my Lord Duke, that if by our endeavours your brother's child be brought to a trial for unchastity you will in no wise aid her at that trial with your voice or your encouragement.'

'A trial!' and 'Unchastity!' the Duke said. 'This is a winter madness. Ye know that my niece—St Kevin curse her for it—is as chaste as the snow.'

'So was your other niece, Anne Boleyn, for all you knew, yet you dogged her to death,' Gardiner said. 'Then you plotted with Papists; now it is the turn of the Lutherans. It is all one, so we are rid of this pest.'

'Well, I will promise it,' the Duke said. 'Ye knew I would. It was not worth while to ask me.'

'Secondly,' the voice said, 'of you, my Lord Duke, we would have this service: that you should swear your niece is a much older woman than she looks. Say, for instance, that she was in truth not the eleventh but the second child of your brother Edmund. Say that, out of vanity, to make herself seem more forward with the learned tongues when she was a child, she would call herself her younger sister that died in childbed.'

'But wherefore?' the Duke said.

'Why,' Gardiner answered, 'this is a very subtle scheme of this gentleman's devising. He will prove against her certain lewdnesses when she was a child in your mother's house. If then she was a child of ten or so, knowing not evil from good, this might not undo her. But if you can make her seem then eighteen or twenty it will be enough to hang her.'

Norfolk reflected.

'Well, I will say I heard that of her age,' he said; 'but ye had best get nurses and women to swear to these things.'

'We have them now,' the voice said. 'And it will suffice if your Grace will say that you heard these things of old of your brother. For your Grace will judge this woman.'

'Very willingly I will,' Norfolk said; 'for if I do not soon, she will utterly undo both me and all my friends.'

He reflected again.

'Those things will I do and more yet, if you will.'

'Why, that will suffice,' the voice said. It took a new tone in the darkness.

'Now for you, Sir Henry Wriothesley,' it said. 'These simple things you shall promise. Firstly, since you have the ear of the Mayor of London you shall advise him in no way to hinder certain meetings of Lutherans that I shall tell you of later. And, though it is your province so to do, you shall in no wise hinder a certain master printer from printing what broadsides and libels he will against the Queen. For it is essential, if this project is to grow and flourish, that it shall be spread abroad that the Queen did bewitch the King to her will on that night at Pontefract that you remember, when she had her cousin in her bedroom. So broadsides shall be made alleging that by sorcery she induced the King to countenance his own shame. And we have witnesses to swear that it was by appointment, not by chance, that she met with Culpepper upon the moorside. But all that we will have of you is that you will promise these two things—that the Lutherans may hold certain meetings and the broadsides be printed.'

'Those I will promise,' came in Wriothesley's buried voice.

'Then I will no more of you,' the other's words came. They heard his hands feeling along the wall till he came to the door by which he had entered. The Bishop followed him, to let him out by a little door he had had opened for that one night, into the street.

When he came back to the other two and unfolded to them what was the scheme of the Archbishop's man, they agreed that it was a very good plan. Then they fell to considering whether it should not serve their turn to betray this plan at once to the Queen. But they agreed that, if they preserved the Queen, they would be utterly ruined, as they were like to be now, whereas, if it succeeded, they would be much the better off. And, even if it failed, they lost nothing, for it would not readily be believed that they had aided Lutherans, and there were no letters or writings.

So they agreed to abide honourably by their promises— and very certain they were that if clamour enough could be raised against the Queen, the King would be bound into putting her away, though it were against his will.

III

In the Master Printer Badge's house—and he was the uncle of Margot and of the young Poins—there was a great and solemn dissertation towards. For word had been brought that certain strangers come on an embassy from the Duke of Cleves were minded to hear how the citizens of London —or at any rate those of them that held German doctrines—bore themselves towards Schmalkaldnerism and the doctrines of Luther.

It was understood that these strangers were of very high degree—of a degree so high that they might scarce be spoken to by the meaner sort. And for many days messengers had been going between the house of the Archbishop at Lambeth and that of the Master Printer, to school him how this meeting must be conducted.

His old father was by that time dead—having died shortly after his granddaughter Margot had been put away from the Queen's Court—so that the house-place was clear. And of all the old furnishings none remained. There were presses all round the wall, and lockers for men to sit upon.

The table had been cleared away into the printer's chapel; a lectern stood a-midmost of the room, and before the hearth-place, in the very ingle, there was set the great chair in which aforetimes the old man had sat so long.

Early that evening, though already it was dusk, the body of citizens were assembled. Most of them had haggard faces, for the times were evil for men of their persuasion, and nearly all of them were draped in black after the German fashion among Lutherans of that day. They ranged themselves on the lockers along the wall, and with set faces, in a funereal row, they awaited the coming of this great stranger. There were no Germans amongst them, for so, it was given out, he would have it—either because he would not be known by name or for some other reason.

The Master Printer, in the pride of his craft, wore his apron. He stood in the centre of the room facing the hearth-place; his huge arms were bare—for bare-armed he always worked—his black beard was knotted into little curls, his face was so broad that you hardly remarked that his nose was hooked like an owl's beak. And about the man there was an air of sombreness and mystery. He had certain papers on his lectern, and several sheets of the great Bible that he was then printing by the Archbishop's license and command. They sang all together and with loud voices the canticle called 'A Refuge fast is God the Lord.'

Then, with huge gestures of his hands, he uttered the words—

'This is the very word of God,' and began to read from the pages of his Bible. He read first the story of David and Saul, his great voice trembling with ecstasy.

'This David is our King,' he said. 'This Saul that he slew is the Beast of Rome. The Solomon that cometh after shall be the gracious princeling that ye wot of, for already he is wise beyond his years and beyond most grown men.'

The citizens around the walls cried 'Amen.' And because the strangers tarried to come, he called to his journeymen that stood in the inner doorway to bring him the sheets of the Bible whereon he had printed the story of Ehud and Eglon.

'This king that ye shall hear of as being slain,' he cried out, 'is that foul bird the Kaiser Carl, that harries the faithful in Almain. This good man that shall slay him is some German lord. Who he shall be we know not yet; maybe it shall be this very stranger that to-night shall sit to hear us.'

His brethren muttered a low, deep, and uniform prayer that soon, soon the Lord should send them this boon.

But he had not got beyond the eleventh verse of this history before there came from without a sound of trumpets, and through the windows the light of torches and the scarlet of the guard that, it was said, the King had sent to do honour to this stranger.

'Come in, be ye who ye may!' the printer cried to the knockers at his door.

There entered the hugest masked man that they ever had seen. All in black he was, and horrifying and portentous he strode in. His sleeves and shoulders were ballooned after the German fashion, his sword clanked on the tiles. He was a vision of black, for his mask that appeared as big as another man's garment covered all his face, though they could see he had a grey beard when sitting down. He gazed at the fire askance.

He said—his voice was heavy and husky—

'*Gruesset Gott*,' and those of the citizens that had painfully attained to so much of that tongue answered him with—

'*Lobet den Herr im Himmels Reich!*'

He had with him one older man that wore a half-mask, and was trembling and clean-shaven, and one younger, that was English, to act as interpreter when it was needed. He was clean-shaven, too, and in the English habit he appeared thin and tenuous. They said he was a gentleman of the Archbishop's, and that his name was Lascelles.

He opened the meeting with saying that these great strangers were come from beyond the seas, and would hear answers to certain questions. He took a paper from his pouch and said that, in order that he might stick to the points that these strangers would know of, he had written down those questions on that paper.

'How say ye, masters?' he finished. 'Will ye give answers to these questions truly, and of your knowledge?'

'Aye will we,' the printer said, 'for to that end we are gathered here. Is it not so, my masters?'

And the assembly answered—

'Aye, so it is.'

Lascelles read from his paper:

'How is it with this realm of England?'

The printer glanced at the paper that was upon his lectern. He made answer—

'Well! But not over well!'

And at these words Lascelles feigned surprise, lifting his well-shapen and white hand in the air.

'How is this that ye say?' he uttered. 'Are ye all of this tale?'

A deep 'Aye!' came from all these chests. There was one old man that could never keep still. He had huge limbs, a great ruffled poll of grizzling hair, and his legs that were in jerkins of red leather kicked continuously in little convulsions. He peered every minute at some new thing, very closely, holding first his tablets so near that he could see only with one eye, then the whistle that hung round his neck, then a little piece of paper that he took from his poke. He cried out in a deep voice—'Aye! aye! Not over well. Witchcraft and foul weather and rocks, my mates and masters all!' so that he appeared to be a seaman—and indeed he traded to the port of Antwerp, in the Low Countries, where he had learned of some of the Faith.

'Why,' Lascelles said, 'be ye not contented with our goodly King?'

'Never was a better since Solomon ruled in Jewry,' the shipman cried out.

'Is it, then, the Lords of the King's Council that ye are discontented with?'

'Nay, they are goodly men, for they are of the King's choosing,' one answered—a little man with a black pill-hat.

'Why, speak through your leader,' the stranger said heavily from the hearth-place. 'Here is too much skimble-skamble.' The old man beside him leaned over his chair-back and whispered in his ear. But the stranger shook his head heavily. He sat and gazed at the brands. His great hands were upon his knees, pressed down, but now and again they moved as if he were in some agony.

'It is well that ye do as the Lord commandeth,' Lascelles said; 'for in Almain, whence he cometh, there is wont to be a great order and observance.' He held his paper up again to the light. 'Master Printer, answer now to this question: Find ye aught amiss with the judges and justices of this realm?'

'Nay; they do judge indifferent well betwixt cause and cause,' the printer answered from his paper.

'Or with the serjeants, the apparitors, the collectors of taxes, or the Parliament men?'

'These, too, perform indifferent well their appointed tasks,' the printer said gloomily.

'Or is it with the Church of this realm that ye find fault?'

'Body of God!' the stranger said heavily.

'Nay!' the printer answered, 'for the supreme head of that Church is the King, a man learned before all others in the law of God; such a King as speaketh as though he were that mouthpiece of the Most High that the Antichrist at Rome claimeth to be.'

'Is it, then, with the worshipful the little Prince of Wales that ye are discontented?' Lascelles read, and the printer answered that there was not such another Prince of his years for promise and for performance, too, in all Christendom.

The stranger said from the hearth-place—

'Well! we are commended,' and his voice was bitter and ironical.

'How is it, then,' Lascelles read on, 'that ye say all is not over well in the land?'

The printer's gloomy and black features glared with a sudden rage.

'How should all be well with a land,' he cried, 'where in high places reigns harlotry?' He raised his clenched fist on high and glared round upon his audience. 'Corruption that reacheth round and about and down till it hath found a seedbed even in this poor house of my father's? Or if it is well with this land now, how shall it continue well when witchcraft rules near the King himself, and the Devil of Rome hath there his emissaries.'

A chitter of sound came from his audience, so that it appeared that they were all of a strain. They moved in their seats; the shipman cried out—

'Ay! witchcraft! witchcraft!'

The huge bulk of the stranger, black and like a bull's, half rose from its chair.

'Body of God!' he cried out. 'This I will not bear.'

Again the older man leaned solicitously above him and whispered, pleading with his hands, and Lascelles said hastily—

'Speak of your own knowledge. How should you know of what passes in high places?'

'Why!' the printer cried out, 'is it not the common report? Do not all men know it? Do not the butchers sing of it in the shambles, and the bot-flies buzz of it one to the other? I tell you it is spread from here into Almain, where the very horse-sellers are a-buzz with it.'

In his chair the stranger cried out—

'Ah! ah!' as if he were in great pain. He struggled with his feet and then sat still.

'I have heard witnesses that will testify to these things,' the printer said. 'I will bring them here into this room before ye.' He turned upon the stranger. 'Master,' he said, 'if ye know not of this, you are the only man in England that is ignorant!'

The stranger said with a bitter despair—

'Well, I am come to hear what ye do say!'

So he heard tales from all the sewers of London, and it was plain to him that all the commonalty cried shame upon their King. He screamed and twisted there in his chair at the last, and when he was come out into the darkness he fell upon his companion, and beat him so that he screamed out.

He might have died—for, though the King's guard with their torches and halberds were within a bowshot of them, they stirred no limb. And it was a party of fellows batfowling along the hedges of that field that came through the dark, attracted by the glare of the torches, the blaze of the scarlet clothes, and the outcry.

And when they came, asking why that great man belaboured this thin and fragile one, black shadows both against the light, the big man answered, howling—

'This man hath made me bounden to slay my wife.'

They said that that was a thing some of them would have been glad of.

But the great figure cast itself on the ground at the foot of a tree that stretched up like nerves and tentacles into the black sky. He tore the wet earth with his fingers, and the men stood round him till the Duke of Norfolk, coming with his sword drawn, hunted them afar off, and they fell again to beating the hedges to drive small birds into their nets.

For, they said, these were evidently of the quality whose griefs were none of theirs.

IV

The Queen was walking in the long gallery of Hampton Court. The afternoon was still new, but rain was falling very fast, so that through the windows all trees were blurred with mist, and all alleys ran with water, and it was very grey in the gallery. The Lady Mary was with her, and sat in a window-seat reading in a book. The Queen, as she walked, was netting a silken purse of a purple colour; her gown was very richly embroidered of gold thread worked into black velvet, and the heavy day pressed heavily on her senses, so that she sought that silence more willingly. For three days she had had no news of her lord, but that morning he was come back to Hampton, though she had not yet seen him, for it was ever his custom to put off all work of the day before he came to the Queen. Thus, if she were sad, she was tranquil; and, considering only that her work of bringing him to God must begin again that night, she let her thoughts rest upon the netting of her purse. The King, she had heard, was with his council. Her uncle was come to Court, and Gardiner of Winchester, and Cranmer of Canterbury, along with Sir A. Wriothesley, and many other lords, so that she augured it would be a very full council, and that night there would be a great banquet if she was not mistaken.

She remembered that it was now many months since she had been shown for Queen from that very gallery in the window that opened upon the Cardinal's garden. The King had led her by the hand. There had been a great crying out of many people of the lower sort that crowded the terrace before the garden. Now the rain fell, and all was desolation. A yeoman in brown fustian ran bending his head before the tempestuous rain. A rook, blown impotently backwards, essayed slowly to cross towards the western trees. Her eyes followed him until a great gust blew him in a wider curve, backwards and up, and when again he steadied himself he was no more than a blot on the wet greyness of the heavens.

There was an outcry at the door, and a woman ran in. She was crying out still: she was all in grey, with the white coif of the Queen's service. She fell down upon her knees, her hands held out.

'Pardon!' she cried. 'Pardon! Let not my brother come in. He prowls at the door.'

It was Mary Hall, she that had been Mary Lascelles. The Queen came over to raise her up, and to ask what it was she sought. But the woman wept so loud, and so

continually cried out that her brother was the fiend in-
carnate, that the Queen could ask no questions. The Lady
Mary looked up over her book without stirring her body.
Her eyes were awakened and sardonic.

The waiting-maid looked affrightedly over her shoulders
at the door.

'Well, your brother shall not come in here,' the Queen
said. 'What would he have done to you?'

'Pardon!' the woman cried out. 'Pardon!'

'Why, tell me of your fault,' the Queen said.

'I have given false witness!' Mary Hall blubbered out.
'I would not do it. But you do not know how they confuse
a body. And they threaten with cords and thumbscrews.'
She shuddered with her whole body. 'Pardon!' she cried
out. 'Pardon!'

And then suddenly she poured forth a babble of lamentations, wringing her hands, and rubbing her lips together.
She was a woman passed of thirty, but thin still and fair
like her brother in the face, for she was his twin.

'Ah,' she cried, 'he threated that if I would not give
evidence I must go back to Lincolnshire. You do not know
what it is to go back to Lincolnshire. Ah, God! the old
father, the old house, the wet. My clothes were all
mouldered. I was willing to give true evidence to save
myself, but they twisted it to false. It was the Duke of
Norfolk...'

The Lady Mary came slowly over the floor.

'Against whom did you give your evidence?' she said,
and her voice was cold, hard, and commanding.

Mary Hall covered her face with her hands, and wailed
desolately in a high note, like a wolf's howl, that reverberated in that dim gallery.

The Lady Mary struck her a hard blow with the cover
of her book upon the hands and the side of her head.

'Against whom did you give your evidence?' she said
again.

The woman fell over upon one hand, the other she
raised to shield herself. Her eyes were flooded with great

teardrops; her mouth was open in an agony. The Lady Mary raised her book to strike again: its covers were of wood, and its angles bound with silver work. The woman screamed out, and then uttered—

'Against Dearham and one Mopock first. And then against Sir T. Culpepper.'

The Queen stood up to her height; her hand went over her heart; the netted purse dropped to the floor soundlessly.

'God help me!' Mary Hall cried out. 'Dearham and Culpepper are both dead!'

The Queen sprang back three paces.

'How dead!' she cried. 'They were not even ill.'

'Upon the block,' the maid said. 'Last night, in the dark, in their gaols.'

The Queen let her hands fall slowly to her sides.

'Who did this?' she said, and Mary Hall answered—

'It was the King!'

The Lady Mary set her book under her arm.

'Ye might have known it was the King,' she said harshly. The Queen was as still as a pillar of ebony and ivory, so black her dress was, and so white her face and pendant hands.

'I repent me! I repent me!' the maid cried out. 'When I heard that they were dead I repented me and came here. The old Duchess of Norfolk is in gaol: she burned the letters of Dearham! The Lady Rochford is in gaol, and old Sir Nicholas, and the Lady Cicely that was ever with the Queen; the Lord Edmund Howard shall to gaol and his lady.'

'Why,' the Lady Mary said to the Queen, 'if you had not had such a fear of nepotism, your father and mother and grandmother and cousin had been here about you, and not so easily taken.'

The Queen stood still whilst all her hopes fell down.

'They have taken Lady Cicely that was ever with me,' she said.

'It was the Duke of Norfolk that pressed me most,' Mary Lascelles cried out.

'Aye, he would,' the Lady Mary answered.

The Queen tottered upon her feet.

'Ask her more,' she said. 'I will not speak with her.'

'The King in his council . . .' the girl began.

'Is the King in his council upon these matters?' the Lady Mary asked.

'Aye, he sitteth there,' Mary Hall said. 'And he hath heard evidence of Mary Trelyon the Queen's maid, how that the Queen's Highness did bid her begone on the night that Sir T. Culpepper came to her room, before he came. And how that the Queen was very insistent that she should go, upon the score of fatigue and the lateness of the hour. And she hath deponed that on other nights, too, this has happened, that the Queen's Highness, when she hath come late to bed, hath equally done the same thing. And other her maids have deponed how the Queen hath sent them from her presence and relieved them of tasks——'

'Well, well,' the Lady Mary said, 'often I have urged the Queen that she should be less gracious. Better it had been if she had beat ye all as I have done; then had ye feared to betray her.'

'Aye,' Mary Hall said, 'it is a true thing that your Grace saith there.'

'Call me not your Grace,' the Lady Mary said. 'I will be no Grace in this court of wolves and hogs.'

That was the sole thing that she said to show she was of the Queen's party. But ever she questioned the kneeling woman to know what evidence had been given, and of the attitude of the lords.

The young Poins had sworn roundly that the Queen had bidden him to summon no guards when her cousin had broken in upon her. Only Udal had said that he knew nothing of how Katharine had agreed with her cousin whilst they were in Lincolnshire. It had been after his time there that Culpepper came. It had been after his time, too, and whilst he lay in chains at Pontefract that Culpepper had come to her door. He stuck to that tale, though the Duke of Norfolk had beat and threatened him never so.

'Why, what wolves Howards be,' the Lady Mary said, 'for it is only wolves, of all beasts, that will prey upon the sick of their kind.'

The Queen stood there, swaying back as if she were very sick, her eyes fast closed, and the lids over them very blue.

It was only when the Lady Mary drew from the woman an account of the King's demeanour that she showed a sign of hearing.

'His Highness,' the woman said, 'sate always mute.'

'His Highness would,' the Lady Mary said. 'He is in that at least royal—that he letteth jackals do his hunting.'

It was only when the Archbishop of Canterbury, reading from the indictment of Culpepper, had uttered the words: 'did by the obtaining of the Lady Rochford meet with the Queen's Highness by night in a secret and vile place,' that the King had called out—

'Body of God! mine own bedchamber!' as if he were hatefully mocking the Archbishop.

The Queen leant suddenly forward—

'Said he no more than that?' she cried eagerly.

'No more, oh your dear Grace,' the maid said. And the Queen shuddered and whispered—

'No more!—And I have spoken to this woman to obtain no more than "no more."'

Again she closed her eyes, and she did not again speak, but hung her head forward as if she were thinking.

'Heaven help me!' the maid said.

'Why, think no more of Heaven,' the Lady Mary said, 'there is but the fire of hell for such beasts as you.'

'Had you such a brother as mine——' Mary Hall began. But the Lady Mary cried out—

'Cease, dog! I have a worse father, but you have not found him force me to work vileness.'

'All the other Papists have done worse than I,' Mary Hall said, 'for they it was that forced us by threats to speak.'

'Not one was of the Queen's side?' the Lady Mary said.

'Not one,' Mary Hall answered. 'Gardiner was more

fierce against her than he of Canterbury, the Duke of Norfolk than either.'

The Lady Mary said—

'Well! well!'

'Myself I did hear the Duke of Norfolk say, when I was drawn to give evidence, that he begged the King to let him tear my secrets from my heart. For so did he abhor the abominable deeds done by his two nieces, Anne Boleyn and Katharine Howard, that he could no longer desire to live. And he said neither could he live longer without some comfortable assurance of His Highness's royal favour. And so he fell upon me——'

The woman fell to silence. Without, the rain had ceased, and, like heavy curtains trailing near the ground, the clouds began to part and sweep away. A horn sounded, and there went a party of men with pikes across the terrace.

'Well, and what said you?' the Lady Mary said.

'Ask me not,' Mary Lascelles said woefully. She averted her eyes to the floor at her side.

'By God, but I will know,' the Lady Mary snarled. 'You shall tell me.' She had that of royal bearing from her sire that the woman was amazed at her words, and, awakening like one in a dream, she rehearsed the evidence that had been threated from her.

She had told of the lascivious revels and partings, in the maid's garret at the old Duchess's, when Katharine had been a child there. She had told how Marnock the musicker had called her his mistress, and how Dearham, Katharine's cousin, had beaten him. And how Dearham had given Katharine a half of a silver coin.

'Well, that is all true,' the Lady Mary said. 'How did you perjure yourself?'

'In the matter of the Queen's age,' the woman faltered.

'How that?' the Lady Mary asked.

'The Duke would have me say that she was more than a young child.'

The Lady Mary said, 'Ah! ah! there is the yellow dog!' She thought for a moment.

'And you said?' she asked at last.

'The Duke threated me and threated me. And say I, "Your Grace must know how young she was." And says he, "I would swear that at that date she was no child, but that I do not know how many of these nauseous Howard brats there be. Nor yet the order in which they came. But this I will swear that I think there has been some change of the Queen with a whelp that died in the litter, that she might seem more young. And of a surety she was always learned beyond her assumed years, so that it was not to be believed." '

Mary Lascelles closed her eyes and appeared about to faint.

'Speak on, dog,' Mary said.

The woman roused herself to say with a solemn piteousness—

'This I swear that before this trial, when my brother pressed me and threated me thus to perjure myself, I abhorred it and spat in his face. There was none more firm—nor one half so firm as I—against him. But oh, the Duke and the terror—and to be in a ring of so many villainous men . . .'

'So that you swore that the Queen's Highness, to your knowledge, was older than a child,' the Lady Mary pressed her.

'Ay; they would have me say that it was she that commanded to have these revels . . .'

She leaned forward with both her hands on the floor, in the attitude of a beast that goes four-footed. She cried out—

'Ask me no more! ask me no more!'

'Tell! tell! Beast!' the Lady Mary said.

'They threated me with torture,' the woman panted. 'I could do no less. I heard Margot Poins scream.'

'They have tortured her?' the Lady Mary said.

'Ay, and she was in her pains elsewise,' the woman said.

'Did she say aught?' the Lady Mary said.

'No! no!' the woman panted. Her hair had fallen loose in her coif, it depended on to her shoulder.

'Tell on! tell on!' the Lady Mary said.

'They tortured her, and she did not say one word more, but ever in her agony cried out, "Virtuous! virtuous!" till her senses went.'

Mary Hall again raised herself to her knees.

'Let me go, let me go,' she moaned. 'I will not speak before the Queen. I had been as loyal as Margot Poins. . . . But I will not speak before the Queen. I love her as well as Margot Poins. But . . . I will not——'

She cried out as the Lady Mary struck her, and her face was lamentable with its opened mouth. She scrambled to one knee; she got on both, and ran to the door. But there she cried out—

'My brother!' and fell against the wall. Her eyes were fixed upon the Lady Mary with a baleful despair, she gasped and panted for breath.

'It is upon you if I speak,' she said. 'Merciful God, do not bid me speak before the Queen!'

She held out her hands as if she had been praying.

'Have I not proved that I loved this Queen?' she said. 'Have I not fled here to warn her? Is it not my life that I risk? Merciful God! Merciful God! Bid me not to speak.'

'Speak!' the Lady Mary said.

The woman appealed to the Queen with her eyes streaming, but Katharine stood silent and like a statue with sightless eyes. Her lips smiled, for she thought of her Redeemer; for this woman she had neither ears nor eyes.

'Speak!' the Lady Mary said.

'God help you, be it on your head,' the woman cried out, 'that I speak before the Queen. It was the King that bade me say she was so old. I would not say it before the Queen, but you have made me!'

The Lady Mary's hands fell powerless to her sides, the book from her opened fingers jarred on the hard floor.

'Merciful God!' she said. 'Have I such a father?'

'It was the King!' the woman said. 'His Highness came

to life when he heard these words of the Duke's, that the Queen was older than she reported. He would have me say that the Queen's Highness was of a marriageable age and contracted to her cousin Dearham.'

'Merciful God!' the Lady Mary said again. 'Dear God, show me some way to tear from myself the sin of my begetting. I had rather my mother's confessor had been my father than the King! Merciful God!'

'Never was woman pressed as I was to say this thing. And well ye wot—better than I did before—what this King is. I tell you—and I swear it——'

She stopped and trembled, her eyes, from which the colour had gone, wide open and lustreless, her face pallid and ashen, her mouth hanging open. The Queen was moving towards her.

She came very slowly, her hands waving as if she sought support from the air, but her head was erect.

'What will you do?' the Lady Mary said. 'Let us take counsel!'

Katharine Howard said no word. It was as if she walked in her sleep.

V

The King sat on the raised throne of his council chamber. All the Lords of his Council were there and all in black. There was Norfolk with his yellow face who feigned to laugh and scoff, now that he had proved himself no lover of the Queen's. There was Gardiner of Winchester, sitting forward with his cruel and eager eyes upon the table. Next him was the Lord Mayor, Michael Dormer, and the Lord Chancellor. And so round the horse-shoe table against the wall sat all the other lords and commissioners that had been appointed to make inquiry. Sir Anthony Browne was there, and Wriothesley with his great beard, and the Duke of Suffolk with his hanging jaw. A silence had fallen upon them all, and the witnesses were all done with.

On high on his throne the King sat, monstrous and

leaning over to one side, his face dabbled with tears. He gazed upon Cranmer who stood on high beside him, the King gazing upwards into his face as if for comfort and counsel.

'Why, you shall save her for me?' he said.

Cranmer's face was haggard, and upon it too there were tears.

'It were the gladdest thing that ever I did,' he said, 'for I do believe this Queen is not so guilty.'

'God of His mercy bless thee, Cranmer,' he said, and wearily he touched his black bonnet at the sacred name. 'I have done all that I might when I spoke with Mary Hall. It shall save me her life.'

Cranmer looked round upon the lords below them; they were all silent but only the Duke of Norfolk who laughed to the Lord Mayor. The Lord Mayor, a burly man, was more pallid and haggard than any. All the others had fear for themselves written upon their faces. But the citizen was not used to these trials, of which the others had seen so many.

The Archbishop fell on his knees on the step before the King's throne.

'Gracious and dread Lord,' he said, and his low voice trembled like that of a schoolboy, 'Saviour, Lord, and Fount of Justice of this realm! Hitherto these trials have been of traitor-felons and villains outside the circle of your house. Now that they be judged and dead, we, your lords, pray you that you put off from you this most heavy task of judge. For inasmuch as we live by your life and have health by your health, in this realm afflicted with many sores that you alone can heal and dangers that you alone can ward off, so we have it assured and certain that many too great labours and matters laid upon you imperil us all. In that, as well for our selfish fears as for the great love, self-forgetting, that we have of your person, we pray you that— coming now to the trial of this your wife—you do rest, though well assured we are that greatly and courageously you would adventure it, upon the love of us your lords.

Appoint, therefore, such a Commission as you shall well approve to make this most heavy essay and trial.'

So low was his voice that, to hear him, many lords rose from their seats and came over against the throne. Thus all that company were in the upper part of the hall, and through the great window at the further end the sun shone down upon them, having parted the watery clouds. To their mass of black it gave blots and gouts of purple and blue and scarlet, coming through the dight panes.

'Lay off this burden of trial and examination upon us that so willingly, though with sighs and groans, would bear it.'

Suddenly the King stood up and pointed, his jaw fallen open. Katharine Howard was coming up the floor of the hall. Her hands were folded before her; her face was rigid and calm; she looked neither to right nor to left, but only upon the King's face. At the edge of the sunlight she halted, so that she stood, a black figure in the bluish and stony gloom of the hall with the high roof a great way above her head. All the lords began to pull off their bonnets, only Norfolk said that he would not uncover before a harlot.

The Queen, looking upon Henry's face, said with icy and cold tones—

'I would have you to cease this torturing of witnesses. I will make confession.'

No man then had a word to say. Norfolk had no word either.

'If you will have me confess to heresy, I will confess to heresy; if to treason, to treason. If you will have me confess to adultery, God help me and all of you, I will confess to adultery and all such sins.'

The King cried out—

'No! no!' like a beast that is stabbed to the heart; but with cold eyes the Queen looked back at him.

'If you will have it adultery before marriage, it shall be so. If it be to be falseness to my Lord's bed, it shall be so; if it be both, in the name of God, be it both, and where

you will and how. If you will have it spoken, here I speak
it. If you will have it written, I will write out such words
as you shall bid me write. I pray you leave my poor women
be, especially them that be sick, for there are none that do
not love me, and I do think that my death is all that you
need.'

She paused; there was no sound in the hall but the
strenuous panting of the King.

'But whether,' she said, 'you shall believe this confession
of mine, I leave to you that very well do know my conversation and my manner of life.'

Again she paused and said—

'I have spoken. To it I will add that heartily I do thank
my sovereign lord that raised me up. And, in public, I do
say it, that he hath dealt justly by me. I pray you pardon
me for having delayed thus long your labours. I will get
me gone.'

Then she dropped her eyes to the ground.

Again the King cried out—

'No! no!' and, stumbling to his feet he rushed down
upon his courtiers and round the table. He came upon her
before she was at the distant door.

'You shall not go!' he said. 'Unsay! unsay!'

She said, 'Ah!' and recoiled before him with an obdurate and calm repulsion.

'Get ye gone, all you minions and hounds,' he cried.
And running in upon them he assailed them with huge
blows and curses, sobbing lamentably, so that they fled up
the steps and out on to the rooms behind the throne. He
came sobbing, swift and maddened, panting and crying
out, back to where she awaited him.

'Unsay! unsay!' he cried out.

She stood calmly.

'Never will I unsay,' she said. 'For it is right that such
a King as thou should be punished, and I do believe this:
that there can no agony come upon you such as shall come
if you do believe me false to you.'

The coloured sunlight fell upon his face just down to

the chin; his eyes glared horribly. She confronted him, being in the shadow. High up above them, painted and moulded angels soared on the roof with golden wings. He clutched at his throat.

'I do not believe it,' he cried out.

'Then,' she said, 'I believe that it shall be only a second greater agony to you: for you shall have done me to death believing me guiltless.'

A great motion of despair went over his whole body.

'Kat!' he said; 'Body of God, Kat! I would not have you done to death. I have saved your life from your enemies.'

She made him no answer, and he protested desperately—

'All this afternoon I have wrestled with a woman to make her say that you are older than your age, and pre-contracted to a cousin of yours. I have made her say it at last, so your life is saved.'

She turned half to go from him, but he ran round in front of her.

'Your life is saved!' he said desperately, 'for if you were precontracted to Dearham your marriage with me is void. And if your marriage with me is void, though it be proved against you that you were false to me, yet it is not treason, for you are not my wife.'

Again she moved to circumvent him, and again he came before her.

'Speak!' he said, 'speak!' But she folded her lips close. He cast his arms abroad in a passion of despair. 'You shall be put away into a castle where you shall have such state as never empress had yet. All your will I will do. Always I will live near you in secret fashion.'

'I will not be your leman,' she said.

'But once you offered it!' he answered.

'Then you appeared in the guise of a king!' she said.

He withered beneath her tone.

'All you would have you shall have,' he said. 'I will call in a messenger and here and now send the letter that you wot of to Rome.'

'Your Highness,' she said, 'I would not have the Church brought back to this land by one deemed an adult'ress. Assuredly, it should not prosper.'

Again he sought to stay her going, holding out his arms to enfold her. She stepped back.

'Your Highness,' she said, 'I will speak some last words. And, as you know me well, you know that these irrevocably shall be my last to you!'

He cried—'Delay till you hear——'

'There shall be no delay,' she said; 'I will not hear.' She smoothed a strand of hair that had fallen over her forehead in a gesture that she always had when she was deep in thoughts.

'This is what I would say,' she uttered. And she began to speak levelly—

'Very truly you say when you say that once I made offer to be your leman. But it was when I was a young girl, mazed with reading of books in the learned tongue, and seeing all men as if they were men of those days. So you appeared to me such a man as was Pompey the Great, or as was Marius, or as was Sylla. For each of these great men erred; yet they erred greatly as rulers that would rule. Or rather I did see you such a one as was Cæsar Julius, who, as you well wot, crossed a Rubicon and set out upon a high endeavour. But you—never will you cross any Rubicon; always you blow hot in the evening and cold at dawn. Neither do you, as I had dreamed you did, rule in this your realm. For, even as a crow that just now I watched, you are blown hither and thither by every gust that blows. Now the wind of gossips blows so that you must have my life. And, before God, I am glad of it.'

'Before God!' he cried out, 'I would save you!'

'Aye,' she answered sadly, 'to-day you would save me; to-morrow a foul speech of one mine enemy shall gird you again to slay me. On the morrow you will repent, and on the morrow of that again you will repent of that. So you will balance and trim. If to-day you send a messenger to Rome, to-morrow you will send another, hastening by a shorter route, to stay him. And this I tell you, that I am not one to let my name be bandied for many days in the mouths of men. I had rather be called a sinner, adjudged and dead and forgotten. So I am glad that I am cast to die.'

'You shall not die!' the King cried. 'Body of God, you shall not die! I cannot live lacking thee. Kat—— Kat——'

'Aye,' she said, 'I must die, for you are not such a one as can stay in the wind. Thus I tell you it will fall about that for many days you will waver, but one day you will cry out—Let her die this day! On the morrow of that day you will repent you, but, being dead, I shall be no more to be recalled to life. Why, man, with this confession of mine, heard by grooms and mayors of cities and the like, how shall you dare to save me? You know you shall not.

'And so, now I am cast for death, and I am very glad of it. For, if I had not so ensured and made it fated, I might later have wavered. For I am a weak woman, and strong men have taken dishonourable means to escape death when it came near. Now I am assured of death, and know that no means of yours can save me, nor no prayers nor yielding of mine. I came to you for that you might give this realm again to God. Now I see you will not—for not ever will you do it if it must abate you a jot of your sovereignty, and you never will do it without that abatement. So it is in vain that I have sinned.

'For I trow that I sinned in taking the crown from the woman that was late your wife. I would not have it, but you would, and I yielded. Yet it was a sin. Then I did a sin that good might ensue, and again I do it, and I hope that this sin that brings me down shall counterbalance that other that set me up. For well I know that to make this confession is a sin; but whether the one shall balance the other only the angels that are at the gates of Paradise shall assure me.

'In some sort I have done it for your Highness' sake— or, at least, that your Highness may profit in your fame thereby. For, though all that do know me will scarcely believe in it, the most part of men shall needs judge me by the reports that are set about. In the commonalty, and the princes of foreign courts, one may believe you justified of my blood, and, for this event, even to posterity your name shall be spared. I shall become such a little dust as will not fill a cup. Yet, at least, I shall not sully, in the eyes of men to come, your record.

'And that I am glad of; for this world is no place for me who am mazed by too much reading in old books. At first I would not believe it, though many have told me it was so. I was of the opinion that in the end right must win through. I think now that it never shall—or not for many ages—till our Saviour again come upon this earth with a great glory. But all this is a mystery of the great goodness of God and the temptations that do beset us poor mortality.

'So now I go! I think that you will not any more seek to hinder me, for you have heard how set I am on this course. I think, if I have done little good, I have done little harm, for I have sought to injure no man—though through me you have wracked some of my poor servants and slain my poor simple cousin. But that is between you and God. If I must weep for them yet, though I was the occasion of their deaths and tortures, I cannot much lay it to my account.

'If, by being reputed your leman, as you would have it, I could again set up the Church of God, willingly I would do it. But I see that there is not one man—save maybe some poor simple souls—that would have this done. Each man is set to save his skin and his goods—and you are such a weathercock that I should never blow you to a firm quarter. For what am I set against all this nation?

'If you should say that our wedding was no wedding because of the pre-contract to my cousin Dearham that you have feigned was made—why, I might live as your reputed leman in a secret place. But it is not very certain that even at that I should live very long. For, if I lived, I must work upon you to do the right. And, if that I did, not very long should I live before mine enemies again did come about me and to you. And so I must die. And now I see that you are not such a man as I would live with willingly to preserve my life.

'I speak not to reprove you what I have spoken, but to make you see that as I am so I am. You are as God made you, setting you for His own purposes a weak man in very evil and turbulent times. As a man is born so a man lives; as is his strength so the strain breaks him or he resists the strain. If I have wounded you with these my words, I do ask your pardon. Much of this long speech I have thought upon when I was despondent this long time past. But much of it has come to my lips whilst I spake, and, maybe, it is harsh and rash in the wording. That I would not have, but I may not help myself. I would have you wounded by the things as they are, and by what of conscience you have, in your passions and your prides. And this, I will add, that I die a Queen, but I would rather have died the wife of my cousin Culpepper or of any other simple lout that loved me as he did, without regard, without thought, and without falter. He sold farms to buy me bread. You would not imperil a little alliance with a little King o' Scots to save my life. And this I tell you, that I will spend the last hours of the days that I have to live in considering of this simple man and of his love, and in praying for his soul, for I hear you have slain him! And for the rest, I commend you to your friends!'

The King had staggered back against the long table; his jaw fell open; his head leaned down upon his chest. In all that long speech—the longest she had ever made save when she was shown for Queen—she had not once raised or lowered her voice, nor once dropped her eyes. But she had remembered the lessons of speaking that had been given her by her master Udal, in the aforetime, away in Lincolnshire, where there was an orchard with green boughs, and below it a pig-pound where the hogs grunted.

She went slowly down over the great stone flags of the great hall. It was very gloomy now, and her figure in black velvet was like a small shadow, dark and liquid, amongst shadows that fell softly and like draperies from the roof.

Up there it was all dark already, for the light came downwards from the windows. She went slowly, walking as she had been schooled to walk.

'God!' Henry cried out; 'you have not played false with Culpepper?' His voice echoed all round the hall.

The Queen's white face and her folded hands showed as she turned—

'Aye, there the shoe pinches!' she said. 'Think upon it. Most times you shall not believe it, for you know me. But I have made confession of it before your Council. So it may be true. For I hope some truth cometh to the fore even in Councils.'

Near the doorway it was all shadow, and soundlessly she faded away among them. The hinge of the door creaked; through it there came the sound of the pikestaves of her guard upon the stone of the steps. The sound whispered round amidst the statues of old knights and kings that stood upon corbels between the windows. It whispered amongst the invisible carvings of the roof. Then it died away.

The King made no sound. Suddenly he cast his hat upon the paving.

KATHARINE HOWARD was executed on Tower Hill, the 13th of February, in the 33rd year of the reign of KING HENRY VIII.

MDXLI–II